BOOK ONE *in the*
CARDINAL TRILOGY

THE SIGN

W.A. SMITH

Print ISBN: 978-1-09836-582-0

eBook ISBN: 978-1-09836-583-7

PROLOGUE

SAMMY WALKED UP THE SIDEWALK TO THE STEPS OF THE red brick townhouse in the northern outskirts of Seattle, Washington, and realized that the front door was half open. It was the middle of October and even though it wasn't quite winter, it was still cold enough for it not to be left intentionally open. Sammy looked down on the porch and noticed that the morning's newspaper was in a pile by the door. The paperboy, whose idea of delivering Mel's neighbor's daily paper was to throw it from the sidewalk to the entryway as he sped by on his moped, would often miss his mark, consequently placing the paper directly in front of Mel's door, not her neighbor's.

Sammy picked up the clutter pile of papers, and noticed the title of an article, 'Guns at Evergreen a Hair-Trigger Topic,' under the newspaper's date of October 19, 2000. He folded the paper as best he could and tossed it so that it was closer to the neighbor's screen door. As he reached for the door handle of Mel's place, he sighed. He could see inside and noticed the disarray in the front room.

As he stepped through the door, he was confronted with a wall of what can only be described as a mixture of marijuana smoke, unclean kitty litter box, and the unpleasing scent of two-day-old pizza.

"What the hell is going on in here?" Sammy wanted to know. He looked around and did not immediately see his girlfriend. He turned and looked behind him to study the yard. Her old, faded red, 1979 Volkswagen Beetle was in the driveway with the door slightly ajar, so he knew that she should be home. He made his way over the dirty clothes and old pizza boxes, and peered into the bedroom just off the living room.

Leaning across her bed in an uncomfortable position, Melanie Forrester was nursing a half empty bottle of beer in her left hand. By the looks of it, she had had several before the one that she was holding. In her right hand, she was holding a joint, having taken a hit off of it seconds before Sammy entered. Sitting on the leather chair in the corner was Joey, who for all intents and purposes was her supplier of all things medicinal, and quite frankly, her enabler. He was your basic dirtbag and actually looked the part. He was wearing the same shirt that Sammy noticed the last 3 times he had seen him. In fact, the same pizza stain was covering the 'S' of the emblem of the Seattle Seahawks.

"Seriously," Sammy uttered in disappointment.

"What?" Mel answered, surprised by his arrival, as she stumbled while trying to get herself in an upright position. Even though she appeared defiant, Sammy could see in her eyes that deep down, she felt at least mildly ashamed.

"You know what," Sammy countered. "You promised me that you were done with all this." Mel had promised to clean up her act several times before, but the most recent time, he actually believed her. The sincerity of the promise almost evenly matched the love which they felt for each other. Apparently, the pull of her addiction was too powerful and had overwhelmed her once again.

Mel could see that Sammy was upset, but in her state of mind, she really didn't want to explain again. Mel knew that he was trying to "save" her, as he called it, and even though deep down inside, she was aware that he did it because he loved her, but she couldn't construct enough will power in herself to allow him to help her. The guilt for relapsing combined with utter shame in the person she had now become, created the emotion of resistance that she could not shake.

"I need it Sammy," Mel retorted in a raised voice, letting her annoyance control the volume in her tone.

"I have been feeling really stressed and anxious all week, and when I ran into Joey, well..." Mel's explanation trailed off as her eyes darted from Joey to Sammy.

At the sound of his name, Joey lifted his head and defended Mel, "Yeah man, get off her back. She is a grown woman and she doesn't need a babysitter, dude."

Sammy sneered at Joey, but didn't say a word to him. As far as he was concerned, Joey had no place being in Mel's townhouse, much less her life.

Sammy was at his wit's end. He loved her so much, but he couldn't continue living like this. Mel was the love of his life, and unfortunately, he was watching the love between them slip away, like a piece of driftwood, floating aimlessly on a winding river.

They had been together for two years; however, it had been 3 long months since she had fallen back into her old habits. Sammy had had enough. There were bouts of times when she was actually like her old self and their relationship was great. Last week was one of those times. Sammy had taken Mel camping over a long weekend. On the second to the last day at the campsite, it rained most of the morning and afternoon causing them to be held up in the tent. They had made love several times during the course of that day and he truly believed that it would be a possibility that he would propose to her in the near future. Unfortunately, that plan would never come to pass.

"Mel, I'm done with all of this. I love you, but you won't take care of yourself and you won't accept my help." Sammy's eyes began to water slightly. He had dreamt of them getting married one day and settling down and starting a family, but he knew deep down in the bottommost regions of his heart that the possibility of that was slipping away.

Sammy's emotions were starting to get the best of him, but he knew he had to try to get his point across any way he could. "I don't want this type of life for you. Can't you see that you are on a direct path to killing yourself. I can't stand by helplessly, watching you self-destruct." As the sounds of his words faded away, Mel stood up and shouted, "Yeah, well, you're such a drag! It's like you're my dad, nagging at me to behave. I'm fed up with... with... this, and you don't care about what I need." Despite sounding like a 5th grader arguing with her parents, Melissa was actually quite intelligent. She almost graduated from the University of Michigan with a Bachelor's degree in Education, but dropped out with a semester and a half to go because she followed her previous boyfriend to Seattle to help him start his business. Unfortunately, the business was growing pot and distributing drugs. Shortly after they moved, he dumped her for a sexy hot redhead.

Sammy had met Mel at a local bar near the college that he attended. Apparently, she was staying with a girlfriend that lived close to it. When he saw her sitting at the bar with a couple of her friends, he fell in love with her instantly. It was love at first sight. The two hit it off right away. Mel was just getting into recreational drug usage after her breakup from her ex-boyfriend, and Sammy believed that he could help her to overcome her addiction. For the first year or so, Sammy was successful in keeping her clean. However, Mel couldn't defeat her demons and began her downward spiral into dependency. Sammy did the best he could, but obviously, by the events unfolding before him, it wasn't enough.

Frustrated and dismayed, Sam answered, "Come on Mel, you know that I've been helping you. Hell, it's been me that has been making sure that you are fed and your bills are paid. When was the last time that you had a job that you actually stayed with for more than a couple of weeks? You have been fired from the last 4 jobs that you've had." Sam paused a moment to grab a stack of bills that was sitting unopened on her nightstand. "I mean, seriously, who gets fired from McDonald's after just one week?"

That was the last straw for Mel. "You don't understand—that manager had it in for me because I was prettier than her," Mel replied. The sound of annoyance in her voice seemed to echo that of the exasperation that Sammy felt for her.

Sammy rolled his eyes at her explanation. The empty beer bottles and the joint were making Mel sound like an utter child. It was her new thing, making excuses for everything that went wrong with her life. It was never her fault.

It was at this point that Joey decided to split. "I'm out of here," he said, as he got up from the chair and brushed past Sammy, lightly bumping Sammy's shoulder as he walked by.

"Later bro," Joey said, as he formed his fingers into a peace sign.

Mel wiped tears from her face, smearing what makeup was on her cheeks. "Wait, Joey, I'm coming with you." She adjusted her denim skirt so that it was almost in the right position, and grabbed her purse.

She looked up at Sammy, and said, "We're done. I can't do this anymore. You don't have to worry about me because, well, because, I, um, can take care of myself." But as Mel went to leave the bedroom, she misjudged the opening in the door and slammed her shoulder in the frame; which made her drop her purse and empty its contents onto the old, stained carpet. Among them were empty wrappers, cigarette boxes, and Sammy's great grandfather's pocket watch. He thought he had lost it over a month ago—he had torn his apartment apart, frantically searching every nook and cranny for it. Even though it should have, the thought of Mel snatching it hadn't occurred to him.

Sammy reached down to pick up the purse, and then with a strained, frustrated voice asked, "You stole my great grandfather's watch?"

Mel was going to deny it and make up some excuse for why it was in there, but she simply did not have the mental energy to come up with a good enough lie. "Yeah, so what? You don't do anything with it, anyways. Besides, I need the money," Mel justified, as if it was a rational explanation.

Sammy grabbed the watch and opened it to make sure that Mel hadn't damaged it in any way. After a quick examination, he quickly placed it in his pocket and picked up the handful of items and stuffed them back in the purse.

Sammy held up the purse for Mel to take, and after a pause, she grabbed it from him and tilted her head in a way so that their eyes locked onto each other.

It was as if you could re-watch the last year of their lives together in the pupils. This moment was a focal point in time and they were cognitively aware of it. He was actually contemplating reaching out and grabbing her to hug her and hold her tight, but the moment passed as Mel turned to leave. "Bye, Sammy," she said, as if the past years had had no meaning.

Sammy just stood there, in the filth and stench, and replied, "Don't do this, Mel, please don't leave like this." His words pleading yet there was finality to them. Mel stole one last glance at Sammy, and then that was it. Mel was gone.

As they drove away, Mel had this sinking feeling that she would never see Sammy again, and somewhere deep in her heart, she knew that she had royally screwed up. Sammy was supposed to have been her husband, and the two of them were supposed to live happily ever after. That was the fairy-tale.

Unfortunately, the wedge of addition had, in that moment, successfully pried them apart. Mel knew that she was making the worst mistake of her life, but as she contemplated it, her compromised mental state was too weak, and she was far too drunk to dwell on it. And not only that, she was extremely pissed off at Sammy, and most of all, at herself.

CHAPTER ONE

"PLEASE HELP ME." THAT'S ALL THAT CLAIRE COULD THINK of to put on the sign. She could go into more detail about why she was in her particular situation, but seriously, who would care. It was around the middle of November and even though the sky was blue and filtered with solid white clouds, it was cold. Claire was used to skipping around from place to place, finding the occasional shelter. But since she had left her foster family a few months back, it was harder to find people who wanted to help out a sixteen-year-old homeless girl.

Despite having literally nothing, Claire never compared herself with the other homeless people. She was smart, enjoyed reading, and was somewhat classy-looking for someone in her situation. She tried to keep herself clean, but it was a challenge. Her long natural blond hair was looking duller due to the dust and dirt of the city sidewalks. She had blue eyes that were a beautiful contrast to her blonde hair, but lately, they appeared dull and sunken. Unlike her mother, she never stole or committed a crime. There was just something deep down in her gut that always prevented her from following through with it. If there was ever a time in which she would be tempted to steal, this was it. A couple days before, someone had stolen her backpack while she slept on a street bench. All that she owned was in that backpack, and waking up to an empty bench where her bag once rested was a real blow. She was wearing ripped jeans that were a little loose on her (probably because she had lost about 5 lbs. in the past week due to lack of food) and a teal cami with a grey cardigan that had a few smudges of dirt embedded in the left arm and around the collar. Obviously, this attire was not cutting it for warmth on this 40-degree day with a wind chill hanging somewhere around thirty-seven degrees.

So, here she was, on a corner on State Street in Chicago, a week before Thanksgiving, feeling detached and alone. Claire was tired, cold, hungry, and just about out of hope. It had been a long and stressful month leading up to this point, and it had taken its toll.

At first, Claire stood silently holding the sign, modeling it after other homeless people that she had seen holding signs. After about an hour or so, she sat down cross-legged with the sign resting in her lap being supported with her knees. Many of the other sign holders would call out to the people walking by, addressing each one almost on a personal level. Conversely, Claire simply stared out into the crowd, not focusing on any one particular person. It was bad enough seeing the reactions of the masses that would actually look at her—a disgusted, uncaring look that showed indifference. However, the majority of the passersby deliberately turned their attention elsewhere, making sure not to make eye contact, a reflex of those who grew up in the big city.

It was now about midday, and all Claire had to show for it was a couple of one-dollar bills and a handful of change. She decided to pull out her grey beanie from her back pocket and place it on the sidewalk and put the money into it so that people could see the donations. A few moments later, out of the corner of her eye, she could see a man slowly walking in her direction. Almost immediately, the hair on the back of her neck rose. She just had a bad feeling about this. Claire slowly shoved the beanie behind her and mentally kept her guard up. As the man approached, she could see that he was rough looking. He had tattoos on his hands, arms and neck. His pants were loose, and exposed about a third of his boxers. He had a cigarette behind his left ear, and she could smell the scent of pot as he approached.

"Hey girl," the man started, "What do you need help with?" He had a shit-eating grin on his face, and then with both hands, grabbed his crotch, and said, "I will help you, if you help me?" Claire was sickened with the notion, and truth be known, a little scared. She forced herself to appear defiant and strong, and replied, "With something that small in size, you need more help than me." She reached behind herself and grabbed the hat with the money and pulled out a dollar. She then held it up for the creep to take. Claire smiled back and then turned it into a frown. The man's face turned red, and he snapped back, "Stupid bitch," and shot out his middle finger while he brushed passed her, almost grazing her knee with his boot. As he walked away, mumbling words that Claire could not make out, she put the dollar back into the hat and let a smirk slip out. She was young, but was maturing rapidly.

A few hours went by, and Claire's hat was slowly accumulating a few more dollars and a couple of pamphlets on how Jesus saves. Whether it was the upcoming holiday season or just the sheer number of people out and about, she was making enough money for today's meal and possibly tomorrow's. Claire looked down at the hat and felt a drop of rain from the sky. The clouds were slowly coming in, and a few of them were dark. By the looks of it, it wasn't going to be a downpour just yet, but it was going to get her damp if it kept up, just like yesterday when it rained and Claire got soaked. At the thought of being cold, lonely, dirty, and now damp, Claire tried to hold back the tear that had formed in her right eye, however, she was unable to do so and it flowed freely down her cheek.

* *

APRIL TURNER LOVED THIS TIME OF YEAR IN DOWNTOWN Chicago. She was raised an hour from the city, and absolutely loved living here. The streets were busy with people shopping for the Thanksgiving season. Everyone knew that Christmas was right around the corner, and you could feel it in the air. April was 36 years old, had brown, shoulder-length hair, and was a book editor for Priscilla Publishing, a publishing company based in Chicago, mainly dealing with romance novels. Her friend, Gina Delaney, was the CEO of Priscilla Publishing, which made it an even better place to work. It had been almost four years since the death of her husband, Nick Turner, and she still missed him. Their daughter, Blake Turner, was fourteen years old, and was a beautiful young lady. She had light brown hair that was long and went to about 12 inches past her shoulders. She had bangs but was in the process of growing them out and she usually accessorized with headbands. Blake wore contacts, but today she was wearing her glasses. They were fashion wear, so they did look cute. Since her father died, Blake and her mother had become even closer. Blake was learning about fashion and designing, so she enjoyed shopping with her mother. With that being said, of course there were occasions when she would disagree with her mother and find her a little annoying, but nothing beyond typical teenage stuff.

So, there they were, on this bustling Friday afternoon, strolling the blocks of downtown Chicago, getting in some early Christmas shopping. Since Blake only had a half-day of school today, April had decided the night before that she would pick Blake up from school at 11:15 a.m. and the two of them would head downtown right away.

"I can't believe that it is almost Thanksgiving, it just seems like yesterday that it was summer," April spoke to Blake, as she raised her sunglasses from her eyes to the top of her head in order to get a better look at an outfit that was displayed in one of the storefronts.

"I know, right?" Blake agreed. "I miss the days of staying at Gina's Lake House and swimming off the dock."

April sighed longingly at the thought of it. It was such a wonderful summer. It was a mixture of work and fun, and they were slowly enjoying life again. It had been a sad four years, but there were more good days than bad days. The memories of her late husband kept her going, and she would always cherish the love that they had for each other. Blake was a blessed reminder of their lives together, and April was so grateful for the beautiful human being that they had produced.

"Will Emily be coming over for Thanksgiving?" April asked Blake, as they continued walking through the downtown streets. Emily Beckett was one of Blake's best friends. They both were freshmen at Jones College Prep High School. Emily had made the junior varsity cheerleading team while Blake didn't show an interest in sports, especially cheering for them. Despite that, Blake supported Emily and even stayed after school with her while she attended practice. Emily's parents were divorced. Her mother lived in Oregon and her father here in Chicago with her. They had split custody and it was amicable. However, her father had her for most of the school year because Emily didn't want to go to Oregon schools. Her parents didn't want to make the divorce worse than it already was for Emily, so they had an agreement. She was supposed to spend the holiday with her dad this year but he would be away on business for the entire week. Emily's mom wanted her to fly out to her ranch in Oregon, but Emily had wanted to stay in the city. Blake and Emily had devised a plan to see if she could spend the long weekend with Blake and her mom but the final decision had not been made yet.

"I still don't know, mom," Blake answered. "Emily's mom really wasn't keen on the idea because she had hoped to spend time with her now that she wouldn't be with her dad."

April grinned at the notion because she could see why Emily's mother didn't want to give up the chance to see her daughter. April couldn't imagine a time in the near future in which she would allow Blake to go with someone else over the holiday.

"Well, you know that she is perfectly welcome if she is able to come," April sincerely said. She liked Emily, and it really would be fine if she could spend the weekend with them, but April knew Emily's mom and she doubted that it would come to fruition.

It was at that moment that April's cell phone pinged—it was a text from Gina. The manuscript that April had been waiting for had just got delivered to the office.

"Great!" April declared to Blake, "The book that I have been waiting for is in; we can pick it up at the office on the way home from shopping." Blake would normally been perturbed by her mother if she worked when they were together but over the last year or so, Blake had learned that her mom really loved her job and was good at it. Her job became a crutch for her when Blake's dad died, and it helped her mom cope with the loss. At least when April was working from home, she was reading most of the time so it wasn't like she was on the phone all the time like other business professional parents.

"Is Wanda working today?" Blake asked her mom. Wanda Hutton was the main secretary at the office. She was about 30 years old and was a character. She kept dyeing her hair, and this month, it was a deep burgundy. Wanda was single and loved it. She liked going out on the town and dating a lot of different guys. She was really pretty, and that is why she was able to get a lot of dates. However, she was kind of quirky, which led to too few second dates. Wanda didn't seem to mind, and she was a fun individual to be around. Blake liked hanging out with Wanda at the office whenever she went there to see her mom.

"Yes, I'm pretty sure she is there today," April replied, with a smile. She too liked Wanda, and really appreciated her for her dedication to the company and her friendship.

"She has been kicking around the idea of coloring her hair again. I think she wants to dye it pumpkin orange," April told Blake.

Blake wrinkled her nose at the thought of the color. "Yuck!" she laughed, and said, "I don't know if I would like it. Wanda has a cute, round face, and I think it might actually look like she has a pumpkin instead of a head."

April smirked at her daughter's assessment of the color. "You're probably right; you are just going to have to delicately explain that to her." Blake nodded her head in agreement. "I will do my best."

The pair was approaching Macy's, and of course, April wanted to go in and shop. She loved going in and seeing all the different departments. With online shopping ripping into the customer base of the department store giants, April still loved walking through the stores and physically touching the items and trying stuff on. When Blake was a little girl, April was hard pressed to get Blake to enjoy shopping but in the last couple of years, Blake was enjoying it more and more. It was something that they both could do and spend the day together.

About forty-five minutes and two full shopping bags later, April and Blake exited the store and continued to walk in search of another shopping adventure. Blake looked over at her mother and declared, "Hey mom, I'm getting kind of hungry. Can we eat soon?" April looked at her phone for the time, and it was almost 2:30 pm. The clouds were starting to thicken and it was looking overcast. "You bet we can," April agreed. "Why don't we go over to the pizza place we love a couple of blocks away? Do you feel like pizza?" Blake excitedly nodded her head in a 'yes', and they started walking in the direction of the pizza place. As they strolled down the sidewalk, April felt a small drop of rain hit her forehead. She instinctively looked up to the sky and another one hit her eyelid. They were only a block away or so from the restaurant, so she wasn't too concerned about it, but she did hasten her step just a little bit.

As she and Blake rounded the corner of the block, April noticed a homeless girl sitting cross-legged with a sign that said "Please help me." As she glanced at the girl on the way by, she mentally noted that she was just a little older than Blake. April hated seeing homeless people, especially when there were kids in the mix. April turned her gaze back to the street and the direction in which she was heading. After taking several steps away from the homeless girl, a clear voice in her head declared, "*Go to her.*" April stopped abruptly and her eyes widened. The voice in her head sounded like her deceased husband, Nick. It was so clear and definite. Blake, taking notice of her mom, asked, "Are you ok, mom?"

The familiar voice that had been absent from her life for the past 4 years resounded in her head again, but this time a little louder, almost commanding, "*Please, go to her.*" She looked back and forth, but did not see anyone that could have said those words, especially in his voice.

Shocked and unsettled, April slowly turned around and looked in the direction of the homeless girl. "I-I don't know," stammered April, her heart pounding, "something weird just happened." Blake grabbed her mother's hand and with a look of increasing concern asked, "Why? What's up?"

April continued to stare at the homeless girl, and noticed that there were a couple of tears gradually falling down her cheek. "I think that we should go and talk to her." April's mind was still reeling from the sound of her husband's voice. Blake followed her mother's stare, and with a hint of disbelief, asked, "Seriously?" Blake couldn't get a handle on her mother's current emotional condition. "Do you know her or something?"

April turned her head towards her daughter, and said, "No, but I think that I need to talk to her." Blake didn't know what was going on, nor had she seen her mother act this way before. The color in her face was a shade paler. "Ok mom, let's go and say 'hi.'" The two of them headed back the way that they had just come. April walked up to the homeless girl, and said, "Hi... My name is April. What's yours?"

The girl moved her head slightly looking up towards the voice, and saw a woman and a young girl, who she presumed was her daughter, standing before her. They were well dressed and she could see that the woman had a genuine look of concern on her face. For a second, the girl thought about making up a fake name, because of her current situation, but something in the way the woman looked at her persuaded her to state the truth.

"Hi there," the girl said, "my name is Claire."

CHAPTER TWO

APRIL REACHED HER HAND IN THE DIRECTION OF CLAIRE IN an offer to help her up. Claire hesitated for a brief second, but slowly stretched out her hand. April gradually pulled her to an upright position, and you could see Claire grimace as the muscles in her legs and knees tightened in protest. She had been sitting in that position for quite a while and her body was a bit sore. While Claire rubbed her knees and calf muscles, she bent down and grabbed her hat with the money in it. She hurriedly stuffed the money in her pockets and then drew her attention back to April.

April took a quick second to examine the appearance of Claire. She was dirty and somewhat dingy but overall not a complete mess. She was, however, a bit underdressed for this weather. Being a mother, April couldn't help notice that she was a little underweight and her skin was a bit pale.

"Is there anyone with you?" April questioned with concern, and then added, "Do you have any family I can call for you?"

Claire didn't think that April was with Child Protective Services or with the police, just by the way that she was dressed, but she could not be too careful. She didn't know if any local law enforcement agency was looking for her and she certainly didn't want to find out. "Why do you want to know?" Claire asked with just a hint of suspicion in her voice.

April detected the concern in Claire's voice and tried to reassure her by saying, "No, no reason, just concern."

For some unknown reason, Claire believed her. She could see the genuine look in her eyes.

"I'm alone," Claire declared matter-of-factly, hoping that this wasn't a set up.

"What is your last name?" April questioned.

Pausing to wipe her nose, Claire said with a hint of caution, "It's Forrester. My name is Claire Forrester."

April gazed in Claire's eyes, and could see that she had probably been through a lot in her short life, and was starting to get curious about her story. At that point, April could feel Blake's hand brushing against her hip. She blinked and became aware that she had not introduced Blake.

"Oh, sorry, Claire, this is my daughter, Blake," April placed her hand on Blake's shoulder, and with the other hand, pointed in the direction of Claire.

Blake smiled and raised her right hand in a wave, and said, "Hi."

Claire reflectively raised her hand in a wave, and responded with, "Hey."

April did not know who this girl was or why she had heard Nick' voice inside her head, but she wasn't going to let this go. It was obvious that Claire was down and out, and definitely could use some help, but what was April supposed to do about it? It wasn't like April was uncompassionate about the plight of the homeless; in fact, she was quite the opposite. She and Blake had volunteered in soup kitchens during previous holidays, and were empathic to their plight. However, she and Blake would go back to their high-rise apartment and continue with their lives and not really give the homeless another thought, until the next holiday.

Blake decided to speak up, and said, "How long have you been out here?"

Claire looked at Blake, and replied, "I've been on the streets for a few weeks, and I've been on my own for about four months or so." She ever so slightly glanced away as a feeling of shame mixed with fear washed over her. Saying it out loud kind of put it into perspective for her.

"That sucks," Blake answered back in a way that a 14-year-old girl would. Blunt honesty.

"Blake," April said, in a voice that let her know that she probably should not have said it in that way.

Claire waved it off, and said, "No, it's ok. She's right. It does suck." There was no need to dance around the circumstances of her being homeless. The sprinkles of rain started to intensify, and it was then that April could see Claire's teeth were starting to chatter.

"Oh, Claire, you must be cold and hungry?" April stated the obvious. "Blake and I were just going to have some pizza for lunch. Would you care to join us?"

Claire wanted to say no, but she was truly cold and hungry. Besides, April and Blake seemed nice enough. She did put "Please help me" on her sign, and if she could get a hot meal out of it, then why not.

Claire patted her pockets as if looking for something, and said, "I'll have to check my schedule but don't think that I have anything going on right now."

Blake snorted a chuckle at what Claire just said, and April had to grin. Even though Claire was in dire straits, she could still make light of her predicament. Claire looked down at her sign and for a second thought about taking it with her. She stared at it for a couple of seconds trying to decide, but she turned her attention back to the mother and daughter, and said, "Lead the way."

As they began the walk, April remembered that she had just purchased a cute scarf at Macy's and she reached in the bag and pulled it out. "Here, wear this. It will help keep you warm till we get to the restaurant. "Oh, ok," Claire stammered, "thanks." As she wrapped it around her shoulders and back like a cape, Claire got a glimpse of the sales tag. Regular price was $159.99, but it was on sale for $99.99. She couldn't believe that April just spent $100.00 for one scarf. It was Burberry, and it was the nicest piece of clothing that she had ever put on. When Claire and her mother did go clothes shopping, it was at the Goodwill, and they never spent more than $20 at one time.

April took the lead as they walked with Claire next to her. Blake was walking slightly behind them. "How old are you?" April asked.

"I just turned sixteen in July," Claire responded. Her birthday was on July 10, and it was one of the worst birthdays of her life, but Claire was not going to bring that up right now.

"I'm fourteen," Blake chimed in, as a way to make conversation. "My birthday is on September 15." Blake said as a way to answer the question that was not asked.

April thought that Claire was close to Blake's age, and she could see they were about the same size, but unlike Blake, Claire had more of a look of maturity about her.

With only about half a block left to go to get to the restaurant, the rain began to fall. April reached for the two umbrellas that were in her briefcase bag, and handed one to Blake. She opened her umbrella and placed it over her head and shared it with Claire. The trio walked the rest of the way at a hurried pace, and made it to the building with the pizza place. April closed her umbrella, and headed to the hostess' stand. Fortunately, there wasn't a wait so they got a table right away. The waitress came over with 3 glasses of water, and asked them what they wanted to drink. Blake immediately ordered a Coke while April ordered a diet Coke. April looked over at Claire, silently saying 'get whatever you want'. "I'll take a Coke," Claire told the waitress. The waitress nodded, and replied, "Here are some menus for you. My name is Cindy, and I'll be back in a minute to take your order."

Blake picked up the menus from the table and handed one to her mom and the other one to Claire. "I always order the meat lover's pizza here," Blake said to Claire, "but look at the menu to see what you want."

"Yes, Claire, please look it over and pick out whatever you want," April instructed.

"Ok," Claire said. Opening her menu, she started looking it over. The menu was 4 pages, and it was amazing to see all the different kinds of pizza that there actually were. There was a BLT pizza, a veggie pizza, all kinds of different meats and cheeses. There was even a tofu pizza. After a minute of intense examination, Claire made her choice. "I'll think I'll have the pepperoni pizza with sausage, if that's ok?" April looked at Claire, and said, "Of course it is, and get whatever you want."

The waitress came back and took their orders. April ordered the Chicken Parmesan, Blake ordered the meat's lovers, of course, and Claire ordered her choice. After the waitress left the table, Claire removed the Burberry scarf and set it on the seat next to her. She looked at her hands and wrists, and noticed how dirty they were. "I'm going to go to the bathroom to wash my hands and stuff," she said to April, but the way she said it was almost a question.

"Sure, of course," April said. "The bathrooms are over there, just on the other side of the hostess' podium," April said, pointing back in the direction of the door through which they had come in.

"Ok, thanks," Claire said.

When Claire was out of earshot, Blake reached over to touch her mother's hand, and said, "So mom, what's with the sudden urge for charity?"

"I'm not really sure," confessed April, "something strange happened when I passed her, and I had to go see her." April didn't want to tell her daughter that she had heard her deceased father's voice in her head as clear as day. She would soon, but April had to figure out what was going on too. "She obviously needs a warm meal and some clothes."

"I get that mom, but we don't know anything about her," Blake replied, with a hint of caution.

"I realize that, dear, but the mom in me makes my heart go out to her," April replied. A few minutes went by and Blake looked in the direction of the bathroom. "I think that I am going to go check on her."

"Ok, but be nice," April told her.

"Of course," Blake chided, "I simply want to make sure that she is alright," Blake said, as she slid out from the booth and made her way to the bathroom. Blake slowly opened the door and saw Claire at the sink, scrubbing her wrists and arms with the paper towel. Claire looked up as the door opened, and saw that it was Blake coming in. "You don't realize how dirty you are until you start cleaning yourself," Claire confessed.

Blake grinned at Claire, and replied, "Yeah, I can only imagine." She then looked at the mirror and at Claire's reflection, and noticed some dirt just above her eyes, and said, "Here, let me help." Blake grabbed a paper towel from the dispenser and moistened it at one of the faucets in the sink. She pumped some of the lavender smelling soap from the box on the wall and started to dab it on Claire's forehead where the smudge of dirt was. As Blake wiped away the dirt, she began to really realize what it might be like to be living on the streets. She tried to imagine not having a bathroom readily available, nor to be able to take a shower on a daily basis. Heck, who knows the last time that Claire had a hot shower.

Blake finished wiping Claire's forehead, and said, "There, that's better." Claire looked at her reflection and looked at Blake's, and said, "Thanks."

The girls returned to the table where April was looking at her phone. As the girls got back into the booth, she asked, "Everything ok?"

"Yes," Claire responded, "I'm good," and then subconsciously looked at her wrists and arms.

"Good," smiled April.

After a few minutes, the pizzas were delivered to the table and they looked delicious. Claire's eyes widened just a little at the presentation. She would get to have an entire small pizza to herself. As they consumed their first slice of the pizza, April asked Claire, "So, I don't want to pry, but what's your story? Why are you on the streets?" You could tell by the way April spoke that she seemed genuinely concerned. Claire paused a second and swallowed her slice of pizza that she was chewing on, and sighed.

"It's kind of a long story," Claire began. She really didn't know where exactly to start. It was like her entire life since birth was a blueprint for how she got to this point. She subtly looked in an upward direction as if she could see in the ceiling of the restaurant a memory that would kick off this story.

"Ok, here it goes." At first, Claire wanted to hold back, but as she started, the words just kind of flowed out like a river whose dam has just opened.

＊ ＊

"MY MOM ALWAYS TOLD ME THAT MY DAD LEFT HER WHEN he found out that she was pregnant," Claire began. "My mother did the best she could for a few years, but couldn't quite grasp the whole 'being a mother' thing." Claire paused and took a bite of the pizza, and chased it down with a sip of Coke. "I mean, she did try, but life was hard for her. She was hooked on drugs and alcohol from the beginning, and it was always a battle for her to find her way." April stared intently at Claire as she talked, immersed in the story that Claire was telling. "I remember once that when I was about 5 or 6, my mom left me home alone for a day and a half. I didn't realize how bad that was at the time, but when she did come home, she hugged me and was crying and telling me she had been in some trouble and that she wouldn't do it again." As Claire recounted that particular memory, Blake looked at her mom as if to say wow. Continuing, Claire said, "But of course, there were many, many other times since that one." At that, April asked, "I can't believe that you never got hurt being that young and by yourself?"

"I know right?" Claire answered her with just a hint of pride. "I remember I accidently broke a couple of things, but I did not get cut or hurt. I remember just playing with my doll all day long and watching TV. If I got hungry, I would just eat some cereal out of the box or maybe some chips." April couldn't fathom how a mother could leave her small child alone. There were just too many things that could go wrong, and without a parent or adult supervision, it could be actually dangerous.

Blake just sat there listening intently as well. It was hard for her to grasp too. No way would her mom have left her alone, in fact, to this day, Blake has to text her mom when she arrives at school, and if April isn't home when she gets home from school, then Blake has to text her mom that she has returned home.

"Where is your mom now?" Blake wanted to know.

"Well, you see," answered Claire, with just a hint of reservation. "She has been in jail for the past 4 years." Claire placed her elbows on the table and elaborated, "The drugs and everything that goes with it finally caught up with my mom. She was arrested several times for shoplifting and breaking into parked cars. After breaking her probation a couple of times, she was put in jail for three months." Claire continued, almost as if she were reading from a teleprompter. "It was then that I was taken away and placed with Child Protective Services and into foster homes. I kept thinking that my mom would pick me up soon and I could go home. When my mom did get out, she found out where I was and tried to leave with me. You can imagine what it was like when the cops showed up and took her away again."

At that point, April asked, "You must have been really upset seeing your mom being hauled off by the police again?" Claire nodded her head in agreement, and continued, "Yes, and that's not the half of it." Blake and April could see in Claire's eyes that the story was not even close to being over.

"A couple of months later, when I was outside at recess eating lunch at school, my mom came up to me when I was at a picnic table next to the playground, and said that I could go home with her. She told me that the judge gave her permission. Of course, she hadn't gotten permission at all. I didn't realize then that she had been drinking and was high on marijuana." Claire blinked back a tear as she spoke, not wanting to give in to the emotion that was welling up inside of her. She had stored this memory away in a deep part of her mind. She never forgot it; but it was always a distant thought of her childhood. Talking about it now and witnessing the reactions of these two strangers made it come to life again. "So, here we were, driving away from the school, not knowing at the time that the teacher had called the police because my mom had not had permission to take me."

April glanced at Blake, and could see that her daughter was listening intently. April could almost guess what was going to happen, but sat on the edge of her seat, letting Claire continue, "When the patrol car turned on its lights and siren, and made a U-turn to chase us, guess what my mother did?"

"What?" Blake asked with wonder.

"She stomped on the gas and tried to outrun the police," Claire replied.

Blake involuntarily let out a little gasp. "Holy cow!" Blake exclaimed, "Are you serious?"

Claire nodded her head in the affirmative. "Yeah, unfortunately."

April chimed in, and asked, "So, what happened next?"

Claire's voice cracked slightly, as she answered, "We raced down the street with my mother driving erratically. She swiped a couple of parked cars, denting and scraping them as she passed. She was coming up to a red light at an intersection and she yanked the wheel hard to the right, to make the turn in front of oncoming cars. Well, her reaction time was slower than what she assumed, so we slammed into an oncoming car with the driver's side of our car." Claire clapped her hands together to make a smacking sound. Both April and Blake blinked, startled by the clap. "The good news was that my mom and I only had minor injuries. The bad news was that the woman in the other car wasn't so lucky. She had several broken bones and cuts on her forehead."

"Oh my God," April muttered, "I am glad that you didn't get seriously hurt." Claire silently agreed with her and reached for another piece of her pizza. "My mother was arrested, and that was the beginning of the end of us. She got serious jail time for that." Pausing to take a bite of her pizza, Claire raised her hand with the slice, and as she bit down on it, a layer of cheese and pepperoni slid off and landed squarely on her lap. Claire sighed and grabbed a napkin to clean up her pants. Placing the now dirty napkin on the table, she said, "She has been locked up ever since."

Claire could see the compassion in the eyes of her dinner companions, and felt almost as if she could lower her guard ever so slightly. Claire concluded the story by saying, "It's been a few years since I last visited my mother in prison. She was obviously clean from the drugs and alcohol, but mentally, she will never fully recover. My mom told me how sorry she was for everything that has happened in my life and that I should move on without her. She told me that I should not come back to visit her, and instead let her go. Of course, I resisted that idea, but she said that I had a decent foster family, and that I should let them raise me. I cried, but deep down I realized that she was doing what she thought was right. She told me that she loved me, and I told her that I loved her, and that was the last time we spoke."

"I'm really sorry about all of this," April said sincerely. "It must have been very traumatic for you…"

"I guess it was. I mean, it just happened, and I had to deal with it." Claire's words sounded more mature than her years. "I've been through a lot and it just seems like the last few weeks have really taken a toll on me." Claire turned her head to look out of the window at the city skyline. The clouds were darker than when they had entered the restaurant, and the rain was now falling at a steady rate. It was as if the weather was a form of measure for the direction Claire's life was taking. Claire turned her attention back to April, and forced her lips to form somewhat of a smile as she declared, "And here we are."

"Yes, here we are," agreed April, smiling back at Claire. The three of them ate in silence for a few moments, as the story of Claire's life lay heavy on their hearts. The waitress approached the table, and asked them if they needed anything. April politely waved her hand and said, "No, I think we're good. Everything was delicious." The waitress left the table and a thought popped into April's mind. Now what? She had bought Claire some lunch, but it was cold and rainy outside. Should she offer Claire money? What good would that do in the long run? April was intrigued by Claire's story, and couldn't picture her daughter, Blake, enduring anything close to that. Before she had time to think more about it, April blurted out, "Would you like to spend the night with us?"

Blake, unsure about what to say, looked at her mother and then at Claire. She then nodded her head in a 'yes' to reinforce her mom's question.

Claire's eyes widened for a split-second, and she blinked once and stuttered, "I–I don't know. You have already bought me lunch, and I really appreciate it. I don't want to impose on you guys."

Following in her mother's footsteps, Blake rebutted, "Please, it will be fun. We can watch a movie or something."

April pressed on, "No, really. It will be fun. I wouldn't feel good if we just left you to fend for yourself in this weather." As if the sky was on April's side, the sound of thunder began rumbling through the restaurant.

Claire really had no reason to decline. In fact, this was a dream come true. She would have a warm, dry place to stay tonight. April and Blake were nice, and seemed like they actually cared.

"Sure, sounds good, why not?" Claire finally declared.

April smiled at Claire's answer and reached for the wallet in her purse to get her credit card to attend to the check. This is going to be fun, April thought to herself.

"Sweet," Blake said, and smiled at Claire.

The waitress came over to the table and collected the check and its payment from April, and left saying she would be right back. The restaurant was getting busier and now there were patrons waiting in the area just inside the front door. After a couple of minutes, the waitress returned with the check, and thanked them for coming in this afternoon.

"Ok ladies, time to go," April said as she slid from the seat and grabbed her purse and shopping bags.

"Oh, Claire, I hope you don't mind, but I have to stop at my office for a little bit before we head back home. Is that ok?" April asked, as she remembered that the new manuscript was waiting for her.

Claire reached for the Burberry scarf and looked at April, and said, "Again, I think I have time to fit that in today."

"I think that we will take a cab to the office," April said, as the rain outside intensified and she thought to herself that she didn't want Claire exposed to more of this weather without the proper attire. The scarf helped, but it was not a coat.

"Sounds great to me," Blake said, as the semi-lazy teenage side of her agreed with her mom's decision. The three of them walked a few steps to the curb, and April hailed a cab. A yellow-checkered vehicle stopped almost immediately for them, and they quickly climbed into the back seat. April gave the driver the address of the office, and then they were on their way.

CHAPTER THREE

THE ELEVATOR DOORS OPENED AT THE 27ᵀᴴ FLOOR OF THE Willis Tower Building where Priscilla Publishing was located. There were offices and cubicles spread through the entire floor. Strategically placed in view of the elevator was the reception desk. Seated behind the counter was Wanda Jennings. She was wearing an earpiece and was talking through it. The streaks of burgundy that filtered her hair reflected brightly due to the office lighting. As April and the girls walked up to her, Wanda noticed them and smiled as she continued talking with the person on the other end of the line. You could tell that the conversation was wrapping up, so April grabbed a few sheets of paper that were for her—they were on one of the paper tray holders on the other side of the counter.

When Wanda finished her phone call, she pressed the button on the side of the earpiece to terminate the connection, and then spoke up with a little excitement in her voice, "Good afternoon, April. How's it going?" Not allowing April to answer, Wanda continued, "The manuscript is sitting in your office on your desk." Then looking at Blake, and doing a happy, quirky wave, Wanda said, "Hi Blake."

"I'm good," said April, now that she could answer.

"Hi Wanda," Blake answered back, "How are you doing today?"

"Busy, very busy. It been kind of a crazy day, but you know me, I love it around here when its chaotic," responded Wanda.

April looked at Claire and back at Wanda, and introduced her. "Wanda, this is Claire. She is a new friend of ours." Wanda gave Claire a quick glance, smiled back at her, and said, "Hello Claire, nice to meet you." Claire grinned at her, and said 'hi' back to her. Her first impression of Wanda was that she seemed really cool and probably was a lot of fun to be around. She was like that one kid you knew back in school that wasn't totally popular, but everyone still liked to be around. That was Wanda.

April led the way to her office, and once inside, immediately went for the manuscript. The office was filled with old and new books on wall units that were custom-made. There were pictures and sculptures mixed in with the books as well. The walls were painted a light grey with black and Tiffany teal accents sprinkled throughout the room. April may have been an editor, but she did have good taste when it came to interior design as well as clothes fashion.

"Wow, this is really nice," Claire said, with a hint of wonder. "It must be really cool to have an entire office to yourself." Claire examined every facet of the office, and then stepped over to one of the books and carefully grabbed it out of its place and looked at the cover. Rubbing her hands over the spine and then slowly flipping through the pages, Claire became more excited as she continued to look over the books. "I realize that it probably doesn't seem like it, but I love reading books. I could read an entire book in the course of one night," Claire said to April.

"Really?" April asked, sounding surprised and excited.

"Yeah," Claire said proudly. "I would prefer to sit in a library all day, than be at either of my foster homes." Continuing, Claire subconsciously swallowed, and then said, "The way that books would take me to different places and people, and make the mundane, humdrum existence of my life much less so..." At that, she kind of laughed, and then sighed. "I think it started when I was left alone by my mom all those times."

Blake grabbed one of the books closest to her, and rapidly rifled through it. "My mom tried to get me to be like her, and wanted me to read a ton of books, but I'm not like her when it comes to this. Don't get me wrong, I like to read but I also like Facebook and YouTube," Blake said matter-of-factly.

April's left eyebrow rose in what could only be the excitement of a book-worm on hearing about Claire's fondness for reading. "What kind of books do you like to read?" April asked curiously.

Placing the book she had in her hand back, and then using her index finger to go across a row of books on another shelf, she replied instinctively, "I like fiction, mainly fantasy fiction. However, I do like most of the classics. *The Adventures of Tom Sawyer, Pride and Prejudice, Little Women,* you know, stuff like that." If truth were told, Claire liked just about anything in book form. She would read books about science and history too. Most of her childhood was spent reading. That part of her life helped her cope with the reality that was her life.

At that moment, Wanda appeared in the frame of the office doorway, and asked April, "Are you here? I know that you are off today, but I have Susan Goodman on the phone. She really wants to talk with you."

Nodding her head yes, April said, "Sure, I have been waiting to get in touch with her." April looked at Blake, and asked, "Is it ok? I'll only be a couple of minutes." Susan Goodman was an author who was almost finished with her latest novel. However, she constantly needed moral support from her editor, April. The book was turning out to be one of her best, and April wanted to make sure that the final chapters would be crafted with as much creativity as the first ones. Susan had a habit of rushing the last chapters just to get done. There were times that April had to encourage her to add more content.

"No problem, mom," Blake replied, adding, "it's ok." Blake was accustomed to her mom being on the phone. It was part of her job. Even though she promised that she would be off today, Blake knew that this was important, so it was totally fine. "I'll show Claire around while you are on the phone."

Blake waved her hand to signal Claire to follow her outside her mom's office. Obediently, Claire followed her out into the hallway and then they proceeded towards the front counter where Wanda's station was. Wanda had settled into her chair and started typing really fast on her keyboard. Blake strolled up to the counter and placed her shoulders on it. "So, my mom tells me that you want to color your hair again?" It was obvious by the sound of Blake's voice that she didn't quite want her to do it. "You know I can't keep one color for too long. It's not in my DNA," Wanda quipped.

"I know it isn't, Wanda," Blake agreed, "But do you think orange is the way to go?" It was the way that Blake questioned that made Wanda smirk. "Your mother put you up to this, didn't she?" Blake purposely blinked like she was offended that Wanda would think that, but Wanda could see that April did say something. Wanda looked over to Claire, and asked her, "What do you think? How would orange look?" Wanda wanted to know.

Claire, who really didn't have an opinion, simply said, "I'm not sure but if you want to do it, go for it."

"You know something, I like you. That's what I've been thinking. Just go for it." And with that she wrinkled her nose in acknowledgment of her opinion.

"I tried," Blake smirked at Wanda, and then turned to leave the station so that the duo could continue with the tour of the office. There was a hallway on the other side of the elevators that they had just used. Walking down through that hallway, Blake pointed out the lunchroom that was recently redone with new appliances and better tables and chairs. They had brought in two new vending machines. One of them housed candy bars and chips. The other one contained gourmet sandwiches and bagels. So, if an associate forgot his or her lunch or someone was too busy to run out to grab something, then it was possible to jet down to the lunchroom and get something decent to eat.

Blake could see that Claire was impressed with the size of the room and the amount of cool stuff that was in there. Mounted on each corner of the lunchroom were big flatscreen TVs. Two of them had news on, from separate networks, while the other two TVs were airing a talk show and a sports channel.

The amount of money that had gone into the room's design and size was seriously impressive.

Blake walked up to a clear-door refrigerator and grabbed two bottles of water. She stretched out her left hand with one of the bottles and handed it to Claire. "Here you go." Claire accepted the water, and said, "Thank you." Blake removed the cap of her water bottle, and said, just in case Claire was wondering, "The beverages in this cooler are free for everyone. It's a benefit of working here."

Claire followed suit and took a drink from her bottle. The girls then proceeded to the next room, which was the copy room. There were several printers—they were the size of washers and dryers. The amount of printed paper that was generated out of that room on an hourly basis was astounding. There were several cabinets mounted on the back wall that contained cases of papers, ink cartridges, labels, and all sorts of forms. Over in the far right corner, bending down with his body halfway into the belly of one of the printers was Henry Coleman. Blake didn't know Henry's last name. Ever since she could remember, Henry was just 'Henry'. He was a little person, about 30 years old, and was the resident tech expert. If anything malfunctioned in that room, Henry could fix it in the blink of an eye... most of the time. Unfortunately, this was not one of those times.

Blake took a few steps closer to the printer that Henry was working on, and said, "Hi Henry."

At the sound of a familiar voice, Henry's head jerked up almost hitting the interior frame of the printer.

"Oh, hey," Henry said, as he recognized Blake. "Long time, no see."

"I know it's been a while. How have you been?" Blake asked. The last time that Blake had talked to Henry was about four weeks ago, when she had visited her mom on a working Saturday, to have lunch with her.

Wiping a small amount of ink from a damaged cartridge, Henry got up, and said, "You know how it is. All work and no play for me," Henry lied.

"Yeah, right," Blake countered. She knew that Henry did work hard, but he also played hard. He was great at his job and everyone liked him. But he didn't let it rule his life. He had a lot of friends and went out quite a bit.

"Ok. Maybe you're right," Henry confessed. "Maybe I do play a little." The pun on his size fell short—the girls didn't get it.

"Henry, this is Claire," Blake said, as she pointed at Claire.

"Pleased to meet you," Henry smiled, and extended his arm to shake her hand, but realized there were still several inkblots smeared across his palm. He apologetically pulled it back and wiped his hands again with the rag. Claire had taken a step closer to accept Henry's hand, but when he pulled it away, she stopped and decided just to say 'hi'.

After a few more wipes with the rag, Henry decided that his hands were clean as they were going to get, and asked, "What brings you guys in here today? I thought that your mom had the day off today?"

"She does," Blake confirmed, "But we just stopped in because she had to pick up something that just arrived today. I think it's a manuscript or something."

At that point, one of the printers next to Henry started to beep in alarm. Henry turned around and rapidly pressed a few buttons and the noise stopped. Nodding his head in satisfaction with the result, he turned his attention back to Blake and Claire. "Do you have any plans for the weekend?"

Claire sent Blake a nervous glance, not really knowing how to answer. Blake took a second to think about it, and then said, "We are going to hang out and watch movies and stuff." Blake didn't want to say anything about Claire because, first and foremost, she didn't want to embarrass her. Secondly, she didn't quite know how to explain it. I mean to pick up a total stranger and invite them into your home for the night was kind of weird.

Picking up on the uncertainty of Claire, Blake grabbed Claire's arm, and said, "Hey, why don't we binge-watch that new series on Netflix? You know, the one that I really want to watch." Claire didn't know if Blake was faking it or not but the gesture was nice. Claire grinned and said, "Yeah, sure. That sounds like fun."

Henry's cell phone vibrated at that moment and he pulled it out of his phone case. His eyes quickly glanced over the content of the text, and said, "Duty calls." He started to walk in the direction of the door when he turned towards Claire, and said, "It was very nice to meet you, Claire. Have fun this weekend."

"Yeah, me too," Claire replied genuinely.

When the door closed, Blake piped up, and said, "Don't worry, Claire, we will have fun tonight. We will watch a movie and have some popcorn." Blake wanted to reassure Claire that things were going to be alright at least for tonight.

Claire was slowly getting excited about the night. Sleeping in a warm place and watching TV seemed trivial, but when you hadn't done it for weeks, it was definitely something to look forward to.

"I just want to thank you guys for letting me spend the night tonight. I really appreciate it." Claire told Blake sincerely.

"No problem," Blake replied.

The door to the copy room opened again, and an associate that Blake didn't recognize walked in to grab papers that she had printed. Blake took that moment to signal Claire to exit the room and continue on with the tour. Just further down the hall was another room—a conference room that contained a long oak table that had six chairs on each side and one on each end. The chairs seemed to be hand-carved and expensive. Blake led Claire into the room and pointed at the chair at the end. Blake went to the chair at the other end and sat down. Facing each other from across the table, Blake picked up a pen from a mug sitting on the table and pulled a blank pad of paper closer to her. Imitating an executive, Blake looked at Claire, and asked, "So, you want to be a writer, tell me a little about yourself?" You could hear the humour in her voice.

Playing along, Claire sat up straighter trying to look more dignified. "Yes, let's see. I'm homeless, and these two complete strangers just picked me up and invited me to their house for the night. I'll let you know how it goes." Both the girls chuckled at that and then Blake began to write something down on the notepad. "Please continue," Blake politely prodded.

"Oh, ok," Claire blinked, and focused her eyes a little more intensely on Blake.

"Um, let's see. Even though I'm a little desperate right now, I still feel like any other teenager. I mean I like to watch TV and read books. If it wasn't for the fact that I'm alone, I could have been somewhat like you." As the realization of what she had just said struck Claire, she spoke out two words that had just hit home. "I'm alone."

Blake could see on Claire's face the impact of what she had just said. To be alone, totally alone. No support team, no one to help you when you need it, no one to lift you up when you are down. Blake could name off about half a dozen or so people that she could depend on just off the top of her head.

"There is no one that you can turn to?" Blake sincerely wanted to know. "You don't have an aunt or uncle somewhere that could possibly help you?"

Claire's stare turned somewhat inward as she reflected on that. It was only her mom when she was younger, and there were no relatives that she could remember. "No, no one really. I mean it's only been my mom and me. After she went to prison, it became a couple of foster families. I've never known any other biological relatives."

"What about the foster families?" Blake asked, as she thought about what Claire said. "Can't you go back to one of them?"

The look that Claire gave Blake when she mentioned foster families drew a concerned query. Blake said, "What? What happened?"

The truth about her last foster family was something that she was not prepared to share with Blake right now. It was the reason why she was homeless and believed herself better off on her own.

"Let's just say that it was bad, and leave it at that for now," Claire muttered, as a hint of fear reflected in her eyes.

"Sure. Ok. I didn't mean to pry," Blake said, as she put the pen back into the mug and pushed her chair back slightly from the table. She didn't get up but she did put her hands on the pad of paper and rested her chin on them, all the while keeping an intent gaze on Claire.

Changing the subject, Claire turned the tables on Blake, and questioned, "So, what do you want to do when you grow up?"

"Well, you see, I really am getting into fashion," Blake honestly answered. "I also like baking, but I've only just started. I've made a few pies and cakes that turned out pretty good." With only 14 years of life under her belt, Blake was just starting to develop some skills and interests, but fashion seemed to be her primary passion.

"That's cool," Claire said.

"Yeah, I think so," Blake agreed, "I've been watching YouTube videos on baking cool cupcakes and things like that. It is fun putting ingredients together and seeing what the final result is."

The two girls sat in the conference room for a few more minutes talking about general likes and dislikes. You could hear giggles and small bouts of laughter coming from the room. Truth be told, it had been quite a while since Claire was this happy.

* *

AS APRIL FINISHED THE PHONE CALL WITH SUSAN, SHE pressed the button on the desk phone that disconnected the call, and smiled. Things were going really well. She liked the direction that Susan was taking with the novel, and it was going to be her best one yet. She rustled a few stacks of papers around her desk, grabbed the manuscript, and then headed out to find Blake and Claire. Walking down the hall, she headed towards the direction of Gina's office. The door was closed but April could see that she was in her office on her laptop typing away.

April knocked quietly on the door, and Gina called out, "Come in."

Seeing it was April, Gina stopped typing, and smiled, "Oh, hi, April. How's it going? I thought that you had the day off?" She then motioned for April to take a seat on one of the chairs facing her in the front of the desk.

"Good," April smiled, "and I do have the day off. I just came here to pick up the new manuscript that arrived today." She lifted the big envelope up from her lap slightly to show it was in her hands.

Gina clicked a few times on the trackpad of the laptop and closed the lid to give April her full attention.

"What can I do for you?" Gina wanted to know.

"We've been friends for a long time, right?" April slowly started.

"Oh shit, you're quitting," Gina's smile turned into a frown.

"No," chuckled April, "I would never leave this job."

Seeing the wave of relief that washed over Gina's face, April continued, "You have known me for a long time, and you were there for me when Nick died." April's voice rose an octave higher at the mention and memory of her dead husband. "Something weird happened today, and I want to tell you about it."

Intrigued, Gina's eyes focused on her friend, and she said, "Yes, go on."

April told Gina about how she and Blake were walking down the street and how she had heard the Nick's voice in her head as clear as day, how they took Claire out to lunch, and added that Claire would be spending the night with them.

"Am I crazy?" April asked. "I could not have heard his voice? Right?"

Gina held out her hands, and reaching out for them, April clutched her friend's hands. "No honey, you're not crazy. I've always believed that we are connected to our loved ones on the other side," Gina answered.

"But I wasn't even thinking about him at the time," April confessed. "I mean, he's always at the back of my mind. I feel his loss every day, but I was just shopping with Blake, having a normal conversation about the upcoming holidays."

Releasing April's hands and then leaning back in her office chair, Gina could only offer this to her friend, "I'm sure that there must be a good reason why he wanted you to meet Claire. Love has a way of finding those that are supposed to be in our lives. See what happens tonight and go from there."

April thought about it for a second, and replied, "I am troubled by what Claire has been through over the last few years. It's not a story that I would wish on anyone. But I don't know her at all."

"I don't know," Gina honestly answered, "I really don't. But you have one of the biggest hearts out of anyone that I know. So if you are supposed to help her in some way, then I'm confident that you will find it and do it."

April shrugged her shoulders, and sighed, "I guess you're right."

"Of course, I'm right." Gina declared, "As your friend and as your boss, I'm always right."

Rolling her eyes, April mockingly agreed, "Yes, you are always right."

Getting up from her chair, Gina stood up and waved April out of her office, "Now get out of here, and enjoy your day off."

"Ok, ok," April said. "I will. Going to go home and set the girls up with a movie while I read my manuscript."

Gina waved her finger in an accusing tone, and said, "No work; have fun."

Waving her finger back at Gina, April said, "You know that reading is fun for me. It's what I really enjoy doing."

Knowing that it was true, Gina's only rebuttal was, "Yes, but there are more things to life than books, sweetie." With that April opened the office door, and exited into the hallway.

Walking down the hallway looking for the girls, April scanned the office space and thought to herself how much she loved where she worked and what she was doing. She was at home here, and it showed in her work.

She came upon the conference room where the girls were, and April opened the door.

"You guys ready to head out?"

"You bet," declared Blake, as she bounced out of her seat.

"Sure," Claire smiled as she too got up from her chair, and headed towards April.

The trio walked down the hallway and to Wanda's desk.

"Bye, Wanda," April said, as they momentarily slowed down the pace to face Wanda.

Looking up, Wanda smiled and exclaimed, "Bye guys!" Looking directly at Claire she finished by saying, "It was nice meeting you again."

Waving and with a hint of a smile, Claire said, "Me too."

Blake pressed the 'Down' button on the elevator, and they waited for only ten seconds before the doors opened. There was no one in there and they got to enter right away. Now facing Wanda's desk, April pressed the button marked 'L' for lobby, and with Blake on her right side and Claire on her left, the doors to the elevator closed and the office scene disappeared from view.

CHAPTER FOUR

THE ELEVATOR DOORS OPENED TO REVEAL THE INSIDE OF
April and Blake's apartment. It was on the top floor and the elevator took them
directly to it. Claire's jaw dropped a little as she stepped out and the full apartment came into view. It was big, at least to Claire. It was an open floor plan
and there was a large, winding staircase towards the back that led to the second
story. It was incredible.

"Wow," Claire said in awe. "This is really nice."

Putting the two umbrellas in a vase next to the elevator, April smiled and
said, "Thanks, we really like living here. We've been here since before Blake was
born so it's been our home for over 15 years now."

Taking the scarf off, Claire handed it to April and said, "Thank you for
letting me use it."

Reaching out to grab it, April thought for a second and pulled her hand
back without the scarf, "You know what? You can keep it. I am giving it to you."

Taken aback, Claire asked, "Seriously?"

"Yes, I want you to have it," April genuinely said.

The look on Claire's face was priceless. You would have thought that
April had given Claire a piece of gold or a bundle of money.

"Cool. Thank you. It will be one of the nicest things I own."

Blake was walking towards the kitchen and she knew that her mother had bought that scarf for herself, but was happy that she was going to give it to Claire. "Besides, it brings out the color in your eyes," Blake started to reassure Claire.

Opening the refrigerator door, Blake grabbed bottled water and asked Claire if she wanted one.

"No thanks, I'm good right now," She responded, as she slowly walked around the apartment taking it all in.

The walls were exposed brick all around and the ceiling must have been 15 to 20 feet high. Just off the kitchen there was a huge dining room table with 8 chairs. It was sectioned off with its own roof with pillars. From there, it opened up into a huge living room that had an L-shaped couch that faced a stone fireplace with a 55-inch TV above the mantel. Examining the staircase she had seen when she first looked at the apartment, Claire noticed that it was twice as wide as a regular staircase. It was hardwood with a carpet runner up the middle as it wound up towards the second floor.

To the right of the staircase, a rounded wooden door was open, and beyond it was what looked like a den. Claire walked closer to it and discovered that it was more than a den—it was a library. It was similar to the one in April's office, but was bigger and contained older books.

While Claire looked around, April set the shopping bags down by the couch and walked towards Blake in the kitchen. She then went to the cabinet that housed her favorite coffee cup and removed it. She picked out a K-Cup from the K-Cup rack next to the Keurig coffee maker, and put it in and closed the lid. Her cup was a ceramic mug that had a picture of her and Blake on it. The picture was taken when Blake was just four years old, and had fallen asleep with her favorite book on her chest. It was a really cute picture. Years later, April had ordered the mug online and submitted that picture to be placed on it. It turned out to be one of her favorite coffee mugs.

When the cup was full and the machine halted its operation, April grabbed it and slowly brought it to her lips to drink it. Before taking a sip, she gently blew upon the hot liquid to cool it down. Taking a sip, April looked at Claire as she walked around the apartment. In the light of the apartment, she could see just how dirty Claire really was.

"Oh Claire," April said with compassion. "Why don't you take a hot shower before we pick out a movie?"

Claire just happened to be standing in front of the mirror that was hanging on the wall near the dining room table, and got a good look at her reflection.

"Sure, that would be great," said Claire, "It's been a little while, you know?" she stated matter-of-factly.

Setting her coffee mug down on the counter, April walked towards the stairs and waved for Claire to follow her. "I'll show you around upstairs, and set up the shower for you." As they proceeded upstairs, Claire asked Blake to grab the bags on the chair and follow them up.

"I think that you and Blake are about the same size, so while you are in the shower, we will find a couple of outfits that you can try on and wear while we wash your clothes for you," April said, as they reached the top.

The stairs led to a grand hallway with two doors on each side. The closest door on the right was April's master bedroom. It had two French doors that opened up to a large master bedroom with its own huge bathroom. It was a beautiful room that had a 'Tree of Life' metal sculpture placed on the wall above the headboard.

The next room on the right was Blake's. It was smaller than April's, but was still big by Claire's standards. It had a lot of pictures on the walls with a few posters of boy bands, and there was one of a coastal scene next to a beach. There was a cute desk with her laptop and iPad on it, and there was also a bathroom with a shower in it. Claire couldn't believe the number of bathrooms in just one apartment.

Across the hall from April's room was a bathroom. It had a garden tub and a shower as well. While it was a different style than the other two bathrooms, it was still elegant. The final room upstairs across from Blake's room was a spare bedroom. It didn't have a bathroom, but it was the same size as Blake's room, with a reverse layout. Instead of where the bathroom would be, there was a La-Z-Boy chair and a coffee table with a medium-sized TV. The entire room had a matching bed frame, long dresser, tall dresser, and two nightstands. There were three paintings in the room, and you could tell they were from the same artist. They were all landscapes with the view being somewhat blurry.

"This place is amazing!" Claire declared. "I can't believe how big it is—it looks like something out of a decor magazine."

"Tell me about it," Blake whined jokingly. "Every time I leave my plate or bowl sitting out, you would think that I committed a sin."

"No," April countered, "I'm not that bad."

Blake rolled her eyes, and said, "Oh no, mom. You're right. You're not that bad," and then with a smirk, glanced at Claire, and shook her head in a 'no'.

"Anyways," April said, changing the subject. "You can use this bathroom." She pointed at the bathroom across the master bedroom.

"Ok," Claire said.

April walked into the bathroom, and showed Claire how to work the shower. She turned it on for her and indicated which knob controlled the temperature. She opened the towel closet next to the shower and pulled out a couple of towels. "Here you go. You can use these to dry off." Claire took the towels and nodded her thanks to April. While exiting the bathroom, April said, "Blake and I will grab a couple of outfits and put them on the countertop for you."

"Thanks," Claire said.

"You're welcome," April replied.

April closed the door to the bathroom and walked into Blake's room. Her daughter was already shuffling through her clothes to find something for Claire. "What do you think of this?" Blake asked as she pulled out a pair of jeans and a sweatshirt. "Sure, honey. I think that would work," April replied. Setting that outfit down on the bed, Blake continued with her search. After going through a few more options, Blake pulled out a different pair of jeans with a sweater. "How's this?" she asked her mom again.

"Yes, that should work," April took a step closer to the closet, and rifled through it herself. After a few seconds, she pulled out a different sweater, and said, "This one might be better."

Nodding her agreement, Blake grabbed that sweater and put it with the jeans in her hands and then grabbed the outfit on the bed. Thinking for a second, Blake went to her dresser and opened a bag that had new underwear in it. She grabbed a pair of socks from the drawer next to the underwear drawer, and took the outfits, and headed to the bathroom. She knocked on the door, and said, "Hey Claire, it's me—Blake. I am just bringing in some clothes for you."

"Cool, thanks, this shower is amazing." It had two different spouts, and you could change the setting on the smaller one to pulsating.

"No prob." Blake said. "Take your time. My mom and I will be downstairs waiting for you."

"Ok, great," Claire said, as she took a second to pick out what shampoo she was going to use from the three big bottles that were stationed on the shelf in the shower. She filled her left hand with the one that had a lavender smell and slowly rubbed it all over her hair.

After about twenty minutes, Claire was finished with her shower, and chose an outfit—the jeans and a sweater. She used one of the towels to wrap her hair up, and headed downstairs. April and Blake were in the living room watching TV, flicking through the channels. April was on the reclining chair next to the couch while Blake was on the couch with her feet up on the ottoman. Claire walked around the far end of the couch and took her place next to Blake. She sat next to her but with somewhat of a distance between them.

"What do you want to watch?" April asked Claire.

"It doesn't matter to me," Claire said, adding, "I'm game for anything."

Blake pushed the button that started Netflix, and began to scroll through some of the movies under the heading of 'Recently added'. After about five minutes of searching, they picked *Pitch Perfect*. It was a good movie because it was fun and it made them laugh. About half-way through, April got up and went over to the kitchen, and placed a bag of popcorn in the microwave. When the first bag was done, she put in another bag, and combined both bags into a red bowl that had white stripes on, and the word 'Popcorn' written on it with popcorn pictured on it.

Walking back to her chair and consuming a handful of popcorn, April handed the bowl to Blake so that the girls could share it. Blake took some popcorn and handed it to Claire. Claire took the bowl and began taking the popcorn one piece at a time. As the movie played on, April would occasionally sneak a look at Claire to see how she was doing. In the beginning, she was a little guarded. But now, three quarters through the movie, Claire seemed a little more relaxed. She was becoming comfortable with her surroundings.

The movie ended around 7:30 pm. Blake got up from the couch, and went to the bathroom that was just off the kitchen opposite the dining room. Claire just sat on the couch, taking it all in. She glanced around and then noticed the 4x6 picture frame on the sofa table next to the couch. It was a picture of April and Blake when she was a small child. Standing next to April was a man that Claire guessed was her husband. He was fairly tall and well-built. He had light brown hair that was normal length for a guy and had deep blue eyes. All three of them were smiling in the picture, but his smile was the most sincere. It was as if he could make you smile just by looking at him. Carefully picking up the picture to take a closer look, Claire examined it intently.

"Is this your husband?" Claire politely asked April.

Smiling at the memory of that picture, April answered, "Yes. Yes it was."

"Was?" Claire asked curiously, but trying not to pry. "Did you get divorced?"

"Ah... No... He died in a car accident about four years ago," said April, with a slight pain in her voice. "His name was Nick. He was driving home from work one winter day, and it was sleeting out. A semi-truck in the other lane lost control and slid into my husband's lane." You could see April's eyes begin to moisten as she explained. "He died on the way to the hospital."

"I'm really sorry, April. I didn't know," Claire said, as she started to apologize for bringing it up.

"It's ok, Claire, you didn't know," April said, as she leaned towards Claire to look at the picture. "That picture was taken when we were on vacation at Mackinac Island in Michigan."

At that point, Blake exited the bathroom, catching the tail end of the discussion that her mom and Claire were having. "My dad and I had just eaten an entire brick of fudge just before we took that picture," she explained to Claire. "My dad wanted to take a picture of us because he said that we both had gained ten pounds, and he wanted visual proof that we had, in fact, done so." that the memory of it made Blake chuckle, as she continued. "So, the three of us stood next to the Fudge Store sign, and tried to give the biggest smiles while rubbing our bellies."

With a giggle and a smile, April interrupted, and said, "Yeah, and then the two of you got sick on the way home that night. Blake's little tummy was upset, and my husband, well, let's just say that we had to make several pit stops all the way home."

Placing the picture back onto the sofa table, Claire looked at Blake, and said, "Sounds like he was a fun dad?"

"Yes he was," Blake truthfully declared. "He was the absolute best."

"He really was," April wholeheartedly agreed. "Nick loved spending time with Blake. He loved spending time with me too." April added. "How he looked forward to coming home from work and having a family dinner with all three of us. He would cook most nights, and breakfast-dinners were his favorite."

Remembering those breakfasts, Blake chimed in, and said, "Oh my God, the scrambled eggs and ham that he would make. He would make a ton of them, and say that we couldn't leave the table until all the eggs were gone." Rubbing her belly like she was mentally trying to physically cram the eggs in there, Blake grinned and allowed herself to revisit that memory.

Claire sat back down on the couch and placed her hands on her lap, taking the stories about Nick all in. She was just going to ask another question about Nick when suddenly, and without time to prepare herself, she let out a big sneeze.

"Excuse me," Claire apologized. Then she sneezed again.

"Bless you," both April and Blake said simultaneously. April took a step closer to the end table next to the couch, and grabbed the box of tissue that was sitting there. Holding the box out towards Claire so that she could take some out, she said, "Here you go."

"Thanks," Claire said thankfully. After that second sneeze, Claire's sinus cavity started to fill up, and she began to feel a little stuffy. No big deal, Claire thought to herself.

Remembering what she was going to say, Claire asked, "What did Nick do for a living, if you don't mind me asking?"

April smiled, and said, "He was an architect. Nick loved walking through downtown Chicago, admiring the older buildings throughout the city. I remember one day when Blake was in first grade and we just dropped her off. We both had taken the day off, and we wandered around block after block with him pointing and taking pictures of all the architectural wonders that were sprinkled all around town."

April walked to a small hutch that was on the wall just inside the living room and pulled out an album. She walked over to Claire, and sat next to her on the couch. Flipping through the many pages, April showed Claire picture after picture of buildings. "You see nothing but buildings." Taking a small pause to flip through more pages, she continued, "Not one of these pictures in here is of the same building." The album consisted of approximately 100 pages, and if one really knew what they were looking for, they could confirm what April had just mentioned—a hundred different pictures.

Claire could see the pride in April's eyes, as she went through the album. "You must be reminded of him whenever you walk through the city." Claire said, realizing why April loved this city.

"Oh yes. Every day, Claire," April said, as she stood up to place the album back into the hutch when a laminated newspaper clipping slipped out from the album, and landed at Claire's feet. Picking it up in order to hand it back to April, she glanced at it, and noticed that it had the words, "Young boy, Nick Turner, saves pregnant teenage girl's life." It was dated May 9, 1982.

"Is this your husband?" Claire asked, pointing at the picture of a six-year-old boy next to a burnt-out car by the side of the road.

"Yes," April grinned with pride, adding, "it is."

"What happened?" Claire asked, almost as though she were asking for permission to read the article.

April took the newspaper article from Claire, and without reading it, recited its contents from memory.

"When Nick was six years old, he and his dad were driving home from the Little League Baseball practice that was abruptly cancelled after they got there, because the coach got suddenly ill. They were ten minutes from home when the car in front of them lost control and flipped over on the side of the road, landing in a small ditch. Almost immediately, the car caught fire. Nick's dad ran to the nearest house to call the ambulance. Nick, being the boy that he was, and not having the sense to not approach a burning car, ran up to the damaged car, unnoticed by his dad. The driver, an eighteen-year-old boy, had died on impact. However, there was a teenage age girl, badly hurt and unconscious, but still alive. Nick crawled inside the car and quickly unfastened her seat belt and helped the girl pull herself out of the car, just before it was totally engulfed in flames."

"Wow," Claire said, fascinated by the events that April was describing. "Did the girl survive?"

April smiled at the question, and replied, "Yes, she did. It just so happened that she was eight months pregnant with twins, and had to give birth to them by an emergency C-Section the next day. Because of the damage to her body that the accident caused, she had to go through several surgeries, and would not be able to have children ever again."

Then April's face turned a little more somber, as she continued, "Unfortunately, she gave the children up because her family situation wasn't the best. Not to mention that she was only sixteen years old, and didn't have the mindset to raise two children. But, ten years later, she got her life in order and tracked down Nick to properly thank him for saving her life on that fateful day. Even though she never got to see her two children, she had managed to turn her life around completely, and she is now the CEO of her own accounting firm. Whenever she travels to a different state, she sends postcards to us. When Nick died, she attended the funeral and promised to continue to mail us postcards. She turned out to be a remarkable woman with a fascinating life. Her name is Addison James.

Placing the album back in the hutch, April stared at a plaque mounted to the wall with the words 'Architect of the Year: Nickolas S. Turner' on it. He had earned that the year before he died. Nick's boss had taken a picture of him at his design desk to be mounted on the plaque. The look of contentment on his face made that picture one of April's favorites. He was doing something that he loved.

Looking over at Blake with a touch of sadness, April could see some of Nick's features in her daughter. She definitely had his nose and the pronounced chin. "If it weren't for Blake here, I don't know what I would have done," April said. "He was my soul mate and it took me years to stop crying myself to sleep every night. I had to be strong for Blake. At least, that is what I told myself so I could get out of bed most mornings." Truth be told, Blake helped April just as much as April helped Blake by being there as a mom.

Wiping away a tear and then focusing on Claire, April said, "Anyways, Nick was my best friend too, so it has been hard getting over a loss like that."

"I can only imagine," Claire responded, her eyes moving from April to Blake. "I never knew my dad. My mother said that he split before I was born, and she never wanted to look for him." There was a slight tickle in her throat and she had to clear it before continuing, "I asked her for a name or a picture of him, but the only thing that I ever got from her was the name 'Sammy'. She had mentioned that she had a nice picture of both of them when they first met, but she had lost it. Apparently when I was a small child, we got evicted a few times and most of our stuff was trashed by the landlord."

The tickle in Claire's throat became more pronounced as she finished the sentence. Looking at the refrigerator, Claire asked if she could grab a bottle of water.

"Yes, of course," April answered, and then decided to probe Claire a little more on what she had just shared.

"Have you ever tried to find your dad?" April asked the obvious question.

Taking a sip from the water bottle, Claire answered honestly, "No. Never." She took a deep breath and carried on with her explanation. "I figured why look for a man who left a pregnant woman? You know...? If he had supposedly loved my mom at one point, how could he just walk away?"

Blake took a seat on one of the island chairs in the kitchen close to where the three of them were standing. She gestured to Claire and asked her to take the remaining chair next to her. April stepped in front of them on the other side of the island facing them, and she put her elbows on the counter with her chin in her hands.

"I don't know, Claire," April responded. "Don't you think that in your situation it might be nice to try to locate him? I mean with your mother in jail, and the fact that you don't have any other family, it could be worth a try?"

Nodding her head defiantly, she replied, "He was not there for me all those years when I was growing up. What makes you think that he would even want to know my name now?" As she finished that last word, her voice cracked. April could see that this was starting to upset Claire, so she decided not to press the issue any further. "Ok, honey. I don't want to push. I am sorry that you never knew a father figure in your life, truly."

Claire found the right tone of voice again, and said, "Don't worry, it's ok. I've been basically on my own for a while now, and I'm pretty used to it. Unfortunately, the last couple of weeks have been really tough, and I found myself sinking deeper and deeper." Thinking about the words on her sign this morning, Claire continued, "Today was the first day that I felt like I had to beg for money." A tear formed in her left eye, and she brought the bottle of water to her face to take a drink in an effort to mask her other hand as she wiped it away.

"Well, I'm glad that we could help," Blake said, smiling and slowly spinning around on the bar stool that she was sitting on.

"Me too," April added honestly. "I am happy to know that you have a warm and dry place to sleep in tonight."

"I know, right?" Claire graciously agreed.

At that, April had a disturbing thought. What happens tomorrow? Do they help her find a shelter or something? She didn't want to bring it up and make it sound like she wanted to toss Claire out first thing in the morning, so April decided that she would think about it at night, and they would deal with it after breakfast.

Blake took her phone from her back pocket to see what time it was. The screen on her phone sprang to life when she hit the home button, revealing the time: 7:40 pm. "It's only quarter to eight mom." Blake said, "Can we watch another movie?" Looking over at Claire for agreement, Blake pushed on. "By the time it's finished, it will only be around ten O' clock"

Because it was a Friday night, and it was too early to go to bed, April agreed, and said, "Sure, I don't see why not?"

"Hey," April said, as she realized that they had not had dinner yet. "Do you want me to put in some chicken nuggets to have while we watch the next movie?" she asked the two girls.

"You know it," Blake said immediately.

April took out the bag of frozen nuggets, and then turned the oven on. She then opened the cupboard to take out a cookie sheet and placed the nuggets on the sheet and set the timer for twenty-five minutes.

"What do you want to watch now?" Blake asked Claire, as they made their way back to the couch.

"Um, let's see," Claire began, as she grabbed the remote from the coffee table and began scrolling through the selections. After a few screens went by, Claire stopped on one movie, and asked, "Can we watch *Hocus Pocus?* I know it is after Halloween, but I love this movie, and it has been a while since I've seen it."

"Sure, that's cool," replied Blake. "I really like that movie too, and we didn't watch it this year, so let's do it."

April nodded in agreement, and then she sat back in her chair, getting into a more comfortable position.

About twenty minutes into the movie, the timer went off, and Blake grabbed the remote to pause the movie. April got up and took the nuggets out of the oven and put them into a medium-sized plastic bowl, and got two small saucers, putting sweet and sour sauce in one and barbeque sauce in the other.

Once settled with the food, Claire pressed the remote and the movie started again. The three of them laughed and giggled throughout the movie. April made some more popcorn, and the time flew by.

"That was really good," Blake said, once the movie was over.

"Yeah, it was," Claire agreed. "Thank you guys for letting me watch it."

Getting up from the chair with the empty popcorn bowl, April smiled, and said, "No problem, Claire. I really had fun too."

Blake got up from the couch and stretched as a yawn forced its way out. "I think that I'm going to get ready for bed."

Claire was tired too, and that sounded like a good idea. As Blake started to walk in the direction of the stairs, Claire put her legs up on the couch, and started to lie across it. Seeing this, April politely asked her, "Are you ready for bed?"

"Yes," she said, grabbing the pillow on the arm of the couch to place under her head.

Realizing that Claire thought that she had to sleep on the couch, April said, "Oh no, Claire. You don't have to sleep down here." Pointing towards the bedrooms upstairs, April declared, "I thought that you could sleep in the spare bedroom."

Remembering how nice the room was, Claire started to resist by shaking her head, "No, that's ok. The couch will be great."

Not taking no for an answer, April gave Claire a look that told her to listen to her, and then she said, "Claire, really, it's fine. It would make me feel better if you slept in the spare bedroom. Seriously, that is why I have a spare bedroom."

Realizing that she was not going to win this battle, Claire gave in, and said, "Ok, thank you."

When they got upstairs, April accompanied Claire into the spare bedroom and pulled down the comforter to the base of the bed. "Here you go... all set," she declared. Blake came into the spare room carrying a nightshirt for Claire. "Good thinking," April told her daughter, "I almost forgot about that."

"I know mom; it's what I do. Take care of the details," Blake chuckled as she spoke.

"Ah hah," April replied, but not necessarily in agreement.

Blake handed the nightshirt to Claire, and said, "You can keep this one. I have a ton of them." Holding the shirt so that she could see what the print was on the front, Claire saw that it was a picture of a band that she hadn't heard of. Despite not knowing who they were, it was still a cool shirt.

"Thanks, Blake, I really appreciate it."

"It's all good," Blake answered.

As April and Blake headed out of the room, April turned to Claire, and said, "Good night, Claire. See you in the morning."

"Good night, April," Claire said warmly, and then she called out to Blake in the hallway, "Good night, Blake."

"Night," Blake softly yelled back in the direction of the spare bedroom. "Sleep in because I'm going to."

When April and Blake were in their own rooms, Claire slowly closed the door to the spare bedroom, and sat on the bed with the nightshirt still in her hands. Looking around the room, Claire couldn't believe how this day had turned out. It felt good to be able to sleep in a nice bed. Damn good. She had had an awesome pizza for lunch, and chicken tenders for dinner. Not to mention the popcorn with the movies. Now here she was, clean and fed. She got up from the bed and changed out of the clothes that Blake had let her borrow. She folded and placed the shirt and jeans on the long dresser, and got under the covers.

She lay on her back looking up at the ceiling with the realization that the bed was really comfortable. It had a memory foam pad on top of the mattress, to add an extra level of softness. As her eyes began to slowly close shut and she surrendered to the exhaustion, her throat was starting to get worse, and little did she know, her nasal cavity was beginning to fill.

Across the hall, April changed into her nightgown, sat on the stool of her vanity, and caught her reflection in her makeup mirror. "What are you doing?" she questioned the woman in the mirror. Rubbing a slight vertical wrinkle in the center of her forehead with her right index finger, she impatiently waited for the reflection to answer back. When she realized that she didn't have an honest answer for herself, she got up and pulled the covers from her bed and tucked herself in. She propped her head up with a second pillow, and reached for the manuscript that she had placed on her nightstand. April was tired, but she wanted to get through a few chapters before finally closing the cover on this day as it were. She kept playing back in her mind the sound of Nick's voice in her head over and over again. April was confident that she had heard it clear as day. Truth be told, she was a little freaked out over it, and maybe that is why she wanted to close the cover on this day. However, after just three chapters, April couldn't fight the Sandman any longer, and set the manuscript aside and turned off the light on the nightstand.

As the night turned into morning, April's memories of Nick transformed into vivid dreams of the years she had spent with her late husband. If there had been anyone else in the room with her that night, they would have witnessed tears of sadness and loss of what they once had and could never experience again.

CHAPTER FIVE

CLAIRE SLOWLY OPENED HER EYES AND SAW THAT THE DIGItal clock showed 8:17 am. Her mind slowly registered that she was not on the streets, but on a soft bed. The memory of the previous day came back to her as she blinked herself awake. She couldn't help but smile at the events of yesterday, and for a brief moment, she felt happy and at peace—almost like a normal teenager.

As she rolled on her back to lift her head up on the pillow, Claire suddenly became aware that she did not feel well. The first clue was the stabbing pain that shot from the right side of her forehead to the left. The second clue was the soreness of her throat due to the fact that her sinuses were almost completely blocked, and she apparently had to breathe through her mouth while she was sleeping. There was no doubt that she was sick.

Claire slowly rolled out of the bed, and her joints and muscles rejected the stunt as they stiffened and tightened up. She staggered into the hallway to the bathroom and quietly closed the door. She looked at the mirror on the bathroom wall, and the image that looked back at her was pale and, as you can imagine, she looked sick.

She rubbed her hands through her hair, and even though it was ruffled up from the pillows on the bed, it was still soft and silky from last night's shower.

Turning on the cold water and letting it run for a second or two, Claire cupped her hands to collect the water and rinsed her face off. Even though her body was cold and her teeth began to chatter, the cold water felt somewhat refreshing. Using the hand towel on the brass towel holder to the right of the sink, she wiped away the remaining drops of water that were clinging to her forehead and face.

The sound of April's bedroom door opening softly could be heard in the hallway bathroom, and Claire opened the bathroom door to say good morning. "Good morning, April," Claire said, as she cleared her throat, and involuntarily wiped her running nose with her wrist.

"Oh my God, Claire," April responded to Claire's appearance. "You look terrible."

"I know." Claire said, matter-of-factly, "I'm sorry," she continued, offering up an apology as if she had done something wrong.

"Oh, honey, don't be sorry," April said, trying to reassure her. "I just meant that you look sick." April went up to her, and placed her hand on Claire's forehead to see if she had a temperature. "You are really warm," April declared. "Let me get you some medicine." April went into the bathroom and opened up the mirror medicine cabinet door, and took out the Motrin bottle. "Do you have any allergies to any kind of medicine?" she asked Claire before she opened the cap of the bottle.

"No. I'm good. At least I'm not aware of anything. I have not had a problem in the past with anything," Claire answered honestly.

April took out two of the orange tablets and handed them to her. She then took a Dixie cup out of the ceramic dispenser that was on the sink's counter, filled it up with cold water, and gave it to Claire, asking her to wash down her pills.

Taking the cup with her left hand, Claire threw the pills back in her throat with her right hand and then washed them down. April took the empty cup from Claire and threw it in the trash. Putting her hand back on Claire's forehead to feel it again, as if the Motrin would have an immediate effect,

April noticed that Claire's teeth were chattering. "Oh my, Claire, you have the chills." She went into her own bedroom and grabbed a soft, light brown throw blanket, and put it around Claire, and said, "Here you go, this should help you keep warm."

Because of the sound of voices in the hallway, Blake got out of bed and opened her door.

Seeing her daughter in the doorway, April said, "Claire woke up sick this morning, and she has a fever."

Blake could see that their guest was not feeling well just by the color in Claire's cheeks. "Holy cow, Claire," Blake said, as she continued to stare at her. "What happened?"

Claire cleared her throat, and answered, "I started feeling a little sick before bed last night. My throat was getting sore but I didn't think too much about it. When I woke up this morning, my head was hurting, I had aches and pains, my nose was stuffy, and I had chills."

"That really sucks," said Blake sincerely, as she grabbed a robe from the chair that was just inside her room. April led the girls downstairs to the kitchen, filled the teapot up with water and turned on the burner of the stove to heat it. "I'm going to make you some tea," April said to Claire as she opened the cupboard and reached for the box of raspberry green tea with honey. "This should help with the sore throat at least," she added. She opened another cupboard door and took out a coffee mug that she placed the teabag in, so that it was ready when the water was hot. Looking in the cabinet above the sink, April searched through the many different medicine bottles and boxes, to see if she had something that Claire could take. She finally chose the Daytime Cold and Flu orange liquid bottle, and set it on the island where Blake and Claire were sitting.

Taking a measuring spoon from the silverware drawer of the island, April poured the recommended amount for Claire, and handed it to her. Claire took the medicine gratefully, and gave the empty spoon back to April.

"I was planning on making you guys a big breakfast this morning, but I think that we should hold off and see how Claire does with some toast and tea first," April said.

"I'm ok with toast and cereal," Blake said, as she got up to get herself a bowl and a box of cereal.

"Toast and tea will be great," Claire agreed. "I'm not really hungry, but I will try to eat something."

After a couple of minutes, the teapot whistled its song of completion. April turned off the stove, poured the steaming water into the coffee mug, and set it on the island in front of Claire. "Here you go. Hopefully, this will help."

Claire took the mug and dabbed the tea bag in the cup about a dozen times to allow tea from the bag to be filtered into the cup. After carefully taking a sip of the hot tea, Claire set it on the counter and cupped her hands around the mug to soak up its warmth.

April made toast for the girls, and only put a slight hint of butter on Claire's pieces because she didn't want to overload it. Blake spread peanut butter and strawberry jelly on her toast.

Claire finished her toast, and then April suggested that she go lay on the couch and get some rest. April ran up to her bedroom and got one of her warm and fuzzy robes so that Claire could put it on over her night shirt to help her stay warm. When Claire lay down on the couch, April took the two pillows and put them under Claire's head, and then covered her with the throw blanket that Claire had brought down with her.

Blake turned on the TV, and the three of them flicked channels for about an hour when Claire slowly started to get up and motioned to April. "April, I think that I'm going to be sick," she said. April jumped out of the La-Z-Boy chair and quickly walked Claire to the bathroom. Claire had barely made it to the toilet when she threw up. After about a minute or so, and after throwing up twice, Claire told April that she thought that she was finished. April had taken out a washcloth from the vanity, and rinsed it in cold water for Claire. Handing it to her, April could see that Claire's color was even paler than before. She was holding her stomach with her left hand because the muscles were now hurting from the act of heaving.

Claire took the washcloth from April, and wiped off her mouth and face. She just sat there for a few minutes on her knees in front of the toilet, waiting just in case she had to throw up again. By this time, Blake had gotten up from the couch and was standing next to her mom outside the bathroom door. She wanted to help, but there wasn't much that anyone could do but wait until Claire was finished.

Claire's stomach wrenched in defiance of its current state, and she groaned in dismay. This was the worst that she had felt in a very long time. Abruptly, the contents of her stomach found their way out with force, and she vomited all over the front of the toilet. Seeing what was dripping down to the floor made Claire vomit even more.

When Claire was finally done, and it seemed like things were settling down, April helped Claire walk up to the La-Z-Boy chair. "April, I am so sorry," Claire said with dismay. "I'll clean it all up."

"Don't be silly. I will clean it up. Just sit there and be still," April told her. "You are in no condition to clean up that mess."

Blake looked in the bathroom in an attempt to help her mom clean it up, but the smell of it made her gag. "Sorry mom, I can't do it," she said, as she held her hand to her mouth and nose to block the stench. Walking away from the bathroom, she sat on the couch next to the La-Z-Boy where Claire was sitting, and gave Claire a concerned look.

"Don't worry, honey," April said, as she went to the kitchen to get a roll of paper towel. "I'll get it."

When April finished cleaning up the bathroom, she took a big, plastic bowl from the cabinet door, and put it on the coffee table next to Claire, and said, "Just in case."

Forcing her pale lips into a half-smile, Claire replied, "Good call."

April then went back into the bathroom to wash her hands and to spray Lysol on the surfaces throughout the bathroom to help eliminate potential germs. Leaving the bathroom, she looked at Blake, and said, "You know, dear, it might be better if you go over to Emily's today to hang out. I don't want you to catch what Claire has."

"Are you sure, mom?" Blake asked, with just a hint of disappointment. "I can stay here with you guys, and we can watch more movies or something?"

Not wanting her daughter to get whatever it was that Claire had, April insisted that it would be better for her not to be here in the apartment in such close proximity to Claire. Blake texted Emily, who told her she could come over and spend the day. She then went upstairs to change her clothes, and was down and ready to go in fifteen minutes.

April used the app on her phone to arrange a car service to pick Blake up and take her to Emily's. The car service was from a company that was sub-contracted by the apartment building, and April found it extremely convenient whenever Blake had to go somewhere by herself. April's mind was more at ease when she used it.

Giving her mom a hug, Blake said, "Don't worry, I'll text you when I get there." She then looked at Claire with apologetic eyes, and said, "Get better, Ok?"

Claire gave Blake a thumbs-up, and replied, "I'll try."

Blake entered the elevator and waved bye to her mom and Claire as the doors closed.

April decided to go upstairs and grab the manuscript from her night-stand and bring it down to the living room so that she could be around Claire, just in case she got sick again. As she walked by the kitchen, April got 20 oz. Sprite from the door of the refrigerator and handed it to Claire. "You need to keep hydrated, so sip on this. It might help your stomach as well."

Taking the soda, Claire said, "Thanks." She put the bottle in her lap but did not open it right away. A few minutes went by, and Claire fell asleep in the chair. April positioned herself on the couch so that she could lie on it with her feet up and her head on the two pillows kept on the arm of the couch. She made sure she faced Claire.

An hour went by, and April was immersed in the chapters of her manuscript. She would sometimes scribble notes within the margins of the pages and highlight certain words where she would recommend a change. The sound of Claire's cough made April set the manuscript aside and look at Claire. Claire's eyes were open, and the coughing sound had turned into a heaving sound. Suddenly, she bolted from the chair and dashed to the bathroom. April followed suit and saw Claire grab the toilet bowl with her hands on either side, and proceed to throw up again. Unfortunately, this time was a bit more intense. During the third bout of heaving, some of the vomit splashed from the bowl, lodging in the ends of Claire's hair. Knowing that Claire would be unable to remove her hands from the rim of the bowl until she was finished, April carefully grabbed the sides of Claire's hair and held them back behind her head so that her hair would not get more messed up.

Tears began to fill in Claire's eyes and roll down her cheeks. As April's hands wrapped around her hair in a way that only a mother's hands do around her child in a situation like this, Claire was overcome with emotion. First, she was sick and felt like utter crap and wanted the churning in her stomach to stop. Second, the way that April was caring for her made her long for something that had only been a daydream for her. She never really had a mother figure who truly cared about her. Now here was April, a stranger who had taken her in for the night and who was now taking care of her. She looked up at April and couldn't control herself, and began to sob. "I'm so sorry for all of this," she said, as the tears started flowing down her face without restriction. Claire just couldn't stop them, no matter how hard she tried.

"Oh, honey," April said, as she wiped the tears away as much as she could. "Don't be sad, it's ok, really. I'm just glad that you are here with me during this. I can't imagine you going through this alone on the streets." The corners of April's eyes began to moisten with tears in response to Claire's emotions. April looked at Claire's eyes, and said, "You have nothing to be sorry for. People get sick every day and it just so happens that today is your turn." Continuing, she said, "Besides, we did have fun last night watching movies, right?"

Forcing a smile through the tears, Claire answered by way of shaking her head, and said, "Yes, of course, it was fun."

They waited for a few more minutes to see if Claire would vomit again, fortunately, she didn't. Claire sat back on the chair, and April cleaned the toilet rim and sprayed Lysol again.

Opening the Sprite bottle, Claire cautiously took a couple of sips and put the lid back on it.

April picked up the remote control and turned on the TV. "Let's flick through channels for a minute to see if there is anything that we would like."

"That sounds good," Claire agreed.

April went through several channels before they agreed on the Hallmark channel, where a movie was just starting.

About half-way through the movie, a thought came to April's mind. *Claire can't leave here today. No way is she well enough to go back to the streets.* She looked at Claire while she was watching the movie, and it was obvious that she was severely sick. Her skin was pale, the color had still not returned to her lips, and her eyes were red and irritated. The aches and pains were increasing in intensity, not decreasing.

This was going to be a long day.

* *

THE ELEVATOR DOORS OPENED, AND BLAKE ENTERED THE apartment. It was 9:30 p.m. and her mother had texted her earlier to let her know that Claire was still going to be there. In fact, it was looking like it was going to be the whole weekend. Not that Blake minded really. She was happy that Claire was going to be with them for the next day or so, but not under these circumstances.

April was waiting for her daughter on the couch, and by the looks of it, was almost finished with the manuscript. Blake gave her mom a look that said, "*Where's Claire?*" to which April simply motioned her hand in the direction of the bedroom upstairs.

"I took her upstairs to the spare bedroom about half an hour ago," April said.

Sitting down right next to her mom, Blake asked, "How was she today?"

Pulling back a strand of hair that was blocking her left eye, April answered, "Not good, sweetie. She got sick several more times throughout the day and could not keep any food down."

"What are we going to do?" Blake asked with concern.

"I don't know," April, responded. "She may have the flu, and if she does, then she will need to go to the doctor's." She set her manuscript down and reached for a coffee cup that she had been drinking from, and took a swig. "I am really concerned for her right now."

"Me too," agreed Blake.

"I will take her to the clinic in the morning if she is not showing signs of improvement," April said as she got up and headed to the kitchen to put her now empty coffee cup into the dishwasher.

Following her mother, Blake got up from the couch and stood behind her.

"You know mom, you are a nice person. Do you know that?" Blake told her.

Surprised by Blake's comment, April asked, "Why do you say that?"

"Because of what you are doing for Claire," Blake explained. "There are not too many people in this city that would do what you are doing for her." Turning around to face her daughter, April put her hands on Blake's shoulders and said, "It just feels right, you know?"

In response, Blake put her own hands on her mother's shoulders, and said, "Yes, but most people out there would do nothing." Blake's hands rolled off of April's shoulders and down her back to form a hug. Hugging Blake back, April squeezed her arms around her daughter and held her close for a few moments. "Thank you, honey, that means the world to me." Turning around to go upstairs, Blake whispered to her mom, "I know it does."

Smiling, April wished Blake good night, and then turned off the kitchen light. Blake retired to her bedroom and closed the door. Looking around the apartment, April made sure that everything was in order and proceeded to go upstairs. She was about to get out of her clothes and get into the shower, but decided to check on Claire first. Quietly walking to the spare bedroom door, April slowly opened it to peer in. Claire was wrapped up in the covers with only her blond hair peeking through, and she was sound asleep. April closed the door and went back into her bedroom.

The hot water from the shower washed away the worries of the day, and April felt more relaxed. Even though she had to clean puke up throughout the afternoon, she felt solace in the fact that she had helped Claire in her time of need. The sadness in the teenager's eyes weighed heavily on her heart. She couldn't imagine having a mother that did not give a damn.

After she was done washing herself and rinsing the shampoo and conditioner from her hair, she grabbed the loofah and poured body wash on it. Rubbing the suds all over her body, she cleaned the sediments of the day off of her. April reached up on the second shelf of the shower stall and removed a Bic razor to shave her legs.

Stepping out of the shower, April reached for the towel and dried herself off. Once dry, April put on a nightgown, and walked to the nightstand next to her bed. Opening a jewelry box, she pulled out her late husband's wedding ring. Letting it roll around in her palm like a pair of dice, April asked the ring, "What is it that I am supposed to do?" Hoping for an answer, April stared at the diamond on the ring in the hope that it would reveal something. But silence was the only answer she got.

With the ring still in her hand, April pulled back the covers and got into bed. She looked at the bedroom door and purposely left it open. She wanted to make sure that she could hear Claire in case something happened in the night.

* *

APRIL AWOKE WITH A START. SHE KNEW SOMETHING WAS wrong but didn't know what it was at first. It soon became clear when she heard Claire yelling and crying from the spare bedroom. April got up right away and headed towards Claire, turning on the hallway light. As she entered the room, she could see that Claire was crying and yelling but was not fully awake. Softly calling out her name so that she wouldn't startle her, April sat down on the edge of the bed beside her.

"Claire, wake up," April whispered.

Claire was sobbing and stammering words that didn't make any sense.

"Claire, wake up," April whispered again.

After a few seconds, Claire's eyes began to focus on April's face and she started to become aware of her surroundings. "What's going on?" Claire asked, confused.

"I think you were having a bad dream," April guessed, as she turned on the lamp on the nightstand.

"I don't remember anything," Claire said, croaking due to the sore throat and wiping the tears from her face and cheeks. Her eyes were glazed over and her face was flushed. April put her hand on Claire's forehead and it was hot.

"Damn," she said, in response to the touch. "You're burning up."

April got up from the bed and went into the bathroom in the hallway to get a cold washcloth to put on Claire's forehead. Letting the water run cold for a few seconds, April soaked the washcloth and then wrung it out. Upon entering the bedroom again, April noticed the time on the clock: 3:06 a.m. She put the cold washcloth on Claire's forehead and went back into the bathroom to get a thermometer and some Motrin. Over five hours had passed since the last dose, and April needed to get Clair's fever down. The digital thermometer indicated that she had a fever of 102 degrees.

April gave Claire three tablets and a Dixie cup of water. She took the pills and sat up higher in bed.

"I don't know what to say," Claire told April. "I'm sorry for waking you up this early in the morning. I have never talked in my sleep. At least I don't think that I ever have."

"It must be the fever, Claire," April explained. "Your temperature is 102 degrees, and we need to get it down."

April moved to leave the room but before she left, she said, "I'll be right back." April then went downstairs to grab a bag of frozen vegetables and a hand towel. Racing back upstairs, she walked back into the spare bedroom and put the hand towel with the frozen peas on Claire's forehead.

"This hopefully will help with the fever," April said.

Holding the peas against her forehead with her left hand and pulling the blanket closer to her neck with the right, Claire just lay there.

"Would you like me to turn the TV on for a little bit?" April asked.

"Sure, I guess so," Claire answered, through her chattering teeth.

April turned on the TV and gave the remote to Claire. Instead of leaving the room, April sat in the Lazy Boy chair and watched it with her for a while. Eventually the two of them fell asleep, Claire in the bed and April in the chair.

CHAPTER SIX

"GOOD MORNING," BLAKE SAID, AS SHE ENTERED THE SPARE bedroom. Her mom was sound asleep in the chair, and Claire was asleep on the bed. She had, at first, gone into her mom's room to see if she was awake, but she was not in there. Hearing the TV in the spare bedroom, Blake had decided to check up on Claire before she went downstairs.

April awoke at the sound of her daughter's voice. The TV was still on, blaring an infomercial about cookware. Wiping the sleep from her eyes, April got up from the chair and stretched her arms in order to get out the kinks. "Good morning, honey," April said to Blake. She then looked over at the bed where Claire was beginning to stir due to the commotion in the room.

Opening her eyes and seeing both April and Blake in the room, Claire pushed the covers from her neck area towards her chest. "Good morning, guys."

April grinned, and asked, "Good morning, Claire. How are you feeling?" As she asked the question, she bent over the bed and felt Claire's head again. It was still warm, not as hot as it had been the previous night but still very warm.

"I feel really achy," Claire confessed. "My stomach is still queasy and my throat is sore." Claire's voice was raspy and tortured.

April stood in front of Claire with her hands on her hips, and declared, "Ok, that's it. We are going to visit the clinic."

Claire wanted to resist and actually started to say something to that effect, but April put up her hand, and said, "Don't even try to say no, Claire. You are in no shape to disagree."

Taking her mom's side, Blake too spoke up, "Don't even try. You look really sick so you should go."

April told Claire to put on the other set of clothes that Blake had given her last night and then asked Blake to get dressed because they were all going to go. Knowing that it would be useless to fight, Claire got up and slowly went to the bathroom. Blake went to her room to change while April went to the master bedroom to change as well.

April used the app to get the car service ready to take them because she did not want them to take a cab. Claire was too sick for that. As they made their way downstairs, you could see how weak Claire was. Merely walking down the stairs seemed like a task for her.

Slowly, the three of them walked outside to the car and got in. April instructed the driver to take them to the clinic.

The drive took about fifteen minutes, but to Claire, it felt like an hour. Her aching body absorbed every bump in the road, and her head was pounding. She couldn't get comfortable at all, and kept moving around in her seat. Her skin actually hurt from the weight of the clothes on it. She just wanted this to be over.

Even though it was a walk-in clinic, April had called ahead and made a quick appointment in the hope that they wouldn't have to wait long. Walking into the building, Blake and Claire took seats in the middle of the room where there were three seats in a row available.

April went up to the receptionist and signed in. Giving her a clipboard with several sheets of paper on it, the nurse asked April to fill it all out. Sitting down next to Claire, April handed the clipboard over to her, and told her to fill out whatever she could. Obviously, the address section would be left blank. Claire filled in about half of the info, and started to get out of her seat to give it to the receptionist. Blake grabbed the clipboard from her, and said, "I'll hand it over." On her way up, Blake's foot got caught in the purse straps of a patient who was waiting. The purse was under the patient's chair, but the straps were sticking out onto the floor. Blake almost fell, but caught herself just in the nick of time. The pencil on the clipboard went flying against the wall.

"Sorry, sorry," Blake giggled, as she set the purse back under the seat. There were a couple of chuckles in the waiting room as Blake tripped. April rolled her eyes in response. Her daughter was at that age when a teenager's body and mind can't quite catch up with their growing. Consequently, Blake was known to trip over her two feet or just bump into a corner of the wall when entering a room. Even though that was not the case here, it was just another example of Blake's clumsiness.

Blake shrugged her shoulders as she returned to her seat.

"I don't need to have you seeing the doctor too today, Blake," April sighed.

"Hey, if I'm going to fall and get hurt, this is the best place to be. Know what I mean?" Blake told her mom matter-of-factly.

"Yes, I suppose," said April.

The three of them waited for about ten minutes, after which the nurse called Claire to the examining room. The nurse stopped them just inside the door, and instructed Claire to step up on the scale. The nurse then flipped the bar across the top of the scale so that she could measure Claire's height. The nurse typed the info into her tablet, and walked them to a door that had a plaque engraved with the number five on it.

After taking her blood pressure and a few vitals, the nurse informed them that the doctor would be in soon.

April and Blake sat next to each other on the chairs while Claire was up on the examining bed. Holding herself up in an upright position, Claire was unaware that she was quietly groaning and swaying uncomfortably back and forth.

The doctor knocked twice on the door before she opened it.

"Hi there," she said. "My name is Dr. Amanda Welch." She held out her hand to Claire.

Shaking her hand, Claire replied to the doctor in her sick and raspy voice, "I'm Claire."

Looking over at April and Blake, Amanda said, "Nice to see you guys again. How are you doing?"

Amanda had known April since high school. They had been friends and hung out in some of the same circles. They had kept in touch in the years following graduation, and when Amanda graduated medical school and accepted a position at the clinic, April and her family started going to consult her as a general practitioner.

"We are good. Thank you for asking, Dr. Welch," April replied.

"Yes, everything is great," answered Blake.

Turning her attention back to Claire, Dr. Welch said, "So, what do we have here?"

Answering for Claire, April said, "Yesterday morning she woke up sick and vomited several times during the day. I gave her Motrin and over-the-counter cold medicine, but obviously it did not work. She had a high fever last night, and as you can see, she is not any better today."

Claire just nodded in affirmative, agreeing with what April had just described.

"Ok then," Amanda said, "Let's take a look."

After a physical examination, Dr. Welch sent Claire up to give a urine sample for the test, and wanted to give a blood sample as well. Because they did not have any record of this patient, they needed to run more tests to make sure nothing else besides the obvious was going on.

Dr. Welch left the room for a few minutes and told them to hold tight, adding that she would be back in a few minutes when she got the results.

Claire decided to lie down on the bed and put her forearm over her forehead, as if she could hold the pain off with it. She never liked going to the doctor's office when she was younger (not that she went often like you should), but she would do anything to feel better at this point.

Comforting Claire as much as she could, April said, "Dr. Welch has been our family doctor for over ten years now. She is really good and will fix you up."

"I hope so," Claire said, forcing a smile.

Because Claire was lying down now, her feet were hanging over the edge of the bed, and Blake could see the bottom of Claire's shoes. Both the soles were worn pretty smooth. The left one had a hole the size of a dime at the base of the big toe, while the right shoe had two holes, one the size of a dime and the other a little bigger than that, possibly the size of a quarter. Rubbing her hand on her mother's thigh to get her attention, Blake motioned with her hand to show April the worn-out shoes.

On seeing the shoes, April's eyes widened, and she made a mental note to figure out what she could do to rectify that situation.

Two knocks sounded on the room door, and Dr. Welch came in.

"Ok, Claire, this is what's going on," she said, as she looked directly at Claire. "You definitely have the flu, and not only that, you have a UTI as well."

Claire blinked her eyes in surprise, and asked, "Really?"

"Unfortunately, yes," Dr. Welch replied. "I will be honest with you. I am a little concerned with some of these levels." Clicking a few spots on the screen of her tablet, Amanda continued, "However, I am going to give you some high power antibiotics to help kill the infections as well as some potent meds to help get you through this flu."

Concerned with the diagnosis, April asked, "What do I need to do for her?"

Looking at April, Dr. Welch said, "Claire needs to get lots of rest, and make sure that she gets a lot of fluids."

"I will be checking up on you tomorrow," Dr. Welch said. "I don't want her out in this weather, so I am going to stop by after my shift to make sure that the medicines are working. "

Surprised by the sincerity of care from the doctor, Claire responded by saying, "Thanks, Doctor."

"It's no problem, Claire. I just want to make sure that you don't get any worse. These meds will definitely help, but with the flu and the UTI, I want to keep a tab on you for a day or so."

Helping Claire off the examining bed, Dr. Welch opened the door to the room and pointed them in the direction of the exit. When April passed her, she reached into her lab coat and pulled out her business card, and said, "Here is my personal cell number. I know that I gave it to you years ago, but I just want to make sure that you still have it. If she takes a turn for the worse or the fever spikes again, please call me immediately. I don't care what time it is. "

"Thank you, Amanda," April said with appreciation, as she took the card from the doctor.

The scripts were available for Claire at the receptionist desk just before the doors that led to the waiting room.

"That will be $40.00 for the office call," the woman in scrubs on the other side of the desk said.

Knowing that they had never had to pay on the way out before, Blake looked at her mom for clarification.

"Claire isn't on our insurance, honey," April said to Blake, as she pulled out her credit card to pay.

"Oh, I get it," Blake realized.

"I'll pay you back somehow," Claire told April, as she cleared her throat, which in turn made her cough.

"Don't worry about it, Claire."

"I know, but..."

Politely cutting Claire off, April said, "It's fine. I don't want you to pay me back. I just want to help you through this."

"Thank you so much. I bet you didn't bargain for all this when you decided to buy me that pizza yesterday, huh?" Claire asked, with a hint of humor mixed with blunt honesty.

Smiling as she put the credit card back into her wallet, April chuckled, and replied, "No, I guess that ended up being more than just lunch."

They stopped at the drugstore on the way back to the apartment to get the scripts filled, and April thought it would be wise to pick up some Gatorade and Powerade for the girls, but especially for Claire. Blake, with a little input from Claire, grabbed a few bags of snacks that they could munch on for the rest of the day. It was clear to April and Blake that Claire would definitely not be going anywhere for the next couple of days. That is if she was well enough to stay with them and didn't have to be admitted to the hospital. April thought to herself that she would be diligent with Claire's medicines so that she wouldn't skip a dose.

Once they arrived home, April immediately gave Claire her medicine and set the timer on her phone for 4 hours from then to give her another dose. Blake and Claire both took positions on the couch, one on each end with their feet almost touching each other. April got one of the Gatorades out and set it on the end table next to Claire. "You need to keep drinking today and get plenty of rest."

"No arguments from me, April," Claire responded. "I feel like I have been hit by a city bus, I'm not moving from this couch for a while."

"Good," April nodded her head. "This will be like a pajama day."

"Yeah, you got that right!" Blake exclaimed, as she grabbed the remote to turn on the TV.

"You guys have fun relaxing on the couch. I am going to be in the den getting a little work done. I'll keep popping in here to check up on you," April said as she went into the kitchen to make coffee before she went into her office.

"April?" Claire asked.

"Yes?"

"I just want you to know how super appreciative I am of you guys for doing this for me. I know that I have been on my own for a little while, but I really don't know how I could have managed out there being this sick. You know?"

April could see the genuine look of gratitude reflecting from Claire's face. "You are very welcome, and I am glad that we went back to say 'hi' to you," April said sincerely.

Blake found a movie for the two of them to watch, and April grabbed her coffee and went into her office.

* *

THE DAY TURNED INTO EVENING, AND CLAIRE WAS STILL feeling pretty crappy, as it were, but at least she could keep food down now. She didn't have much for lunch—just a few crackers and some toast, and truth be told, she did sneak a few cookies that Blake gave her. She still got the chills periodically throughout the day, but her teeth didn't chatter. Her temperature was still high, but it was now only 100 degrees. Claire was still achy and her muscles were sore. April had given her a bag of honey lemon cough drops after lunch, and it was now almost empty. It was 6:30 pm and April was in the middle of microwaving a bowl of chicken noodle soup for the girls when Claire got up to go to the bathroom and felt dizzy. She grabbed the edge of the La-Z-Boy chair, and fell awkwardly into the chair as the room continued to spin.

"I'm really dizzy," Claire said to April, with the sound of concern increasing in her voice.

April went over to her and crouched down on her knees to be at eye level with Claire. She could see that Claire was having a hard time trying to focus on one thing. After about a minute, the room righted itself, and Claire could sit upright in the chair.

"That was really weird," said Claire, as she was now able to fully focus on April's face.

Blake slid over from the far side of the couch to sit closer to Claire. Giving her mom a concerned look, she took the half-drunk bottle of Gatorade and handed it to Claire. "Maybe you should take a sip of something?" Blake offered.

Claire took the bottle from Blake and took a sip. Still having to go to the bathroom, Claire got up slowly to see if the room would react in the same way as it had a minute ago. April gently grabbed Claire's arm and escorted her to the bathroom as a precaution.

After she was done, April stayed close to her as she walked back to the couch. April decided to text Dr. Welch to let her know about the dizziness to see what the doctor thought.

April's cell phone beeped sixty seconds later with the doctor's response: it was probably the medicine in her system. But the doctor wanted to know if it happened again. Dr Welch also said she would be coming over tomorrow to check up on Claire. Texting back a thank you for her quick response, April set her phone down on the coffee table next to the couch.

"Well, isn't this an interesting turn of events?" April asked Claire.

"This really sucks. I have never been dizzy like that in my life before," Claire said truthfully. "Even when I was a kid, I would spin around until I fell to the ground dizzy, but I was never that dizzy."

"Let's hope that it doesn't happen again," Blake said as she looked at Claire.

"Yeah," Claire agreed.

April's cell phone beeped again with a text message. Retrieving it from the coffee table. April read it on her way to the kitchen. It was a picture of Wanda with her orange hair. April chuckled at it and then showed it to the girls. Even though April had feared the worst, it didn't turn out too bad. In fact, the color was really cute on her. It was at that moment that April realized that it was Monday the next day, and that she had a meeting at work while Blake had to go to school. What about Claire? She should definitely not be left alone when she was this sick. April quietly sent a text to Wanda saying her hair looked fantastic, and that she would not be in tomorrow. She added that Claire was sick with the flu, and that she couldn't be left alone. After pressing send on that text, she went to a thread of texts between her and Gina, and sent her the same thing saying she wouldn't be in on Monday due to Claire's illness and that she would call Gina in the morning for more details.

April went back into the living room and sat on the couch next to Blake and asked, "Alright, what are we going to watch now?"

"Why don't we watch some YouTube videos?" Blake offered.

"Sure, that's cool," Claire said, as she reached for a blanket that was on the couch—it was the one she had been using all day long. She tucked it into the corners of the Lazy Boy chair and pulled it up to her chin. Blake laughed at the image, and said, "Look mom, a Claire burrito."

April chuckled and suggested another option, "How about Claire chimichangas?"

Seeing where this was heading, Claire played along. Smirking just a little, she whispered, "Claire Carnitas."

"Right?" Blake chuckled, with a nod in her direction.

They settled into watching various videos about a variety of things. April was amazed by the amount of stupid stuff that was on YouTube. There were a lot of videos of kids being crazy and stupid, which still racked up tens of thousands of views. Over an hour went by, and April decided that she had had enough of the videos for now. She went into the kitchen to make some tea, and sat on the kitchen island, looking at emails on her phone.

The night was starting to wind down, and April gave Claire her last dose of medicine for the day. Blake walked with Claire upstairs to get ready for bed, just in case she would become dizzy again. Blake took a shower in her room and it was decided that Claire should wait to take one in the morning just to be on the safe side. April didn't want her to become disoriented in the shower with the possibility of falling on the wet tile floor.

"Good night, Claire," April said, while she hovered around the bedroom door. "I'll set you up with another set of clothes in the morning." Stepping into the room closer to Claire, April sat on the bed next to her, and continued, "Hopefully tomorrow you will feel better and you can eat because you are looking way too thin."

April was telling the truth—over the last couple of weeks, Claire's diet had been frugal at best. And the past couple of days of her being sick and not being able to keep anything down had really made her face and body seem sunken.

"I hope so too, April," Claire replied.

"Well, get some sleep tonight so that you regain some strength," April instructed her, as she patted the top of the blanket on the bed reassuring her.

"I will. It's not like I'm going to run a marathon or anything," Claire quipped with a grin.

"No, I suppose not," April smiled and then exited the room, leaving the door a crack open.

Before she retired to her own room for the rest of the night, April opened her daughter's bedroom door and called out, "Good night, Blake; don't let the bed bugs bite."

"Good night, mom."

"Hey, honey, did you have homework due tomorrow?" April asked. After all that had happened with Claire over the weekend, she had forgotten to question Blake about it ahead of time.

"I did, but I finished it when I went to Emily's house on Saturday," Blake reassured her mom. "You know it is not like me to forget about my school work," she added. You could tell that Blake was kidding just by the way she said it.

"Yeah, right," April raised her eyebrow in response, "There are times my dear."

Closing the door to Blake's room, April headed to her room for the night. Once there, she took a shower and put her hair up in a towel so that it would be dry and ready to be prepped in the morning.

Getting into bed, she noticed that Nick's wedding ring was next to her pillow. She remembered that she had held it the night before. She picked it up and held it in her palm for a couple of seconds before placing it back on the nightstand. Subconsciously, April caressed and spun her own wedding ring that had been securely housed on her ring finger since the day she got married. It had been four years since Nick's death, and she had not had the strength to remove it. She knew deep down that she should take it off, but in her mind, she had continued to feel married.

Maybe someday she would take it off, but for tonight, it remained on her finger.

CHAPTER SEVEN

BLAKE WALKED DOWN THE STAIRS WITH HER BACKPACK and purse, and headed straight to the kitchen. Even in her room minutes before she came down, she could smell the sweet scent of breakfast.

"Good morning, mom," Blake said cheerfully to her mom, as April set a plate filled with eggs, bacon, and toast in front of her.

"Morning, sweetie," April said. The Keurig coffee maker finished filling a mug of coffee that April was making for Blake.

"Here you go," said April, as she handed it over to her daughter.

"Where's Claire?" Blake wondered. "Is she still upstairs?"

"Yes, she is. I just checked on her, and she is sound asleep," April said, as she buttered a piece of toast and started to cut a grapefruit for herself.

Seeing that her mom was still in her robe, Blake asked, "Are you not going to work today?"

"No, I decided to work from home today to keep an eye on Claire."

"That's probably a good idea," Blake agreed. "I've never seen anyone that sick before, you know?"

Pouring a spoonful of sugar on her grapefruit, and then taking a spoon to dice into it, April replied, "I just feel like someone should be here in case she gets worse." You could hear the concern in her voice.

"So is she going to stay here another night then?" Blake asked, with a grin.

"More than likely, honey," April said. "I really don't see her well enough to go outside tonight or to be in some shelter," she continued, with a little emotion in her voice.

"I agree, mom," Blake set her fork down and put her hands up showing that she agreed.

"I was just hoping she was, that's all," Blake said, as she picked her fork back up to continue consuming her breakfast.

April finished her grapefruit, and made herself a cup of coffee in her favorite mug, and sat there with Blake until she finished her breakfast. Grabbing her stuff for school, Blake headed to the elevator doors. "Bye, mom. Have a great day," she said before her mom could say it.

"Have a great day, darling. Text me when you get there," April responded.

"You know I will," Blake said, as the elevators closed.

April continued to drink her coffee while she cleaned up the mess in the kitchen. Once Claire was awake, April thought that she could make her whatever she wanted for breakfast. April grabbed bottled water from the fridge and went into her office. She purposely left the door open so that when Claire came down, she could see her.

April had made several calls to the office. She had a detailed conversion with Gina about her weekend. Gina, of course, was fully supportive of what April was doing. There were a couple of calls from Wanda about meetings and conference calls that she had arranged for the next couple of days for her. April had just disconnected from a call with another editor in her office when she heard a sound in the living room by the stairs.

Claire had woken up, and had made her way downstairs.

"Good morning, Claire," April called from the office. "How are you feeling?"

Walking towards the den, Claire peeked into the office, and said, "Good morning. I feel a little better, but I am still really achy, and I still have a headache."

She was in her nightshirt and robe with that throw around her. She did look a little pale but the color was starting to return to her cheeks. April removed the earpiece from her ear, and set it on her desk. She picked up her phone and headed towards Claire.

"Are you hungry? What would you like for breakfast?" April asked.

"To be honest, I am a little hungry."

"Good," April said. "Do you like eggs?"

Nodding her head, she answered, "Yes, I could eat some eggs."

"Perfect, let me get some out, and I'll make them," April said, as she and Claire made their way to the kitchen. April cracked about 4 eggs in a bowl and added a splash of milk and started whisking them. She got out a pan from the cabinet, placed it on the burner, and started it. Pouring the egg batter in the pan, she went to the other counter and grabbed a couple pieces of bread and placed them in the toaster.

"So, Claire," April began, "I know that you are a little better, but I think that you should stay here another night or so." Claire looked at April's eyes, and April could see that Claire was somewhat shocked by the offer.

"Really?" Claire sheepishly asked.

"Yes, absolutely," April declared. "You are not well enough to go back to the streets or to even a shelter. Besides, I want to talk to you about it."

"Ok?" Claire asked. She was happy that she was staying for another night but didn't know where the conversation was going to go.

April finished making the eggs. The bread had just jumped from the toaster a few moments ago. So she prepared the plate, placed it in front of Claire, and sat next to her on the island.

"I would like it if you stayed here for a night or two so that you are all well before you leave," April began, as Claire slowly started eating her breakfast.

"Thank you," Claire said, as she took a bite out of a piece of toast.

"But where will you go after that?" April asked no one in particular, as if she was trying to pull a suitable answer from the air.

"I'll be fine on my own," Claire said, but you could tell that she not only was trying to convince April, but truth be told, she was trying to convince herself too.

With a look of thoughtfulness, April tried to come up with something else. "I know that you are a tough girl and all, but I would feel so much better if you had a decent place to go to, especially at this time of year." Trying to think of something, April said, "Is there a foster family that you can go back to?"

Claire dropped her fork in an involuntary response to the words 'foster family'. Her eyes widened, as she couldn't control an outburst, "No, I can't go back there."

Surprised by Claire's reaction, April said, "Ok, ok, honey. I didn't mean to upset you."

April was not necessarily a shy person, and she was good with people, so she cautiously pressed on. "Why, Claire? Is there a reason why you don't want to go back to foster care? Won't it be better than being alone and fending for yourself?"

Looking in her mind's eye at a recent bad memory of her last birthday, Claire really didn't want to say anything to April. But she did want her to understand the reason behind her current situation on the streets.

"Ok, April," Claire said, as her shoulders dropped a little and she started her testimony. "Please don't tell anyone about this because they probably wouldn't believe me anyways." April could hear the bitterness as she spoke, and nodded her head in an affirmative, and said, "Of course."

Turning her barstool to face April, Claire let loose with her explanation. "I am from Seattle, Washington. That is where I grew up. After my mother was put in jail four years ago, I bounced around to different foster families until I got placed with the foster family of Roger and Carrie Bower. I was with them for about six months until the day of my 16th birthday. They had a son who was 8 years old, and his name was Stephan. The Bowers had fostered kids before, so everything seemed fine for me when I went there. They were nice enough, but I always got the impression that they really didn't want another kid. I don't know why they had applied to be foster parents, but they never truly accepted me."

Stopping to take a sip of orange juice, Claire continued. "So my 16th birthday was on a Saturday morning, and it happened to be the same day that Stephan had an early morning soccer game. So he and Carrie went to the game, and Roger and I were going to join them after he got home from work. He was a doctor, but would work the midnight shift at the hospital once a month, usually over a weekend. The Bowers lived on a small ranch that had three cows and two horses, so I stayed home to feed the animals and take care of the minor chores before Roger got home, so that we could leave right away."

April was listening intently when her cell phone went off. April quickly rejected the call, and switched it to 'Do not disturb'.

"Go on," April said.

"So, here I was, at the house, waiting for him to get home. When the car rolled into the driveway, I could tell that something was wrong. He came in quickly, and had to slam on the brakes so as not to hit the closed garage door. He stumbled from his car and came in through the front door. He called out my name and I came running downstairs. As soon as I entered the kitchen, I could smell the alcohol on his breath. I knew that he liked to drink from time to time but nothing like this; he was totally drunk. He asked me if I was ready to go, and I told him that we shouldn't go because he had obviously been drinking."

A tear formed in Claire's eyes as she continued to recall her birthday.

"He instantly got pissed. He told me to mind my own business, and to do as I was told. I got really scared and I didn't know what to do. He became enraged at my indecision and he yelled at me to get my ass outside." Blinking hard and recalling the memory, Claire continued, "When I saw the state he was in, it brought back memories of my mom coming home drunk and then driving away in her Volkswagen Beetle totally intoxicated. I knew that he was just an accident waiting to happen."

April couldn't believe what Claire was saying. It was supposed to be a special birthday, and here she was, dealing with a very adult situation.

"As I went towards the door outside, I noticed his car keys on the counter, so I swiped them on my way out and threw them into the bushes surrounding the house. Holy cow did that piss him off even more! He grabbed my shoulder and spun me around to face him, and smacked me hard across my face."

"What!" April gasped.

"I was shocked, and the pain from the slap made me slightly disoriented. Before I could stop it, he hit me again on the other cheek, and pulled me back into the house. He threw me on the floor, and kicked me on my side. I screamed out in pain and began to cry hysterically. I was yelling for him to stop. He grabbed me by my neck and forced me into an upright position. There was this look in his eyes that I have never seen before. I begged him to let me go."

More tears began to flow from Claire's eyes as she continued.

Roger dragged me to the bedroom and threw me on the bed. He was wearing hospital scrubs, and he started taking his shirt off. He said that he was going to teach me a lesson, and then began pulling his pants off. The only thing that he was wearing was his underwear. He jumped on the bed and began to call me names. His hands began slowly caressing my legs. He then began to pull his underwear down with both hands, because now he was on his knees straddling me; pinning me down. Fortunately, my hands were free for a moment as he did that, so I quickly grabbed the lamp on the nightstand and smashed him in the face with it. "

Claire grabbed her napkin to wipe the tears from her face.

"Oh my God," April said softly.

"He yelped in pain and fell off the bed. I scrambled off the bed and ran out of the house and down the gravel driveway until I got to the road, too scared to turn around to see if he was chasing me. I kept running until I finally managed to hitch a ride with a truck driver. The good thing was that the truck driver was a woman in her fifties, and turned out to be really nice. She noticed the bruises on my face, and could see that I had been crying. Realizing that something bad had just happened, she said that she was heading towards Springfield, Illinois, and I asked if I could join her. Because of her, I ended up in Chicago. As I was getting out of the truck, she gave me all the cash that she had on her, which was like fifty bucks, and then wished me safe travels. That was my 16ᵗʰ birthday," Claire concluded.

April stood up from the barstool and held her arms open for Claire. The tears in April's eyes made them look clear and reflective. Upon seeing April's tear-filled eyes, Claire's emotions got the better of her, and she crumpled into April's welcoming arms and squeezed April with a hug. Embracing April, Claire sobbed into April's housecoat. April squeezed Claire a little tighter and rocked her for a few moments.

Claire broke the embrace of the hug, and sat back down on the stool. "Wow," she said, as she brushed away more tears with her wrist. "I haven't told anyone that. I don't know what Roger said to the police or to Child Protective Services, but I can only imagine."

"Why didn't you go to the police?" April questioned.

"Come on, April, you know why," Claire chuckled cynically. "Who do you think they are going to believe? A well-respected doctor or a sixteen-year-old girl, whose mother has been in and out of prison with a rap sheet the size of a toilet paper roll?"

Even though April couldn't believe that there was nothing that could have been done, she did see where Claire was coming from.

"To answer your previous question, that is why I cannot go back to the foster family," Claire said.

"I can't believe that you had to endure that," April said apologetically.

"I am scared to go back into the foster care system," Claire replied, matter-of-factly.

April really felt for Claire. Not only was Claire's mom in prison but her foster father who was supposed to care for her, had almost raped her.

Looking deeply, willing herself to put her trust in April, Claire pleaded, "Please do not call Child Protective Services on me."

"I won't, Claire, I promise," April said, before she had time to think.

"I know how it sounds," Claire said. "A runaway girl living on the streets is accusing her foster family of criminal acts in a sorry attempt to hide something that she actually did, but I can honestly tell you that nothing is further from the truth. It happened exactly the way I just described, without any exaggeration, I promise."

There was no way to be hundred percent certain that Claire was telling the truth, but April just had a gut feeling that she was. It was as if Clare's facial expressions were unable to speak a lie, and her account of what she was saying had happened, seemed brutally honest.

"I don't think that at all," April tried to reassure her, "I am horrified at what you had to endure."

April couldn't even imagine what would have happened, if this had happened to Blake... What if she was somehow put into the foster care system and ended up with a foster father like Roger? Something had to be done, but not at Claire's expense. April had to think about reporting this, but for now, it would have to wait.

"I know, right?" Claire said, "I just want you to know that I am truly a good girl. I mean, I don't do drugs, I haven't stolen anything, and I basically stay to myself. It's just that life keeps throwing me curveballs, and I'm desperately trying to hit the ball so I can get to a base, you know?"

April had to smile at that analogy. Claire was pretty mentally mature for her age.

Claire turned her attention back to her plate to finish her breakfast. April left her alone for a few minutes, as she looked at her phone to get back to the person that had called during Claire's story.

Taking the last bite of eggs from her plate, Claire set the fork down on the plate and said to April, "Those eggs were really good. Thanks for breakfast."

"Glad you liked them. I try to make them like Nick did, but his way will always be better."

"Well, don't worry, April, yours are great," Claire said, as she pushed herself up off the stool with the help of the counter.

"Do you want to watch TV?" April asked.

Claire thought about it for a second, and then asked, "No, not really, but can I read one of those books in your office?"

Glancing towards the den, April smiled, and said, "Of course you can, come on in, and you can take a look at what I've got."

Once inside, Claire got a better look at the library, and she was awestruck. She thought the books in Claire's office at Priscilla Publishing were great, but they didn't compare to the ones here. The bookshelves went high up to the ceiling, and the ceiling went up to the height of the second floor. There was a sliding staircase that April used to get to the books on the higher shelves. It was simply amazing. There were hundreds and hundreds of books in that room.

"Wow, April, this library is totally awesome!" Claire exclaimed.

"I know. It's been a passion of mine for the past ten or so years," April said, with pride dripping from every word.

"Look at whatever you like," April instructed Claire. "Please be careful of the books over on that shelf though," she said, pointing at a shelf that was separated from the others and had its own separate shelving unit. "You see, those are really old and the binding on some of the books is very weak."

Seeing Claire's reaction, April continued, "You can touch them but just be careful, that's all."

Claire looked in wonder at the room for several seconds, and started looking at the titles. Eventually, she picked out a book, and asked April, "Can I read this one?"

April didn't have to see the title, and instantly said, "Yes, of course, I said whatever you like, you can read."

The den had April's desk with two chairs in front of it, so that if she had clients or guests, they could sit in front of her while she worked on her computer. There was a couch behind the desk, and a La-Z-Boy with a small coffee table. Claire sat on the edge of the couch for a second to open the book and flip through the pages.

Two hours later, April was typing away on her keyboard on her desk with the earpiece in her ear. She was editing a few chapters from one of her many clients, and she was lost in the world of that particular novel. Claire, who had stayed in the den with April, was now lying on the couch, and was several chapters into the book that she had picked out.

The sound of the book falling to the floor made April turn around, and she saw that Claire had fallen asleep, and the book had slipped out of her hands. Smiling, April quietly walked over to the couch and picked up the book. She set it next to the coffee table, and grabbed a plaid blanket that was folded nicely on the end of the couch and pulled it over Claire.

Even though Claire was starting to feel better, she was still sick, so she definitely needed her rest. April left her office and quietly closed the door in order to not disturb Claire. She then went upstairs to get dressed as she was still in her nightgown and robe. Picking out a wool skirt, a wintergreen short-sleeved blouse, April added a pair of nylons to go with the outfit. Once dressed, she sat at her vanity and turned on the curling iron. She put on her makeup while she waited for the iron to get hot, and then curled her hair. April wasn't planning on going out tonight but she wanted to be presentable, just in case.

April went back downstairs and sat on the La-Z-Boy in the living room. She turned on the TV, but muted it. She decided to call Wanda about a few things. Picking out Wanda's name from her 'Favorite' icon in her contacts list, she touched the picture.

"Yes, boss?" Wanda's voice asked, as the line connected.

"Can you reschedule Tony Landon's meeting with me from Tuesday to Wednesday?" April asked.

"I'll call him right now, and call you right back," Wanda replied.

"Wanda?" April asked.

"Yes, boss?" Wanda waited for the next order.

"I was just wondering if you are still planning on coming over for Thanksgiving dinner this Thursday."

"Of course, I am," Wanda confirmed. "I will be bringing over my famous cheesy potatoes."

"Good, I just wanted to make sure," said April.

"You got it, boss. I'll call you back in a minute when I get a hold of Tony." With that, the phone call ended.

Thanksgiving was only four days away, and April's thoughts turned to Claire. April had told Claire that she could stay with them for another day or two, but that would end a day or so before Thanksgiving. Could she let Claire go just a day before the holiday? Should she keep her until after the holiday? Another thought hit April's mind—Claire was only sixteen and still a minor. Would she get into trouble for housing a runaway?

But then the memory of what Claire had had to endure with Roger and Carrie came back in full force, and April could not allow her to be placed in a home like that again.

She couldn't believe that one lunch with a homeless girl had now turned into... what? It was all because of Nick's voice... Why did he want her to help Claire anyway? It was very confusing; however, April had already made up her mind. She was going to let Claire stay for the week.

The office door opened, and April saw Claire walking out of it with the book in her hand and the plaid blanket around her.

Yawning, Claire said, "I must have fallen asleep."

"Yes, you fell asleep about an hour or so ago. I didn't want to wake you because you still need your rest," April said, as she got up from the chair.

Seeing that April was dressed, Claire looked at the clock in the kitchen to see what time it was. The clock revealed that it was 12:27 p.m.

"How are you feeling?" April wanted to know.

"Tired and still a little cold. I don't feel queasy from the eggs I had for breakfast, so that is a good thing," Claire surmised, as she stretched her arms.

"Well, that's good at least," April answered, "Have you been dizzy again since yesterday?"

"Nope," Claire replied truthfully.

"Good," April breathed, "Why don't you take a shower and put on some clean clothes. I will pick out a couple outfits from Blake's closet for you so that you will have a clean set of clothes."

"Sounds good," Claire said, setting the book she was reading on the skinny round table that was just outside the office and near the staircase.

"I will make us some lunch when you come down," April said, as she realized the time.

"Ok," Claire replied, as she walked slowly, but steadily up the stairs.

April rummaged through the kitchen to get a few ideas on what to make for lunch. She finally decided to make grilled cheese and ham sandwiches with tomato soup. She put the soup in a pan, and started to cook it on low heat. By the time Claire was done with the shower, the soup would be ready, and all April had to do was to make the sandwiches.

Claire took about fifteen minutes in the shower and another ten minutes to blow-dry her hair. She didn't want to leave it in a towel this time, so she made an effort to blow-dry it and brush her hair. April had picked up a pair of jeans and a pretty olive blouse. Looking in the mirror before she went down, Claire saw a fine, young, clean, and well-dressed lady staring back at her. This was the first time in a while that she felt human.

When she made her way downstairs and to the kitchen, April had the soup on warm to keep it from boiling, and she had the square pan heated, ready to go for the sandwiches.

"Grilled cheese sandwiches are my favorite," Claire informed April.

"Mine too," April declared, honestly.

April and Claire had finished the first grilled cheese sandwiches when the buzzer by the elevator door went off. April went up to it and used the intercom to ask who it was. The bellman at the elevator entrance said that a Dr. Amanda Welch was there, and wanted to know if she could come up.

"Yes, of course. Please send her up," replied April.

Dr. Welch walked into the apartment with her doctor bag, and said 'hello' to April and Claire.

Looking at Claire, she could see that the worst was over, and that she was getting her color back.

"I was in the neighborhood and thought I would drop by for a quick visit to see how my patient is," she said, as she opened her bag to take out the stethoscope.

"I think that I am getting a little better," Claire said, as the doctor approached her.

"You are starting to look better. Let me see if you sound better." She put the headset of the stethoscope into her ears, and applied the chest piece on Claire's back.

"Take a deep breath," Dr. Welch politely commanded.

Claire took a deep breath, and then the doctor told her to do it again.

Moving the chest piece to the front and on her chest, she commanded Claire to take a deep breath again.

A couple of breaths later, Dr. Welch sighed and said, "It's still a tad bit raspy."

She put the stethoscope away, and took out a digital thermometer. She put the probe tip into Claire's mouth, and told her to make sure that it was under her tongue and towards the back. A few seconds went by and the thermometer beeped. The number on the screen read 99.9 degrees.

"It's still a little high, but it's going down," the doctor informed the duo.

"Were there any more dizzy spells?" she asked Claire, as she put the thermometer back into the doctor's bag.

"No, ma'am," Claire answered, respectfully.

"Good. It was probably all the antibiotics we put into your system, but I wanted to make sure that it wasn't something else. "

Looking at April, Dr. Welch said, "It is still very important that she gets lots of rest and liquids for the next couple of days. I don't want her to go back to school until Wednesday. She will be weak for at least a day or so. "

Claire looked sheepishly at April, but didn't say anything.

Dr. Welch pulled out a paper pad from her bag, and started to write.

"I'm going to write you this note stating that you may return to school on Thursday, November 24, which is Thanksgiving, so basically I'm saying that you need to have the rest of the week off from school."

Claire took the note from the doctor, and said, "Great, thank you."

"You're welcome. Just get some rest and continue getting better," Dr. Welch replied, as she picked up her bag and headed towards the elevators. April walked her to the door, and thanked Dr. Welch for coming over.

"It was no problem," Dr. Welch said. "Let me know if you need anything else from me."

"Ok. I will."

The doors closed, and April went up to Claire.

Claire looked at April and handed her the note. "I don't think that I am going to need this."

April sighed, and said, "No, I guess not," wondering how Claire would ever get back to school.

"You know, Claire," April began. "Thanksgiving is only a few days away, and Dr. Welch said that you need to rest for a day or so before you will fully recover. So, I was thinking that would it be ok if you stayed here with Blake and me through Thanksgiving."

Claire couldn't believe what she was hearing. It was one thing to have a stranger spend a night or so, but now it was going to be a solid week, not to mention, she would be having Thanksgiving dinner here.

Trying to be rational, Claire said to April, "Are you sure? I mean you will have me here for a whole week?"

"I was thinking this morning that I wanted you to stay for the next couple of days because you were sick, but then that would lead right up to Thanksgiving, and I certainly couldn't live with myself if I let you go before one of our fantastic Thanksgiving dinners," April said, as a counter to Claire's argument.

Claire couldn't help but smile. She couldn't believe that this nice lady would do that for her, especially when she knew of her troubled past.

"I would love to, April," Claire began, "but I don't want to be a burden. I mean I am super grateful for all that you have done for me this far, but I don't want to impose."

"You aren't. Believe me. It would be a pleasure for Blake and me to have you stay here for another week. Besides, that will give us time to figure out what you should do."

"Only if you are really sure about this?" Claire asked, for the final time.

"Yes, I am absolutely sure," April smiled, and gave Claire a quick, little hug. "This will be fun."

CHAPTER EIGHT

IT WAS THANKSGIVING MORNING, AND THERE WAS A LOT TO do. Claire had just recovered from the flu and her UTI was all but gone. However, it did take a lot out of her, and it took all three days leading up to the holiday. She must have lost ten pounds; but the sad part was that she really didn't have it to lose.

April was laying the plate settings on the dining room table, and she mentally went over the final guest count. Setting the plates down, she named them as she counted: me, Blake, Claire, Gina, Wanda, dad, and mom. Emily couldn't come because her mom wanted her to spend the holiday with her. She had flown out on Wednesday to Oregon, and would be returning late on Sunday night. Placing the final plate on the table, April went into the kitchen to help the girls with breakfast.

Blake was getting the ingredients out to make her famous French toast pancakes. Claire had asked Blake if she could help with breakfast, and of course, she said 'yes'.

"I have never really baked before," Claire admitted, as she looked over the ingredients on the counter.

"It's ok, Claire, I got you," Blake responded to her cooking partner.

April watched the girls intently as they embarked on their breakfast mission. You could tell that they were both having fun. It was nice to witness the interactions of the two girls. Blake did not shun Claire away for being homeless. Most kids Blake's age would be hesitant about befriending a girl like Claire—someone off the streets—but not Blake. She was kind to her, and treated her with respect.

For Claire, Blake was like that best friend that she never had growing up. Claire would laugh and giggle with Blake when they would watch YouTube or play video games. April had had a hearty laugh a night ago, as she could hear the girls screaming and laughing at each other—apparently, they were getting beat up by the other team in some first-person shooter game that they were playing online. It was refreshing to hear laughter coming from her daughter again.

"Ok, Claire," Blake began, "please blend the contents of the bowl with the mixer right there."

"You got it," Claire obeyed, but before she put the arm of the mixer down in the bowl, she turned it on. Blake started to mouth the word 'No' just as Claire put the rotating arm into the bowl.

Instantly the flour, egg, vanilla, and cinnamon exploded in all directions from the bowl.

Everything in an entire five-foot radius became covered in wet flour. April only got a little bit on her clothes because she was just clear of it. Unfortunately, both girls were in the blast zone.

Blake looked at Claire. All she could see was a flour-covered silhouette of her, with pieces of eggs running down her face. There were only two eyes blinking in shock showing through a blanket of flour.

"Shit," a shocked Claire let slip out.

"Shit, shit," she repeated a little louder, staring in disbelief at the mess she had just created. Claire was turning her head from side-to-side, looking at the flour debris, when a big clump of flour fell from the ceiling and landed squarely on her head.

Blake couldn't help it. She burst out laughing. "Oh my God!" Blake yelled out, as she began to laugh even louder. The sight of a shocked Claire blinking in surprise, and Blake's outburst of laughter made April laugh too. Seeing that April wasn't mad at the mess that she had just made, and the sound of Blake now laughing hysterically, caused Claire to start laughing. Here they were, covered in flour, crying because they were laughing so hard. Blake tried to take command of her laughter, but when her mom let out a snort while she was laughing, all bets were off. Pounding the table and trying to get air into her lungs, tears of laughter were falling from Blake's eyes. Of course, the more they tried to stop laughing, the worse it got.

About five minutes later, the three of them calmed down, and began the tedious job of cleaning themselves up as well as the entire kitchen.

"Oh man," April said, handing a dishtowel to each girl as they started the process of wiping the flour out of their hair. "I haven't laughed like that in a very long time."

"Me neither," agreed both Blake and Claire.

They cleaned up what they could, and finished making breakfast. Still somewhat covered in flour, they sat and devoured Blake's pancakes. After breakfast, the two girls had to take a shower in order to totally rid themselves of the pancake batter. April only had to change her clothes because she did not get totally covered in the pancake batter.

When Claire and Blake returned to the kitchen, April showed them how to prep a turkey for the oven, and then placed it in the bottom oven for it to start baking. Blake and Claire prepared the green bean casserole while April made her favorite fruit salad.

Once they were done with preparing the rest of the dinner, they took a minute to sit down on the couch, and turned on the Macy's Thanksgiving Day Parade.

"This is a tradition for us," April told Claire about the parade.

"When Blake was little, Nick and I would take her to the parade; and he would put little Blake on his shoulders, so that she could see the entire parade."

Blake continued the story when her mom paused, "You see, ever since my dad died, we haven't been able to bring ourselves to physically go there and watch it, so we prepare the dishes and the turkey, and then watch it on the television."

"Oh, I see," replied Claire, as she could understand the feeling of loss.

"But we make the best of it," April said happily.

"Yes, we do, mom," Blake confirmed.

Looking over at Claire, April said, "We will make this year special because Claire is joining us."

"You got that right, mom," Blake immediately agreed.

Claire smiled at Blake, and then said to her and April, "This past week has been truly special, and I will never forget all that you two have done for me."

Claire added, "I might not be alive today, if you hadn't taken care of me."

That hit April a little hard because Claire had a point. What if she was still on the street and couldn't get the antibiotics right away or even at all. She might be dead on the sidewalk somewhere.

April blinked away a tear that had begun to form in her eye. "Let's just say that everything happens for a reason, and that maybe it was us being here when you were sick that was what was meant to be."

The buzzer of the elevator rang, and it was April's parents arriving. They had wanted to get there a day earlier but her dad had had to take the company jet to fly to Vancouver for a last-minute meeting, and wasn't able to fly back until late last night. He was the Executive Vice President of Operations for Anixter International, based out of Glenview, Illinois. Anixter International was a fortune 500 Company that supplied communication and security products throughout North America. April's mom was a realtor for a small real estate company near Glenview but she only worked part-time. They lived in the village of Northfield, which was about forty-five minutes away from April's apartment.

April buzzed them up, and the trio waited at the door for them to come up. Claire was just a little nervous because she was about to meet Blake's grandparents, and she had never known what it was like to have grandparents. Not to mention the fact that she was a homeless teenager who had been living with their daughter for the past week or so.

Unknown to Claire, April had called her parents the night before and had already explained the entire situation. To their credit, they were proud of their daughter for taking in this poor girl. April asked them not to ask Claire too many questions because she didn't want her to get uncomfortable. April's mom could see where April was coming from, and said that they would keep their curiosity at bay. However, April shouldn't have worried because her parents were good people, and they had raised a remarkable daughter. The last thing they would ever want to do would be to make Claire feel uncomfortable or unwanted.

The elevator doors opened to reveal Joseph and Anne Walters.

"Happy Thanksgiving everyone," Joe shouted, as he stepped off the elevator. He was carrying a couple of big shopping bags that he set on the floor next to the elevator, and turned his attention back to everyone in the apartment.

"Grandpa and Grandma," Blake exclaimed, as she stepped forward to hug them.

"Happy Thanksgiving, dear," Anne said to her daughter, April, as Blake was still hugging her grandpa.

"Happy Thanksgiving, Mom and Dad," April smiled, as her mom went in for a hug.

After hugging April, Anne noticed Claire standing there, and went up to her, and said "Hello, Claire, I'm Anne Walters and this is my husband, Joseph." After the introduction, she gave her a welcoming hug.

"Nice to meet you," Claire said to Anne. She could see how nice Anne was, and by the look in her eyes, she seemed like a genuine person. Hearing his first name, Joseph looked at Claire, and said with a big smile, "Glad to meet you too." And he too gave her a hug. Claire could tell that he was a professional, but he seemed light-hearted and fun to be around. Claire's nervousness started to subside.

They all spent the day talking and laughing and watching the football game. Joe and Anne would engage in conversation with Claire, but it wasn't forced or phony. By the time the other guests arrived for dinner, Claire was almost totally at ease with them. Claire was starting to understand why April was the person that she was. April's parents cared about people and the environment. Even though it appeared that they had a ton of money, they still cared about things that anyone would, and they didn't take anything for granted. Anyone could see during the conversations of the day that they too dearly missed April's husband, Nick. He was the son that they had never had. Joseph and Nick went on several fishing trips together, and had the time of their lives. April's parents missed him terribly.

Before dinner, Blake had taken Claire up to her bedroom, and let her pick out any dress or skirt that she wanted. At first Claire had resisted, and didn't want to wear a dress, but Blake was quick to point out that April insisted on it for every major holiday. Giving in, Claire picked out a green and blue plaid skirt with a black sweater. Blake was wearing a gold, one-piece dress with a shiny gold necklace. Blake sat Claire down on her vanity stool, and told her that she could use whatever makeup she wanted. Claire's color was almost back to its original tone, but her skin was just a shade paler than what it should be. Since she'd got here, Claire was definitely cleaner, and the homeless look about her was all gone. Because she had been sick the entire time, no one had thought about makeup since she had never left the house to go anywhere.

Claire dabbed a little blush on her checks and skittishly started to apply the eyeliner. Blake reached over Claire's shoulders, and said, "Here, let me help you."

"Thanks," Claire said, looking a little ashamed.

"Don't worry about it; I'll show some tips on applying makeup," Blake reassured her.

"My mom didn't really show me how to use makeup, you know?" Claire explained, with a thoughtful look in her eyes.

At that moment, Blake realized how good she actually had it. She had a mother who spent countless hours with her teaching her how to apply makeup, what to use and when to use it. Her mother supplied her with everything that she needed when it came to that department. Now here was Claire who had never had that mother-daughter moment when it came to learning the art of applying makeup.

Finishing up with a light application of lipstick, she smiled at her handy work, and said, "There. All done."

Claire looked in the vanity mirror, and breathed out, "Wow, I look good."

Blake didn't put too much on, but what she did really enhanced Claire's natural beauty.

"Tomorrow morning, we will take a little time, and I'll go through some of the basics with you if you don't mind?" Blake told Claire.

"That would be great," Claire said thankfully.

Claire stood up from the vanity and took a few steps towards the door.

Before they left her room, Blake opened the top drawer in her dresser, and pulled out an old wood box. She removed its contents and handed it to Claire. Lying across her hand was an old white pearl necklace.

"No, I shouldn't," Claire bucked the thought of wearing the fancy jewelry.

Making a sad puppy face, Blake pleaded "Please, wear it for me."

Knowing that she was not going to win this argument, Claire gave in and allowed Blake to put it on her. Claire looked in the mirror at the pearl necklace, and it was exquisite. Each pearl radiated brightly in its own luster. She carefully caressed the pearls along the strand, and found them to be almost as smooth as glass.

"Besides, they are a family heirloom my mother gave to me because they were my great-grand mother's, and I thought that they would look good on you," Blake quickly said, as she bolted out of the bedroom and headed downstairs.

"Why you..." Claire said to Blake, as she went to chase after her.

The girls ran about halfway down the stairs but slowed to a gentle walk when they saw April looking disapprovingly at the speed of their approach.

However, the look of disapproval turned into one of amazement when she saw Claire and what she was wearing. "Claire, you look beautiful," April said, as the girls walked to the dining room table where she was with Anne. Talk about a transformation from a week ago. Standing before her was not the dirty, homeless girl who was nearly at the end of her rope, but a beautiful, young lady who was wearing makeup and was dressed up in fancy clothes. It was simply breathtaking.

"Thanks," Claire smiled shyly, as she wasn't used to getting compliments.

Then Anne noticed the pearl necklace that Claire was wearing, and said, "The family pearls look amazing on you."

April turned her attention to Claire's neck. She glanced behind Claire, and saw that Blake was smiling. Raising her hand to touch the pearl necklace on Claire's neck, April agreed with Anne, and said, "You're absolutely right, mom—they look beautiful on her."

"It was my idea," Blake proudly declared.

"Well, good choice, my daughter, and you look beautiful too," said April, looking at both girls, side by side.

"You really don't mind me wearing them today?" Claire sheepishly asked about the pearls.

"Definitely not," Anne spoke with affection.

"Seriously Claire, you look great, and I don't mind it," April echoed Anne's sentiment.

Even though Claire wasn't used to wearing any kind of skirt, she felt classy for the first time in her life. Being here in this apartment with this family and all the nice people made her yearn for something more.

The buzzer on the elevator chimed, and it was Gina and Wanda. They came up to the apartment, bringing in more food for the holiday dinner. Wanda was wearing an orange cocktail dress with a tiny trim of brown on the bottom hem of the dress. It totally complimented her recently dyed orange hair. She looked quite pretty.

Gina was wearing a black dress that fell just to the top of her knee. She was wearing black nylons and she looked classy.

"Happy Holidays everyone," Gina declared, as she handed a bottle of expensive wine that she had brought with her to April.

"Happy Thanksgiving," April said, as she graciously took the bottle of wine, and set it next to the electronic wine opener on the kitchen counter.

Wanda set the cheesy potatoes down on the counter and took off her coat. Seeing the girls by the dining room table, she smiled and said, "Hey, hi, girls, Happy Thanksgiving."

She went over to Blake and gave her a big hug. Then she stepped up to Claire, and said, "Hi, again, Claire," and then gave her a hug too. Claire hugged her back, and she replied, "Hi, Wanda, Happy Thanksgiving."

Both Gina and Wanda made the rounds, and said hello to everyone in the apartment. They had known Joseph and Anne Walters for years, so they were almost like family—just like April and Blake were.

April had politely instructed the girls to grab the rest of the food that was warming in the oven, and Joseph had taken his position at the table near the turkey, preparing to carve it. He opened the silverware drawer and took out the set of knives that he had given Nick years ago. The knives were a set that he had bought when he was in Asia during a business trip—he had gifted them to his son-in-law on Nick and April's first Thanksgiving as a married couple. For the past four years, Joseph had specifically used this particular set to carve the turkey because it reminded him of his son-in-law.

Once everything was placed on the table with organized precision, April directed everyone to their seats and she herself remained standing.

"Before my dad opens with grace, I would just like to say a few words," April said to the guests now seated around the table. Everyone turned towards April in polite anticipation.

"First of all, I would like to thank all of you for sharing this holiday with us," April started.

Placing her hands on the edge of the dining room table for emotional support, she continued, "I am truly blessed to know each and every one of you, and I am thankful to have you in my life."

Signaling her dad to proceed, April sat down and put her hands on her lap.

Standing up, Joseph cleared his throat as he started to say grace.

"Dear Lord, today we give thanks for our many blessings. As we pray for those in need... We give thanks for our family and friends, as we pray for those who are lonely. We give thanks for our freedoms, as we pray for those who are oppressed. We give thanks for our good health, as we pray for those who are ill. As we give thanks for our comfort and prosperity, we share our blessings with others on this day of Thanksgiving. May the love of God enfold us, the peace of God dwell with us, and the joy of God uplift us."

Joseph paused for a brief second, and then ended with, "We thank you for taking care of our beloved son, Nick. Even though we miss him each and every day, we celebrate the fact that he is with you watching over us. Also, thank you Lord for those of us that are new to this table today." Looking at Claire, he continued, "We welcome you, Claire, to celebrate with us, and we are happy that you have recovered from your illness and are healthy enough to be here today."

Claire's face immediately turned a color almost as red as the cranberries sitting in the dish on the table. She definitely hadn't expected to receive that kind of welcome, and was not used to being the center of attention.

Joseph finished grace with an "Amen".

"Amen," responded all the guests around the table.

Blake tapped Claire's shoulder, and offered her a fist bump. After a second, Claire realized what Blake was after, and raised her fist to make contact with Blake's. The knuckles on each of their hands gently came into contact with one another, and Blake let out another "Amen."

Claire smirked at Blake, and they both turned their attention to the dinner awaiting them on the table.

"Dig in, everyone," April directed, as she removed the napkin from the ceramic turkey-shaped napkin holder, and placed it neatly on her lap.

Everyone started to fill their plates with the dishes that were closest to them on the table, and then began passing the dishes around. Claire knew what was going to be served because she had helped prepare some of the dishes, but nothing prepared her for the sight that was the Turner Thanksgiving Day feast. Never, in her entire life, had she been a participant in a dinner like this. She didn't realize it, but she was staring at the food with a childlike wonder.

"Please pass the mashed potatoes," Blake asked Claire, as she handed the green bean casserole bowl that she just emptied on her plate to Wanda, who was sitting on the other side.

"Sure thing," Claire replied, as she grabbed it from the left side of the table, and passed it to Blake.

Blake took the spoon out of the bowl and used it like a shovel, and dug a pile of potatoes onto her plate.

"Want some plate with your potatoes?" April sarcastically questioned her daughter.

"No, I'm fine," Blake grinned back at her mom.

The next thirty minutes witnessed everyone eating and drinking and engaging in polite discussions. Wanda was a blast just by the way that she said things. Her knack for just living life with no real worries was refreshing. When they finished dinner and were all still sitting at the table, April spoke up and said to the table as a whole, "Ok, everyone, I would like to go around the table and have you tell us what you are thankful for."

Joseph started, and said that he was thankful for his wife and his family. Anne went next and mentioned how she was thankful for her husband and her daughter and granddaughter. Gina was thankful for a good friend and editor like April. Wanda said that she was thankful for her job (because both her bosses were sitting at the table) and for her little dog, Archie. Blake looked at her mom and smiled, and said that she had the best mom in the world and added how much she appreciated her. She looked at Claire and spoke about how much she enjoyed having Clair stay with them.

Claire smiled, and using that as a cue for her turn, she said, "I am thankful for the day that April and Blake turned around on that sidewalk and came up to me and offered me lunch. I have enjoyed every minute since that moment." Taking a second to collect her thoughts, she continued, "I don't know what I did to deserve all this, but I will be forever grateful. You have shown me kindness and sincerity when I needed it the most. You nursed me back to health when I was sick with the flu, and let me stay here all week so that I could recover." Looking directly at April, she concluded, "Thank you so much for welcoming me into your home."

Not expecting that heartfelt testimony, April's cheeks flushed a little, and she looked at Blake.

Blake was smiling from ear to ear, and you could tell that she was excited to be a part of what they were doing for Claire.

"Thank you so much, Claire, for that," April said, as she looked into Claire's eyes. "I am so glad that you agreed to come with us to lunch that day, because you have really touched our lives as well. I can't believe that it has only been a week since that day, and it has been a pleasure for me to help you out."

Blake grabbed Claire's hand and held it chest high in solidarity, as April continued, "To follow up with that, I would like to say that I am thankful for everything that has happened in my life that directed my path to all of yours. I am so grateful for all your support, especially in the last four years. My life was changed forever, and I don't know how I could have managed without all your love and strength."

"Here, here," Joseph said, at the conclusion of April's speech.

"I would like to make a toast," Joseph began, as he reached for his glass, and waited for everyone else to do the same.

"To family, to friends, and to those friends that are considered family," Joseph raised his glass and said, "Cheers."

"Cheers," everyone said in unison, as they clinked each other's glasses and took a drink.

"Who is ready for dessert?" April asked.

Everyone signaled that they were, so April went into the kitchen to fetch the pies that were in the fridge. Claire followed her into the kitchen to help with the plates. Before April opened the fridge door, she looked at Claire, and said, "That was really beautiful what you said."

"I meant every word of it. You and Blake have been so awesome to me, and I can't believe that I am here with you guys on Thanksgiving," Claire spoke with sincerity.

April raised her hand and rubbed Claire's left upper arm, and said, "Well, believe it." And then she smiled as she opened the refrigerator door to retrieve the pies.

After dessert, everyone just sat around the table stuffed beyond belief. Gina, Wanda, and April were discussing clients and novels. Claire was sitting next to Blake as they both were heavily engaged in conversation with Blake's grandparents. The chiming of the clock on the wall next to the dining room indicated that it was now 8:00 p.m., and Gina and Wanda decided to call it a night. Saying their goodbyes to everyone, they made their way to the elevator, thanking April and everyone for a great night. April wished them good night and told them she would see them on Monday. She had taken Black Friday off as she and Blake were going to go shopping.

Joseph and Anne decided to move to the couch where it was a little more comfortable, in order to give more time to digest the wonderful diner, before they departed for home. April and the two girls joined them in the living room.

"You know something, April?" Joseph asked his daughter, with a look of serenity on his face.

"What's that dad?"

"I truly think that the Thanksgiving feast is getting better and better each year," Joseph said, patting his puffed-out stomach.

"You think so, do you?" April joked, as she answered.

"Of course," exclaimed her dad. "I am in awe of the amount of food that you prepare and how beautifully it is prepared, not to mention that you make me proud of the woman that you have become."

"Wow, thanks, dad."

"It's true honey. You followed your dreams and worked hard, and look at what you have got to show for it. You have an amazing daughter that you are doing an excellent job of raising, and you have the career that you always wanted," Joseph declared as he reached for his wife's hand, as if he was channeling her feelings as well.

April flushed slightly, as her dad praised her. She had very loving parents and she had a great childhood growing up with them, but hearing the words of praise from her father is something that every daughter in the world secretly yearns for.

"Yeah, mom, you're the best!" Blake said, jumping on the 'praising April' bandwagon.

Claire looked at April, and nodded her head affectionately, and said, "Yes, April is the best."

Everyone in the room could feel how grateful Claire was for being there. This Thanksgiving was like the ones she used to dream about, spending the whole day with family and friends as you dedicate the day to cooking, cleaning, and watching football.

Anne looked at her husband, and released his hand to point at the bags by the elevator doors, and said, "I think it is time to get the bags."

Joseph grinned, and replied, "Quite right my dear." He got up from the couch and walked over to the elevator and walked back to the couch, but stopped in front of Claire.

"Claire," Joseph began. "Even though my wife and I just met you today…" he paused to sneak a glance at April, before continuing, "we have immensely enjoyed this holiday with you, and would like to give you a little something." He set both bags down in front of her, and proceeded to sit back down next to her and his wife.

"Really?" Claire said in a shocked voice. "Why?"

Anne spoke up and explained further, "You see Claire we have the opportunity to give you a couple of items that you are in need of, and we would be honored to help you out."

Although she really wanted to see what was in the bags, Claire hesitated and motioned to April, "April has done so much for me already, and I think that she knows how much I appreciate it. But I'm not here to collect as many handouts as I can." Claire was trying to get her point across—that she did not want to take advantage of April and Blake's acts of kindness.

"Oh, sweetie," Anne countered, "It's not a handout, it's a hand up. We can see that you are a good person who has been encumbered by bad circumstances. Joseph and I would like to help you out just a little."

"Open them," Blake impatiently ordered Claire because she wanted to see what her grandparents had gotten her.

Claire bent down and grabbed the bag closest to her, and proceeded to remove the tissue paper. In the bag were three shoe boxes. She took the top one out and opened it, and discovered an awesome pair of gray and orange Skechers Flex Appeal 2.0 tennis shoes. The look on her face said it all.

"These are for me?" she couldn't believe that she was going to get a brand new pair of shoes.

"Sure are," Anne answered. "All three boxes are yours."

Claire reached into the bag and pulled out the second box, and in that box was a Tiffany Teal pair of Converse Chuck Taylor All Star Low Tops. When she saw the shoes, she almost squealed with excitement. "Seriously you guys, these are amazing," Claire said, her face lighting up like it was Christmas day.

Blake was seriously happy for Claire, and was glad that her grandparents did all this for her.

"One more box," Blake gleefully informed Claire.

Claire took out the last box from the bag, and eagerly opened it. "No way," she exclaimed as she pulled out the right boot of a pair of Insulated Nordic Casual leather boots, with a tag on them that made it known that it was waterproof.

"Those are awesome," Blake blurted out, smiling from ear to ear.

"My God, you guys, this is too much. Thank you so much," Claire said, as she stood up and then asked, "Is it ok if I give you a hug?"

"Of course, you can," Anne answered, as she pushed herself up from the couch, and spread her arms wide to receive Claire's embrace. Joseph got up to receive his hug as well.

April sent a look over to her parents, as if to say 'well done'. She knew that she could count on her parents to deliver. When April had talked to them on the phone the night before, she had mentioned that she and Blake had noticed that Claire's shoes had holes in them and that she didn't have any clothes to her name either.

Stacking the boxes of shoes to her left, Claire pulled the second bag closer to her and slowly began to remove the tissue paper. This bag was significantly lighter than the first one, but it was approximately the same size. There was more tissue paper in this bag, which created a big pile of tissue next to her as she worked her way closer to the bottom of the bag.

The last piece of tissue paper was removed revealing an iPhone 7 box.

"No way!" Claire screamed, "You have got to be kidding me!"

Pulling out the box, Claire held it up for all to see.

"Way cool!" Blake said gigging with delight, "You got a phone!"

Claire turned to Anne and Joseph, stammering in shock, "I can't believe it. Why would you do this for me?" Claire wanted to know.

Joseph addressed the entire living room with his answer, "You see, Claire, in my business, communication is key to everything. I thought it was important for a young lady who is trying to make it in this world all alone to have access to some sort of communication. I mean, everything is on the web, and how is a person supposed to function without it?" He paused a second to take the box from Claire and opened it. He turned on the phone and waited for the display to come to life. He tapped it a couple of times and then began typing.

"So, we got you this phone so that you will not be left in the dark and will be able to get in touch with anyone that you need to. Oh, by the way, we are taking care of all the billing, so you don't have to worry about ever having to make a payment."

The phone had already been activated. Joseph was now placing his and Anne's contact information in the phone.

"You now have our numbers, so I am kind of expecting a few updates from time to time to see what's going on," Joseph said, with a polite smile.

Joseph handed the phone back to her, and she accepted it as if it was made out of glass. She looked around the frame of the phone to choose the button that turned it on. After a couple of seconds, the white Apple logo appeared on the screen and it took a while to fully load itself.

Tears of surprise, tears of joy, just tears in general were making Claire's eyes wet. She hugged Anne and Joseph again, and as she did, she kept saying, "I can't believe this."

Blake asked Claire if she could see her phone and Claire handed it to her. "This will be cool. We can text each other now whenever we want."

"You know it," Claire said to Blake, as they sat by each other on the couch, and started to experiment on the new device.

April was relieved because Claire had new shoes that didn't have holes in them. The phone was a surprise for April too, as she hadn't known that her dad was going to do that for Claire, but he was the Vice President of a communication and security company, so it would be just like him to do something like this for her. God, she loved her parents.

April's parents stayed for another hour, and then decided that they had better get going. After all, Joseph had an important video conference call in the morning, and unfortunately, it was with a client in California.

"Good night, everyone," both Joseph and Anne said pretty much at the same time.

"Love you, Mom and Dad. Thanks for everything," April said, as she hugged them again.

"Happy Turkey Day," Blake said to her grandparents, and then added, "I love you guys."

"We love you too," Anne replied to Blake, and blew her a kiss.

The elevators closed, and April went back to the La-Z-Boy in the living room and pulled the footrest up and let out a satisfying sigh. "What a wonderful night," she said to the two girls who were about to sit back on the couch.

Claire, who was still in shock over the gifts she had just received, opened the shoeboxes again just to look at them. "I still can't believe it. I mean I just met them today. I didn't know that there were people like them out there in the world."

April grinned and said, "Those are my parents. They are very compassionate. I only suggested a pair of shoes because I noticed that yours had a few holes in them. It's just like them to go above and beyond."

Claire's eyes widened in amazement as she put the shoe boxes aside, and then took out her new phone. She tapped it to open the camera app, and waved for Blake to get closer to her, extending her arm out to hold the phone to take a selfie of the two of them.

"Nice," Blake said, approving the picture.

Looking at April, Claire approached the La-Z-Boy chair, and asked April, "Do you mind?"

"Of course not," April said, as she adjusted the hair falling on her forehead and prepared for the selfie. Claire reached out with the phone, and they both smiled as Claire took the picture. Claire showed the picture to April—it was a remarkably nice picture of the two of them, especially because they were both dressed up and Claire was still wearing the family's pearl necklace.

"I love it," April declared. "Please text it to me. I would love to have it."

"Sure, you bet," said Claire with delight.

Once Claire had April's cell number, she texted the picture to her.

"Can I take one of just you, so that I can save it as your contact picture?" Claire asked April.

"Absolutely," April said, as she sat a tiny bit straighter to pose for the picture.

"Thanks," Claire said, as she assigned the newly acquired picture to April's contact info.

"Oh," April told the girls in the room, but addressed Claire. "I forgot to mention this, but you are coming with us to do some Black Friday shopping."

Taking a moment to realize what April meant, Claire looked a little puzzled, and asked, "What?" and then added, "you have already done so much for me. I couldn't have you take me shopping. Besides, it is a mother-daughter thing for the two of you, and I don't want to intrude."

April put her hands on her lap, and explained, "Listen Claire, Blake and I have already discussed this today, and we would love for you to come with us so we can help you get a few more outfits that you can call your own." Not waiting for Claire to resist further, April added, "Besides, Blake and I love shopping for not only each other, but for other people too." April's voice then took on a serious tone, as she concluded, "Please let me do this for you."

"Yeah, we have to find outfits to match your new shoes," Blake said, as if the world depended on finding the perfect set of clothes.

"I don't know what to say..." Claire began.

"Just say yes," April prodded.

"Well, yes?" Claire slowly replied.

"Sweetness," blurted Blake, as she held up her hand to give a high-five to Claire.

Claire paused for a second for dramatic effect, and then whipped her hand out to smack Blake's hand.

"Yeah, girl," Blake shouted.

"Yeah, girl," Claire repeated, not quite as loud as Blake but sounding just as excited.

April pushed herself up from the chair, and yawned, "It's getting late. We all better get to bed so that we can get up early tomorrow."

Blake and Claire agreed as they were starting to feel the after-effects of the turkey dinner, and were pretty tired. That was the most that Claire had eaten in one sitting in a very long time. Her stomach was extremely happy, but unfortunately, very full.

Blake got up from the couch, and felt exhausted, "Sounds like a good idea—I'm beat."

"Good night, ladies," April said, as she walked to the stairs.

"Good night," Claire said to April, as she picked up the boxes to take them upstairs.

"Night, mom," Blake said to her mom, as she reached down to help Claire with her stuff.

* *

CLAIRE STEPPED OUT OF THE SHOWER AND PUT ON another nightgown that Blake had let her "borrow," which meant that she could keep it. April had gone into her room and had closed the door, so Claire didn't have to worry about disturbing her if she made a noise in the bathroom across from her bedroom door. Claire was about to go into her room, but decided to make a pit stop in Blake's room.

Claire quietly knocked on the bedroom door that was slightly open.

"Come in," Blake said, as she waved Claire in.

Blake was lying on the bed and was propped up by her favorite reading pillow. Actually, she used the pillow more for YouTube or for watching TV. Nonetheless there she was, using it to look at her phone.

Blake gestured at Claire, asking her join her on the bed, and Claire lay down next to her.

"What's up?" Blake asked.

"Can I just say how totally cool you have been to me over this past week? Here I am, a total stranger, and your mother just invites me to your home. Most girls would have been jealous or weird around me but you have been a real friend to me."

Blake turned her body and to totally face Claire, and replied, "You know, I didn't fully understand why my mom stopped that day to go back to you, but I am glad she did. You are pretty cool yourself, and I am glad that you have been here all week. Even though you were sick and puking your guts out for half of it, but hey, I still had a great time."

"Me too," giggled Claire.

"Besides," Blake continued, "I think that you have given my mom a purpose again."

"What do you mean?" Claire asked.

"I think that she has been going through the motions lately. I mean she has been wonderful at taking care of me, but the first couple of years after my dad died, she was lost. I could see it in her eyes. Over the last two years, she has been getting better, but she's still not quite her old self." Pausing to think of the right words to make her point, Blake then said, "But over the last week, I have noticed a look in her eyes that hadn't been there in years. She has found a purpose in you. I know it's not pity—it's just that there is a spark in her eyes now. A purpose."

Claire rolled on her right side to look at Blake face-to-face, and sarcastically asked, "So, I'm a purpose?"

"Yes" Blake blinked. "You're a 16-year-old, blonde, blue-eyed Purpose. A purpose without a clue."

They both giggled at that.

Claire looked at Blake and asked with a serious tone, "Can I tell you something?"

"On purpose?" Blake laughed.

"Yes on purpose," Claire smirked.

"Shoot," Blake grinned.

"I know it has only been a week, but you are like one of the nicest girls that I have met. I never really had friends, you know. I realize it sounds a little corny but when I was growing up, I was bounced from place to place, and by the time I made friends, I would be shipped out. The friends that I did make were always guarded because I was a foster kid. The brothers and sisters were nice enough, but most of them were indifferent. "A tear escaped from Claire's right eye and rolled down her cheek, making a tiny splash on the bed cover.

"Now it's my turn to say something," Blake said, as she used the blanket on the bed to wipe away Claire's tears.

"I know that you have had a hard life, and for that, I am really sorry. But I just want you to know that you are a pretty cool girl. When my mom went back to you, I was like 'what the hell are you doing' but now that you've been here for this week, I can honestly say that we have grown attached to you."

Blake grabbed the tiny throw pillow just above her head and wrapped her arms around it.

Sounding mature for her age, and extremely motherly, Blake added, "Don't worry Claire. It's going to be alright—you're going to be alright."

"How do you know?" Claire asked dubiously.

"I just know," Blake responded with certainty.

"But how do you know?" Claire really wanted to know.

"Claire," Blake said, "You have a purpose here."

Both girls smiled and continued talking for another forty-five minutes before they fell asleep on Blake's bed.

CHAPTER NINE

THE STREETS OF DOWNTOWN CHICAGO WERE PACKED with people on Black Friday. April and Blake were used to it. They had lived here all their lives. Claire, on the other hand, had not.

"This is crazy!" Claire exclaimed, as the hundredth person bumped into her as she kept up with April and Blake.

"I know, right?" Blake agreed, as she herself maneuvered between pedestrians.

April was leading the way through the chaos with the expertise of a ship's captain. Her ability to weave in and out of the wave of people was remarkable. Partly because she had a plan for where she wanted to go first, and partly because she was a mother guiding her young through the treacherous jungle as it were.

"Which store are we going to first?" Blake asked her mom, as she almost walked into a light post.

"We are going to go to Macy's, of course," April answered. "Then I thought that we would go to Nordstrom Rack, Marshall's, Carson's, and then end up at Burlington Coat Factory, where we can look for a decent coat for Claire."

"Wow, April." Claire said, as the list of stores just recited seemed a little daunting.

"My mom doesn't mess around with her shopping," Blake told Claire honestly.

April wasn't a shopaholic, but she did enjoy spending time with her daughter looking for good deals, and she did appreciate a great looking outfit at a great price. April was a bit more excited this year because they were taking Claire, and it felt good to be able to buy a few things for someone who would truly appreciate it and who absolutely needed it.

Blake had let Claire borrow a coat, and of course, Claire was wearing her new tennis shoes that April's parents had given her. Thank goodness too, because the amount of walking that the three of them would be doing today would have probably done her old shoes in.

Claire followed April and Blake through the onslaught of people and even though it was a trek through block after block of people, Claire was having fun. It was the first time in her life that Claire had gone shopping like this. It was definitely an adventure. Claire's reflection in the shop's windows mirrored a beautiful, young lady who was happy, and who was allowing herself to smile.

As they entered Macy's Department Store, a car horn sounded just behind them. A white Mercedes E-Class wagon slammed on the brakes and barely avoided crashing into a black Saab 9-3 that had darted out from a parking spot.

Claire stopped to look in the direction of the car horn—that's when she noticed a homeless person standing at the curb begging for money. She involuntarily stopped to stare as the realization hit her. It was hard to believe that just a week ago that was her.

Claire turned away from the homeless woman, and said to April and Blake, "Sorry guys, it's just that I can sympathize with her, you know?"

Knowing how hard it was for Claire to be on the streets, but probably not understanding what it must have been like to be that person actually standing there, April appreciated Claire's compassion for someone else who was in her situation.

April reached into her wallet and pulled out a $20 bill and gave it to Claire. "I know that it's not a solution to her problems, but maybe you can brighten up her day with this."

Claire blinked in reaction to April's kindness, and said, "Yes, it will definitely brighten up her day, and you can't imagine what this will do for her mental health right now." She walked over to the woman and handed over the money. The woman looked at it, and his eyes got wide. "Bless you child."

"Bless you too," Claire replied. "I just want you to know that you simply have to believe that things will work out. Just have faith. It's working for me," Claire said to her, and walked back to April and Blake. "Thank you for that. It felt really good," Claire told April,

April smiled and confessed, "Yes, I know how good it can feel," and then turned around to continue their trek to Macy's.

"Don't worry, April," Claire said to her, as they walked through the front doors and into the store. "I'm not going to do that to every homeless person. It just kind of hit me, you know?"

Chuckling, April said, "That's good because I think that I would run out of money really soon if you did." It was sad and frustrating though that so many people were homeless in the city. April didn't know how to fix the problem, but she at least had reduced the homeless population by one.

April led the way to the women's clothing section and began browsing through the rows of racks.

Blake pulled out a couple of shirts and held them up to Claire's chest to see how they looked. Claire wrinkled her nose at the yellow one, but really seemed to like the purple one. April was looking at a rack that was next to the one that Blake and Claire were at, and noticed a cute sweater. She held it up for Blake to see, and Blake nodded a yes.

After about fifteen minutes of picking outfits, April and the girls went to the dressing rooms to try on what they had selected. Claire really liked almost everything that she tried on. However, there was a red blouse that had a strange neckline, and Claire thought that it was uncomfortable.

Blake was the same size as Claire, so it made trying on clothes that much easier. Blake decided to try on the red blouse that Claire hadn't liked, and discovered that she liked it. There was a shirt that Blake had picked out for herself, but she didn't like the way it looked once she had it on. She thought that it would look good on Claire, so she put it on the hanger and hooked it to Claire's dressing room door and politely commanded her to try it on.

April had discovered a few good outfits for herself and was in the process of trying them on as well. She did grab a few dresses for work, but ultimately they didn't make it to the purchase pile.

Claire had about five different outfits that she felt looked good on her and that were comfortable. There was a sixth outfit that Blake had chosen for her that fit well, but Claire wasn't a fan of. Blake insisted that it should remain in the good pile for consideration.

"Which one should I get?" Claire asked April, as she came out of the fitting room for the final time.

A little confused, April asked, "Which one?"

"Yeah, which one do you want me to have?" Claire asked again, as she didn't know which was the one outfit that April wanted to buy for her.

"All six of them, Claire," April said with conviction.

"No, I can't let you buy me all of these," Claire began. "It's too much."

"Listen, Claire," April began, "I'm not taking no for an answer. You need new clothes and since we have Blake with us to help with picking out what looks good on you... We are doing this." April held out her hand to deter Claire from debating her further, "Let me do this for you."

Waiting until April was done, Claire said, "Why won't you let me pick out just a couple then?"

Blake grabbed Claire's pile and put it into her own pile and replied to the question that was directed at her mom, "No, we are getting all of these. You look amazing in all of these, and we know that you need your own stuff. This is what I am good at, so just suck it up."

"All right, but I will eventually repay you guys for all of this," Claire said with gratitude.

April put her arm around Claire's shoulder, and said, "Ok, someday you can repay us if you like, but don't worry about it today." Taking her other arm, she wrapped it around Blake, April gave them both a quick squeeze, and said, "Let's go and get checked out. We still have more places to go to."

April took her pile of outfits, and then the three of them headed for the registers. The lines were long and they burned thirty minutes of shopping time just standing around to get rung up. With bags in hand, the three of them headed outside to hit the next store.

* *

"THAT COAT LOOKS AMAZING ON YOU!" BLAKE COMPLI-mented Claire, as they exited Burlington Coat Factory. It was their last stop, and Blake had found the winning coat of the day. It was a camel-colored, leather jacket that had a winter lining with a faux fur collar and hood. April had the sales clerk remove all the tags and sensors, so that Claire could wear the coat out of the store. All three ladies shopping bags in both hands—they really couldn't have handled carrying another bag, even if they had wanted to.

"It does look really cool," Claire smiled, as she agreed with Blake's assessment of the coat.

"Everything that we got today for you looks wonderful on you, Claire," April said, as she moved her hands to twist the bags in a half circle to indicate the items in the bags.

"I am blown away by everything today," Claire told her shopping partners honestly.

"It was our pleasure to help you shop and to set you up with your own clothes," April told Claire.

"Besides," Blake cut in, "I got to use my fashion knowledge to pick out some totally amazing outfits for you, if you don't mind my saying say."

Nudging Blake with her elbow in appreciation, Claire replied, "I couldn't have done it without you."

"Right?" Blake asked.

As they continued on their way down the block, April got a whiff of cinnamon rolls coming from her favorite bakery.

"Hey, you two, let's get some muffins to take home with us from Cindy's Cupcakes," April suggested as she turned her attention to the bakery.

"Oh yeah!" exclaimed Blake. Looking at Claire, she said, "You haven't had a cupcake until you've had one of Cindy's! They're to die for!"

Claire was getting hungry and the thought of a baked goodie made her stomach growl.

"Sounds good to me," Claire agreed.

"Good. Let's go," April said, as she made her way to the bakery.

Every time you opened the door at Cindy's Cupcakes, your nose was consumed by several scents of deliciousness. The first scent that attacked your olfactory senses was that of cinnamon. Following closely behind, the warm smell of fresh bread baking in an oven would hit you. Then the smell of a heavenly mixture of chocolate, honey, and sugar would lead you on.

"It smells great in here," Claire said, as she stepped through the door of the bakery. Once inside, she noticed how warm and inviting it was. There was a bulletin board with a 'Help Wanted' sign, an ad for a music lesson, and a cozy room for rent neatly pinned on it. On the other side of the bulletin board, was a stone gas fireplace that was on and contained a hot, flickering flame. The whole décor of the establishment was based on a log cabin with exposed support beams. It felt like you had just strolled into a log cabin in the woods.

"Hi there. Welcome to Cindy's Cupcakes," the young woman behind the cupcake showcase said.

"Hello," April replied.

"Hi," Blake and Claire said, almost simultaneously.

There was a line of about ten customers, so they walked to the end of the line and began to look at the many different kinds of muffins and cupcakes in the showcases. As April examined each section to see what she wanted, she received a text on her cell phone. Taking her phone out of her purse, she looked at the screen and let out a grin.

"Its Crystal," April informed Blake.

"Is she back yet?" Blake questioned.

Other than Gina, Crystal Evans was April's best friend. April and Crystal met in the fourth grade and had been friends ever since. Crystal, a beautiful black woman, could have been a model. However, she went into criminal justice and became a police officer. After six years of walking a beat, she became a plain-clothes detective solving cases throughout Chicago. Many people underestimated her because of her beauty, but she had a black belt in karate, and a brown belt in judo. If you had to use a single word to describe her, it would be 'badass.'

Crystal and her boyfriend Tripp Davis had saved up for an entire year to book a vacation in the Cayman Islands. It had been about five years since she went on a full vacation anywhere so this was truly a special trip. She had just texted April to inform her that they were boarding the plane, and would arrive late tonight.

"No, not yet. But she is boarding the plane right now. They should be in later this evening." April told Blake.

April told Claire all about her best friend Crystal.

"She sounds like a cool person," Claire admitted, as she listened to stories of Crystal.

"She is totally rad. I've known her my entire life and she is like an aunt to me. In fact, I call her Aunt Crystal most of the time," Blake added.

"Yes, she is like the sister that I never had," April conceded. "Ever since Nick died, she has been someone that I can rely on."

April texted Crystal back and told her how she couldn't wait for her return and to have a safe flight. April decided not to mention Claire right now—she would do it tomorrow, when she called Crystal. Crystal had planned to come over this Sunday for dinner, in order to tell April and Blake all about her vacation.

"What can I get you guys?" the clerk asked, from behind the counter.

April decided to get a dozen donuts for them to eat on the way home, and then had each girl pick out something special, like a flavored muffin or a cinnamon roll. April and Claire each chose a muffin while Blake decided to get a cinnamon roll with extra frosting.

Since they had too many shopping bags to handle, and couldn't eat the donuts and walk at the same time, April found a bench about half a block down, and the three of them settled down on it.

April opened the bag, and offered it to Claire and Blake before she took out one for herself.

"I'm beat," Claire realized, feeling her energy drain as she continued to sit on the beach.

"Me too," Blake agreed, as she stretched her legs out a little more, and then put her arms around her mom and Claire on the bench because she was seated in the middle.

"This was super fun though," Claire said to both of them. "Thank you both again for all of this," Claire said, as she motioned to the bags by her legs.

"I had fun too," April told Claire.

"It was totally fun and we picked out some cool clothes for Claire," Blake said, and held up her fist to Claire for a fist bump. The two girls touched knuckles, and both made a little explosion sound as they opened their fists in a wave.

"You two are cute," April observed.

"You're cute," countered Blake immediately.

April squinted her eyes at Blake, showing a subtle irritation with her for repeating her words. At times, Blake would make it a habit to repeat what April just said. For instance, if April said 'That's cool,' then Blake would say 'You're cool' back to her. Most of the time it was fine; but there were a few instances in which April thought this behavior was not appropriate.

Blake looked at Claire so that Claire could ascertain what Blake had just said.

Hesitating for a second, Claire slowly said to April, "You... are... cute?"

Blake laughed at Claire's nervous sounding voice, and April couldn't help but grin.

"Yes, Claire, I'm cute... But so are you," she said, reaching across and touching Claire's nose with her index finger. Then April pinched Blake's left cheek, and happily declared, "You're cute."

Blake stuck out her tongue and turned her head to the left, which made Blake's tongue run over the top of her mom's hand and across her knuckles.

"Yuck!" April screamed, as she quickly pulled her hand away from Blake's face.

Blake let out a loud chuckle at her mom's reaction. Claire let a tiny gasp slip out as she saw the look on April's face as she wiped Blake's saliva off of her hand.

"Blake, that was gross." April sounded mildly annoyed.

Blake started to say, "You're gr..." but then thought better of it, and merely said, "I know, mom."

April shot her a stare, as if to say 'Don't finish that sentence' and then squinted her eyes.

They sat there for a few more minutes consuming most of the donuts in the bag.

"Ok girls, let's hit the road," April suggested, as she bent down to retrieve her shopping bags and stood up.

"Sure, you got it," Blake said, as she followed her mother's movements and grabbed her own bags.

Claire got up and said, "Ok. Let's do this."

April made the executive decision to hail a cab instead of hauling all of their loot across the several blocks between them and the apartment. The cab pulled up, and the driver got out and opened the trunk of the car. He helped them with their bags and then hurriedly got back in the driver's seat and started the meter. Blake gave the driver the address of the apartment building and then they were on their way.

Blake opened the bag of donuts and took out a custard-filled white-powdered donut, and took a big bite out of it, smearing white powder and filling across her lips and cheek. A drop of custard fell out of the donut and splattered on her right pant leg. Blake grabbed April's hand and used it as a napkin to wipe off her pants.

"Blake!" April declared. Blake couldn't help it—she burst out laughing.

Claire didn't see exactly what had happened but by the sounds of it, Blake was at it again. Claire didn't want to laugh, but the sounds of April's turmoil and Blake's laughter made Claire smirk and giggle.

"I can believe you did that!" April said, trying not to laugh herself.

"You can't? Seriously?" Blake joked.

"I take it back. Of course, I believe it," April said, trying to sound annoyed.

April opened her purse and rifled through it until she found a trial pack of wet wipes. She took one out and opened it. Using it to clean up the custard from her hand, April then took out another wipe and handed it to Blake.

"Thanks, mom," Blake said, as she began cleaning off her face and lips.

"You're very welcome, my messy little child," April said matter-of-factly.

The cab driver pulled off to the curb, and they got out and reclaimed their shopping bags. April paid the cabby and they headed into the building.

Once they got up to the apartment with all their loot, April told Blake and Claire to put the bags on the couch so that they could go through them again to see all that they had got. April began to take the clothes out of each bag and place them in piles on the couch, sorting them by whose outfits they were.

"I must say we did really well today," April said, as she held up individual pieces of clothing to examine them.

"Yeah, we did," Blake nodded as she allowed her body to fall onto the couch. Claire flopped down next to her and the two of them went through the piles of clothes that April had organized.

April went into the kitchen to make herself a cup of coffee. "Would either one of you guys like a cup of coffee?"

"Yes," said Blake.

"Sure, please," Claire answered.

April took out two more k-cups and set them on the counter to wait their turn in the coffee machine. April took out her favorite mug and grabbed two more plain white ceramic mugs for the girls. When the coffees were done, April picked up a mug in each hand and walked into the living room and handed them to the girls.

April went back to the kitchen to get her mug, and then called out to the girls in the living room, "Hey, how about we break out the leftovers from yesterday and have dinner soon?

"That sounds good," said Claire, as she blew on her coffee to cool it down.

Blake nodded her head to agree, and then said, "I could eat Thanksgiving leftovers for a solid week straight and I wouldn't ever get sick of it."

After a few minutes of relaxing in the living room and talking about their shopping experiences today, the three of them went to the kitchen and took up several containers of Tupperware and began fixing their own plates. Once all the meals were heated up in the microwave, they sat down at the dining room table and started to eat.

"I love the cheesy potatoes," Claire remarked, as she took a big bite of them off her plate.

"Me too," Blake agreed, as she put a big spoonful of cheesy potatoes in her mouth.

April took a sip of coffee and then picked up her fork to pick up a piece of turkey. "What do you want to do tonight?" she asked the girls.

"I don't know, but I'm good with just staying in," suggested Blake.

"Yeah, that sounds good to me," agreed Claire. Even though she had spent most of the week cooped up in the apartment recovering from the flu, the thought of spending another night with April and Blake sounded like fun. Besides, she was exhausted from all the shopping that they had done today. She wasn't used to the fast pace and hadn't realized just how tiring it could be. Claire had never been shopping like that in her entire life; to go out and spend the better part of a day going from store to store and trying on all the clothes was like a dream come true.

After they finished dinner, Blake and Claire cleaned up the table, and April went to the junk drawer in the kitchen and took out the UNO cards. "Hey, you guys want to play UNO?"

Claire put the last of the plates in the dishwasher, and said, "Sure, but you are going to have to show me how to play because I have never played it before."

"It's pretty easy, but of course I will show you," April said to Claire.

"Yeah, it's fun," Blake added. "We played UNO most of the summer, and as I recall, I won most of the games."

April gave Blake a somewhat dirty look, and said, "That may be true, but that was then and this is now, so I am feeling pretty lucky tonight."

"We'll see," Blake said mischievously.

Over the next two and half hours, they played UNO, and Claire was the overall winner with the most wins. April won three games; Blake won two, while Claire won four games. She actually won the first two games of the night, and Blake chalked it up to beginner's luck.

Blake decided to go upstairs for a little bit while April and Claire stayed in the living room. April got out her laptop and was looking through a bunch of emails. She sat down on the La-Z-Boy and pulled the lever to raise her legs up. Claire got out a book from April's office library and was reading on the couch with her head on the armrest and her body spread out across the couch. The book that Claire was reading was by one of the first authors whose book April had edited when she was promoted to editor. It ended up being a three-book series about a young woman who was a maid at an elite high-rise hotel in downtown New York and who had witnessed a double murder when she was cleaning a room. The journey of this young lady from getting away from the murder, and then making it to the courthouse to testify was riddled with intrigue and thrills. The author was Mandy Stonewell, and she had written four other series of books—a total of nineteen books in all. She had become a well-known author throughout the U.S., and she was based out of Chicago. She became one of Priscilla Publishing's star authors and was among those who had helped it become the publishing firm that it was today. So, here was Claire reading this particular author for the first time and enjoying the book so far. She was about fifty pages into the book, when Blake came downstairs and joined them in the living room.

Blake was holding a hairbrush in her left hand and her iPad in her right hand.

"Hey mom, when you get a sec, can you brush my hair like you usually do?"

April looked up from her laptop and noticed that Blake had the brush in her hand.

"Sure honey, give me one minute while I finish typing this email," April said as her fingers danced across the keyboard.

Blake sat down cross-legged in front of the La-Z-Boy and played with her iPad until her mom was ready. Claire could see part of the screen of Blake's iPad, and it showed a fashion app which allowed you to create various designs for clothes and dresses. There were different avatar models that showcased your designs when a user finished creating them. By the looks of it, Blake had a couple of dress designs that she was working on. Catching Claire's stare at her iPad, Blake said, "I've been working on these for the past couple of days, and I'm almost done. I am just trying to capture some more inspiration before I can say that I am 100% satisfied with it." Claire looked impressed, and said, "They look good to me. I like the silver one with the black necklace the best."

Looking intently at that particular design, Blake commented, "I do too, but I think that I am missing a little something—I don't know what yet." Blake mulled over her design for a few more seconds, and then noticed that Claire was holding a book.

She looked at Claire, and asked, "What are you reading?"

Claire looked up from her book, and said, "It's called *Maid of Honor.* It's about a maid who sees a murder and everything that ensues after that."

"Cool," Blake said only mildly interested. She did like to read, but not as much as Claire.

Claire grinned at Blake, and continued, "It's an action thriller, and it's Mandy Stonewall's first novel of the series. I have not read any of her books yet, and I thought that I would start reading them in the order that she wrote them."

"Cool," Blake said again, but with a grin this time.

Claire couldn't help but smile at her, and after a slight pause, she said, "You're cool."

"Yes. I'm well aware of it," Blake quipped.

April closed the lid of her laptop and set it on the side table next to her chair, and said, "I'm ready."

Blake handed her mom the brush and tilted her head back just a little so that it was in the proper position. Ever since she was a little girl, Blake's mom would sit her down in front of her and brush her hair. After Nick passed away, April and Blake would often sit together in this position—the mother and daughter duo would share special moments and remember what an amazing man Nick was.

April began by running her fingers through her daughter's hair from the top of the forehead down to the ends. She did this several times and then worked in the brush. After several minutes of brushing, April quietly started to hum. Most of the time, April wouldn't realize that she was humming until either Blake would say something or start humming herself to imitate her mom.

Claire glanced over at April at the sound of her humming and was captivated by the moment. April's hum kept rhythm with the brush strokes—it sounded like she was playing a musical instrument. Claire was mesmerized by it. Claire's own mother had never spent any time with her. After a few seconds of staring, Claire blinked and brought her attention back to her book. She found herself feeling ashamed for pitying herself.

Claire received a text on her phone and she slightly flinched in response. She looked at the screen and it was a text from April's mom asking her about her day.

"Who's that?" Blake asked.

Claire smiled, and said, "It's from April's mom, asking me my day of shopping went."

"That's cool of her," Blake answered. "Why don't you take a picture of the clothes you got—grandma would love to see them."

"Yeah, that sounds like a good idea," Claire agreed. She got up and ran upstairs to the spare bedroom, where she had put her shopping bags before dinner. After several minutes, Claire came back downstairs with about six pictures on her phone of the outfits, and of course, the winter coat.

Claire answered Anne in a few sentences telling her how much fun she had had, and how thankful she still was for the phone. She looked at April and Blake. It was such a good scene of the mother and daughter together. Hit by an idea, Claire positioned the phone in front of her like she was still texting, but aimed it at the duo. She clicked a picture of April in the middle of brushing Blake's hair. April had the brush in her right hand, and with her left, she was holding a long strand of hair as she brushed it. Claire quickly examined the picture and was pleased with the result.

Claire set the phone down on the coffee table, and opened the book back to where she had left off. The novel was getting good and she wanted to finish the book before the end of the day. She had just finished the chapter that she was on, when April said to Blake, "All done, honey."

Blake got up from in front of the chair, and said, "Thanks mom. That felt good."

April sat there for a few seconds with the brush in her hand and looked at Claire reading. Claire hadn't realized that April had caught a glimpse of her as she watched April brushing Blake's hair, and that April had detected a look of longing in Claire's face. April knew at that moment that Claire probably had never had a mom who brushed her hair.

"Claire," April called out.

Looking up from the book, Claire answered, "Yes?"

"Your turn," April said with a smile, as she waved the brush and pointed at the floor where Blake was just seated.

Claire's eyes met April's, and she allowed herself to bask in the warmth of them. She blinked after a second, and said, "Ok."

She closed the book, set it next to her phone on the coffee table, and sat down in the same position that Blake had just been in. Her heartbeat increased and her breathing became labored as if she was about to embark on a roller-coaster ride. Claire suddenly became aware of how nervous she was and couldn't fully understand it. As the nervous energy in Claire's body found its outlet, she began to subconsciously rub her hands together.

April reached up to Claire's head and began running her hands through her long blond hair. After a few strokes, April could feel Claire's shoulders relax and the tension release. After a minute or so, April added the brush and followed the same routine that she had done with Blake.

Claire sat there allowing her mind to be fully immersed in the moment. She couldn't believe that something so simple as brushing someone's hair could mean so much.

Blake sat on the couch where Claire had sat, and watched her mom and Claire intently. It was nice of her mom to offer to brush Claire's hair and to see them both sitting there put a smile on Blake's face. A thought came into Blake's mind, so she spoke up, "Hey mom, why don't you give her a French braid? I think it would look cool with her long blond hair."

April looked down at Claire as Claire turned her head to look at April.

"Sure, that would be great," April said. "Do you want one?" she asked Claire.

In all of Claire's life, she had never had a French braid. In fact, she didn't even know how to make one. Feeling even more excited, she said, "Yes, I would love one, if you don't mind?"

"No, of course not, it would be my pleasure," April responded, as she continued brushing. After about ten minutes of brushing, April started braiding—taking strands from the top of the head and weaving them in an inter-locking pattern.

Just then, Claire received another text. Her phone, which was on the coffee table, beeped, and Blake looked at the screen. Because Claire had not set the privacy notification, Blake could see that the text was from grandma, who was commenting on Claire's outfits.

Looking at the phone and then at Claire, Blake said, "It's grandma, she says that you will look amazing in the clothes that you got."

"Ok," Claire said, "Can you text her back for me and tell her thank you. You know what my password is to unlock the phone."

Blake typed in the password, and the screen opened up to where Claire last left the phone—it was a picture of Blake and her mom brushing her hair. She almost said something out loud, but suddenly thought of an idea. She quickly texted grandma back and waited for a moment, then took a picture of April braiding Claire's hair. It was an amazing picture. April had a look of determination on her face while Claire had a look of genuine joy. Blake immediately sent the picture to herself, and then deleted it from Blake's phone. She was going to do something special with it, but did not want Claire to see it just yet.

April was half-way through the braid when she began to hum. Claire noticed it right away, and looked over at Blake. It took Blake several seconds to become aware and she saw Claire looking at her. Blake was about to say something to her mom about it but noticed a tear in Claire's eye. This was a moment in time that Blake realized that Claire had never experienced before—an act that only a mother and daughter could share. Blake tilted her head and smiled at Claire. In that moment Blake and Claire understood the gravity of the situation, and what it meant for Claire.

April finished the braid and declared, "All done."

Blake got up from the couch and guided Claire to the mirror on the wall. Looking at the reflection, Blake said, "Sweet, that looks really good, mom."

Claire turned her head from right to left to see as much as she could at the back. April got up from the chair and pulled a hand mirror out of the hutch next to the mirror on the wall.

"Here, look at it like this," April instructed Claire, as she held the hand mirror behind her head so that the reflection revealed the braid clearly."

"Wow, it looks amazing," said Claire excitedly.

The braid was done with such delicate precision that it almost didn't look real—almost as if someone had made a wig specially designed for her. Claire took the end of the braid and set it in front of her right shoulder, so that it rested comfortably there.

"Let me take a picture of it," Blake said, as she pulled out her phone. She snapped a couple of shots from the back to get the full effect of the braid, and then she pulled her mother closer so her reflection could be seen in the mirror, along with Blake and Claire. Holding the phone at waist level, Blake pointed it up towards the image of the three of them. It was like she was taking a picture of a portrait of the three of them hanging on the wall.

Claire looked at April in the reflection of the mirror, and said to her graciously, "Thank you so much April. It really means a lot to me. I love it."

Turning her head and looking at Claire directly, April said, "You are very welcome, Claire. I am so glad that you like it. It's been a little while since I've done a braid like that. I used to do more of them for Blake when she was smaller, but I don't do them that often anymore."

"Yeah," Blake interjected. "She used to do all kinds of different braids. They were cool. I just like her brushing my hair now more than braiding it." Looking at her mom, she quickly added, "That's not to say that I don't ever want one again, in fact, by the end of this weekend I can see myself rocking a braid. Right, mom?"

Grinning at her daughter, April responded, "Maybe if you're good and don't lick my hand like you did on the street bench, then we might be able to work something out. "

"Not going to guarantee it, but it does look promising," Blake said jokingly.

"Only time will tell, my dear," April said, with a hint of mischief.

April and Blake stepped into the kitchen while Claire stood in front of the mirror for a few more seconds.

"God I love it here," Claire said to herself in the reflection. She gingerly placed the palms of her hands on the back of her head to caress the braid in awe. Claire couldn't help but smile as she followed the other two into the kitchen.

* *

THEY HAD DECIDED TO RENT A NEW MOVIE ON THE APPLE TV, and of course, had made popcorn to go along with it. When the movie finished, all three just sat around the living room doing their own thing. April was on her phone texting a variety of people—Gina, Wanda, and of course, her parents. Blake was switching between texting her friend, Emily, and working the fashion app on her iPad. She was telling Emily about Claire, and how she had stayed with them, and Emily was kind of shocked and texting her concerns about it. Blake was doing her best to ease any misgivings that Emily had, and was trying to explain how cool the situation was. Claire was nose-deep into her book, only a few pages away from finishing it.

It was late in the evening at this point, and it was nice just to sit around together. April's phone rang, and she saw that it was Crystal.

"Hi, Crystal!" April said excitedly, as she answered the phone. "Are you back in town yet?"

"Yes, finally," Crystal said, sounding exhausted.

April got up from the chair and headed to her office so that she could talk to her friend without disturbing Blake and Claire. She closed the door about half way, and sat in the office chair behind her desk.

"So tell me all about the vacation, and don't leave any of the good parts out," April said cheerfully.

"Well, you know." Crystal began. "It was incredible. You don't realize how much you truly need a vacation until you are on it."

Over the next ten minutes, Crystal engaged in a full day-by-day synopsis of the daily events of her vacation—most of them ended up with drinks and dancing throughout the night.

When she was done detailing her vacation, she asked April how she had been.

Taking a deep breath, she began, "Good, but I have something to tell you."

By the sound of April's voice, Crystal knew that it must be something important.

"Ok?" Crystal questioned cautiously.

April cleared her throat, and began, "Last week, Blake and I were shopping in downtown Chicago, and we came across this sixteen-year-old homeless girl."

"Yeah?" Crystal asked.

"We walked past her, and after a few steps, I heard it," April continued, in a tone that Crystal hadn't heard before.

"What did you hear April?" Crystal wanted to know.

Taking an audible breath, she replied, "I heard Nick's voice. I did, Crystal. I know I did."

"Nick... your Nick? What did he say?" Crystal asked, trying to hide her disbelief.

"He asked me to 'go back to her'. He said it twice. I knew instantly that he wanted me to go to the homeless girl and I did." April started to tear up talking about it. Just to recount Nick's voice made it real again in her head.

You could hear the concern in Crystal's voice as she spoke. "What happened then?"

With a hint of a chuckle, April said, "I introduced her to Blake, and we took her out to lunch."

"Ok, so you took her out to lunch. How did it turn out?" Crystal asked, not knowing the rest of the story.

"Well, you see," April continued. "We ended up taking her home to spend the night, and she has been with us ever since," April said, finishing the last part of the sentence at a faster speed.

"You what!" exclaimed Crystal, as she voiced her concern. "Are you crazy?" The detective in her was suddenly taking charge. "Do you realize how problematic most of those people are? Because I do."

April was aware that she was about to get a lecture from her friend.

"You brought a complete stranger into the same house as your fourteen-year-old daughter? You don't know if she is on drugs, or she steals, or any number of bad things that she might be mixed up with."

April knew that Crystal had a point, but Crystal had not spent the past week with Claire and didn't know how sweet and normal she actually was.

"Listen, Crystal, I know that you care for me and Blake, and I appreciate it, but, you don't know Claire like we do. Not to mention the fact that I heard Nick's voice. I mean, Crystal, I am not kidding when I tell you that I heard his voice as clearly as I am hearing you right now." Crystal could hear the emotion in her voice, as April tried to explain, and she got chills from it.

Crystal tried to remain calm on the phone with April. "Ok, sweetie, what does Blake think of all this?"

"She and Claire have been getting along splendidly. I mean, it's been great having her here." April paused a second before she continued, "But I have not mentioned anything to Blake about hearing Nick's voice. I didn't want to freak her out because quite frankly, I can't explain it."

April then told Crystal how she had spent the week with Claire, how she had taken care of her when Claire had gotten really sick, and how Claire got along famously with Blake. Finally, she told her about what her last foster dad did to her on her birthday and how she had been running ever since.

Feeling only moderately calmer, Crystal said, "I don't know. I want to run her name and information through the computer to see what it brings up. I want to find out if she is telling the truth."

April suddenly got defensive and almost snapped. "She is telling the truth!" At the tone of her own voice, she immediately said, "Sorry, Crystal, I didn't mean to yell at you. I know that you care and it probably is a good idea to check her out to make sure, but there is something about her that I can't put my finger on, and I honestly believe her."

Not letting her friend's tone upset her in any way, Crystal continued with the discussion, "Look, I'm not judging you or her, really, I just want to err on the side of caution, and make sure that things are what they seem... That's all."

Letting out a heavy sigh, April said affectionately, "I know, Crystal. I hear you. It's been a fascinating week, and it has been so because of Claire. I don't know where to go from here."

Taking a moment to think about what to do, Crystal began going over things mentally in her head. After a few seconds of silence, she spoke up, "I got an idea. Why don't I come over tomorrow so that I can meet this Claire and we can talk? I just want to see who this person is and where she is coming from." As if she was anticipating April's next words, Crystal continued, "And don't worry, I'll be nice. It won't be an interrogation; not really."

"Sure, that would be ok, but she has been through a lot, so just be nice," April somewhat pleaded.

"You have my word. You are my best friend and I trust you, but with that being said, I also have a duty to protect you. And that's what I'm going to do," Crystal said.

"Ok. At what time do you want to come over tomorrow?" April asked.

Crystal was supposed to spend the day with her boyfriend, Tripp, and his parents, but she could make some time for April in the morning.

"Why don't I come over at 9:00 a.m., and we can have breakfast at your house. I can get to know Claire while we eat, and it will feel more inviting that way," Crystal suggested.

"Perfect. Sounds like a plan," April agreed.

"Great, see you at 9:00 a.m." Crystal said.

"Thanks, Crystal, you're the best," April responded, as a way of good–bye, and tapped the red circle to end the call.

April stared at her phone for a second, as if it was going to replay the entire conversation back for her, and then she clicked the screen off and went back into the living room.

April was almost on the couch when Claire closed the book shut and declared proudly, "All done."

She got up from the couch, stretched and noticed April a few steps away. "April, that book was so good. I can see why you wanted to edit it. I can't wait to read that next one, if that's ok?"

Smiling at Claire's reaction to the book, April answered, "Of course, it's ok." And then she added, "What was your favorite part of this book?"

Only taking a second to think about it, Claire responded, "The part where the FBI agent at the end was really working for the cartel and how the maid almost got killed. The action and suspense was a killer."

"I know, mine too," April agreed honestly.

Seeing an opening to talk, Blake glanced up from her iPad, and asked, "How's Crystal doing?"

"Good Sweetie. In fact, she is coming over tomorrow morning to have breakfast with us." April tried to cover the nervousness in her voice by sounding excitement about her friend's visit. Not detecting anything out of the ordinary, Blake said, "Cool beans," and then directed her attention to Claire and said, "I can't wait for you to meet Crystal tomorrow. She is awesome! She is going to love you!"

Smiling, Claire responded, "I hope so." And then said it again with a hint of nervousness; "I hope so."

"She is going to love you," Blake reassured her. "Trust me. She is super cool."

Claire felt assured, but she was still a bit nervous. "Ok if you say so."

To make Claire feel better, and to reassure herself too, April said, "Yes, she is going to like you very much."

The three of them lingered around the living room for a few more minutes before it was decided that they should close the door on this day as it were.

Claire and Blake started to go upstairs when Claire stopped at the base of them and turned to April, and said, "April, I really, really want to thank you and Blake for everything that you have done for me today and actually for the entire week." She grabbed the tip of her braid and continued, "I mean it. I hope that you truly know how grateful I am. I had so much fun today that it kind of feels like a dream."

April whole-heartedly knew that Claire meant every word. She could see it in her eyes. "You are so very welcome Claire. We enjoyed ourselves too."

Blake grabbed Claire's hand, and said, "You are really cool, and you are special," and then added jokingly, "Like me," and she pulled Claire up the stairs as she started to run.

"Good night, April," Claire shouted behind her as she quickly was pulled towards the upper landing.

"Good night, girls," April called out, and then allowed a chuckle to escape from her throat.

* *

THE WHITE WATER FROM THE WAVE CRASHED ON THE SIDE of the canoe, and it splashed up and smacked Blake on the face and neck. It felt so refreshing, she couldn't help but smile. It was a beautiful Sunday afternoon, and she was with her mom and dad canoeing on the Au Sable River in Grayling, Michigan. They had decided to rent a canoe on their way back from Mackinac Island and they were about an hour into the trip, and it was spectacular. Blake was in the front with April and Nick behind her in the middle and back of the boat. There were no other canoes near them, and it was as if they had the entire river to themselves. Blake looked at the clear water, and noticed that her reflection was that of a fifteen-year-old girl. She didn't think anything of it because she was having the time of her life with her parents.

As they rounded a bend in the river, Blake could see lily pads in the path of the boat up ahead. Blake paddled a little harder to get to them faster because she wanted to pluck one out of the water to give to her mother. April and Nick were talking about how much fun that they were having, and how great it was to have gone to Mackinac Island. Nick turned his attention to see what Blake was doing, and said to her, "So you want a lily pad, do you?"

"Yes, dad, can I grab one?" Blake asked innocently.

"Of course, you can, but you better let Claire get it for you," Nick told his daughter.

"Claire?" Blake began to ask, as she looked behind her to question her dad, but then she saw Claire sitting directly behind her with her own paddle, as if she had been on the boat the entire time.

"Hi, Blake," Claire smiled, "Your dad wants me to help you get the lily pads." She then set her paddle down and slowly stood up on the canoe so that she could balance herself.

"Be careful, sweetie," Nick said to Claire, as she attempted to get into position.

"I will," she fearlessly told Nick.

Claire bent down over the front left side of the canoe next to Blake and extended her right arm out to grasp the lily as they went by.

All of a sudden, the river became rough and the lily pads floated just out of Claire's reach. With a look of determination on her face, she reached out farther to grab it. Just then, a tree that was under the water floated up in front of the boat, causing the canoe to slam into it. Claire abruptly lost her balance and fell out of the canoe and into the rough waters of the river.

Screaming, Blake reached for her and barely got a hold of her hand, but the roughness of the water was increasing by the second and the sun was now blocked by a row of dark rain clouds. Suddenly, a loud clap of thunder echoed through the river valley, and it started to rain.

"Help me, Blake!" Claire screamed, as both girls could feel Blake's grip starting to slip.

"Oh God! No!" Blake screamed, as tears streamed from her eyes, mingling with the rain water.

Blake could hear her parents yelling and screaming, but they weren't helping. Sneaking only a second to look in their direction, Blake noticed that they both now had seat belts fastened around their laps and shoulders, and they were desperately trying to release them, to no avail.

Nick could see Blake losing her grip on Claire, and he said to her in a loud clear voice "Do not let her go. Do you understand? Don't let her go! I love you so much, Blake, and I know that you can do it!"

Blake turned her full attention back to Claire, and she could see the look of fear in her eyes. It was the fear of being let go.

Both girls were crying, and the weather acted as if its sole purpose was to separate them. The water churned, the rain intensified, the sky blackened. Day was now almost night because of the amount of dark clouds that were blocking the sun.

Blake's heart was pounding, her arms and hands were hurting, and she was puffing rapidly to force more air into her lungs.

Then, without a hint of warning, a big wave splashed over the bow of the boat drenching both girls with a sheet of water. The sheer force of that wave effectively dislodged Blake's grip on Claire's hand, and both girls let up a chilling scream.

"No! Claire! Come back!" Blake screamed at Claire, who was now being forcibly washed away at an alarming rate.

"Don't let me go, Blake!" Claire pleaded, as she was dragged further away from the canoe.

Nick and April were still trying frantically to break free from the seat belts. April was crying and yelling at Claire, but the wind and rain were drowning out the sound of her voice. However, Blake could hear her dad's voice loud and clear, as if she was wearing ear buds and his words were the only sound allowed to flow through them. Nick called out to Blake one final time, "Blake, don't let her go!"

Her head shaking from crying, Blake yelled to Claire, "Don't go!"

"Don't let me go, Blake. Don't let me go!" Claire yelled again as the water swiftly took her further and further away.

Blake could barely see Claire now as the distance between them doubled with each passing second. Off in the distance, she could barely hear Claire. "Don't let me go! Please don't let me go!" It was almost like a whisper now.

Blake began to cry harder when Claire went out of her sight. She was still leaning over the side of the boat when another wave crashed on the bow, and drenched her with water, causing her to be washed out of the boat. She was falling into the river, but just before she broke the surface of the water... Blake awoke with a start.

Blake jerked on the bed as if she had fallen and then landed on the bed. Her face was wet from crying, and her heart was beating rapidly. The dream felt so real. Her face and forehead were soaked from a mixture of tears and sweat. It took her a few seconds to fully realize that the dream was over, and she was in her bed.

"Claire?" Blake said out loud, and she bolted from her bed and stepped into the hallway. She cautiously opened the door to Claire's bedroom, and peered inside to make sure that she was still there.

Sleeping silently on her bed was Claire. Blake quietly tiptoed into the room and put her face close to Claire's. She could see that she was breathing normally, and her belly was slowly rising and falling, like it was supposed to. Blake stared at Claire as the memory of her dad's words in the dream washed over her. 'Don't let her go,' he had told Blake, and she started to cry as she realized that she had not heard his voice in over four years.

Blake stood over her for a couple of minutes to reassure herself that Claire was ok. She wiped the remaining tears off her cheek with the fabric of her nightshirt and carefully left Claire's room.

Still shaken from the nightmare, Blake walked passed her room and decided to enter her mother's room.

April had not woken up from the sound of Blake crying because her bedroom door had been closed, and she did not hear the commotion. Blake walked over to her mother's bed and tried to sneak under the covers. April awoke instantly and saw that it was Blake.

"Blake, are you ok?" April was surprised by her daughter' arrival in her bed.

"No, mom," Blake muttered. "I had a really bad dream," she said, letting out a small whimper.

"Oh, honey," April said gently, "Come under the covers."

Blake tucked herself into the covers next to her mom and put her arm around her. April could feel the wetness of the tears that were starting to flow again.

"What is it?" April questioned with affection.

"It felt so real," Blake began. "You, me and dad were in a canoe and we were having a great time. But I wanted to get a lily from the river, and then Claire appeared next to me. Dad wanted her to get it from the water instead of me." April turned her head fully in the direction of her daughter so that they were face to face.

"So, she bent over the canoe to grab it, and the water and the sky turned bad and she fell in. I grabbed her hand, but the waves and rain were too much, and I lost my grip." Blake used the pillow that her head was on to brush away the tears on her cheek. "Dad kept telling me 'Don't let her go'. He kept saying it. Then as she was washed away, both Claire and I were crying, and she too kept saying 'don't let me go.'"

Blake paused, trying to remain calm. "I mean I heard dad's voice telling me not to let her go."

April could feel her own tears rolling out of her eyes and onto her checks. She could almost feel the emotions that Blake was explaining.

"Blake." April began. "There is something that I've been wanting to tell you for the past week, and I didn't know how to until now."

Confused, and still upset from her nightmare, Blake replied, "What is it?"

Taking a deep breath, April said, "The day that we met Claire holding the sign..."

"Yeah...?" Blake urged.

Blinking a tear away, she confessed, "I heard your dad's voice in my head telling me to go to her. I heard it as clear as day."

Sniffling a sob, Blake whispered, "What? You heard daddy's voice?"

"Yes, honey, I did. He wanted me to go to her, and I did," April declared, feeling as if the truth had just set her free.

Blake could tell that her mom was telling the truth, and she realized that it was her dad's voice that she had heard loud and clear in the dream. Feeling a little unnerved, Blake asked her mother, "Why didn't you tell me?"

"Well, for one thing, I was kind of in shock, and I didn't know what to do. I didn't want to make you anxious, in case I was losing my mind or something. It kind of freaked me out, so I wanted to see where things went," April explained as best she could. Now that Blake had had this dream about her dad and Claire, April's decision to go back to Claire seemed validated.

"What does this mean?" Blake asked, a little confused and unsettled.

April rolled her daughter onto her right side, and she cuddled up to her wrapping her arm around her.

"I don't know, sweetie, I really don't know," April answered honestly.

The two of them lay in bed together, deep in their own thoughts about what had transpired, not just tonight with the dream, but over the entire week with Claire.

April thought of something, and lifting her head to whisper in Blake's ear, she said, "I think I know what we have to do."

CHAPTER TEN

CLAIRE'S EYES SLOWLY BLINKED OPEN AS SHE BECAME AWARE of the bedroom around her. The room was bright because it was 8:00 am and the sun was shining through the bedroom windows. The comforter was halfway off the bed with a corner of it touching the floor. Because of this, the left side of Claire's body had been left uncovered through most of the night. With each passing moment, her mind was registering that almost half of her body was, in fact, cold. As Claire attempted to grab the comforter with her right hand to pull it back over her body, she realized that she had tucked her hand under her head during the night, restricting the blood flow to her hand. In other words, her hand was numb.

As Claire moved her arm, she did not have any control over it from the elbow down. Her mind willed her hand to move the blanket, but it simply landed on her chest with a thud. "Dammit," Claire said out loud. Claire tried to lift it again, but it only managed to move slightly. Using her left hand, she grabbed the right arm and picked it up. She could feel the right arm in her left hand, but still could not feel any sensation in her right arm.

This is wonderful, Claire thought, as she poked at her useless arm. There were indentations in her hand and wrist where the weight of the head had caused a mark. After a few jabs, she could feel a tingling sensation as the blood slowly returned to her hand. After a minute or so, the numbness all but subsided, and

Claire stretched both her arms above her head and allowed a yawn to escape her lips. She looked around the room and examined all the clothes and shoes that she had acquired over the last couple of days. She still felt like she was in a dream. April and Blake had both been so amazing to her, and she was truly fond of them.

Claire put on her robe and left the bedroom to go and see if Blake was up. She peered into Blake's room and discovered that she was not there. Thinking that she must have gone downstairs, Claire started walking in the direction of the staircase. That was when she heard voices coming from April's room. It sounded like Blake was talking to her mother. Claire stopped by the entrance, and softly knocked on the bedroom door.

"Good morning, Claire," April said. "Come on in."

Claire opened the door and saw Blake lying next to April on the bed. By the look on their faces, she guessed that they must have been having a serious conversation, so Claire said, "Good morning... I didn't mean to interrupt you guys. I'll go and take a shower."

"No, Claire, it's ok. Why don't you come over here and take a seat?" April instructed, as she pointed at the side of the bed next to her.

"Yeah, come on in," Blake smiled. "We were just talking about you."

Claire took a few steps and sat where April had motioned with her hand.

Blake adjusted her body so that she was seated with her back resting against the headboard of the bed, and waited for her mom to begin. April grabbed the corner of the blanket on the bed and put it over her and Claire so that both or their legs were covered.

"I want to ask you something, and I want you to be honest with me," April said, with her voice laced with just a touch of suspicion.

"Ok?" Claire answered, unable to hide the nervousness from her voice.

"How do you like it here?" April asked, with a smile forming on her face.

Claire blinked at the question, and then smiled, and said without hesitation, "I love it here." "This past week has been the best week of my life." Thinking back to all the new clothes and stuff in her room, she continued, "And it's not because you guys have bought me nice things." After the words left her lips, she quickly amended, "...all of which I absolutely love."

Cutting in, Blake interjected, "You love them because I helped you pick them out, and of course, you look amazing in all of them."

Pausing to smile at what Blake had just said, Claire kept going, "I love it here because of the way you have treated me all this while. You have been so nice to me, not to mention that you guys took care of me when I was sick. Not everyone would have done that for a stranger. Not only are you super nice to me, but you have also treated me like I belong. That is not a feeling that I have experienced in a very long time." When Claire said the word 'belong', her voice cracked with emotion.

April reached across and placed Claire's hand in hers. She could feel the indentations on her hand, and gave her a quizzical look.

"Oh," Claire said looking down at her hand. "I fell asleep on my hand and I woke up with it completely numb." She explained.

"I see," April said, as she brought up her other hand and began rubbing Claire's hand between hers so that it would help smooth out the indents in her skin.

Bringing her attention back to what Claire had previously spoken about, April said, "I do have to say that Blake and I have grown extremely fond of you over the past week." Pausing to glance over at Blake, April winked, and then continued, "We find ourselves at a crossroads because we have been talking this morning, and we aren't exactly sure about what to do."

Claire looked up from her hand that was in April's, and asked, "What do you mean?"

"Well," April began, "Blake and I really would like it if you would continue to stay with us."

Claire turned her head to look at Blake's face, and saw her smiling from ear to ear. Then she quickly returned her gaze to April and asked, "Are you serious?"

"Yes, of course," April replied with conviction. "I don't know exactly why, but I think that you are meant to be here with us."

Blake put her hand on her mother's shoulder in a show of support. Last night's dream was still fresh in Blake's mind, and after her mom's confession to Blake about hearing her dad's voice directing her to Claire, it felt right to see what they could do to have Claire continue her stay.

"I would love to stay here," Claire said, not trying to hide the excitement in her voice. "But do you think that I'll be able to?" she asked.

"Well, we are going to try our best," April said, earnestly. "Crystal is coming over this morning for breakfast, and we are going to ask her what steps we can take to make this happen."

Thinking about the conversation between herself and Crystal the night before, April realized she would have to do her best to convince her best friend that this was the best course of action.

Feeling a little nervous, Claire asked April, "Wouldn't Crystal have to report me to Child Protective Services because she is a police detective?"

"She wouldn't do that," Blake said defiantly, and then after a second or two of thought, asked her mom, "She wouldn't, right?"

Seeing how nervous both girls were becoming, April put on a big smile, and said, "No, of course not, she is my best friend, and I'm sure that she will listen to what we want, but we may have to really make our case and try to convince her."

Blake got up from the bed and went over to the side where Claire was sitting. Pulling Claire up off the bed, she said, "Let's go get ready. I will pick out your outfit today so that you can look your absolute best for Crystal."

Claire responded by saying, "You don't have to pick out my clothes for me—I am almost a grown woman." She then pulled Blake towards her, and the two of them crashed on the bed. Claire grabbed Blake's midsection and rolled her over, causing Blake to be underneath her, and then began tickling her.

Blake let out a big scream that was immediately followed by uncontrolled laughter as the tickling increased in intensity. Blake tried to make her stop, but Claire persisted, and Blake was unable to defend herself against the onslaught of Claire's tickle attack.

"Stop! Stop! Please!" Blake begged through the laughter. "Mom! Help me!" Blake yelled through gasps of air. April leaned across the bed and decided to join forces with Claire, and began tickling Blake as well.

Blake's voice rose to a shriek, and she yelled, "No! Stop mom!" She tried to say more but the words just wouldn't come out. Blake was desperately gasping for air when April and Claire halted their tickle attack. April held out her palm to give a high-five to Claire. Claire saw the raised hand, and gave her a high-five.

Blake lay there on the bed for a several moments, trying to get her lungs filled with air again.

"Very funny, you guys," she said, as she took in a deep breath.

"I had fun," April said, enthusiastically.

"Me too," agreed Claire.

Blake got up from the bed and stood between her mom and Claire, and declared with a grin, "You two suck."

"You suck," Claire retorted with a smile.

"Oh, I see how this is going to go," Blake said, pointing a finger at Claire. Using that same finger, she pointed it at her mom, and said accusingly, "And you, I needed you, and what did you do? Nothing. Wait, that's not true. You were worse than nothing. You jumped on the tickle band wagon, and double teamed me."

April shrugged her shoulders, and said innocently, "I have no idea what you are talking about."

"Uh, huh," Blake said, sheepishly.

Claire looked at Blake, and reiterated, "You don't have to pick out my clothes, and I am perfectly capable of choosing my own attire."

"True," Blake agreed, "but I do it better than you."

"Yeah?" questioned Claire.

"Most definitely," answered Blake.

April motioned for the girls to leave her room, "Let's get dressed so that we can be ready for Crystal."

The girls began to leave the room when Blake grabbed Claire's arm to stop her, and said, "Oh, by the way, I have something for you." Then she quickly put her index finger in her mouth and then put it in Claire's ear.

"Oh gross!" Claire yelped, as she flung her hand up to her ear to wipe away the saliva.

Giggling uncontrollably, Blake took off running to her room to get away from Claire.

"Oh, you're done," joked Claire, as she gave chase.

April watched the two run out into the hallway towards Blake's room. Blake almost got the door closed in time to prevent Claire from entering, but Claire was a second too fast, and jammed her body between the door and the doorframe.

"Oh crap!" yelled Blake, as Claire forced her way into the bedroom tackling Blake onto her bed. Claire managed to get on top of her with her legs on either side, with Blake facing her. She grappled for a few more seconds and secured Blake's wrists with her hands against the top of the bed, pinning her down.

"I think someone needs a car wash," said Claire.

April had followed them to Blake's room, and was standing in the door-way watching.

"What's a car wash?" April wanted to know.

"This is a car wash," Claire answered as she stuck out her tongue and began spraying Blake with her spit.

"Come on!" giggled Blake, as she tried to free herself from Claire's grasp.

April had to laugh, it was fun to see them horsing around.

In between sprays on Blake's face, Claire would ask, "Who gives the best car washes?"

Not stopping until Blake answered, Claire kept spraying.

Finally, Blake gave in and yelled, "You do! Ok? Little Miss Blonde Claire does! Now get off me so I can wash my face!" Blake laughed.

Satisfied with the answer, Claire cautiously let Blake go and got up from the bed. Now that Claire was not blocking her view of the doorway, Blake saw her mom standing in the doorway watching the whole thing.

"Again, she doesn't help me," Blake said of her mom sarcastically.

"You reap what you sow," April retorted.

"Reap? Sow? What the heck does that even mean?" Blake asked quizzically.

April sighed, and with a giggle simply said, "Never mind. Get up and get dressed."

Claire smiled at her handy work, and left Blake's room to go to her bathroom where she could take a shower. Blake spent a few moments wiping and cleaning off Claire's spit from her face.

"Mom," Blake began as she walked over to her closet.

"Yes?" April replied.

"I just want to let you know that I believe that we are making the right decision having Claire stay with us." Blake said, as she rifled through her closet to see what she wanted to wear today.

"You think so?" April said, thankful for the reassurance.

"I know so," Blake said proudly, as she pulled out a peach-colored blouse.

Blake looked back into her closet, and declared, "Now, what else can I find for Claire?"

"Hi Crystal!" Blake said, as she lurched forward to give her a big hug. "So glad that you are back from your vacation."

"I'm not," Crystal said, only half-jokingly returning Blake's hug as she remembered the tropical weather that she had just returned home from.

When Blake finished hugging her 'Aunt Crystal', April gave her best friend a big smile and a hug, and said, "Welcome back."

Behind April was Claire, standing in nervous anticipation. She was wearing a new pair of jeans that she had got while shopping with April and Blake, but the top was a peach blouse that Blake had picked out from her closet. Blake chose a soft, white, fluffy scarf to accessorize it with that she wrapped loosely around her neck. Claire had used Blake's curling iron, and created long, flowing, loose curls that made her long blonde hair wavy. Blake had let her borrow a black plastic headband with peach and white roses embroidered on top with fake diamonds mixed throughout. Blake had taught Claire how to put on makeup properly, and she had done a good job on her own this morning. Blake had only had to blend in the foundation a little more.

April turned and pointed at Claire, and said, "Crystal, this is Claire."

Crystal went up to Claire, proceeded to give her a hug, and said, "Hi Claire."

Claire was a little taken aback by how beautiful Crystal was. April had mentioned that she could have been a model, and she was not kidding. Crystal had long, flowing, black hair, and her skin was extremely smooth and silky looking. She had intense brown eyes that had the power to pull you into them, and you felt like she could see your thoughts. Crystal wasn't overly intimidating, but one got the feeling that those eyes could shoot laser beams at a person if she wanted them to.

Smiling and hugging her back, Claire said, "Hi Crystal, so nice to meet you. April and Blake have said nothing but nice things about you."

Crystal released the hug, and then with her hands on each of Claire's arms performed a visual inspection of Claire's body.

"Aren't you a pretty little thing?" Crystal seriously declared, as she finished with her eyes focusing on Claire's.

Blushing, not quite knowing what to say, Claire simply said with a grin, "Thanks."

Taking Claire by the hand and heading towards the dining room table, Crystal said with genuine interest, "Come on, honey, and tell me all about yourself."

Blake sat next to Claire, and April took a seat closer to Crystal and across from Claire and Blake.

As Claire looked into Crystal's brown eyes, she could feel her nerves slowly start to dissipate.

"Don't worry dear." Crystal said disarmingly, "I don't judge people on their circumstances. I just would like to know how this all came to be."

Claire told Crystal about her childhood with her mom. Most of it comprised what she had already told April and Blake, but she added a few extra details that she remembered as she spoke. Crystal continued to smile and take in everything that Claire was saying. She had excellent memory recall, a perk of her job, so when a person was detailing a story or explaining events of a crime, Crystal could detect small inconsistencies that indicated that the person was lying or at least not telling the whole truth. Fortunately, Crystal was not detecting anything that would make her suspicious of what Claire was telling her.

Claire finished with the story of her life, but brushed over the incident with her last foster family and Roger.

"Can I ask you something that may upset you but I need you to clarify it for me?" Crystal asked Claire with a hint of suspicion.

"Sure," Claire replied, not quite knowing where this was going to go.

"It's about your last foster family," Crystal began.

Claire instantly became nervous, and you could see the color flush out of her cheeks.

"What about them?" Claire asked nervously. No one could see, but the hairs on the back of her neck had begun to rise.

"Well, why did you leave them?" Crystal asked, as she pulled out a clasp envelope from her bag.

Claire looked over at April for help. April remembered what Claire had told her about Roger and how he hit her and tried to rape her.

"No, please, I don't want to say it in front of Blake," Claire winced at the thought of it.

Blake looked from April to Crystal and then at Claire.

"Why?" Blake asked with increasing concern.

Again, Claire begged not to confess what had happened, "Please Crystal, don't do this."

April looked at Crystal with concern for Claire and said, "Let's not do this now."

Crystal opened the envelope and flipped it to the third page. Taking a deep breath, Crystal looked at the words on the page, and said, "According to the police report, you smashed a lamp over Roger's head and stole his wallet that was his great-grandfather's as you ran away."

Angry tears flowed from her eyes as she stood up in defiance. "That's not true!" Claire yelled in a defensive tone. She glanced at April, who shook her head, urging Claire to tell Crystal the truth about what had occurred.

Blake grabbed Claire's hand for support, and said, "It's ok. You can tell us."

Claire's eyes rolled up in the direction of the ceiling and a sob escaped from her mouth.

"Why?" questioned Claire, "No one is going to believe a sixteen-year-old's version as opposed to that of a doctor, right?" Claire asked Crystal in an accusatory tone.

"I just need to know what the truth is from you, I'm sorry but this report paints a bad picture." Crystal calmly said to Claire.

"Fine," Claire said, giving in.

She turned to Blake, and looking only at her, she told her side of the story.

"He came home from his hospital shift drunk on my 16th birthday... We were supposed to meet Carrie, my foster mom, and Stephan, their son, at a soccer game," explained Claire.

Blake's eyes were starting to moisten with tears due to Claire's show of emotion.

"So, when I took his car keys away, he hit me hard and then forced me into the bedroom. I tried to fight him off, but he managed to get on top of me and started taking off his clothes. I will never forget the look in his eyes, you know?" Claire wiped tears off her cheeks and looked back at Crystal.

"He wanted to rape me, but I managed to grab the lamp and hit him on his head. I took off running and didn't look back," Claire said. Sitting down at the table, she buried her head in her arms and crying.

"Oh my God," Blake said, looking at her mom.

After a few moments, Claire lifted her head up, and with mascara running down her face, she looked at Crystal, and grimly said, "He tried to rape me. I'm telling you the truth."

"And as for his stupid wallet," Claire said coolly, "I didn't steal it. He probably hid it or threw it away, so that he could make up something to explain why he got hit in the head and why I ran away."

"I'm really sorry this happened to you," Crystal said compassionately. Speaking to the whole group, she continued, "I wanted to see what really happened because when I looked up her info, this police report from Seattle came up." She held up the report in her left hand. "Claire, I didn't do this to hurt you. I did it as a friend of April and Blake."

"So, what now?" Blake wanted to know. "Because mom and I have made the decision that we want Claire to stay with us."

Crystal blinked at being blindsided, and gave April a sideways glance, asking if this was true.

"Crystal," April began defensively, "We have grown very fond of her, and we feel that fate has brought her to us."

"Yeah," interrupted Blake, as she nodded her head for emphasis, thinking about the dream she had about her dad.

Pressing on, April said, "Not to mention that she has been through a lot in her life, and we want to give her a nice place to stay with people that care about her."

Crystal wasn't prepared for this new revelation, and mentally tried to figure out what could be done. "April, I don't know if you will be able to because she is a ward of the state of Seattle."

Blake spoke up, "She can't go back there, and she just can't. What are they going to do for her there? Treat her like crap because they think that she stole some rapist's wallet!" Blake's eyes were becoming more intense, as she continued, "Put her in another foster home? Or will she be placed in some juvenile detention center where kids who commit crimes are placed. Is that what you are implying here?"

The tension in the room could be cut with a knife, and Crystal could see how important this was to her best friend, especially because she knew that April thought that she had been directed to this girl by her dead husband.

Crystal stared at Claire. "Listen, Claire. I want to help you. I really do. I am not the bad guy here." As she told her that, she used her right arm to pull April in closer to her. "April is my very best friend and I trust her. The detective in me needs to know all the information, that's all. I wouldn't be a good friend if I didn't do my best to protect them."

Crystal reached across the table and offered her hand to Claire. "We will figure this out together." Then looking at April and Blake, she said, "Together."

Claire was starting to calm down just a little, and reached out for Crystal's hand, "I'm sorry Crystal, I just don't want to go back to Seattle. When April and Blake told me this morning that they wanted me to stay here, I just got excited. My whole life has been one disappointment after another. I have never felt so content and wanted in my entire life as I do right now." Claire wiped away the remainder of the tears on her face, which smeared more of her mascara, and then added, "And I have only been here a week."

Squeezing her hand as an indication of support, Crystal said, "Ok, Claire, I can see that all of you want this. The question is: how can I do this without causing a shit storm?"

Crystal looked through the sheets of paper involving her case.

Getting out of her chair and walking behind Crystal, and giving her a big hug, Blake said, "Thank you for doing this for us, Aunt Crystal."

"I love you, Blake," Crystal told her affectionately. "I just needed to make sure that this was in the best interest of both of you guys, you know?"

"It is," Blake insisted. "And I love you too." Looking over at Claire, she raised a fist for a fist bump. Smiling at Blake's gesture, Claire slowly raised her fist and bumped it against Blake's. "There it is." Blake smiled as she opened her hand, imitating an explosion.

"Come on upstairs and I'll fix your face up," Blake instructed Claire, noticing the black stains running down her face.

Rubbing her fingers where her mascara probably was now, she wiped her cheeks, and said, "God, I must be a mess."

Claire got up to leave the table, and Crystal looked up and said, "Claire, hold on a sec." Crystal stood up and gave Claire a hug. "Honey, it's going to be ok. I promise," she said, and Claire could see that Crystal meant it, and the hug was a way for Crystal to signify that she didn't want any hard feelings between the two of them.

"I hope so," Claire said, with a touch of apprehension. "It's... it's like I have never felt so wanted as I have felt here with April and Blake. You know what I mean?"

Remembering something from her own childhood with her father, Crystal could honestly say that she did. Her dad had walked out on her and her mother when she was very young, and Crystal had always felt that her mom had blamed her for some undeserving reason. This had left a tear in their relationship. By the time Crystal was in high school, the resentment that her mother held for her was like a physical brick wall, and she felt totally alone even though she lived with her mom.

Crystal said, "I do know, honey, I really do."

Blake and Claire went upstairs to clean up Claire's face.

Crystal glared at her friend and said, "You kind of ambushed me here."

"I know. I didn't plan on it, honestly," April said, apologetically, "I didn't have time to tell you, but Blake had a vivid nightmare about her dad and Claire last night."

Crystal looked intently at April, and said, "Ok?"

April pulled Crystal a tiny bit closer and lowered her voice so that the girls wouldn't hear.

"Apparently, the four of us were on a canoe and we were on the Au Sable River and Clair had fallen out of the boat. Blake held her by the hand, but Claire slipped from her grasp. Blake heard Nick's voice vividly, urging her not to let Claire go. He told her several times, *not to let Claire go.*"

"So, are you saying that Nick was talking to Blake too?" Crystal asked, a little bewildered.

April paused for a second looking upstairs in the direction of the girl's bedrooms.

"I don't know for sure, but she was really upset by it. You've got to admit how uncanny it is that she had the dream the night before you came over to talk about possibly taking Claire back to Seattle."

April looked back at Crystal, and said, "Because she was so upset last night after the dream, I told her about hearing Nick's voice the day that we met Claire."

"What did she say?" Crystal asked, inquisitively.

"She thinks that he is trying to tell us something and wants Claire to be here."

"But why?" Crystal prodded.

"We don't know. This week has been like a whirlwind, and I feel that Claire really needs us too," April explained, trying to wrap her head around it.

Crystal could see that her best friend really believed that she had heard Nick, and that Blake too had had some sort of communication from her dad. Crystal had never seen April like this, and it was concerning to her.

"Ok, April, you have my complete support. I will do whatever I can to make sure she stays here, no matter what."

Breathing in a sigh of relief, April hugged her friend, and said, "Thank you, thank you, thank you."

Crystal broke away from the hug, and held up her hand to stop April in mid-sentence. "Don't thank me yet. There is plenty of work to do before this is a done deal."

Nodding her head in agreement, April responded, "Ok, ok, but thank you so much."

"You're welcome," Crystal said, affectionately. "Besides, I'm not doing it just for you; I'm doing it because Blake feels just as passionately about this."

At that point, the girls came down the stairs. Claire's face was now cleaned up and looked good as new.

"So, what's for breakfast?" Crystal asked with a big smile on her face. The question was directed more towards Blake than any other person in the house because she knew that Blake liked to cook breakfast.

"How about some scrambled eggs, toast, and pancakes?" Blake responded almost immediately.

"Sounds great to me," Crystal said, as she got up from the table and headed to the kitchen.

Blake waved at Claire, asking her to follow Blake into the kitchen, and said to Crystal, "We got this." Then she motioned for Crystal to take a seat at the island.

Claire stopped walking just before entering the kitchen, and questioned Blake, "Are you sure? Don't you remember the last time we were cooking in the kitchen together?"

Blake grinned at the memory, "Yes, of course I remember, but that was then, and this is now. So I feel confident that we will be successful."

"Ok, then," Claire surrendered and stepped into the kitchen. Blake promptly handed her a red-and-white checkered apron with a smirk, and said, "Just in case."

"Of course," Claire grinned, accepting the apron.

Blake instructed Claire on just what to do, and the two of them had fun mixing and preparing the ingredients. There was a casualty though because just as Claire was cracking the final egg into the bowl, it slipped out of her hand and landed with a splat on the floor. Other than that, no major mess ensued.

While the girls were working in the kitchen, Crystal was telling the group about how much fun she had on her vacation. April had taken the seat next to Crystal on the island, and was listening intently and only occasionally interrupting her with a question or comment.

"Do you remember when your mom and dad took us on a Disney cruise when we were in 6th grade, and we snuck off the boat at the Port in the Bahamas, and we almost didn't make it back to the ship before it departed?" Crystal asked, laughing at the memory.

"Yes." April said, as her eyes widened at the thought. "I can't believe that we made it in time. The staircase had started to move up, and we sat there crying near the crew member until it came back down."

"Did your parents ever find out?" Crystal asked, quizzically.

"Nope," April said with pride. "To this day, they still think that we were hiding in the ballroom on the main deck."

Blake stopped what she was doing and looked at the two women, and said, "You never told me that."

"Yeah, well, if we ever take a cruise, we will be stuck together like glue," April informed her daughter.

"Uh huh," Blake said, with a smirk.

A few more minutes went by and breakfast was ready to be served. Blake directed her mom and Crystal to the dining room table and brought over the four plates filled with food. Claire was still in the kitchen waiting for the final round of bread to toast in the toaster. When it popped up, she grabbed them, and put them on the plate and took her place at the table.

"This looks amazing," Crystal said admiringly. "I wish that I could cook like this. I mean, I can catch murderers, find identity thieves, and I can even catch a few bank robbers, but when it comes to making a delicious breakfast like this, I'm a complete loser." She emphasized on the word 'loser', and it sounded silly.

"Well, I agree with the first part, but I can honestly say that you are not a loser," April chimed in.

"Maybe not a total loser then," Crystal said begrudgingly.

The four of them sat at the table enjoying the food when Blake asked Crystal, "So, what do we have to do so that Claire can stay here with us?"

"Well, I think first and foremost, I need to contact the Seattle Police Department, and inform them that I have found Claire and that she is safe and sound." Consuming a bite of toast, Crystal continued, "Second, I think that I will call Duncan O'Rourke, who is a close friend of mine at Illinois Child Protective Services. I am going to have him call Seattle, and tell them that he has found a temporary home for Claire." Pausing to think about her plan a little more, Crystal took a fork full of pancake and devoured it. Looking at Claire, her eyes lit up with an idea, "I could tell them that Claire is part of an investigation here in Chicago, so I need her here."

"That sounds like a good plan to me," agreed Blake.

"You would do that for me?" Claire asked, candidly.

Crystal smiled, and said, "Yes, yes, I would."

Crystal's job was all about analyzing a person's face and body gestures. She could also detect variances in speech patterns that would reveal untruthfulness or lying. As she spoke to Claire, Crystal could not detect any telltale signs of deceit. According to Crystal's training, she felt that Claire was telling the truth. Besides, Crystal was beginning to see what April and Blake saw in Claire—she was your basic regular teenage girl who seemed honest and genuine. There was nothing in her past to indicate that she had gotten into trouble, except for the Seattle Police report. But if what Claire said was true, then that report was false.

There was something else about Claire that Crystal could not quite put her finger on though. Nothing bad or criminal, but her sixth sense picked up on something that was subtle. She felt confident that in time she would figure it out but right now it eluded her.

"Thank you so much," April said to her friend, as she got up from her seat to get some coffee. "This really does mean a lot to us."

Flipping through the pages of Claire's file, Crystal replied, "I will try my best to make sure everything goes according to plan. As she looked through the file, a thought occurred to her and she directed it towards April, "You know something? You need to have her start school here in Chicago because the last time that she attended was before summer."

"You're right," agreed April. "She was sick for a solid week, and then it was Thanksgiving. We only just decided this morning to figure out if she could stay here. Of course, that would be the next course of action."

Blake's eyes lit up with the realization, and she said to Claire, "Yay, you get to go to school with me. This is going to be awesome!"

"Claire is a little older, so she obviously won't be in the same grade," April said matter-of-factly, "but, yes you two will be going to the same school."

For a split-second, Claire was a little nervous about going to school because she had not been to school in almost six months, including the summer vacation time before the fall semester. Not to mention that the last couple of schools had just been alright because she had only spent a year in each school, having moved to different foster families.

"Sweet," Claire half-smiled, attempting to sound sarcastic. But then a genuine smile found its way out, and it was obvious that she was happy. "It has been a while since I have been to school, but my grades were pretty good. I should be ok to jump right it."

"According to your transcripts here, you were at 3.7 GPA. That's really good, Claire." Crystal said, admiringly.

"Wow, Claire," Blake praised her. "You're smart."

Feeling a little bashful, Claire said, "I'm not that smart. I just like to read a lot and I spent most of my time doing homework. I didn't have many friends, so I concentrated on my school work."

Blake could see that Claire was getting a little uncomfortable with her past school experiences, so she switched gears. "Claire, you will get to meet my friend, Emily, because she flies in from Oregon tonight. She is coming over tomorrow morning."

"Cool," Claire said with a smile, remembering the pictures of Emily that Blake had shown her over the course of the past week. "She seems really nice, at least in pictures."

"Yes, she is really cool. She has been my best friend all through grade school up till now," said Blake. As soon as she said that, she quickly amended her statement. "Besides my new best friend," she said, meaning Claire.

Picking up on what Blake was saying, Claire offered her a little solace, "Blake, don't worry about offending me. Seriously. I know that you and Emily are best friends, and I would not do anything that would jeopardize that. I have made it known to you that you are my best friend, but I don't want you to have to choose me over Emily. I just want you to continue with what you normally do because even though I am eternally grateful for the opportunity to be here, I don't want my presence here to disrupt your life or your friendships in any way."

April glanced at Crystal with a look of adoration towards Claire, and couldn't believe how mature this girl was, especially knowing what she had been through.

Blake had to grin at that, and it made her like Claire even more. "You know something, Blondie," responded Blake, jokingly, "I respect what you just said, but I can have several best friends, and I hate to tell you this, but you are definitely one of them now. So, you better get used to it."

Thinking back to the conversation that they had the other day in Blake's bedroom, Claire enthusiastically said, "I thought I was your little blonde purpose?"

Smirking at the memory of that, Blake agreed, "Yes, you are my little blonde purpose, but you are one of my best friends now." Thinking of one more thing, Blake questioned earnestly, "Maybe it's your purpose to be my best friend, ever think of that?"

Contemplating Blake's words, Claire offered this as feedback, "It's a possibility." She then held up her fist for Blake this time. Blake's eyes widened and blinked with excitement because of the offer. Raising her own fist to make contact, Blake said, "That's what I'm saying, Claire Bear." Their fists bumped and they followed it up with their familiar movement to show an explosion.

April had to giggle at the two girls. It had only been a week, but the bond was evident. It was heartwarming to see how nice Blake was to Claire, and vice versa, for that matter.

The three ladies spent the next hour or so at the dining room table talking to Crystal. Claire could see why Blake liked her so much. It was kind of a rough first meeting, but Claire was opening up to her and was slowly letting her guard down.

Crystal glanced at her watch and knew that she had to get going. Getting up from the chair, she said, "It's been so nice joining you guys for breakfast."

Going up to her and giving her a big hug, April said, "I'm so glad that you came this morning and I cherish you as a best friend."

Blake followed her mother, hugged Crystal, and said, "Thank you so much for helping us out with Claire. You are my favorite aunt." Thinking about that for a second, Crystal replied, "Um, I am your only aunt, but nice try."

Claire added, "Thank you again for helping me to stay here. I will do whatever you want me to do." Suddenly, Claire thought of something and found herself voicing her concern to Crystal. "Oh, I just had a thought. Is there a foster child with Roger and Carrie now? I mean, Roger tried to rape me—what if there is another girl there and he tries to do the same with her?"

Crystal stared at her for a second, and answered, "You know, Claire, that is a very good question. Since you managed to escape and run away, no one was there to inform the authorities about the attempted rape, and so, there would be no reason to suspend his fostering license." Realizing that there was potential for further abuse in her previous foster family, Crystal said, "I will find out when I call Duncan, and he can ask Seattle for me." She then reached out to give Claire a hug, and said, "Don't worry, I will do my best to find out for you, and don't worry, I will do whatever I can to support you."

As Crystal made her way towards the elevator, she said, "Goodbye, Turners, I will give you a call on Monday and let you know what I find out." Crystal stepped into the elevator and disappeared when the doors closed. As she descended to the lobby, she jotted a couple of notes in Roger Bower's file. If he did try to rape Claire, then she was not just going to let him off the hook. Even though Seattle was not in her jurisdiction, she was still going to get the son-of-bitch, one way or another.

Blake clapped and said, "Well, that went well." She then looked over at her mom, and asked, "Do you really think Crystal can help Claire stay with us?"

Without hesitation, April replied with a grin, "If anyone can, it's Crystal." She looked at Blake and Claire, and said with conviction, "Yes, I know she will."

The three of them headed towards the kitchen, and Claire sat on the bar stool near the island, and spun it around in order to take in the full view of the apartment. "You know something?" she asked April.

"What honey?" April asked.

"It just hit me that I might get to stay here," Claire said, unable to suppress her smile. "I can't believe it, you know? I have never felt more at home in any place in my life. I never could have dreamt a week ago that a mother and her daughter would come up to me to offer me lunch and a place to stay."

To be honest, April couldn't believe it either. "Well, it comes as a surprise to us too. It's not like we go around just taking in any person we might meet on the street." April did not want to tell Claire what exactly it was that had led her to Claire, so she said, "But I can say that it was fate that brought us to you."

"So what do you guys want to do now?" Blake asked, speaking about the rest of the day.

April thought about it for a few moments, and suggested, "Well, I have a few things that I have to look at over in my office, so if you two want to hang out and play video games or whatever, then we can meet up for lunch."

"Sounds good to me," Blake said, looking at Claire. "Do you want to play *Justice League*? I feel like kicking your butt again."

"Oh, I don't think so," Claire challenged, as she gave Blake a look as if to say, 'Bring it on'.

* *

THE GIRLS HAD A FUN-FILLED DAY, PLAYING VIDEO GAMES the rest of the morning while April filled her time with emails and prepared a slide presentation for a meeting that she had to facilitate on Monday morning. When it was lunchtime, April prepared ham and cheese sandwiches with a pot of mac and cheese. And after lunch, they sat around the living room talking and watching a little TV.

April had called her parents and told them about her plan to have Claire stay with her. Of course, they were supportive. After that conversation, Anne texted Claire and told her that she was happy that Claire was going to be staying with April, and was looking forward to seeing her again soon.

For dinner, April decided to take the girls out, so they went to a nice Italian restaurant. On the way home, they walked by some of the buildings that Nick had taken pictures of, and April pointed out to Claire some of his favorite designs. The evening was chilly with a slight wind, but it was a nice walk. Claire was wearing her new coat and the Burberry scarf that April had given her on the first day they met. When they got back to the apartment, Blake made hot chocolate, and the three of them sat at the island enjoying it.

Holding her cup with both hands to warm them, Claire took a sip and said to April, "Would it be ok if I grabbed the second book in the series that I'm reading? I would like to start it tonight when I go to bed."

"Of course, Claire. You can go to the office and grab whatever book you want at any time," April said fondly. She liked having someone in the house who enjoyed reading almost as much as her, and it felt good to be able to discuss books with Claire.

Blake smirked and said with a touch of sarcasm, "Hey mom, is it ok if I go into your office to grab... never mind, I don't want to read a book."

Annoyed, April rolled her eyes, and said, "Brat." And then added, "You know, sweetie, it wouldn't hurt you to pick up a book once in a while?"

Blake looked offended but then debated her side of the argument, "Yes, but I could get a paper cut if I picked one of those books up. I could become crossed-eyed looking at pages all day instead of at a computer screen; I might even get ink poisoning from the letters on the page. I mean, my God, mother, I could get an infection and die."

"Wow," April said, "just wow."

Claire laughed at Blake. It was funny to see how Blake handled her mother whenever she tried to get her to read more.

April got out the UNO cards, and asked if they wanted to play a few games before they got ready for bed. Looking at Blake, April said, "Oh, I'm sorry, will the ink on the cards cause an allergic reaction to your skin?"

"Funny, mom," Blake replied, "I have built up an immunity to UNO cards, don't you remember?"

"Oh yeah, that's right. You have a selective allergy to ink. How could I have forgotten?" April grinned, as she pulled the cards out of the box and began dealing. After about four games, it was unanimously agreed that it was time to call it quits and everyone made their way to bed.

Blake yawned and stretched her arms. She just got really tired, and she had a bit of a headache. So, before she went upstairs, she took two Motrin from above the kitchen sink.

Claire went to what was now considered her bathroom upstairs, and brushed her teeth and then prepared the shower. She looked in the mirror before taking off her clothes, and almost didn't recognize the image before her. The face looking back at her was not the one from a week ago. This face now had a healthy glow and not only had makeup, but it was properly applied too. Her hair still had a wavy curl to it that exhibited a healthy shine. Finally, the look in her eyes had changed. It was as if someone had removed all the pain and anguish that had built up over the years, and replaced it with a contentment that she had never experienced. Claire couldn't help but smile.

She stepped into the shower and began to wash herself. Halfway through the shower, Claire started to feel cramps coming on. It has been such a whirl-wind for her over the past week that she forgot that her time of the month was approaching. *Great,* she thought to herself, and then remembered that her backpack which had been stolen a couple of weeks earlier had had the feminine products she needed.

When Claire was finished with the shower and dried herself, she put on her nightshirt and went to Blake's room and knocked on the door.

"Come in," Blake answered. Her body had started to ache just a little, but she hoped the Motrin would kick in soon. She was at her desk and looking at a picture of her and her dad. Unknown to Claire, Blake was still affected by the dream that she had had the night before, and it made her yearn for her dad. When she noticed the picture at her desk, Blake picked it up and stared at it.

Claire, noticing that Blake was holding the picture, asked, "Can I look at it?"

"Sure, of course," Blake replied, and handed her the picture frame.

The picture was of her dad and her sitting together in a Mexican restaurant, and they both were wearing sombreros. Blake was about eight years old.

"Cute picture," Claire said admiringly. "It must be hard for you to live without him?"

"It is," Blake said honestly. "I miss him every day."

Claire handed the picture back to Blake and she set it back on the desk next to a man's wallet. Claire noticed the wallet, and gave Blake a quizzical look.

Blake picked up the wallet and opened it to show Claire. Inside was Blake's dad's driver's license.

"Days before my dad died," Blake began, "he took me to the Secretary of State, on his 37ᵗʰ birthday, so he could renew his driver's license. It was a Friday afternoon when we went and he took me to get ice cream afterwards." She paused a moment, and then said, "It was one of the last pictures taken of him alive, and we received it the week after his funeral. Can you imagine what it was like to get that in the mail?"

Claire examined the license. The first thing that stood out to her was that Nick seemed as if he was really happy. Usually, license pictures can make the person look as if they are posing for a mug shot, but not Nick's. The look of joy was obvious. Maybe it was because Blake was with him and was making him laugh. Whatever it was, it created a perfect picture of him. Claire read the license as if it was a book, trying to cling onto every word, almost as if she was going to get quizzed on its contents afterward. His license number was T134-7835-1992; he was born on January 18, 1976; the license expired 3-25-2017; and it displayed April's and Blake's current address. Printed across the top of the license were the words, "Jesse White – Secretary of State" and then it had a red color symbol the shape of the state of Illinois with the word 'Donor' printed in the middle of it. Underneath his picture was Nick's signature. Claire didn't know that it was because he was an architect, but his handwriting was incredibly neat.

Claire handed the wallet back to Blake, and said, "It's cool that you have that of him."

Blake set the wallet back on the exact spot that she had picked it up from, "Yes, it is."

The two girls sat in silence for a few moments, each caught up in their own separate thoughts.

"I have a question for you?" Blake said to Claire.

"Ok?" Claire answered.

"Have you ever thought about looking for your dad?" Blake asked, reflecting on her past experiences with her own dad.

Blinking her eyes in shock over the question, she almost blurted out a defiant 'no', but she thought about it for a second, and replied, "I have never really thought about it, to be honest with you. I mean I have never known who he is, so it's not like I miss him." Claire glanced back at that picture of Blake and her dad, and continued, "I don't have any memories like you and your dad sitting in that restaurant. The only thing that I know about him is that his name is Sammy, and he left us before I was born. So I don't miss what I have never had."

"You don't ever want to look for him?" pressed Blake.

Sighing, Claire grabbed the ends of her long, wet blonde hair, and began twirling them between her fingers. "Even if I wanted to, the only thing that I know about him is that his first name is Sammy, and that my mother had a picture of her and him together at some bar. However, she said that she lost the picture when I was a little girl."

Beginning to realize how problematic this was, Blake said, "God, that sucks that you don't have anything to go on."

Sitting down on the bed facing Blake's desk, Claire said, "I know. That is why I really haven't thought about trying to find him. I never had dreams of him riding in on a white horse and claiming me as his daughter as we ride off to his house in the mountains of Seattle."

"Maybe Crystal can help you try to locate him?" Blake said, thinking of Crystal's detective abilities.

Grinning, Claire joked, "Are you trying to get rid of me already?"

Backpedaling, Blake immediately responded, "No, God no. I want you here with us." Claire could hear the sincerity in her voice. "I was just thinking how I miss my dad, and I thought that if we could find yours for you then you might be able to experience fatherly love too—that's all."

Claire stretched out her arms behind her and leaned back further on the bed looking up at the ceiling. "Thanks for thinking about me, but I don't know about trying to find a man who would leave his pregnant girlfriend and not care to try to find his child."

"Yes, of course," Blake gave in. "We will focus on you staying here with us, ok?"

"Sounds like a plan," Claire agreed and exhaled a breath of air. Despite being defiant about not wanting to locate her dad, there was a tiny place in her heart that longed to find him. Claire was not fully aware of it mentally, but it was there. Maybe one day she would overcome her bitterness, and give in and start the search. But tonight, she was very happy staying with April and Blake.

Claire went to get up from the bed and the cramps in her belly made her remember the reason she had walked into Blake's room in the first place.

"Blake, I hate to ask you this, but can I borrow a couple of pads? I'm about to start my period, and the only pads that I had left were in my stolen backpack," Claire asked bashfully. She wasn't used to being around other girls in this situation, and of course, she did not have a mother figure to help her with this either. Claire didn't know the proper etiquette to use in dealing with this.

"Oh my, of course," Blake said, as she went into her bathroom and grabbed a few Stayfree pads from the cabinet and handed them to Claire.

"We will go to the drug store tomorrow, and get you set up with some stuff," Blake told Claire matter-of-factly.

"Thanks, Blake," Claire said, as she took the pads and headed towards the bedroom door.

She turned around just before leaving, and said smiling with gratitude, "When I say thanks, I mean thanks for everything."

Blake smiled back and got into bed. She looked over at the picture on her desk one final time and turned out the light on the nightstand. As she pulled the blanket up over her shoulders, she wondered if she would dream of him again tonight.

CHAPTER ELEVEN

EMILY BECKETT WAS A LITTLE CONCERNED FOR HER BEST friend, Blake Turner. It had been over a week since that homeless girl had turned up at her apartment, and even though Blake had been texting her, she got the feeling that there was something that Blake was hiding.

So, when Blake texted Emily to come over on Sunday suggesting that she could hang out with her and Claire, she jumped at the opportunity to meet this girl. Emily wasn't the overly jealous type, but she didn't want some stranger taking advantage of her best friend.

When the elevator doors opened to reveal Blake's apartment, Emily was a little surprised at what she saw. Emily had had a preconceived notion that the girl would look scummy and rough, and would have a look about her that conveyed worthlessness. However, when Emily saw Claire standing next to Blake, she was visibly taken aback. Standing next to her friend was a pretty, blonde girl with new clothes and a polished look. The look on her face was welcoming and sincere.

Stepping towards Emily to give her a hug, Blake embraced her and then looking at Claire, she introduced, "This is Claire."

"Hi Emily," Claire smiled welcomingly.

"Hi," Emily said, sounding a little shocked. "How's it going?"

"Good," Claire replied, "How was Oregon?"

Pausing for a second, Emily wondered how Claire knew that she was in Oregon. But then she figured that Blake must have talked about her to Claire.

"Good," answered Emily. "It's warmer there than it is here."

"Well, that's cool," Claire said. "I lived in Seattle for most of my life, so it's close to Oregon."

"Yes," Emily agreed. "But it rains more there."

"Yes, it does," agreed Claire.

Blake said, "Why don't we head out and get a little shopping done, and then we'll eat lunch at the burger place next to Cindy's Cupcakes?"

"Sounds good to me," Emily said.

Blake and Claire got their coats and scarves, and proceeded towards the elevator. Because April had left to meet with Crystal and Gina for coffee before Emily arrived, she wanted Blake to text her on their way out. Blake told Claire to text April instead. She figured, Claire would have to get used to texting April when she left—she was certain that the texting rule would be applied to Claire too.

Claire pulled out her phone and typed in 'Leaving now' with a smiley face emoji.

Within ten seconds, Claire's text tone went off. It was a text from April stating, "Have fun and be careful."

Even though Blake found texting her mom every time tedious, Claire thought it was cute. It just meant that April cared for them, and wanted them to be safe.

As the girls walked the streets of Chicago, Emily questioned Claire on her story and how she ended up with the Turners. Claire gave her the short version, but did tell her about her mom being in jail and how April and Blake had found her on the streets. She obviously didn't mention anything about her foster parents. She didn't know if Blake would tell her, but didn't think so, at least, not right away.

Claire liked Emily, but there was something guarded about her. She didn't know what it was, but she wasn't making a big deal about it. She had only just met Emily, and didn't want to do anything that would cause friction between Blake and her.

After they left the clothing shop where Blake bought Claire a cute top, Emily purchased a sweater and matching shoes, and Blake discovered the perfect pair of jeans, they decided to go to the independent pharmacy a few doors down.

Emily went over to the makeup section just to look while Blake took Claire over to the feminine aisle to get some of the basics. After looking over several different brands, Claire settled for a box of the brand that Blake had let her borrow last night. Blake then took her over to the deodorant aisle and grabbed one that she thought that she would like.

Joining Emily by the makeup aisle, Blake and Claire examined the wall of cosmetics. Blake arbitrarily picked out several lipsticks, foundations, mascaras, nail polish, blushes, and brushes. Claire didn't think too much about it until Blake implied that it was all for her.

"Seriously, Blake, it's ok, I don't need all that," Claire said, refusing the items.

"Oh, no," Blake rebuked. "Yes you do. I told you last night that I was going to set you up, and I meant it. Plus, I have strict orders from my mom to make sure all the necessities are covered."

Emily glanced at Claire and then at Blake. She couldn't believe that Blake was going to buy Claire all that stuff. She had just bought her a shirt and now all this stuff. It just felt to Emily that they were going overboard for some girl that they had just met. She didn't say anything, but Claire caught a glimpse of Emily and could pretty much guess what she was thinking.

Suddenly feeling ashamed, Claire said to Blake, "No Blake, it's ok, I don't need it."

Detecting the change in Claire's voice, she said with more authority, "No, Claire, this is what I am getting for you and that's final." Blake took the basket of cosmetics and feminine products to the counter to pay.

Blake placed the drug store bag in her bag with her jeans, and headed out of the store. She knew something was up with Claire, but didn't know exactly what was bugging her.

"Let's get some lunch," Blake said, as she led the trio in the direction of the burger place.

The girls made small talk on the way to lunch. Claire began to feel a little more reserved around Emily, only using a few words to answer specific questions.

Claire knew that they were getting close because she could smell the sweet scents emanating from Cindy's Cupcakes. From what Blake had previously mentioned, the burger place was next to it.

When Blake and April had taken her to get donuts there, she had not noticed the burger place. It had a red and white sign with a cartoon face taking a bite from a burger. The place was called "Rick's."

Blake and Emily took the lead entering Rick's, with Claire close behind them. It was bigger than it appeared from the outside, and it had about twenty round tables. Emily picked a table at the right corner, and the three of them chose their seats. The menus were already placed on the table, so the girls picked them up and looked through them.

Just like the pizza place that April and Blake had taken Claire to, the menu was huge and displayed a variety of burgers that ranged from a regular house burger to a burger that had all the ingredients and toppings infused within the burger itself.

"Wow," Claire said, adding, "these look delicious." Looking over at Emily, Claire asked politely, "Which one is your favorite?"

"Oh," Emily said, "Um, I usually get the mushroom burger with Swiss."

"That sounds yummy," agreed Claire, and continued to search for one that she could decide on.

"I like the burger with the pulled pork infused in it," Blake said to Claire as she pointed at a picture of it on the menu.

"That looks good too," Claire said with indecision.

The waitress came over and dropped off three glasses of water. She said that she would be back in a minute to take their orders.

Blake made a few remarks to Emily about how they had been there in the past, and the fun that they had had through the years. She told Claire a story about when they were little girls eating here with Emily's parents, and how the guy seated at the table next to them got sick and threw up all over the floor next to Blake's seat. In response to the smell of vomit, Blake had puked all over the guy, and Emily's parents had had to take her home to clean her up. It wasn't funny then, but now, years later, it was.

The waitress came back to the table and the girls gave her their order.

Emily ordered the mushroom and Swiss, Blake ordered the infused pull pork, and, at the last second, Claire decided to get what Blake ordered. Claire and Blake didn't notice, but Emily rolled her eyes at Claire's choice. It just seemed to Emily that Claire was following Blake like a lost puppy.

By the time that Claire finished the last bite of burger, she was full to the brim. She had just ingested about a full pound of beef, not to mention the pork.

"I am really stuffed," Claire said happily. "That was probably the best burger that I have ever had."

"I'm sure it was," Emily said, candidly.

Claire glared at Emily because the way she said it, came across as a little crass. Blake glanced over at Emily, and detected a little tension.

Before Blake could say something to her friend, Claire boldly said, "Yes, it was."

The waitress came back, took the dirty plates, and left the check. Blake dove into her purse and took out the credit card that her mom let her use. She set it down on the table. The waitress was just about to take it, when Emily said, "Wait, I can pay for mine." She took out some cash and put it next to the bill.

Blake looked at Emily and said, "It's ok, I got it." But Emily just shook her head, and looking at Claire, she said, "I got mine." It was like she was saying she had money and Claire didn't.

The waitress took the credit card and the cash, and left.

"What's up with you?" Blake asked, sounding a little confused. "You've let me pay before."

"Nothing," Emily replied bluntly. "I just can pay for my meal; that's all."

Claire knew exactly what Emily meant—that she had the ability to pay and Claire didn't. Claire became immediately aware that Emily either resented her or was jealous of her. But she couldn't possibly figure out why Emily was jealous—afterall Claire was homeless, with no family to speak of, and nothing to her name.

"Seriously, Emily," Blake continued, "I don't understand why you didn't let me pay?"

Emily shrugged her shoulders, and replied, "'Drop it. It's done. Don't worry about it."

Blake shook her head and didn't know how to respond to that. The waitress came back with the receipt, and Blake signed her name on it.

The girls then walked out of Rick's, and Blake started to walk in the direction of Cindy's Cupcakes. It was a tradition for the two of them to grab some cupcakes or donuts after they had dined at Rick's. They were always too full to eat them there, but they would each take a bag home for later. It didn't matter if it was Emily's parents or Blake's, they would stop no matter what.

Blake noticed Emily hesitating, and turned towards her. "What? You're not getting cupcakes now?"

Acting a little aloof, Emily replied, "No, I better get home, my dad is expecting me soon so that we can hang out."

Emily really didn't mean to sound rude, but when she spoke the word "dad," she said it in a different tone. And although she didn't intend to, Blake felt that Emily had implied that she still had a dad, and Blake and Claire did not.

"No problem," Blake replied crossly. "Just go."

Claire couldn't believe that Emily had said what she had, especially knowing that Blake didn't have a dad anymore. Claire was perturbed by Emily due to the way that she had treated her, but to dismiss Blake like that was uncalled for.

But just before Emily turned to leave, Blake grabbed Claire's hand purposefully, and led her into the cupcake store.

Once inside, Blake looked at Claire, and apologized, "I am really sorry about that. I don't know why she did that." Claire could see that Blake was hurt by it and didn't understand what had happened.

"I think that she was jealous or resentful of the fact that you have been paying for me," Claire said as she sized up the situation. "Believe me, I have been to several schools in my life, and when the new girl steps into someone's life, there is always someone else who gets their nose out of joint."

Going over the events of the day, Blake tried to think rationally about her own behavior and couldn't come up with even one time when she had ignored Emily or implied that she was choosing Claire over Emily.

Claire knew it was going to take time, and that she didn't want this incident to cause a rift between Blake and Emily. "Later tonight, you should call her and talk to her about this," Claire instructed Blake.

"I don't know," Blake said, with a touch of annoyance. "She was mean to us for no reason."

Thinking about it for a moment, Claire said, "Well, maybe you should find out what that reason is, and explain to her that I am not a wedge trying to separate you from her."

"Maybe you're right," Blake said, caving in. "It's just... I don't know. We have been friends forever, and for her to imply that about my dad...."

"That is why you two need to talk it over," Claire pressed.

"Ok, ok," said Blake.

While Claire and Blake waited in line, Claire was doing the best she could to keep an open mind. Despite what Blake had said and done while buying her stuff today, the way that Emily had looked at her at the drugstore did make her feel ashamed about not having any money.

Finally, it was their turn, and they got a variety of donuts, cinnamon rolls, and cupcakes. It took up two bags and Blake gave one of the bags to Claire to carry.

It was decided that they had done enough shopping for the day and so they headed back to the apartment.

* *

APRIL, GINA, AND CRYSTAL SAT AT THEIR FAVORITE BOOTH in the coffee shop a few blocks from April's apartment. It had become a routine for the three of them to get together on Sundays for coffee. However, this was the first Sunday that all three had gotten together in about three weeks.

For April, the last week had been a whirlwind of emotions. Her mind was still reeling from hearing Nick's voice in her head, and how worried she was when Claire was terribly sick for those first few days, not to mention Blake's dream reinforcing the idea that Claire should stay with them.

Gina and Crystal were her two best friends and she felt confident that they would help her try to figure this out.

Crystal took a sip from her glass mug, and said to April jokingly, "Talk about a wild week. I mean, I leave to go on a vacation, and you take in a stray, homeless girl."

"I know, right?" April replied. "It's not like me to do something like this, but I didn't have a choice," she added, referring to Nick's voice commanding her to go to Claire. "But, today, I can't imagine myself letting her leave. I mean, I have grown so fond of her in the last week that it's almost scary."

"Well," Gina said, "Just be careful. I know that Nick has led you here, but I just don't want to see you, or Blake, hurt."

"Believe me, I am aware," responded April.

Just then a handsome guy walked into the coffee shop and took a seat at the counter. He was about April's age, and Crystal noticed right away that he was not wearing a wedding ring. Despite the fact that he was wearing a heavy coat, you could tell that he was slender and was somewhat muscular. His clothes indicated the presence of money, and his demeanor was that of confidence. He had a professional-looking backpack with a unique business symbol on it. It was like a 'W' or an 'M' within a circle, with some words in it, but she couldn't make out what it said. It looked like he had a laptop and other business essentials in the backpack. When he talked to the waitress behind the counter, his voice was warm, and he seemed to have a pleasant demeanor.

Crystal elbowed April, and looked in the direction of the guy.

"What?" questioned April, not understanding what Crystal was getting at.

"Why don't you put yourself back into the dating pool again? I mean, it's been four years, and even though I miss Nick dearly, I think that he would want you to be happy again," Crystal said affectionately.

Gina quickly put in her two cents, and added, "Oh yes, you definitely should go over there and talk to him."

Sighing and then taking a sip of her coffee to ignore what her friends were suggesting, April said softly, "No, Crystal. I'm not ready." She held up her left hand to show her wedding ring, and asked, "Do you think that if I was ready, I wouldn't have taken this off?"

Not taking her eyes off her friend, Crystal grabbed April's left hand and held it. "Honey, it's been four years. Four years! As your friend, I am asking you to reconsider the possibility of putting yourself out there." Looking at Gina for support on this, Crystal continued, "You are a beautiful, bright, and yes... young woman who has a lifetime ahead of her."

Trying to think of a counter argument, April said, "What about Blake?"

"What about her?" Crystal countered. "Are you worried that she wouldn't understand that you are lonely and would like to have another companion? She is fourteen years old, and in a few short years, she will be leaving the nest, and then you will be really alone."

Crystal released April's hand, and April thought about what she had just said. "I'm not lonely, I've got Blake, even if it's for a few more years as you put it, I've got you guys, and I have my career," April told them.

"Yes but..." Gina began jokingly, "but what if I were to fire you right now? Then you would only have Blake and your friends, not your career."

Seeing where Gina was taking this, Crystal added, "Yeah, and what if we dumped you as friends today? Then you would only have Blake."

Gina broke in, and said, "And you know, Blake will go off to college soon, and then she won't look back. She will probably go off to some elite New York fashion college, and will never return to her spinster mom back in Chicago."

April had to chuckle, and then she said, "I am really glad that you guys have thought my entire life through for me. I better walk up to that total stranger right now and tell him to sweep me off my feet before I grow gray hairs tomorrow."

"That's the spirit!" Crystal declared, getting up from her seat to allow April to get through.

"Sit down," April laughed. "I was just being facetious." April turned her attention to her cup of coffee and, after taking a sip, said, "Listen, I really appreciate that you love me and want the best for me but now is not the time. Seriously, I'm ok, and if I promise to keep at least one eye open to the possibility of finding someone, will you stop harassing me about it?"

Taking what she could get, Crystal conceded, "Yes, but the one eye has to be open and with mascara applied. Do I make myself clear?"

"Crystal clear," April said, smiling at her own pun.

Crystal brought two of her fingers up to her eyes and then pointed them at April's eyes.

"I'm keeping my eyes on you, Turner," Crystal warned with a smirk.

April imitated Crystal's two fingers in a mocking manner, and then said, "I wouldn't have it any other way."

The handsome guy with the backpack turned away from the counter with his cup of coffee and headed towards the door. April didn't get a good look at his face—all she could see was his side profile, that too only for a split-second. He walked out of the coffee shop and disappeared into the wave of people walking by.

Crystal sighed, and said, "Well, you just missed your opportunity to find true love."

April grinned sheepishly, and said, "Oh well, maybe next time."

The three friends talked some more, and the waitress filled their coffee cups two more times before they got up to leave. Outside, the sky was overcast, but not too dark. Even though the forecast didn't call for any snow, there were a few snowflakes floating slowly down from the sky.

April took out her scarf, wrapped it around her neck, and tied it into a fashionable knot.

"It's was so good to hang out this Sunday. I love you guys—you are my best friends," April said, giving Crystal and Gina a hug. "Thank you for being so supportive."

"It's what we do," Gina replied, with a smile. "See you tomorrow at the office," she added, and then they departed, heading their separate ways.

April began her trek through the streets of Chicago with a grin on her face. She had the two best friends that any woman could ever ask for. They had been there for her through most of her life, and they continued to show their support.

As she rounded the corner that would bring her apartment building in sight, she noticed a homeless woman and her husband or significant other standing next to her. April stopped and stared for a few seconds, but she did not hear Nick's voice in her head. April didn't fully understand it, but she was now committed to seeing this thing through with Claire.

The streets were bustling with people still shopping post Black Friday. There were plenty of sales that lasted through the weekend, and the city was in full Christmas shopping mode. It was a sight to see. About fifty feet ahead of her, a guy hailed a cab and when he got in, April recognized the backpack from the coffee shop. She only caught a glimpse, but she was almost certain that it was him.

Thinking about what her friends had said about putting herself out there again, April's mind swirled with the possibility of what that might look like. What would she do first? Go on a dating website and set up a profile? Then what? Just go on arbitrary dates with guys she didn't know? Dating random strangers looking for the same thing or possibly looking for more? This was precisely why April wasn't ready for yet. There was too much uncertainty.

April picked up her phone and texted her mom, asking her what she and her father had planned for the day. Anne replied that they were going to the movies and then going out to dinner. April told her mom to have a great time and that she loved her. It was so nice to have parents who still enjoyed each other's company and who still liked to go out on dates.

Claire was sitting on the couch by herself reading the second book in the series.

"Hi, Claire," April said, "I didn't think that you guys would be home this early."

Claire set down the book and gave April a look that said, 'me neither'.

"What happened?" April asked, as she sat next to Claire.

"Well," Claire began, "It was fine in the beginning, but I think that Emily became weird about me being around."

"What do you mean 'weird'?" April wanted to know.

"It's like she resented my presence. Blake paid for my lunch and bought me a shirt, and I think that Emily thinks that I am here just to sponge off you guys," Claire said. "You know that isn't the case right?" Claire asked April bleakly.

"Oh God, of course not," April replied. "We are the ones who brought you here, and who want you here. It's our pleasure to help you with clothes and things like that. We don't expect you to pay for anything. You're still a teenage girl, after all."

Claire told April that she had felt a little ashamed earlier. "She kept giving me looks, and made me feel like I was a burden. I felt ashamed about having to depend on you for all this help. Don't get me wrong, I am in Heaven here and I couldn't have wished for anything better. You and Blake mean the world to be, but I just got the impression that I should be contributing somehow."

"Listen, Claire," April replied, the mother in her taking over. "You are only sixteen years old, and have had a terrible time up till now. No one expects you to pay for stuff or work to 'pay' for anything. I am so glad that we can offer you a stable place to live and help you get back to school." April paused a second to think about what she was going to say next. "Speaking of school, that is your job. All I ask from you is that you do the best you can in school and do all your homework. That is the only 'payment' I want from you, ok?"

Claire nodded her head in agreement, and April added, "Seriously, don't feel like you are a burden. Just be the beautiful, warm, and compassionate young lady that you are."

Feeling better now, Claire said, "Thank you, April, that really means a lot." And then thinking about Blake, Claire told April what Emily had said about her dad.

"It was a low blow, especially coming from her supposed best friend," Claire said. "I haven't seen Blake that upset since I've been here."

"Is Blake in her room?" asked April.

"Yes," Answered Claire. "I told her to call Emily and confront her about this because I didn't want them to ruin their relationship because of Emily's feelings towards me. It's the last thing I want."

"That's a mature idea," April said approvingly, "Do you think that she is on the phone now with her?"

"She might be," Claire guessed. "Blake mentioned that she was going to call her in a few minutes when we got home, and that was fifteen minutes ago."

Looking at her phone for the time, April said, "I better not go up there until she comes down, huh?"

"That's probably a good idea," agreed Claire.

Remembering the visit to Cindy's, Claire motioned to the bags on the island, and said, "We got cupcakes today, would you like some?"

"Yes, that sounds yummy," April said eagerly, "Care to join me?"

Setting her book down on the coffee table, Claire got up, and replied, "You bet."

April and Claire took their positions at the island and they each took turns picking out what they wanted from the bag.

Taking this time to talk to Claire, April asked with a measure of genuine concern, "So, what do you like to do? What do you want to be when you grow up?"

After she finished her bite of cupcake, Claire responded, "You know, up until this week, I would have answered that question totally differently." Pausing to wipe a few crumbs from her lips, she continued, "I mean, last week before we met, I would have said that school was a waste of time, and that my life didn't have much meaning. But today, I feel like I have a chance to change my story."

Getting up to get a cup of coffee, Claire asked April if she wanted one. When April nodded, Claire took out two mugs, and continued, "I guess if I have to say right now what I like in school, it would be reading and writing. I do like English, but I haven't really decided what I would like to do or what direction I would like to take."

"Well, you still have time to figure out what you want to be in life," April said. "That is the good part of high school—that you don't have to know right away. Besides, when you start taking your classes this week, you might find something that you enjoy."

Claire did like school in general, but she was a little nervous about starting this school in Chicago. If Emily was any indication of what some of the students were like, then she was not going to enjoy it.

"I hope you're right, April," Claire said, as she brought the coffees over to the island and set April's down in front of her.

"I am, sweetie," April said, as she picked up her cup and blew on its hot contents.

April and Blake spent the next fifteen minutes seated at the island, talking about school and other things. April told Claire about the time when she was in school, and how she and Crystal had so much fun. April got Claire to discuss some of her friends back in Seattle, but it seemed like Claire didn't have many friends—clearly as a result of moving around so much. She didn't want to get too close to anyone because invariably she would have to leave, or something would happen, and friendships would fall apart.

"Eating all the donuts, I see," Blake declared, as she walked down the staircase towards the kitchen.

"Yes," blurted Claire, jokingly. "Your mom just ate the last one."

"Oh, I believe it," Blake said seriously.

"Hey!" April retorted with a grin, "This is my first one."

When Blake settled down on the stool next to Claire, April asked her about Emily. Realizing that Claire had explained what had happened earlier, Blake answered, "I think that we are in a better place now." Blake reached into the bag and pulled out two donuts. "It's just that she acted really strangely today, and I have never known her to be jealous of anyone before, and for her to bring up her dad was totally uncalled for."

"So, what did she say?" April pressed her daughter.

"She didn't understand how we could take in a stranger and then basically make her a part of the family within a week. I told her that Claire is a good person and that we really want to help her." Blake took a big bite of the donut, and had to finish chewing it before continuing, "She said that she really didn't mean the 'dad' comment the way it sounded, and reflecting on it, she was really sorry for the way that it came out. She sounded sincere about that, so I did forgive her."

"Well, that's good," said April approvingly.

Blake reached across and took a sip of Claire's coffee, and said, "We are ok. I told her that Claire wasn't going anywhere and that if she wanted to still be my friend, she would have to accept this fact. She still has some reservations about it, I'm sure, but in the end, she agreed that our friendship was too important to mess up, and that she would try and give Claire a chance."

Claire reached across and took a bite of Blake's donut, and said, "Like I said before, I don't want to come between you and your friends. You mean a lot to me, and I don't want to cause any distress with your friends."

Blake grabbed for her donut back from Claire with a smirk on her face, and said, "Don't worry, Claire Bear, you aren't causing me any distress. And as I said earlier, you are my friend too—and whether my other friends can accept it or not is their choice."

Blake nodded her head in a defiant gesture to signify that her point had been made.

"Well, I'm proud of you my daughter," April said boastfully. "It is always the best route to take—to stand up for what and who you believe in, and to talk things out."

Blake nodded her head again, agreeing with her mom. "Truth be told, it was Claire's idea for me to call her and work things out," Blake confessed.

"Well, that's what friends are for," April said, looking at Blake and Claire.

Claire smiled and patted Blake on the shoulder. "Anything I can do to help out," she said, and taking the donut from Blake's hand just as she was about to put it in her mouth, Claire took off running towards the staircase.

"Oh, no, you didn't?" Blake exclaimed, as she took off after Claire, almost knocking over Claire's coffee cup in her haste to jump out of her seat.

April chuckled as the two girls ran upstairs towards Claire's bedroom. "When you two finish chasing each other, why don't you help me get out the Christmas totes so that we can decorate the apartment tonight?"

Claire stopped in her tracks, which allowed Blake to bump into her on the top of the stairs. "Sweet, sounds like fun. It's been a long time since I helped anyone decorate."

April could see a longing in Claire's eyes, but didn't want to press for any more details because she didn't want to make her feel worse about her past. "I'll start getting the totes from the closet, and you can separate them out in the living room," April directed.

"Let's do this," Blake said to Claire, as she pushed past her on the stairs and headed to her room.

"Where are you going?" Claire asked.

"I have to pee first," Blake said matter-of-factly. "When you got to go, you got to go."

"Obviously," Claire chuckled.

April began stacking the totes up in neat piles as Claire started hauling them from the storage closet to the living room. As she took out the totes, she purposefully left one in the closet. Blake arrived a couple of minutes later, and helped with the remaining totes. When all the totes had been moved, Blake took out her phone and opened a music app that played Christmas music.

As Claire opened up the first tote, she gazed at its contents, and said, "Wow, April. You have beautiful stuff." Most of the decorations were purchased from the same company over the years. Everything matched and looked as if it had just come from a department store window.

"Thank you," April replied. "We have been adding to this collection for years. Nick and I first started it the year that Blake was born. It became a tradition to buy several pieces each year, but I haven't gotten anything new since he died."

Blake looked at her mother and thought of something. "Maybe we can go this year and buy something new to add to our collection?"

April could hear the hopefulness in Blake's voice. "You know something… that just might be a good idea." But she didn't elaborate on it any further. Last year, April had almost gone to that shop to buy something, but at the last moment, she found that she couldn't go inside. She knew it was silly, but there was something about going in there without Nick that felt wrong.

It took the trio about two hours to finish. April took the time to tell Claire about some of the sentimental ornaments and guided her on where to put certain decorations.

The Christmas tree took the longest. Even though it was a pre-lit fiber-optic tree, April liked to place a lot of ornaments on it to fill in all of the gaps.

When Blake had put the final ornament on the tree, Claire said, "This place is breathtaking. It is like we are in a Christmas village." All three of them sat on the couch and admired what they had just accomplished.

"We certainly love Christmas," April agreed with Claire's observation.

As Blake sat on the couch, she placed her head on the back of the couch. After a few minutes, her eyes began to close.

April, noticing her daughter's tiredness, said, "You better get to bed—you have had a long day."

"Yeah," agreed Blake. "It was both mentally and physically exhausting," she said. April could only imagine what Blake had gone through as she dealt with the situation with Emily.

As Blake and Claire headed for the stairs to retire for the night, Claire gazed down at the Christmas tree and all the decorations, and thought, 'I still can't believe that I am here'.

* *

APRIL'S ALARM WOKE HER UP PROMPTLY AT 6:00 A.M. SHE HAD taken a shower the night before, and had laid out her clothes in preparation for

Monday morning. This was going to be a busy day for her, but she was excited for it to begin. April had completed the presentation that she had to make today, and had made a list of things that she needed to accomplish today.

One of the items on that list was to call the school and find out how she could go about getting Claire started. Crystal was going to help her with this, and she had her friend from Social Services contacting her today. April had his name written down in her phone—it was Duncan O'Rourke.

April got dressed, applied her makeup and curled her hair. She texted Blake to see if she was up, and got a response saying 'I'm up' and that was it. Normally, April would have yelled down the hallway, but she didn't want to wake Claire up.

Having checked herself one last time in the vanity mirror, April went downstairs to make breakfast for Blake before school. When she was about half-way down the steps, she smelled the scent of coffee.

Standing in the kitchen was Claire, wearing her nightgown and robe, with her hair a little disheveled. Clearly, Claire was awake and by the looks of it, was attempting to make breakfast.

"Good morning, Claire," April said, a little surprised. "What are you doing up this early?"

"I heard Blake's alarm go off, and decided to get up and see if I could make breakfast for you guys." They had talked the night before and had discussed that Claire would stay in the apartment all day, while April and Crystal could figure out the school situation.

"Why thank you, Claire," April said, "You didn't have to get up and do this though. It's pretty early."

"No worries," replied Claire, "I wanted to do it."

Claire had begun cracking the eggs into a bowl, and was getting ready to whisk them together. She opened the refrigerator and pulled out the half gallon bottle of milk. She took out a measuring cup and poured the amount she wanted into the cup and then dumped it into the bowl.

As she whisked the eggs, Claire looked at April, and said, "I like that outfit you have on today. You really look elegant, yet professional."

"Thank you, Claire," April said appreciatively. "You look stunning, too."

Knowing she was in her nightgown, Claire grinned, and said, "Yeah, I'm going for morning chic."

"Well, it's working for you," April confirmed with a smile.

Claire took out a pan from the cabinet, and put it on the stove. She turned the dial to medium temperature and waited for the pan to heat up. She then took a few moments to search for the cooking spray and when she found it, set the spray can on the counter next to the stove.

Claire handed the cup of coffee that she had made for her a few minutes earlier, and then set one for Blake on the table next to April.

April took a sip of coffee, and then asked, "Are you sure you are going to be ok by yourself today?"

Claire smiled indulgently because she could detect a 'worried mother' vibe coming from April. Claire had been staying there for over a week now, but today would be the first day that she would be alone for most of the day. To Claire, it was no big deal. She was used to being alone. But she knew that April cared about her, and that to Claire, it must be like leaving her kid at school for the first time.

"I'll be perfectly fine, April," Claire comforted her. "I won't go anywhere, and I'll be fine by myself."

Despite knowing that Claire had been on her own for several months, April was still a little concerned. "I know you will, I just worry. That's all. It's not that I don't trust you, because I do. It's just in my nature to be a little worried."

On her way towards the kitchen, Blake said sarcastically, "I think that I'll be like thirty years old, and I'll still have to text her when I'm on my way to work."

"Good morning to you, too," April sneered.

"Good morning everyone," Blake greeted with a smile, "Claire is cooking breakfast this morning? How cool is that?"

"Yes, I am, and you're going to like it whether it is good or not," Claire joked, as she poured the whisked eggs into the now heated pan. She got a spatula from the drawer and began stirring the yellow liquid in the pan.

When the eggs were done, Claire divided them out onto three separate plates and then put the pan in the sink. She put bread in the toaster and now that it was up, she smeared butter on each slice and put them on a plate in the middle of the island.

"This is good, Claire," April said, referring to the eggs. "You did a nice job."

Talking with a forkful of eggs in her mouth, Blake agreed, "Yeah, you did well."

"Thanks," Claire said happily. "I'm glad they turned out well."

They finished breakfast, and April and Blake got ready to leave.

"Remember, if you need me for anything, you have our numbers in your phone," April said for the third time this morning, but Claire smiled and replied, "Sure thing. I got it."

Turning to her mother in exasperation, Blake said, "Claire is not an infant mom, I think she's got this." Then turning to Claire for a fist bump, she asked, "You got this, right?"

Grinning and bumping Blake's fist, Claire said, "Right!"

"Ok, ok, I get it," April told Blake. "Let's get going."

April and Blake left the apartment. Claire then cleaned up the kitchen and put the dirty dishes in the dishwasher and cleaned the counters. She then went upstairs to her room and made her bed. When she was done, she examined her room and still couldn't get over the fact that this was her room. After a few moments, she decided to get cleaned up and take a shower. She opened her closet door and there were now several outfits to choose from. Not only were there clothes from when they had gone shopping on Black Friday, but Blake had also given her several pieces from her own closet.

Claire picked out a pair of black leggings and a purple sweater. She wasn't used to wearing leggings, but she wanted to try them out today, especially since she was going to be home all day.

After her shower, she blow-dried her hair, and then decided to put on some makeup. She thought to herself that she needed the practice and did want to try some of the stuff that Blake had bought for her from the drug store. She still had cramps from her time of the month, and it was good that she would be home all day. Normally her emotions would be all over the place thanks to the hormones, but fortunately, today she felt normal.

When Claire finally made it downstairs, it was a little after ten in the morning, and she had the whole day ahead of her. Sitting on the chair next to the couch, Claire thought about what she should do today. There was obviously going to be a lot of reading completed today, because she was halfway through the second book, and she wanted to finish it. She had already planned to clean all the bathrooms in the house. April didn't ask her to, but Claire wanted to do something to show her appreciation for staying with the Turners.

As Claire opened her book to start reading where she left off, a thought occurred to her. Feeling confident from her successful breakfast, she would prepare dinner and have it ready when April and Blake got home tonight. She didn't know what she wanted to make yet, but she would look on the internet for ideas and go from there.

The day felt like it flew by. Claire had read most of her book and then decided to clean the bathrooms. After that, she Googled for recipes, and finally decided to try a baked chicken recipe. She looked in the freezer to make sure that she had chicken. She took it out to thaw and gathered the rest of the ingredients and placed them together in the refrigerator.

Claire was lying on the couch, finishing up the last few pages of the book when her phone rang. She didn't recognize the number, but decided to answer it anyways.

"Hello?" Claire said.

"Hi Claire, it's me, Crystal. How's it going?" Crystal asked warmly.

"Oh, hi," Claire answered, "It's going good. I'm just about to finish a book that I started yesterday. What's up?"

"That's good," Crystal said cheerfully. "You are definitely staying with the right family if you like to read."

"I know, right?" agreed Claire, looking in the direction of April's library.

"Well, I spoke with my contact in Social Services, and we would like to stop by this afternoon to talk to you and have you sign some paperwork so that you can legally stay with April," Crystal said with no concern in her voice.

"Yes, sure. I am here all day. What time are you thinking about coming?" Claire asked.

"Well, I know that he already talked with April earlier about school, and that's no problem, but he does want her to be there, so I'm going to say around six o'clock."

"Sounds good to me," Claire said, "Thanks Crystal for everything you are doing to help me."

"It's no problem. I know that April wants the best for you, and I am here to support her and her decision." Pausing for a moment, Crystal added, "And I want to support you too."

Crystal could almost hear Claire smiling through the phone line. "See you at six o'clock, Claire."

"Ok, bye Crystal," Claire said, as she hung up.

Claire was starting to feel a little scared. It wasn't that things weren't working out. It was the opposite. It was that things were going great. That is why she was scared. It was usually when things seemed like they were going well that they fell to pieces.

Claire finished her book and then went to grab the third book in the series. She read a few chapters and then stopped to begin dinner. It was time for Blake to return from school. She was eager to tell her about Crystal's conversation and ask her how Emily had treated her in school today.

Claire was just placing the chicken in the casserole dish when Blake came out of the elevator doors.

"I see you didn't burn the place down," Blake said jokingly.

"I did, but the fire department came and put out the fire," Claire retorted.

"Nice one," Blake said, adding, "Say that to my mom when she comes home."

Knowing that April probably wouldn't find that funny, Claire grinned and said, "No, that's ok."

Blake examined Claire's choice of clothing, and commented, "Nice outfit, Miss Claire."

Looking down at her chest and leggings, Claire said, "Thanks. I dressed myself today."

Blake smiled and gave a thumbs-up, and said, "Good job. But don't get used to it."

Claire then asked Blake how school was and how Emily had been. Blake told her that school was school, and Emily was fine, but there was still a little resentment there. Blake didn't know if it was coming from her or Emily but it was manageable.

"Give it time," Claire offered, "Take it from me, you don't want to put a wedge in any friendship unless you absolutely have to."

Taking what Claire said to heart, Blake replied, "Sure. Ok. I will."

Claire then told Blake about how Crystal and Duncan were coming over tonight to talk with her and April about getting the paperwork started so that Claire could stay with them.

"Sweet," Blake said, enthusiastically.

"I'm trying not to get my hopes up, but it does look promising," Claire said, cautiously.

Blake sat down on the island and noticed what Claire was doing. "So you are making dinner now too!" Blake said, with an excitement that was infectious.

"Yes, I wanted to make myself useful around here, so I found a chicken recipe on the Internet, and decided to have a go at it," Claire replied.

Blake got up from the island and looked at the recipe on Claire's phone. It did look delicious. Blake offered to help her, but Claire refused. She wanted to do this on her own. Blake went upstairs to her room for a little bit while Claire finished combining all the ingredients with the chicken and then put it in the oven. Claire had texted April to see what time she was going to be home, and April texted back saying 'Around 5:30 pm'. Crystal had already texted April about the meeting at six with her and Duncan.

Blake came down and headed to the couch to do some homework and to hang around Claire. After she cleaned up the countertop, Claire sat next to Blake on the couch and opened the book to the page where she had left off.

After an hour or so, April came home and walked out of the elevator. The first thing that she noticed was that Blake and Claire were on the couch reading and doing homework. The next thing that April noticed was the smell of something wonderful coming from the kitchen.

"Hi guys," April said. "Something smells amazing in here."

"Welcome home, April," Claire said, warmly. "I made dinner for us. I hope you like it."

Claire and Blake got up and set the table. April sat down while the girls set everything up for dinner.

Claire brought in the casserole dish and it looked delicious. "Wow," April said, adding, "That looks amazing."

"Thank you, I hope it tastes as good as it smells," Claire replied.

The dinner turned out great, and Claire felt proud of herself for thinking about making it. They joked and laughed during dinner, and April informed the girls that her presentation was successful. Blake and Claire managed to get the plates and dishes cleaned up just before Crystal and Duncan arrived.

Crystal introduced Duncan to all three of them, and right off the bat you could tell that his guy was straight out of Ireland. He had red hair and possessed a thick Irish accent. He appeared to be nice, but you got the feeling that he meant business.

Duncan held out his hand to each one of them, and taking Claire's hand last, said warmly, "So, this lassie is Claire?"

"Yes," she replied. "I'm Claire."

"Nice to meet you, Claire," Duncan said, "shall we have a seat and we can get to work?"

They all sat down at the dining room table and Duncan opened his briefcase and removed several folders. Giving Crystal a look, he said, "This wouldn't be possible if it weren't for this one here." Pausing a moment to let Crystal smile at her achievement, Duncan continued, "It seems that there were some issues related to the way you left the Bowers." Before Claire could react to his comment, Duncan kept going, "I was made aware of this by Crystal, and I'm not here to challenge you in any way."

April could see the relief in Claire's eyes when she didn't have to go over the terrible circumstance that forced her to run away.

Opening the files, he took out several pieces of paper and a couple of pens. "I have spent the day going over a mountain of paperwork and having intense conversations with Seattle Social Services as well as the Seattle Police Department and Claire's new high school here in Chicago."

April spoke up, "Mr. O'Rourke, I just want to say that I really appreciate all the work and time that you put into this today. I know that this is out of the ordinary, but I can tell you with one hundred percent certainty that this is very important to Blake and me. Claire has entered our lives and we believe that it was fate that brought her to us." April paused a moment to grab both Blake and Claire's hand, and then said, "We are willing to make sure that we provide a nice place for Claire to thrive, and that she continues with her education."

Duncan could see that Claire would be well provided for with the Turners, and even if he hadn't meet April face to face, he would have agreed because of Crystal's recommendation.

"Well, thank you for that, Mrs. Turner. I can see that you will provide an environment in which Claire can do well. Because of the nature of this, I need you to fill out some forms," Duncan said.

"Certainly," April replied, "Just show me where I need to sign."

There were several forms that April had to sign. There were a few more that she and Claire both had to sign. One of the forms was from the Chicago Police Department that basically said that Claire was part of an investigation, and that April would provide a place for her until it was completed. Crystal's signature was already inked at the bottom. Leave it to her best friend to make this happen so quickly.

Duncan pulled out the last form, set it down in front of April, and said, "This is the financial form."

April almost signed it, but something caught her eye, and she asked, "What's this for?"

"It's for the amount that you will get every month from Child Services, the foster parent agency here in Chicago, for becoming a foster parent," Duncan said matter-of-factly.

April set the pen down, and declared, "I don't want money for this."

Duncan's eyes didn't hide his surprise, and said, "It's all legal, and this is the normal payment amount from the State when it comes to housing a foster child."

April put her hands together on the table and replied with conviction, "Duncan, I appreciate it, but I'm not doing this for the money." She looked at Claire, and proceeded, "I make plenty of money to support an addition to this family, and I wouldn't feel right about taking money from the State because of my decision to help her. We want her here, and she won't be a financial burden, I can assure you."

Claire's heart skipped a beat, and her eyes instantly began to tear. No one had ever said anything like that about her. Claire truly believed that no one else would ever do that for her.

"April," Claire began. "It's ok for you to take the money. I won't think that you are doing this merely to get a check." Claire wiped tears from her cheeks as she finished.

"Seriously, I don't want it. I just want you to know that I really want to do this for you," April said, "and that from now on, you will be part of this family and we will face the future together."

"You know it!" Blake blurted out, agreeing with her mother.

Duncan looked at the women sitting at the table and took the unsigned financial form and placed it back in the folder. "Ok then, Mrs. Turner, no financial assistance per your direction."

"Correct," smiled April. "We're good."

Duncan nodded his head in agreement, and took out one more file.

"This is for Claire to be registered in classes starting tomorrow. I already spoke with the school, and I have everything set up. Based on her previous transcripts, we have placed her in classes that we think she will be able to handle. She can pick up her class schedule tomorrow at the counselor's office. If, for some reason, you begin to have issues with them, please let your counselors know. Alright?"

"Ok," Claire said, not trying to hide the smile on her face. "I will."

He had both April and Claire sign the form, and it was now official. Claire would be staying with April and Blake. Duncan took the signed piece of paper and placed it properly in the folder. He looked at the women at the table, and said, "Well, this has been the most peculiar case that I have ever been involved in, but it's now official." Turning his attention to Claire, he said, "It's extremely rare that a family will go to such lengths to obtain a child such as yourself, and I sincerely hope that you will cherish this opportunity. They seem to care for you a great deal and believe me when I say, that is half the battle."

Claire went up to Duncan, and shook his hand. "Thank you, Mr. O'Rourke. I most definitely will. I know that this is a great opportunity for me and I don't plan on ruining it."

Duncan smiled and said. "Oh lassie, I can see that you are grateful. Just keep out of trouble, and you will make me happy."

Crystal stood up and hugged April and Blake. "Well, we did it. Now it's up to you guys to make sure that you keep this girl healthy, happy, and content."

"We will Aunt Crystal, we will," Blake said, grinning from ear to ear.

Crystal went up to Claire and gave her a big hug. "Welcome to the Turner Family," she declared. And then she whispered something into her ear, "We will work together to make sure that Roger Bower pays for what he did to you, I promise." Claire looked into Crystal's eyes, and that was when she knew that Crystal truly believed her, and she felt relieved that someone would trust her.

"Thank you," Claire whispered back. "Thank you."

With that, Duncan and Crystal headed out and left the apartment.

Blake ran up to Claire, and gave her a hug, "Welcome to the Turner Family!" she yelled as she shook Claire in her arms.

April went up to the two girls and put her arms around them, and said, "I can't believe that we pulled this off, but we did it."

Claire was smiling, laughing, crying, all at the same time. It was an emotional moment.

She looked at April and Blake, and with intense gratitude declared, "This is home."

CHAPTER TWELVE

TREVOR THOMAS QUIETLY CLOSED THE DOOR TO THE JANI-
tor's closet on the third floor of the high school. It was early Tuesday morning,
about half an hour before class. Accompanying him was his friend and team-
mate, Jordan Stiles. Trevor was a power forward for Jones College Prep High
School basketball team. Soccer season had just ended, and now Trevor was on
sport number two of a three-sport year. After basketball, he undoubtedly would
be a part of the varsity Lacrosse team.

On this day, Trevor was about to make a decision that would forever
change his career in sports as well as his life. You see, Trevor was a junior this
year, and was one of the popular kids because he was good looking and a jock.
Uncharacteristically though, he was somewhat of a nice kid who didn't get into
too much trouble.

Jordan played point guard on the team, and he was pretty much Trevor's
sidekick. Wherever Trevor went, Jordan wasn't far behind. He was a few inches
shorter than Trevor, but a tad bit bulkier.

So, here they were, waiting in a janitor's closet for the one thing that
would alter his future forever.

"Trev, are you absolutely sure you want to do this?" Jordan questioned Trevor.

Trevor adjusted his belt and said, "Yeah, sure. You heard the coach. We are on track to get to the finals this year, and he wants us to do whatever it takes to be the best."

Jordan gave a nervous laugh, and then said, "Yeah, but I thought he was thinking more about exercise and diet, not this…"

"Come on, Jordan," Trevor began, sounding a little irritated. "You know the pressure that I am under to play well. I mean if it's not coming from the coach, it's coming from my dad."

When Trevor's dad, Rodney Thomas, attended the same high school some twenty years ago, he was considered the most popular kid in school. He dominated every sport that he played, and was awarded a scholarship to attend Baylor University for football. Unfortunately, midway through the first year, he injured his right knee, and due to the severity of the injury, was let go from the team. Since a football career was off the table, he focused on school and graduated with a Bachelor's in Finance. Rodney eventually found himself working for Avison Young as a capital market analyst. Despite having a lucrative job that provided him with money, Rodney Thomas still dreamed of the life that might have been if he had been able to continue with football. When Trevor was born, Rodney saw his son as a vessel through which he could relive his glory days.

Ever since Trevor was a little boy, his dad pushed him into sports and wanted him to be the best at it. Rodney had paid for training camps and had bought the best equipment. Trevor's basketball coach and Rodney had been best friends growing up, and they were teammates on the Lacrosse team. So, most of Trevor's life had been spent watching, practicing, playing, and breathing a cornucopia of sports.

Trevor's mother, Darlene Thomas, used to be a cheerleader for Baylor University. When she met Rodney, it was love at first sight. Even though she was crushed that Rodney would not have a football career, her disappointment faded as he quickly became successful in the finance world. Darlene had graduated from Baylor with a degree in communication. She eventually found her career as a Communication Director for a Chicago lobbying firm based somewhere downtown. Even though she was busy like her husband, she still managed to find time for their only son. Because Darlene had been a cheerleader for Baylor, she was used to the sports world, but she did not want her husband to push Trevor as much as he was pushing him. They had spent a great deal of time arguing about this very fact, but to no avail. Rodney wanted his son in as many sports as possible, and that is what was going to be. On Trevor's sixteenth birthday, it was Darlene who pushed to get him the car that he really wanted—a bright-red Ford Mustang. In a way, it was like she was trying to make up for her husband's ambitious goals for their son.

There was a subtle knock on the closet door. Trevor opened the door, and a nerdy-looking kid entered. His name was Owen Adler. Owen was a senior, and your basic loner. He only had a couple of friends, and didn't socialize that much. However, Trevor did convince him to do some of his homework last year, so that Trevor could maintain a good enough grade point to stay on the team. Now, a year later, they were not friends, per se, but business partners. Trevor now paid him to do some of his reports and homework.

But today, Trevor had recruited him for something else entirely.

"Do you have it?" Trevor asked anxiously. Owen's dad was a pharmacist for a major pharmacy just on the outskirts of downtown Chicago. Because he had been working at the same store for over twenty years, he was well known in the community and was trusted by doctors. However, what most people didn't know was that Owen's dad ran a side business with some of the drugs that he stole from his own pharmacy. What started out as a way just to help pay for a new car, grew into a bigger racket. Unfortunately, he pulled his son Owen into it so that he could expand into the high school market.

"Yeah, but are you sure about this?" Owen asked nervously. Most of the students that he supplied to were your basic stoners and potheads. Trevor was different; he was one of the star jocks in the school. If something went wrong or if he got caught, it would cause an uproar.

"Of course, I'm sure," replied Trevor. "Besides I'm not going to tell anyone about it, and I certainly won't tell anyone who I got it from."

Owen wasn't too sure about that. He could easily see that if something went wrong, Trevor would rat him out in a New York minute. Owen had always given in to peer pressure, so he reached into his pocket, and pulled out a Ziploc bag. Trevor took the bag from Owen and unsealed it. Inside the bag were about 12 capsules of Anabolic steroids. The capsules were a mixture of red and orange color with tiny black writing on each one.

"Sweet, Owen, you're the man!" exclaimed Trevor, as he patted him on the shoulder. "This is going to be awesome."

Owen cleared his throat to indicate his payment. "Oh yeah, sorry dude," Trevor realized, and pulled out a plain white envelope of money and handed it to him.

"Remember, starting out you have to find the right dosage cycle that fits your body," Owen warned. "I have put a piece of paper with a graph and some advice. If you start seeing any of the mentioned side-effects, stop taking the capsules, and let me know. I can try to figure something out for you." It wasn't like he cared about Trevor, but he didn't want something bad to happen to him, leading to the steroids being traced back to Owen.

"Will do, doc," Trevor said, with little to no apprehension.

"I mean it, Trevor," Owen said a little more seriously, despite knowing that Trevor didn't seem to care.

Owen cracked open the closet door to see if anyone was around and quickly slipped out and into the hallway, walking at a fast pace to put some distance between himself and Trevor and the closet.

Still in the closet, Trevor unzipped his backpack and concealed the Ziploc bag in a secret pocket that he had one of the hot-looking girls from history class sew in last year. The pocket's original intention was to hide homework and money, just in case it was searched. However, he did hide a bag of marijuana last year for a senior on the hockey team, when the senior had had his locker searched. That had led to Trevor getting in the good graces of his senior.

Jordan looked up at his friend and captain, and didn't know what to say. He was a little scared for his friend, but Trevor was Trevor, and he did what he wanted.

"Let's split, dude," Trevor said with a grin, and carefully opened the closet door. He and Jordon slipped out without notice, and the two walked down the hallway without a care in the world.

They went down to the main cafeteria and met up with some of the other teammates. They would usually hang there before class talking about all sort of things that teenage boys talk about: cars, sports, girls, and of course, sex.

Trevor, and his now ex-girlfriend Brie Dixon, had broken up just three weeks ago. They had dated for four months before the breakup. There was no main reason for why they had called it quits, but if you could narrow it down to one single thing, then it might be that Trevor had just lost interest. The newness had worn off, and things were just becoming a habit. Not only that, but Brie was hesitant about having sex with him. Brie was a cheerleader for the varsity squad, and she was popular with most of the junior class. She had many friends and her GPA hovered consistently around 3.5. Her parents were still together, and they had money. Because of that, Brie could act spoiled at times, and often came across as snobbish. She was, of course, skinny with long brown hair.

Both she and Trevor were still friends, but they had hardly spoken since the breakup. Brie really missed being with him, and she secretly hoped that they would get back together soon.

Brie was in the cafeteria with a couple of her girlfriends when Trevor and Jordan strolled in. He looked especially happy today and Brie wondered to herself if he had found another girlfriend. Her group of friends was close enough for Brie to overhear some of the conversation that Trevor was having with some of his teammates, and it didn't seem to Brie that he had found someone.

Trevor had just finished telling one of his buddies about some amazing three-point shots he had sunk at the first basketball game of the season, when he noticed Brie sitting relatively close to his group. He looked over at her, smiled, and nodded his head as if to say 'hi'. Brie smiled back and put up her right hand in a wave, and said, "Hi". Trevor grinned and turned his attention back to his group of buddies.

Brie followed suit and turned back to her group, but only half-listened to what they were saying. Maybe Trevor missed her, and was possibly thinking about getting back with her. It was just a simple hello but Brie wondered again if there could be more. More and more students began filing into the cafeteria and the hallway leading to it. Then the first bell rang to alert students to get to class. Slowly, the students began walking to the classrooms for their first class.

For Trevor, Jordan, and Brie, their first hour was Biology with Mrs. Clemens. She was an older lady, with about fifteen years of experience as a full-time teacher. She knew her stuff, and was one of the student body's favorite teachers. Mrs. Clemens enjoyed all sciences, but was the leading instructor for biology.

The biology room was arranged with fourteen rectangular tables that had two tables pushed together to form one square table that sat four students with two on each side.

Trevor sat in the corner table in the back of the room with Jordan, Casey, Paul, and James. Conversely, Brie sat at the table that was near the teacher's desk with Rose, Shelly, and herself. The fourth chair had been empty since the beginning of the semester. All the other desks were filled with students.

The second and final bell rang, indicating the beginning of class—it meant that students had better be at least inside the classroom and ready to take their seat when that bell rang.

Brie opened her biology book to the chapter that was on the board, and out of the corner of her eye, kept glancing in the direction of Trevor's table. Did he want her again? She wondered to herself, as Mrs. Clemens cleared her throat and began class.

Claire pressed the 'Send' button on her text to April that read: "Made it to school. Thanks for everything. Have a great day." April had asked Claire to send a text when she made it to school. Of course, Blake had already sent a message the moment they had walked into the building, but Claire knew that April would appreciate it if she too sent a message. A moment later, April responded saying, "Thank you, have a great first day of school." Claire smiled at the phone's screen and then put her phone in her back pocket.

"Hello, Miss Forrester," Mrs. Patricia Falk said to Claire, as she entered the counselor's office. Mrs. Falk was the head counselor of the school, and was the one who had been on the phone with Duncan O'Rourke the day before.

"Hello," Claire replied politely.

"I would like to officially welcome you to Jones College Prep High School," Mrs. Falk said, with the peppiness of a high school cheerleader. "I think that you will find this school a great place to learn as well as make friends."

"Thanks," Claire said, with a smile. To be honest, Claire was excited about going back to school. Even though she had been moving from school to school her entire life, Claire felt right about attending this one. Blake had talked it up to her the previous night, and with any luck, this might be the one that she would stay in for a while.

Mrs. Falk smiled back, and then proceeded with a five-minute discussion about the rules and policies of the school, and had Claire sign several forms. When she was finished, she handed Claire her class schedule and gave her a map of the school. Her first class was Biology with Mrs. Clemens.

"Follow me, Miss Forrester, I'll take you to your first hour," Mrs. Falk said, as she bounced out of her chair and signaled for Claire to follow her into the hall.

Because the first class of the day had already begun, there were a couple of students racing through the hallway in an attempt to get to class. The two of them walked at a steady pace, and Mrs. Falk pointed at various items or banners to indicate an upcoming event or to simply inform her about the school itself. There were several posters taped to walls and classroom doors that had the school emblem printed on them. The emblem was a navy and white circle with the head of an eagle poking through the center.

As they rounded a corner, Mrs. Falk pointed at the huge trophy showcase that housed the various sports trophies that were earned by the school over the past thirty years. "These are the trophies that our sports teams have won over the last thirty years," Mrs. Falk explained. 'We not only pride ourselves on providing a fine education to our students, but our athletics department is one of the best in our district." You could hear the school pride dripping from every word that Mrs. Falk spoke.

"Wow, that's cool," replied Claire, bringing her right hand up to the glass in an unconscious attempt to touch one of the trophies. As she looked from one trophy to another, she wondered about what it must be like to be on a team, much less a winning team. Even though she never wanted to play a sport, there was a tiny part of her that still wondered what if?

Claire turned her attention away from the trophies, and continued following Mrs. Falk down the hallway. They eventually made their way to the biology room, and Mrs. Falk knocked on the door before entering.

There was a brief pause while Mrs. Clemens looked through the glass slit of the door, and recognized Mrs. Falk.

"Come in," she said.

Mrs. Falk opened the door, and Claire followed her into the classroom.

"This is Claire Forrester," Mrs. Falk said to Mrs. Clemens, but loudly enough so that the class heard the introduction. "She is a transfer student from Seattle, Washington."

"Hello, Claire, my name is Mrs. Marie Clemens, and I will be your teacher this semester for biology," Mrs. Clemens introduced herself, and then pointed at the only set of tables that had an open chair. "I guess that will be your seat."

Since the desk was close to the teacher's desk, she didn't have to walk too far to get to her seat.

Claire sat down and set her bag on the floor under her feet, and then set the class schedule and school map in front of her on the desk.

The girl seated across from her, Rose Garcia, almost immediately extended her hand, and said, "Hi. I'm Rose." Rose's parents had emigrated from Mexico to America when she was only two years old. Her dad studied law at the University of Texas, and when he passed the bar exam, he moved his family to Illinois, and passed the bar there as well. He was now a divorce lawyer in a law firm near downtown.

"Hi, I'm Claire," she introduced herself, thinking that if first impressions were accurate then she and Rose would soon be friends.

To Rose's left sat Shelly Clark. She was a red-haired Irish girl with a thick accent. She raised her hand in a wave, and said, "Hi, Claire, I'm Shelly." Claire grinned and waved back. Like Rose, Shelly seemed cool too. Her dad ran a local Irish pub in downtown Chicago, and it was quite successful. Seated to Claire's right was Brie Dixon. When Claire looked at her Brie introduced herself. Even though Brie didn't do anything that would constitute as 'mean' per se, she came across as indifferent. Claire responded back with an "I'm Claire," and left it at that for now.

Mrs. Clemens reached into a cabinet next to her desk, and took out a biology textbook. Going over to Claire's desk, she handed it to her.

"Ok class, let's pick up where we left off," Mrs. Clemens told everyone.

"We are on Chapter six, page 132." Rose informed Claire.

Claire started to flip through the pages after thanking Rose quietly.

Unknown to Claire, Trevor was staring in the direction of her desk, specifically her. As soon as she had entered the class, Trevor found himself unable to take his eyes off of her. There was something simple but intriguing about her. Sure, she was extremely cute and had long blonde hair, but the depth of her blue eyes had him mesmerized.

After a few minutes, Brie glanced over at Trevor to see if he was looking in her general direction. He was, unfortunately, looking directly at Claire. Brie stared at him for several moments trying to get his attention, but he was totally focused on Claire. A seed of jealousy was now planted in Brie, replacing the earlier attitude of indifference towards Claire.

Unaware of what was happening next to her, Claire focused on listening to Mrs. Clemens' lesson. Brie's face expressed irritation, and on noticing this Shelly checked out who Brie was staring at. It was Trevor, and he was gazing at Claire. Knowing the relationship between Brie and Trevor, Shelly understood that this wouldn't bode well for Claire.

Trevor continued to stare at Claire for a few more moments until he saw Brie looking at him. Their eyes locked onto each other for just a fraction of a second, but Trevor knew that she had caught him gawking at the new girl. He quickly turned his attention back to the teacher and pretended to listen to her. Picking up his pencil, he wrote a few words down on his notebook and nudged Jordan to look at it. Jordan glanced at the page of the notebook, which said, "New girl is hot."

Jordan let out a little chuckle as he nodded to his buddy. "I can see it, Trev," Jordan whispered. "I think that you should introduce yourself after class."

"Oh, I plan on it," Trevor replied, with a boyish grin on his face.

Time went by rather quickly for Claire, and when the bell rang signaling the end of class, she sat there for a moment glancing at her schedule to see where the next class was.

Shelly and Rose got up, and immediately started talking to Claire. "So what class do you have next?" Shelly asked.

"I have English Lit," Claire replied, locating the second class on the piece of paper.

"Cool, I have it too," said Rose.

"I have Algebra II," Shelly said, about her second hour.

"What do you have?" Claire asked Brie, who had just then got up from her chair.

"I've got World History," Brie replied, as if reading from a phone book. She was kind of glad that she didn't have the same class as Claire because Trevor was in World History with her for the next hour.

"Oh, ok," said Claire, now realizing that Brie didn't seem to like her. Claire had been to plenty of schools and knew that not everyone would want to get to know her and that no matter how much she tried, some things might just not change.

"You can follow me for the next few hours if you want..." Rose made Claire an offer.

"Thanks Rose, that would be great," Claire smiled.

Claire, Rose, and Shelly headed out the door, and the three walked down the hallway. It was a coincidence that Brie was heading in the same direction as the three, but she was about ten feet behind them. Trevor and Jordan passed her and strolled up to Claire.

"Hey, Claire," Trevor began, "I just wanted to say 'hi' and introduce myself."

Stopping at the sound of her name, Claire turned around to come face to face with Trevor.

"Oh, hi," Claire replied with a smile, as her eyes widened at the sight of him. He was a good-looking guy and was wearing a letter jacket. She knew that he was probably a jock, but he seemed nice.

"I am Trevor, Trevor Thomas," he introduced himself.

"I'm Claire."

Glancing over at his right-hand man, Trevor said, "This goofball is Jordan Stiles."

Jordan looked over at Claire, and gave her a peace sign, "What up, Claire?" Jordan said, as an introduction.

"Hi, Jordan," Claire replied politely. It was obvious that it was Trevor that was the lead in this.

"So, what sport do you play?" Claire asked Trevor, noting his lettered jacket.

"Actually," Trevor grinned, "I play all of them." He didn't seem to sound boastful about it—it was actually the truth.

Shelly spoke up, and said, "It's true, team captain Trevor here plays like three sports."

"Really?" Claire asked, a little impressed.

"She's right," Trevor said, tooting his own horn. "I just got finished with soccer and now basketball season just started. In the spring, I will be on the Lacrosse team."

"Impressive," Claire said. "Are you like the school jock or something?" she asked jokingly.

"Yes," Trevor said, "yes, I guess I am."

It was at that moment that Brie caught up with them, and looked right at Trevor. "Hi Trevor, how's it going?"

Trevor looked from Claire to Brie, and said, "Good, real good," And then keeping eye contact with Claire, he asked Brie, "How's it going with you?"

Brie could already tell that Trevor was really into Claire, and that only made her dislike the new girl even more.

"Good," Brie simply replied, and then left to head to her next class.

"So," Trevor asked, without skipping a beat, "What class do you have next?"

"She has English Lit with me," Rose spoke up happily.

Trevor nodded, and then asked, "Hey, let me scan your schedule to see if we have any other classes together."

Claire handed him the schedule sheet and after a few seconds, he said, "Hey, we have Political Science, computers, and the same lunch hour together."

"Cool. I guess I'll see you in Political Science then," said Claire, with a grin.

"Yeah, see you," Trevor replied, as the group walked together for a few more steps, and then Trevor and Jordan separated from them and went down the north hall.

When they were out of earshot of the guys, Shelly turned to Claire, and exclaimed, "Wow, Claire. Trevor was totally into you."

Claire smiled on the inside but said, "No, I don't think so. He was just being nice to the new girl. I never was one to hang around with the sports crew, you know what I mean?"

"Be that as it may, but he looked like a lost puppy. I've had him in several classes over the past couple of years, and I think that he is smitten," Shelly said to Claire as she waved bye, and turned the corner to head to her next class.

Claire followed Rose further down the hall, and Rose began talking. "Just so you are aware, Brie used to be Trevor's girlfriend up to like a few weeks ago." It came out as a statement, but was, in fact, kind of a warning.

Claire suddenly realized why Brie didn't seem to like her—it was quite clear.

"That's awesome. I don't need to be caught up in a love triangle on my first day," Claire said irritably.

Rose tried to reassure Claire. "No, don't worry. It's been over for like a month now. It's not like that they are going out now."

Claire was still doubtful, but decided right then and there that if Trevor tried to pursue a relationship with her, she would politely decline and would make it clear that she just wanted to be friends.

"This is us," Rose said, as she turned into the last classroom at the end of the hall.

The pair walked in and Rose motioned for her to take a seat in front of her. It just so happened that it had been empty since the semester had started. When the final bell rang, the teacher entered the classroom and shut the door. Mr. Gus Reed was the English Lit teacher, and he looked remarkably young for his age. He had a tightly shaved beard and he wore a sports jacket with jeans. He had graduated from the University of Iowa with a Master of Arts in Literary Studies.

"Ok, class," Mr. Reed began. "Let's pick up where we left off with chapters three and four." He sat at his desk and pulled out the novel *The Awakening* by Kate Chopin. As he opened it, he noticed Claire getting out of her seat to join him at his desk.

"Hello," Mr. Reed said, "You must be Claire."

Claire smiled, and replied, "Yes, I am."

"I am Gus Reed, your English Literature teacher, and I would like to welcome you to our school." He pulled open the bottom left drawer from his desk, and after a couple of seconds of looking for something, he pulled out a copy of *The Awakening*.

"Here you are, Claire. I have a few extra copies that I keep in my desk, just in case a student forgets their book at home." Mr. Reed handed the book to Claire and she accepted it with a grin and a thank you.

Once she sat down, Mr. Reed began again, "Ok guys, chapter three. So, when Leonce returns from Klein's hotel, he is cheerful and talkative. But because it is late, Edna is already asleep. Nevertheless, he tries to talk to her anyways. Why does he seem upset by it?"

Only about six hands rose in the air, and Claire's hand was among them.

Mildly surprised, Mr. Reed called her out. "Ok, Claire."

Without opening the book, Claire answered, "Well, you see, Mr. Reed. Leonce views his wife as a sort of amusement. He really doesn't view her as an equal partner in the marriage. Because he comes home from the hotel probably a little drunk and somewhat talkative, he expects Edna to chat back with him, and wants her to take an interest in the things that concern him. He views her sleepiness as a kind of indifference to him personally. After he finally goes to sleep, she goes out on the porch and cries until the mosquitoes force her back inside. It shows how insensitive he is to her."

"Very well put, Claire. I see that you have already read this book," Mr. Reed said, with satisfaction.

Nodding her head, she answered, "Yes, I read it a couple of years ago."

"Good, Miss Forrester, I'm glad that you won't have to catch up in this class," he said, and then asked another question, and called on another student to answer.

Rose tapped Claire's shoulder when Mr. Reed turned around to write something on the chalkboard, and whispered, "This class is going to be fun for you."

Claire agreed with her and whispered back, "English is my favorite subject."

Just by the way that Mr. Reed was teaching, Claire thought that this would be one of her favorite classes. Claire obviously loved to read, and this teacher really knew his stuff, not to mention that he was very charismatic and had a way about him that made you want to get entrenched in the world of the story.

Claire was called on a couple more times, and Mr. Reed was impressed with her knowledge of the novel as well as the insightfulness of her answers.

When class was over, Rose showed Claire the general direction to the Political Science class, but she herself had to go in the opposite direction. Rose did say that she would meet her in the cafeteria for lunch after her class.

Claire found her classroom without any issue, and as she entered the room, she noticed the instructor sitting at her desk. Mrs. Randall looked up as Claire approached her, and said, "Oh, hi, you must be Claire Forrester?"

Claire stopped at the desk, and replied, "Yes, that's me."

"Nice to meet you, Claire. I'm Mrs. Olivia Randall," she said, as she extended her hand to Claire. Mrs. Randall was a middle-aged woman that looked like she came right out of Congress. She looked extremely professional, and when she spoke, you got the feeling that she worked in politics.

"Hi, Mrs. Randall," Claire responded appropriately, and then added, "I'm a transfer student from Seattle, Washington."

Mrs. Randall smiled and welcomed Claire to the class. She handed her the textbook for the class and a few forms to go over. Mrs. Randall then directed her to a seat that was not assigned to anyone, which was towards the back of the class.

Claire went over to her desk and sat down. Only about half of the class had arrived, but there were still a couple of minutes remaining before the bell. There was no one in the class that she recognized from her other two classes, but she knew that Trevor would be coming in soon. About thirty seconds before the bell rang, Trevor strolled into class, and upon seeing Claire, gave her a small wave, and said, "Hi, new girl." The way that he said it was charming and you could tell that he had a smile on his face when he said it. "Hi, again," Claire said, waving back. Trevor took his seat, which was about two seats left of Claire.

Class started, and Claire found the page that she was supposed to be on. This wasn't one of her favorite classes, but she knew that she would have to spend more time on it just to get caught up.

The chapter they were on was about how the United States Constitution came into existence, and who our founding forefathers were. It was filled with dates and names of people who signed the document and how each of them became involved in its creation. Claire enjoyed the history part of political science, but she really didn't get into the whole dynamic of the branches of the government, and how each of them operated.

As class went by, Claire noticed a few times that Trevor glanced back towards her. It was one of those times that his eyes caught hers and locked for a second or two.

Great, Claire thought to herself. She thought that he was handsome, but still had reservations about even thinking about getting involved with him. She definitely wasn't looking for a boyfriend right now.

Class ended, and Claire remained in her chair, looking at her textbook for a few moments as the other students in the class made their way to the door.

Many of them had lunch after class, so they were excited to get out and head to the cafeteria. When the classroom was just about empty, Claire looked up in the direction of Trevor's seat and saw that it was empty. *Good,* she thought to herself, and then stood up and collected her things from the desk. As she left the classroom and entered the hall, she almost ran into a boy who was standing just outside the door.

"Oh, sorry," Claire began, as she looked up. Their eyes met, and she saw that it was Trevor.

Trevor had been leaning up against the wall of the hallway, obviously waiting for her.

"About time you came out," Trevor said to her with a grin.

Claire sighed, and her eyes blinked a couple of times, "What are you doing, Trevor?" Claire asked, with polite uncertainty.

Innocently putting his hands up, Trevor replied, "What? Can't I show the new girl to the cafeteria?"

Claire started to walk down the hallway, and Trevor paced himself right next to her on the left.

"Look, Claire," Trevor said, as he continued to match strides with her. "I am just trying to get to know you—that's all. I know that you are new to the school, and I would like to be your friend." Trevor's words were so convincing that Claire was beginning to believe it.

"Ok, then," Claire answered Trevor with a smirk. "You can show me to the cafeteria, but I am going to have lunch with Rose and Shelly." Claire was trying to get the upper hand and dictate how things were going to go down.

"No problem," Trevor replied smoothly. "I am going to eat with my teammates anyways, but until we get there, I am all yours."

Claire had to smile at that. This kid was certainly a charmer. Maybe it wouldn't be so bad to be friends with the popular kid for once. "Ok, Mr. Basketball Player. Tell me about yourself."

Trevor gave Claire a brief synopsis of his life of popularity at this high school. It wasn't too boastful, just informational really. Things like how he had played sports all his life, and was undoubtedly going to get a scholarship from a well-known college to play ball.

Knowing that the lunchroom was coming up quickly, Trevor asked Claire, "Tell me something about yourself besides the fact that you are from Seattle." He had overheard that fact during her first hour introduction.

Claire had to think about it for a second because she didn't want to get into any depressing detail about her life up to this point. As the lunchroom doors approached, she answered, "I like to read books and I am staying with a freshman named Blake Turner and her mom, April."

Trevor stopped a couple of steps from the lunchroom door, and turned to face Claire. "So, I know that you are from Seattle, you like books, and you are staying with a family that goes to school here. I think that we know quite a bit about each other in just a short amount of time. Don't you think?"

"I guess so," Claire said, as she stared into his eyes trying to get a handle on him.

"Claire!" Shelly and Rose declared, as they waved her over to their table.

"Time's up," Claire playfully said, as she waved bye to Trevor and walked towards her two new girlfriends.

As she walked away, Trevor called out with a smile, "I'll see you later, friend," and for a few moments, kept his gaze on Claire.

* *

"SO, HOW WAS YOUR FIRST DAY AT SCHOOL?" APRIL ASKED Claire with sincere interest.

Claire and Blake had just entered the apartment, and they were talking about their day to each other.

"It was actually pretty good," Claire answered with a smile. She told April about how she loved her English literature class, and how she met two nice girls who would probably turn out to be her good friends.

"Oh, honey, I am so glad that you had a good day." April was happy that Claire had had a good day, because it sometimes could go the other way when it came to new kids starting in the middle of the year.

"My day was amazing," Blake said to her mom, answering the question that had not been asked.

"How was your day?" April asked daughter, a little sarcasm dripping off each word.

The corners of Blake's mouth went up into an exaggerated smile, and she replied again, "My day was amazing."

"It's awesome that you had an amazing day," April said, with the same exaggerated smile.

Blake decided to quit this friendly banter with her mom before it continued through the night.

"Oh, yeah, and mom. Guess who wants to be friends with our Claire?" Blake spoke up while she and Claire settled on the stools of the kitchen island.

"Who?" April asked, with a hint of curiosity.

Claire started to say something to interrupt Blake, but Blake cut in, and said, "The most popular boy in the entire eleventh grade class. Trevor Thomas, the captain of the basketball team. That's who!"

"Really?" April asked, with a hit of surprise mixed with pride.

Claire gave Blake a look as if to say, 'thanks for that,' and then sighed, as she answered April, "Yes, but I think that he just wants to get to know the new girl, because I am a novelty right now."

Blake put her elbows on the counter and ran her hands through her hair to readjust the plastic headband that she was wearing. "That's not how I heard it, Claire Bear," Blake said to her. "There were some girls talking by my locker, and they said that one of their friends saw him constantly staring at you in political science class."

"No, he wasn't constantly staring at me, he only glanced at me a couple of times because, like I just said, I am the new girl, and he is fascinated with the new toy in the toy box. That's all."

But as she explained it to Blake, Claire wondered if there had been more times when he had turned back to look at her, and she hadn't noticed. She quickly banished that thought because she didn't want to believe that they were more than just innocent glances.

"Think what you want, but I think that he is smitten," Blake told her.

April listened to the girls banter back and forth for a few moments, and she interjected, "Listen Claire, you are a bright and beautiful young lady, and it shouldn't be a surprise that someone like this Trevor would want to get to know you."

Claire snorted, and then let April in on a little secret as she put it. "I've been to several schools over the past few years, and you know what is a constant in all of them? Jocks. And you know what is a constant among all jocks? They only care about themselves."

Disagreeing with Claire's assessment, April tried to reassure her that this wasn't always the case. "I don't think this is always true. I have had jock friends in high school, and most of them seemed like good guys."

Claire merely shook her head and used her right hand to pull a strand of blond hair that had just fallen in front of her eyes, and tucked it in behind her right ear. "Believe what you want, April, but I've seen it several times, and I am just going to proceed with extreme caution."

"Ok, ok, but don't allow yourself to miss out on happiness just because of past events. That's all I'm saying," said April, politely counseling Claire.

Claire knew that April wanted her to experience all the good things that high school had to offer, and that she just wanted her to get to know new people and have a good time. "I will, April. I promise."

April was happy with the promise, and the three of them sat by the kitchen contemplating what to make for dinner. They looked up a couple of ideas from one of April's cookbooks, and finally decided on Chicken Parmesan. Blake took the lead and with Claire's help, whipped up everything that they needed and then placed the casserole dish in the oven.

While Claire and Blake cleaned the counter, April asked, "Do you guys have any homework?"

"Of course, I have homework in just about every class, except for English Lit," Claire said, with just a hint of agitation.

Blake, equally agitated, spoke up, "Yes, I always have homework, but it is only in math and history."

"Why don't you start your homework and I'll set the timer for dinner and call you when it's ready. How does that sound?" April asked.

"You got it mom," Blake replied, as she gathered her bag and then grabbed a bottle of water from the fridge.

"Sounds like a plan to me," Claire agreed.

The girls headed to their respective rooms, and April decided to go to her office to send out a few emails before dinner. Before she knew it, the timer was going off alerting her to the fact that dinner was ready.

"Come on, girls," April yelled, "dinner is ready."

Blake and Claire came out of their rooms and headed for the kitchen. Just as Claire entered the kitchen, she received a text. Claire grinned after reading it and said, "It's from your parents, April. They want to know how my first day of school was." Claire loved the fact that April's parents cared so much about her. She wasn't used to adults caring about how her day was or how she was doing in school.

"Tell them that I say 'hi,'" Blake said.

"I sure will," Claire said, and then pretending to read out the text she typed, she said aloud, "Blake asked me to say that she doesn't deserve grandparents as nice as you guys, and that Claire is awesome."

Blake turned sharply to see if Claire was really sending that, and on seeing Claire smirking, she said, "Very funny." She then took out her own phone and began typing. After a several seconds she stopped and put her phone back in her pocket. A few moments later, Claire's text tone went off, and she looked at the message. It was from Blake and it read, "Blake rules and Claire drools. Lol." Claire rolled her eyes, and said, "You drool."

Blake, now satisfied with her retort, focused her attention on dinner. April took out the oven mitts from the drawer, and pulled out the Chicken Parmesan and placed it on hot pads that she had taken out when the timer went off.

"This looks great," said April, as she gazed at the contents of the dish before her.

"I know, right?" Claire said a little boastful. She was proud of herself and Blake for being able to prepare dinner. Claire had never had the opportunity to learn how to cook elaborate dinners, and she was really starting to enjoy it. She and Blake had made breakfast for Crystal the other day, and that had turned out great, and now this Chicken Parmesan was about to be another success.

Claire helped April set the table, and Blake went to the fridge to get drinks for everyone.

Once they were seated and began eating, April's phone buzzed. "Hello Gina," April said, answering the phone.

"Hi, April, sorry to bother you at home, but I just wanted to tell you the good news," Gina said, with excitement spilling out of every word she uttered.

"What is it?" April asked anxiously.

"Are you sitting down?" Gina asked.

"As a matter of fact, we just sat down for dinner," April confessed.

"Oh, sorry. I'll be quick. Does the name Monica Towers mean anything to you?" Gina asked, already knowing that April was completely aware of who she was.

"Yes?" April replied. Monica Towers was a famous romance novelist, who created a series of novels, *Legal Trouble*, about an intense romance between two divorce lawyers, Jane Jersey and Jason Gibbs, who became lovers while they were opposing counsel. Monica's books sold over a million copies each, and were highly anticipated with each release. There were five books in the series, and it was rumored that she was going to start the sixth book in the spring.

"Well, she just switched from Lenox Publishing to Pricilla Publishing effective tomorrow," Gina said, like a little kid who didn't get caught swiping her mama's cookies from the cookie jar.

"Holly shit!" April exclaimed. "Are you for real?"

"Not only is it for real," Gina elaborated, "but she specifically asked for you to be her editor."

"Holly shit!" April exclaimed again. "Why me?" April seriously wanted to know. Almost immediately, she asked, "Why is she leaving Lenox?"

Now by this point, both Blake and Claire were listening intently to what was going on, looking at April with eager anticipation.

Gina's voice changed to a more sober tone as she replied, "That's the sad part." Gina explained, "Monica called me directly just an hour ago and told me that she had caught her editor and her husband having an affair. She apparently walked in on them having sex in Monica's bedroom. According to Monica, the affair had been going on since the release of her second book."

"That's horrible," April said. She couldn't imagine her husband Nick cheating on her when he was alive. Her heart went out to Monica and for what she must be going through right now.

"But why me?" April asked again.

Gina cleared her throat, and replied, "She told me that she had contacted some of your authors and asked them what kind of editor you were. All of them gave you rave reviews. The consensus was that you cared for them on a level that most editors didn't. You got to know them, and showed compassion for what they were feeling. You could bring out the best in them without being overbearing.

"Wow," April was astonished. She felt humbled by the way her authors had described her.

"Damn right, wow," Gina said. "You are going to be Monica Tower's new editor."

Gina urged April to celebrate tonight. She informed her that she would set up an appointment for April and Monica, so the duo could meet and go over the next step to be taken.

When the call ended, April let out an excited gasp. "Guys, I am going to be editor to Monica Towers!"

"Oh my God, that is so awesome!" Claire said right away, knowing immediately who Monica Towers was.

Blake did not really know who she was, but knew that she must be someone famous.

"Coolness," Blake said, truly excited for her mom.

April's face was flushed from the excitement of it all.

"Isn't Monica going to be working on her next book soon?" Claire asked, as she knew about the series.

"Yes, and I am the one who is going to be editing it," April said with pride.

"I am really happy for you, April." Claire said with a smile, as she used her fork to stab a piece of chicken and put it on her plate.

After dinner, Blake and Claire went up to Blake's room to finish their homework together. April surmised that once they were done, they would play video games together for a little while. April decided to pour herself a glass of wine and settle in her office for a little while. She decided to call her mom and tell her about the opportunity to edit Monica Towers' book. Anne was thrilled for her daughter, and told her that she was, of course, proud of her. April's dad was working late, and her mom said that she would tell him when he got home.

While she was on the phone with her mom, April received a text from Wanda congratulating her. Wanda knew that this was a big deal, not only for April, but for the company as well. April texted Wanda and joked that she better get a good night's sleep tonight, because tomorrow was going to undoubtedly be a busy day for both of them. Wanda's replied that she would be up to the task no matter how many Zzzs she got tonight.

April decided to do some research on Monica Towers, so that she would have a better idea about the kind of writer Monica was. April pulled up the most recent interviews of Monica, where she was being questioned about the characters and what was next for her series. There was nothing to indicate that there was anything wrong with her marriage, however. In fact, she had mentioned several times that she and her husband were still madly in love, and she considered him her rock.

An hour went by before April even realized it, and she stood up from her desk and stretched her arms up in the air. She carried her empty glass to the kitchen, and then decided to go upstairs to check up on the girls. When she was about halfway up the stairs, she could hear them yelling and laughing at the game console.

"Hey, you two, what are you doing?" April asked, as she stepped into Blake's room.

"I'm kicking the snot out of Claire, that's what I'm doing," Blake giggled in response, referring to her character on the monitor.

Claire had somewhat of a defeated look on her face, and said, "Yeah, well, if little Miss Cheats-a-lot didn't cheat, the score would be in my favor." Almost to prove Claire's point, Blake did a maneuver that allowed her character to grab a hold of Claire's character, and hold him in a headlock and knee him in the head several times. No matter what Claire did, she could not break her character free until the entire move was completed.

"See? See, April. This is what I'm talking about," Claire whimpered with a grin. "It's like I can't move until I die." Claire released the controller, as if she was about to surrender. Then when her character didn't die but only had a few points of life left, she quickly picked the controller back up and resumed battling Blake.

"Did you get all your homework done?" April asked, as she sat on the edge of Blake's bed.

"Yes, we did," answered Claire honestly, twisting her controller as if she could physically move the character with her hands.

"Dammit!" Claire blurted out, when her character fell over and died.

"And that is how it's done," Blake said, schooling Claire after winning the match.

Claire set down the controller, feeling defeated, and faced April to ask her a question. "Have you ever met Monica Towers before?" Claire was happy that April had bagged the opportunity to work with Monica. Claire had not read any of the *Legal Trouble* books yet, but she knew that they were popular and already made a mental note to start reading them when she was finished with the *Maid of Honor* series.

"No, I haven't," April answered honestly, "I'm a little nervous actually. She is a big-time author, and now I am getting to work with her at a time when her world just got flipped upside down with a scandal. I am just a little apprehensive."

Blake turned off the gaming console, and spoke up, "Mom, you are an awesome editor, and when Monica meets you, she will realize how great you really are."

"I totally agree," Claire joined in Blake's assessment. "I am really happy for you, and I know that you and Monica will work well together."

April put her hands on Claire and Blake's shoulders, and said, "Thank you, I appreciate this. I will try my best to help Monica with this book, and I am glad that I have your support."

April told the girls not to stay up too late, and she left Blake's room to go take a shower and get ready for bed. Claire remained with Blake in her room for another twenty minutes before she retired to her room to get herself ready for bed as well. Of course, she had every intention of reading a few more chapters of *Maid of Honor,* so that she could finish the series and start Monica Tower's books.

CHAPTER THIRTEEN

BLAKE AWOKE FROM A DEEP SLEEP, AND WAS AWARE THAT something was amiss. It was still dark in her room, so she knew that it must still be early in the morning. Blake lay on her back for several seconds trying to figure out why she had woken up so abruptly. She turned her head to the right to see the time on the clock which displayed 3:16 am. That's when she realized that she was covered in sweat. Her head was drenched, and it was almost like someone had snuck into her room and poured a container of water on her. Her chest was soaked, and the sheet of the bed was saturated.

"What the heck?" Blake said out loud, as she slowly removed the wet sheet that was covering her and pulled it off the bed. She got up and went into her bathroom, and turned on the light. Sure enough, she looked as though water had been poured on her head and the top half of her body.

Blake grabbed a towel and began to dry off. Turned from the bathroom, she looked down at her bed and noticed a wet stain on the bed where she had been lying. Surprised by how much water had soaked into the bed, she began using the towel to start wiping the mattress. After a couple of swipes back and forth, in an attempt to dry as much of the bedsheet as possible, Blake noticed that she didn't feel sick. She actually felt fine except for being completely covered in her own sweat.

At first, Blake didn't want to tell her mom about it because it was early in the morning, and she felt fine. But, if her mother found out when she woke up, and discovered that Blake hadn't come to her in the night, she would probably be upset with her. Blake quietly opened her bedroom door and walked over to her mother's room. The door was open about half-way, and she slipped through without touching the door at all. Blake softly put her hand on her mom's shoulder and whispered, "Mom. It's me, Blake."

April awoke instantly and blinked her eyes as they focused on her daughter. "Blake, darling. What is it?" April asked, realizing that it was still too early to be up.

"Sorry mom, I didn't want to wake you," Blake began. "But I just thought that you should know that I just woke up to a big puddle of sweat all over my head and on my bed."

April propped herself up and turned on the lamp on the nightstand next to her bed. She looked up at Blake, and noticed that her hair was disheveled and damp.

"Are you ok?" April asked, wondering if she felt sick.

"I feel fine, except for that I was soaked in sweat, and my pillow and bed are drenched," Blake explained as she used the towel to further dry her hair.

April got out of bed and put her hand up to Blake's forehead to see if she had a fever. She only felt slightly warm, but it could have been from Blake wiping it off with the towel. "I don't think that you have a fever, but I will use the thermometer to double check just to make sure. The two of them went into the bathroom in the hallway that was closest to Claire's room because that is where she had last put the thermometer away. April removed it from the medicine cabinet and told Blake to hold it in her mouth until it beeped. After several seconds, the thermometer beeped, and Blake removed it from her mouth. April took it from her to read the display herself: 98.9.

"Well, your temp is up only slightly but it's nothing that should be cause for alarm. I am going to give you some Motrin, just in case though. I don't want it to spike up," April said, taking out the Motrin bottle from the medicine cabinet and giving Blake two tablets. Blake grabbed a Dixie cup from the ceramic cup holder in the corner of the sink and poured cold water into it. She downed the two tablets and then tossed the cup into the trash can.

April and Blake went into Blake's room, and Blake showed her the wet spot on the bed.

"Holy cow, Blake," April said, surprised by the amount of dampness on the sheet. "That is really soaked. Are you sure you are feeling ok?"

"Yeah, I am. I'm just tired, but that is because I was awakened from a deep sleep. I mean, I don't feel like I have to throw up or anything, and I don't feel like I have any cold symptoms," Blake replied, feeling a little bewildered. "I never had a night sweat like this before."

Thinking back to the chicken dinner that they had consumed, April wondered if it was food poisoning. "Do you think it was from the chicken?" April asked, as if Blake might have an idea about what it was.

"I don't think so, but I'm not sure. I don't feel nauseous so that is why I don't think that is it," Blake answered to the best of her ability.

Claire's bedroom door opened as Claire walked out and stepped into Blake's room. "What's going on?" Claire asked, a little worried. "Is everything ok?"

April looked over at Claire, and replied, "It's Blake, she woke up soaking wet, covered in sweat."

Claire's eyes moved from April to Blake, and she now noticed the dampness of Blake's hair and nightgown. "Are you ok?" Claire asked Blake, realizing that she could be potentially sick.

"Yeah, I'm fine. I was just covered in sweat, as if someone poured a bucket on me," Blake then pointed at her bed, and showed Claire the soaked spot on the bedsheet.

"Wow, that is really wet," agreed Claire. "Want to sleep in my bed tonight, and we will clean that up in the morning when we get up before school?" Claire asked Blake.

"Sure, that would be great, I really don't feel like making the whole bed right now anyways, and it has to dry up before we put a new sheet on," Blake said, thankfully.

Blake opened the third drawer in her dresser, and took out a dry night-gown and told Claire that she would be right in after she changed. Claire went into her room to wait for Blake while April took off the sheets to uncover the wet spot, so it could dry. April would show the girls in the morning how to take care of the spot with fabric cleaner if the mattress was stained.

Before Blake left her room for Claire's, April felt her forehead one more time, and then kissed her on the forehead. "Good night, honey. If you get sick or feel worse, wake me up immediately."

Looking at her mom through tired eyes, Blake said, "I will mom. Good night," and then let out a small yawn.

"Good night, Claire," April called out to Claire in the hallway.

"Good night, April," Claire responded, peeking through the open bed-room door.

The girls settled in Claire's room and April went back to bed. She wondered what had happened to Blake, and worried about what the morning might bring. It took her about half an hour to finally fall asleep again.

* *

CLAIRE'S PHONE ALARM WENT OFF AT 6:00 A.M., AND SHE reached out to grab the phone on the nightstand to turn it off. Blake was lying next to her, and was starting to make moaning sounds. Claire turned to face her to see if she was wet from sweat. Fortunately, she was completely dry.

"Good morning," Claire said to Blake, as they were face to face on the bed. Blake's eyes opened and smiled at how close Claire's face was to hers.

"Good morning to you, Claire Bear," Blake replied. "What time is it?"

"It's time to get up and start our day—that's what time it is," Claire answered with a grin.

"Thank you, Mrs. Obvious," Blake retorted.

"It's 6:00 a.m.," Claire said. "By the way, how are you feeling? You didn't sweat again last night," she added, pulling the covers off herself.

Taking a few seconds to perform a mental analysis of her body, Blake yawned and answered, "I feel fine. I don't feel sick or anything. I am just a little tired, but that is probably from waking up in a puddle of sweat."

"Good morning, girls," April called out, as she knocked on Claire's door. "How are you feeling, Blake?"

"Good, mom," Blake said, as she got out of bed. "I was just saying to Claire that I feel fine. I didn't sweat again last night."

"That's good, honey," April said, as she lifted up her hand that was holding the thermometer, and motioned for Blake to open. "I just want to check your temperature this morning to make sure that you don't have a fever."

Sighing, Blake stepped closer to her mom and took the thermometer from her and placed it in her mouth. After a few seconds, she pulled it out and read it herself, but showed her mom anyways. "98.8."

"That's good," April replied, relieved. "That was the weirdest thing with you sweating last night."

"I know, right?" Blake said matter-of-factly.

"Let's check out your bed, Blake, and then you guys can get ready for school," April said, as she turned to exit Claire's room.

They went into Blake's room, and April had the girls help her strip the entire bed, sprayed a fabric cleaner on it and then left it to dry off during the day.

"Blake, why don't you jump in the shower while Claire and I make breakfast and get things ready to go?" April suggested.

Running her hands through her sweat-dried hair, Blake nodded her head in agreement, and went into her bathroom. April and Claire both hurried up and got dressed, and then went downstairs to get breakfast ready.

Claire made it down first, so she was cracking the eggs into a bowl when April walked into the kitchen.

"You don't mind scrambled eggs, do you?" Claire asked, almost as if she thought she could put the yolks back into the eggshells if April didn't want them.

"Sure, that sounds good," April, answered. "I'll get out the bread for toast."

The two of them had breakfast ready and on the plate waiting for Blake when she finished showering and came downstairs. Walking into the kitchen, Blake took a whiff, and said, "That smells good, you guys."

April gave Blake a once-over to see if she still looked ok, and she did. "Claire made most of it," April informed Blake.

"Looks yummy, Claire," Blake said truthfully.

"Thanks, Blake. I think that I am getting the hang of this cooking thing," Claire said, enthusiastically.

Claire and Blake finished their breakfasts, and quickly cleaned up their plates and loaded them into the dishwasher. April finished what was left of her coffee, and placed the mug in the dishwasher.

"Hey, I just want to let you know that I may be a little late tonight because I am not sure how this whole Monica Towers thing is going to go today," April informed the two girls. "Make sure you guys text me when you get home from school today," she added, as if she had to state what had been carved in stone in Blake's mind for years.

"Always do," Blake and Claire replied simultaneously. Blake grinned at Claire—she was fitting right into the Turner household.

Blake held up a fist, and Claire immediately tapped it with her own fist and made the hand explosion sign.

April let out a little snort, and said, "Fine. But you two won't be so cocky if I have to call you when I don't get a text. You know how I worry."

"Won't ever happen now that I've got backup," Blake insisted, as she gestured towards Claire.

"Ok, you two, you better get going to school," April said as she grabbed her purse to make sure that she had everything that she needed before she headed out to the office.

"Bye, mom," Blake blurted out as she headed towards the elevator.

"Bye, April," Claire called out. "Good luck at work today."

"Bye, you two, I'll see you tonight." April said, waving as the girls entered the elevator.

April decided to take a look at her desk in the library to make sure that she hadn't forgotten anything. She replied to a text that Wanda had just sent her, replied to an email from an author that she hadn't heard from in a few weeks. April then left the apartment and headed to her office.

As she walked on the sidewalk that led to her office, April realized that she was walking with more of a skip in her step. She was very excited to be Monica's editor, but was surprisingly calm despite the potential pressure that it would undoubtedly generate. It was almost the first of December, and the weather was trying its best to let April know that. Even though it was partly sunny out, the twenty-mile-an-hour wind made the thirty-four-degree temperature feel much colder than what it was.

By the time April made it to her building, her cheeks were rosy red, and her hands were quite cold. April rubbed her hands together in the elevator on the way to Pricilla Publishing. As soon as she stepped out of the elevator, Wanda gleamed at her and with a big smile, and said, "Hi boss. Congrats on the Monica thing. You totally deserve it!" You could tell that Wanda was genuinely happy for April.

"Thanks Wanda, it's definitely going to be exciting around here for a while," April replied candidly.

"You got that right," Wanda agreed, as she touched a button that connected her with a line that was calling into the switchboard.

"Hello, Priscilla Publishing. How may I help you?" Wanda spoke into her mic.

April motioned with her hand that she was going to be in her office and began walking in that direction.

She was just about to turn the handle of her office door when Gina yelled out, "Hey, how's everything going with my favorite editor?" She said it jokingly, but it was mostly the truth.

"I'm good. Ready to get started with Monica Towers," April admitted with a grin.

"Good," Gina said. "This is going to be one of the best deals to come to Priscilla Publishing in a long time."

"No pressure or anything," Gina said. But they both knew that April would do her best, and it was going to turn out very well.

April entered her office and immediately went to work. She was working on a couple of other manuscripts and was gearing up for the meeting with Monica at the end of the week. Before she realized, it was lunchtime, and Wanda interrupted to ask if she wanted her to get her something.

"Yes, please. What are you going to get?" April asked, not really knowing what she wanted.

"I was thinking about getting a sub from that place next door," Wanda replied. April thought about that for a few moments, and then wrinkled her nose at the idea. "Can you grab me a grilled chicken salad from Papa's?" Papa's was a restaurant on the bottom floor of the same building as Priscilla Publishing. They mainly made burgers and pizzas, but they did do a great grilled chicken salad.

Wanda nodded and took out her phone from her pocket so that she could place April's order.

As Wanda closed the door of April's office, April's cell phone rang, and it was Crystal.

"Hi, Crystal. How's it going?" April hadn't spoken to Crystal since Monday, but she had thought about calling her at some point today.

"Good. Busy. You know me. Investigating local drug rings, solving murders, dealing with stolen puppies..." Crystal said jokingly, but it wasn't too far from the truth. "How is everyone doing?" She had been working a case and it had kind of consumed her over the last couple of days, so she wanted to touch base to see how Blake and Claire were doing.

"Everyone is doing great," April said, thinking about Claire's first day of school and how well it seemed to have gone, "Claire's first day went very well, and I think that she made some friends too, by the looks of it. There is even a jock who apparently showed some interest in her, but she says she wants to keep her distance," April revealed, and Crystal could already hear motherly affection spilling out of April's words.

"That's good, April, I am glad that she is fitting it," Crystal said. She truly believed that Claire had an excellent chance of succeeding in life if she stayed with the Turners. Crystal was at her desk at the station, and was working on her computer. "Just between you and me, I have been doing some digging into Roger Bower—Claire's previous foster dad." April could hear Crystal typing on the computer as she spoke.

"Oh yeah?" April asked, sounding a little surprised.

"Of course," Crystal said, lowering her voice. "You didn't think that I would just drop the whole attempted rape thing, did you?" April could tell by the sound of Crystal's voice that she truly believed Claire's version of what had happened those many months ago.

"I guess that I didn't think that you could because you work in Chicago," April said thoughtfully.

"I am in contact with the Seattle Police Department, and they are going to open an investigation into Roger Bower," Crystal revealed. April was glad to hear this because ever since Claire had confided in her about the attempted rape, April couldn't get the sick feeling out of her mind—she was shocked that Roger would try to harm Claire, and wondered what might have happened if she hadn't managed to flee his grasp. Claire could have been raped, or he could have even killed her! April shook her head, as she tried to get that thought out of her head.

"They are going to perform surveillance on Roger starting tomorrow," Crystal said, with a hint of excitement. "Can't wait to see what this asshole does," she added, coolly.

April had to agree with her friend. It would be nice to see justice served in this situation.

"Please keep me posted," April requested.

"You know I will," Crystal said candidly. "By the way, how is Blake doing?" Crystal asked, changing the subject from Claire to Blake.

"Actually," April began, "She is fine, but she woke up around 3:00 a.m. today, soaking wet with sweat. When she got up to go to school, she was fine."

"What do you think it was?" Crystal asked.

Sighing, April didn't have an answer, "I don't know. She didn't have a temperature this morning and she was feeling fine. Maybe it was from the chicken that we had for dinner last night."

"Well, I hope that she isn't coming down with the flu or anything," Crystal hoped. "I hear that there is a bug or something going around. You don't think that she got it from Claire, do you?"

April thought about it for a second, and then said, "I don't think so. She would have shown symptoms days before this." But April couldn't help but wonder if it was the beginning of the flu.

"It is around her lunchtime, so I am going to text her to see how she is feeling," April said to Crystal, as she put her phone on speaker so that she could text Blake.

I think that she is alright, but I just worry about her sometimes. You know how I get."

"Yes, I do," Crystal agreed, "but I'm fine with how you are because you are a great mom and Blake is an awesome kid."

"Thanks, Crystal. I really appreciate that," April said, with a hint of bashfulness.

"It's all true, my friend," Crystal replied.

They talked for a few more minutes, and April got the text reply from Blake. It simply said, 'I'm good' with a thumbs-up emoji. April let out a small breath that indicated that she was relieved. "I just got the text from Blake saying that she is fine," April told Crystal.

April could almost hear Crystal's relief through the phone speaker as she said, "Good, it's probably nothing and she will be ok."

"I hope so," April said, apprehensively.

Crystal and April ended their conversation with the possibility that Crystal might drop by the apartment tomorrow night to see Blake and Claire.

April set her phone down and almost immediately it rang again. It was her mother this time.

"Hi, mom," April said. "How's it going?"

"Good honey, how's it going with you?" Anne asked her daughter.

"Good mom, just extremely busy today but good," April answered by putting her phone on the speaker so that she could type an email while she was talking with her mom.

"I just wanted to ask you if you and the girls want to come over and spend the day with us this Saturday," Anne was excited to see her daughter as well as Blake and Claire.

Pausing to think about whether she had any prior engagement, April said, "Sure, I don't think that we are doing anything this weekend. Let's make it a date."

"Great, we can take the girls shopping downtown and have lunch at our favorite café. I was thinking about making the meatloaf recipe that you like so much for dinner. We can have mashed potatoes with it and then some steamed vegetables. How does that sound?" Anne asked cheerfully.

"Sounds great, mom. I'm sure that Blake and Claire will be excited to see you," April said, knowing that the girls would love to see her parents again.

"Perfect. I'll let your dad know so that he doesn't make any other plans. Can't wait to see you," Anne said sincerely. "I'll have your father send Derek to pick you guys up around 10:00 am. Is that good?"

"Sounds great to me," April said, making a mental note of the time.

April was excited to go to her parents' house. It was a big house with a huge yard. April liked going back to the house where she grew up. Her parents had kept her bedroom exactly the way she left it when she went off to college. There were still some of her high school books on the shelves throughout her room. Even back then, she loved reading.

There was a small knock on the doorframe, and Wanda came in with April's salad. "Here you go boss," Wanda said, handing April a round container and a large beverage.

"Thanks, Wanda. I really appreciate it," April said gratefully, as she opened the salad and the ranch container to pour it on her salad.

"No problem, April. It's what I do," Wanda said. As she started to leave the office, April asked, "Why don't you eat lunch in here with me?"

Smiling, Wanda turned back towards April, and sat at her desk in a chair that was facing her. "Sure, don't mind if I do."

The two of them talked and ate for the next twenty minutes or so, until April got a text from Gina, who she wanted to see April in her office as soon as she was available. April texted back saying she would be 'right there' and took the last bite of her salad and then threw the container in the trash.

"Duty calls," April said to Wanda, as she stood up to leave.

Wanda got up and walked out with April but took her remaining lunch back to her desk with her.

April knocked on Gina's door and slowly opened it. "You wanted to see me?"

"Yes, come in," Gina waved her in, and April sat down on the closest chair.

"I set up your meeting with Monica Towers for this Friday," Gina began. "She is excited to meet you, and is eager to get back to work."

"Ok, that's good. That will give me an extra day to prepare and check out more of her books," April said, thoughtfully. "What time did you set it up for?"

"She wanted to meet at 9:00 a.m. so the two of you could spend the day getting to know each other, and see what your thoughts were about the outline of her new novel," Gina replied.

"Sounds like a plan to me," April said, as the reality of working with Monica set in.

"Good. Between you and me, I think that she is looking for a company that is going to be there for her and won't let her down. Remember, it wasn't only her husband, but her trusted editor that screwed her over—so it was a double blow for her."

"Don't worry, I'll take care of her," April told Gina, and she knew she would. April was a very compassionate woman who cared about everyone, so she would be the best choice to help Monica with the transition.

April left Gina's office and headed towards hers. She still had a lot of work to do but as she strolled into her office, the reflection of her face on the glass door revealed a smile that would not be easy to get rid of.

* *

CLAIRE, SHELLY, AND ROSE SAT AT THEIR DESK IN BIOLOGY class before the first bell rang, talking about a variety of things. Since they had just met yesterday, Shelly and Rose were eager to get to know Claire, and they were like three peas in a pod. By the end of Claire's first day, it was obvious that the three of them would be good friends. Because Claire had been through several different foster homes, making friends at school was difficult for her. The few friends that she did make were nothing like Shelly and Rose.

Rose was joking about something on YouTube, making Claire and Shelly giggle. At that point, Brie strolled in and glanced in the direction of Trevor's chair before taking her own seat. Her other tablemates were giggling and smiling as she took out her biology book. Brie looked at the group and for an instant almost felt like she was the new girl.

"What's so funny?" Brie asked, almost as if they were laughing about something that concerned her.

Rose told her that it was about a YouTube video, and how funny it was. Brie seemed to show interest, but not too much. Shelly made a comment about it and then Claire added a few words. By the look on Brie's face and her body language, she really didn't care about Claire's commentary.

The bell was just about to ring when Trevor and Jordan slipped in through the door. Trevor was leading, and on their way past Claire's table, he whispered, "What up, new girl?"

The look on Brie's face went from indifference to disdain.

Before Claire could respond to Trevor, Rose grinned and spoke up in a sarcastic tone, "Nothing, honey, what's up with you?"

Trevor grinned at Rose, made eye contact with Claire, and gave her a nod, and said, "Hey."

Claire didn't want to be rude, so she grinned at him, and replied, "Hey."

Knowing that Claire was toying with him, he began to whistle as he headed to his seat. Claire was intensely aware of the tension that was coming from the seat next to her, but before Claire could say anything to Brie, Shelly asked Brie a question about last night's biology homework. It was at that point that Mrs. Clemens started class.

During the entire hour, Brie kept glancing over towards Trevor with a look of bitterness. Conversely, she would hardly look at Claire at all. Thank God for Rose and Shelly sitting at her table because it might have been far worse if she didn't have friends like those two.

When the bell rang, Brie quickly collected her stuff and headed out the door. As for Claire, Shelly, and Rose, they talked for a few more moments and then as a group headed out the door. Claire had only taken about three steps into the hallway when she felt the presence of someone directly behind her.

"So, Claire, my friend. How are you doing today?" Trevor's voice rang softly in her ear, as she spun around to see who it was.

"Hey," Claire said, repeating her greeting from an hour before.

"Hey," Trevor imitated her back.

"So, again I ask, how are you?" Trevor asked with a little more commitment.

Giving in, Claire sighed, and said, "Good, how are you?"

"Me?" Trevor said pointing at himself. "I'm good, just walking and talking with my new friend." Trevor was certainly turning on the charm.

Claire turned around to make a comment to Shelly and Rose, when she noticed them splitting and leaving her alone with Trevor. Claire's first thought was how she was going to repay them for leaving her alone with him. She had told them that she wasn't interested in Trevor, but they were excited for the potential of what could be between the two of them.

Before Claire could object to anything that Trevor was about to say, his eyes turned a little serious, and he said, "Listen, I just want you to know that I only want to get to know you, and that I am a nice guy."

Claire's inner voice was screaming at her to walk away, but the sixteen-year-old girl who had the captain of the basketball team courting her made her stay. "Here's the thing, Trevor. I don't want any trouble or drama by being your friend. Do you understand? I've been through a lot, and that last thing I need is trouble." She didn't go into details about her past, but she could tell that Trevor seemed genuine. She finished her question with another question for him. "Are you trouble?"

Trevor put his right hand on his chin as if pondering whether he was troubled. "Well, friend, I can tell you for sure that I don't believe that I am, but, you need to get to know me so that you can find out for sure."

Smooth, real smooth, Claire thought to herself. "Ok, here's what I think that we should do." Claire could see Trevor's eyes light up but didn't say anything until Claire was finished. "Let's take it slow, and we can begin to build our friendship over the next few weeks. Does that sound good to you?"

Taking what he could get, Trevor nodded and replied, "You drive a hard bargain, but I accept your terms." Trevor held out his hand for a handshake as if they were agreeing to a verbal contract.

Claire hesitated for a moment, and then brought her hand up to shake his. "Deal," Claire declared.

"Now, let me walk you to class so that you aren't late."

"Ok," Claire grinned, and the two of them headed towards English Lit.

When they got there, Trevor looked her in the eyes, and said, "See you in Political Science," and he left her at the entrance of the classroom, but he waved to her before he turned the corner of the hallway.

Claire quickly waved back and then walked into class. This whole thing with Trevor was moving way too fast, and she knew what direction he wanted it to take. She just had this feeling that he wasn't going to take 'no' for an answer. Claire was firm on her resolve, but there was a feeling in the pit of her stomach that she had not felt before. Was it passion? She immediately disposed of the thought. She had never had a real boyfriend before, and she was in unfamiliar territory.

Class began, and Claire submerged herself in her book. She had read the chapters at home last night just so that she could familiarize herself with the specifics again. Mr. Reed had called on her several times during class, and Claire could tell how much he appreciated her for knowing the material.

When class ended, she headed to her locker to grab her political science book and ran into Blake on the way. "Hey Blake, how are you feeling?" Blake stopped at Claire's locker, and said, "Great, never better," Blake looked completely fine as if nothing had happened the night before. "Good, glad to hear it," Claire replied, "What class do you have now?"

"I have pre-algebra. What's next for you?" Blake asked, as she held up her math book.

"I have political science," Claire said.

Thinking about it for a second, Blake asked, "Is that the class with Trevor?"

A sheepish grin sprang onto Claire's face for an instant before she could take control of it, and answered, "It just so happens that it is."

"And how is Trevor today, Claire Bear?" Blake asked, in a devilish tone.

"Trevor is good, as far as I can tell," Claire said, trying not to show any emotions one way or another.

"Trevor is really good?" Blake prodded playfully. "Like, really, really good?"

Claire pushed Blake and said, "Quit it. You know how I feel about this."

"Yes, I know, just playing," Blake said, candidly. "I just want you to be happy and have fun."

Claire took out her political science book and turned to Blake. "I know you do. I am so happy to be here, and I am making friends. I just want to be careful when it comes to boys, that's all."

"I get it," Blake said. "Seriously, I do." Blake thought about what had happened with her Clair's foster parents and the incident with Roger. She instantly felt bad for being so pushy with Claire.

"Claire, I'm sorry. I don't want to push you," Blake said. Claire could sense a shift in her tone and put her right hand on Blake's cheek, winked, and said, "It's ok."

Blake winked back at her and then smiled as she said, "Ok then, I'll see you in an hour for lunch."

"You got it," replied Claire, as she closed her locker and headed for class.

* *

CLAIRE WALKED INTO THE LUNCHROOM WITH TREVOR and Jordan walking just behind her. Blake was sitting next to Emily, and they were talking about something that had happened in the class before lunch. They were friends, but there was a little rift still between them. It was going to take a little time to get back to where they were. Blake waved Claire over to the table. She sat across from them as Trevor followed her to the table and sat next to her.

Jordan continued to another table where a few of the basketball players were. Shelly came in next and sat on Clair's other side.

"Hi guys," Shelly said to the entire table. Looking at Claire, Shelly asked, "How goes the second day so far?"

"Really good, honestly," Claire replied, truthfully. "This school is amazing and most of the students here seem really nice." Shelly knew that she was specifically thinking about Brie, but didn't want to say it out loud with Trevor sitting next to her.

"So, Trevor," Shelly questioned. "How's basketball going?"

"You know how it is with the coach," Trevor said. "Train more, work more, score more." That pretty much summed up Trevor's relationship with high school sports.

Shelly wrinkled her nose at the harshness of the motto. "Sounds like a ton of fun."

"Fun?" Trevor asked sarcastically. "Sports are supposed to be fun?"

At that point, Rose came walking into the lunchroom, and sat next to Shelly, but when she slammed her body next to her, it caused somewhat of a domino effect, causing Shelly to slam into Claire, and Claire into Trevor.

"What's happening?" declared Rose, with a big smile. "I just got an 'A' on my history quiz, so I am happy with life right now."

Moving closer to Shelly and off Trevor's right side, Claire said to Rose, "Good job, that's cool."

"The best part is that I didn't even study. I kind of forgot about it," confessed Rose.

"Well, that's even better," admitted Shelly.

Trevor got up and went to get some food and asked Claire if she wanted anything while he was up there. She said that she would go up and get it, but Trevor said, "No worries, I got you this time."

Claire started to get up, but Trevor motioned her to stay put. He went towards the kitchen and disappeared in the group of students.

"Wow," Rose said to Claire, but for the benefit of the entire table. "What's up with that?"

Claire sighed. "He says he just wants to be friends, but I think he wants more." Claire nervously bit her lower lip as she said it out loud.

Rose and Shelly looked at each other with a devious smile.

Claire saw the look and bumped Shelly with her shoulder. "Seriously, you two. I just want to be friends. I am not looking for anything more."

"Ok, we get you," Rose said. "You can never have too many friends, right Shelly?"

"You are correct," Shelly agreed.

Blake received a text—it was April asking her how she was feeling. She decided to tell Claire so that she could change the subject, and direct it away from Trevor. "It's mom," Blake said to Claire. "She wants to know how I am feeling."

Claire loved the fact that April truly cared about her daughter. Claire knew that Blake viewed April as overbearing at times, but it was far better than the alternative.

Blake typed on her phone, and texted "I'm good" and a thumbs-up emoji. She set her phone down on the table and turned her attention to Emily. Claire could tell that Emily still had issues with her, but at least she wasn't as vocal about it.

Trevor returned with two trays of food, and handed one to Claire. "Here you go."

Claire took the tray, and said, "You didn't have to do that, but thank you."

Trevor smiled and said, "No worries." He remained standing and scanned the room until he found his teammates across the room. "Well, ladies," Trevor said. "It's time for me to hang with the boys," he said, giving Claire a long glance as he left.

Claire followed him with her eyes until he sat down next to Jordan. He started to turn his head, and Claire quickly looked away and focused her eyes on Blake.

"So, Blake," Claire said to get her mind off Trevor, "have you designed anything else lately with that app that you have on your iPad?"

Blake's eye's gleamed with excitement as she answered, "Now that you mention it, I have been working on a couple of dress designs." She pulled out her iPad and clicked on the app. A moment later, it sprang to life to reveal a black dress with lace and a bow. Claire took the iPad from Blake and looked at the design. "That's really cool."

Shelly really didn't know Blake, but Claire had told her a little about her when she told her that she was living with Blake and her mom. Looking at the iPad that Claire had in her hand, Shelly said, "Wow, Blake, that is really good."

"Thanks, it is something that I have been working on in my spare time," Blake said. She swiped the screen to the left, and another dress design came to life on the screen, but this time it was a green and navy plaid tennis skirt, matched with a black blouse with pearls. It was very similar to the dress that Claire had worn for Thanksgiving, but it had more of a party dress vibe to it.

"You designed this one too?" Rose asked, reacting to the professional looking design.

"Of course," Blake said, frankly. "I've done a ton of designs, but I think that I am really starting to develop a sense of fashion. When I first began, it was more about messing around with clothes, seeing what looks good, but now I am envisioning how they fit and look, and what items work with different designs. If that makes any sense?"

Claire could see that her two new friends were really impressed. "Keep up the good work," Shelly instructed Blake. "You definitely have fashion sense, unlike my friend here," Shelly said, looking at Rose.

"What?" Rose acted offended. "You don't like my sweatpants and sports bra looks on the weekends?"

"Um, no," giggled Shelly, trying to erase that visual from her mind's eye.

Blake put her iPad away and finished the rest of her lunch. Emily talked with her for a few more minutes and decided to leave the lunchroom. Lunchtime was almost up so the girls gathered up their trays and trash, and headed towards the exit.

"See you after school. I'll meet you by my locker," Blake told Claire. Her locker was the one closer to the exit.

"You got it," Claire told Blake, and all four of them went their separate ways.

* *

TREVOR AND JORDAN FINISHED LUNCH AND THEN WENT to the bathroom down the hall of the lunchroom. This was Trevor's second day on the steroids, and as far as he could tell, they hadn't started working yet. He had decided to take smaller doses throughout the day so that meant that he had to take a dose after lunch. Of course, he couldn't let anyone see him taking any kind of pills, so Jordan and he decided that he would take the afternoon dose immediately after eating lunch and before 4ᵗʰ period. Hiding in the stall, Trevor carefully pulled out the Ziploc bag from the secret pocket of his knapsack. Taking one of the capsules out, he pulled bottled water from his bag, and took a swig of it to wash the steroid down.

Jordan had stationed himself outside of the stall, just in case anyone walked in and tried to open the stall that Trevor was in. The stall door opened, and Trevor walked out. "All set," he said, and then the two of them abandoned the boys' room and headed for class.

* *

THE BELL RANG AT 2:25 P.M. INDICATING THAT SCHOOL WAS over for the day. Students began pouring out of the classrooms like ants running away from water. Some kids simply ran as fast as they could, as if they were sprinting towards a finish line. Others walked as if they didn't have a care in the world, and it didn't matter if they were first or last out of the building.

Brie stuffed all the books that she needed to take home with her that night in her cheerleading duffle bag and headed towards the gym. She had practice from 2:30 p.m. to 4:00 p.m. every day after school. On her way to the gym, she rounded the corner, and noticed that Claire was at a freshman locker with the girl named Blake. She and her mom were the ones who had taken in Claire. It seemed like every time that she looked at Claire, more and more animosity was building up in her. Deep down she knew that she and Trevor were done, but she couldn't shake the jealousy that was slowly consuming her.

Brie watched Claire and Blake exit the school, and she continued her trek to the gym. Walking into the locker room, she met up with a few of the other girls and changed into her cheerleading uniform.

On Mondays, Wednesdays, and Fridays, the freshmen cheerleading squad practiced in the same gym with them at the same time. One group took the near end, while the other group practiced on the far end. Since today was Wednesday, the freshmen took their places on the far end of the gym.

About forty-five minutes into practice, the two groups stopped for their ten-minute break. The girls just sort of scattered throughout the bleachers. Brie took out her water bottle from her bag, and took a seat next to a couple of the freshmen girls, just one row up from Stephanie and Lindsey who were juniors like her. They were talking about a class, and Brie heard them say 'Claire'.

Her interest in the conversation now peaked; Brie turned her attention to them. "So, what about Claire?" Brie asked, pretending to be sincere.

"Oh," Lindsey said, "I was just saying that Claire seems really smart. I have her in English Lit, and she knows a lot about books. She helped me with my homework today, and she didn't need to look in the book at all." Stephanie and Claire have only one class together, which was Algebra 1, and it was the last class of the day. Stephanie nodded her head in agreement. "I just had her in my last class and she seems really nice."

Brie, becoming more frustrated with Claire's popularity, asked, "What do you know about her? All I know is that she just transferred from Seattle."

Stephanie and Lindsey didn't have much more to add to that. "I think that she is staying with a freshman or something," Lindsey commented.

Brie tried to contain her jealousy, but said under her breath, "I don't know what the fuss is all about!" She was about to say something else when a voice to her right asked, "Are you talking about Claire Forrester?"

Turning towards the voice, Brie found that it was Emily, the freshman cheerleader. She could tell by the sound of Emily's voice that she was not a member of Claire's fan club.

"Actually, we are," Brie confessed. "Why do you ask?"

Emily moved a little closer to Brie, as if she was going to confess a sin. "My best friend is Blake Turner, and it is her and her mom that took Claire in." Brie looked at Emily as if to say, 'go on' and then Emily continued, "I don't understand why they did it. Ever since she came into their lives, Blake has focused mainly on her." Brie could hear the frustration in Emily's voice, and she wanted to know more.

"Why did they want a foster kid from Seattle?" Brie asked, not fully understanding.

Emily grimaced as she spoke the next words. "They found her on the streets of Chicago. Literally."

"What do you mean?" Brie questioned, a little confused.

"Claire was a homeless girl living on the streets of downtown, here in Chicago. She had been homeless for like four months or something." Emily was speaking to Brie like she was spilling some big secret. "Blake's mom walked up to her and basically took her home. Kind of like a stray dog."

Brie couldn't contain her surprise. "Holy shit! Are you serious?"

"Yes, totally. Blake came over the night after they brought her home and told me about it. At first, it was supposed to be just for one night, but apparently, she got the flu and was really sick, and ended up staying there for the entire week," Emily said, pausing to collect her thoughts. "Then she stayed for Thanksgiving, and they took her shopping all day on Black Friday. The next thing I know, Blake and her mom are now her foster parents. It happened very fast, and it was kind of weird. Blake and I got into it when I questioned her about it, and now our friendship is in the gray zone." Emily's voice cracked with emotion, and Brie realized how hard it was for her to experience this.

"I can't believe it," Brie exclaimed. "Claire is a homeless girl." This was information that Brie would have never guessed about Claire.

"Wait a minute," Brie said to Emily, "I thought that she transferred from Seattle? Is that a lie?"

Emily had pulled out bottled water and was taking a sip from it. "That's the kicker too," Emily replied, wiping the excess water from her lips. "She is from there, but she ran away from her foster family four months ago."

Brie's eyes widened even more. "Wait, so you mean to tell me that not only is Claire homeless, but she is a runaway too?" This was almost too much for Brie to handle. This trove of information had just made her day. Hell, it even made her week. The jealousy that she felt for Claire evaporated almost immediately because she knew that Trevor wouldn't want anything to do with a homeless street girl.

"Emily. Thanks for the information. It just made my day," Brie gleamed cheerfully.

Seeing how excited Brie was about the news, she became a little apprehensive, and lowering her voice, she said, "Please don't tell anyone that I told you. I don't want Blake to find out that I said anything. I don't really like Claire, but I want my relationship with Blake where it was earlier."

"Don't worry, I won't tell anyone," Brie lied. "It will be our secret."

Taking Brie's statement at face value, Emily said, "Ok, then."

The coach blew her whistle and the cheerleaders went back to the gym floor. Brie's cheering after the break became more enthusiastic as her thoughts kept churning over her newly acquired information. When practice ended, the coaches passed out brochures to the girls about the upcoming bake sale to help raise money for the team trip to Washington, DC, in the spring.

Coach Debbie handed Brie the brochure, and said, "Here you go." Brie took the brochure and performed a quick scan of its contents. As she looked at it, a thought popped into her mind. She knew exactly how she was going to 'out' Claire as the loser that she truly was. She wondered briefly if it would be too mean, but that thought quickly disappeared as her plan took shape. This is going to be epic, Brie thought to herself as she left the gym.

CHAPTER FOURTEEN

CRYSTAL AND APRIL SAT ON THE COUCH IN APRIL'S LIVING room, waiting for the girls to return home from downtown. It was Thursday night, and Crystal wanted to stop by and check up on Claire and Blake. It was dinnertime, and the girls were on their way home. Shelly and Rose had wanted to take Claire and Blake to get some malt after school. April said it was fine just as long as they were back in time for dinner.

"I can't believe how well Claire is doing," April told Crystal. "If you would have told me two weeks ago that I would be taking in another teenage girl, I would have said that you were nuts, but, look at us now. She has blended right into this family."

Even though Crystal was concerned at first, she had to agree with her friend. "I can't believe how well-adjusted she is despite all the trauma that she has been through her entire life."

"Not to mention how good she is to Blake," April added.

Crystal nodded and said, "Yes, and I think that Blake is good for Claire too. They definitely bonded as friends, and Blake is really fond of her."

Thinking about what led Claire to April in the first place, Crystal asked, "Have heard any more voices, if you know what I mean?"

Knowing that Crystal meant Nick's voice, she slowly shook her head, and replied, "No, nothing. I haven't heard anything since the day I first saw Claire."

"Well, maybe this is what was supposed to happen. You helped a girl, almost saved her life, when she was down with the flu, and now you are helping her by giving her a stable place to live while she gets through school," Crystal reasoned.

"Maybe," April responded. "All I know is that Nick wanted her here, and here is where she is going to stay." Looking at her friend, April smiled, and said, "And thanks to you, she can stay here. I know that you really worked your magic for this to happen. I am really grateful for that."

Brushing aside her thanks, Crystal said, "As I said before, you are my best friend and I would do anything for you. This was really important to you and I could see it in your eyes."

The elevator doors opened as Blake and Claire returned home.

"Hi, Aunt Crystal," Blake smiled, as she walked up to her and gave her a hug. "How's it going?"

"Good honey, how's it going with you?"

"I'm good," Blake said.

"Hi, Claire, good to see you again," Crystal said, going in for a hug. "Good to see you too," Claire said. She was getting used to engaging in hugs with just about everyone, and was enjoying it immensely. Throughout most of her life, she had never had that closeness with any family, especially one with members who supported each other emotionally. Such a simple gesture a hug was, but it made such a big impact.

"How is school?" Crystal asked Claire politely.

"Very well," Claire answered, truthfully. "I am making friends, and I am not behind in my classes. It just feels like I am picking up where I left off."

Crystal could hear the excitement in Claire's voice, and she was glad that Claire's transition had been stress-free. "Listen, if you ever need anything, just pick up the phone and give me a call." Then, glancing over at her best friend, she said, "And you don't even have to tell April."

Claire grinned and said, "Ok, I will, Crystal."

"Ha, ha," April responded to Crystal's comment. "Yeah, well, I call Tripp all the time and tell him stuff about you."

Crystal chuckled at her friend's retort, and said, "No, you don't. I have his phone tapped, just saying."

April wasn't sure if Crystal was kidding—with her, you never knew.

"I was thinking about ordering pizza for all of us, and we can talk and maybe play some UNO?" April suggested.

"Sounds great to me," Blake said, sitting on the couch next to Crystal. She put her feet up on the coffee table and crossed her arms. "I feel like kicking Aunt Crystal's butt again."

"Oh, it's on," Crystal threatened.

"Cool. Let's do it," Claire said. "I've got some homework, but it's not much. I can definitely do it after dinner."

April looked at Blake, and asked, "What about you? Do you have homework?"

Blake did have homework, quite a bit, truth be told. "Yeah, I've got a little, but it can also wait until after dinner."

It was unanimous, so April took out her phone and used the food app to order the pizzas and breadsticks. Blake got up from the couch, and went into the kitchen to retrieve the UNO cards from the drawer.

Forty-five minutes later, the pizzas arrived, and they paused the game so that they could all eat. Crystal took the pizzas into the kitchen, and put them on the island. "Dig in everyone."

Blake grabbed the paper plates from the kitchen cabinet, and set a pile of them next to the pizzas. She then put two pieces of pizza on her plate and took a couple of breadsticks. Claire followed behind her and put a couple of pieces on her plate. Claire and Blake sat next to each other while April and Crystal sat next to each other on the opposite side of the table. Claire sprinkled Parmesan cheese on her first piece and had just taken a bite out of her first piece of pizza when Blake reached over and grabbed a mushroom off Claire's second piece and then shoved it into her mouth.

"Seriously?" Claire chuckled. "You are picking off of my pizza."

"It just looked good," Blake said, giggling through her explanation.

After a minute or two, Blake got up to get water. She asked if anyone else wanted one and they all did. When Blake got back to her seat, she noticed that there was a breadstick on Claire's plate and one missing off her plate.

"Well played, Forrester," Blake said.

Claire was about to take a bite from the breadstick when Blake said with a grin, "I licked my breadsticks before I put them on my plate."

Reflexively, Claire dropped the breadstick on the table, and said, "Gross." Almost immediately, she knew Blake was kidding. Claire was just about to pick up the breadstick when Blake grabbed it from the table and licked it. "Oh my God!" Claire exclaimed, trying not to laugh.

April sighed at her daughter. Typical Blake. "Blake, seriously."

"You're serious," Blake quipped, trying not to laugh.

April gave her daughter a look like you better not say another word.

Claire picked up a piece of pizza and took a bite out of it. She got some sauce on her lips and asked Blake to pass her a napkin. While reaching for the napkin, Claire grabbed Blake's hand instead and used that to quickly wipe her face.

Pulling her now sauce-stained hand away, Blake let out a snort. "Look what Claire did mom," Blake complained as she wiped her hand with the napkin that she was going to give to Claire.

"From where I am sitting, that was justified," April smiled.

"Oh, here we go again, taking Claire's side," Blake pretended to be offended.

Crystal just sat there taking it all in. It was fun to witness the interaction between the two girls. Blake was genuinely having fun.

April and Crystal got up to get some more pizza, and Claire got out of her seat to get another glass of water, and to grab one more slice of pizza. That left Blake alone at the table.

Fortunately for Blake, Claire got back to the table first and sat down. April and Crystal were still at the island picking out more slices when Claire picked up the glass Parmesan cheese shaker and shook it over her pizza. Unknown to Claire, Blake had sabotaged the shaker by loosening the lid. So, when Claire shook it, the top of the shaker flew off, and all the Parmesan cheese in it poured into a pile on top of her pizza. Holding the now empty shaker in disbelief, Claire blinked at her single piece of pizza totally buried in a pile of Parmesan.

"What the!" Claire began, as Blake erupted in a fit of laughter.

Crystal and April looked curiously, and saw the pile of cheese on Claire's plate.

Tears of laughter were pouring out of Blake's eyes, as Claire tried her best to excavate her pizza from the pile of cheese. She took her fork and was delicately scraping as much of the Parmesan off as possible.

"Blake," Claire declared to the entire group. "You are a menace to society. Do you realize that?"

Catching her breath, Blake looked at Claire, and smiled, "Listen Claire Bear, you can never have enough cheese in your life."

"Yeah, you think so?" Claire asked, trying a bite of her newly recovered pizza.

"I do, I really do," Blake said mischievously.

After they finished eating, the four of them resumed the UNO game. Three more games later, April suggested that they quit so that Claire and Blake could do their homework. Blake had won all three games, and was feeling rather pleased with herself.

"I had fun tonight," Claire told Crystal. "Thanks for everything."

Smiling and hugging as she left, Crystal said, "It's my pleasure. Just keep doing well."

Blake hugged Crystal, and said, "Bye, Aunt Crystal. It was fun kicking your butt."

Crystal didn't release Blake from the hug, but began squeezing her tighter.

"Oh, crap, Aunt Crystal, let me go," Blake gasped. "I just ate, and you are going to make me barf."

Squeezing her for a few more seconds, Crystal finally released Blake from her grasp, and said, "Who's kicking whose butt?"

"Yeah, that's right, leave," Blake playfully taunted. Crystal made a move towards the door, but with cat-like reflexes, stepped towards Blake and smacked her on her butt.

"Wow," Blake chuckled, and made a move like she was going to do something to Crystal in retaliation, but decided against it, and then turned and ran upstairs.

Claire waved bye to Crystal, and then ran up after Blake.

"Thanks for coming over. It is always fun when we get together," April said, as she walked Crystal to the elevator.

"No problem," Crystal smiled, "Keep me posted on the inner workings of the Turner family."

April nodded and replied, "I always do."

With that, Crystal stepped into the elevator, and was gone.

April decided to go upstairs, take a shower and pick out her clothes for the meeting with Monica the next day.

When she got upstairs, she noticed that Claire was in her room and Blake was in hers. They both had books out and were beginning their homework.

April turned on her shower and went to the sink to brush her teeth. She opened her closet and took out a nightgown and her comfortable teal robe. April had a lot on her mind, but the thought of a long, hot shower put those thoughts on the backburner.

When she was finished, she dried herself off and put on her robe, searching in her closet for an outfit that displayed professionalism but style.

April sat at her vanity, and slowly brushed her hair. It felt good to take the time to take care of herself like this. She did have a lot of reading left to finish tonight, but it was still early in the evening, and she had plenty of time.

April left her bedroom to check on the girls, and discovered that Blake had left her bedroom and was in Claire's. By the sound of it, Claire was helping Blake with her homework.

"How's it going in here?" April asked as she walked in and sat in the La-Z-Boy.

"Good," Claire said. "I am just helping Blake out with pre-algebra homework."

April could see that Blake didn't fully understand it, but Claire was doing her best to help her with it.

"I am going to be reading in my room to prepare for my meeting with Monica tomorrow, so when you finish with your homework, come in so I can talk to you for a minute."

"Will do," Blake said, not looking up from the math problem she was trying to solve.

"No problem, April," Claire said, giving April a look that said Blake's homework was probably going to take a while. As April walked by Claire sitting on the bed, she put her hand on Claire's shoulders to show support and gratitude for helping Blake. Claire looked up at her and smiled warmly.

April left Claire's room and went to her room to settle in for a while.

As the evening winded down, April only heard about two bouts of frustration coming from Blake with her algebra homework. Claire was extremely patient with her, and when Blake was finally done, she did have a better understanding of the equations that were on her homework. Blake decided to stay in Claire's room while she worked her civics and US history homework. Claire finished her homework while Blake was fighting her way through algebra. She was sitting on the La-Z-Boy reading the last book in the series that she was on. Blake looked over at Claire reading, and asked, "How come you like reading so much?"

Claire looked up from her book and turned her head and faced Blake. "It has always been a way for me to leave my reality for a while and visit places and times that were always more exciting than my own," Claire explained. She turned her body around so that her legs were lying across the arm of the chair so that she could face Blake better. "I could always see that story unfold before me through the words. It is almost like watching TV, but in my mind. It is hard to explain, but I always felt free when I read. Does that make any sense?"

Blake shifted her body so that she was sitting cross-legged on the bed. "I suppose so. I know that my mom loves to read, and I see that you love it as well. Not so much for me, though. I was just wondering what all the excitement was about."

Claire thought for a moment and used 'fashion' as a comparison. "Think of it like this. You like fashion, right?"

"Right," Blake agreed.

"So, when you are designing, you are caught up in the world of fashion. You spend time looking at the various styles, you combine fabrics, you can mentally see where you want to go with an outfit or dress," Claire argued.

"Ok? Go on," Blake urged, trying to see where Claire was going with this.

"Well, during the time that you are designing, that is your world—a world that you have created via your designs. That is what reading is like for me, and I am sure it is similar for your mom." Claire said, as she concluded her explanation.

"So, when I get lost working on a design, that is what reading a book is like to you," Blake said, making the comparison.

"Precisely," Claire agreed, seeing that Blake understood what she was saying.

"Ok, I get it. I was just wondering..." Blake said.

"No problem," Claire turned her attention back to her book while Blake continued with her homework.

An hour went by and Claire still had her legs hanging over the arm of the chair, but she didn't care. The book was getting so good that she didn't want to spend the time repositioning herself—she just wanted to keep reading. Claire had just finished the second to the last chapter when she looked over at Blake, and saw that she had fallen asleep on her bed. She lay with her body across the top of the bed and her head was resting on the open US history book. She had her civics book cuddled in her arms, almost like a teddy bear. It was the cutest thing that Claire had ever seen. She quietly pulled her phone out of her pocket and texted April. "When you get a sec, come in my room but be very quiet." About thirty seconds later, Claire's bedroom door slowly opened and April quietly tiptoed inside. She walked over next to Claire and they both stared at Blake sound asleep.

"Oh, my gosh," April gushed, "Isn't that cute?"

Claire nodded her head and whispered, "I know. As soon as I saw her like that I wanted you to see it."

April smiled at Claire, and then took out her phone to take a picture. She took three pictures from three different angles. "Text them to me if you don't mind," Claire told April.

"Certainly," April said, "These are definitely keepers."

They just kind of stared at Blake for a few more moments, and Claire said, "I have only one more chapter to go, and then I am done with the series."

"Good job, Claire," April proudly said. "You remind me of myself when I was a little girl. I would read constantly."

"Thanks, April, that means a lot to me," Claire said seriously. "I enjoy it a lot."

April took a step towards Blake to wake her, but Claire stopped her, and asked, "Is it ok if I wake her after I finish this chapter? I will help her finish her homework, I promise. I just want her to rest for a little bit more."

April agreed and looked at Blake one more time. God, she was growing up fast. It felt like yesterday that she was only two years old, sitting on her lap, playing horsey.

April went back to her room while Claire finished the book. About fifteen minutes later, April could hear Claire's gentle voice saying, "Hey Blake, time to get up. You fell asleep." In her mind, April could almost see Claire carefully nudging Blake to wake her up.

"Oh, crap," April heard Blake say in a tired voice, "I still have to do my Civics homework."

"I'll help you so that you can get it done faster, if that's ok?" Claire asked.

"Cool, thanks, Claire Bear," Blake said, as she turned to the chapter in the civics book that she was working on.

April turned her attention back to her book and got lost in the story once again. A half-hour passed, and Claire and Blake appeared at her bedroom door. Blake still had a red mark on the right side of her face from where she had slept on her book.

"Are you all done with your homework?" April asked Blake.

"Yes, I am now, thanks to Claire," Blake said with appreciation. "If it wasn't for her, I probably would have bombed my algebra homework," Blake confessed honestly.

"Did you thank her for helping you?" April wanted to know.

"You bet I did," Blake replied. "I told her that she was the greatest."

Claire shook her head, "It was really no problem, and I will help you anytime, Blake."

April looked at the clock next to her bed. "You guys better get to bed soon, it's getting late."

Blake tried to suppress a yawn but failed. "You got it, mom."

Because Blake yawned, Claire followed suit and tried to stifle a yawn, but was unsuccessful. "I was going to start another book, but I think that I'll watch a few minutes of TV before turning in."

"Good night, you two," April said, as Blake came over to hug her goodnight.

"Good night, mom," Blake replied.

April waved Claire over and gave her a hug as well. "Good night, Claire. Thanks for helping Blake finish her homework."

Claire hugged April back, and smiled as she said, "Good night, April. See you in the morning, and I don't mind at all helping her."

Blake and Claire each retired to their rooms to get ready for bed. April picked up where she had left off in her book. Before she knew it, an hour had passed, and her eyes were getting heavy. She closed the book and set it on the nightstand. Tomorrow was going to be a very interesting day, and she was excited about it. Turning off the lamp next to her bed, April thought to herself just how much her life had changed in the past two weeks—from taking in a foster kid to joining forces with Monica Towers. April chuckled to herself as she thought that her life up to now would make a great plot for a novel.

* *

"HELLO, MONICA," APRIL STOOD UP FROM THE CHAIR IN THE conference room, and offered Monica Towers a handshake. It was exactly 9:00 a.m. as Monica entered the room. Gina stepped in behind her.

"Hello, April," Monica replied with a smile, as her hand firmly grabbed April's, and returned the handshake. "It's good to finally meet you."

"Likewise," April answered honestly. "I have been an admirer of your work for some time now."

"Thank you, I appreciate that," Monica said, as she took the seat next to April's. Gina walked to the head of the table and put down her iPad and a couple of file folders as she sat down.

Monica had long, flowing, blonde hair that went down to the middle of her back. She was 35 years old, and didn't seem to have any wrinkles at all on or near her face. She had magnificent light green eyes, and when she spoke, it was as if each sentence had been previously written and edited before being said out loud. Her fingernails looked as if she had just visited an expensive nail salon, and they were dipped in pink with the tips painted white.

April was just about to open with a pre-planned dialogue that she had mentally prepared the night before about how glad she was that Monica had chosen her and Priscilla Publishing when Monica took the lead and began to speak. "April, I would like to start out by saying I know that you are aware why I left Lenox, and I don't want it to be the elephant in the room. It did and does really hurt, and it will be quite a while before I will be able to sit down for any length of time and not think about it. I would like you to know that I am going to put my heart and soul into this next book, and I don't want you to walk on eggshells around me. You can ask me anything and we can talk about anything. That is how we will get to know each other, and I believe that is how you will get the best work out of me too."

April immediately knew that she liked Monica. She was the kind of person that April liked to be around.

"Thank you for that, Monica," April replied. She crossed her hands in front of her and placed them on the table and said, "I am honored that you have personally chosen me to be your editor, and I will be completely honest with you at all times. I like to help my author with their creative process, but I don't take over the project." April was looking directly at Monica, and could see that she was receptive to what was being said.

The meeting lasted for quite a while, and when it was winding down, Gina picked up her tablet and folders, and said, "I know that this will be a great transition from Lenox to Priscilla." Gina was very pleased with how the meeting went, and the addition of Monica Towers to Priscilla was surely going to make her year.

April and Monica stood up from the conference table as Gina headed out of the room. When the door closed, Monica turned her attention to April, and confessed, "April, I want to confide in you about why I really chose you as my editor."

April's eyes widened slightly but she answered, "Yes, of course, please do."

"You see, I am aware that you lost your husband four years ago, and I am terribly sorry about it," April nodded her head to accept Monica's condolences, but did not quite know where this was heading.

"When I walked in on my husband and my editor in bed together, it was as if a car crash had taken my husband too. Even though he was still alive, in my heart he was dead to me. I lost him in that moment."

April could see the sorrow in Monica's eyes, and in that moment realized that they both had something in common. They had both lost their husbands.

"I am deeply sorry that he did that to you, and if you will allow me, I will try to help you through it. If you just need someone to talk to when you are having a bad night, please call me. Seriously, I have spent many nights asking why this happened to me, and if it weren't for Gina and my friend, Crystal, I don't know what I would have done."

"Thank you for this," Monica said to April, as she leaned in to give her a hug. April hugged her back, and said, "You are very welcome."

The two of them left the conference room, and April told her that she was going to call her tomorrow to go over the book outline that Monica had given her during the meeting.

April walked down the hallway to Gina's office and knocked on the doorframe as she stepped through the recently opened door.

"That went well," April smiled as she spoke to Gina.

"Yes, it did," replied Gina, as she sat in her chair. "Monica Towers is now part of Priscilla. What a weird turn of events, wouldn't you say?"

April agreed, and said, "I think that we are going to work well together."

Gina pointed a finger playfully at April, and said, "You better because there is a lot riding on this. You thought that readers were eager to see the next novel before this happened..." Gina paused for dramatic effect. "They will be lining up for miles to see what she comes up with for the next story, especially after having her heart crushed by her husband's infidelity."

April held up her hands, and said, "Don't worry my dear friend and boss. I am going to help her so that this will be the best book yet."

"That's my April," Gina exclaimed. "Did I ever tell you that you're my best editor? Seriously, you are the best." Even though it came across as brownnosing, Gina was serious about the sentiment.

"I know," April simply said, as she walked out of the room and headed towards her office.

* *

TREVOR WOKE UP BEFORE HIS ALARM WENT OFF AND GOT up from the bed right away. One thing about the steroids was that he felt that he had more energy. It was Friday morning, and there was a game tonight. Trevor removed the pills from the secret compartment in his backpack, and instead of taking two pills for his morning dose he decided to take three. Over the past couple of practices, he thought that he had had more stamina, but he didn't know if it was the steroids working, or the idea of starting the steroids that made him feel that way. Whatever it was, he liked it.

He jumped in the shower and when he was getting dressed, he heard his phone beep. A few droplets from his wet hair dripped onto his phone screen as he peered down to see who it was.

It was Brie asking him if they could meet up before class. Trevor really didn't want to, but he knew that she would keep bugging him until he talked to her. He had a pretty good idea what it was about, and he already knew what he was going to say. Trevor did like Brie, but that ship had sailed, and now he had his sights set on Claire. Trevor texted Brie back and answered "Sure" and then typed "Let's meet in the hallway by the gym."

Trevor put his phone in his pocket, not waiting to see if Brie replied, and then headed to the kitchen for breakfast. His dad was out of town, but had told him the day before that he would be back to watch his game. Trevor never worried about it—his dad came to every game. He had never missed a game in Trevor's whole life. It had snowed the night before. There was about an inch of new snow on the driveway and as Trevor looked outside, he could see the snow plow truck heading towards his driveway. Trevor put two pieces of toast in the toaster, and then put a breakfast hot pocket in the microwave. Because Trevor wasn't devoting his full attention to what he was doing, he accidently pushed the three-minute button on the microwave instead of the two-minute button.

The toaster popped the toast up just the way that Trevor liked it, with only a few brown spots throughout. He took out the tub of butter from the fridge, and with a swipe of the knife, had his toast buttered.

The microwave chime sounded indicating that his hot pocket was finished, and he quickly opened the door and took out the plate. At that moment, his phone beeped, and he automatically checked it. It was Brie answering him back. Distracted by the text, he didn't see that the hot pocket exterior had ripped open, because of the extra minute of cooking, and had expelled about half of the melted cheese all over the outside of the hot pocket. Trevor reached for the hot pocket and firmly grabbed it, and immediately yelped in pain as the melted cheese burned his hand. In a rage, he threw the hot pocket across the kitchen, splattering it on the far wall. Because he was now furious, he took the plate that the toast was on and flung that too. The porcelain plate broke into several pieces and flew in different directions all over the kitchen.

"God damn it!" Trevor yelled, now thoroughly pissed off. He quickly stepped over to the sink and ran his hand under cold water. The spots on his fingers where the cheese had made contact were bright red and blisters were starting to form.

"Great, just fucking great," Trevor said out loud. He knew he had a game tonight and he had just burned his dribbling hand. After a few minutes of running cold water over it, he dried his hand off and put band-aid on the blisters.

The remains of the hot pocket slowly dripped from the wall and onto the floor, combining with some of the pieces of the broken plate. Trevor opened the fridge and took out the plastic gallon of orange juice and drank directly from the bottle. After drinking about a third of the bottle, Trevor put the orange juice back into the fridge and then grabbed his keys off the counter. He stomped by the mess on the kitchen floor and opened the door to the garage. He jumped into his red Mustang and slammed the door shut with more force than needed. Trevor put the key into the ignition and sat there for a few moments trying to calm down. He took a few deep breaths and then turned the key. He backed out slowly, but then sped out of the driveway with a velocity that was not appropriate for the weather conditions. He raced off in the direction of Jordan's house.

Darlene was in the upstairs bathroom when she heard the sound of a plate shattering. By the time that she raced down the stairs to see what had happened, Trevor's Mustang was pulling out of the garage and out of the driveway. She surveyed the kitchen to see the broken plate as well as what was left of the breakfast Hot Pocket on the wall and floor.

"What the hell?" Darlene questioned out loud, and wondered what the circumstances were that led to this mess. She wasn't going to text or call Trevor when he was driving so she made a metal note to ask him about it when he got home this evening.

* *

BRIE GOT TO SCHOOL BEFORE TREVOR, AND WAS LEANING against the frame of the door that led into the main gym. She was nervous and somewhat anxious about this meeting. She knew that they were pretty much finished as a couple, but no way would she let Claire have him. What he saw in her Brie didn't know, but she was going to try to get him back one final time.

Brie could hear him approach before she saw him because she recognized his voice as he spoke to Jordan. Brie wanted to talk to Trevor alone. It frustrated her that he couldn't even speak to her without his sidekick.

"Hello, Trevor," Brie said, with her lips pursed in a straight line, as she looked in Jordan's direction. "I wanted to speak to you alone."

Trevor gave Jordon a look, and Brie could have sworn that she saw Jordan's eyes roll before he said, "I'll bounce. See you in class."

When Trevor turned his attention back to Brie, she noticed a look in his eyes that she had not seen before. Not only did he not seem to want to be around her, it was like he despised her.

Before Trevor could open his mouth, Brie said, "Look Trevor, we had been going out for a while before we broke up, and I hope that you don't make a mistake by jumping to the new girl just because she is new and has long blonde hair." Trevor's eyes narrowed and he was about to say something, but Brie put her hand up to stop him, and continued, "You and I had a good thing going. I don't fully understand how it ended, but it doesn't mean that it can't start again. I care deeply about you, and we were amazing as a couple. I don't want you to get mixed up with that Seattle trash."

It was Trevor's turn to erupt. "Brie, for once in your perfect little cheer-leader life, just shut up because you don't know what you are talking about." If Brie had been standing behind him, she would have seen the hairs on the back of his neck stand up. "Yes, we did have a good time together, but that is over and done with. Do you understand?" he asked. Brie started to say something and Trevor cut her off and exclaimed, "I mean it, Brie, do you understand?"

Trevor was treating her like she was six years old, and she was getting pissed. Again, she tried to repeat what she had just started to say when Trevor cut her off again, but with his arms waving in the air. Brie's lower lip began to tremble ever so slightly as the feeling of getting yelled at began to take its toll.

Brie folded her arms in front of her, and snapped, "Yes, I fucking under-stand, ok?"

"Good," Trevor said matter-of-factly, with very little emotion now.

Brie wanted desperately to tell Trevor about Claire being a homeless girl on the streets of Chicago and a runaway from Seattle, but he was going to find out about it all soon enough.

"Fine," Brie quipped. "All I wanted to do was to warn you, but you know what? Forget it. We're done. We aren't friends anymore, and when things turn to shit with Claire, don't come running back to me!"

Brie turned away from Trevor so fast that her ponytail almost smacked him across the face.

Even though Trevor acted like he didn't care, the fact of the matter was that deep down he did care about Brie, but what he felt for Claire trumped other feelings. It was a combination of the fact that she was the new girl in the school, and the excitement of someone different that was driving his emotional state. Of course, and unknown to Trevor, the steroids that he had just begun taking were causing his psychological state to morph into highs and lows.

As he walked away, Trevor's thoughts turned towards two very separate topics. The first one was Claire. The second one was the game tonight.

* *

CLAIRE KNEW THAT SOMETHING WAS WRONG WITH BRIE during Biology class. She had this miserable look on her face, and she did everything in her power to not look in Trevor's direction. Whatever had happened, Claire suspected it was not good. For his part, Trevor too was avoiding the table at which Claire and Brie were seated. The class had just started, and Claire sat back in her chair and tried to mentally prepare herself for what was probably going to be a very long and nerve-wracking hour.

Thank God for Shelly and Rose because they too noticed that Brie was even more unpleasant than usual, and they did their best to make the time go by without any potential drama. When it came time for the experiment portion of the lesson, Shelly got up and put herself between Claire and Brie. Rose also tried to keep the attention off of anything related to Claire by asking more questions of Brie about what was supposed to happen in the lab.

With just a few more minutes left of class, Claire inadvertently caught a glimpse of Brie staring at her. The look was that of disdain. Claire was about to say something along the lines of 'What the hell is your problem' but the teacher came up to address the results of the lesson with all of them.

The class bell finally rang and the students immediately started to file out. Trevor and Jordan bolted right away, but took the long way around the classroom, avoiding Brie's table. Claire glanced at Brie as she watched the duo leave, and Claire could tell that she was hurt. In a weird sort of way, Claire felt sorry for her. Even though Trevor and Brie had separated before Claire's arrival, Claire did feel a sense of responsibility for the current state of affairs.

After the two boys left the room, Brie's facial expression turned from hurt to defiance. Brie turned to Claire as if to say something but all she did was smirk and then left the room.

"What the hell?" Claire said to Rose and Shelly. "I literally have done nothing to her, and she loathes me. I don't get it. I know that she thinks that I am trying to take Trevor away from her, but that is totally not the case."

Shelly faced Claire, and said, "We know. You are totally awesome and we know the truth about what is going on." Rose jumped in, and said, "She is just jealous and can't function knowing that someone else may have a chance with Trevor. Don't worry about her. She is just a bitter, bitter girl."

Claire only felt mildly reassured but it was nice to have new friends like Rose and Shelly. The funny thing was that Claire could see her and Brie as friends if the whole Trevor thing never happened. Obviously, that was not going to come to fruition any time soon.

The rest of the day flew by. Usually Trevor came looking for Claire at lunchtime, but today he was nowhere to be found. Even though Claire's heart fluttered slightly when he was nearby, she didn't mind not seeing him today because of the drama that had apparently happened. Claire had spent lunch with Shelly, Rose, Blake, and even Emily participated with the group. It wasn't like

Emily was now on the Claire train now, but she was at least civil to her. During lunch, Shelly had asked if Claire was going to go to the basketball game tonight. She really hadn't thought about it, but it was finally decided that they would all go. Of course, Emily was already attending because she was a cheerleader, but the others—Shelly, Rose, Claire, and Blake—decided to meet at the game.

Now it was almost the end of her last class of the day—Algebra I. Claire didn't especially like math, but she was average at it. The teacher was nice enough and allowed time for the students to get most of their homework completed in class.

When the bell rang, Claire stayed for an extra minute to finish up the last equation on the sheet, which meant that she didn't have to bring her math book home for the weekend. Claire put her now finished math problems in her book, and then headed towards the door. Standing smack in the middle of it was Trevor.

Claire's reaction said it all, and Trevor joked as he noticed the look on her face, "What? Not happy to see me?"

Claire turned her surprised facial expression to one indicating tension. As she walked up to him, she asked, "What happened between you and Brie today?" Claire could see Trevor's shoulders tense up as he prepared to answer. "She wanted to talk to me this morning, and started giving me shit about you. I told her that she and I have been over for weeks now, and that it was truly over." Surprisingly, Trevor sounded mature, and it made Claire look deeper into his eyes.

"Is that all?" Claire questioned.

"Yes, that is pretty much it. She didn't like the fact that I want to get to know you," he said. Both Claire and Trevor started walking down the hall towards Claire's locker.

Claire used her right hand to wrap a strand of blonde hair that had fallen across her line of vision, as she said, "Look, Trevor, I must admit that I too would like to get to know you, but I really don't need any more drama in my life. I mean, I can handle Brie, and I am not asking for any kind of interference from you, but I don't want to be the girl in the middle."

Trevor nodded his head in agreement, but said, "Claire, I said it before, and I'll say it again. I want to get to know you. I think it's obvious that I like you so don't worry and just let me get to know you."

They had reached her locker, and after she placed her math book in the locker, Trevor unexpectedly grabbed her hands and held on to them as he faced her. "Claire, I like you a lot. I would like to get to know you, and I want to hang out with you. If you don't want me, just let me know now and I will leave you alone."

Claire had never had a boyfriend before, so when Trevor grabbed her hands, it was something that she was unaccustomed to. In that moment, with their hands touching, as he looked into her eyes with longing, Claire's heart skipped a beat. A voice deep down in her gut whispered that she should walk away from him right now and be done with all of it, but the teenage girl whose hormones suddenly awoke took over, and Claire said as she smiled, "Ok Trevor. You win. I want to get to know you too, but I want to take it slow. I want a friend first."

Still grasping her hands and not letting go, Trevor smiled and answered, "You got it, Claire. I promise." He then held up his hands still attached to hers and tried his best to perform the Boy Scout salute.

"I promise," he laughed, as his fingers wrapped around hers in a weird sort of way.

Claire chuckled too, and then she noticed the Band-Aids on some of his fingers. "You ok?" she asked, as she used one of the fingers that were wrapped in his to indicate the Band-Aid.

"Yeah. I'm good," Trevor declared. "I had an altercation with my break-fast this morning and I'm still not sure who won."

Claire smirked at his answer and realized that he still had a hold of her hands.

"So, friend," Claire wondered, "When do I get to have my hands back?"

Trevor pretended that he didn't know what she was talking about, making it a point to hold his hand linked to hers in front of his face.

"Oh, yes, I see what you mean," he said. Quickly bringing his right hand that was holding her left hand up to his lips, he gave her hand a quick kiss. He then released both hands and gave her a smile.

It took Claire a second to realize what had happened, as she unconsciously touched the spot of the kiss with her right hand. "I'll see you tomorrow," Trevor said as he turned to leave.

Claire remembered the plans made at lunchtime, and said to him, "I'll see you tonight because a group of us will be going to the game."

Trevor turned back to face her, and smiled, "Totally awesome, I'll be the one scoring the most."

It came out as a joke, but somehow Claire knew that it was based on the truth.

Across the hall, hidden by a group of students, Brie witnessed the entire encounter between Trevor and Claire. She saw him grab her hands and then kiss one of them. She knew at that point that Monday was going to be the day that her plan took shape. She couldn't allow Claire's charade to continue any longer.

* *

BLAKE AND CLAIRE WALKED INTO THE GYMNASIUM ABOUT fifteen minutes before the start of the game. It took them a minute or so to locate Shelly and Rose. They were about midcourt and approximately three rows up from the floor.

"Hey, guys," said Claire, as she stepped up onto the bleachers towards them.

"Hi, Claire," Rose said, as she waved at Blake and Claire. "Glad to see that you could make it."

Claire sat down with Rose on her right and Blake on her left. As she looked out across the gym, she suddenly realized that this was her first time attending a basketball game. She couldn't help but smile at all the excitement that was being generated throughout the gym. The players from both teams were wearing their shooting shirts as they ran their practice plays, basketballs were bouncing all over the court as several players shot at the hoop at the same time, and the cheerleaders were practicing their routines while they yelled and jumped with enthusiasm, shaking their pom-poms in each hand.

Shelly and Rose pointed at various players, and gave Claire the rundown on each. They would giggle and laugh as they described them by using cartoon names. Claire was having so much fun with her new friends that she couldn't believe this was happening to her. To think that a few weeks ago, she was homeless and alone, and tonight she was with two great girls, not to mention her best friend, Blake.

Blake had been to several games in the past, usually to support Emily, but tonight, she was there with Claire and her new friends, and it felt more exciting. Blake watched the freshman cheerleaders in order to catch Emily's eyes. Blake waved at her until she saw her, and Emily gave her a quick smile to indicate that she had spotted Blake.

The music over the loudspeaker lowered in volume as the announcer said that the game was going to start in five minutes. He went over a few advertisements to satisfy the sponsors who had paid money to help with the team. Claire was looking at the court almost as if she was watching a tennis match. Her head turned from the left to the right, taking it all in. As her eyes focused on center court, she noticed a player staring directly at her. It was Trevor—he must have been looking for her in the bleachers, and he had found her. Their eyes zoomed in on each other, and it was almost as if no one was around her and Trevor, and they were the only two people in the entire gym. Claire smiled and gave him a tiny wave. Trevor smiled back and then nodded an acknowledgment as he shot the basketball towards the net without really looking. Surprisingly, the ball hurled towards the net, and actually bounced on the rim a couple of times before falling to the floor without entering the basket. It was still an impressive shot. A few onlookers saw Trevor almost make the shot, and then applauded their approval.

The Jones College Prep High School Eagles were playing against their rivals at Payton College Prep High School. It was going to be a tough game because the two teams were pretty evenly matched, but the Eagles were down their best senior player. All eyes were on Trevor to pick up the slack as the players on both sides were introduced to the crowd.

The first string players came out onto the court taking their places for the tip ball. The Eagles won the tip and scored the first basket of the game. The crowd went wild with applause as the score turned from 00 to 02.

At the end of the first period, the Eagles only gave up the lead twice and now led by four points. Trevor was on fire and only missed 2 of his 8 shots on basket.

As the game went on, Claire found herself eagerly anticipating the times that Trevor went in, which was most of the time. He would only be taken out for short periods of time, and was the player with the most playing time thus far. Shelly had gone to the concession stand and bought popcorn and snacks for all four of them. When she got back to the bleachers, one of the Eagle players had stolen the ball from the Payton player and sprinted back to the basket and quickly completed a layup. Just about everyone stood up and cheered. One of the fans almost knocked one of the popcorn tubs from Shelly's hand, but Blake caught it out of the air before it could spill.

"Great catch!" Shelly exclaimed to Blake, totally impressed with the catch.

"Thanks," Blake giggled after the shock of her catch. "I can't believe that I caught that."

Claire saw what Blake had done, and raised her fist for a fist bump. Blake fist-bumped her and smiled at her. "Nice," Claire said and then turned her attention back to the game.

At halftime, the Eagles were down by two points. The game had been tied with seven seconds to go before the half when a Payton player threw the ball to midcourt to another player who was unguarded sprinting towards the basket thus making an easy layup.

The cheerleaders took the court to showcase their routines to the delight of the crowd. Claire caught a glimpse of Brie, but Brie didn't pick Claire out of the crowd. If Claire didn't know any better, she would have thought that Brie was a bright and happy person as she smiled and cheered. Of course, cheering was a form of acting, and Claire knew that Brie's demeanor would suddenly change if she had spotted her watching Trevor play. After the Varsity Cheerleaders performed, the freshmen cheerleaders made their way to the floor and performed their routine. Emily was among them and when the routine was finished, Blake said to the group, "I'll be right back. I am going to go and talk with Emily for a few minutes."

"Sure thing," Claire said.

Claire was happy that Emily and Blake were at least seeing eye-to-eye again, even though Claire knew that Emily viewed her as a mild annoyance now instead of a full-fledged enemy.

With ten minutes to go for the second half to start, Rose, Shelly, and Claire sat there eating popcorn and talking about the game. Of course, the topic kept flowing back to Trevor, and how well he was playing tonight. Claire got the distinct impression that her friends wanted Trevor and her to be a thing.

Blake returned to her seat as the tip off to the second half started. As she stepped up to the third bleacher, her shoe caught the edge and she tripped. Blake almost fell, but Claire was right there and grabbed a hold of her arm just below the shoulder. "Thanks," Blake said, as Claire pulled her back fully upright. "No problem," Claire said, happy that her reflexes were quick enough to catch her. Claire asked how Emily was doing and Blake remarked that she was actually doing well and all seemed really good.

With all eyes on the Eagles, the second half of the game was a nail-biter, to say the least. Unlike the first half, the score's leaders flipped more times than pancakes at IHOP. The Eagles would take the lead and then Payton would score and then be up by a point. This continued until Payton was up by six going into the last period. Claire noticed a gentleman in a sports jacket talking to the head coach and the players of the Eagles and they kept looking at Trevor. Claire didn't realize at first, but it was Trevor's dad, Rodney. By the look on his face, he seemed overly concerned about the score and the way that things were turning out.

With only five minutes left in the game, Trevor was coming in for a layup and a Payton player fouled him as he leaped to take the shot. The ball didn't go in but it meant that Trevor got to shoot free throws. However, the foul was a little more aggressive than what the Payton player had intended, and Trevor got knocked to the floor with the Payton player landing on top of him.

Trevor immediately recovered from the fall and got right up to the Payton player and pushed him in the chest. "What the hell, man!"

The Payton player knew he had fouled Trevor, but was not going to let him push him, so he pushed Trevor back. Trevor instantly got really pissed and pushed him back harder, which caused him to trip over his own foot and he fell to the floor.

The referee called a technical on Trevor. The Eagles coach started yelling from the sideline that it was the Payton player that should get the un-sportsman like conduct, not Trevor. By the time that it was sorted out, Trevor shot his two free throws; making both of them, and then the Payton player got to shoot two technical foul shots, making one of two, and then Payton got the ball again.

Trevor had to sit out for a couple of minutes, and when he got back in, there was only fifty-five seconds left in the game. It went back and forth for a couple of plays, and there were only seven seconds left in the game with Payton up by two. They had the ball and had to inbound it. The game was virtually over, but the Eagle defense prevented them from allowing them to inbound it at close range so the Payton player had to pass it to the only available player that had the best chance of accepting the pass. As the Payton player threw it in, Trevor somehow managed to tip the ball with the fingers on his right hand, which changed the trajectory of the ball's path and the Payton player missed the pass. The ball bounced on the floor at midcourt as several players from both sides scrambled to get it. Trevor raced for the ball as the seconds ticked by. He grabbed the ball at the midcourt line with two seconds left. Because he had been sprinting at full tilt to retrieve the ball, he was unsteady and didn't have time to set up for the shot. Trevor threw the ball in the air a half second before the buzzer sounded. The ball soared through the air at an unnaturally high arch. The buzzer went off as the ball's flight began its descent. The ball hit the rim, bounced about six feet in the air straight up and then swished directly through the center of the hoop. The Eagles won the game by one point!

The crowd in the bleachers erupted in a combination of applause and screams of joy. The Eagles bench cleared and the team raced to Trevor, and everyone was dancing and jumping around him, celebrating the win. All the Eagle cheerleaders, varsity and freshmen, ran screaming onto the floor as well. Claire found herself screaming at the top of her lungs with excitement. The four of them were jumping and laughing, and couldn't believe how great this game was.

"I must say," Claire yelled to Shelly and Rose over the noise of the crowd, "This was the best first basketball game ever!"

Shelly looked at Claire and replied, "This was your first basketball game ever?"

"Yuppers," Claire said. "I have never been to any kind of a school sports game before. I wasn't in any sports growing up, and there was not a need to really go." As she thought back about it, it brought up memories of her mom. Claire wondered how she was doing, and deep down, she missed her mom. Despite all of her shortcomings, her mom was her mom and there was a part of Claire that wanted her to be in her life.

Blinking the memory away, Claire turned her attention back to her friends. The four of them sat there for several minutes waiting for the chaos to settle down and allow more people to leave the gym.

The team had gone to the locker room to change, and when they came out, the remaining crowd cheered again for the home team winners.

Trevor walked to the part of the gym where his dad and coach were talking. He saw Claire still sitting on the bleachers and held up his finger to indicate to hold on a second and that he wanted to see her.

As Trevor approached his dad, Rodney let out a little yell and said with pride, "There's my boy!"

He held up his hand so that his son would give him a high five and then hugged him.

"Great job today, Trevor. You keep this up and you will be a shoe in for the full ride scholarship that we talked about." It was obvious to Claire that Trevor's dad was proud of him, but she got the feeling that he wanted his son to be the best. A few minutes went by as the coach and Rodney talked to Trevor, and then Trevor said something along the lines of "See you when I get home."

While Trevor was talking to his dad, Claire and the group got up from the bleachers and slowly walked on the court, keeping a fair distance between them and Trevor so as not to appear like they were waiting. Trevor flung his basketball bag over his shoulder and walked towards Claire.

"So, Claire," Trevor began, "did you enjoy the game?"

"It was awesome," Claire exclaimed. "This was totally exciting and we had a really fun time."

After a second, Claire added, "Not to mention, I don't believe that you made that shot at the buzzer! That was so sweet!"

Trevor knew that it was just dumb luck that he made that shot, but he jokingly played it off like he knew it was going to go in. "I knew all along it was going in." he lied.

"Sure you did," Claire smiled, calling him out on his lucky shot.

Trevor smiled and said, "Hey listen, I am really glad that you came to the game tonight."

"Me too," Claire said sincerely. "I must say that it was really fun." Almost as an afterthought, Claire added, "You are pretty good at it."

"Pretty good?" Trevor questioned with a raised eyebrow. "Just pretty good?"

Claire pretended to sigh and give in to him. "Alright, then," she amended her reply, "pretty great—how's that?"

Trevor put his hand on his chin as if he was thinking about his answer, and then he declared, "Yes. Pretty great sounds about right."

Claire giggled at that and the two of them talked for a few more minutes until Trevor said that he better get going because he was meeting the team at Coney Island for some hotdogs to celebrate the win.

There was an awkward pause between the two of them as if one of them should say something other than 'bye'. After a few seconds, Claire spoke up, "Have a good night, and I'll see you on Monday."

Trevor smirked and said as a goodbye, "See you Monday, New Girl." With that, he turned around and walked out of the gym. Claire stood where she was for a few moments, allowing her eyes to follow him out of the gym. When she turned around, she saw Shelly, Rose, and Blake all standing there, quietly looking at her with puppy dog eyes.

"Ok, ok," said Claire sheepishly. "Let's hit the road." The girls were giggly about what was happening between Claire and Trevor, but they truly wanted Claire to be happy.

Claire couldn't believe that she was falling for the jock of her class. This was something that she would have never done in the past. Being here in Chicago, living with Blake and April, was making Claire feel more confident about herself and her life.

CHAPTER FIFTEEN

IT WAS EARLY SATURDAY MORNING WHEN BLAKE WOKE UP. It was 6:24 a.m. and for a brief moment, Blake thought that she had to get up for school. As reality slowly sank in, she remembered that it was a Saturday, and that she did not have to go to school. As Blake sat up, she realized that she had a headache. It wasn't a terrible migraine or anything but her head was pounding slightly.

Blake got out of bed and went into the bathroom to use the toilet and then brush her teeth. She noticed that she was just a little bit achy as well. *Great,* Blake thought, *I better not be sick.* She was about to take a shower when she thought that she would see if Claire was up yet. Blake slowly opened Claire's bedroom door and discovered that she was still asleep. She quietly closed the door and then went towards her mother's room to see if she was awake.

As she approached April's room, Blake heard her mom's alarm going off. She must have set it for 6:30 am. Blake opened the door just as her mom was turning off the alarm.

"Morning, mom," Blake said as she jumped into bed next to her.

"Morning, daughter," April replied, wiping the sleep from her eyes. April pulled the covers down towards the end of the bed so that Blake could get underneath and cuddle with her mom.

"How did you sleep?" April questioned.

"Good, but I think I woke up with a headache," Blake answered honestly. "It's not bad, but I do feel a little achy."

April looked at Blake's face and didn't really think that her color was off. She then put her hand on Blake's forehead to see if she was running a fever but she didn't seem to be.

"When we get up, why don't you take some Motrin, maybe that might help," April suggested, as she ran her hands through Blake's hair.

"I will," Blake answered.

The two of them lay underneath the covers for a few minutes as April continued to run her hands through Blake's hair. It was almost hypnotic to Blake as she closed her eyes and almost fell back asleep. April heard footsteps in the hallway and knew that it must be Claire.

"In here," April shouted in the direction of the hallway.

Claire stepped through the door wearing a light blue gown that really brought out the blue in her eyes. April motioned for her to join her and Blake on the bed. Claire climbed in beside Blake and said, "Good morning, guys. How's it going?"

"Good," April answered, "My alarm went off and Blake just came in. How did you sleep?"

Claire had dreamt of Trevor last night and the dreams were pretty awesome. It was summer time and they were walking hand and hand in a park. The birds were chirping as they walked and talked. When they arrived at their apparent destination near a crystal clear pond, Trevor swung her around to face him and then he started kissing her. There they were embraced in passionate kisses as other park goers walked by, not paying any attention to them. When he finally stopped, he told her that he loved her and how much his life was better with her in it. As Trevor leaned in for another kiss, Claire woke up. The smell of flowers and the heat from the sun was still emanating from her mind.

"Real good, actually," Claire answered April with the dream sequence still playing through her mind.

April had been working late the night before and hadn't had the chance to talk to the girls when they got home from the basketball game.

"So, how was the game last night?" April asked Claire.

"Oh my God, it was amazing," Claire said excitedly, as she remembered it. "It was my first game and we all had so much fun."

Blake shifted her position, sitting up in bed, at a better angle so she could speak to both Claire and her mom. "Yeah, and Trevor scored the winning basket at the buzzer. It was from half court and it went in!" Blake recounted the basket as if it just happened.

April could see the twinkle in Claire's eyes at the mention of Trevor's name.

"So, Claire. How's it going between you and Trevor?" April asked, hoping things were going well.

"Well, I think that he likes me. He has been trying to get to know me since my first day of school. I think that I like him, but he is the jock of our class so I'm uncertain about all this."

April could see the conflict in Claire as she spoke.

Claire's expression turned a tad more serious as she asked April, "Can I talk to you about something?"

Without skipping a beat, April replied, "Of course you can."

Blake heard the tone in Claire's voice, and sat up a little bit in order to show that she too was going to listen intently to what Claire was about to say next.

Claire cleared her throat, and started, "Because I moved around a lot, and never really took the time to get to know the other kids in my class..." Pausing for a moment to collect her thoughts, she continued. "...and I spent a lot of time reading books, you know?"

April nodded her head to indicate that she was listening to what she was saying and to continue.

Claire's face was kind of turning a light shade of red, like she was embarrassed about something but she continued and said, "I... I... I never really had a boyfriend before..." Claire then looked down at the bed like she had just confessed to a sin.

April gave Claire a warm smile, and then said, "Oh Claire, that's alright. I was a senior in high school when I got my first serious boyfriend." Then looking at Blake, April amended, "And no, it wasn't your father."

Blake blinked a little in surprise, "Oh really, mother? And who was this first boyfriend of yours?"

April gave Blake a wave as if to dismiss her question. "We are not talking about me right now. We are discussing Claire."

April turned her attention back to Claire, "Look, sweetie, there is no timeline for dating. Your heart will tell you when it is time. What does your heart say about Trevor?"

Claire had to mentally check in with her heart to listen to what it was telling her. On one hand, she was nervous about getting involved with the most popular boy in school. But on the other hand, she had never before felt the kind of longing that she now felt for him. She had begun to think about him more and more, and couldn't seem to focus on other things. Of course, the dream of Trevor last night surely didn't help matters.

"I think my heart is telling me to give him a chance," Claire couldn't stop herself from grinning as she replied. "I have never felt this way about a boy, and I was so nervous about where this might lead. I have been closed off to people in general for so long that I am scared for putting my heart out there. I have been let down my entire life and I think that I am apprehensive about diving in with someone that might cause another tear in my heart," she confessed.

Her words were powerful and weighed heavily on everyone's minds. April could see that this was a focal point for Claire, and she didn't want to let this opportunity to help Claire go by.

"I hear what you are saying, and I know that you have been through a lot emotionally, but what I can offer you is this." April took one of Claire's hands in hers, and continued, "A person's heart is truly a remarkable thing. It can be torn to pieces in a few seconds or it can be destroyed over years and years, but for some reason, a heart can be mended by one act of kindness or the discovery of love."

April paused to let that sink in, and then continued, "So, Claire, your heart may have taken a beating over the last sixteen years, but that doesn't mean that it is damaged. You just need to listen to where it is taking you and allow it to guide you. You are a remarkable young lady with so much ahead of you, so if the direction that your heart is taking you is towards Trevor, then it's ok to listen to it."

Claire blinked back a tear because she had never had a conversation like this with anyone. "Wow," Claire whispered, adding, "thank you." Turning to Blake, Claire said, "Your mom is awesome. Don't ever forget that." Blake too was impressed by what her mother had just said. "I know she is," Blake told Claire.

April didn't know where the words had come from, but she suspected that they were based on her feelings for Nick. Her heart had been torn apart for years now, and maybe deep down, her own heart was trying to tell her something. The memory of Nick made April reach out and give both girls a hug. The three of them just sat on the bed for a few minutes lost in their own thoughts.

"We better get up and get ready to start our day. Remember, we are going to my parents this morning."

"Sweet," Blake replied, as she slowly got out of bed. "I can't wait to go. I love being at their house."

Claire stood up and turned to April, and said, "Thanks again for everything."

"You are very welcome," April replied. "That is why I am here."

As Blake reached for the bedroom door to open it a little further, April caught a glimpse of her arm and noticed a big bruise on it.

"Blake," April gasped, "What did you do to your arm?"

Not knowing what she was talking about, Blake looked at her arm and noticed the bruise.

Thinking for a second, and then realizing what it was, she replied, "Oh, it must have been when Claire caught me last night at the game."

"Caught you?" April asked.

"Yeah," Blake said, "I was coming back to the bleachers, when I tripped and almost fell. Claire, with her cat-like reflexes, grabbed my arm just before I slammed my face into the bleachers."

Claire looked at Blake's arm and was amazed at how big the bruise was. "I'm sorry, Blake, I didn't know that I grabbed you that tightly."

"No, Claire, it's ok, my face would have been smashed if you hadn't stopped my fall," Blake reassured Claire.

April stepped closer to look at the damage. There was a hand-sized bruise on her arm.

Blake, seeing her mother's concern, said, "Mom, it's fine, really. It doesn't even hurt. I'll be fine."

Concerned, April wondered what she could do for the bruise, and then remembered that Blake had complained about having a headache as well.

"Are you sure you're ok? You do have a headache too," April asked.

"Mom," Blake said bemused. "I am fine," she said, enunciating all three words slowly so that her mother would take the hint and not worry about it. "The headache was probably due to the game last night. I mean with the music and the loud fans all night, it's no wonder I have one.

"Ok, darling, if you think that you're fine," April gave in, still sounding unconvinced.

"Yes, mother, I'm fine," Blake said, as she headed out of April's bedroom towards her own.

* *

"HI, DEREK," BLAKE WAVED, AS SHE APPROACHED THE BIG, black SUV that he was standing next to. Derek Burke had been working for April's dad for the past six years. He had started with the company when he had just turned seventeen. Derek's dad was one of Joseph's good friends. He had suddenly passed away from a blood clot two days after Derek's sixteenth birthday. Joseph had hired Derek a year later as a part-time errand boy so that Derek could make some money and Joseph could kind of keep an eye on his late friend's son.

Derek was a senior in college, and was studying Psychology with a minor in Sociology. He had become a driver for the company because he liked being around people and seeing the city. It was a good gig for him because it was part-time, but Joseph paid him well. Derek had driven Blake and April over the years, and a couple of years ago, Blake had had a little crush on him even though he was almost ten years older. The crush had faded, but Blake still thought Derek was handsome, but he was almost like a big brother to her now.

"Hello, Miss Turner," Derek said directly to Blake, sounding like a flight attendant. "How is your day today?" He took her hand as she opened the door to gently place her inside the vehicle.

"Great," Blake smiled, as she nodded like an aristocratic lady getting into a carriage. They had performed this same ritual for the past year or so, and it was their thing.

April and Claire were a few steps behind Blake as they approached the vehicle. April gave Derek a hug, and said, "Hi Derek, good to see you again." Then she put her hands on Claire's shoulder, and introduced her, "Derek, this is Claire." April paused for a second as she thought about what she was going to say, and then added, "She is my foster daughter."

Derek blinked in mild surprise but said with a warm smile, "Pleasure to meet you, Miss Claire." He held out his hand to shake it and then kept the hold as he carefully guided Claire into her seat.

"Nice to meet you too," Claire replied, with a warm grin.

Derek then walked April to the other side, and opened the door for her and guided her into the seat directly behind his.

The city streets were covered in two inches of fresh snow so far this morning, and the forecast indicated that two to three more inches were due before evening. Derek was a careful and cautious driver, and he was used to driving in the worst Chicago weather. As they began the forty-five minute trek to the Village of Northfield, April told the girls to keep an eye out for the Christmas decorations that people were putting up in their yards. Once they got out of the city, the falling snow began to intensify, and it was like they were driving in a snow globe.

"Wow, this is really beautiful," said Claire admiringly, as she gazed out of the SUV window. Even though it does snow in Seattle, the amount of snow was nothing in comparison to Chicago.

"It definitely can be," agreed Derek. "I like the snow because it makes people slow down and helps them remember what is important in their lives."

Blake looked at Derek and commended him, "Well put, my friend." Derek looked in the rearview mirror, and gave Blake a quick grin of acknowledgement. "It's good to take time to cherish what you have. Don't sweat the small stuff."

Blake knew that Derek still thought of his dad every day, and if Blake really thought about it, that was why they got along so well... because they had both lost their dads, and it was like a two-person support group.

Turning to Claire, Blake said aloud, "My dad used to take me and my mom to the park when it snowed, and we would try to build a huge snowman." Reliving the memory, she grinned as she spoke, "I would roll a big ball of snow until I couldn't physically push it anymore, and then my dad would push it to a spot where I wanted it. We did this until we had all three parts of the snowman's body. Of course, my mom would bring the best clothes for it. Our snowman ended up being the best dressed in the entire park."

April smiled and sighed as she recalled the memory as if she were watching it on television.

"You know, it was your dad's idea for me to bring the clothes to dress it up because..." April blinked in realization, as she remembered, "because, he said he hoped that a homeless person would come across the snowman and take the clothes for warmth."

Blake looked at her mom and then at Claire. "Oh my God, I forgot about that. We always tried to make two snowmen—one man and one woman—so that there would be clothes for each."

The irony did not escape Claire—even years ago the Turners did what they could for the homeless. Claire thought about the pictures throughout the apartment and the photo albums that Blake had shown her over the last few weeks, and it almost felt like she knew Nick.

"I wish I could have met him," Claire said honestly. "I bet that I would have really liked him."

Without skipping a beat, Blake replied, "Yes, you would have. He was totally awesome." As she looked over at Claire's smile, Blake added, "Of course, he would have really liked you too."

Then, without warning, Claire suddenly found herself wondering about her own dad, and what he must have been like. Would he have built snowmen with her? She quickly pushed the thought back to where it had come from, and turned her attention back to Blake and her dad. April thought about what Claire and Blake had said, and recalled the moment when she had met Claire, with Nick's voice guiding her to Claire. April wished that she knew why it was so important for Claire to be here. It was obvious that April and Blake both were growing extremely fond of Claire, and that they liked having her around, but was that the only reason?

The drive ended up taking almost an hour and ten minutes because it was slow going as they approached the Village of Northfield. As they drove through the subdivision of April's parents' home, Claire got the distinct impression that they were not in Kansas anymore. The sub was a gated community, and each house looked like a mini mansion.

"You grew up here?" Claire asked April in wide-eyed wonder.

"Yes, I did," April answered trying to sound humble. "My parents had bought this house when I was very young, like two or three years old, and that is where they have lived ever since. It is the family home."

The SUV went through the gate, travelled down a couple of blocks, and then stopped at a huge house at the end of a cul-de-sac. The word house was too loose of a description. It was a mansion that was made entirely of grey/white cobblestones with dark oak trim and shutters. It was exquisite.

The Turners had already decorated the outside of the house and yard for Christmas, and it was almost like looking at a Thomas Kinkade Christmas painting. The newly fallen snow had covered the roof of the house, giving it an almost fairytale look to it as the snow began to slowly overtake the gutters. The resulting effect gave the impression that it was a gingerbread house and an angelic being had frosted the roof with pure white frosting.

"Holy shit, April," Claire let slip. "Is this the North Pole?" She immediately put her hand over her mouth to signify that she did not mean to swear.

Smirking at Claire, Blake said, "It does feel that way, doesn't it?"

Derek pulled the SUV into the driveway, and stopped at the archway between the house and the garage. He got out of the vehicle and opened the doors for the occupants, and helped them get out of the car. The door leading to the house opened up to reveal April's parents.

"Good morning," Anne greeted them, as she stepped into the snow to hug her daughter.

"Hi, mom," April replied happily, as she embraced her mother. "The place looks beautiful as always."

Joseph was standing behind his wife as she hugged April. "You know how we love our Christmas holiday," He said, spreading his hands out to indicate the house and yard. "Pretty soon it is going to look like we have Santa on the payroll." He held out his hands for his daughter to give him big hug. "Don't change a thing," April said about the decorations. "It reminds me of my childhood and how much fun we used to have as a family during the holidays."

Both Blake and Claire received their hugs from Joseph and Anne. After Anne was done hugging Claire, she looked her over from head to toe, and said, "Living with April and Blake looks good on you."

Claire smiled, and replied, "I agree wholeheartedly." If you looked at a picture of Claire when she had first arrived at April's a month ago and a picture of her today standing in front of Joseph and Anne's house, you would see quite a contrast. The Claire of today had a glow about her. She was clean, of course, but there was a look of elegance about her. If you didn't know her back story, you would assume she had been raised in the finer part of town.

Blake asked her grandparents with a grin, "Yes, but don't I look good too because Claire is with us?"

Smiling, Joseph replied, "Yes, my dear little Blake. Having Claire living with you looks good on you too."

Blake put her arm around Claire, and said, "Two peas in a pod, I say."

Claire grinned and in a joking tone, asked her, "Do you? Do you really say that?"

Blake, faked being offended, and answered, "Yes, I say it all the time." Of course, this was the first time that she ever used that phrase, but it was fun to watch the two of them banter.

Joseph turned to Derek and asked him a few questions about how school was going and how things were going with his family. After a few moments, he asked Derek if he could come back later in the evening to take April and the girls home. Derek said that he would be there, of course, and would be ready whenever they were set to go back.

Anne led them into the house, and Blake took Claire on a tour. The house had six bedrooms, with all of them housing their own bathrooms with showers. Five of the bedrooms were upstairs while the huge master was located on the main floor. One of the upstairs bedrooms had been April's when she was growing up, and the Turners had left everything in it untouched. The room was a shrine to the love that they had for their daughter, and the time they spent raising her. April once overheard her dad saying to a reporter who was interviewing him for an article in *Fortune 500* magazine that his greatest achievement was being a father to his lovely daughter, April.

Claire was in awe of the size and elegance of April's parents home. It brought back memories of when she had first entered April's apartment, and had been awestruck then. But here she had the same feelings times five!

Blake took Claire to the billiards room. There were two regular-sized pool tables with green tops and one huge, elegant pool table that had a red top. There was a bar in the corner with three hand-carved booths adjacent to it.

"This place is amazing," Claire said, as her voice cracked with awe.

"I know, right?" Blake responded. "And I haven't shown you the indoor pool and spa area yet."

Claire gasped in excitement, "This place has an indoor pool?"

"Of course, it does," Blake said, cheerfully. "Maybe later, if you feel like it, we can go for a swim?"

"That would be amazing," Claire couldn't stop smiling at how incredible the house was. Every room that they went into revealed one fantastic thing after another.

Blake and Claire met up with April and her parents in the Great Room. There was a huge stone hearth wood-burning fireplace that was the centerpiece of the room.

"Your house is so amazing," Claire said to Joseph and Anne. "I am in shock at the size of it."

Anne put her arm around her husband, "Thank you Claire. It has taken us years to get it to what you see today, but it sure has been a fun and loving journey."

The five of them sat by the fireplace enjoying the warmth of the fire. The discussion soon turned to stories of April and her childhood, and the adventures that the three of them had had. After about half an hour, it was decided that they would go into town to shop and look at the town's Christmas decorations.

Because Joseph had sent Derek home, Joseph decided to take his new Jeep Grand Cherokee into town. Blake had called shotgun so it was Joseph in the driver's seat with Blake in the front passenger seat. Even though it was only a mile to downtown, snow and cold prevented them from walking there.

Joseph pulled into the parking lot for the Three Tart Café and Bakery. Because it was a little past noon on a Saturday, the lot was almost full. Fortunately, Joseph found an empty spot on Mt. Pleasant Street, parallel to the café. It was located about six car lengths from the front of the building. As they walked towards the door, the oversize snowflakes that were falling from the sky firmly attached themselves to the hair and clothing of the group. Once inside, they brushed the snow from their coats and scarves.

There were three couples ahead of them so they had a little time to decide what they wanted from the menu. There were many delicious looking sandwiches along with hot paninis. When it was their turn, Blake ordered the Grown-up Grilled Cheese. April ordered the Tuna Melt, Anne ordered the Chicken Rosemary, and Joseph ordered the Roast Beef sandwich. Everything looked really good to Claire, and it took her a few extra seconds to decide what she wanted. Eventually, Claire ordered the Mozzarella Pesto sandwich.

Finding a table by one of the light wood French doors, the Turners sat down and began enjoying their lunch.

Taking a sip from her hot chocolate, Blake looked at her mom, and said, "I can't wait to show Claire the shops in town. I bet that she likes the old bookstore the best."

Claire's eyes perked up at the mention of a bookstore, and asked quizzically, "Bookstore?"

April nodded her head, and said, "Yes, it is a really old bookstore that I used to shop at when I was a little girl. I think that is where I first developed an interest in reading." April suspected that Claire would love it, and she couldn't wait to take her there.

Blake took a bite of her grilled cheese, and then said, "I can't wait to take her to the fashion clothes shop. I bet you I can find you a really cute outfit." Claire was getting used to Blake browsing for different kinds of outfits for her. Claire was your basic jeans-and-sweatshirt kind of girl, but over this past month and with Blake's help, she was acquiring a taste for some of the finer things that fashion had to offer.

Finishing lunch, they decided to head out in the direction of the fashion store for two reasons. First, it was closer. Second, if they went to the bookstore first, they would never get April and Claire to leave it before the other stores closed.

Blake was in her element at the fashion boutique, and had a lot of fun picking outfits for Claire. Fashion was truly something that Blake excelled in. Of course, there were many outfits that Blake tried on and fell in love with. April was enjoying shopping with both the girls, and it was an added bonus to be with her mother as well. She remembered shopping here for school clothes with her mom. Joseph was not much of a fashion shopper, but he loved being with his wife, daughter, and grandchild so much that it really didn't matter where he was, he was just happy to enjoy their company.

A full hour went by, and they were still knee-deep in clothes shopping. Blake had picked four really cute outfits for Claire and two for her mom too. Anne was thrilled as she watched the girls try on clothes, and would giggle at the faces that Blake made at the few times that Claire would attempt to find her own clothes.

When they finished the fashion show and decided on several outfits, Joseph quietly instructed the sales clerk to give him the bill.

"Dad," April said gratefully, "You didn't have to buy all of this. I can get it."

Shrugging off his daughter's words, he said, "Listen honey, I don't get to spend much on you anymore, and I am glad to do it."

"Thank you, anyways," April said again.

Claire and Blake gave Joseph a hug, and thanked him graciously.

As the group left the clothing store and walked down the street, a thought occurred to Claire. She wanted to do a couple of things for April and Blake for Christmas, but she didn't have any money. It wasn't like she had planned on spending a lot, but there were a few meaningful gifts that she wanted to give them. Claire walked closer to Anne and managed to get close enough to whisper that she wanted to ask Anne something in private when she got a chance. Anne shook her head, acknowledging Claire's request, and they both waited for a suitable opportunity.

The next shop was a Christmas ornament store located a few doors down the street. The inside looked like a log cabin, but contained several rooms, all of which showcased Christmas items. While Blake and April veered off to the room on the right, Claire hung back with Joseph and Anne. Joseph walked around one of the showcases, and Claire spotted her opportunity to talk with Anne then.

"I really hate to ask you this, but I don't know what else to do," Claire whispered to Anne as Claire picked up a red cardinal ornament.

"What is it, dear?" Anne asked, wondering what Claire was so concerned about.

Claire didn't like asking for things and almost felt ashamed for asking. "Well, there are a couple of cool things that I would like to get April and Blake for Christmas, but I don't have any money of my own. I mean, they both get me whatever I could ever want and need, so I'm not saying that I don't have anything because they actually have provided me with all that I could ever need." Claire was almost rambling, stalling to get to the point.

"I... I mean... May I borrow some money so I can get them something for Christmas?" Claire blurted out. It was harder than she thought because she didn't want to seem ungrateful for all that she had received thus far.

Anne let out a sigh of relief and with the warmest smile that Claire has ever seen on a person, said, "Oh my gosh, of course you can, sweetie." Anne could see how difficult it was for Claire to ask, but she completely understood her dilemma. "I totally understand and I would be happy to help you," Anne said, giving Claire a quick reassuring hug. "What do you have in mind?" she asked. Claire whispered what she wanted to get April and Blake, and Anne blinked at the thoughtfulness of the gifts. "That would be perfect. They are going to love it."

Anne thought about it for a minute, and told Claire, "You know, why don't we secretly get together next week after school, and I will pick you up and we will go shopping together."

Claire grinned and whispered, "You would do that for me?"

"Yes, of course. It would be my pleasure to go with you," Anne replied honestly. "I'll text you on Sunday night with a day that I can be in town, and we will go. How does that sound?"

Claire nodded her head, and said, "Thank you so much." Claire set the cardinal down back on the shelf, and then added, "I just want you to know how much I truly care for April and Blake. I don't know what my life would have been like right now if it weren't for them. They welcomed me into their home and never looked back. I owe them my life, you know?"

Anne let out a tiny gasp of emotion at the sincerity of Claire's statement. She waved her hand at her eyes to dry a tear that had escaped. "Claire." Anne began, "you are a remarkable young woman, and don't let anyone tell you any different. Ok?"

Claire didn't know if she was supposed to answer, but she said, "Ok, I won't." Just then, Joseph walked up and asked Anne if she had found anything that she wanted. Discreetly wiping what was left of her tears from her cheek, she turned towards her husband and smiled. "Not yet but I am trying my best."

As Claire turned to look at more ornaments, she realized that the moment that she just shared with Anne was her first 'grandmother moment'. She had never had a grandmother figure in her life, so this must be what it was like to have one. April was a few steps away and noticed the look on Claire's face.

"Are you alright?" April asked, curious about why Claire was upset.

Claire's eyes focused on April and what she was asking, and she replied with a twinkle in both eyes, "Yes, very much so. I think that this is the happiest that I have ever been."

"I'm really glad that you are," April said sincerely. "It just looked like something was bothering you."

"Just the opposite, I assure you, April," Claire affirmed. "I was in the middle of a thought that made me reflect, that's all."

"Ok, then," April earnestly, and then waved Claire in her direction. "Come with me, I want to show you something."

Claire eagerly followed April to the adjoining room, stopping at the area in front of a fake fireplace. Hanging on a wall to the right was a peg section of Christmas stockings. Blake walked up behind Claire and pointed at the stockings. "Claire..." Blake began before April could speak, "since you are going to be with us for Christmas, it is important that you pick your Christmas stocking."

Claire looked up at the wall, and then looked at April.

"You see, Claire, it is a Turner tradition that we place our stockings on the mantle of the fireplace on the night of Christmas eve, so that Santa can see them and fill them for Christmas morning. When we put the decorations up, I left the tote with Blake's and my stocking in the closet. Our stockings have our names on them, so we would like you to pick one out so that we can have your name embroidered on it."

Claire looked back at the wall, and said, "Wow, that's is cool. Thank you. I have never had a stocking before."

Before Blake could think about what she was saying, she blurted out, "Really?"

Claire kept looking for a stocking, but in a voice that was a little lower, answered, "Yes, you see, my real mom didn't believe in Christmas, so we never really celebrated. I think that she was upset that she couldn't get me anything worthwhile for Christmas, so she never bothered to hype up the holiday." Claire paused to focus on a stocking that caught her eye. "Then, when I was in foster care with my previous foster family, they celebrated Christmas, but it was a few presents on Christmas morning, however, we never had stockings."

April knew that Claire had had a bad childhood, but listening to the stories of her past, and of how she had never really celebrated Christmas made her heart go out to her. April had already been preparing to make this Christmas a good one for her, but hearing about her past Christmases made April want to give her the best one Claire had ever had. Of course, it wasn't just about the gifts. It was about spending time with each other and creating lasting memories.

"Well, Claire, this year, we are going to change all that," April declared matter-of-factly. "It's time for you to experience a Turner Classic Christmas."

Claire scanned the wall for a few more moments, and then found the stocking that she wanted.

"What do you think of that one?" she pointed at a green one with white trim and a green and white plaid design on the stocking itself.

"Perfect," Blake answered. "It will match the scarf that my mom gave you the first time we met."

Claire looked at it again and Blake was right, it did resemble her scarf.

"Yes, it does," agreed Claire. "That is the one I want then," Claire said proudly.

April got the attention of the sales clerk, who located a pole with the hook on it so that she could grab it and lower it down to Claire. She held it in front of her to examine it more closely. Happy with her decision, Claire held onto it like a teddy bear for a few seconds, and then turned to April. "Thanks again."

"You are very welcome. I can't wait to see it on the mantle," April said.

By the time that they left the ornament store, April had purchased the stocking for Claire, and a beautiful snowman ornament that Blake picked out.

Even though it was snowing and the wind was picking up, Claire and Blake were having a blast shopping. It was fun ducking in and out of the many shops that littered the downtown area.

It was finally time to visit the infamous bookstore from April's childhood. Claire got her second wind and was virtually leading the way with the rest of the group trying to keep up. April could see the same excitement in Claire that she had had when she was a little girl. Blake, on the other hand, was not as excited to go shopping at a bookstore, but she was happy that Claire was enthusiastic.

"This place is awesome!" Claire said in delight. "I am so excited."

Claire went up and down the aisles taking it all in. She would occasionally stop and pull out a book and then put it back and continue looking. April and Claire found themselves talking about some of the books that she had found. April's parents looked around for books that interested them, and they were enjoying themselves just watching how excited April and Claire seemed to be. Blake was only half interested until she found a new book about New York fashion. She removed it from the shelf and began flipping through the pages and then cozied up with it in a La-Z-Boy that was located in a corner on the main floor.

Fifteen minutes later, Claire noticed Blake sitting in the chair with her head buried in the book. Claire walked a little closer and then pulled out her phone and snapped a few pictures of her. Claire put her phone back in her coat pocket and then strolled up to Blake in the chair.

"So, Blake... What are you reading?" Claire questioned, as she squeezed herself in the chair with Blake.

Feeling like a sardine, Blake positioned her butt so she was a little more comfortable and then showed Claire a page with a silver dress in it. "It's a book about the last two years of New York fashion shows." Claire could tell that Blake was really fascinated with the designs that she was looking at.

"Looks cool," Claire said admiringly. "I am totally impressed with your ability to recognize fashion. The way that you can see outfits in your head is remarkable."

"Thanks, Claire Bear," Blake said, adding, "it means a lot to me that you think that I know what I am doing."

"Of course, Blake. Over the past month that I have been with you I have learned more about clothes and makeup than I have in my entire life. I am amazed by how you truly care about trying to get me up to par with all of this stuff."

Blake grinned at Claire, and said, "It's what I do—take care of Claire."

Claire put her hands on the arm of the chair and pushed herself out of it, "Well Blake, you do it well." Claire put her fist up to Blake for a fist bump and Blake immediately bumped her fist, almost as if she had been expecting it. "Boom," Blake said.

"Boom," Claire answered back, and then headed towards a table near the cash registers that had books that were newly out this year. She glanced through the titles and picked one up. It was about a long lost daughter of a billionaire who was reunited with her parent on her twenty-first birthday.

April came up to her and Claire said out loud without realizing that she was speaking, "Maybe my dad is someone like this." As she held up the book, April glanced at the title. Claire suddenly felt childish for even bringing it up. "Oh God. I'm sorry April. I didn't mean to sound so coy about it." Claire quickly put the book back on the table and started to walk away. April put her hand on Claire's shoulder, and said, "It's ok, Claire. It's only natural to want to know about your dad." April studied Claire's eyes to try to see if she could read what was going on in her head.

"I know, April. I know it is," Claire began bashfully. "It's just that I am really happy living with you and Blake, but for some unknown reason, I have had an occasional thought rise up and I briefly wonder about him." Blake overheard the conversation between April and Claire, and she got up from the La-Z-Boy and walked up next to them, listening.

"But then I get very apprehensive about it. What if I do locate him and he doesn't want me. What if he does want me? Will I have to leave you guys?" Claire was becoming frazzled and a little anxious. "I mean, what if he is a drug addict or even something worse? What if he is in prison— like my mom? Can you imagine that?"

"Claire," Blake interrupted, trying to calm her down. "Don't freak out about something that you don't have any information on yet. Besides, if you ever want to look for him, that would be fine. My mom and I would support you."

Claire let out a breath that she hadn't realized she had been holding in.

"Thanks for that, Blake," Claire said, "But here I am having thoughts about me finding my father when you have lost yours. I still remember what Emily said to you when I first met her, and it still bothers me that she would have even implied that to you. I don't want you to think that of me."

Blake sighed, and then explained, "That is not the same. You have never had a dad so you don't know what it is like. I had an awesome dad that loved me with his entire heart. I will always have the knowledge that I was loved and wanted. Now that he is gone, I miss him every day but I will never wonder about him because I had him in my life. So, don't feel bad for wanting to find out about yours."

April was so extremely proud of Blake—she sounded so mature as she spoke to Claire on such a sensitive subject.

"Blake is right," April told Claire. "We will support you, no matter what you decide. You will always be welcome in our house. So don't worry about having to leave if you don't want to."

Claire really didn't mean to cause this much drama over a book, but now she didn't have to worry about losing the Turners no matter what happened if she ever wanted to look for her dad.

"You two are totally awesome, and I am so glad that you found me." Claire said now more relaxed about the situation. "I don't want you to think that I am an emotional mess about this. It just sort of hit me today. If I decide to look for him it's not because I am looking for anyone better than you two. I want you to know that."

"We do," said April, earnestly.

"We know, Claire Bear," Blake said reassuringly, trying to lighten the mood.

Joseph and Anne were listening from around the corner but didn't want to interfere. But now that the discussion seemed to be over, they approached the girls, and Joseph said, "Are you guys ready to go so that we can get home and make some dinner?"

"Sounds great to me," Blake said eagerly.

"Me too," agreed Claire.

Blake put the fashion book back on the shelf and the five of them headed towards the door.

The walk back to the car was quite entertaining. Blake had made a snowball and chucked it at Claire. Of course, Claire retaliated and threw a handful of snow at Blake and then put another handful down Blake's coat. At one point, Blake was walking with her hands in her coat pocket and slipped on an ice patch next to a snow bank. She tried to catch herself from falling but the hands in the pockets prevented her from reaching out to break her fall. Consequently, Blake fell head first into the snow bank.

Claire burst out laughing at the sight of Blake covered in snow. Blake held out her hand so that Claire could help her up. Claire reached out her hand to assist Blake, but Blake grabbed Claire's hand and pulled her down onto the snow bank. Now, both girls were covered in snow from head to toe.

Blake jumped on Claire and yelled, "I'm the queen of the snow pile!" Claire tried to get out from underneath Blake, but because she was partially buried in snow, could not.

"Let me up!" Claire said, through bouts of laughter.

"Make me, Blondie," Blake teased, as she pulled snow from the pile, and spread it all over her chest and face.

Blake released Claire and allowed her to get up. Claire looked like Frosty the Snowman in the greenhouse. A snow-covered, melted mess.

When they got to the car, Claire and Blake were soaking wet. Joseph had started the car about ten minutes before they got to it with an app on his phone, so it was toasty warm when they entered the Jeep.

April opened the back of the jeep and pulled out a grey thermal blanket so that Blake and Claire could wrap themselves up in it. "Here you are, my little wet burritos," April said, as she tucked the blanket over Claire and Blake almost as if she was tucking them in bed.

When they got back to the house, April and Anne prepared dinner while Blake and Claire changed into their bathing suits to warm themselves up by swimming in the pool. Joseph always kept the temperature high because Anne always liked it like bath water.

Blake jumped in first with Claire not far behind. Claire swam the length of the pool and got out of the shallow end and then ran around to the deep end to jump in again. Blake just stayed in the pool, relaxing and swimming. Claire swam to the shallow end again and got out, but instead of going all the way back to the deep end, she stopped halfway at the spot in the pool where Blake was and then jumped in right next to her; causing the splash to engulf Blake.

"That was super cool of you," Blake said joking. "Too bad that I was already wet."

Defending her stunt, Claire simply said, "Yeah, well now you're even wetter than a few seconds ago."

Then she splashed Blake again using her hands to push it towards her face. Blake dove down under water and swam under Claire, grabbed her foot and yanked her under water. Both girls came up from beneath the water laughing.

Claire and Blake swam for another fifteen minutes, and then Blake said, "Hey, why don't we go sit in the hot tub for a few?"

"Let's do it," Claire agreed.

The six-person hot tub was built into the floor in the corner of the pool-house, with steps leading to them.

"Oh," Claire said, as she stepped down into the hot tub. "This is really hot."

Blake was right behind Claire, and offered, "You will get used to it after a minute or so. It's awesome."

Blake was right. After a couple of minutes, Claire was in total relaxation mode, and she was sitting with her back against the wall and had both of her arms on the stretched out on the rim of the hot tub.

"I think that I am in Heaven," Claire said matter-of-factly with her eyes closed, soaking in the moment.

Blake was sitting across from her, but then moved to a seat that allowed a person to be in a more reclined position. "It truly is," Blake answered. "We used to come here more just after my dad died, but because of work and school lately, we don't come here as often as we did earlier."

Thinking of April, Claire opened her eyes, and said, "It must have been really hard for your mom when your dad died."

"It totally was," Blake replied, candidly. "She had lost the love of her life within a split-second, and we didn't even get to say goodbye. She spent the first two years focusing solely on me and making sure that I was ok. Then she kind of dove back into her editing career to fill in the void, you know?"

Blake wasn't getting emotional about the conversation, just the opposite. It felt good to talk to someone about what she and her mom had gone through.

"We still think about him every day, but we are getting along without him. It's still hard around the holidays and birthdays, but as you saw during Thanksgiving, it's slowly getting better."

They sat in silence for a few moments, letting the hot water soak into their skin and the steam of the water dissipate on their faces. "Can I ask you a question?" asked Claire.

"Shoot," Blake said, openly.

"I don't want to upset you with this question but would it be ok with you if your mom wanted to start dating?" Claire asked affectionately. "Your mom is a classy, bright, and beautiful woman who possesses an enormous heart. Would she ever consider trying to find someone else to share her life with?"

A year or so ago, Blake would have told Claire a solid 'No'. But now that she was older and into her teenage years, becoming more aware and mature, Blake had to think about it for a few moments.

"You know," said Blake thoughtfully, "as her daughter, I would hope that the answer is 'yes'. I mean, I'm not that girl that wants her mother to be alone her entire life just because she doesn't want her mom to be with anyone other than her dad. But I am afraid she might get her heart broken again." Blake looked at Claire with concern, and continued, "What if he leaves her or if he turns out to be an ass or something?"

Claire blinked when Blake said the word "ass" because she hardly swore.

Smirking at Claire's reaction, Blake kept with her explanation. "I wouldn't mind a father figure around, but it still might be weird for someone who wasn't my actual father to take me to a daddy-daughter dance. Just saying."

"Besides," Blake said gleefully, "she's got you right now, so I think she has all she can handle." The humor was very evident in her tone as she spoke.

"Ah, no, not really. I am here so that I can help her deal with you. Not the other way around."

Blake smirked at Claire's retort, and said, "Believe what you want, Claire Bear. I know the truth."

"You're the truth," Claire said to Blake, smiling.

"Yes, yes, I am," Blake said, smiling back.

Claire and Blake relaxed in the hot tub for another ten minutes and then decided to get out.

April and Anne had just walked into the pool house when they were getting out.

"I was just coming in to tell you that dinner is going to be ready in about fifteen minutes so you should get ready," April said, as she went up to the girls. "I take it that you are warmed up and toasty now?" April asked.

"Totally," Claire answered. "I was telling Blake that this place is like Heaven. It must have been so cool to grow up here."

Remembering the fun that she had had in the house, April said, "Yes, it was a very enjoyable time in my life, I can honestly say." Then, looking at her mom, April said, "Of course, it just wasn't about the house, I had two great parents who encouraged me to go after my dreams, and so I did. It took me away from them but this place will always be my home away from home."

Anne smiled and praised April, "She was a remarkable child who brought great joy to our lives. We never really had to worry about her." Thinking back, Anne amended, "But there were a few times when April and Crystal got into trouble that caused us a little grief..." Anne let the sentence trail off as if she had more to say on the topic but thought better of it.

April, not wanting to elaborate on things that she and Crystal may or may not have done, changed the subject back to dinner, "You girls better get dried off and dressed."

"You got it, April," Claire replied as she accepted the towel that Anne was now offering her.

"Thanks, Anne," Claire said, as she caped the towel around her back.

"Sure thing, mom." Blake said. "I am getting a little hungry. Swimming with Claire takes a lot of energy so I need my sustenance."

"Yeah?" Claire questioned.

"Yup, it sure does," kidded Blake.

"Come on, Blake. Let's go," Claire motioned for Blake to lead the way back to the bedroom where their clothes were. "Don't want you to pass out from being overworked or anything?"

Claire followed Blake out of the pool area and disappeared into the house.

Anne turned to April, and commented, "You are surely doing a good thing for Claire, you know? She looks happy, healthy, and confident, thanks to you. Can you imagine what might have happened to her if you hadn't plucked her from the streets when you had?"

"Thanks, mom," April said to her mother fondly. "You and dad made me that person that I am today, but, no... I can't imagine where Claire would be right now. I try not to think about what would have happened if she got sick with no one to take care of her." April shook her head at the thought.

"It is hard to think of her not staying with us. She and Blake are like best friends now, and I am thankful that Blake and Claire have found the connection that they have developed. It's nice to see both of them interact with one another."

April and Anne made their way to the kitchen to prepare finish prepping for dinner. Anne was removing the meatloaf from the oven when Claire and Blake walked in.

"Wow, that smells amazing," noted Claire almost immediately. "All of this looks delicious," Claire followed up as she scanned the dining room table.

"Grandma makes a mean meatloaf," Blake said to Claire. "My mom tries to reproduce it at our apartment, but there is something in the way that Grandma makes it that makes it turn out better. We can't explain it."

Not taking offense at all with her daughter's statement because it was true, April merely said, "Unfortunately, she is correct."

Joseph came in from the Great Room, and joined the ladies in the kitchen. Once everything was on the table ready to go, Joseph paused for a few moments to say grace. When he was done, Blake dove right in grasping the tongs next to the meatloaf platter and hastily picking out the nearest two pieces.

At the conclusion of dinner, everyone seated at the table was stuffed beyond belief.

Claire sat back in her chair and put her left hand on her belly. "I am stuffed. Thank you for that wonderful dinner. I think the last time I ate that much in one sitting was at Thanksgiving dinner."

"Glad you enjoyed it, honey," Anne said to Claire gracefully. "It's one of my all-time favorite recipes, and I loved making it for April when she was a little girl."

April got up from the table and said, "Come on girls, help me clear the table so that we can rest our bellies for dessert in the Great Room. Everyone stood up as Blake and Claire started picking up the empty plates. Joseph went into the Great Room to start a fire and they all met in there by the hearth of the fireplace.

As Claire took a spot by the fire next to Blake, she told everyone, "Thank you so much for everything today, you guys. I am so grateful for everyone in this room. You all have been so welcoming to me, and I hope that you know how appreciative I am..." Claire looked at each person in the room. "I just wanted to express my gratitude again to all of you."

Anne spoke up and said kindheartedly, "First, you are very welcome, but it is us who should be thanking you for being such an amazing person. It's our pleasure because you are part of our family now. No longer should you consider yourself as an outsider. You are a member of the Turner family." Anne paused to look at her husband, and he smiled back at her and then turned to smile at Claire.

Anne continued her speech by saying, "We think of you as another granddaughter, Claire. Joseph and I have been talking, and if you would like to call us Grandma and Grandpa, we are fine with that."

Claire looked at Blake to see her reaction to that, and of course, she was grinning from ear to ear.

"I would love to," Claire said amazed with the sudden turn the discussion had taken. "But are you sure? I've only been living with April and Blake for a month, so if you think it's too soon for that, I would completely understand."

"Claire," Joseph began, "We are sure. I would love it if you called me 'grandpa.'" Sneaking a quick glance at Anne, he continued, "We know that you never had grandparents in your life, so we would love to be your grandparents."

Claire got up from the hearth and gave Joseph and Anne a hug. "I don't know what to say, but it means the world to me that you are willing to do that for me. I never had this in my life, so thank you from the bottom of my heart."

April loved her parents, and they always managed to surprise her with their sincerity and compassion. For them to suggest that to Claire not only meant the world to Claire, but to April as well. It made her proud to be their daughter.

By the time the night ended, Blake had affectionately called Claire 'granddaughter' a couple of times to politely tease her but Claire knew that Blake was thrilled with her grandparents for allowing her to call them 'grandma' and 'grandpa'.

The car ride home took a little longer than the trip there because the roads were worse than they were earlier. However, Claire didn't mind at all. She spent most of the time lost in her thoughts. This was the happiest she had been in her entire life. She couldn't believe that this was the way it was supposed to be—a family that truly wanted her and a set of grandparents who cherished her. When they arrived at the apartment and the SUV pulled up to the curb, Claire looked out the side window and declared, "We're home."

CHAPTER SIXTEEN

"GOOD MORNING," APRIL SAID TO BLAKE, AS SHE STROLLED into the kitchen. It was 6:15 a.m. on Monday morning, and Blake had already taken a shower and was dressed for school.

"Is Claire up?" April asked as she put a k-cup coffee in for Blake.

"Yuppers," Blake answered. "I heard the shower going when I left my room to come down here," Blake replied, as she planted her butt on the bar stool of the kitchen island waiting for breakfast to be served.

April removed the mug from the coffeemaker and carefully set it on the island next to Blake.

"Do you have any tests this week?" April asked, curious like any mother would be about tests and quizzes.

"Yes," Blake said, almost sneering at the thought of it. "I have a test in Civics tomorrow, and I have a quiz in Earth Science on Wednesday."

April turned the stove on to warm up the pan for scrambled eggs, and asked, "Are you ready for them?"

Blake had just pulled her phone out to type a text to Emily and paused to answer. "I'm pretty sure I know it. I just have to study for Earth Science tomorrow night." Blake turned her attention back to her phone, and immediately began texting.

By the time the eggs were finished, Claire had made her way to the kitchen.

"Good morning, everyone," Claire announced to April and Blake. She took the barstool next to Blake and then grabbed Blake's coffee and took a sip.

"Hey," Blake complained, sounding only mildly offended. "Get your own."

"Oh, I will," Claire smiled, "but the coffee from your mug always tastes better."

Blake grabbed her mug and glanced in it as if to look for the reason why it possessed a better taste. She then reached in her school bag, took out her iPad, loaded up the fashion app, and brought up a design that she had been working on.

"What do you think of this?" she asked Claire, as she tilted the screen in her direction.

"Holy crap, Blake, it looks totally cool," Claire said impressed. "That dress is beautiful."

"Thanks," Blake said gratefully. "I've been working on this for the past week or so. I spent an hour last night just adjusting the hem line."

"Well, whatever you did, I like it," Claire said, sounding truly impressed with Blake's fashion sensibilities. For someone who was only fourteen years old, Blake had an eye for design that rivaled all the well known designers, at least in Claire's opinion.

April scooped up the eggs from the pan and placed them on the plates on the counter. She handed Blake and Claire a plate, and then put the rest on her plate.

"Thanks for breakfast," said Claire, as she shoveled in a forkful of eggs.

"Yeah, thanks mom," Blake said, as she took a bite of toast and continued to examine the dress that she had designed.

"You guys are very welcome," said April, as she smiled at the two girls. April was pleased with how things were turning out and how natural it felt for Claire to be there. It was almost like she had been living with them for years instead of weeks.

Claire got up to get herself a cup of coffee. "What do you have planned for today?" she asked April, as she waited for her coffee to brew.

April finished chewing her eggs, and answered, "Well, I have a meeting with another new author. This is her first book, but early indications are that it will be well-received." April took a sip of coffee once it was finished, and then continued, "I also have a conference call with Monica Towers about setting an outline for the sixth book. After that, I will be going over some manuscripts that have been sitting on my desk for several days now."

Claire nodded thoughtfully. "Sounds like you have an action-packed day," and then added, "it must be so exciting to edit authors and help them shape their books. I would love to do that."

April grinned at Claire's statement. "Yes, I am lucky that I got into a career that I absolutely enjoy," April paused, and then added, "I don't know what I would be doing if I wasn't an editor. I never had a backup plan."

Blake looked up from her iPad, and smirked, "Good thing you didn't need a backup. I would hate to be the daughter of a doctor or a lawyer."

"I don't know, Blake," April started to joke, "I think that I would have made a great psychiatrist. I mean I have been dealing with you for years now."

"Very funny," Blake replied bemused. "My mind is so in tune with the world that I could be a piano and you wouldn't even notice."

April looked at Blake for further explanation on what she meant, but did not get any.

Claire enjoyed the banter between Blake and April. She realized that she had never experienced anything close to the relationship that April and Blake shared. April, of course, was motherly and a compassionate person, but there was a special bond between the two of them. It was almost like they were best friends too. April actually wanted to spend time with her.

Claire took a bite of her eggs and removed her phone from her back pocket. Shelly had sent her a text. Claire read it and then asked April, "Would it be ok if I went downtown with Shelly after school for a couple of hours? She needs to pick up a few things and wants to know if I can go with her."

"Sure, of course," April answered. "Just text me your location, and also when you are on your way home. I just worry—that's all."

Claire nodded her head, and replied, "Thanks, and I will," Claire typed her response on the keypad, and then set the phone on the counter next to her plate. April caught a glance at the lock screen on her phone, and it was a picture of Claire and her—the picture that she had taken of the two of them on Thanksgiving night when she had received the phone. April smiled to herself. She really did care for Claire and had grown incredibly fond of her in such a short amount of time.

The girls finished their breakfast, and after they put their plates in the dishwasher, headed out for school.

"Have a great day at school," April said to them as she headed towards the apartment office to retrieve a printout before she headed to Priscilla Publishing.

"Bye, mom, see you tonight," Blake said, as she stepped into the elevator.

"Bye, April, thanks for letting me go tonight. I'll see you later," Claire managed to get in before the elevator doors closed.

* *

BLAKE WAS TIRED. REALLY TIRED. IT WAS THE SECOND period, and she was halfway through gym class. Over the last couple of months, it was basically the same routine. Compete twenty five jumping jacks, do 30 situps, try to do twenty pushups, and then run laps around the gym. Usually Blake did ten laps, but here she was, on the third lap and her lungs felt like they were going to explode and her limbs felt fatigued.

"Are you alright?" Emily asked from behind her. Emily was already on her fourth lap, and was coming up on Blake doing her third. Blake was practically at walking pace.

"I'm pooped," Blake admitted. "I don't think that I can finish the laps," she said, her face redder than usual. She sounded winded.

Emily walked with her to the sideline, and approached Mrs. Fields, the gym teacher.

"I'm sorry Mrs. Fields, but I can't finish the laps. I am really tired today," Blake said as she bent down and put both hands on her thighs. Her breathing sounded labored.

Mrs. Fields ran a tight ship, but she was a compassionate teacher. She knew when to drive the students beyond to get more out of them, but she also could tell by looking at Blake that she needed a rest.

"Ok, Turner," Mrs. Fields said. "Go grab a water and have a seat on the bleachers." It wasn't like Blake to try to get out of doing the activities, so Mrs. Fields knew that this wasn't a ploy to get out of working out.

Blake gave Emily a 'thumbs-up' as Emily returned to the gym floor to continue with her laps.

The cold water felt good going down as Blake sat there regaining her strength. Blake felt totally fine today, and didn't think that she was getting sick. Her throat was fine and she didn't even have a headache. She was just exhausted.

When everyone else had finished with the laps, Mrs. Fields brought out the playground balls and then divided the class into two teams. She had always made up the teams by saying this half of the room or by handing out different color shirts so that no one would ever be picked last.

The game was dodge ball, and it was the least of Blake's favorite games to play. However, it was also one of the least tiring games to play because you could mainly stand in one or two spots on the floor and try to swerve out of the way of incoming balls. Blake was relieved because she physically didn't feel like dribbling a basketball up and down the court or running drills around orange cones. Dodge ball would do just fine today.

Even though Blake did try, she would occasionally let a ball hit her so that she could be out for the rest of that particular match.

By the time gym class was over, Blake felt like her normal self again and her color was less flushed than it was twenty minutes prior.

As they were changing out of their gym clothes in the locker room, Emily asked Blake if she was feeling better. "Yeah," Blake said, as she grabbed for her winter green sweater and began placing it over her head. "I just felt a little weak and really tired, but now I'm perfectly fine."

"Well, that's good," Emily smiled. "You looked a little flushed there for a minute."

Blake reached in her locker and pulled out a green and white headband that matched her outfit, and positioned it on her head and then said. "I'm all good now. Nothing to worry about."

The two friends walked out of the locker room and headed for the gym door.

"Hey, Blake," Emily said. "Do you want to go with me to Cindy's Cupcakes after school?"

Blake could see the sincerity in Emily's face, and she knew that Emily was trying to get them back to where they were as friends earlier.

"Yeah, sure," Blake replied. "Sounds like fun. I'll text my mom at lunch and I'm sure it will be fine."

"Cool," Emily smiled at Blake's answer, and then they parted ways to head to different classes.

Blake went to her locker to get her math book. On the way there, Rose stopped her in the hallway to ask her a question. "Hey, Blake," Rose began as she stopped Blake. "How's it going?"

Blake had only talked to Rose a couple of times because she was seated with Claire, but Rose was nice to Blake and she seemed really cool.

"Good," Blake answered, now standing in front of her. "How's it going with you?"

"Good, real good. Hey, I was wondering if maybe sometime we could sit together during lunch and go over a couple of ideas for dresses for the Winter

Formal? I think that I want to go, but I don't have any idea about what would look good on me. I don't like to dress up, and I know that fashion is your thing."

"Of course," Blake beamed as a smile formed on her face. "I would love to."

"Cool, thanks," Rose said. "Maybe sometime this week?"

"Whenever works for you, Rose," Blake replied, honestly. "I'm good any time."

"Sweet, Turner," Rose said cheerfully. "I appreciate it," Rose said, as she smiled and walked away in the direction opposite to where Blake was headed. *Wow, that was cool,* Blake thought. Winter Formal was still over a month away, but it was time to start planning what she and Claire would be wearing. It was then that she realized that she and Claire had not discussed it, so she didn't know if Claire would want to go. Of course she will go, Blake thought. Trevor would definitely be going, and Blake couldn't imagine him not asking Claire.

Blake got to her locker, collected her math book and headed towards her third hour class.

I can't wait for lunch to talk to Claire about the Winter Formal. Blake smiled inwardly and found herself already starting the dress designing process in her mind.

* *

AS FAR AS SCHOOL DAYS WENT, THIS ONE WAS GOING ALONG pretty nicely. During first hour Biology, Claire and Shelly teamed up to do an experiment, while Brie and Rose were partnered up. Brie seemed to be in an uncharacteristically good mood during the entire hour, and Claire wondered about it in amusement. When the bell rang to release the class, Rose and Shelly told Claire that they were going to meet her by her locker after her third hour so that they could walk to the lunchroom together.

Second hour with Mr. Reed was, of course, awesome. They had started reading a book that Claire had always wanted to read, but had not had the time. English Lit was her favorite class and it showed. She earned straight As on all the homework, and could write brilliant, well thought out essays about the story and its characters.

Third hour was more challenging for Claire. Political Science was clearly not her favorite class, but she was holding her own. She had to work a little harder at it, but she was maintaining a B average. During class, Trevor was his regular charming self and had on a couple of occasions made Claire abruptly laugh out loud. Claire knew that she liked him and had lowered her guard down when it came to him. When the class ended, Trevor and Claire walked slowly out of the door together, and had stopped just a few steps outside of class in the hallway.

"I have a scheduled ten-minute meeting with the coach right now, but I will see you when I get done," Trevor told Claire.

"Sounds good," Claire smiled. "Shelly and Rose are meeting me at my locker anyways, and then we are going to go to lunch so that's cool."

Just a split-second before they parted, Claire got the feeling that Trevor was pausing—pausing for a kiss? She couldn't be sure but there was definitely a look in his eyes like he wanted to go in for a kiss.

Not wanting to seem awkward, Claire kept going in the opposite direction. As she walked down the hallway, a boy she didn't know came up to her, and said, "Here you go," and handed her a handful of change. He didn't stop or say anything else, and kept going.

How odd, Claire thought as she looked at the coins in her hand, amounting to eighty-three cents. Thinking that he had her confused with someone else, she kept going towards her locker. About halfway there, she ran into Shelly, who was making her way to Claire's locker.

Just as Claire came up to Shelly, a blonde senior girl, who Claire had recognized as one of the cheerleaders from Friday's basketball game came up to her, and handed her about five quarters.

"Here, you need this more than I do," the cheerleader smirked as she walked away.

Noticing the dumbfounded look on Claire's face, Shelly asked, "What was that about?"

Claire raised her hand to show Shelly the coins in her hand. "I don't know," she said, confused. "That is the second person to just hand me money."

"I wished that would happen to me," Shelly kidded. "It has mostly been people wanting to borrow money from me." Shelly shrugged it off until another kid came up to Claire and laughed saying, "Don't spend it all in one place," and proceeded to almost throw the coins at her.

"What the hell is going on?" Claire demanded in a raised voice as she was becoming annoyed, but as Claire and Shelly rounded the corner to her locker, she got her answer.

Taped to her locker was a neon orange poster board with a picture of her in the middle. It looked like it was taken in Biology class without her knowledge. Surrounding her picture were brochures and flyers about homeless shelters and runaway facilities in the Illinois area. Spelled out in big, bold letters were the lines, "Please donate your spare change to Claire Forrester! She is a runaway, homeless girl, begging for money!"

Claire stopped in her tracks and was mortified. "Oh my God!" Claire exclaimed, her mind reeling from what she was seeing. It was like she was dreaming and was naked in class and wondered what had happened to her clothes.

"What is that?" Shelly questioned as she read the sign. "Is that true?"

Claire leaned against the locker next to her, as if all the air was let out of her body. "Yes," she whispered. "It's true."

At that very moment, Rose came running up to Claire's locker with one of the flyers in her hands. "What is this shit?" she asked. You could tell that she was really pissed at the person who was responsible for it.

"It's true," Claire said again, as tears began to cascade down her cheeks. In a deflated voice, Claire began to explain her life. She told them about her mother being a junkie, and how she was currently in jail. She told them about her dad who didn't want her. She told them about how she had to run away from Seattle, but she left out the part about almost being raped. Continuing her explanation, she revealed how April and Blake Turner had discovered her on the streets down and out, and how they had welcomed her into their home even though she was severely sick with the flu for several days, and probably would have died alone in the streets if it weren't for them.

Just as she was finishing up her story, a sophomore boy who had seen the poster board in another hallway, approached Claire with a handful of change. Before he could open his mouth to say a snide remark, Shelly in her deep Irish accent yelled, "Fuck off!" and slapped the coins right out of his hands. Shocked by the intensity of the slap, he paused there for a second looking at the coins rolling about the hallway floor.

Rose gave the kid a sneer, and snapped, "Hey, can't you hear? Piss off! We are having a moment here!" The kid did an about-face and quickly disappeared in the direction in which he had come, rubbing his bruised hand.

Shelly was the first to speak after Claire had finished. "Claire, this doesn't change a thing about how we feel about you. You are a really cool person, and we like you no matter what. Please don't be ashamed."

Nodding her head in agreement, Rose reiterated Shelly's statement. "Truly, Claire, you are our friend, and we will support you. I just can't believe that you have been through so much." With that thought, Rose wondered, "Hey, who the hell would do this to you?"

Claire's first thought was that it might be Emily. She was the only other person besides Blake in the entire school who knew her situation and how she had come to be with the Turners. But why would Emily do this now? She and Blake were almost back to where they were earlier, and she was actually civil to Claire now.

"It was Brie," a female voice spoke up. Audrey Vince was in the same grade as Claire, but Claire didn't have her in any classes. She had only said 'hi' to her once or twice before.

"What?" Claire asked, as if she had not heard the name correctly.

"It was Brie Dixon," Audrey repeated. "I saw her tape on the poster just before the bell rang. I was late for the third period and had to go to my locker, and she had just taped up the sign. She was with another one of the cheerleaders and I heard them say that this was the last one. I think that there might be more throughout the hallways."

"That bitch!" Shelly yelled. "I'm going to kick her ass!" She was now beyond pissed that Brie would do this to Claire.

"No, you're not," Rose declared matter-of-factly. There was a brief pause as Shelly looked at Rose quizzically, as if to ask, *why not?*

"You're not going to kick her ass... I am!" Rose exclaimed, almost spitting out the words.

Claire was still in a state of shock and mortification. She couldn't believe that this was happening to her. Now everyone in the entire school would know that she had just been homeless, wandering the streets.

With tears still escaping from her eyes, she held up her hand between Shelly and Rose. "No. I need to take care of this." Claire took a moment to wipe the tears from her face, and then she tore some of the brochures and flyers from the poster board, and then began walking in the direction of the lunchroom. Shelly and Rose walked directly behind her, as if to show that they had her back.

When Claire was almost near the lunchroom, Blake came running up from behind, and in an exasperated voice, asked, "Claire, I just saw the sign. Are you ok?"

"No," Claire replied honestly, as Blake stopped her to hug her, "but I'm going to be soon."

Blake followed Claire, Shelly, and Rose into the lunchroom as Claire scanned the tables. Brie was sitting at her usual table, and was with some of her cheerleader friends. Brie's back was facing the entrance, so she didn't see Claire walk in.

As Claire and the trio behind her approached Brie's table, the cheerleader sitting across from Brie noticed Claire, and signaled to Brie that someone was approaching.

Brie had just turned around to face Claire when Claire threw the flyers and brochures at her.

"Very funny, Brie!" Claire yelled. "What the hell is your problem?" Claire seriously wanted to know.

"I just don't like liars," Brie replied, smugly.

The tears were still flowing down her cheeks but Claire's eyes were wide with anger and disdain.

"Or is it that you don't like me talking to Trevor!" Claire countered. "I mean, what the fuck, Brie. I have done nothing to you. I didn't take Trevor from you! You two had been broken up weeks before I even got here." Claire paused to take a quick breath and continued, "Besides, he has been pursuing me. Get the picture?"

"Yeah, well..." Brie stammered trying to defend her actions, "you lied about who you are!"

"Did I? Did I?" Claire blurted out. She looked at the students seated on the surrounding tables and yelled out to the entire lunchroom. "Hey everyone, gather around. I've got something to say."

The lunchroom immediately became quiet except for the shuffle of students moving closer to Brie and Claire. If there was going to be a fight, there was definitely going to be an audience.

"Listen up, everyone. Here is the deal," Claire spoke up with a determination that she didn't quite know she had in her. Maybe it was the confidence that April and Blake had helped her develop over the past few weeks, or maybe it was her terrible past that she couldn't seem to run away from. Whatever it was, Claire was letting it all out.

Looking directly at Brie but yelling to the entire lunchroom, Claire began, "My name is Claire Forrester and I was homeless. Is that what you want to hear?" Brie was about to say something but Claire held up her hand and cut her off.

"That's right everyone, I was scared and alone on the streets of Chicago for four months! I stayed at shelters whenever I could, but there were times when I didn't know where my next meal was coming from!" Claire's voice was getting louder as she confessed the story of her life.

"Do you know why I got in that situation?" she asked the crowd. "Let's see, my dad left my mom when she was pregnant with me. And my mom was a junkie most of my life! She was in and out of jail several times when I was a little girl, and now she is serving some serious prison time in Washington for almost killing someone in a car accident. She doesn't even want to see me because she thinks that my life will be even more messed up than it was!"

Brie tried to jump in, but Claire yelled at her, and said, "No. You don't get to talk right now! You wanted everyone to know, and I'm letting everyone know."

By now, the entire lunchroom was entranced by the discussion that was unfolding. If it wasn't for Claire's voice, you could almost hear a pin drop.

"So, here I was down and out on the streets of Chicago, alone and hungry, scared out of my mind, not knowing what I was going to do," Claire said, pausing for a brief second to wipe more tears from her fierce eyes. She turned and looked at Blake.

"That was when April and Blake Turner found me and took me in. They bought me lunch and then let me spend the night. The next day I got the flu, and if I wasn't with them, I probably would have died on the streets!"

Claire's voice almost became a sob. "I might have died. Do you understand?"

There was a slight rumbling that came over the crowd as the reality of her plight sank in.

"So, total strangers welcomed me into their lives and I can't believe how lucky I am. Would any of you do that? Would you?"

Claire paused to give Blake a hug in front of everyone. "I can't imagine my life today if they hadn't found me," Claire said again, in case anyone still didn't get it.

Claire glared at Brie, and with a voice that resounded throughout the entire room said, "So, thank you so much for making fun of me. I hope that you made everyone laugh so that they can feel better about their lives. God, I wish for once that girls like you would get a fucking clue about the realities of life!" Claire turned her attention to the crowd, and said in a slightly lower voice, "I refuse to have you or anyone else make me feel like I am anything less than human."

If anyone in the room had considered teasing Claire, those thoughts were now gone. The stares of disdain were now focused on Brie and Brie alone.

The color drained from her face, and for the first time since Claire had arrived, Brie felt ashamed... really ashamed. It became crystal clear that Brie should not have acted like this. Mortified by her own actions, Brie sat there, speechless and alone. The other cheerleaders had slowly moved away from her, and she was now the focus of intense scrutiny.

Rose and Shelly were completely shocked by what they had just witnessed with their new friend, Claire. Shelly slowly put her hand on Claire's shoulder in a show of support. Rose followed suit, and it was at that moment that Claire realized that she had two really great friends who would be there for her.

Claire slowly turned around and embraced her friends. Blake gave her another hug, and the four of them turned away from Brie and started to walk out of the lunchroom. When they got about halfway to the door, the entire room erupted in applause for Claire. Brie was so embarrassed that she stood up and ran in the other direction as fast as she could.

In the group of students in the lunchroom was Emily. She had witnessed Claire's entire tirade, and realized that she was the one who was basically responsible for Brie's actions. If she hadn't told her about Claire, this never would have happened.

Emily came up to Blake and Claire as they stepped out into the hallway, and was about to apologize for her role in what Brie had done, but Blake saw her first and stopped her with a venomous look in her eyes. "Don't even talk to us right now!" Blake exclaimed. "How could you?" Blake was so upset with her friend that she raised her voice. "Seriously, Emily, it's like I don't even know you anymore!"

The only words that Emily could get out before Blake turned away from her were, "I'm sorry."

The four of them walked back to Claire's locker and removed the poster board.

"I'll go and get the others," Rose said, as she darted towards the north side of the school.

Shelly and Blake stood next to Claire as she ripped the flyers and brochures into little pieces.

"Why do people have to be so mean?" Claire said to the shredded paper as it hit the floor.

"Why?" she demanded, again to no one in particular.

Shelly leaned against the locker and sighed as she spoke. "I don't know Claire, I really don't. Maybe it makes some people feel better about their shitty lives if they show that there are others out there that have it worse."

"Apparently so," Claire tried to grin at Shelly's analysis. "I haven't done anything to her, like at all. I tried to get to know her, but right from the beginning she has had this chip on her shoulder against me."

Rose had come back a few minutes later with three more signs and a handful of flyers. "I think I got it all."

"Thanks, Rose," Blake said. "I hope that no one will come up to her again."

Rose looked at Shelly, and said with a protective gaze, "Well, if anyone is stupid enough to approach her, we will put them in their place."

"Damn right," Shelly agreed. "Bring it on."

Fortunately, Shelly and Rose didn't have to worry about that because the students that did approach Claire were coming up to show support. A few cheerleaders even came up to Claire to say that they were sorry about the things that had happened to her and told her to ask them if she needed anything.

It was then that Trevor came up to Claire's locker. "Are you alright? I went to the lunchroom after my meeting and everyone was talking about what happened. I can't believe that Brie would do that." He was sounding more and more angry as he spoke.

Claire looked at him with big, unyielding eyes. "So, now you know about me... and where I came from. What do you think of me now?" Claire bashfully looked at Trevor, as though she had committed a crime.

"Yeah, sure I do," insisted Trevor. "This doesn't change the way I feel about you, ok?"

Claire smiled at Trevor, and asked, "Are you sure? How would that look, you dating the homeless girl?"

Even though it sounded kind of funny, Claire was very serious with this question.

"It will look just fine," Trevor said with conviction. "Besides, you're not homeless now? Right? You have a nice place with Blake Turner and her mom. So, in reality, you have a home."

Claire liked how Trevor rationalized her predicament, and was comforted by his words. Even though she put Brie in her place in front of half the student body, Claire still felt embarrassed and unsettled.

Lunch hour was winding down. Claire, Blake, Shelly, Rose, and Trevor had chosen to sit on the floor by Claire's locker to finish out the remaining time left. A few minutes before the bell rang, Claire turned to the group and said numbly, "Do you guys mind if I leave for the rest of the day? I just want to go home and rest."

Turning to Shelly, she said, "I'm sorry, can I take a rain check for afterschool?"

"Sure, of course," Shelly said. "We are here for you—so do whatever you need to do."

Blake wanted to go with Claire, but Claire told Blake that she had better stay in school. Claire promised Blake that she would go straight home and text her when she got there. Trevor wanted to drive her home, but all Claire wanted to do was to be alone.

Claire told the office that she wasn't feeling well, but news of what happened had already made its way there. The vice-principal told her that she could go home and that he was going to investigate what had happened.

Because it was cold and snowing out, walking all the way to the apartment was out of the question so she had a car come from the apartment building to pick her up.

It was 12:30 p.m. when she got home and she texted Blake right away before she forgot. Claire decided to make herself a cup of hot chocolate and fell on the living room couch crying. As the memory of the sign on her locker reared up, Claire began to cry even more.

Claire wrapped herself up in the blanket and turned on the television. Her emotions were on a roller-coaster ride, and all she wanted to do was hide.

The sound of the elevator doors opening made Claire look away from the screen, and she saw April walk into the apartment. Claire didn't know but Blake had called her mom from school and told her what had happened. April had left work to head straight home. April was holding a handful of mail that she had retrieved before entering the elevator. On top of the pile was a postcard from St. Louis from Addison James. It had been a few months since she had got a postcard from her, and it was a nice surprise receiving it today. April made a mental note to text her later, but as she set the mail down on the side table, all she wanted to do was to be there for Claire.

April had this look of compassion and comfort on her face, and Claire could tell that April knew. Claire was about to get up, but April sat down next to her and held her. Claire was going to say something, but only sobs came out.

"It's ok, honey," April reassured her. "Let it out."

Claire wrapped her arms around April, and held her tight. "Why? Why did this have to happen?" Claire sobbed. "Am I that terrible to be around?"

Not releasing her hold on Claire, April squeezed her even more and whispered in her ear, "Absolutely not. You are a wonderful person and a beautiful girl." After a few moments, April finally released Claire, and wiping the tears from Claire's cheek, she said, "Listen to me. I know that you are a beautiful, smart, confident, and brave young lady who was dealt a bad hand in the beginning of her life. But over the last month, I have witnessed you overcome your past and start a new chapter in your life." April paused to wipe a tear from her own eye that was making its way down her face. "You are one of the bravest women I have ever met, and I am honored to have you here with me. And as for Brie, she will someday realize that the way she treats other people will reflect on her as a person. Life has a way of coming back to bite you in the butt when you treat others badly."

Claire chuckled at April's analogy, and said, "I hope you're right. It just seems that girls like her always win." Claire leaned back on the couch, and said, "It's not that I want to win all the time, but I would like to be allowed in the game, you know?"

"Don't worry, Claire. I totally believe that you are in the game and you know what? You are winning. You have a few really good friends at school. You have this Trevor boy that likes you. And, of course, you have Blake and me."

Claire loved the way that April could listen to her and comfort her with words of wisdom and compassion. Claire's heart was opening up for the first time in her life in regards to family and friends and it all felt like a dream, almost like she was living someone else's life, but she wasn't. This was her new life.

As Claire sat there next to April, a thought occurred to her. "April, aren't you supposed to be at work?"

April gave her a sideways glance and said, "Blake called and told me what happened. I cancelled my appointments for the rest of the day and came straight home."

"I'm sorry," Claire began to apologize.

"Don't give it another thought," April said compassionately. "This is what I do. I take care of my kids, so don't even worry about it."

Claire immediately picked up on the word "kids" and knew that April considered her one of her own. Being a foster parent wasn't a job to her, but just a continuation of what she had already been doing—being a parent.

April got up from the couch and headed for the kitchen. "I have just the thing that will help you through this." Claire looked at April in slight wonder, as April opened up the freezer and pulled out a gallon of Rocky Road ice cream, and then collected two spoons from the drawer.

"When I was a teenager and was sad or distraught, Crystal would come over and we would sit in my bedroom and devour an entire gallon of ice cream." April took up the spot next to Claire on the couch and handed her a spoon. "Desperate times call for desperate measures, so dig in."

Claire grinned and accepted the spoon. April held up her spoon and they both clinked them together before diving into the newly opened gallon. April reached for the remote control and selected a movie that she had purchased years ago. "If you don't mind, I've got just the movie for us to watch to get our minds off of this."

Claire took a spoon full of ice cream and replied, "Sure, whatever you want."

April smiled and pressed play on the movie. It was *Breakfast at Tiffany's*.

Blake walked through the elevator doors, and the first thing that she saw was her mom and Claire together on the couch wrapped in a blanket with an empty gallon ice cream container on the coffee table in front of them.

Blake set her school bag down and immediately took up the spot next to Claire on the opposite side of where her mom was.

"How are you doing?" Blake asked Claire, as she looked at her and then at the empty ice cream container.

"Better now," Claire said, realizing that she was no longer as upset as she had been when she first got home. Then glancing at the empty ice cream container, she said, "Your mom has a way of making things better."

Smirking, Blake agreed. "Yes, mom and Rocky Road have helped me with my early teenage years."

Blake's tone turned more serious and she said, "By the way, I think that Brie got into trouble with the school for that stunt she pulled. I saw her being walked out of the office by the vice-principal after the fourth hour, and word around the school is that she may have gotten suspended."

April was relieved that at least the school took what Brie did seriously. "Well, I hope that she learns her lesson through all of this."

"Me too," Claire said, "I don't feel like handling more drama from her. And I hope she doesn't retaliate against me."

Blake offered, "I don't think she will. I bet it would be worse for her if she did."

"I hope so," Claire sighed, "I hope so."

The three of them sat together on the couch, all wrapped up in the same blanket for another hour just flicking through channels. Then, Blake received a text and she looked at the screen.

"No, I don't think so," Blake said, sounding angry. Looking at Claire, she said, "It's Emily, and she is downstairs, wants to come up and talk to Claire."

Blake was about to text her back stating something like 'no f---king way,' but Claire turned to April, and said, "I'll talk to her."

Blake looked at Claire, and boldly said, "You don't have to talk to her because you think that she is still my friend, because she is not... anymore."

"I mean, seriously, I don't even want to see her again considering what she did to you," Blake said, obviously hurt by Emily's involvement in the incident and what she considered a violation of their friendship.

Deep down, Claire really didn't want to talk to Emily, but there was something in that discussion that she had with April that made her think that she should hear her out.

"Blake," Claire sighed. "Text her back and tell her to come up. I want to hear what she has to say for herself."

Blake gave Claire a look as if to say 'are you crazy' but conceded and sent the text.

April started to get up from the couch to give Claire and Emily some privacy, but Claire held her hand and said, "Please stay, I want you here with me."

"Ok, I will," said April, sitting back down in the same spot.

A couple of minutes went by and Emily entered the apartment. She knew that she had lost whatever friendship she had with Blake, but knew that she had to try to explain that she never expected this to happen or that she was involved in any way. Emily stood in front of the couch and it was almost like standing in front of the Spanish Inquisition.

Looking directly at Claire, while trying to avoid Blake's stare, she began, "Please, Claire, believe me when I say that I am truly sorry." Emily felt like a little girl whose hand was caught in the cookie jar.

"I didn't mean for any of this to happen," Emily said remorsefully. "It was during practice last week that she was talking to another cheerleader about you, and was wondering about your story. I don't know why I spoke up, but I did." Emily's eyes were focused on Claire as she spoke. "I told her about you being homeless and how you had run away." As she explained what happened, Emily became more and more embarrassed by her actions. "I didn't tell her to be mean to you or to have this happen. I guess, I was caught up in my own jealousy which made me think it was alright to tell Brie about you."

Emily then glanced at Blake too, and said with every ounce of sincerity that she could muster, "I am so sorry."

Blake started to say something not so nice to Emily, but Claire squeezed her hand, making her stop.

She looked at Blake and then turned to Emily, and asked, "What did you have to be jealous about? Right from the beginning I told Blake that I didn't want to cause any distress among her friends."

"I don't know," Emily began. "I... I just felt that she wanted to spend more time with you, and I felt left out," Emily said, trying to vocalize what she had felt towards Claire. But as she tried to explain, the rationale felt stupid and petty to Emily. "I couldn't understand why Blake was so taken by you. We had been friends for years, and then when you came, it was like all she could talk about was you."

"Emily," Claire said, as she stood up from the couch. "I was so eager to meet you because Blake told me all about your friendship over the years. You can't imagine what it is like to be placed in one foster home after another, and then to have to run away to escape some really scary shit," Claire's voice was rising in intensity. "To be on the streets, cold and alone, not knowing where your next meal is going to come from was very frightening. Can't you understand that? I can't imagine where I would be right now if it wasn't for them," Claire said, spinning around to gesture towards April and Blake. "You should be proud that your best friend would do this for someone. How would you feel if it was you in my position? To be able to finally be with a nice family and go to a school where I made a couple of really cool friends, and then to have someone like Brie throw my past in my face, and be mean enough to tell the entire school!"

Emily realized in that moment that she had been a bitch to Claire, and that she had never had a good reason to be so mean. "You're right, Claire," Emily confessed. "I should've been nicer to you. I'm sorry." Then Emily looked at Blake, and asked, "Can you forgive me? I still want you as my friend."

Blake was still upset from the incident with Brie and the way that Emily had acted towards Claire from the beginning. She was unsure if she still wanted to be Emily's friend.

"I don't know, Emily," Blake said honestly. "I need time to think about it."

"Oh, ok," said Emily, sounding hurt. She hoped that at least there was still a chance to save their friendship.

"I better go," Emily said, turning her attention back to Claire. "Again, I am sorry about telling Brie about you, Claire. I didn't expect any of this to happen."

Claire only nodded and then April spoke up, "Thanks for coming over, Emily. I'll walk you out."

When April and Emily got to the elevator doors, Emily turned to April, and said, "I am really sorry, Mrs. Turner, I hope that they can forgive me..."

"I'm sure they will—just give them both some time. You have been Blake's best friend for years so I'm sure you guys will find your way back," April reassured Emily as she entered the elevator. "Be careful going home."

"I will. Bye, Mrs. Turner. Thanks," Emily said, as the doors closed.

Claire and Blake hung out watching YouTube and playing video games. Both of their phones were blowing up from students wanting to show support to Claire. Because April had left work early, she spent a little time in her home office catching up on emails and doing some manuscript reading. But she checked on the girls more often than usual. It was an emotional day for all three of them.

April was extremely proud of how Claire had handled Brie, and hoped that her past wouldn't cause her more heartache. Claire needed to escape the stigma of being homeless and be allowed to grow into the person that she was meant to be. As April thought about that, it occurred to her that because of her, Claire would have a chance to be anything that she wanted.

It was getting late so April went to tell the girls 'good night'. When she came up to Claire's room she could hear Claire talking to Blake.

"You don't know what it meant to me that April came home today from work to comfort me," April overheard Claire say. She could hear the heartfelt conviction in Claire's voice. "Seriously, Blake. I never had that. Ever. To have her come up to me and just hug me and tell me that it was going to be ok... I just want you to know that your mom is the best, you know what I mean?" Claire said.

April heard Blake reply, "Yeah, I know. She is the best mom ever, and I am really lucky to have her." And then she joked, "But if you tell her that, I will deny it."

April smiled and blinked away a happy tear. She paused for a few moments to not make it look like she had overheard their conversation and took a few steps back. Now, stepping towards the door, April called out, "Good night, young ladies, it's time for bed."

"Good night, mom," Blake said as she got up from Claire's bed to head towards her room.

"Night, April," Claire said, getting up from the bed. "Thanks for everything today. I really appreciate it."

"You are very welcome, sweetheart," April replied. "I hope that you are feeling at least a little better and ready to face the day tomorrow?"

Claire sighed, and tried to give April a positive grin. "I hope so."

* *

THE NEXT FEW DAYS AT SCHOOL PROVED TO BE OVER-whelming for Claire. She never would have guessed that she wouldn't have gotten teased. In fact, contrary to her expectations, she had kids coming up to her wish her well, and saying they were glad that she was living with the Turners. Apparently Brie did get suspended for three days. She was scheduled to return on Friday—the last day of school before Christmas break.

Tuesday afternoon, April received a phone call from the school, wanting to know if she would be available to attend a meeting with the Principal and Brie with her parents on Friday morning at 8:00 a.m. April didn't have anything scheduled (but would have rescheduled it if she had) and accepted the meeting. April had heard through the grapevine that the school had taken the incident between Claire and Brie seriously, and not only was Brie suspended but there could be further repercussions as well.

Claire had redeemed her rain check with Shelly, and had Anne Turner pick them up, and all three of them went shopping on Thursday after school. Of course, April didn't know that her mother was with them—she thought it was just Claire and Shelly going out. Thanks to Anne, Claire had completed her Christmas shopping, and all she had to do was wrap up the gifts.

It was now Friday morning, and April had gone to the school with Blake and Claire. Because class started at 7:20 a.m., Claire had gone to her first hour and would be called down for the meeting. April had found a seat in the commons area and decided to wait there for the meeting to start instead on one of the chairs by the principal's office. There was something about sitting in those chairs that made it seem like you were in trouble. April was in the middle of a phone call with Wanda when she saw Brie and her parents enter the school at the far end of the hallway. The office was at the halfway point between the door entrance and where April was sitting. April could tell from her vantage point that Brie's parents didn't look too happy. They led their daughter through the hallway without saying a word to her. Brie had a frown on her face, and it was obvious that the past few days had probably been rough on her.

April felt sorry for Brie's parents. She couldn't imagine Blake doing something like this and to have to come to the school to discuss further disciplinary action. April took a few moments to finish what she had called Wanda about, and then hung up the phone.

"April," Claire quietly called out from the hallway facing the other direction on her way to the office. Claire walked up to the commons area, and April asked, "Are you ready for this?"

"As ready as I'll ever be," Claire said half-heartedly. "I just want this to be over."

"Me too," April agreed. "Let's go hear what they have to say."

April led the way through the entrance of the office door. April and Claire followed the secretary down a hallway that led to the principal's office. Brie and her parents had just sat down in front of the principal's desk and as they walked in, Principal Hayward stood up and did the introductions.

"Obviously, we all know why we are here today," Principal Hayward began. "It seems that Brie here instigated an incident that we at this school consider to be bullying," he explained. Brie looked at Principal Hayward at the mention of her name, but didn't say anything.

"The Disciplinary Committee decided to suspend her for three consecutive days with today being her first day back. This meeting was set up so that Brie could apologize to Claire for her actions, and to discuss further possible punishment in this matter." Principal Hayward paused and looked at Brie to indicate that this was the time for her to apologize.

Clearing her throat, Brie looked bashfully at her parents and then at Claire. "I am so sorry that I did this to you," Brie said, beginning her apology. "To be honest, I don't know why I took it that far. My jealousy got the better of me, and I just didn't think about the consequences of my actions."

Claire was looking at Brie straight in the eyes as she was delivering her speech. Even though it sounded rehearsed, it did come across as sincere.

Continuing, Brie said, "But I know now how stupid it was to do that to you. Will you accept my apology?"

Claire had already decided that she would, just to be able to put this whole ordeal behind her. But she also wanted Brie to understand how much it hurt.

"Before I accept it, I just want you to know how much you hurt me. I mean, Brie, I am just like you. A teenage girl just trying to make her way through life; hopefully graduating high school and making friends along the way." Claire was on a roll and didn't want to stop. "To go through what I have been through in life, and then to have someone throw it in my face... it made me feel like I wasn't worthy of even existing. Do you get the picture?"

Brie slowly nodded her head, and Claire finished saying, "Yes, I do accept your apology. I hope that you truly realize that teasing people who are less fortunate than you is probably not a good idea."

After that, Brie's parents apologized to April for their daughter's actions and promised her that it wouldn't happen again.

Principal Haywood then pulled out a file folder, and took out a piece of paper from it. It was a form that Brie's parents had to sign in order for Brie to enlist in a five-hour bullying course that would be conducted for an hour after school for five days. Because this was the last day of school for Christmas break, it would start during the first week after Brie's return.

Once they signed the form, Principal Hayward's gaze turned even more serious.

Because this incident was categorized as a bullying offense, the Athletic Director and I have a meeting later on today to possibly remove Brie from her cheerleading spot on the team.

Brie's eyes opened wide and you could see that she was devastated by this revelation.

"Please, no," Brie pleaded to Principal Hayward. "I promise not to be mean to anyone again." Brie's eyes began to tear up, and Brie's parents were obviously mad about this.

"Look," Principal Hayward interrupted. "We take bullying very seriously in this school, and unfortunately Brie's behavior on Monday may warrant this outcome."

Claire could see the anguish in Brie's eyes with this new announcement, and for some weird reason, Claire felt sorry for her. Brie had been a bitch to Claire right from the beginning and now, as they both sat in the principal's office discussing a suitable punishment for Brie, Claire felt sorry for her.

As Brie's parents tried to reason with the principal, Claire came up with an idea. At first, she thought it was a stupid idea, and she didn't want to bring it up. But as the look of anguish intensified on Brie's face, Claire just blurted it out. "Instead of kicking her off the squad, why can't she just spend a couple of days serving people at a soup kitchen?"

Brie's parents and Principal Hayward stopped speaking, and looked at Claire. April spoke up for the first time, and said, "I think that would be an appropriate punishment, and it will help Brie to understand the plight of the less fortunate, wouldn't you agree, Mr. Hayward?"

After a few moments of thought, Brie's parents welcomed that idea because it meant that Brie could stay on the cheerleading team. Principal Hayward seemed a bit skeptical but then realized that it might be just the thing to help Brie see the error of her ways.

By the time the meeting was over, it was decided that Brie would complete the bullying classes and then report to a soup kitchen for two eight-hour days. She would then have to write a four-page essay detailing what she learned from both days, and why it is wrong to make fun of those less fortunate than herself.

On the way out of the office, Brie stopped Claire just outside the door, and said seriously, "I am sorry for all of this."

"I know," replied Claire reassuringly, "I just want all this crap between us to be over." Brie thought better of saying anything else and decided to let things stay as they were. Brie's parents thanked April and Claire, and apologized again for their daughter's behavior and headed down the hallway towards the exit while Brie headed in the direction of her locker. Since there were only ten minutes left in the first hour, Principal Hayward said that they could just wait until the second period to go back to class.

April and Claire walked slowly to the commons area. "I am so proud of you," April began. "Making the suggestion of the soup kitchen was a great idea."

Claire couldn't help but smile. It was a good idea, and hopefully Brie would learn something from spending time with homeless people.

"It just came to me, and for some reason, I kind of felt sorry for her," Claire explained to April. "I don't know why. What she did to me was horrible, but when the principal wanted to kick her off the team, I didn't think it was right."

April looked at Claire, and said, "Do you know why you felt that way? It's because you are a compassionate person and you want to see the good in people."

Claire grinned at April, and said tenderly, "I hope that you are right about that. I try not to get into trouble, but for some reason, stuff like this happens to me."

"Trust me, Claire, I'm right about you," April said, with conviction.

April said goodbye to Claire, and told her that she would see her when she got home from work.

Claire told April that she would be right home after school, and added that Blake would be making dinner with her tonight. Blake had found a recipe that she wanted to try, and Claire, of course, had offered to help her prepare it.

The bell rang out from the speakers on the walls of the hallway, and April made her way through the sea of students. Claire watched her as she disappeared through the door and thought to herself how awesome it was to have April in her life.

CHAPTER SEVENTEEN

"WAKE UP CLAIRE!" BLAKE YELLED EXCITEDLY, AS SHE launched herself over the side of Claire's bed and landed directly on top of her. "It's Christmas morning and Santa was here!"

"Holy cow, Blake," Claire wheezed as the weight of Blake on her belly prevented her from taking a breath. Looking at the clock on the nightstand, and pulling the covers over her face, Claire said, "It's only 5:15 a.m."

Blake stayed on top of Claire. "It's time to get up, Claire. Time to open presents." The happiness in Blake's voice reminded Claire of Christmas movies that she had watched where all the kids would be racing down the stairs to see all of the gifts. Even though Blake was fourteen, she sounded like a little girl who couldn't contain her excitement.

Blake then pulled the sheet and blanket off of Claire. "Let's go Claire Bear!"

"Ok, ok," Claire smiled as she too was getting excited. This was the first Christmas in a long time that she was actually looking forward to, not just because of the gifts, but because of the way that she felt about spending it with April and Blake.

Claire reached for her robe and then took a moment to straighten her hair with her hands. Both the girls headed towards April's bedroom, and then they quietly opened the door.

Blake tiptoed quietly to one side of the bed while Claire followed suit on the other side. Blake held up fingers counting down from three to one. "Merry Christmas!" they yelled at the same time.

April had woken up when she heard Blake waking up Claire but pretended to be asleep when they came in. "Merry Christmas, girls." April greeted them as she suddenly opened her eyes. She sat up in bed, and as Blake and Claire climbed in alongside her, she asked, "Are you ready to see if Santa has been here?"

Of course, both girls were ready to go. April got out of bed and headed for the door.

"Alright then, let's head down." It was tradition that the entire family would go down the stairs together. Blake let Claire lead the way, and when they got down about halfway, Claire couldn't believe her eyes. All the Christmas lights were on, and there was a pile of presents under the tree. Of course, in actuality, they each had about ten presents, but to Claire, it felt like the room was full.

Blake had told Claire that it was customary for them to open one present at a time, going from person to person, so that each gift would be seen by all. Claire liked that idea, and Blake handed Claire a gift that was wrapped in green and red wrapping paper, and the tag on it said, "To Claire from Santa."

Most of the gifts had labels that said they were from Santa, but there were a few that said from Blake and April.

The first gift that Claire opened was an outfit that she and Blake had seen while shopping a couple of weeks ago, and it looked awesome on her. "Thank you, this is beautiful. I love it," Claire said sincerely.

Blake grabbed a box that had her name on it, and began to open it. It was a pair of shoes that April had discovered, and thought that Blake might like.

"Wow, these are really cute," Blake said, "Thanks, mom, Um, I mean Santa."

After Claire and Blake had opened several gifts, Claire pulled out one that she had wrapped, and handed it to April.

"This is from me," Claire said with excitement. "I hope that you like it."

April unwrapped the box and removed the top. Inside, in the middle of tissue paper was another little box. April smiled at the small box and opened that one. Inside was a locket with a picture of Blake on one side and Claire on the other.

"Oh, my, Claire," April said graciously. "I love it." The locket was in the shape of a butterfly, but the wings opened up to reveal the pictures on either side. April put the locket around her neck and asked Claire if she could latch it up for her.

April looked at it in the mirror, and said, "This is perfect, thank you."

Claire was really happy that April liked it. She had seen it and thought it would be a neat idea.

Blake removed a rather large rectangular box from the back of the Christmas tree and handed it to Claire. "This is from me," she declared.

Claire set the box down on the floor and began to tear away the gift wrap. The box was pretty heavy so Claire was careful when she took the top off the box. Inside was a large crystal picture collage frame. There were ten pictures of Claire, Blake, and April from when she first arrived. However, the middle picture was larger than the others, and was that of April brushing Claire's hair and making that French braid.

"Oh my," Claire began, as she held back a tear. "This is amazing," Claire said, looking at Blake and April, and then turning her gaze back to the main picture. "I love this picture. I didn't even know that you took it. Thank you so much," Said Claire, memories from that day rushing back to her. It felt like a year ago when, in fact, it had only been a month since April had brushed Claire's hair. It was such a simple gesture, but it meant so much to Claire.

"You are welcome, Claire Bear. Now you can put this on the wall in your room," Blake said, as she held up her fist for a fist bump. "You're the best," Claire said.

"Oh, I am well aware of it," Blake chuckled, as she replied.

Claire got up and located the present that she had gotten for Blake. "Merry Christmas, Blake. I hope you like it."

Blake sat the box down in front of her, and slowly began to unwrap it. Claire had bought Blake the fashion book that she had looked at in the bookstore in the village of Northfield on that day when they had gone to see Anne and Joseph. Underneath the book were three fashion magazines straight out of New York.

"Wow, thank you Claire," Blake cheerfully said. "I can't believe that you got this for me."

Blake immediately started flipping through the pages as she remembered some of the designs.

"You're welcome," Claire said. "It's the only book that I could get you that you would appreciate." The irony wasn't lost on Blake, but she didn't care. The fashion book was fantastic. "You know something?" Blake began, "I think that you might be right, but I don't care. I love this book."

Of course, with the opening of the first presents, all three of them had taken pictures with their cell phones, and Claire and Blake were snapping selfies with each other.

When all the presents were unwrapped, there were piles of clothes littering the floor in front of the tree as well as books, some jewelry and cosmetic gift sets.

April got up from where she had been sitting on the floor and walked up to the mantle.

"Time to look in our stockings," April carefully took them off the hooks and handed Blake and Claire their stocking.

Both girls sat cross-legged on the floor with their stocking in front of them. Claire slowly began taking each item out as Blake simply dumped the contents of hers on the floor.

Claire pulled out gift cards to her favorite stores. There were little things like hair clips, a nail trim set, make-up, and of course, candy. There was one little box that was wrapped up in silver wrapping paper with a gold bow on it. Quizzically, Claire held it up and then opened it. Inside was a debit card with Claire's name on it.

She looked at April for an explanation.

"That is your own debit card. You can use it to make credit purchases or you can take cash out. I deposited $200.00 on it so that you can go out with your friends. I thought it would be nice in case you wanted to go shopping or to the movies, or whatever you wanted."

Claire just stared at the card in disbelief. "Seriously, you did that for me?"

"I know you don't like asking for money, so I thought that it would be better if I deposit money in it every week like I do for Blake. That way, you will always have funds on you in case of emergencies or just to buy something. It's a good way to have access to money without carrying cash all the time." April paused for a moment, and then continued by saying, "Plus, it's a good way to build up credit for yourself."

Claire couldn't believe it, but she now had her own card with her own money.

"Thank you, April. I am in shock with all of this," Claire said. She had never had a Christmas like this, and she felt like she was dreaming and would wake up at any moment.

April instructed the girls to leave the piles of torn wrapping paper and the gifts on the floor for a while so that they could enjoy Christmas morning longer. April and Nick had started this tradition when Blake was four years old. Instead of cleaning up the mess and making it as if it was gone in a flash, Nick had read that if you leave the mess, it makes the magic of Christmas Day last longer.

As April headed to the kitchen to put in the breakfast quiches, Claire asked Blake if she would help her hang her picture collage in her room. As the girls went upstairs, April thought to herself what a great Christmas this was. This was the first time since Nick had died that she and Blake had smiled and laughed throughout the entire morning. Because of Claire, this Christmas felt special and new. April smiled at the thought of Nick's voice calling her to Claire those weeks ago. Maybe this is what he wanted. To open their hearts again and allow for the sadness of his loss to be replaced with the joy of helping a girl who needed a family.

Whatever the reason, April was glad that Blake had established a close friendship with Claire, and loved how they were now a family.

"Hey mom," Blake called from Claire's room. "Come take a look at this." April preheated the oven and then went upstairs. The girls had used command strips to affix the collage to the wall.

"Looks great," April said sincerely. "It's the perfect spot for it." As April looked around Claire's room, it became evident that it was definitely not just a spare bedroom anymore. Between the clothes that Blake had given her during Claire's first week and the clothes that she had received from April and her parents, the room looked like a teenage girl's room. Blake and Claire had put some pictures and other things up on the walls. They had even put some Christmas decorations up and there was a tiny little Christmas tree on her dresser. It was now clearly Claire's room.

April went back down to the kitchen to get the quiches and began making herself a cup of coffee. April then headed to the living room where the pile of gifts still lay scattered around the floor, and sat on the couch as she waited for the girls to come down. It was snowing outside and it was colder than usual for December. April grabbed the blanket on the far side of the couch and wrapped herself in it. She had just gotten herself tucked in when her cell phone went off. April had to remove the covers in order to reach the phone.

"Merry Christmas, mom and dad," April said as she answered the phone. Her parents knew that Blake would have woken up early, and would be up by now.

"Santa was here and the girls just finished opening their gifts," April said, as she reached for her coffee mug to sneak in a sip.

"Merry Christmas, honey," Anne said as Joseph exclaimed, "Merry Christmas!" in a Santa-like voice.

"We can't wait to see you guys today." Anne declared, as she took over the phone conversation. "I think that girls will like what we got them."

April knew what her parents had got each of the girls for Christmas, and yes, they were going to freak. Looking upstairs to see if the girls were on their way down before she spoke, April said, "I think that this might be one of the best Christmases that Claire has ever had. It seems that she didn't get many gifts in the past, and that her previous foster parents weren't into the holidays like we are. It makes me happy to see her happy."

You could almost hear April's mother smile over the phone, as she said, "You know dear, it's your kind heart and loving nature that will make this day special for Claire as well. I am so proud of you for taking her in and helping her out. It's kind of what the season is all about."

"Thanks, mom," April said, graciously. "I learned from the best."

It was at that moment that Blake and Claire were making their way to the living room.

"It's Grandma and Grandpa on the phone," April told them, as she put the phone on speaker.

"Merry Christmas!" Blake yelled to make her voice heard from the distance between the bottom of the stairs and the living room.

"Merry Christmas!" Claire said in a raised excited voice. "I can't wait to see you today!"

April, Blake, and Claire were going to go over to April's parents house for Christmas Brunch.

"Us too," Anne said truthfully. "We love spending Christmas day with family."

Blake and Claire told them what they got for Christmas, and then ended the call saying they would see them in a few hours. April hung up the phone and sighed a happy sigh as she leaned back on the couch and put her feet on the coffee table.

Claire and Blake went to the kitchen to get coffees for themselves, and joined April on the couch.

"You know, April," Claire began, as she carefully sipped the hot coffee, trying not to get any drops on the couch. "This is by far the best Christmas I have ever had," Claire said, as if she was stating it for the record. "Being here with you and Blake," Claire paused to find the right words, and continued, "... being here has meant the world to me, and I don't think that I can possibly tell you enough how much I appreciate being here."

"We are so glad that you are here with us," April said, glancing at Blake. "It's been a joy to have you around." April then held up her coffee mug in order to make a toast. Taking a moment to realize what April was doing, Blake raised her mug and Claire followed suit.

"To family. Merry Christmas," April declared, as she clinked Blake and Claire's mug.

"To family," Claire said earnestly, as she looked at April and then Blake.

"Merry Christmas, everyone!" Blake toasted, as she brought her coffee up to take a drink.

The three of them sat snuggled up on the couch while they waited for the quiche to get done. Blake would sneak pieces of Christmas candy when April wasn't looking. Claire gathered the clothes and gifts she got for Christmas and organized them into a pile. April could see by the expression on Claire's face that this was the most that she ever received for Christmas.

After they had devoured the quiches, April told them that they better get their showers done so that they could get dressed and ready to go. The car wasn't going to pick them up for another two hours, but April didn't want to rush getting ready.

When Claire got out of the shower, Blake had laid a dress out on her bed for her to wear. It wasn't one that she had gotten for Christmas and she didn't think that she had seen it before in Blake's closet. It was a beautiful vintage red dress that had black lace for the sleeves and shoulders. It was ruffled from the waist down to just below the knee. And knitted throughout the bottom portion of the dress was a white pattern of a village and trees covered in snow. It was remarkable. Still wet from the shower and with her towel wrapped around her, she went into Blake's room and asked suspiciously, "Where did this come from?"

Blake was sitting at her vanity and turned at the sound of Claire's voice. "Isn't it amazing?" Blake asked, blissfully dodging Claire's question. "You will look totally awesome in it."

"Yes... Blake, it is awesome, but where did it come from?" Claire asked again, pretending to be irritated.

"Um... well... you see." Blake stammered, "I got it for you." Before Claire could say anything, Blake interrupted her. "You looked so beautiful at Thanksgiving dressed up in that skirt and sweater. So I wanted to get you something that would tell the world that Claire Forrester can wear the hell out of anything that Blake puts in front of her."

Blake got up and took the dress from Claire and held it against Claire's body, and turned her around so that she could see it in the mirror. "Right?" Blake asked. "Amazing, isn't it?"

"Besides," Blake continued, as she reached into her closet and pulled out a dress of her own. "I got one for me too." The dress that Blake pulled out was a black dress that, like Claire's, went down just past the knee. It was all black, but it had white snowflakes speckled throughout the entire dress. There was a thick green ribbon with white snowflakes that tied in front like a bow that acted as a belt.

"Wow, Blake," Claire said in awe. "That is beautiful!"

"I know, right?" I saw them both downtown a week ago, and I said to myself that I had to get them for us." Blake got closer to Claire and whispered, "Mom doesn't know that I got them. We are going to surprise her when we walk downstairs."

Blake put her dress in front of her and stood in front of the mirror with Claire.

"Well?" Blake asked. "Are you ready to put that dress on and make this the best Christmas ever?" The excitement in Blake's voice was infectious, and Claire was still overwhelmed by the dress.

"Thank you, Blake, this is wonderful, and I appreciate you helping me with all this 'being a lady' stuff. You have never once thought of me as any less because I didn't know how to put makeup on or want to be dressy." Claire was looking at Blake through the reflection in the mirror. "Thanks to you, I now want to be that girl that has style and class, but can be a little edgy when she wants to be."

"Don't worry, Claire. I've got your back," Blake said faithfully. "I am good with all this fashion stuff, and I can't wait to see you in that dress, so quit stalling and put it on already." Blake turned to go into her bathroom, and then whispered to Claire, "After you get your dress on, come in here, and I will help you with your makeup. I know that you are pretty good at it now but I want to try something that will go with the dress."

"Aye, aye, Captain," replied Claire, as she brought her right hand up in a mock salute.

Claire peeked out of Blake's bedroom door to make sure that April hadn't come upstairs and then bolted across the hallway to her bedroom. By the time Claire had blow-dried her hair and slipped on the dress, it was fifteen minutes later.

Claire snuck back over to Claire's room and when she entered, she saw that Blake was just finishing up. Blake was stunning, not just in her dress, but she had put on a blended green and grey eyeshadow that matched the green ribbon belt perfectly. Blake also wore a green headband that had black snow-flakes instead of white ones.

"Blake, you look like a model," Claire said. "Seriously, it is like you walked straight out of a magazine. How do you know how to do all of this?" The amazement in Claire's voice was evident and Blake's abilities never ceased to amaze Claire. Blake was only fourteen years old, but she had a knack for design and fashion, that was for sure.

"Thanks, Claire," Blake replied, but then turned the compliments towards Claire. "I knew you would kill in that dress," Blake said. "As soon as I saw it, I knew it was you," Blake told Claire to take a seat at her vanity, and then got to work. She looked at Claire's face for a few moments as if she were an artist looking at a blank canvas waiting for inspiration to hit. Then Blake picked up the eyeshadow and got to work.

Within ten minutes, Claire too looked like she had just stepped out of a picture in a magazine. Blake had gotten red lipstick that matched Claire's dress perfectly, and had tried new mascara. The end result was breathtaking.

"God, I'm good," Blake smirked, as she checked her handy work. Blake then took out the pearls that Claire had worn on Thanksgiving and handed them to Claire. "You know that this will complete the whole outfit."

Unlike last time, Claire accepted them and majestically put them around her neck. She knew that April and Anne wouldn't mind, and actually she wanted to wear them. She began to feel like a princess, and even though she was getting used to wearing makeup now and dressing up in nice clothes, it still made her feel like she was living someone's else's life. At the very least, she was in the middle of a dream, that she didn't want to wake up from.

Blake took out her phone and called her mom.

"Yes, my daughter, what's up?" April asked, wondering why her daughter would call her from upstairs.

"Are you in the living room?" Blake wanted to know.

"No, I'm in the kitchen. Why?" April questioned.

"We've got something to show you, so go into the living room and look towards the staircase." Blake instructed her mom.

"Ok," April said as she walked the few steps into the living room facing the staircase. "I'm ready."

"Ok, bye," Blake answered as she hung up the phone.

April stood like a statue looking towards the top of the stairs. She couldn't believe her eyes when Blake and Claire came into view.

Both girls walked side by side down the stairs, and when they got halfway down, Blake grinned, waved her hands at Claire and then herself, and yelled out, "Ta... Da..."

"Oh my God, you guys," April began, awestruck. "You're stunning!" April looked from one girl to the other, and couldn't believe her eyes.

"I bought both dresses last week, and I just surprised Claire with hers." Blake offered as an explanation. "Of course, I discovered this little number on my way up to pay for Claire's dress, so I had to get it too," Blake confessed as she spun around to show off the entire dress.

"I just wanted to surprise you with this, mom. You were so pleased with how we dressed up for Thanksgiving that I wanted to do that again," Blake said, as she spun Claire around to show off her dress as well.

April was smiling from ear to ear, delighted by how elegant the girls looked. "This is the best Christmas present that I could ever have. I am so proud of both of you."

April took several pictures of the girls on the staircase and then wanted to get a couple of them in front of the Christmas tree. "Oh my, these pictures are awesome, you guys," April declared as she flipped through the screen on her phone.

"Come on, mom, get in here," Blake said, as she waved her mom over by the tree.

"I'm not ready yet," said April, looking at the bath robe that she was wearing.

"It's fine, get over here," Blake quipped. "Come on."

"Ok," April smiled and got in between Blake and Claire. April held the phone up high and took a picture of the three of them.

"Cute one, mom," Blake said about the picture. "When you get dressed, we will take some more of you with each of us."

"Sounds like a plan," April said, as she headed towards the stairs. "I'm going to take a shower and get ready."

Blake and Claire sat down on the couch, and turned on the TV to see what Christmas movies were on. Claire started texting Shelly and Rose to wish them a Merry Christmas. Claire sent them a couple of pictures of her in her Christmas dress. Of course, they both loved it and thought that she looked beautiful. Claire then sent a text to Trevor and wished him a Merry Christmas. It took about five minutes before he responded, but he did text back wishing Claire a Merry Christmas also.

Claire smiled and actually couldn't wait to see him again. They didn't have exact plans yet, but the last time they had talked, they had discussed that they would get together over Christmas break.

Forty-five minutes later, Claire and Blake were deep in conversation about some YouTube video when April came downstairs.

"Wow, mom," Blake exclaimed as April stepped into view. "About time you take after me," Blake joked as she gazed at her mom.

April was wearing a solid green dress with a longer than normal white pearl necklace.

"You look great," Claire smiled at April.

"Thank you," April smiled as she modeled her dress for the girls. "I had to make sure that I at least look almost as good as my girls."

"Well, you are beautiful, and now I can see where I get some of my fashion talent from," Blake said warmly.

Blake remembered to take pictures of April with her and Claire in front of the tree. She also wanted to get a picture alone with her mom and then took a picture of just April and Claire.

It was time to leave for April's parents' house, so they got on their coats and scarves, and Blake and Claire helped April get the gifts ready to take with them.

"Ok, you guys, off to grandma's house we go," April started to sing as she entered the elevator. Blake rolled her eyes. "Oh God, please don't sing, mom," Blake said holding her hands over her ears.

Claire joined in the singing with April as the elevator doors closed.

"No way!" Claire exclaimed as she opened the gift from her 'grandparents'. Inside the box was a MacBook laptop. "Are you serious right now?" Claire asked, as she pulled the super thin laptop out of the box.

"Merry Christmas, Claire," Anne said as Claire got up from the chair that she was sitting on in the Great Room, and gave both Anne and Joseph a big hug.

"This is awesome!" Claire shouted out in reaction to opening up the screen. "I can't believe you got me a computer!"

"We figured that you needed your own computer for school, and of course, social media type of things." Joseph said, as he couldn't help but smile at Claire's excitement.

"Thank you so much!" Claire declared giving them both another hug. She sat back down and turned on the computer and waited for the screen to come to life. She set it on the table next to her in order to see what Anne and Joseph got Blake.

Blake's gift was a Christmas box with a lid that had a big red bow on top. Blake carefully lifted the lid off and pulled out the top layer of tissue paper.

"Holy crap!" Blake shouted out. "No, you didn't?"

"Yes, we did," Anne answered. "Merry Christmas Blake!"

Inside the box was 'Kevyn Aucoin—The Essential Brush Collection' as well as a very expensive bottle of French perfume. Blake had discovered the bottle at the mall several months ago when she was out shopping with her grandparents for the day.

"This is totally awesome!" Blake said, as she jumped up and hugged her grandparents. "I can't believe you got these for me. They are really expensive."

"It makes us happy that we can spoil you girls from time to time," Anne replied as she handed a gift to April.

April opened it. Inside was a really old and extremely rare book that she wanted to buy at an auction that she had attended with Gina over the summer, but was outbid by a woman who was there on behalf of her client. April blinked in surprise.

"That was you?" April asked, stunned as she remembered how the woman was on her phone with her client, who she now realized was her dad.

"Yes, it was," April's dad admitted. "I asked one of my interns to go there and outbid anyone in order to get that book. You had talked about trying to get it for weeks before going there so I knew that you really wanted it."

"You are amazing parents," April said lovingly as she hugged and kissed them. "I love you so much." You could detect the emotion in her voice as she told them that she loved them.

"We love you too, honey," Anne and Joseph said at the same time.

After they finished opening up a few more presents, it was time for brunch so they all headed to the dining room. Claire was amazed by the amount of different food that was presented. It was like going out to a fancy restaurant, but it was there in the Turners' house.

They all talked and laughed during brunch, and Anne commented on how beautiful the girls looked at least five times.

After brunch, they all gathered in the Great Room by the Christmas tree for some coffee and hot chocolate. April showed Claire the old book and told her the story behind this particular edition. Blake dabbed a bit of her new perfume on her neck and wrist, and the sweet fragrance slowly spread across the room.

Blake received a texted from Emily wishing her a Merry Christmas. Claire caught a glimpse of the screen, and saw that it was from Emily.

"Have you talked to her since last Friday?" Claire inquired.

"Nope," Blake replied steadfastly. "I didn't really want to text or talk to her today either."

Claire noticed Blake's intense stare as she looked at her phone screen, trying to decide what to do.

"Text her back and wish her a Merry Christmas," Claire urged Blake.

Blake sighed, and then said, "I don't know Claire. I'm still really mad at her for what she did. I don't want to forgive her yet."

"You don't have to forgive her yet, but you can still wish her a Merry Christmas," Claire suggested. Emily was not Claire's favorite person in the world either, but technically she wasn't involved in the Brie situation even though her info was definitely the catalyst for the incident.

Blake continued to look at her phone for several moments before she shut the screen, without typing anything, and then set the phone down on her lap. Looking at the Christmas tree across the Great Room, Blake contemplated Emily's text. After a few moments, she picked up her phone and then texted Emily back, simply saying, "Merry Christmas".

Claire didn't say anything else about it, but she was glad that Blake did acknowledge Emily. Maybe one day they would repair the damage to their friendship. Deep down Claire knew that her arrival at the Turner's was the main reason for the rift between them, even though it wasn't her fault.

Claire really cherished the time that she spent with April's parents because they were such nice people and they treated her with respect and dignity right from the very first day that they met. Claire was typically shy around older people because they intimidated her, but not Anne and Joseph Turner. She could tell them anything, and they didn't judge her. In fact, they were interested in what she had to say and would engage her in conversation.

As the afternoon turned into evening, the five of them sat in the Great Room listening to Christmas music as they talked. Claire was sitting in between Anne and Joseph on the couch while April and Blake sat on the couch across from them. Trevor had texted Claire during brunch and they had continued over the next couple of hours. They texted about what they had got for Christmas, and Trevor told her that he was going to have a get-together with some of his friends at his house for New Year's, and wanted to know if she could come. She informed him that she would have to ask and get back to him.

"So, April," Claire began, "Trevor is going to have a get-together with some friends at his place for New Year's and wants to know if I can go?"

April's first reaction was 'no'. She was still kind of thinking that she was the parent of a fourteen-year-old, not a sixteen-year-old too.

"Let me think about it, ok?" April said cautiously. "I just want to make sure his parents are going to be home, and that everything will be supervised."

"Ok," Claire said, as she texted Trevor April's conditional answer.

At first, Claire thought that Trevor would be mad about April's answer, but a few seconds later, he texted back with, "No problem, I'll have my mom call yours tomorrow."

Claire smiled and told April Trevor's response. April could tell that Claire really wanted to go and she was probably going to let her, but she wanted to make sure that his parents were there.

It was almost 9:00 p.m. when April, Blake, and Claire left to go home. It had been a remarkable day for all three of them, but for Claire it had been almost magical. It started with the sight of all the presents under the Christmas tree, followed by the delicious brunch at April's parents, the gift of the MacBook laptop, and the entire family just sitting around talking. Just talking.

By the time they got back to the apartment, all three of them were whipped from the festivities of the day.

Blake headed to the bathroom upon entry, while April and Claire went to the kitchen. It was now 10:00 p.m., and even though they were tired, April decided to pour three glasses of eggnog.

Blake joined them in the kitchen, and April held up her glass to toast. "To a great Christmas!" she said, as they clinked glasses.

"To the best Christmas of my entire life," Claire said sincerely. "You two are the best."

"Yeah we are," Blake agreed shamelessly, and grinned as they clinked glasses again.

After a few minutes, Blake and Claire gave April a hug, and wished her a Merry Christmas as they went upstairs to bed. April put the dirty eggnog glasses in the dishwasher, and then stood in front of the Christmas tree for a few moments. *Merry Christmas, Nick, thank you for everything,* April thought as she pictured Blake and Claire and how they had both immensely enjoyed this holiday. April slowly walked up the stairs enjoying the last few moments of Christmas. As it turned out, this was the first Christmas since Nick passed away that did not end in April crying.

* *

"HAPPY NEW YEAR!" TREVOR'S MOM EXCLAIMED, AS SHE opened the door. Claire, Shelly, and Rose were standing outside the front door in the frigid cold. "Come in," she said, waving them in. Once inside, she took their coats and put them in the hallway closet. "Everyone is in the living room," she said, guiding them towards the sound of the voices.

There were about ten people already there, and most of them were jocks or cheerleaders. Trevor noticed Claire and leaped off the La-Z-Boy that he was sitting in and went up to her.

"Hey, Claire," Trevor said excitedly. "I'm glad you could make it." He grabbed her hand and guided her towards the living room. "Let me show you around," he said. Shelly and Rose followed Claire and Trevor, as he took them on a quick tour of the house. It ended with them in the kitchen. "Grab something to drink," he said, pointing at the counter that had stacks of red solo cups and three punch bowls, each one containing a different colored liquid.

Claire poured herself a drink from a bowl filled with the orange-flavored liquid. Before she took a sip, she put it up to her nose to smell it. There was no scent of alcohol, so she promptly took a sip. It wasn't like she was a prude or anything, but April let her go to this party under the condition that there would be no drinking, so Claire wanted to make sure that she didn't consume any alcohol, whether intentionally or otherwise.

As the clock ticked closer to midnight, the group of guests grew in size from ten to twenty, and it was getting louder. There were a few boys in front playing an online computer game while most of the party was in the living room and kitchen watching the TV as the countdown to midnight continued.

Claire and her friends were having a great time, and to Claire's surprise, she was getting to know a couple of the cheerleaders, and they actually seemed really nice.

Trevor's mom was constantly roaming around the rooms, making sure things were on the up and up, but also talking with most of the girls because they had apparently known her for some time. She was nice to Claire, and came up to her several times to talk to her.

Trevor's dad, however, was a different story. Claire could tell that even though on the outside he seemed friendly enough, on the inside, she couldn't tell. It almost seemed like he was hiding what he was truly feeling on the inside. Claire didn't know if she was being paranoid, but it seemed like he was short with Claire. Claire was sure that he knew that she had been homeless, and maybe that is why she felt apprehensive, but she didn't want to bring it up with Trevor, especially on New Year's.

With only two minutes to go, couples started to pair up for the final countdown. Trevor had left her side a few minutes ago to get a drink but hadn't returned yet. With sixty seconds left, he strolled in the living room and came up to Claire. He handed her a cup and had one for himself. As the final ten seconds ticked down, Trevor held his cup to hers, and said as he looked into her eyes, "Happy New Year." But before they could take a drink, he slowly went in and kissed her on the lips. Even though Claire secretly wanted the kiss, she was still surprised by it. They held the kiss for ten long seconds before separating. Claire's face flushed slightly, and she became warmer than she was ten seconds ago. Before she realized it, he went in for another kiss and they held it for twice as long.

"Wow," Trevor declared, when the kiss was over. "That was cool."

Claire smiled and subconsciously put her fingers to her lips, as if rubbing in the kiss so it couldn't be wiped away.

Just then, Shelly and Rose came up to her, and yelled, "Happy New Year!" and pulled her away to celebrate with the others as the music grew even louder and people cheered.

Claire, Trevor, Rose, and Shelly sat around for the next hour until the girls had to go. Shelly was spending the night at Rose's house, and Claire was going to go back to the apartment. Shelly's mom had come to pick them up. Before she left, Trevor grabbed Claire and found a secluded spot in the den where no one was.

"I had a great time tonight," he said to Claire.

"Me too," Claire smiled as she hugged him. They kissed again, and Claire turned to leave.

"Claire," Trevor said, as her back was towards him. She turned around, and he kissed her again.

"Have a good night," Trevor said smiling, as he headed towards the living room.

Shelly and Rose were standing by the door watching the whole thing. "Way to go, Claire!" Rose cheered as she brought her hand up for a high-five.

"Yeah, Forrester, talk about starting your year off right!" Shelly giggled.

Claire sighed but couldn't help but smile at her friend's excitement. "Ok, ok, let's go," Claire said, trying to hide her own emotions. Rose started singing the song "Trevor and Claire sitting in a tree..." as they got into Shelly's mom's car.

* *

WHEN CLAIRE GOT BACK TO THE APARTMENT, APRIL AND Blake were sitting on the couch watching TV, drinking sparkling grape juice and eating potato chips.

"So, how was it?" April asked, signaling to Claire to sit down next to her.

"It was really fun," Claire began. "I talked with several girls from our school and then we all sat around after the ball dropped. "

"That's great," April, answered. "Did you get a kiss from Trevor when the ball dropped?" April asked with a sly smile on her face.

Unable to control a grin at the sound of the word 'Trevor' and 'kiss', Claire gave her answer away with her facial expression. "Yes, yes we did."

Blake said, "Oh yeah! I'm really happy for you Claire Bear!" She put her arm across April so that she could fist-bump Claire. As Claire's fists met Blake's, April grabbed both of their closed fists and held them together with her hand. "You two are so cute," she said as she laughed and then let go of the fists. The three of them stayed up for a few more minutes until Blake couldn't keep her eyes open any longer and fell asleep.

"Let's get to bed," April said, as she tapped Blake on the shoulder to wake her up. "Happy New Year, girls," April declared for the last time. Turning to Claire, she said, "I'm glad you had a great time at the party."

"Thank you, and thanks again for letting me go. I really did have fun," Claire graciously said.

"You're welcome, honey," April told Claire.

All three of them went upstairs and into their respective bedrooms. April had just gotten into bed and was about to turn the light off when she noticed a shadow approaching her door. It was Claire.

Claire peeked through the door, and asked, "Is it ok if I talk to you real quick?"

"Of course, come on in," April said, as she sat up in bed.

Claire came up next to April's bed and sat on its edge. "I just want to tell you that my New Year's resolution is to be the best foster daughter ever. I can't tell you how much it means to me that I am here, and I want to thank you for helping me rewrite my story. If it weren't for you, I would either be in the streets right now or something worse. I know that I have thanked you time and time again, but I needed to say it once more," Claire finished. April was truly touched by Claire's heart-felt proclamation. "Claire..." April began, as she took Claire's hand. "You are a fine young lady and I am happy beyond words that you are here with Blake and me." April paused a moment and then said, "This is going to be your year. I can feel it. So, keep doing what you are doing by going to school and enjoying the time with your friends. Great things will come your way."

"Thanks, April," Claire said as she tried to hold back a yawn. "I will try my best."

"Ok, then," April said, concluding the conversation. "You are one tired girl, so you better get to bed."

"Good night, April," Claire said as she hugged her and headed for the door.

"Good night, Claire," April said, smiling at her.

April turned off the light on her nightstand and placed her hand on her pillow. As she thought about what she had just said to Claire, April fell asleep thinking that this was going to be a good year for the Turner family.

CHAPTER EIGHTEEN

THE MONTH OF JANUARY BLEW BY AS IF CLAIRE WAS EXPERI-
encing the entire time in 'fast forward'. She and Trevor were officially dating
and she was becoming more and more popular by the day. Ever since the con-
frontation with Brie, Claire was well known throughout the school. Students
wanted to meet the girl who had stood up to a cheerleader, and to show support
for what she had been through. Conversely, Brie was shunned most of the time,
and a lot of her friends had deserted her. Despite all of it, Claire didn't' let the
popularity go to her head. She still was best friends with Shelly and Rose, and
never let anything get between them.

Claire also spent some time with April at her office. April had introduced
Blake and Claire to Monica Towers a few days after New Year's. Claire was
thrilled, and had asked Monica several questions that were well-thought-out,
and reminded Monica of herself when she was Claire's age.

Because Claire liked spending time at Priscilla Publishing, she and
Wanda had struck up quite a friendship. Wanda let Claire work the phones on
several occasions, and even instructed her on the software aspects of the computer system that the entire office ran on. Once after school, Blake and Claire
had visited April, but spent most of the time with Wanda in the cafeteria while
she ate lunch. Everyone at the office fully accepted Claire and treated her like
they would Blake.

It was Friday, January 20, and the Winter Formal was just around the corner. Trevor, of course, was taking Claire. April was taking the girls dress shopping after school this afternoon. Blake already had several dresses being held for them, and even though April was the parent, it was quite obvious who was going to be in-charge tonight.

Claire was walking hand in hand with Trevor on their way from her locker to her 5th hour class.

"I won't be able to go to the game tonight because April and Blake are taking me dress shopping," Claire informed Trevor apologetically. "I have grown accustomed to watching you score the majority of the points," Claire said.

"I know, it's like scoring points is my favorite new hobby," Trevor said jokingly. "No worries. We are playing against Lincoln Park High School, so it should be an easy win for us.

Jones College Prep High School basketball team had been undefeated so far this year, and the coach was ecstatic. He knew that this particular set of players were his best chance to date of getting to the championships, so he wasn't taking any chances. He had increased practice durations as well as extending practices to every other Saturday. Of course, Trevor's dad was totally on board with this as he and the coach talked constantly.

On Monday this week, Claire noticed that Trevor's muscles were getting bigger, and that he was losing weight, but gaining muscle mass. Needless to say, Trevor was becoming more of a hunk than he already was.

As Claire and Trevor rounded the corner near Claire's class, a senior named Brett, who was distracted by a text on his phone, bumped into Claire's shoulder causing her to spin around. But fortunately, he didn't knock her to the ground.

"Hey, asshole!" Trevor blurted in instant rage. "What the fuck?"

Startled by Trevor's aggression, Brett held up his hands, and said, "Sorry, dude." He stammered to both Claire and Trevor. "I didn't mean it."

Claire was taken aback by Trevor's outburst. "It's ok, Trevor, really, I'm fine," Claire said, trying to defuse the situation.

Trevor pushed Brett on his shoulder, causing Brett to take a step back. "Watch where you're going next time! Got it?"

"Yeah, no problem man," Brett answered carefully. Then looking at Claire, Brett said, "Sorry."

He walked away nervously, as Claire looked at Trevor. "What the hell was that about?" Claire asked harshly. "You didn't have to rip his head off," Claire had caught a glimpse of anger in Trevor's eyes as he was yelling at Brett, and it rattled her for a moment.

Trevor suddenly realized that Claire was upset with him, so he quickly changed his demeanor. "Sorry, babe," Trevor apologized. "I don't like to see my girlfriend hurt, that's all," His words dripped with charm as he spoke.

"I get that," Claire said, "but you don't need to get physical with everyone that I run into. Know what I mean?"

"Yeah... Yeah... Sure thing. I get it," Trevor promised, as he smiled and went in to kiss Claire.

"I just want my girl bruise-free," Trevor joked, but the way he said it, she couldn't really tell if he meant it.

"I'll see you after class," Trevor said, as he kissed her again and headed towards the other end of the hall for his next class.

Claire stood in the same spot for a few moments watching Trevor leave. As he walked towards his class, he seemed like the same old Trevor that she had been with over the last month. He waved 'hi' to several classmates as he walked, and gave a high-five to one of his basketball teammates just before he entered his class.

Maybe Trevor thought Brett had bumped into her more forcefully than he had, and that is why he acted the way he did. *That must be it.* Claire thought to herself as she walked into the classroom and focused her thoughts on World History.

As Claire took her seat at the second desk from the back, she noticed Brie walking into the classroom and sitting down at her seat in the front right corner. Since the new semester had started, Claire had Brie in two classes, World History and Chemistry. Claire didn't know that the office had planned it out, but in both classes they just happened to be seated on opposite ends of the room.

Claire sat there with her book open on her desk, secretly peering in Brie's direction. It had been a month since the lunchroom incident, and neither of them had said a word to each other. It wasn't like Brie was furious with Claire— it was just that Brie thought it was better not to try to have a conversation with Claire. Besides, Brie was becoming more and more depressed, so she didn't want to cause a scene with anyone.

As class went on, Claire was becoming more excited at the thought of going shopping with April and Blake after school. She enjoyed spending quality time with both of them. Even though April was putting in longer days due to working with Monica Towers, Claire still spent time with her, whether it was sitting with her in the apartment office while she worked as Claire read on the couch, or those times when April got home late, and they would sit at the island having a late snack discussing the events of the day.

As for Blake, she was in full design mode, researching dresses and shoes for the Winter Formal. Claire didn't know what made Blake more psyched, looking for her dress, or searching for the perfect one for Claire.

Because Claire was lost in thought, she didn't fully hear the question that the instructor had posed.

"Well, Miss Forester?" the teacher asked, waiting for the answer.

Blinking her attention back to the reality of World History, Claire sheepishly grinned, and said, "I'm sorry, can you repeat the question?" There were a few good-hearted snickers from some of the students, but nothing that would imply teasing.

"Of course, Miss Forester. I love spending my class time asking the same questions over again," the teacher said, with a touch of sarcasm.

Fortunately for Claire, she knew the answer and promptly recited it almost word for word from the book.

"Very nice, but next time, please pay attention to what I am saying."

"Of course," Claire said, even though she knew that she didn't have to answer her.

Molly, the girl sitting directly behind Claire, tapped her on the back once the teacher had turned her attention to the chalkboard, and said, "Nice one, Claire." Molly had been out for the past week because her grandmother had passed away, so she and her family had to fly to New Mexico to attend the funeral and take care of her things. Claire had only talked with Molly a couple of times before that since the new semester started, so she knew her, but really didn't know her that well.

Claire turned around and gave Molly an appreciative grin. "Thanks, that was close."

Molly smiled in return. "Can I ask you something?" Molly asked in a whisper.

"Sure?" Claire replied, wondering what it was.

"You seem really smart and I am having a hard time with this class trying to remember all the dates and stuff. I am trying to catch up from the week that I was gone and was wondering if you could help me study sometime?" Molly was asking if Claire could tutor her.

"Yeah, no problem," Claire said, shaking her head yes. "I would love to. Maybe we can get together at my house over the weekend for a couple of hours?" Claire offered.

Molly's face lit up, and replied, "Cool, thanks a lot." Claire turned back around to listen to what the teacher was saying. *This is really awesome,* Claire thought to herself. Never in her entire life had she had kids that wanted to be around her or hang out with her. As Claire turned her attention towards the front of the class, she glanced over at Brie and in some part deep inside of her brain, couldn't help but feel sorry for her.

* *

TREVOR HAD JUST CHANGED INTO HIS BASKETBALL JERSEY, and was in the locker room placing his stuff in the locker when the coach came up to him.

"Trevor," the coach began. "I want to talk to you for a minute." He then sat down on the bench next to the lockers and gazed at his clipboard.

"Your dad and I have been talking, and we know that you can take this team all the way. It's quite a feat for a junior to be in the position that you are in. If we can make championships this year with you leading the team, you are almost guaranteed a full-ride scholarship! Do you hear me?" the coach asked excitedly. "Just keep focused on what is important and keep your eye on the prize. Do you know what I mean?"

At first, Trevor thought that the coach might have found about the steroids but that didn't seem to be the case. Then it dawned on him. Was he talking about Claire? Trevor was spending a lot of time with her, and he suspected that his dad was uncomfortable with his choice of girlfriends. Even though his dad didn't say anything to him directly, there were moments that Trevor picked up on that made it seem that his dad was skeptical.

Trevor looked intensely at the coach's facial features to see if they would reveal his true meaning. Unable to ascertain exactly what he was trying to say, Trevor asked, "So you want me to practice harder and work out more?"

"Yes, that's part of it," the coach conceded, "but it is also the mental part too. Staying sharp and focused is what turns basketball players into stars."

Feeling agitated, Trevor turned away from the coach, and said, "No problem boss." He then headed out the doors to the basketball court. As he ran through the drills with the other players on the team, Trevor thought to himself that he needed to pay Owen Adler another secret visit. He was due for another round of pills, plus he was going to see what else Owen could supply that would take him to the next level in his training.

* *

"THAT'S THE ONE!" BLAKE EXCLAIMED, AS CLAIRE STEPPED out from behind the dressing room curtain. This was the fifth dress that Claire had tried on, and it was spectacular. It consisted of a sleeveless shimmery, jeweled upper bodice that flowed into layers of luminous lavender and satin that draped to the floor.

"Not bad, if I do say so myself," Blake said boastfully, admiring Claire's dress.

Blake couldn't decide between two dresses so she kept trying one on and then the other, over and over again, so that she could look at them at different angles. Finally, she decided on a gown that was made from satin with a full skirt that swayed along almost to the floor. The upper portion of it was encompassed in a silver and royal blue beaded material that flowed from a sweetheart neckline, very much like a princess.

The sales lady, Gayle, kept coming over to check on Blake and Claire, suggesting possible shoe choices or other accessories. As Claire was standing beside Blake admiring the dress in the mirror, Gayle strolled over and said to April, "Both of your daughters look beautiful. I think we have discovered the perfect dresses." Of course, Gayle had no way to know that Claire was April's foster daughter.

"Yes, I believe that you are right," April agreed with confidence. "They are stunning."

As Claire stood there, listening to the conversation, she noticed that April didn't correct Gayle. April didn't need anyone to make a distinction between biological and foster—to her, Blake and Claire were both her daughters.

Claire did an intense examination in the mirror before her. On her left was Blake's reflection. She was smiling at both Claire and April, and was beaming with pride as a result of her dress choices. Claire could see that Blake was not only happy with the dress itself, but with how they looked on each of the girls individually. It was like Blake was a 'dress whisperer' and could 'hear' what the dress was telling its wearer. Claire could sense that Blake was kind of an old soul and even though at times she did act her age, she had a maturity that was beyond her years.

Now Claire turned her attention to her reflection in the mirror. She was beginning to accept that she had rapidly changed from a scared little girl to one who was refined and confident. As Claire continued to examine the mirror, she noticed that April was staring into the mirror as well. There was a moment when Claire made eye contact with April, and for a second, their eyes locked. Claire's heart skipped a beat as she struggled to mentally assess the emotion that she was feeling at that exact moment.

Blake had not noticed April looking in the mirror or Claire's reaction to it, so she didn't realize that when she turned and grabbed Claire's hand to take her over to the shoes section, she had interrupted a moment that Claire had not experienced since she was a toddler.

"I know just the right shoes for that dress," Blake declared with pride and determination, as she led her foster sister over to the shoe rack that was two aisles over. "Whoa!" Claire giggled as Blake dragged her across the store barefoot. Claire had to almost tip toe along in order to keep up with Blake's eager pace.

"What do you think of these?" Blake asked as she gazed at the shoes.

The shoe had a half-inch heel and matched the top portion of Claire's dress. Not only that, but it had a translucent sheen.

Claire blinked in awe at how magnificent they were. "Holy cow, Blake, these are perfect," Claire picked up the right shoe, and looked it over while Blake searched through the boxes stacked in front of them to find her size.

Blake pulled out the correct size, and offered Claire the box. "Try them on... Cinderella." Even though it was meant as a jest, Claire did really feel like Cinderella. Claire slid them onto her bare feet and carefully took a few steps towards the mirror, shakily. Despite the heels, they were very comfortable and looked sophisticated and stylish.

"They are amazing," Claire whispered in admiration. "I'm at a loss for words," Claire added, as she stopped and ogled at her footwear. April caught up with the girls, and was taken aback at Blake's choice of shoes for Claire.

"Those are simply striking," said April. "The entire ensemble is exquisite and you look like a princess." Then April added, "Both of you are my princesses. The two of you are so beautiful." April almost couldn't contain herself. "I have to get a picture of you two," April pulled out her phone and snapped a few pictures. Blake put her arm around Claire's shoulders, as Claire placed her arm around Blake's waist. Even though the girls didn't have their hair styled the way they were planning to for the Winter Formal, the picture was darling—with Blake in her headband and Claire in her ponytail.

By the time they checked out with bags in hand, it was 6:35 p.m. "I'm starving," declared Blake, as if she had read her mom's mind.

"Me too," April admitted. "Where do you want to go?"

"It doesn't matter to me, just as long as we can eat soon," Blake said, trying to sound whinier than how she felt.

"I'm up for just about anything," agreed Claire.

The temperature was way below freezing so they obviously they didn't want to walk a significant distance in order to eat.

"What about this sushi place?" April asked, pointing at the restaurant that was two stores down from where they were standing.

"I don't know," Claire said honestly. "I don't like raw fish." The thought of anything raw subconsciously forced Claire's nose to twitch.

"Not all sushi is made from raw fish. There are many different kinds of sushi that contain no fish at all," April said to Claire in order to properly inform her about this possible dinner idea.

"Are you up for something different? I think that you might like it if you try it?" April suggested.

Claire paused to think about the idea of sushi, and then putting on a brave face, she said, "I'll try it, April. Just as long as you promise me that I don't have to eat raw fish."

April smiled at Claire's slight discomfort, but knew that Claire was about to try a new experience.

"Of course, honey. I wouldn't think about making you eat something that you didn't want to try," she said, adding, "let's go in and we can look at the menu, and I'll show you what I mean."

The three of them went inside and were taken to a table that was in the middle of the dining room. Claire picked up the menu and discovered that April was correct—there were several sushi dishes that didn't contain any raw fish or animal. As she scanned the menu, she found sushi dishes under the heading of 'fish-free' that included California Roll, Tamago, PLS, Unagi, Epic bacon roll, and Dragon roll, to name just a few.

"You're right, April," Claire said, pointing at that part of the menu. "These don't have fish, and they seem decent."

Blake informed Claire that she liked the Dragon roll, but Claire seemed more interested in trying the Epic bacon roll. Blake had to show Claire how to use her chopsticks, and it took her several attempts to master the wooden stick utensil. Blake had given Claire a piece of her Dragon roll to try. Even though Claire did like its taste, she was glad that she had chosen the bacon roll. To Claire, it was the sushi that most resembled something familiar to her.

Finishing her last bite, Blake leaned back in her chair, and said, "I am stuffed." Claire smiled at her in agreement, and said, "Me too." Claire slowly picked up her last piece of bacon roll with her chopsticks and engulfed the whole thing in one big bite.

Claire finished chewing her last bite, and looked at April. "Thank you for suggesting this. I probably would have never tried it if it weren't for you."

Before April could answer her, Claire added, "Of course, I would rather have chicken strips or pizza, but this was good just the same."

April had to grin at Claire's honesty. "It is nice to try new things, and I'm proud of you for trying it."

"Yeah, me too," Claire said, truthfully. "You guys have exposed me to many new experiences since I have been living with you, and I am grateful." Claire took a sip of water to wash down her last bite of sushi. "I can't believe that I am here with the both of you, eating sushi, and trying on beautiful dresses for a school dance."

Blake grinned at Claire, and said a little jokingly, "Don't forget about the shoes."

"Oh yes, the shoes. Didn't mean to leave those out of the list," Claire said, politely mocking Blake.

"Darn right," Blake smiled.

"You know something, Claire," April questioned with a look of anticipation. "This is only the beginning. I believe that you will go through many different life experiences over the next few years that will help shape you as a person." Then looking at Blake, April concluded, "It is my hope that you will let Blake and me be a part of that with you."

Claire was thrilled when Crystal had allowed her to stay with the Turners. But, now, hearing April speak about her being a part of the Turner family over a longer period of time made Claire realize that April and Blake were more than likely the last foster family that she would have. April was basically telling her that this was not a short-term gig in her mind. Claire was going to be a permanent addition to the family.

Claire saw the same look that April had given her in the mirror at the dress store. Claire stared at April for a few seconds and she realized that there was silence because April had stopped speaking.

"Yes, of course, April," Claire said affectionately. "There is no other place I would rather be." Claire looked at April and Blake, and raised her fist for a fist bump. "Am I right?" Claire asked Blake, as she bumped fists.

"You are correct, Claire Bear," Blake said, happily bumping Claire's fist. "You are going to be my fashion mannequin for a very long time."

Claire laughed, and then said, "Oh boy, what am I getting myself into?"

Later that night, Blake was in her room flicking through the channels, trying to find something decent to watch before she went to bed when Claire knocked on the door.

"What's up?" Blake asked, turning her attention away from the screen.

Blake had her Winter Formal dress hanging on the hanger over her bathroom door and Claire looked at it, admiring it again.

Blake noticed that Claire had this bashful look on her face.

"I can't thank you guys enough for getting me the dress today," Claire began, "I love it. Really." Blake could sense that Claire wanted to tell her something else.

"But?" Blake asked curiously.

"No... There is no 'but," Claire insisted. "It's just that... I... um... I..."

"Spit it out," Blake said.

"Ok... um... I don't know how to dance," Claire said, looking at Blake as if she had confessed to doing something wrong.

"Oh," Blake answered, and then realizing that the dance was coming up in a week said, "Oh. I see. How is it that you don't know how to dance?" Blake asked quizzically.

Claire sighed, "It's not like I went to a lot of dances growing up. My mom didn't exactly spend quality time with me, so I never had the opportunity. Even when I was in middle school, I never went to any of the dances."

Seeing that Claire was quite concerned about this, Blake smiled and said gleefully, "Don't you worry. Blake's School of Dancing is now open for business." Blake hopped off the bed and picked up her phone from the nightstand where it had been kept for charging.

It took Blake a few seconds to find the song that she wanted, and then she pressed play. Walk the Moon's song *Shut Up and Dance* began to play as Blake turned Claire around to face her.

"Ok... Show me what you got," Blake said, as the music filled the room.

Claire started to move her arms and shoulders and was stepping through the song almost like she was walking.

"Um," Blake said, thinking about where to start first. "Try using your hips more. A lot of the flow comes from the hips." Blake began to swing her hips with the beat of the music and her body just flowed with it. Then she raised her arms and it complimented the movements of her hips and feet.

"Wow," Claire blinked, "you are really good. Where did you learn how to dance?"

Blake grinned and said, "Believe it or not, it was my mom."

Blake grabbed Claire's arms so that she could guide them through the movement.

"My mom and dad were really good dancers. Apparently, they used to go out dancing all the time when they met, and would go out dancing and leave me with my grandparents or Aunt Crystal."

"Really?" Claire sounded surprised, as she concentrated on Blake's movements.

"Yeah, really," Blake said, as she danced around Claire in a circle.

Blake had Claire copy her movements as she performed several basic moves. After a few minutes, Claire was starting to get the hang of it. Because Blake had the song selection on repeat, *Shut Up and Dance with Me* played over and over. During the third rendition of the song, Claire was laughing and was starting to get into it. Blake got on the top of her bed and pulled Claire up there with her.

They were part dancing and part jumping and giggling.

"What's going on in here?" April asked, as she peered through Blake's door having heard the music across the hall.

"I'm teaching Claire how to dance," Blake said from the bed.

April looked at Claire. "You don't know how to dance?"

Claire jumped down off the bed to talk to April. "No, I never learned how to."

Glancing over at Blake, April grinned at her, and then said to Claire, "We are going to have to change that." April then grabbed Claire's hand and held up her arm so that she could spin her around.

"Yeah, mom!" Blake exclaimed, as she jumped off the bed, "Let's teach Claire how it's done!"

April, Blake, and Claire spent the next forty-five minutes showing Claire all sorts of moves as the three of them danced all around Blake's room, laughing and giggling.

* *

APRIL OPENED HER EYES AND THE FIRST THING THAT SHE realized was the smell of sausage and bacon cooking. It was Saturday morning and she hadn't set her alarm the night before. Allowing her eyes to focus on the room, April became aware that the girls were making breakfast.

As she walked down the stairs towards the kitchen, the aroma of a rich cup of coffee battered her senses, and she noticed a slight burning smell of bread in the toaster. Both girls were still in their pajama pants and T-shirts as they bustled about the kitchen preparing what looked like a huge breakfast. Not only were there eggs, bacon, and sausage, on the table, but Blake was in the middle of mixing batter for her special pancake recipe.

"Good morning, girls," April acknowledged as she tried to stifle a yawn. "What is all this about?" April asked, gaping at all the food that was in the process of being prepared.

"We just wanted to surprise you and make you breakfast this morning, that's all," Blake said, cheerfully. "It's our way of showing you how much we appreciate you."

Claire had just removed the bacon slices from the frying pan, and shook her head in agreement with Blake's explanation. "Yeah, we wanted to tell you 'thank you' for the dresses yesterday, and show you that we appreciate everything that you do for us."

"Why, thank you very much," April smiled appreciatively. "This is a wonderful gesture," April took a seat at the dining room table as Claire and Blake finished preparing breakfast. Blake was the last to sit down and retrieved the salt and pepper from the cupboard to put on the table.

"Everything is delicious," said April, in between bites of pancakes and scrambled eggs.

"Thanks, mom," Blake replied, as she took a drink of orange juice.

"Thanks, April," Claire said, as she paused between the words 'thanks' and 'April'. There was a brief moment of hesitation—April did pick up on it, but decided not to address it. It was like Claire was going to call her something else but then remembered April's name.

"So, what are your plans today?" April asked both girls.

"I think that I am going to kick the crap out of Claire in *Justice League*," Blake responded matter-of-factly.

Claire smirked at Blake, and then turned to April. "After I defeat 'Little Miss Blakey Pants', I am going to have Molly from my World History class come over today so I can tutor her. Is that ok?"

"Yes, that will be fine," April said, "Am okay with both things."

"Funny, mom," Blake complained, "But wait till Claire is crying in her room because she loses to me and then you will have to pick up the pieces." Blake began to giggle at the last part of her sentence because Claire was making a funny face at her.

Claire took a bite of toast, and asked April, "What are your plans today?"

"I thought that I would get some reading done and then later I want to organize my office here in the library," April responded as she mentally tried to remember some key elements from the list she had written up last night, that was still lying next to her nightstand.

"Would you like help with your office?" Claire asked eagerly. "When I get done with Molly, I can help clean and move stuff around if you like."

"Sure, darling, that would be great. I could use the help," April answered earnestly. "Thank you."

"No problem," Claire said, delighted at the thought.

Seeing how enthusiastic April and Claire were about cleaning the office; Blake couldn't help but put her two cents in. "Hey mom," Blake said. "Can I help too with the office? Oh, wait, I mean, can I be anywhere else besides the office?" Blake grinned as she amended her statement.

April sighed and then thought of a good retort. "Or, you can clean and organize my office while Claire and I go shopping for clothes."

"Yeah. That would be the day," Blake smirked, as she stuffed a forkful of pancakes into her mouth.

Just then April's phone started to ring.

"Hi, Crystal," April greeted as she answered. "How are you doing on this fine Saturday morning?"

"Pretty good," Crystal replied. "How are my best friend and her two girls?"

"Terrific. We are almost finished with an awesome breakfast that the girls made." April said as she reached for the last piece of bacon on her plate. "What have you been up to?" April asked.

"Well, funny you should ask." Crystal replied suspiciously. "I want to talk to you guys today. Can I stop by later?"

"Of course, you can," April said, becoming slightly nervous. "Is everything ok?"

"Yes. Don't worry. I just want to talk with you and Claire about my investigation, that's all," Crystal said with a touch of mystery.

"Ok," April was becoming more anxious by the second. "Is it bad news? April questioned.

Blake and Claire were now listening intently to April's conversation because April's tone had changed and when they heard the words, 'bad news', it made them turn their full attention to her.

"I'll stop by later this afternoon, and I'll bring some of Trip's famous no bake cookies," Crystal said, as she tried to reassure April.

"Ok, see you then," April replied, as the call ended and she set the phone down on the table.

"What was that about?" Blake asked her mom.

"It was Crystal. She wants to come over to talk to us about the investigation," April told the girls.

"What investigation?" Claire sounded concerned.

"Don't freak out, but Crystal has been part of an investigation looking into your previous foster dad in Seattle," April began slowly. "She just wants to keep us updated on what is going on. That's all."

Claire didn't know what to say at first. The thought of that man made her want to throw up, literally. However, a sense of satisfaction blanketed over her as she realized that Crystal had truly believed her and wanted to follow-up and do what she could to help provide justice.

"What else did she say?" Claire asked nervously.

Seeing how Claire was reacting, April went up to her and put her arm around her.

"Don't worry, honey, it's going to be ok. Crystal just wanted to keep you updated about what she is doing so far. Nothing is going to change the fact that you are staying here. You are not going anywhere."

Blake agreed with her mom. "It will be fine."

"I hope so," Claire said. She couldn't help but feel apprehensive.

After breakfast, Claire won every game of *Justice League,* and Blake was jokingly complaining that Claire had cheated and wanted a rematch.

Molly came over around noon and Claire introduced her to April and Blake. Claire took her upstairs to her room and they spent the next couple of hours going over the chapters that she had missed when she had gone to her grandmother's funeral. Claire had prepared cue cards for her, and they actually helped. By the time she left, Molly had a good grasp on two of the three chapters, and thanked Claire for helping her out. Claire was pleased that Molly had asked her for help the other day in class. She thought this might be the beginning of a new friendship.

Claire walked over to April's office, and took a peek inside. April was lying on her couch reading a hardcover book. Claire stood there for a moment watching April read. There was something about the look on April's face as she intently read the pages. Claire realized that she must demonstrate a similar expression as well. Both of them enjoyed submerging themselves in the worlds created by the written word. Claire couldn't imagine living with anyone else. It was like April was handpicked specifically for her, as a way to make up for her dreadful childhood years.

Claire quietly entered the office and walked towards April.

"Hey?" April said, noticing that Claire was in the room. "How did everything go with Molly? She seems like a sweet girl." April placed her bookmark on the page that she was on, and sat up to talk with Claire.

"Actually, it went really well," Claire said. "I made her cue cards and we went through a couple of chapters so she has caught up now." Claire took a seat on the office chair and turned it around to face April.

"Good, good for you. It sounds like you are making some good friends," April noted thinking of the popularity she had received after the Brie incident.

Claire agreed with April. "Yeah, it's been a wild month, you know? I have never had this many kids want to get to know me and sincerely want to be friends. It's crazy."

Claire asked April about the book that she was reading. April picked up the book and began telling Claire about the plot. Before they knew it, thirty minutes went by as April and Claire continued talking about books in general and some of the manuscripts that had recently come across April's desk.

Feeling hungry, April suggested that they get some lunch, and Claire went up to call Blake.

Blake was on her iPad when Claire knocked on her bedroom door. "Come in," Blake called out from her bed.

"What do you want for lunch?" Claire asked Blake, as she entered her room. "April and I can't decide, and it's pretty much up to you." Claire jumped on the bed next to Blake to get a better look at her iPad. "What are you working on?" Claire asked with genuine interest.

Blake handed Claire the iPad, and said, "Just another design that I have been messing around with, nothing too special." Claire looked at the screen, and said, "This is really cool. I think that you should wear it one day. It would look great on you."

Blake looked at her design again, and shrugged. "I don't know. I was thinking about this for you."

"Well, whoever gets to wear it, I'm sure it will look fabulous on them," Claire said, as she moved to get off the bed. "Let's go and have lunch." Claire then grabbed Blake's arm to pull her up from the bed.

"Ok, ok, why don't we have homemade tacos?" Blake suggested.

"Yeah," Claire agreed, thinking that that was a good idea. "Tacos sound good."

The two girls left Blake's room and headed downstairs. Claire could hear April talking to someone, and at first thought April was on the phone. But when they got halfway down, she could see that Crystal had just arrived. She brought with her a Tupperware container of homemade cookies that she set on the kitchen counter.

"Hi, Crystal," Blake said, as she ran down the rest of the stairs. Blake went up to her and gave her a hug. Looking up at her, Blake said, "So what's this about an investigation?"

It was just like Blake to get straight to the point.

Before Crystal replied, she waved Claire over and gave her a warm hug. "Hi Claire," Crystal began. "Nice to see you again." The softness in Crystal's voice put Claire at ease.

"Good to see you too," Claire began. "So, how's it going?" It was Claire's way of asking what was going on.

The four of them took seats in the living room around the couch and La-Z-Boy. Blake took a seat on the La-Z-Boy and she sat there with her elbows on her knees and her hands cupping her face, looking intensely at Crystal.

"Go on," Blake prodded Crystal.

Crystal grinned at Blake's show of support for Claire.

"Ok guys, I didn't mean to make you all nervous, but I wanted to touch base with you on a few things that have been happening." April adjusted her position on the couch and glanced quickly at Claire.

Continuing, Crystal said, "Seattle PD have had Roger Bower under surveillance for the past month or so, and it would appear that he has been active on online chat rooms. They have had an undercover officer posing as a fifteen-year-old girl make contact, and he has been making some pretty disturbing statements." Crystal cleared her throat and kept going. "Roger Bower made comments about what he would do for her if they ever got together, which concerned us deeply. Of course, he is being somewhat vague but we have seen behavior like this a million times before. Roger seems to have a predatory disposition, and they are going to set a trap for him."

Claire was relieved that it wasn't something on the case that would prevent her from staying with April and Blake.

"So, are you saying that he might finally end up in jail?" Claire asked cautiously. "Will he get in trouble for what he tried to do to me as well?"

"Oh yeah, honey. Don't you worry?" Crystal said decisively. "That ass is going down."

April let out a smirk caused by Crystal's last statement.

"Do you really think that it will be over soon?" April asked Crystal.

"Listen, they are in the process of obtaining a search warrant for his house and property for his grandfather's wallet. If it is there, then it is proof that he lied on an official police statement. Furthermore, they are going to seize his computers and phones. Just the little they already know about his search histories and the information on the computer will be enough to put him away for a while," Crystal sounded very confident that it was all going to work out.

Crystal slowly got off the subject of Roger by asking the girls how they were doing in school and what was new in their lives. Blake went up to the bedrooms to get the dresses that they had bought for the Winter Formal to show Crystal.

"Wow, those are beautiful!" Crystal declared. "I can't wait to see them on you."

April remembered that she had taken a picture of them at the store, and she handed her phone over to Crystal so that she could see. "You two are breathtaking," Crystal remarked staring at the screen.

"Thanks, Crystal," Blake said, opening up a shoebox that she brought down with the dress. "What do you think of these?" she asked, holding up the shoes next to the dress.

"Totally awesome," Crystal nodded her approval of Blake's choice.

As Claire and Blake took the dresses and shoes back upstairs, Crystal leaned in closer to April so that she could hear her without speaking too loudly, and said, "You know, Nick would have loved seeing Blake in a dress like that." Crystal observed, "He was a really great dad and loved Blake with all his heart."

April nodded and smiled at the mention of Nick's name. "God, he would have. He would have loved going to daddy-daughter dances with her," April said, blinking at the thought of it. "He was a really good dancer and would have been that dad that took lots of pictures and took her out on the town." April then looked at Crystal, and said matter-of-factly, "Now that he is gone, you have to be the one that interrogates the boys that Blake will bring home."

That caused Crystal to laugh, and then she said, "You know it. When her date walks in, I will be sitting with my badge on and wearing my shoulder gun holster looking all threatening and stuff."

April had to laugh at the image of Crystal, looking all badass and intimidating the hell out of any potential boyfriend of Blake's.

Blake and Claire came back down to the living room. "Hey, Crystal?" Blake said, "We were just about to make homemade tacos, can you stay and join us?"

"You bet I can," Crystal grinned. "I never turn down free tacos."

April and Blake went into the kitchen to start the ground beef. Crystal and Claire stayed out in the living room as Crystal talked to Claire. April could hear that Crystal was engaging Claire in discussion about school and she was asking her how Trevor had been. By the time the ground beef was ready, Crystal had Claire laughing and talking a mile a minute. April really appreciated the way that Crystal cared for Claire and how she wanted her to be successful.

After lunch, Crystal had to get going, but before she left, she told Claire that she was proud of her for how well she had been doing with the Turners. "Don't worry about Roger Bower anymore. We are going to bring him to justice. Mark my words," April said, as she hugged Claire. "Thank you for everything and for believing in me," Claire replied.

"You are welcome, sweetie," Crystal said, as she went to hug April and Blake on her way out.

"Good bye all," Crystal said, as she waved.

"Bye, Crystal. You're the best," April told her as the elevator door closed.

Blake and Claire took seats at the island as April took a cookie from the Tupperware bowl that Crystal had brought over. "God, these cookies are awesome. If I'm not careful, I am going to eat the entire bowl."

"Not if I can help it," Blake announced, as she took a couple of cookies for herself.

Claire took a cookie as well, and after she finished eating it, she said, "I won't lie... I was a little nervous about what Crystal was going to say today."

"Me too," agreed Blake. "But, we have to remember that Crystal wouldn't do anything that would jeopardize your stay here. I mean she knows how much better it is for you to be here."

"Crystal has been my best friend my entire life and I can tell you that since her first meeting with Claire that she would do anything to help her. She knows that we care about you," April said looking at Claire, "and that we want the absolute best for you."

Blake jumped in and echoed April's sentiments, "Yeah. We want the best for you. That is why I am here to make sure you are dressed well." Blake put her index finger on her chin, as if contemplating, and then said, "That reminds me, I have to pick out your clothes for tomorrow," Blake joked to Claire.

Claire playfully nudged Blake on the shoulder, and countered, "Can I wear the pink pants and the red shirt like you always wear?" April snorted at Claire's retort.

"Ha, ha, very funny Claire," Blake said jovially. "Be careful what you wish for, I just might leave that outfit out for you tomorrow."

Claire thought about that for a second. "It won't bother me. I'll wear that for the whole day."

After they finished eating some of the cookies, Blake and Claire went upstairs to watch a movie on Netflix in Claire's room. April thought that she would give Gina a call to see how she was doing. Apparently, Gina was thrilled with the progress that April was making with Monica Towers.

Afternoon turned into evening. April was sitting on the couch in the living room on her laptop when the girls came down. Blake was carrying a hairbrush.

"Would you mind?" Blake warmly asked her mother.

"Of course," April smiled, as she closed the cover of the laptop and placed it on the coffee table.

"Who's first?" April asked.

"Me, of course," Blake blurted out as she took the familiar position on the floor in front of her mother with her back towards her. Claire sat on the La-Z-Boy, patiently waiting her turn. Blake turned on the television and selected the YouTube app so that the three of them could watch videos while sitting there.

When April finished Blake's hair, she called Claire over to her. "Your turn," she told Claire, who sat crossed-legged in front of her and let her shoulders relax. Claire loved having her hair brushed by April. It was such a simple thing, but it meant so much to her. When April finished with Claire, she handed the brush to her and then went to pick up her laptop.

Claire looked at the brush in her hand and then turned to April, and asked, "Would you like me to brush your hair?

"Um, sure," April said, smiling at Claire as she set the laptop back on the coffee table. "That would be really nice."

Claire began brushing April's hair in a fashion similar to how April had done earlier. April had to admit that it was relaxing just sitting there having Claire brush her hair. As Claire slowly brushed April's hair, it almost became hypnotic and therapeutic for her. When she finished, April turned around and said, "Thank you. That felt wonderful. Now I know why you guys like it so much."

"You're welcome, April," Claire grinned. "I love it when you do it for us. I wanted to return the favor."

"Well, I would like more of those," April said, as she ran her fingers through her own hair.

"You bet, April," Claire replied, as she smiled and sat in the La-Z-Boy.

When the night was over and the girls went upstairs to get ready for bed, Claire said good night to April and Blake and went into her bathroom to take a shower. As she stood there under the hot water, her thoughts traveled back to the events of the last two nights. How she had gone dress shopping with April and Blake. She kept remembering the image of locking eyes with April in the mirror at the store, and how she couldn't put a finger on what she had felt then. How Crystal had come over with news, and the feeling of nervousness Claire had felt about what Crystal was going to say about the investigation, and then finally how April had brushed her hair and vice versa. All of these thoughts swirled around in Claire's mind as she dried herself off and wrapped a towel around her head.

Claire climbed into bed and decided to read for a little while before officially calling it a night. She tried to relax her mind but she was feeling anxious, and couldn't quite put her finger on why. Claire fell asleep with the book on her chest and the nightstand light still on.

* *

CLAIRE WALKED INTO THE APARTMENT AFTER SCHOOL, and for some reason, she was alone. Blake was already home. As the elevator doors opened, she caught a glimpse of the inside of the apartment and knew something was terribly wrong. Inside were about five to six police officers, and they were bustling around as if looking for something.

As soon as Claire took a step into the apartment from the elevator, she was aware that there were two police officers behind her, one on each side. They closed in behind her so that if she had decided to turn back into the elevator, they would be able to prevent her from doing so.

Sitting at the dining room table were Blake and April, and you could tell that they were upset. When April saw Claire, she tried to get up from the chair, but there were four officers around her and Blake, who prevented her from standing up.

A woman detective approached Claire, and asked, "Are you Claire Forrester?" Of course, Claire thought that the detective already knew the answer just by the smug look on her face.

"Yeah. Why?" Claire bravely demanded. "What's going on?" Even though Claire was scared, she put on a defiant persona.

"I'll be asking the questions around here, if you don't mind," the detective snapped back at her.

They sat Claire on the couch, and she could barely hear April and Blake's voices coming from the dining room.

"Did you know that you have a warrant out for you?" the detective asked Claire, almost taunting her.

"Yes, but Crystal... Um, I mean Detective Evans... Crystal Evans of Chicago Police told me that it was all taken care of," Claire stammered, trying to make sense of what was going on.

"Oh no," the detective countered, "Detective Evans does not have jurisdiction in Seattle." It was almost as if this detective was delighted that she was here confronting Claire.

"But... Roger tried to rape me!" Claire tried to explain. "And I never stole his wallet!" Claire yelled, becoming more anxious and confused.

"We both know that didn't happen, right Miss Forrester?" the detective pressed, accusing Claire of lying. "You are just an ungrateful teenage bitch who didn't appreciate what the Bowers did for you."

"No!" Claire screamed as she tried to get up from the couch, but the two police officers behind her put their hands on her shoulder preventing her from standing.

"No?" the detective teased. "The correct answer is yes."

Claire couldn't believe this was happening. She turned to look at April and Blake, but there were more police officers in the room now, and their bodies were obstructing the view.

"You know, Claire," the detective grinned menacingly and said, "April is going to be in some trouble with the law because of you."

"Why?" Claire demanded, not believing this was happening. Her heart was pounding and tears were beginning to flow.

"Because it's against the law to harbor a fugitive, especially a minor," the detective said darkly. "And you little Miss Know-It-All are a minor and a fugitive," the detective began to laugh, as if the situation that Claire was in was actually funny.

Claire's thoughts were scrambled because her emotions were going haywire.

"But, but, there is paperwork by Chicago CPS. They filled it out. We are legal," Claire stammered, hoping that the detective would believe her.

"I told you, Claire!" the detective suddenly raised her voice and pointed her finger at her, "Chicago doesn't have the authority!"

As Claire continued to explain her situation, two police officers walked by, leading April and Blake out of the apartment in handcuffs.

"No! Please! Wait," Claire jumped up and tried to get to them.

"Claire!" Blake yelled as the cop pushed her through the apartment and headed for the elevator.

"Blake! Don't go!" Claire yelled after her.

"Please let us go!" April pleaded with the cop. Then she tried to look at Claire and yelled, "Claire! I'm sorry! Please don't go!"

The cops were pushing April and Blake towards the elevator, and the detective looked directly at Claire, and asked, "So... Claire... Why should I let you stay here? Why?"

April and Blake were forced into the elevator, and Claire looked at April. Both of them were crying, but through the tears, Claire caught April's eyes and it was the exact look that she saw in the mirror of the dress shop and she began to realize what it was.

"Why? Why should I let you stay?" the detective yelled again, almost in a rage.

"Because...I...," Claire tried to answer.

"Because, what?" the detective interrupted. "What? Because you...?"

The elevator doors began to close. Claire needed April to hear this before the doors closed.

Claire had one last chance to tell everyone why. Keeping her eyes locked on April's, she shrieked, "Because... I..."

Claire was abruptly torn from the scene of the living room as everything disappeared and she was suddenly lying in her bed under the covers. April and Blake were standing over her. "Wake up, Claire," April was saying, as she softly put her hand on Claire's shoulder to wake her up.

"Wake up, Claire," Blake said, a little concerned.

Claire's heart was pounding from the nightmare. Beads of sweat were coalescing on her forehead as she tried to catch her breath, as if the wind had been knocked out of her.

"Claire? Are you alright?" April asked softly, knowing that Claire had just woken up from a nightmare.

"You were yelling and screaming," Blake offered, explaining why they were in her room. "You were really loud and it sounded like you were being attacked or something," Blake said, trying to explain the ruckus in her bedroom.

Claire's eyes focused on April and Blake, and she realized that the police in the apartment was just a part of a nightmare she had seen. "Oh my God!" Claire exclaimed breathlessly. "You're here?" Claire sat up from her bed and held her arms apart so that she could hug both of them at the same time.

"It's going to be ok now," April, said soothingly. "The nightmare is over."

"What happened?" Blake wanted to know.

Claire started to recite the dream as if she had just watched a movie. However, she was breathing heavily, as though she had just run up a flight of stairs. She told them about how when she got home, the police were already there, interrogating both of them. Claire went into the part about how the detective was really mean to her and would not listen to her when she was explaining how Crystal had taken care of everything.

"The police officers had both of you handcuffed, and were taking you away to the station. The detective kept asking me why I wanted to stay but she wouldn't let me say." The frustration of that part of the nightmare cut deep in Claire's memory. "I just had to tell you guys..." Claire paused for a second, as if she couldn't put into words what she was feeling.

"I mean, you were being taken away and I wanted to tell you before the elevator doors closed," Claire said.

"Tell us what?" April asked, bewildered, wondering what Claire was trying to tell them.

Claire looked at April and Blake, and her eyes widened with the complete realization of what it was.

"Oh my God," Claire said, as if talking to herself.

"What?" April asked anxiously.

"Oh my God," Claire said again, but this time it was almost a chuckle. Claire then looked at April, and said, "I just had to tell you guys that... that... I love you." Claire's eyes rolled up just a little to try to prevent tears from slipping out of her eyes.

The look in the mirror at the dress shop between her and April was that of love. The moment at breakfast when Claire had hesitated before saying April's name was because she had almost called her 'mom'. When the police officers in her dream wanted to take them away from her, Claire knew in that moment that she had to tell them that she loved them.

Claire began to cry happy, emotional tears at her epiphany. "I couldn't let you go without letting you know that I love you—both of you," Claire said. April had to wipe a tear away as she smiled at what Claire had just told them.

"Oh, Claire, we love you too," April confessed, as she put her hand on Claire's cheek, and then pulled her close again for another hug. Blake joined in the hug. "We love you," Blake echoed her mom's sentiment.

Claire had moved out from under the covers, and was now sitting on her knees on the bed. "I have never felt this way before, and I think that it took me by surprise. I mean, I loved my mom, but I was really young and didn't know anything else. When I went to my previous foster families, I was never this attached, not even close," Claire said, smiling as she spoke. The emotions of realization overwhelmed her. "But here, with the both of you, I have found what I should have had years ago—a family that I love." Claire didn't want to stop talking. "When I thought that you two were going to be ripped away from me, it became clear what my heart was feeling. I needed to tell you that I love you."

April knew that when she had first met Claire, there was an instant connection. A fondness that was undeniable. At the time, she didn't know if it was because Nick's voice had drawn her to Claire, but, as time went by, April was subconsciously aware that she too was feeling love for this girl. When April caught the mirror's reflection of the girls at the dress shop, she too realized the truth. That she loved both of them. And that was the look that Claire had seen on April's face—the look of love for her two girls.

"I am so happy that you feel this way," April told Claire. "You know that we have wanted you since the beginning, and I am thrilled that you have accepted us into your heart," April said, pausing for a moment as if she was translating what her heart was telling her to say. "I think that from the beginning, we knew that there was something special about you, and that is why we wanted you here with us. I immediately felt this connection with you and fondness that I couldn't explain. So, here we all are, finally expressing what our hearts have been trying to tell us."

Blake knew that Claire was her best friend and to hear her express her emotions this way was uplifting. She considered Claire as a sister, and this revelation tonight only made that bond stronger. However, it was 2:45 am, and she was emotional because of Claire's proclamation, and she was tired.

"Claire, I love you too. I mean it. You are like a sister to me," Blake said affectionately, "but it's like three in the morning. I promise that I will love you just the same after we get more sleep."

All three of them broke out in laughter at Blake's comment.

Then, on a serious note, April asked, "Are you ok to go back to sleep after your nightmare? Do you want me to stay up with you?"

Even though Claire was still riding an emotional roller-coaster after the traumatic events of her nightmare, she felt like a weight had been lifted off of her soul, and divulging her love for them had given her power over her dream.

"I'm ok now," Claire said gratefully. "I feel a lot better."

"Ok, sweetie," April said, as she got up from the bed. "See you in the morning." Then pausing for only the briefest of moments, she added, "Love you." When she said it, the words were genuine and heartfelt.

"Love you too," Claire grinned, as she replied. This was the first time, in probably her entire life, that she truly, genuinely, meant it.

CHAPTER NINETEEN

THE DAY OF THE WINTER FORMAL HAD FINALLY ARRIVED. The school was buzzing with excitement as the class hours flew by. Claire was actually feeling giddy and couldn't stop smiling. She and Trevor were caught kissing by the lockers, but because it was the day of the dance, they just received a verbal warning for excessive show of affection.

Blake was in full fashion mode, and had actually assisted four other girls besides Claire, Rose, and Shelly. Word had gotten out that Blake was the 'go to' girl for the hottest fashions, and Blake was relishing every moment of the attention.

At lunch, Claire was joking and laughing with Trevor when Shelly and Rose jumped up from behind them causing Claire and Trevor to jump, startled.

"Hey guys," Claire said, as the two friends sat down across from Claire and Trevor. "How's it going?"

"Great," Rose declared. "I got an "A" on my math test, thanks to Shelly here who stayed up all night with me to study." Rose nodded her head in Shelly's direction as Shelly grinned and said, "Damn right it was me. She wouldn't let me leave last night until she understood it all. I had to drink 2 Monsters to stay up, and guess what? That's right. I was up all night long!" Shelly jokingly complained, as she pretended to look like she was wired. "Now I am about to crash and I have three more classes to go."

Rose shrugged as if Shelly's predicament was of no consequence, "That may be so but... I got an 'A' remember?"

Blake walked up to the table talking to a girl—a freshman that Claire and the rest of the gang didn't know. Blake was showing her a picture of the dress that the girl had apparently purchased on Blake's advice.

"I think that you can use these shoes with it, and I'm thinking about this necklace," Blake said to the girl, who had taken pictures of her closet and the shoes.

"Cool. Thanks, Blake. I didn't know what would look better. Since my mom died, my dad tries, but he is really no good at this kind of stuff," she said. Her mom had passed away when she was six years old, and her dad had raised her by himself. He had done an amazing job, but at times like these, there was no replacement for a girl's mom.

"No problem, it's what I do," Blake replied happily, as she took a seat at the lunch table. The girl waved bye and headed towards the other end of the lunchroom.

"Still working, fairy Godmother?" Rose teased Blake, as she nudged her with a smile.

"Actually, yes I am," Blake said, holding up her iPad to show the dress on the screen. "This one is for Michelle Young, a girl from my gym class."

"It's not as good as my dress," Rose joked, "but it should work for her."

Blake smirked and nudged Rose back. "And yours will definitely work for you. I love how it looks on you." Blake swiped the screen on the iPad and brought up the picture of Rose in her dress that Blake had taken three days earlier.

Claire listened to her friends talk about the dance as she leaned up against Trevor's shoulder and looked across the lunchroom. Most of the students just blended in the crowd, but as she focused on a group in particular, Claire realized that Brie was one of them. Luckily for Claire, Brie didn't notice Claire watching her. Brie was talking to a student named Russell Quinn, and it looked like Brie was a little nervous. Russell was a fairly tall kid for his age. He stood approximately six foot high, and he was a tiny bit gangly. He was one of those kids who had had a growth spurt, but unfortunately, his mind hadn't caught up with the length of his limbs. He wasn't klutzy per se, but he was a little clumsy. Claire only had him in one class so far, and she was indifferent to him. It seemed to Claire that Russell was only partly popular because his parents were extremely rich, but because Russell was kind of awkward, his popularity wasn't as high up the chart as it might have been otherwise. Not to mention that he had the tendency to be a jerk from time to time.

So Claire couldn't help but listen to the conversation that Brie and Russell were having. As they talked, it became clear to Claire that Russell had asked Brie to the Winter Formal and she apparently had said 'yes'. They were discussing arrangements for tonight. Even though Claire was still upset with Brie for doing what she had to her, Claire couldn't help but think in the back of her mind that Brie could do better.

Claire turned her attention back to her friends at her table because she didn't want Brie to see that she had been listening in on her. Claire had just turned her eyes away when Brie happened to look at her table. She missed the fact that Claire had eavesdropped on her conversation with Russel, and instead, she only saw Claire's head resting comfortably on Trevor's shoulder. Brie blinked as a feeling of regret washed over her—regret for the split with Trevor, regret for the way she had treated Claire, and regret for the position that she found herself in at this particular time in her life. The past two months had taken their toll on Brie as she began to fully realize that rut that she was now stuck in.

Russell Quinn was definitely not on Brie's short list of suitors that she would have wanted to take her to the dance, but there wasn't exactly a line of guys hitting up her phone, begging her to go with them.

Brie forced a smile on her face as she walked away from Russell and the group of students that she was in, and headed to the lunch line to pick out what she was going to have for lunch. She was just about to pick up a tray, when two freshmen nerds, who were conducting a fake light saber battle, inadvertently bumped into Brie and knocked the phone out of her back pocket. The phone, of course, landed on the corner edge of the buffet counter, which caused the screen to crack.

"Great, just fucking great," Brie mused.

Brie gave the two freshmen a totally pissed off stare but she decided not to yell or say anything to them because she didn't want to be judged again for making a scene, even though this time probably it would have been justified.

Brie angrily picked up her phone and with a huge sigh, put it back into her pocket and reached for a lunch tray without saying another word.

* *

BLAKE AND CLAIRE WALKED DOWN THE STAIRCASE OF THE apartment to the excited eyes of about a dozen people. April's parents were at the apartment when the girls got home from school. A few minutes after that, Crystal and Tripp had shown up eager to see the girls in their dresses. Now, as Claire and Blake walked slowly down the stairs, they could see that Gina, Wanda, and Monica were here as well.

"You two look amazing," Joseph declared, with a proud smile on his face. It brought back memories of when April was a teenage girl, and had dressed up for her dances and proms.

It took about half an hour for everyone to get the pictures and poses they wanted with Claire and Blake. A few minutes before five-o-clock, Trevor showed up with a beautiful wrist corsage that matched her dress. Of course, April had purchased a boutonniere for Claire to present to Trevor. There were several pictures taken in various poses.

Claire's phone rang, and it was Shelly informing her that she and Rose had just arrived with their dates, and were on their way up. Of course, when they got to the apartment, there were even more pictures taken.

Just before the group was about to leave for the dance, Joseph took Trevor aside, and because there wasn't a father figure in the lives of the Turner girls right now, took it upon himself to give Trevor 'The Speech'.

The talk didn't take long, and Joseph wasn't too intimidating, however, Trevor did get the feeling that Joseph wasn't playing around and that he should be on his best behavior.

As the girls and Trevor headed to the elevator, Joseph wanted to make an announcement.

"I just want to say that all of you look simply remarkable, and it makes me happy that I am here to be a part of it. Also, as you know, Derek is downstairs waiting to take you to dinner and then the dance. However, it won't be in my black Suburban. I got you all a limousine for tonight so that you can enjoy the ride to and from the dance." Joseph paused a moment to let the party of dancegoers thank him for the limo, and then he said, "Oh, by the way, dinner is already taken care of, and I think you will find it delightful."

The group thanked Joseph yet again and made their way down to the lobby. When they walked outside, Rose and Shelly gasped at the sight of the limo.

"Holy cow!" Rose exclaimed. "This is awesome! Look at the size of this car!" The limo was a beautiful white, super long stretch car that had colored lights glowing from the undercarriage of the vehicle. It had soft, leather seats that felt more like couches then actual car seats. There were two monitors on each side of the car with one larger monitor towards the front. There were two separate bars in the limo and they were stocked with all sorts of sodas, juices, waters, and sparkling white grape juice. Of course, every drop of alcohol had been removed.

The limo stopped at a very elegant and expensive restaurant. They had reservations, of course, and the appetizers were promptly served almost immediately after they took their seats.

The group enjoyed great conversation, and even though Blake was the only one that didn't have a date, she was having a blast. Blake was the only freshman present, but that didn't seem to matter. Shelly and Rose considered her not only Claire's foster sister, but a friend as well. Blake was truly one of the team.

Dinner was brought out quickly, and Claire surmised that Joseph had probably instructed the restaurant to make sure that the group was well taken care of, so that they wouldn't be late for the dance.

After dinner, they all piled back into the limo and headed towards the school. It had begun to snow lightly, and everything looked beautiful. The way the city lights reflected the snowflakes in the distance just added to the romantic feeling of the night.

The limo pulled up to the school, and the group piled out. It was just two minutes after 7:00 p.m. and the dance had just begun. Students were pouring into the school. There was a classroom just before the gym that was set up as a coat check, so that the students could have a proper place to store their winter coats and scarves.

When you walked through the door of the gym, you entered through a tunnel that was designed to look like ice. Once through, it opened up into a magical winter wonderland themed room that made you feel like you were actually at the North Pole. The school had hired local sculptors to carve ice blocks into beautiful statues that were positioned all around the outer rim of the gym. Holographic projectors had been placed strategically around the corners of the dance floor that made it look like you were dancing on real snow. There was a popular local band that was setting up on stage, but in the meantime, a DJ was jamming out in a booth next to the stage as he picked out songs to play.

The group made their way towards a round table that was close to the dance floor, and placed their purses and cell phones down. Even though the music was playing, there were only a handful of students actually on the dance floor. Claire was just about to pull the chair out to sit when Rose and Shelly grabbed her hand, and Shelly said, "Oh no, you don't. Let's get this party started!" Rose pulled Claire as Shelly pulled Trevor to the dance floor as their dates followed suit. The group started to get down with the music as Claire waved Blake over to join them. Blake ran up next to Claire and began showing what she could do.

Halfway through the song, Rose commented to Blake affectionately, "Wow freshman, you can really dance."

"Thanks, Rose," Blake smiled, as she spun and put her arms up with the music.

Claire was having a great time. She was holding her own on the dance floor. Trevor was a good dancer and was keeping up with the entire group. After ten minutes, the DJ decided to change the mood with a slow song. The couples began to pair up, and Trevor stepped up to Claire and put his arm around her waist. Because Claire and Trevor hadn't practiced any kind of slow dancing, Trevor just led Claire through a box step, mixing it with a spin from time to time.

As the dance continued on, Claire and her group were having a blast. Shelly and Rose's dates were really nice guys, and Rose's date was an amazing dancer. Claire's feet were beginning to hurt as she realized she had been danc-ing continuously for the past hour. Claire and Trevor decided to sit a couple of songs out while they got something to drink from the punch bowl.

"God, you're beautiful tonight," Trevor said, as he smiled at her and raised the crystal cup up to take a sip.

"Why thank you, you don't look too shabby yourself," Claire said, paying him a compliment back.

As Claire looked at Trevor under the spotlights of the gym, she noticed that his jawline was even more pronounced. His neck was getting a tad bit thicker, not because he was gaining weight, but because he was gaining muscle. Trevor had taken off this tuxedo jacket about fifteen minutes ago, and you could see the muscles straining under his dress shirt.

God, he's hot, Claire thought to herself, as she stood next to him.

Just then, another slow song began, and Trevor took her cup from her and set it down on the small table next to the punch bowl. "Shall we?" he asked, as he grabbed her hand and led her to the dance floor, not waiting for her to answer.

This time, he had her entire body wrapped around him, almost like they were hugging, and then began to slowly sway back and forth. Claire laid her head on his shoulder, and began to quietly hum to the music. As they slowly moved in a circle, Trevor moved his head slightly to whisper in Claire's ear.

"I love you," Trevor said softly.

Startled by his words, Claire raised her head up so that her eyes were locked into his. She could tell that he meant what he had said. She kept her eyes gazing into his, taking a few moments to intensely examine all the parts that made up his pupils.

Claire smiled and replied back tenderly, "I love you too." Claire then put her head back onto his shoulder as the song continued. As they swayed, Claire's mind began to race. She was elated that her boyfriend had said the three words that all girls want to hear, but at the same time, Claire was feeling apprehensive. She had just announced to April and Blake that she had loved them, and it was the first time in a long time that she had felt that way towards anyone.

Now, here at the Winter Formal, Trevor had expressed his love for her, and she wondered if she truly did love him back. It had been only a month since they had been going steady, and even though she really liked him and loved spending time with him, did she genuinely love him?

Claire's head began to feel like it was filled with helium as the song ended, and she wanted to sit down for a minute. Trevor and Claire walked off the dance floor hand and hand. As they approached their table, Brie and Russell just happened to be walking towards them. Both couples had to stop in order for one of them to get through the chairs that were placed around the tables. Claire softly pulled Trevor's hand to signal that they would stop, thus allowing Brie and Russell to pass.

As Russell looked up, he noticed Trevor, and put his hand up for a high-five. Trevor really didn't care for Russell but he had known him since grade school, so they were kind of acquaintances. Trevor gave him a high-five back just to be nice, as Russell exclaimed, "Hey Trevor, how's it hanging?"

Claire could see Brie cringe as Russell spoke, but didn't say anything. She had this sickened look on her face, as Russell engaged Trevor in conversation. Claire could only guess that Brie didn't want to be with the only two people in the entire school that had literally turned her life upside-down within a course of a couple of weeks.

"What's up, man?" Trevor answered politely, trying to make this encounter as short as possible.

Russell grabbed Brie's hand with excitement and held it up as if it was a prize that he had just won. "Just dancing with the hottest chick here." Then he looked at Claire, and joked, "No offense."

Brie shot Claire a quick look of embarrassment, implying that she was sorry for Russell's words.

Claire found Russell repulsing. She knew that Brie did as well. Claire simply grinned and replied, "None taken."

Claire waved the couple through, and as they passed, she thought that she caught a faint whiff of alcohol on Russell's breath. It was very faint, but during her time on the streets, Claire had developed a keen sense of smell, which she had learned to trust.

Once Claire and Trevor made it to their seats, Claire asked him, "Did you smell the alcohol on Russell's breath?"

"No," Trevor replied, honestly. "I didn't, but I would be drinking if I had to take Brie to this dance." Trevor's tone instantly changed, and it was like a switch turned on, and he was spiteful.

Claire gave Trevor a dirty look. "Wow, mean much?" Claire asked, completely surprised by the manner in which Trevor's emotions had just turned.

Trying to grin, Trevor backpedaled, and said, "Look, I mean I am still mad at her for what she did to you, that's all. I love you now, so I don't really care about her and her date."

Claire looked at Trevor for a few more seconds, and then turned her attention to the table. She picked up her cell phone and began flipping through all the pictures that she had taken so far tonight. There were a ton of pictures of her and Trevor posing for the camera and then some that were action shots of them dancing. There was one of her and Blake on the dance floor and it was a super cute one. Thinking about Blake, Claire scanned the room to see if she could locate her. After a few seconds, she found her on the dance floor dancing with a sophomore boy. They were cute together, and you could tell that they were just dancing for fun.

It was now a little past 9:00 p.m., and the band had been playing non-stop for the past hour-and-a-half. Claire, Shelly, Rose and Blake were all on the dance floor jumping and bouncing to the fast-paced song that the band was playing. Trevor and the guys had sat down at the table a few minutes ago because clearly they couldn't keep up with the girls.

The band had just announced that they were going to take a twenty-minute break, but that they would be back to close the dance. After a brief moment of silence, the DJ started to take requests from the students and began to play a song that Claire really didn't care for. Hot and tired, she and Blake headed towards the table, but before they got there, Blake said to Claire that she had to go to the bathroom.

"I'll go with you," Claire offered, and then told Trevor that she would be right back because she was going to walk with Blake to the bathroom. Trevor was in the middle of a discussion about a new video game that had just been released with the guys that Rose and Shelly had brought to the dance. They had been playing it for the past few days. Trevor nodded an acknowledgment to Claire, and continued talking.

Claire and Blake walked out of the gym and headed down the hallway towards the bathroom.

Brie was tired and severely agitated. Her date with Russell hadn't worked out the way she had hoped, and all she wanted was for it to end. Russell had snuck in a flask of whiskey, and had had most of it. Even though he wasn't totally wasted, he was getting louder and acting more like a jerk than usual.

After sitting at the table alone for twenty minutes while Russell danced around clumsily, Brie decided that it was time to go. She got up and with a solo cup full of soda in her left hand, headed out of the gym. She was on her way to the coat check just past the bathrooms when she heard a voice calling out to her from behind.

"Hey, Brie, wait up." It was Russell. He had noticed her walking out of the gym and wanted to know what was up.

"What's going on? Where are you going?" Russell asked, slurring a bit over his words.

Brie sighed and couldn't hide her disgust any longer. "Look Russell," Brie started. "I'm tired and I don't feel good, so I want to go home." Brie felt fine except for the pounding in her head that was caused by being with Russell for a lengthy amount of time.

"You can't go yet," Russell demanded. "The dance isn't over, and we didn't get a chance to kiss yet."

Brie almost threw up in her mouth at the thought of kissing him.

"Ah, no," Brie stammered, "this date is over, and we are not going to kiss."

Brie turned away from Russell to head back towards the coat check, when he said, "No, wait!" He then reached out to grab Brie's shoulder to stop her. Unfortunately, he misjudged the distance, and he could only grasp the sleeve of Brie's dress. The sleeve tore, causing Brie to spin back around facing Russell, which in turn made her lose her grip on the solo cup, which fell to the floor, its contents spilling all over her chest.

Shocked at the force with which Russell had pulled her, and the cold liquid on her dress, Brie instinctively took a step back. Her heel caught the edge of the puddle of soda on the floor, making her lose her footing. She fell down on the floor, landing on her right knee with a thud.

Witnessing what had just happened, Russell took a step towards Brie to reach out in order to help her up, but as he stepped towards her, his dress shoe landed squarely in the middle of the puddle, causing him to fall face first, and he landed hard on Brie. The heel on Brie's shoe snapped due to the weight and pressure of Russell's body. His hand landed on Brie's tiny purse that contained her cell phone and makeup, causing it to empty all over the floor.

Brie cried out in pain as Russell lay on her, twisting and convulsing, trying to push himself off of her.

Claire and Blake were walking down the hallway towards the bathroom. From the far end of the hall, it looked as if Russell had grabbed Brie and thrown her to the ground and then jumped on her. Claire and Blake had witnessed it from halfway across the hall.

"Get the fuck off of her!" Claire yelled, as she ran up to them. Blake was right behind her, shocked at what she saw. Claire got to them within seconds and pushed Russell off of Brie, which sent him rolling on the floor.

Brie was lying on the floor, drenched in soda, dress ripped, and tears running down her cheeks. Looking at Russell with wide eyes, Claire exclaimed, "What the hell were you doing?"

Russell jumped up off the floor and took a step towards Brie to help her again, trying to explain what had happened. "I, I was trying to..." he started to say, but before he could say another word, Claire stepped between Brie and Russell, and held up her hand to stop him.

"You know what? I don't want to hear it," Claire declared, as she lowered her hand towards Brie to help her up. Brie slowly accepted Claire's hand and Claire pulled her up. By now, several students had seen the commotion, and begun to gather in the direction of where this had all happened.

Russell turned and started walking away. At that point, Claire noticed Brie's broken shoe and cell phone screen, and yelled at Russell, "Hey, Ass hat?"

Russell figured that he better turn around to acknowledge Claire.

"What?" he asked meekly.

Claire held up Brie's shoe and cell phone, and forcibly asked him, "You are going to pay for these, right?" Despite her words constituting a question, Russell got the impression that it was a demand.

"Yes, but the phone was already...," Russell said, as he tried to explain that Brie's phone had been broken several hours before and that he had not broken it, but he thought better of it. Seeing the fierce look on Claire's face, he mentally calculated that a new pair of shoes and a cell phone screen repair would involve far less hassle than the alternative.

"Yes, I will take care of both," Russell relented, and then asked, "Can I go now?"

Satisfied with his answer, Claire dismissed him with a wave, "Yeah, get the fuck out of here."

Blake stood there through the entire incident with her mouth open. She was so proud of Claire for what she had just done.

The three of them stood there in silence for a few moments, allowing the shock of the incident to subside. Brie looked at Claire, and whispered, "Thank you."

Brie turned back towards the coat closet and with her broken shoe in one hand, and her purse and cell phone in the other, started to limp away only wearing one shoe. Brie had tears flowing down her cheeks, which was causing her mascara to run. Her face was distorted by the emotions of despair that she felt. She was at the lowest point in her life.

Claire saw the look on Brie's face, and she knew that she was deflated and broken. At that moment, everything that Brie had done to Claire shattered into pieces and was swept away from Claire's mind. Claire thought back to her time on the streets, and realized this is how she must have looked the day that April and Blake had found her.

In a moment of clarity, Claire called out, "Hey Brie, wait."

Brie stopped walking, and then slowly turned towards Claire.

As they faced each other, Claire held out her arms and stepped towards Brie, wrapping her up in a hug. Brie wanted to resist, but her emotions got the better of her, and she let her arms fall to the side, allowing Claire to hug her. Claire had a flashback of the day when she was throwing up with the flu, and

April had instinctively known that it was the worst time of Claire's life. In spite of only knowing Claire for twenty-four hours, April had hugged her to let her know that everything was going to be ok.

Still embracing her, Claire told Brie, "The shit between us is over, ok? I forgive you, and I want us to be friends." Pausing only briefly, Claire finished by offering, "We're good now."

Claire held the hug for a few more seconds, waiting for a response from Brie. When she didn't say anything, Claire started to release her, but suddenly, Brie raised both arms, still holding her purse and cell phone in her hands, and wrapped her arms tightly around her. She was sobbing and Claire could feel the wetness from the tears on her own shoulders.

"Ok," Brie answered, as the weight of the world just got taken off from her shoulders by Claire's words.

"Ok," Brie said, again as she nodded her head.

After a few moments, Claire released Brie, and took in her appearance.

"Don't take this the wrong way," Claire said, as she wiped a tear from her own eyes, "but you look like shit."

Claire and Brie both began to laugh, as the students who were around started chuckling too.

"Come on," Claire said, grabbing Brie's hand. "Let's go get you cleaned up." Turning to Blake, and pointing at the stain and the rip in Brie's dress, Claire asked her, "Can you help Brie with this?"

Blake was surprised that Claire had forgiven Brie, and that she was going to be friends with her. But she quickly realized that Claire had made up her mind and this is what she wanted.

"Ok... umm, well, ok, we're doing this," Blake said matter-of-factly, deciding how to deal with the situation that she and Claire were now in. Remembering that Claire had asked her a question, Blake answered, "Yes, yes, of course. Come on Brie, follow me." Blake took Brie's hand from Claire and led her to the bathroom.

Claire walked a few steps behind, watching Blake talk to Brie, telling her that it was going to be ok.

Blake instructed Claire to find some seltzer water, and then asked another girl who just happened to be walking by to go to the Home Ec. Room to grab the sewing kit that Blake knew was in one of the cabinets.

As Blake worked on Brie's dress, Claire moistened a piece of paper towel and helped Brie wipe the makeup off her face. It took several minutes, but by the time they were done, Brie ended up looking almost good as new. Blake had removed most of the stain off Brie's dress with the seltzer water, and had sewn enough of the shoulder to hold it in place for the rest of the night.

The three of them walked back into the gym like they were Charlie's Angels. They walked up to the table at which Trevor, Rose, and Shelly were sitting, and each took a seat. Trevor had this look of 'What the hell is she doing here' as Rose and Shelly looked bewildered.

"Look guys," Claire explained, "Brie and I just made up, and I would like us to be friends. Actually, I would like all of us to be friends." Noting the stunned looks around the table, Claire continued, "So, please help me make the rest of this evening a night that we won't forget, ok?"

Even though Rose and Shelly were protective of Claire, it was evident that something had happened in the hallway to change her feelings for Brie. They considered Claire to be their best friend, and so if Claire was ok with Brie, then they would be too.

"You got it, Claire," Shelly conceded. Rose nodded her head in agreement.

Trevor leaned in to whisper into Claire's ear, and asked, "What the hell?"

Claire looked at Trevor and whispered back, "I'll explain later." Blake got Brie something to drink, and placed a napkin in her lap, you know, just in case.

The group sat there for several minutes until *Shut up and dance with me* started playing over the speakers.

"Claire!" Blake exclaimed enthusiastically, "it's our song!" Blake jumped up from the table and grabbed her hand, saying, "Come on!" As she moved to the dance floor, Claire waved at everyone at the table to join them. "Let's dance everyone!" Claire yelled as she found an empty spot on the dance floor and began dancing.

Everyone at the table got up, but Brie thought that she should stay. Rose and Shelly noticed that Brie was still sitting at the table, and they quickly went to her and grabbed her hands. "You too." Shelly smiled as they pulled her to the dance floor and deposited her right in the middle of the group.

Blake and Claire surrounded Brie as they danced, and Brie began to dance with the group. The entire group raised their arms, danced and laughed throughout the song.

After that, the band got back on stage, and decided to start things off with a slow song. Claire and Trevor began to dance as a couple as Blake and Brie sat back down at the table.

Claire explained to Trevor what had happened with Brie and what Russell had done. Even though he understood why Claire had saved Brie, he still couldn't wrap his mind around why Claire would want to bring Brie into the fold. "I don't know, Trevor. It just felt like something I needed to do. You weren't there, and didn't see what I saw."

Trevor just shook his head and continued to dance with Claire. As they danced, Claire glanced towards the table where Brie was sitting and then decided to wave Brie onto the dance floor. Knowing it was still a slow song that was playing, Brie shook her head so that Claire could finish it with Trevor. Claire stopped moving and waved Brie on the dance floor again. Reluctantly, Brie walked towards them.

"What are you doing?" Trevor whispered to Claire.

"Trust me," said Claire, and then welcomed Brie to be the third dancer. Trevor was in the middle with Brie and Claire on either side. The three of them finished the dance, and went back to the table.

The dance was almost over, and students began to slowly wander out of the gym. There were just a few couples left on the dance floor.

They were all sitting at the table with Brie next to Claire. There was a single long crack on Brie's phone screen, from the top right corner to bottom left. She could still use it. Claire noticed that she was texting her mom to come and get her.

"Don't worry, we can take you home," Claire told Brie. We have a limo that is big enough for all of us, so it won't be a problem."

Brie stopped and asked, "Are you sure? My mom won't mind coming to get me."

"Seriously, it's no trouble at all. We've got plenty of room," Claire said, as she looked around the table and everyone agreed.

"Well, ok then," Brie hesitantly said.

As they walked down the hallway, unknown to the group, a student snapped a picture of all the girls as they had unintentionally spread across the length of the entire hallway. The student had captured them as they were approaching, and as luck would have it, every member of the group was smiling at the same time—even Brie. It would later turn out to be a remarkable picture in the student yearbook.

After everyone else had been dropped off, the only person left in the limo besides Claire and Blake was Brie. Blake lay across the seat like she was on a bed, and used one of the pillows in the limo to prop her head up. "That was an amazing night," Blake said, closing her eyes pretending that she was sleeping.

"Yes, it was," Brie said, looking at Claire. "You know, I didn't really thank you for what you did." Then after pausing for a few seconds, Brie asked, "Why did you help me anyways? Especially after what I did to you?" It was a fair question, and Claire didn't understand the reason fully herself.

"To be honest, I just had to help you. I mean I saw Russell push you to the ground and then fall on top of you. Something in me just wanted to spring into action," Claire said, looking at Brie and trying to think of the right words. Without looking up, Claire continued, "When I saw the look on your face when you turned around to leave, it brought back memories of what I used to be. I saw who I was in your eyes."

"Thank you, Claire, for everything," Brie said honestly.

"You're welcome," Blake chimed in. "I mean, the dress didn't fix itself you know," Blake pointed out with a grin.

"Oh yes, thank you," Brie smiled knowing that Blake had been a big help. "Seriously, to both of you, thanks."

When they got to Brie's house, Brie's mother was by the door waiting. Brie had texted her saying she would be coming home with Claire and her friends in the limo, and that she would explain everything when she got home. Brie wanted Claire to go up with her for a minute so both girls got out while Blake stayed in the limo.

Blake could see the three of them talking just inside the entrance of the door, and could only imagine what Brie's mother must have been thinking. Here Brie was with the girl who she had gotten in trouble for bullying, and now they had just spent the last part of the Winter Formal together, and Claire had helped her out of a potentially difficult situation with Russell.

After a few minutes, Blake noticed that Brie was coming back to the car with Claire and she was carrying a bag.

"Everything ok?" Blake asked, looking at Brie and her bag.

"Yeah, it's all good. Brie is going to spend the night with us tonight," Claire offered as an explanation. "I texted April and asked her, and said that I would tell her about it when I got home."

"Ok, cool," said Blake, as she laid back down on the car seat. By the time the limo got to the Turner apartment, Blake was fast asleep.

* *

IT WAS 11:00 A.M. ON SATURDAY MORNING, WHEN THE GIRLS finally woke up. The night before when they got home, Claire had explained everything to April, and thanked her for letting Brie spend the night. Claire and Blake spent a few minutes telling April how great the night had been, and that they had had an awesome time. Because Blake was whipped, she went up to bed a few minutes after that. Claire and Brie talked to April a little while longer, explaining what had happened with Russell, and how Claire and Blake had fixed Brie's dress and makeup and finished the night out. April was glad that everything had turned out well, and that they all had had a great time.

Claire and Brie had stayed up talking and watching TV until 3:30 a.m., when they had both fallen asleep. Claire had told Brie all about her childhood and how bad it actually was. Brie got a glimpse of the struggles that Claire had had to endure, and began to fully appreciate how kind and compassionate Claire truly was, despite all the obstacles that she had faced throughout her life.

April made breakfast when she heard the girls moving around upstairs.

Blake came down first, and she looked exhausted.

"Good morning, darling," April said. "How are you feeling?"

"Sore and tired," replied Blake, slowly sitting on the bar stool near the island. "My feet are killing me, and my whole body is sore. I must have danced the entire night." Even though she was complaining about the pain, there was a hint of pride in it, not regret.

"Here, have some breakfast and coffee. It may help to get some food in you so you can regain some energy," April suggested, as she placed the plate of eggs and toast in front of Blake.

"You got it, mom," Blake grinned, as she dug into the eggs with her fork.

A few minutes later, Claire and Brie came down looking almost as tired as Blake. They sat at the table after they got their plates from the kitchen, so Blake picked up her plate and joined them at the table. After breakfast, Brie thanked them again, and told Claire to call her later that day if she wanted. Claire said that she would and that she was glad that Brie had spent the night.

As the day wore on, the girls just wanted to stay home and veg. All three of them ended up in the living room later in the afternoon. Blake was seated in the La-Z-Boy with her feet up, letting her body recover from the rigorous dance moves that she had put it through. April had her laptop on, and was going over some notes on the new novel that Monica was working on. Claire also had her laptop on, and was working on an essay that she had to write for school. It wasn't due until Wednesday but she wanted to get it out of the way.

Claire's phone went off—it was Trevor texting her asking her what she was up to. Claire texted back saying she was just hanging out with April and Blake today. He told her that he was going to hang out with the guys at Jordan's house outside of the city. Jordan's house had about twenty acres of property that included a huge pond and a wooded area. Jordan was getting a group of people over to play hockey on the frozen pond, and then they would go riding on the snowmobile. Claire told Trevor to have a great time, and to call her when he got back home.

Claire got up from the couch to make herself a cup of coffee. She asked April if she wanted one, and of course, April did. Claire was about to ask Blake but noticed that she had fallen asleep on the chair. Claire quietly went into the kitchen and made two cups. She handed April hers as she sat back down on the couch.

"How is grandma doing?" Claire quietly asked April about the phone call that she had received from Anne before she sat on the couch to work on her laptop.

"Oh, really good. She couldn't stop talking about how beautiful you two looked yesterday," April said, as she blew on the hot coffee attempting to cool it down.

Claire smiled and said, "I still can't believe yesterday happened. The whole day was remarkable, and it seems like a dream." Claire thought about the great time she had had with her friends, and how she had saved Brie from Russell, and how she had befriended Brie. Then she remembered that Trevor had told her that he loved her—she had not mentioned it last night as Brie was with them.

"Oh yeah, there is something that I wanted to tell you last night, but with Brie around, I didn't want to mention it."

"Ok? Shoot," April told Claire curiously.

"Trevor and I were dancing to a slow song about two hours into the dance when he whispered in my ear that he loved me," Claire said, looking a little bashful, as she told April this. But she also knew that she could tell April anything, without getting her upset.

"Wow," April said, sounding a little surprised. "What did you say?"

"I told him that I loved him too," Claire replied simply.

"And do you?" April asked warmly, wanting to get to Claire's true feelings.

"I think so," Claire told her. "I really like him, and as you guys know, I have been through a lot... and I was just able to tell you guys that I love you." Claire looked longingly into April's eyes. "I know that realizing that you love the family you are with is different from loving a boyfriend. It's just that my feelings for him are intense, and he is my first serious relationship, you know?" Claire stopped the explanation as she wrestled with her thoughts.

April grabbed Claire's hand, and said, "If you love him right now, that's great, but you will know when you do for absolute sure. It's ok not to really know yet," April offered her advice. "It's only been a month of you guys dating, so you don't have to rush into the true love part of the relationship if you aren't ready."

"I think I love him so I'm going to leave it at that for a while," Claire concluded, thanking April for listening to her and then went back to her essay. April grinned at Claire's response and turned her attention back to the notes that she was working on.

Blake woke up about an hour later, and they all decided to go out to dinner because no one really wanted to cook.

After dinner, the three of them were walking through the streets of downtown on their way back to the apartment. Even though it was cold outside, there were no clouds in the sky, and the sun was shining. It was April's idea to walk home from the restaurant, so that Blake could get her muscles limber after being sore all day.

As they walked by a wedding dress shop, Blake surprised April with a question. "Do you think that you will ever want to marry again, mom?" Blake had noticed the mannequins in the window dressed up in a tuxedo and a wedding dress.

Shocked by the question, April stammered, "I... I don't know, honey. What made you think of it?"

Blake shrugged and looked at the window showcase. "I know that dad has been gone for over four years now, and you are still kind of young. I just want you to know that I wouldn't be opposed to it, if you found the right person."

April wondered if Blake had been thinking about this for a while. It just seemed to come out of nowhere. "All I can say is that if the right person comes along, I will entertain the idea," April replied, half joking.

"Ok mom. I just wanted to know if you would be open to it, that's all. You are an awesome mom and a beautiful woman, and I just want to see you happy again," Blake said looking at her mom.

Claire didn't want to chime in on this moment between mother and daughter, so she just stood there listening.

"I am happy," retorted April. "I am in a good place in my life right now. Sure, we both were sad when your dad died, but I think that I can finally say that I am not depressed at the loss that I have felt. It is still there, but I am dealing with it."

"Ok. I just felt the need to tell you that I would be open to it," Blake confessed, as they continued the walk towards home.

It was dark when they made it home, and all three were cold and tired. The girls went to bed early, still exhausted from the dance. Claire had called and talked with Trevor for quite a while, and he had told her about his day of fun with the boys. At the end of the call, he told her that he loved her, and she replied with an 'I love you too'. After that, Claire called Brie to ask her about her day. Apparently, when Brie got home from Claire's house, there was a gift bag on her porch that contained a pair of new shoes and a gift certificate for a free cell phone screen replacement.

April stayed up watching a little TV, processing the events of the day. She wondered what had possessed Blake to broach the subject of her dating again. April didn't think that she was sending out mixed signals about a desire to date.

April turned off the TV. And she reached to turn off the light on the nightstand, she noticed her wedding ring on her finger. She stared at it for several long moments, she waged a battle in her mind. Finally, with her right hand, she took off the ring and placed it securely in the drawer on the nightstand. As she turned off the light, it was like she was closing the back cover of a book that she had just finished. She was now ready for a new story to begin.

* *

APRIL'S ALARM CLOCK WENT OFF AT 6:00 A.M. ON MONDAY morning. She turned it off, and continued to lay on her bed for several minutes thinking about what the day ahead. There were several conference calls scheduled until noon, and then she and Gina were going to have a business lunch with another potential author.

She got in the shower after picking out her clothes, and then blow-dried her hair and proceeded to apply her makeup. Before she got in the shower, she texted the girls to get up and get ready for school. As she looked at her phone, she realized that only Claire had answered her back.

April could hear Claire blow-drying her hair, and knew that she was up and getting ready. April texted Blake so that she would get up and get ready for school.

Once April was finished, she went into Blake's room to wake her up. When she turned on the light, she blinked in surprise. Blake was awake, but just barely, and she was extremely pale and looked weak.

"Blake!" April exclaimed, racing to her bedside, "what's wrong?"

"Mom..." Blake began whispering, "I... I can't get out of bed. I am really weak and I don't feel good. My body is sore all over."

"Oh my God, honey," April said anxiously, as she pulled back the covers.

"Claire!" April yelled. "Come here, quick!"

Claire raced across the hallway into Blake's room, and saw April next to Blake's bed. There was something obviously wrong with her.

"Holy shit," Claire said as she looked at Blake. "What happened?"

"I don't know!" April said in a panic. "She woke up like this!"

April was on the left side of the bed, and Claire went to the right.

"I'm sore," Blake said, as tears began to form in her eyes. She was scared and didn't know what was happening to her.

April and Claire managed to get Blake in an upright position, but she was weak and hurting all over.

"That's it," April exclaimed. "I'm calling 9-1-1." April ran to her bedroom to get her phone.

Claire just sat next to Blake trying to comfort her. "It's going to be alright," Claire said softly. "We are going to get you to a hospital."

Blake was frightened because she had never felt this way before and she knew that something wasn't right. April raced back to the room on the phone with the operator. She had just given her address, and was updating the woman on the other end on Blake's condition. April tried to keep her composure for Blake, but her voice sounded frantic while talking with the operator.

The ambulance arrived within minutes, and it took a few more for them to make it up to the top floor. One of the paramedics raced upstairs towards Blake. The other two were working on bringing the stretcher up the stairs.

The paramedic that got to Blake first was named Jill. As she hooked up sensors and wires up to Blake, she asked her about her symptoms and other related questions. It was obvious that Blake was very weak and in distress.

The stretcher arrived and after a few minutes got Blake settled in. They had an IV line hooked up to Blake's arm. They didn't know what was wrong with her yet, but her vitals were not where they should have been. Jill told April that they were taking her to Chicago Med where an ER doctor was waiting for them.

Tears flowed down April's eyes. Claire too couldn't believe this was happening to Blake and began to cry. The paramedics loaded Blake into the truck, and allowed April and Claire to ride along with them. The hospital was ten minutes away, but it felt like it took an hour. Blake was really pale and looking more fragile by the minute.

Finally, the ambulance arrived and Blake was taken immediately to a waiting ER doctor. April told Blake that she loved her and that everything was going to be ok. April and Claire were told that they had to stay in the waiting room until the doctor could look at Blake.

The duo took a seat. April got out her phone and called her parents.

"Mom," April began, sobbing as she spoke. "It's Blake... She's sick."

CHAPTER TWENTY

CLAIRE SAT IN THE WAITING ROOM, WONDERING IF THIS was all a bad dream. It all just seemed so surreal. Blake was on the other side of that door being looked at by the doctor, and all they could do was wait.

Anne and Roger had just arrived, and April had tears in her eyes as she explained what had happened. Anne sat down next to Claire and gave her a hug.

"Blake looked so sick," Claire told Anne, tearing up again. "I felt so helpless."

Anne tried to comfort Claire as Roger comforted his daughter and tried his best to find out what was happening.

It was now about 8:00 a.m. and school had already started. Claire texted Trevor, Shelly, and Rose about what had happened, and that she obviously wasn't going to be in class today. Roger called the school for April and let them know that Blake was in the hospital and that Claire wasn't going to be in today either.

Claire texted Brie and let her know what was happening with Blake. Then Claire decided to text Emily to let her know about Blake. Claire figured that Emily had been Blake's best friend, and that she should be made aware of what was happening.

Crystal showed up and gave April a big hug. "How is she?" Crystal asked.

"No news yet. It's been over an hour and we still don't know anything," April answered, sounding frustrated.

Trying to comfort her best friend, Crystal said, "This is the best place that she could be. The doctors here are some of the best in the entire country. She is in good hands."

"I know, but I can't stand not knowing what the hell is going on with my daughter," April replied anxiously.

Around 9:30 a.m. a doctor came to the waiting room, and asked to speak to April.

"Yes? I'm April Turner. How's my daughter?" April asked, getting up from her chair.

"Hello, Mrs. Turner. I'm Dr. Powell, and I am the one in charge of your daughter's case," Dr. Powell began.

"All I can say, for sure, is that Blake is really sick, and we are running a battery of tests to determine what is wrong with her. We have been giving her fluids and are conducting blood work in an effort to see what's going on. We should have some preliminary results fairly soon."

"You don't have any ideas as of yet?" April asked, scared of the answer.

"I can't say until we are sure of what's going on. I will have a better under-standing of what is going on shortly. I promise that I will let you know as soon as we do," Dr. Powell said, as she turned to go back to Blake.

April's mind was racing and was hoping that it wasn't anything serious. Now she was pacing back and forth, not knowing what to do. There were several vending machines at the far end of the waiting room and April realized that neither she nor Claire had any kind of food that morning.

"Claire, do you want to come with me to get something out of the vend-ing machine?" April asked, as she pointed over to the far side. Claire could see the look in April's eyes and knew that doing anything to get her mind off Blake for even a few seconds would be good.

"Sure," Claire indicated, as she got up from her seat and walked with April to the vending machines.

As she stood there, a man appeared next to her, and set down his backpack. Because of the sound it made when it hit the floor, April turned her attention to it. As she looked at it, she instantly realized that she had seen it before. April's eyes quickly glanced up towards the owner of the backpack, and discovered it was the hot guy from the coffee shop all those weeks ago.

"It's you," April's words slipped out when she realized who it was.

The hot guy, somewhat startled by April's voice, turned to face her. "Yes, it is I," he said jokingly, as he looked at April trying to figure out if he knew her. As he looked into her eyes, a feeling washed over him that he had never experienced before. It was a combination of fascination, intrigue and intoxication, all rolled into one.

Feeling embarrassed at her outburst, April looked up at the hot guy's eyes to explain what she meant. But before she could start her explanation, a spark of emotion ran from the top of her head to the bottom of her toes. She had only experienced that feeling once before, and that was when she had met Nick for the first time.

April was speechless for a few seconds as she gazed into his eyes.

The hot guy patiently waited for April to collect her composure.

"Oh, God, I'm sorry," April began. "I'm being rude. My name is April Turner. I'm sorry about that."

The hot guy gave a charming smile and held out his hand, and said, "My name is Mason Steele. Nice to meet you." Then he thought about what April had said earlier, and asked, "Have we met before?"

Feeling childish, April said, "No... Not really. I just saw you at the coffee shop a few weeks ago, the one that is actually a couple of blocks from here. I remembered the symbol on your bag."

"Oh, ok, that makes sense," Mason chuckled. He then explained that the symbol was his company's logo.

"What do you do?" April asked.

"I have my own computer company. I do web design, equipment installation, and programming," Mason answered with a smile.

Claire came over and saw April and Mason talking. Realizing that Claire was standing right next to her, April said, "Mason, this is my daughter, Claire."

"Hi, nice to meet you," Claire smiled, looking at Mason and then at April.

"Nice to meet you too," Mason replied, holding out his hand for Claire to shake it.

"So, is everything ok?" Mason asked sincerely. "What brings you here?"

April told Mason about Blake and how they were waiting to hear about her condition.

"I am sorry to hear that. I hope that she is ok," Mason told April. "If there is anything I can do, feel free to ask."

Seeing the quizzical look that April was giving him, Mason said, "I will be around the hospital for a while, I am in charge of installing the computers on the new wing, and I have the contract on working on the software for the new server that I put in a few weeks ago."

"Well, Mr. Steele," April said, "thank you. It was nice to meet you."

"The pleasure was all mine, April," Mason said, as he chose what he wanted from the vending machine and turned to leave. "Oh and it was nice to meet you, too, Claire. I hope that your sister will be ok."

"Me too, and thanks," Claire waved as he walked away.

"Oh my God," Claire sounded excited. "That guy was totally into you."

April was watching him leave when she said to Claire, "No, he wasn't."

"Yes, yes, he was. And by the look in your eyes, I can see that you are into him too," Claire said as her eyes were widening with happiness for April.

April couldn't get over the feeling that she had just experienced with Mason. When their eyes had met, it was like she had been zapped by an electric current. It sounded clichéd, but it was true.

Claire and April walked back to the waiting room, hoping to hear some news soon.

Mason sat at the computer terminal and took a bite from the vending machine breakfast bar. His thoughts were still on the woman that he had just met. It had been a while since the divorce, but he wasn't ready to dive into the dating pool again. However, after meeting April just now, he could think of nothing but her. He couldn't get the image of her face out of his mind. Even her voice sounded like an angel's voice to him.

Get a grip, Mason told himself. The woman was at the hospital because one of her daughters was really sick. He did notice that she wasn't wearing a wedding ring, but it wasn't like he could go up to her, and say, "Hey, I know that your daughter is sick and you are waiting to hear what's wrong with her, but would you want to go out with me?" Mason chuckled at the absurdity of the thought. He couldn't shake the feeling that she was going to need him, and he vowed to himself that he was going to be there.

Mason picked up his phone to text his sister, Charlie. Her name was actually Charlize, but he had referred to her as Charlie ever since he was a little boy. As he typed the three words that would make his sister call him later that night, he chuckled. "I met someone."

* *

"I AM REALLY SORRY TO HAVE TO TELL YOU THIS, BUT BLAKE has leukemia," Dr. Powell said. She had asked April to come to her office so that she could discuss the diagnosis with her. April had taken her parents and Claire into the office with her.

"What?" April asked in disbelief. Then as the word 'leukemia' sank in, she began to cry.

"No, please no," whispered April, between tears. Her parents grabbed April's hands for support. Claire was standing behind them, numb with shock at the news.

"How could this have happened?" April asked, totally dumbfounded. As the reality of the news began to sink in, a horrible thought crashed into her mind, "Is Blake going to die?"

Dr. Powell was one of the best oncologists in the entire state, having participated in hundreds of discussions with parents on informing them about their child's leukemia diagnosis. Dr. Powell was compassionate, however, she didn't sugarcoat it. She treated every patient as if they were her own child, and was diligent about helping each and every patient.

"April," Dr. Powell began, "I know that this is difficult for you and I want you to know that I am going to be totally upfront with you. Blake has what we call acute lymphocytic leukemia. Unfortunately, this kind of leukemia progresses fast, and the symptoms may worsen more quickly than other chronic leukemia." Dr. Powell paused to hand April some info that she had prepared for her about the kinds of leukemia and their progression. Dr. Powell folded her hands on her desk, and said, "Her symptoms may have included things like getting tired or fatigued more easily or more often. She may have had aches and pains or have been achy or sore. Some of the kids may bruise easily. Sometimes the patient suffers from night sweats or has chills. Most of the time, it is thought to be the flu or a cold because they share the same symptoms."

April turned to look at Claire, as the doctor was finishing up with the description of the symptoms. "Oh my God, she had these." Thinking back, April recalled the night when Blake had woken up soaked in sweat, the morning that she saw the bruise on her arm, and the weekend when Blake had been sluggish and sore.

"Why didn't I take her to the doctor?" April exclaimed to herself. "This is all my fault."

"Mrs. Turner, there was no way you could have known that these individual symptoms could lead to leukemia. Because of the type that she has, the intensity of the symptoms can worsen suddenly, and this is what can occur sometimes."

As Claire listened to the doctor, she too felt guilty about not seeing Blake's symptoms for what they were. Blake was her best friend, and it was hard to think about what would come next.

Joseph asked the doctor, "So what's next? What is the next step?" His words were filled with concern and uncertainty.

"Blake will have to undergo chemotherapy as soon as possible. Because she has extremely low counts of healthy blood cells, we are going to give her blood and platelet transfusions to help prevent bleeding. She will receive antibiotics to help prevent infections, and we will give her medications to help control side-effects," Dr. Powell gave a straightforward answer. She then looked directly at April, and told her, "Because of the type and severity of the leukemia that Blake has, her only chance of survival is a bone marrow transplant."

April found the news overwhelming. She tried to stay strong in front of her parents and Claire, but the doctor was saying words like 'severity' and 'only chance'. April felt as if she was wearing a lead blanket, and it was a struggle to breathe. Her baby girl, Blake, was dying.

"Can I give Blake my bone marrow?" April suddenly asked, wondering if she could be a good match because she was her mother.

Dr. Powell shook her head, and said, "Parents of the patient are always a half match. This means that four out of eight HLA markers match. Only matching half of the HLA is problematic, and there are added risks. Because of this, I recommend that we initiate trying to find Blake a perfect match. Due to how sick she is, she needs the HLA markers to be at one hundred percent."

April became even more discouraged by this news, but again tried to appear strong.

"We are going to submit Blake's DNA information on the 'Be the Match' database, and attempt to locate a match. Hopefully, someone who has all her markers has already been tested and will be a good match."

Dr. Powell spent the next half hour answering questions that April and her parents asked. Claire just stood there, trying to listen as intently as she could, and retain every bit of information as well. Blake was about to go through hell, and Claire was going to be there for her.

"Can we go and see her now?" April asked Dr. Powell.

"Yes, you can. She is resting and the medications have started to work to help relieve some of her symptoms," Dr. Powell said, leading them out of her office and down the hall. They had moved Blake to a private room on the fourth floor because she would need to be in an environment that would pose the least threat of catching infections as she started chemo treatment.

Blake was lying in bed and was asleep. She still looked pale, but not like she was in distress the way she was when she was brought in.

April walked up to her bed and stood next to her. She looked up at the ceiling trying to control her tears. How was she going to tell her baby that she had cancer? How was she going to explain to her that she had to go through chemo?

April knelt down next to her and put her hand on Blake's forehead. "Blake, honey, It's me... mom." Blake's eyes slowly opened, and she looked at April with a curious expression.

"Hi, mom," Blake said, lifting her head slightly. "What's going on? What happened to me?"

Blake could see that her grandparents were standing behind her mom, and Claire was now stepping closer to the bed, but on the other side. She could see by their faces that something was wrong.

"Um," April began, trying to find the right words. "You are sick, honey. Very sick." Tears involuntarily started to flow from April's eyes, as she fought to restrain them.

"What is it?" Blake asked again, sounding even more worried.

"You have leukemia," April told her. "You need a bone marrow transplant."

The news hit Blake like a boulder. "No, mom, please, no," whispered Blake, as she began to feel light-headed.

"I know, baby girl," April consoled her, "I know." April grabbed Blake's hand and held it as they cried. Blake could hear her grandparents behind April saying words like, 'We are going to do everything to make sure you get the help that you need. But Blake could only make out half of what they were saying. She had this sick feeling in her gut that she was going to die.

Claire was still standing on the other side of the bed, tears rolling down her face as she watched a mother tell her child that she had cancer. Blake raised her hand for Claire to take it, and Claire slowly reached for it. "Blake," Claire said but couldn't manage to say anything else. Blake knew that Claire was in shock, just like she was.

April then told Blake about her line of treatment, including the fact that they would start chemo and give her antibiotics.

"I'm going to lose my hair?" Blake whined, as the thought occurred to her. Blake knew the answer. She knew what it meant to go through chemotherapy. The thought of going bald and feeling like absolute crap made her even sadder.

"Why me?" Blake cried, as she pictured her near future involving chemo and radiation. "I can't do this," Blake exclaimed. "I don't want to do this." Looking at her mom, she pleaded, "Isn't there anything else that I can do? I mean, aren't there pills or something that I can take?" Blake knew deep down that there wasn't any other option, but she was in denial right now, and her mind was trying everything to think its way out of cancer.

"Oh, honey, I wish there was. I need you to be strong, ok?" April told her. "I am going to be here with you every step of the way, and we are going to fight this together. Do you hear me?" April's tears were turning from sad to defiant. "We are going to beat this."

"I'll try my best," Blake finally offered, as she wiped the tears from her cheeks.

"Ok, honey," April said, "I am going to hold you to that."

The morning turned into afternoon as the reality of Blake's situation weighed on everyone. Claire called Rose and Shelly during their lunch hour at school to let them know. After that, she called Trevor but it went to voicemail, so she left a message informing him about Blake, and asking him to call her when he got the message.

April's parents had just come back from the cafeteria, and they suggested that she and Blake go get something to eat, and that they would stay with Blake. April wasn't hungry, but thought that she could go down with Claire and have at least a cup of coffee.

When the elevator doors closed, and they were heading down to the cafeteria, April began to cry. She couldn't help it. It just came flowing out of her like a river coming down a mountain. Of course, Claire too began to cry. She was standing behind April in the elevator, so she wrapped her arms around her, and put her head on her right shoulder.

"I am so sorry, April," Claire said, as she tried to comfort her foster mom. "I can't believe this is happening."

"Me neither, Claire," April sadly agreed. "Me neither." When the elevator came to a stop, Claire released April and they both tried to wipe the tears off their faces.

Claire decided to grab a chicken wrap and a bag of potato chips while April just got a cup of coffee. It had been a long day and she knew that caffeine would help her make it through the rest of the day.

Because the cafeteria was busy, Claire chose a table towards the far end of the room. There were only about three available tables to choose from, so Claire picked the one closest to the window.

As they sat there, April began telling Claire stories about when Blake was a little girl and all the things that she did. It was a light-hearted moment. April even giggled thinking about the time when she was out of town, and Nick was in-charge of taking care of Blake. Little Blake had told her dad that she had washed her hair in the shower, and had wrapped it up in a towel. For some reason, at that age, Blake didn't like washing her hair in the shower. April had called to check up to see how things were going, and Nick said that everything was great, and that Blake had just got out of the shower. Something made April ask Nick to check underneath Blake's towel. When he did, Blake's hair was completely dry. Nick was surprised that Blake would lie to him, so he took Blake to the kitchen sink and washed her hair himself, but he used his manly smelling shampoo. That was the last time that Blake lied about washing her hair.

Claire had almost finished eating her chicken wrap when a voice over her left shoulder said, "It's you." The voice belonged to Mason. He was looking at April. He had jokingly said the same words that she had said to him just a few hours ago.

"Yes, it's me," April answered back trying to remember exactly what he had said to her.

"Hi, Mason," Claire said, remembering his name.

"Hi, Claire," Mason said with a smile. "Good to see you again." Then he turned his attention back to April.

"How's your other daughter?" Mason asked, truly concerned.

April glanced over at Claire, who nodded. It was almost as if April was asking Claire for permission to tell Mason about Blake. Claire could sense that Mason was a nice guy.

"Not good," April explained, sadly. "We just found out that she has leukemia."

"Oh my, I am so sorry to hear that," Mason said, sincerely. "If there is anything that I can do, or anything you need, please let me know."

As Mason stood and spoke to April and Claire, a family of four took that last open table that he was heading towards until he had stopped to say 'hi'.

Mason looked around the room and didn't see any open tables. Claire realized what was going on, and then asked Mason, "Why don't you join us since there aren't any open tables?" April looked at Claire to mentally ask what she was doing, but as she looked at Mason, she found herself willing him to sit with them.

"Ok, only if it isn't an imposition," he asked April, hesitating to sit until April approved.

"Of course, yes, you may," April said after a pause, "Please, have a seat."

Mason took the seat between April and Claire. On his tray, he had a basket of boneless wings and a side salad. He took a sip from the fountain pop cup and turned to April.

"Thank you for allowing me to join you. I hate standing and eating. I tend to wear most of my dinner when I do that," Mason smiled, as he attempted to make April smile.

"You're welcome," April replied, as she drank the last remaining drops of coffee from her cup.

Claire's phone rang: it was Trevor. She looked at April, and said, "It's Trevor. Can I take this?"

Knowing that Trevor was still at school and was calling between classes, April nodded and Claire picked up the phone. "Hey, hold on one sec," Claire said, as she got up. Excusing herself from the table, she walked towards the corner of the cafeteria where she could talk to him.

Mason smiled as Claire walked away. "She is a beautiful girl. You must be really proud of her." April was just going to agree but something told her that it was ok to tell Mason about Claire.

"Yes, I am. She is a remarkable young lady, but Claire is my foster daughter. She kind of just popped into our lives a couple of months ago, and we have been quite taken by her. It is a long story, but there was just something that Blake and I saw in her that made us want to help her."

"Wow, good for you. I'm really glad to hear that," Mason said, with genuine appreciation. "The world needs more caring people like you."

"Thank you," April said, blushing ever so slightly.

"So, the child admitted to the hospital is your biological daughter?" Mason asked.

"Yes, her name is Blake, and she is fourteen. She is the only biological child that I have," April informed Mason. "What about you? Do you have any children?"

For a moment, April thought that she saw a flash of despair shooting through his eyes, but it was gone almost as soon as she saw it.

"Unfortunately, no. I don't," Mason answered truthfully. "I never had the opportunity to do so."

April could tell there was more to the story, and for some reason, she wanted to know it. However, she didn't want to pry right now, and secretly wished that she would get the opportunity to find out.

Knowing that April wasn't wearing a wedding ring, Mason wanted to find out if she was married or what the deal was with Blake's father. He didn't want to appear rude or hasty, but he desperately wanted to know. He thought of an opening and decided to go for it.

"I was married for six years, but we ended up divorced. It has been about five years since then." Mason said, telling April more about himself. "How about you? Are you still with Blake's father?"

April instinctively looked down at her hands, at her wedding ring, but then she remembered that she had just removed it the other day. That is why Mason was asking about Blake's father— because she wasn't wearing a ring.

"No, my husband passed away four years ago. He was killed by a semi-truck that slid into his lane on a winter night," April told Mason. "It's just been Blake and me ever since." Then she added, "Of course, we discovered Claire a couple of months ago, so it is now the three of us."

"I am sorry to hear about your husband. It must have been a challenge raising a daughter by yourself after the loss of someone you loved?" Mason asked gently.

"Actually, it was hard at first," April said, looking into her empty coffee cup. "I was dealing with grief while trying to console my daughter to help her overcome the sorrow that she felt over the loss of her father. There were times when I would look at Blake and see Nick, my husband, in her eyes, and would break down."

April looked up from the coffee cup, and met Mason's eyes. "I realized that I would always have a piece of him living through my daughter. It made me happy to know that he would always be here."

April's eyes moistened at the thought of Blake had just been diagnosed with leukemia, "Today I just got this terrible news about Blake and..." April's voice trailed off. "I'm sorry, Mason. I don't mean to project me grief onto you." The idea of possibly losing her daughter made April's heart ache. She had lost her husband, and now, her heart was feeling anguish over even the mere thought of losing Blake.

"April," Mason said, "It's fine. Really. I can't imagine what you must be going through, and I hope that she will get through this." Mason gave April a smile. "Besides, I know a little about grief, so I don't mind helping you deflect some of it."

"Thank you, Mason. I appreciate it," April tried her best to smile through the sadness she was feeling.

Claire came back to the table and could see that April and Mason were in the middle of a discussion, so Claire did her best not to interrupt.

April turned her attention to Claire, and asked, "How is Trevor?"

Claire told April that Trevor was obviously shocked by the news, and couldn't believe it.

The three of them sat at the table for a couple of more minutes, and April looked at Claire and said, "We better get back to Blake." The three of them stood up.

"Thank you for letting me crash your table," Mason said with gratitude. "I am glad that I could sit with you for a little while."

April held out her hand to Mason. "Nice seeing you again. Mr. Steele."

"Likewise, Mrs. Turner," Mason replied respectfully, but with a hint of charm. "I will be around, so if you want to talk or have me return the favor and have you eat at my table. Just let me know."

"Ok, thank you," April said, as she turned and led Claire out of the cafeteria. Mason sat back down at the table, and couldn't divert his eyes away from April's direction until she walked through the double doors. He didn't fully realize it, but he was grinning from ear to ear.

* *

AS THE WEEK WENT BY, IT WAS LIKE CLAIRE WAS IN A NIGHTmare that she couldn't wake up from. She had missed the first couple days of school, but went back on Wednesday. She didn't want to be there, and couldn't focus on her homework. Shelly and Rose were extremely supportive. They made it bearable for Claire to make it through the sixth hour. Trevor was also there for Claire as well, but all she wanted to do was to be at the hospital with Blake.

After school on Thursday, Claire went immediately to the hospital to see Blake, but when she got there, Blake wasn't doing well, and they wouldn't let anyone see her right away. The nurse told Claire that it would take a little while. April had taken the entire week off, and was basically living at the hospital. You could tell that she was fatigued, but nothing was going to prevent her from spending as much time with her daughter as possible.

Claire went to the waiting room lounge because she knew that April was there. When she got there, April was sitting on a couch facing one of the wall-mounted televisions. April was sitting there watching TV, but not really paying attention to it. Claire could see that April was lost in thought.

"Hi, honey," April said, as Claire approached her. "How was school?"

Claire sat next to April, and handed her a coffee that she had got from the Starbucks next to the hospital on her way in.

"To be honest," Claire began, "I'm just going through the motions. I don't want to be there when I know that Blake is in here. I can't concentrate, and it feels like the wind has been taken out of my sails." Claire had a lot of catching up to do in school. Normally, she wouldn't have minded doing extra homework, but all she wanted to do was to spend time with Blake.

"I know how you feel," April confessed, "I'm still in shock. My life has been turned upside-down, and I am trying hard to stay positive but when I see my daughter lying on that bed, knowing how sick she is..." April let her words trail off, as she tried not to think about it.

The two of them sat there for a few minutes in silence watching a talk show that was playing on TV. Claire bent down and took out a book from her bag and began to read. After about an hour, Claire fell asleep and her head rested against April's shoulder.

"Mrs. Turner?" the nurse asked looking at April. "You can go see Blake now."

April gently nudged Claire to wake her up, and said, "Claire, we can go see Blake."

Claire opened her eyes, and got up. "Ok, good," Claire said, as she collected her book and bag, and headed to Blake's room with April. The room was slowly filling up with flowers and 'get well' balloons from associates from Priscilla Publishing as well as kids from Blake's class.

Blake looked tired and weaker than she had yesterday. Blake had been wearing her glasses since she had arrived in the hospital, and was cleaning them when April and Claire walked into the room. April pulled up the chair next to her as Claire decided to sit on the bed on the other side. It had been her place to sit for the past couple of days.

"Hi, baby," said April. "What's going on today?"

Pulled herself up a little more in bed, Blake replied, "I have been really nauseous today, mom. I couldn't even keep water down. The nurse changed my IV, and I'm starting to feel a little better." April could tell that Blake was still shaky from the nausea. "I'm sorry, honey," April said, trying to comfort her.

Blake got a serious look on her face, and asked, "Mom, how am I going to handle chemo tomorrow? I am getting sick just with the medications that I am on for the symptoms—I don't know if I can handle it." The worry in Blake's voice was evident.

Before April could answer, Claire spoke up and said, "No worries, Blake, you got this." Blake looked at Claire sitting next to her, and asked, "I don't know, Claire Bear. I know I have to, but I feel like crap. How can I go through all this? Plus, I am going to lose my hair. You know how I am." With each passing minute, Blake was getting more and more frustrated and scared of her future.

"Because Blake," Claire replied, "I am going to be here to help you through it." Claire held up her fist for a fist bump. Blake grinned and slowly raised her hand with the IV in it. Claire carefully bumped it and let Blake slowly put her hand back on the bed.

Thinking about what Blake had said about losing her hair, Claire had an idea. "Hey, why don't I cut my hair to support you?" she suggested. It was a kind gesture. Blake and Claire knew that best friends of cancer victims would sometimes shave their heads or cut their hair really short to show support for their loved one battling cancer. Claire loved her long blonde hair but she would shave herself bald in an instant, if it meant showing support for Blake.

"No," Blake said curtly. "I love your hair. Please don't cut it." Blake didn't want Claire to sacrifice her hair for her illness. Even though it was a beautiful thought, Blake simply couldn't allow it.

"But I want to do something to show that I am supporting you, Blake," Claire said, defiantly.

"I know you do, and I truly appreciate it, but I refuse to have you cut your hair. I will just have to think of something else that you can do," Blake said, as her mind searched for a good idea.

Blake picked up her iPad to begin her search for anything that Claire could do besides take shears to her long blonde hair. After a few minutes, Blake set her iPad down and grabbed the bowl next to her bed as she felt like throwing up. Claire set down her phone to help Blake. After Blake was done, Claire got a washcloth to help wipe off the droplets that had splashed from the side of the bowl onto Blake's face. April removed the bowl and called for the nurse to let her know.

The nurse came in and looked at the IV and then told Blake that the medication should be helping soon. She then took the bowl away with her when she left the room.

Blake sat there with her head on the pillow trying to make the feeling of nausea subside. She put her wrist on her forehead trying to rid her mind of the queasiness that was working its way up from her belly.

After a few minutes, the medicine began to work, and Blake slowly felt her stomach getting back to normal.

Suddenly there was a knock on the door, and Claire turned her head to see who it was. Emily and a couple of Blake's friends were standing there.

"Come on in, girls," April waved as she got out of the seat next to Blake. Emily and the two girls stood at the foot of the bed.

"Hi," Emily said to everyone in the room. "Hey guys," Blake said, trying to perk up. "What's going on?"

April decided to excuse herself so that Blake could have some time alone with her friends. She told Blake that she and Claire were going to grab some dinner and would be back. Claire followed April out of the room and the two of them headed towards the elevator.

As they waited for the elevator to reach their floor, April asked Claire, "How are things between you and Emily?"

After the Winter Formal when Claire had forgiven Brie, the damage that Emily had done was now kind of a moot point. Claire hadn't really thought about Emily after that, but when Blake fell sick, she texted Emily to tell her. Ever since then, Emily had made it a point to text Claire every day to see how Blake was doing and to ask if she could do anything.

"Good," Claire answered, "since Monday, we have been talking and texting a little. I am pretty much over the drama between us, and I just want us to be friends."

"I am so glad to hear that," April said as the elevator doors opened. "I know that it was Emily's fault that the Brie got her hands on that information about you, but I don't believe that she knew what was going to happen, nor do I believe that she would have told Brie, knowing what Brie had in mind."

"I know. I just want us to be ok with one another. I want Blake to know that there are lots of people that care about her," Claire finished, as she entered the elevator.

The two of them left the hospital and headed towards a restaurant that was only a block away. It was extremely cold out there, but it wasn't snowing. By the time they got there, both April and Claire felt frozen.

April chose a booth towards the middle of the room and they both sat down, taking their scarves and coats off.

The waiter came over to the table with two glasses of ice water and dropped off menus for them. April ordered two hot chocolates right off the bat. April then picked up the menu and began scanning the pages. She looked over the top of the menu and said to Claire as her eyes filled with tears, "Blake's starting chemo tomorrow." It was as if she was reading the words—as if they were printed on the menu.

Claire looked away from her menu, and tried to comfort April. "I know. I can't believe this is happening to her. I'm still in shock."

"I can't lose her, Claire," April said, lowering her voice. "I can't." Claire could only imagine how April was feeling. It was devastating to Claire, and she had only just met Blake a few months ago. Blake was the best friend that she should have had growing up, but never did.

"You won't," Claire said with a certainty that she herself really didn't possess. "Blake is a strong girl who has taken after you, April, and if there is anything that I have learned in the past couple of months, it is that you are strong. I admire you for what you have gone through with the loss of Blake's dad, not to mention that you openly took in a teenage girl off of the streets and made her feel welcome and loved. You did that," Claire paused to find the words that would complete her thoughts. "If Blake sets her mind to something, then she does it. We just have to be there to show her that she can get through this."

The waiter came back to take their order. When he did, his eyes lingered longer at Claire than they did April. Neither Claire nor April noticed it. He began to write down the orders. April decided to get a Cobb salad, while Claire went for a burger and fries. The restaurant was starting to fill up as more and more customers poured in.

April picked up her spoon and began to stir the marshmallows into her hot chocolate. After a minute, the marshmallows were completely blended, but she kept stirring, her mind skipping to Blake in the hospital room. April's phone beeped. It was a text from Crystal asking for an update on Blake.

April set her spoon down, and texted that Blake was slated to start chemo tomorrow. Crystal then texted back asking if there were anymore encounters with 'Hot Guy'. That made April snort. Claire looked up from her phone, and eyed April quizzically, "What's up?"

"Oh, it's just Crystal asking if I have seen Mason again this week. She has been telling me over the last couple of days to try to find him," April said.

"I like him," Claire said, for the record. "There is something about the way that he looks at you that makes me think that you should go talk to him." Claire could sense that April was attracted to him, and that she needed a little prodding from her foster daughter as well.

Before April could mount a defense, Claire continued, "I'm not trying to push you, April, but I think that you deserve to find happiness."

As if Crystal had a listening device and had just heard what Claire had said, she sent a text back to April saying, "I think that you should try to meet with him and take him out for coffee."

"God," April smirked, after reading Crystal's text. "It's like you two are reading from the same book or something. She is telling me the same thing."

"Well that's good. You are like the best woman in the world. That's all I'm saying," Claire smiled at April.

A few minutes later, the waiter dropped off their food, and gave Claire another quick glance, as if he was checking her out. This time, both of them caught him doing so. April shot him a glance that let him know that if he looked at her that way again, he was going to forfeit his tip. His eyes quickly darted away from the two women at the table, as he jetted back in the direction of the kitchen. Claire had to smile at April. It felt nice to have a mother figure in her life. "Thanks, mom," Claire said half-joking.

April grinned and looked at the retreating figure of the waiter, and said, "You're welcome honey."

April took a few moments to reply to Crystal to inform her that she hadn't seen Mason in a few days, but would try her best to see if she could bump into him tomorrow or the next day.

April and Claire hurried and ate their dinner. There was an unspoken agreement between them that they had to get back to the hospital.

While they were standing at the front counter to pay for their dinner, Claire told April that she had to go to the bathroom before they left. April said that she would meet her by the entrance when she finished paying for dinner.

As Claire opened the door to the bathroom, there was a woman with her four-year-old daughter trying to fix her hair. Apparently, the girl didn't want her hair up in a ponytail, and the mom obviously did. Claire grinned at the battle that was raging between the woman and child. The girl was screaming and crying that she didn't want it up and that she hated her mom. The mother, even though she was smiling through her frustration, kept trying to brush the girl's hair back so that she could get her child's hair into a ponytail.

Claire thought of an idea, and after she exited the bathroom, she walked up to April, and said, "I have an idea but we need to stop at home first before we go back to the hospital." April gave Claire a curious glance as they walked out on the cold, snowy sidewalk while Claire told April all about her plan.

* *

APRIL AND CLAIRE WALKED INTO BLAKE'S ROOM JUST AS THE nurse was taking away her dinner tray. Because Blake hadn't felt good most of the day, she had just had a cup of chicken noodle soup and some Saltine crackers. She was managing to keep it down, so at least that was a good sign.

Emily and the girls had left about ten minutes before April and Claire arrived. Emily had been devastated by the news earlier that week, and had been to the hospital every day to see Blake.

April and Claire stood by Blake's bedside, and April asked Blake how she was feeling after eating the soup. Blake told her so far, so good, and gave her mom a thumbs-up sign. April pulled out her bag and said to Blake, "I've got something that I want to do for you."

Curious, Blake looked at the bag, and asked, "Ok?"

April pulled out Blake's favorite hairbrush and headbands that Claire had wanted to pick up on the way back to see Blake.

"Mom..." Blake sighed, as the emotion of what it represented swelled up in her. "I love you."

April had a flashback of a six-year-old Blake sitting on her lap, smiling from ear to ear as April brushed her hair. Now, April stood behind a hospital bed, next to monitors and IVs and began brushing her sick daughter's hair. April took her time, humming mid-way through her task, as she got caught up in the moment. For thirty minutes, April kept softly brushing Blake's hair. It was as if she knew that when it was over, she might never get another chance to ever do it again. April was smiling when she finally finished, but there were tears in her eyes. Claire had just sat there in the chair next to the bed, watching, mesmerized by the beauty of it all.

April reached for her bag and removed a couple of different headbands for Blake. After careful selection, Blake chose the one that had a swirl of blue and yellow fabric. She put it on her head and looked into the camera of her cell phone to see how she looked. Claire got up and grabbed one of the other headbands and put it on. She then stepped behind the head of the bed and knelt down so that she could pose with Blake.

When Blake saw Claire step into the screen of the phone behind the bed, she exclaimed, "Oh my God, that's it!"

Stunned by Blake's reaction, April blinked in surprise. "What's it?"

Smiling as if she had won first place in a fashion design contest, Blake just thought of the perfect idea.

"Instead of cutting her hair, Claire can wear a headband that matches my head coverings. We can get them made out of the same fabric and plan which ones we will wear on a daily basis." Blake's excitement was infectious, and Claire couldn't help but laugh. "That's an amazing idea!" Claire said agreeing with Blake. She smiled and did several poses with Blake, showing off their headbands. "And you know what?" Claire began, "we can get several of them, so that all of Blake's friends can wear them as well. Blake can post which ones she is going to wear and then her friends can wear the same ones during school."

April felt invigorated by Blake's sudden change of attitude. As she watched Blake and Claire take selfies together, April took the remaining headband out of her bag and put it on as well. "I could get used to wearing these."

Blake looked at her mother wearing the headband, and said, "You look really cute, mom. Will you wear a matching headband too?" Blake asked, knowing that her mother usually didn't like wearing them.

April joined Claire behind the head of the bed and told Blake candidly, "I am going to wear one of these everyday, from this day forward until you are better. That is my promise to you."

"Me too," Claire declared, enthusiastically. "We are going to support you and let everyone know that we are there for you."

"I love you guys," Blake whispered with excitement. She picked up her iPad and began searching for headbands and scarfs that she would be interested in wearing. By the time April and Claire left for the night, Blake had placed an online order for seven head coverings with seven matching headbands.

CHAPTER TWENTY-ONE

THE CHEMO TREATMENTS WERE STARTING TO KICK BLAKE'S ass. The first couple of rounds weren't that bad, but now on the third day, she felt like absolute shit. She had vomited several times, and was exhausted. Blake felt like she had just run a marathon, and obviously hadn't won. The doctors were keeping a close eye on her to make sure that some of the other side-effects like febrile neutropenia (low white cell count combined with a fever), anemia, and extreme vomiting didn't occur. They were also keeping an eye on her liver to make sure that it was handling the toxins like it should.

Because of the strong chemotherapy treatment that Blake had to endure due to the aggressive nature of her leukemia, Blake's hair began to fall out soon after chemo started. After the second day, Blake noticed a few strands on her pillow and bedsheet. The doctors told her that it would soon start to detach in clumps.

It was late on Monday morning, and Blake was alone in her room. April was at the office for a couple of hours and didn't yet know the severity of Blake's side-effects. Claire was at school. Even though she wanted to be with Blake every minute of the day, she still had to suffer through her classes.

Blake lay as still as possible in her bed, afraid that any sudden move-ment would cause the feeling of nausea to wash all over her stomach. She was completely miserable. She slowly reached for her iPad and began working on her fashion app. *Maybe designing something will help get my mind off of this crap,* Blake thought to herself, as she pulled up a design that she had started a day or so ago.

After a few minutes, Blake couldn't keep her eyes open any longer and fell asleep with her iPad on her chest. She slept through her nurse coming in to change her IV bag and take her blood pressure. When the nurse came in with her lunch, Blake only woke up for a few minutes and then went back to sleep. She wasn't hungry anyways, and the sight of food made her stomach churn.

It was almost 11:30 am when Blake woke up with a start. Before she realized what was happening, she was vomiting all over herself with her iPad taking a direct hit. Blake was light-headed and felt really queasy. Her hands stumbled around trying to find the control so that she could push the nurse call button. As she pushed the button, Blake began to cry. She was covered in vomit and so was her iPad. Because she felt nauseated, she couldn't begin to try to clean herself off without wanting to vomit again, so she just lay there covered in her own vomit.

The nurse came in right away and discovered what had happened. She tried to comfort Blake as she quickly started to cleanup. The nurse called for an orderly to help her with changing Blake's sheets and bedding. It only took a couple of minutes for Blake to be cleaned up and to look good as new. "It's ok, sweetie," the nurse told Blake as she placed a cold moist washcloth on her forehead. "It happens quite a lot as the chemo progresses." The nurse was really nice, but Blake didn't want to make small talk, especially the way that she was feeling today, so Blake turned her head to the side and just stared at the monitor that was next to her bed.

The nurse tucked the covers into the side of the bed, and then left the room. Blake just let tears run down her face and drip helplessly to the floor.

She lay like that for several minutes till she heard a voice say, "Hi, honey, I'm back." It was her mother at the foot of her bed. As Blake turned her head to face her mom, April saw the look of utter dismay on her daughter's face.

"Blake," April said, as she knelt down next to her, "what's wrong?" Blake's face was pale from vomiting, and the area around her eyes was red and swollen.

"I threw up all over myself a few minutes ago and I feel like crap, mom," Blake said harshly. "I'm so weak and tired, I can barely do anything," Blake continued impatiently. It was like when you were sick with the flu and no matter what you did, you couldn't get comfortable or get in a position where you could relax. Blake was encountering something similar. She didn't know what to do. She felt like pacing, but was too weak to do so.

April could see the despair and frustration in her daughter's eyes, and wished she could wave a magic wand and make it all go away. "Why don't we watch a movie or something to get your mind off of how you're feeling?" April reached for Blake's newly cleaned iPad and handed it to her.

"I don't know, mom," Blake sighed undecidedly, "I don't feel like doing anything, but I want to do something. Does that make any sense?"

"Yes, it does," agreed April, because she felt something similar—not knowing what she could do to help her daughter.

Eventually, Blake decided to pick out a show on her iPad. April moved her chair against the hospital bed and leaned in so that they both could see the screen. Blake tapped the play button on *Harry Potter and the Chamber of Secrets*, and then the movie started. April allowed herself to sit back and let her shoulders down. It felt good to sit next to her daughter and try to get their minds off of her illness, even if it was for only a couple of hours.

With only ten more minutes until the end of the movie, Claire walked in. She had come straight from school and was carrying her book bag.

"Hey, guys," announced Claire, as she walked in. "How's it going today?"

Blake cleared her throat and told Claire about the bad day that she'd had. Claire put her book bag down just inside the room, next to the door. She took her usual place next to Blake on the bed and examined her face. Claire noticed that Blake's skin did look somewhat pasty.

"I'm sorry, Blake," Claire said, apologizing. "I wish that I could have been here today for you," Claire hated being away from Blake, knowing how sick she was.

Blake told Claire that they were almost done watching Harry Potter. Claire swung her legs up onto the bed and gently crawled in next to Blake. The three of them then finished watching the remainder of the movie.

Claire spent the next ten minutes going over current events in the school. Everyone was coming up to Claire to wish Blake a quick recovery. Rose had told Claire that she was going to stop in to see Blake after school, but first she had to go home and help her mother with something before going to the hospital.

April stood up from the chair and stretched. She had been sitting on it for over three hours and her butt and legs were numb.

"Hey, I have an idea," Claire said to Blake. "My laptop is in my bag. Do you want to play *Overwatch*?"

"Yeah, sure," Blake answered. "It's been a week since I last played."

Claire got up and grabbed her bag by the door and pulled out her computer. She placed it on the tray next to the bed and then placed it in such a way that Blake could reach the keys without inconvenience.

April knew that they could play that game for hours, so she told them that she was going to go down to the cafeteria to grab something to snack on since she hadn't had time to have lunch.

"Do you want me to bring you anything?" April asked Claire, as she picked up her purse from the floor next to the chair.

"No. I'm good," Claire said, as she turned on the laptop. "Shelly gave me one of her energy bars after school, and I ate it on the way here."

"Ok," April said, as she opened the door. "If you need anything, just text me."

"Ok, will do," Claire nodded and then turned her attention to Blake and the computer, but, just as she stepped out in the hallway, Blake called to her. "Mom?"

April turned around, and asked, "Yes, honey?"

"Text me when you get there. You know how I worry," Blake teased.

"Funny," April smiled, as she let the door close behind her.

April walked slowly through the hallways of the hospital on her way to the cafeteria. She weaved in and out of the crowd, barely paying attention to the direction that she was heading in. It felt like she was on autopilot; the plane was flying towards an endless horizon. It was amazing how a person's life could change in an instant. Blake was dying of cancer and April was the mom doing her best to help support her.

The cafeteria was crowded so it took her a few minutes to get through the lines to select what she wanted to eat. As she waited in line to pay for her turkey and Swiss sandwich, her phone went off. April balanced the tray and managed to answer the phone. It was Monica.

"How's Blake?" Monica asked with genuine concern. April had been with Monica earlier that morning for a quick meeting. April and Monica were more friends than business associates now.

Setting her tray down by the cashier, April whispered into the phone, "Not so good, but can I call you back in a little bit? I'm paying for my food at the hospital cafeteria."

"Absolutely, just call me back whenever you get a chance," Monica said.

April paid for her food and proceeded to search for a seat in the outer corner of the room. There just happened to be an empty booth next to the trash can, and she walked towards it. She was about ten feet away from it when she heard a voice from behind her say, "Hi, April."

April turned in the direction of the voice and discovered that it belonged to Mason. He was sitting alone and had apparently just started consuming his dinner. He was sitting at a table with only two chairs, but his backpack was occupying the other chair.

"Oh, hi, Mason," April said, smiling as she recognized him.

Mason glanced at the tray that she was holding and quickly asked, "Would you care to join me? I still have to return the favor from the other day."

April paused for a moment but then answered, "Yes, of course." Mason smiled at her reply and then reached for his backpack and moved it to the floor next to him.

Once April was seated, Mason looked at her and asked delicately, "How's Blake doing?"

April sighed and confessed that today was not a good day for her. She told him how sick Blake had been all day, and that her hair was starting to fall out.

"I'm really sorry, April," Mason replied compassionately. "I know how bad chemo can be starting out, especially for children." Mason took a fork full of salad and then continued, "If there is anything that I can do to help her, please let me know." April could sense that he sincerely wanted to help her in some way or other.

"Thanks, Mason," April replied. "That means a lot." Both Mason and April sat for a few moments in silence as they ate.

"So, tell me a little about yourself," Mason said, "I only know that you have Blake and Claire, but that is about it. What do you do for a living? What are your hobbies?"

April started with how she was a book editor with Priscilla Publishing. She mentioned her childhood with Crystal, her best friend. That led to how her parents were still alive and how totally awesome they were. She then began talking about Nick.

Mason listened intently, soaking up all the information he possibly could about this beautiful woman before him. He wanted to know everything about her, even about her deceased husband.

"So, tell me," Mason questioned candidly, "How did you and your husband meet?"

April chuckled at the memory and then began the story. "Well, it was Black Friday 2001, and I had just spent the day shopping with Crystal. We had departed and gone our separate ways, and I was in the process of walking back to my tiny little apartment when I saw these shoes in a department store window. My hands were full of all of my previous purchases, but I was determined to see that pair of shoes," April's smile widened as she recalled the memory.

"I tried to open the door by using my foot to push it open from the bottom. Unfortunately, the sidewalks were slick from the snow and ice that had fallen the day before. So, as I raised my right foot up to push the door, my left foot slipped out from under me and I fell squarely on my back."

April took a quick bite of her turkey sandwich and kept going with the story. "As you can imagine, some of my bags flew from my hands and I looked like a turtle that was upside down. Suddenly, a man reached for my arm to pull me up. After he got me back upright, I looked into his eyes and at that moment, I knew, I knew that I was going to marry him."

"Wow," Mason smiled humorously. "You literally fell head over heels for him."

April blinked in surprise. Of the hundreds of times that she had told that story over the years, no one had ever used that analogy.

"Yes," April smiled gleefully. "I guess I did."

She then told Mason how Nick had just moved to Chicago after he had just gotten out of a serious relationship. He relocated to the Windy City because he had received a job offer as an entry-level architect working for a firm downtown. He had just graduated from UCLA and was ready to take on the world.

April concluded her narration with details of the accident that killed Nick and how she had been raising Blake ever since. She decided not to tell him about how she actually met Claire and the story behind it. Maybe someday she would get the chance, but she didn't think it appropriate for today.

"That's me in a nutshell," said April, as she took a sip from her coffee cup. "How about you? What's your story?" April had just spent the better part of twenty-five minutes telling Mason about herself so she was eager to learn more about him.

Mason drummed his fingers on the table and said, "Let me see, where to begin?" he joked as he thought what would be a good starting point.

"I am the oldest of two. I have a younger sister named Charlize. She is five years younger than me, but she is my best friend," Mason smiled at the sound of her name. "She lives in Eugene, Oregon, with her husband Jake, and she has a little boy who is three years old, Alexander." April could sense the pride in every word that Mason was saying. He was obviously proud of his sister and family.

Continuing, Mason said, "Charlize just accepted a position at the University of Oregon as a professor in the History Department, so I couldn't be more proud of her. She has worked really hard to get that stage in her life, and it took her a while get over the grief of our mom and dad's deaths."

His tone changed though when he mentioned his parents. "When I was twenty years old, my father passed away. It was hard for me then, but I got through it. It was tougher on my sister because she was younger than me." Mason was looking deep into April's eyes, almost like he was trying to have her see the memory that he was recalling. "Unfortunately, two years after my dad died, my mother passed away as well."

April could see the hurt in his eyes, even though he was doing his best to hide it from her.

"I think that was how my sister and I became so close, because we lost both our parents within a relatively small amount of time and we were the only ones left," Mason explained the reason for the close bond that he felt for his sister.

April involuntarily touched his hand when she said, "I am sorry to hear about your parents." She slightly adjusted her hand to remove it from his, but it seemed like her brain wasn't letting the nerve endings in her hands move fast enough.

Mason blinked once at the sudden contact, but kept his composure and continued with the story.

"Now for the meat and potatoes of my life," Mason joked, but you could tell that something important was about to be revealed.

"When I was fourteen years old, I was a forward in my school's soccer team. I was going for a shot at a goal when I was pushed from behind. I slid towards the goalie as he was in mid kick to stop my shot. His foot landed squarely on my privates, and I immediately knew that I was in trouble," Mason paused to let the gravity of the situation sink in.

April's face conveyed a look of shock and concern. "So, what happened?"

Mason grimaced at the memory but continued in spite of it. "I was in the hospital for two days and when the dust cleared, the doctor informed me that I would never be able to produce any biological children of my own."

April now realized what he meant when he said "never had the opportunity" to have children.

"I am so sorry," said April. "I can see why you are excited when you talk about your nephew." It was evident that Alexander was the closest he had come to having a child of his own."

April thought of something, and asked, "I don't want to sound uncaring about your predicament, but couldn't you adopt? I mean I have Claire now as my foster daughter. Couldn't you do something similar?" It was a valid question. Many men and women were adopting these days because of one reason or another.

Mason cleared his throat, and answered, "Yes, of course I have. But when I first got married, my wife knew about my condition and said that when we were ready, we would adopt. But a couple of years went by and some of her friends were getting pregnant, and I believe that she was jealous of them. Here she was tied down to a man that could never fulfill her wish. We even talked about insemination, but it was becoming apparent that she resented me."

Mason took a sip of his fountain pop, and concluded, "It took a couple of bitterness-filled years, but she finally ended it with me. She eventually found what she was looking for in the arms of a heart surgeon in New York City."

Mason grinned at what he said next. "I think that they have four children now and she is the head of the local PTA." There was something in the way that he spoke those words that revealed that he was over it.

"Would you ever want to foster or adopt any kids of your own?" April asked matter-of-factly.

Mason smiled at the question and didn't hesitate. "Yes, of course I would. I love children and would love to be a father." He paused, thinking of the best way to explain it to April. "When I got divorced, I was just going through the motions for several months. I thought about adopting, but then I had the opportunity to date a few women and I thought to myself that if I met that special someone, maybe we would both be ready to start a family. Unfortunately, those dates didn't pan out, and here I am, several years later."

April was fascinated by Mason's life's story. She truly felt sad for him and the fact that he couldn't have his own kids. She was mesmerized by his voice and the sincerity of the emotions that he was relaying.

Lightening up the mood, Mason held up his hands, and said, "Don't get me wrong; I am happy with the direction of my life. I have a wonderful sister, an awesome nephew, and my own business that is thriving. It's not like I am desperately searching for the first woman that comes along and bats an eyelash at me. It's just that I am holding out for the *one special* woman who wants to be my partner and lifelong friend and who also wants to be a mother, no matter how it happens."

When Mason stopped speaking, April just sat there in silence for a few moments, taking in everything that he had just said. Her heart went out to him and she couldn't shake the feeling that there was something special about him. April was totally intrigued by Mason Steele.

She glanced at the clock that was on the wall behind Mason, and realized that she had been talking to Mason for over an hour.

"Wow, I can't believe it's been an hour," April said, surprised with herself for losing track of time. She picked up her phone and texted Claire to see if Blake was still ok. Claire responded several seconds later saying Blake was starting to feel a little better, and that she had kicked ass at *Overwatch*. Claire also texted that Rose had stopped by just after April had left to go to dinner, and was just getting ready to leave.

April sighed with relief to hear that Blake was feeling a little better.

"Everything good?" Mason asked, trying to detect if the sigh was caused by good info or bad.

"Yes, well, at least reasonably good," confided April. "Blake is feeling better than before. She was playing an online game on her laptop with Claire."

Mason perked up at the mention of the laptop. "That's great. Glad to hear that she is gaming. It's a good way to get your mind off of the reality of life, at least for a little while."

April grinned and then agreed with Mason's assessment. She pushed her chair back and began to stand up. "Thank you for your company and the use of your table. I think that makes us even now," April said gratefully. "I better get back to Blake."

Mason instinctively got up from his seat when April did, and replied, "Sure thing. The pleasure was all mine." As he watched April pick up her purse and gather her trash tray to put away, Mason asked, "I know that you don't know me that well, but would it be ok if I came with you so that I can meet Blake? I don't want to intrude, but I would love to meet your daughter."

April would normally not think it would be a good idea, but she had just spent the last hour with him and felt like she had known him for months. He was sincere and compassionate.

April paused to consider his request, and he did his best to assure her that he only had the best intentions. "It would be an honor for me to say hello to her, and I won't linger, I promise. I know that she is sick and won't feel up to small talk."

April agreed and the two of them walked out of the cafeteria together. When they got to Blake's room, April went in first and Mason remained in the hallway.

"I'm back," April said, as she walked in. Claire was lying next to Blake and the two of them had just finished playing *Overwatch* and were now watching YouTube videos of *Overwatch* gameplay.

Claire and Blake both looked up from the laptop screen, and Blake grinned and said, "Hey, mom."

Claire smiled at April, and then noticed Mason just behind her still in the hallway. Claire's eyes lit up and she smirked, "So... April? How's it going? How was dinner?" Blake turned her head to look at Claire because the way that she was asking April sounded suspicious.

"Blake, honey," April began, "I want you to introduce you to someone that I met here at the hospital..."

Before April could say his name, Claire let out a somewhat loud, "Hi, Mason, come on in."

April gave Claire a mischievous look, but then smiled as she looked at Blake.

"Blake, this is Mason Steele. I met him on your first day here," April said, by way of explanation.

Blake's eyes widened ever so slightly, and she gave Mason a wave. "Hello, Mason. I'm Blake. Nice to meet you." She then looked over at Claire, and whispered, "He's the one you mentioned?" The whisper was loud enough for both April and Mason to hear.

Mason could tell that Blake was sick. Her skin was pale and she looked exhausted. "Hello Blake. It's an absolute pleasure to meet you," Mason replied sincerely. After a brief pause, he then turned his attention to Claire, "Nice to see you again."

"You too, Mason, what's up?" Claire smiled.

April didn't know it, but her cheeks were turning a light shade of red. She felt like she was bringing a new boyfriend home to meet her parents for the first time.

Mason turned his attention back to Blake in an effort to answer Claire's question. "Your mother and I have had several conversations over the past week, and I just wanted to meet you in person."

Blake could tell that he really liked her mother. Blake could also tell that she really liked him.

"So, Mason, Claire tells me you are into computers. Do you play online games?" Blake questioned, with a smirk on her face.

"It just so happens that I do," Mason confessed. "I'm not a full-fledged gamer per say, but I can hold my own." Blake could tell by the way Mason was talking that he was probably pretty good at gaming, but didn't want to admit it.

"What else do you do?" Blake asked innocently, but laced with curiosity.

"I install computer systems and work with software applications." Mason began to explain. "I have a big job right now installing computers on the new wing of this hospital."

Blake was having fun interrogating her mother's "boyfriend", as if she were the mother figure.

"Sounds like fun," Blake told Mason. "I like computers, but fashion is my passion. I like to design dresses and put together outfits." Mason was taken by Blake's personality and ability to communicate well with adults. Here she was, sick in a hospital bed, but was holding her own with him.

Blake picked up her iPad and opened her fashion app. She tapped a couple of buttons and then showed the screen to Mason.

"You designed that?" Mason was impressed with what he saw on the screen.

"Yes, I did," replied Blake honestly. "I want to make this so that Claire can wear it for prom." Claire had had no idea until just now and looked at Blake in surprise. "Really?" Claire asked in surprise.

"Yeah. I didn't want to tell you yet, but I might not be able to get it the way I want it before then, so I just wanted to let you know," Blake explained.

"Cool, Blake. You are totally awesome," Claire said, surprised by the design.

Mason looked at April, and then said to the room in general, "Thank you so much for allowing me to meet you, Blake," Mason began. "I just want you to know that I will be thinking about you and I hope you get well soon." He turned to face the door, but stopped to ask Blake a question that had just occurred to him, "Hey, do you know how to play chess?"

Blake replied, "No, not really. I only played it once or twice but I have pretty much forgotten everything."

"Good," Mason declared. "If you are up to it, and if it's ok with your mother, I would like very much to stop by and teach you. Would it be ok if I did that?"

Blake liked Mason from the moment that he spoke his first word. He seemed totally genuine and made her mother smile. She wasn't too keen on playing chess, but it would be a good reason for him to be around.

"Sure, I would love to," Blake turned to her mother, and asked, "Is it ok if he comes back to teach me chess?"

April's mind raced at the possibility of seeing Mason more often. "Sure, it's ok with me."

"Settled," Mason grinned. "I will stop by tomorrow sometime to see how you are feeling." Mason paused and then said, "Also, if there is a time that you are too tired or simply don't want to, please let me know. It won't hurt my feelings. I know that this chemo stuff really sucks."

Blake snorted at the way that Mason said the last sentence. "Cool, I'll see you tomorrow."

Mason waved at Blake and Claire on the way out, and said, "Goodbye, ladies."

April walked Mason out into the hallway, and when they were out of earshot of the girls, she said, "Thank you for doing this for Blake."

Mason really wanted to spend time with Blake. She was a delightful young lady and Mason could see that she got most of her personality traits from April.

"Of course, April," Mason said, assuring her. "Both of your girls are amazing. I should be the one thanking you for allowing me to spend time with them, especially during this unsettling time with Blake's illness."

April liked the idea of Mason being around, but she was nervous because of the way she was feeling towards him, especially when her heart was in deep turmoil due to Blake's cancer diagnosis.

April said goodbye to Mason. As he walked away from her and down the hall, she couldn't take her eyes off of him. She finally turned away from his disappearing silhouette, and stepped back into Blake's room.

* *

IT WAS WEDNESDAY AFTERNOON, AND CLAIRE WAS SITTING with Trevor during lunch. Shelly, Rose, and Brie were sitting on the other side of the table. Ever since the Winter Formal, Brie was now considered their friend, and hung out with them. Silently, Trevor didn't like the fact that the group was all chummy with Brie, but he was cordial to her, and didn't let his true feelings show. It was like he was waiting for Brie to say something bad about him, and then Claire wouldn't want to be his girlfriend any more. Trevor was becoming more irritable when she was around. He didn't realize it, but the steroids were altering his moods.

For instance, the three of them were talking about Blake and how they were planning on distributing the matching headbands. It seemed to Trevor that every conversation that they had was about Blake's illness. Even though Trevor could be caring and compassionate, he was becoming more annoyed with how Claire's time and energy was being hijacked by Blake's condition. He just wanted some quality alone time with Claire, but for the past week and a half, she had been distracted and worried.

As Trevor took a bite from his burger, he heard Claire say that she was going to meet Brie at the hospital today after school.

"Wait, what?" Trevor interrupted the conversation. "Are you going to the hospital again tonight?"

Claire looked at Trevor like he had a third eye, and said, "Ah, yeah, why?"

Trevor got this pouty, pissed off look on his face, and said with a hint of defiance, "We are supposed to be going to Jordan's tonight, remember?"

Claire had to search her memory for a brief moment to try to remember why they were supposed to go out to Jordan's. Then the reason became clear, as Trevor said, "The bonfire? Remember?"

Jordan's parents were out of town enjoying a tropical island vacation. Because there was no school on Thursday and Friday this week due to Records Day, Jordan and Trevor had planned this party three weeks ago.

"Oh yeah," Claire replied, as she remembered, "Can't I come later in the night? After I see Blake?"

Trevor flashed a look that Brie saw, but Claire didn't fully notice because she was right next to him. For a moment, it looked like Trevor was going to flip out. Then he composed himself, but was still very irritated. "I guess so." He said as he looked away from Claire.

"You guess so?" Claire answered back. "I'm sorry I forgot about this party, but in my defense, my foster sister was diagnosed with cancer!" Claire's voice was rising in volume as she finished her sentence. "It's not like I am trying to bail on you because I don't want to go. I have to be with Blake right now."

Claire couldn't believe that Trevor was pissed off about this. She gave him a look that conveyed how irritated she was.

"Look, Claire," Trevor explained, "I'm sorry, but forgive me if I just want to spend time with you. You are my girlfriend, after all."

Claire pursed her lips as her brain came up with a response. "I get that, Trevor, I really do. Believe me, I want to spend more time with you too, but you have got to cut me a little slack here. Don't you realize that I am a mess right now?" Claire's words were filtered with emotion. "My best friend in the entire world is dying of leukemia, and I am trying to be strong for her. I am watching her get sicker and sicker, and there is nothing that I can do to help her. Do you know what that is like?"

Trevor knew that no matter what he said, it would seem like he was the bad guy. Maybe he was, but he didn't like to share Claire with anyone. He decided to let it go, so he said, "Ok, I get it. I'm sorry. I just love you too much." Trevor then transformed his face, with a charming smile.

Even though Claire was still frustrated with Trevor's behavior, she slowly began to ease up on him and then said, "I love you too. I just have to be with Blake as much as possible."

Trevor clapped his hands softly. "No problem babe, I'll go solo to the party, but I won't like it."

Claire gave him a faint smile, "Thanks, I'll go to the next one, I promise."

Trevor seemed satisfied with that and he changed the subject by telling the group about how much he had been working out and how much muscle mass he now had.

As Claire listened, she wished that Trevor had chosen to go with her to the hospital, instead of going alone to the party.

* *

TREVOR PULLED HIS CAR INTO JORDAN'S DRIVEWAY AN hour or so before the party was scheduled to start. He sat in his car with the motor running for a few moments, thinking about his conversation with Claire. He really did love her, but he was getting tired of her spending time with everyone else except for him. He cranked up the radio and pounded his steering wheel several times.

He let out a few quick breaths to calm down, and then turned off the vehicle. Before he opened the door, he reached in the backseat and grabbed his backpack, the one with the secret pocket. After school, he sent a text to Owen stating that he wanted to meet at Jordan's house. Owen was pulling in the driveway just as Trevor was getting out of his car. Owen pulled up behind Trevor's car. Trevor jumped into the passenger's seat with his backpack, and then shut the door.

"What's up?" Owen asked with concern. He could see that Trevor was getting bulkier.

Trevor smiled at Owen, and said with a hint of mischief, "I need more stuff. That's what's up."

Owen's eyes blinked in shock as he mentally calculated what Trevor should have remaining. "How much do you have left?" Owen questioned.

"Enough for the weekend, and that's about it." Trevor replied, truthfully.

"Wait," Owen said, "this weekend?"

"Yup, this weekend," answered Trevor, sounding bold. "Is that a problem?"

"Well, Mr. Captain of the Basketball Team, you should have a couple of weeks' worth stuff left at least." Trevor could see that Owen was becoming more irritated with the situation, but Trevor didn't care. He was at the top of his game and he looked the part.

"Listen, Owen," Trevor said, pointing his right index finger at him. "How about you give me what I need and save the shit for someone that cares. I am telling you that I want more, and will be paying you for it, so don't be a douchebag. Got it?"

Owen hated dealing with Trevor now. He was becoming a liability, but there was nothing that Owen could do about it. *God... jocks suck!* Owen thought to himself. *I'm going to stick with the fucking burnouts after this.* The two of them sat in Owen's car in total silence for several seconds. It was as if Owen was trying to build up enough nerve to confront Trevor and refuse his demands. Unfortunately, he caved in. "Ok, ok asshole," Owen said, "I only have a little on me right now, but I'll get you more on Monday. Ok?"

Trevor smiled, acting as if he was a little boy in a candy store whose mother had just given in to his cries for more candy, he said, "Fuck yeah!" Trevor pulled out a wad of cash from his wallet and handed it to Owen. After counting it, he placed it into the inside chest pocket of his coat and then pushed the glove box, causing it to fall open. He removed a Ziploc of steroids and handed it to Trevor.

"See you Monday," Trevor said gleefully, but with a hint of threat. He secured the drugs into his secret pocket and then got out of the car. Owen just watched Trevor leave his car and walk towards the front door of Jordan's house.

How the hell am I going to get myself out of this? Owen thought as he put the car into gear and drove away from Trevor as fast as he could.

The hour before the party, Trevor was still irritated with Claire for not coming. He was the captain of the basketball team, and probably the best athlete in the entire school. He wasn't accustomed to not getting what he wanted.

However, as the party got started, Trevor felt his mood changing. He was having fun with the guys, and was becoming the life of the party. Half of the kids were outside in the snow, sitting around the bonfire, while the other half was inside, drinking and eating. About an hour into it, Jordan and Trevor made their way into Jordan's dad's billiard room. That room was always locked up when his parents were out of town, but Jordon had found out where his dad had hidden the key. So, here the two of them were, sitting at the bar, looting the liquor cabinet.

Jordon removed a fifth of Jack Daniels, and cracked it open. He poured a little into each of their solo cups and began sipping the mixture of Jack and Coke. Trevor had tried whiskey before with Jordan, but was still surprised with how it burned going down.

When Trevor's cup was half empty, Jordan poured more Jack into it but no Coke.

As the two of them sat there, Jordan looked at Trevor and asked, "Hey, have you banged Claire yet?"

It was the typical teenage boy question. Trevor really hadn't made out with her for any length of time but he didn't want Jordan to know that. "No, not yet," but then he gave Jordan a devilish smirk and added, "But I'm going to tap her on Valentine's Day." Jordan chuckled at Trevor and said, "Oh yeah? What do you have planned?" By the way that Jordan was talking, the liquor was starting to take effect. His words were getting louder. While he waited for Trevor to answer, he took the bottle of Jack and drank directly from it. Truth be told, he was showing off to Trevor.

Trevor's eye's gleamed with excitement over the challenge, and answered, "I am going to take her out to dinner at a fancy restaurant and then drive her to the Navy Pier. There is a place there where I used to park and make out with Brie. I am going to start out slow, but then we are going to go all the way."

Trevor smirked at what he had just told Jordan, and then suddenly snatched the bottle from his hands and took a long, hard chug. Even though it burned his throat terribly, he hid it from Jordan, and then slammed the bottle down on the bar.

"Holy shit, dude!" Jordan exclaimed, "You're the man!" The two of them sat there laughing and giggling about the plan to bang Claire.

Now that Jordan was drunk, he had a thought and could barely tell it to Trevor. He was giggling as he told Trevor, "Hey, why don't you take Claire to a soup kitchen for Valentine's Day?" Then he exploded in laughter.

Normally, Trevor would have defended his girlfriend. He knew that it was wrong to think that way. However, having been irritated with her earlier that day, and having had the amount of alcohol that he had consumed, Trevor erupted with laughter. "That's so fucking funny!" Trevor exclaimed, as he tried to keep from pissing his pants.

Just then, a couple of cheerleaders who just happened to be walking by the billiards room, heard the commotion caused by the two drunk friends and decided to join them. One of them was wearing black tights with a sexy blue sweater while the other one had form-fitting blue jeans with a flannel, long-sleeve shirt. However, the top three buttons were undone.

"Hey, girls," Jordan slurred, still giggling from what he had said about Claire. "What's happening?"

One of the cheerleaders saw the bottle on the bar top and asked, "Can we join you?"

Without skipping a beat, Jordan exclaimed, "Hell yeah!" and then patted his hand on the bar stool next to him. One of the cheerleaders sat next to Jordan, while the other one sat closer to Trevor. Both girls were fully aware that Trevor was dating Claire, but, fortunately for them, her name never came up.

CHAPTER TWENTY-TWO

"CHECKMATE," MASON TOLD BLAKE, MATTER-OF-FACTLY. HE had moved his bishop which caused her king to be either taken by it or his rook.

"Damn it," she said, staring in disbelief at the board in front of her. "Not again?" It was the third time in a row that Mason had won, and she actually thought this time that she had him on the ropes.

"It's ok, Blake," Mason consoled, "you are doing remarkably well for someone who just learned how to play a few days ago."

"You think so?" Blake asked, as she began setting up the chessboard for another round.

"Yes, of course I do. You have a real talent for this game. It is refreshing to play with a rookie like yourself who actually thinks about the strategy of each move, instead of just moving pieces arbitrarily just to move them." The look of pride in Mason's eyes was undeniable.

This was the third day that Mason had visited Blake, and she had picked up the game rapidly. The second day, she hadn't felt that well, but they did manage to get in a couple of games before he decided to leave and let her rest.

However, today Blake was a little more energetic, and wanted to spend more time playing chess.

When they were halfway through the fourth game, April was walking up to Blake's room and heard Mason inside. She stopped before entering, and listened just outside the room next to the doorframe. April stood there, smiling at the banter between Mason and her daughter. It was evident that he enjoyed his time with her as he instructed her on the nuances of chess moves. He would make her giggle as much as she made him laugh.

After a few minutes, April entered the room, acting like she had just gotten there.

"Hi guys. How's the chess teaching going?" April asked, as she took off her coat and placed it over the chair next to Mason.

"Great. Your daughter is doing very well. One of the best students I have ever had—and I am not just saying that. It's very true." Mason started to get up from his seat, but April put her hand on his shoulder. "No, don't stop. You two can finish your game. You don't have to quit on my account." Mason gave April a quick smile and placed his butt back on his chair.

It was a Sunday afternoon, sometime between lunch and dinner. April had been there first thing in the morning, but had gone home for a couple of hours to shower and get cleaned up. Claire had been with her and had stayed there after she left. Brie and Emily had come to visit Blake for a while, so the three of them were talking and spending some time with Blake. After Blake ate her lunch, she instructed the girls to go down and get food for themselves. Mason had then stopped by to play chess.

Over the last few days, April and Mason had managed to run into each other either before he played chess with Blake or after. They had spent a few hours in the cafeteria again and had even talked on the phone earlier this morning.

After ten minutes, Blake proudly shouted, "Check." Mason pretended to be surprised by it but knew that that was the direction that Blake was going to be heading in. He quickly moved his king to another position that was safe from her attack, and then continued. Blake could almost taste victory as Mason performed a few moves that Blake thought were clumsy. However, three moves later, Mason let out a sigh, and then, as he moved his knight, he said, "Checkmate."

The look of surprise on Blake's face was priceless. "What the hell?" Blake questioned. "No... Seriously, what just happened?" The look of dismay mixed with determination made Mason grin.

"I'm done," said Blake as the fourth loss to Mason took its toll on Blake's pride. She pulled the covers from her stomach closer to her shoulders. She looked at Mason, and smiled as she asked, "Can you come back tomorrow?"

Mason had a lot scheduled for Monday, but mentally was already trying to rearrange his schedule to accommodate Blake's request. "Sure thing, Miss Turner," Mason said, bowing to accept her request. "I'll text you when I am on my way. I have a meeting in the morning, but should make it here around lunchtime."

"Sure, no problem, But you don't have to hurry or anything. It's not like I'm going anywhere." Blake said, reminding everyone that she was stuck here in this room.

Mason smiled at Blake and then softly grabbed Blake's foot with his right hand. "See you tomorrow, kiddo."

April told Blake that she was going to walk Mason out and that she would be right back.

The two of them walked slowly side by side down the hallway towards the elevators.

"Blake is really doing well at chess," Mason offered. "She is a wonderful girl and smart as a whip, I must say."

April grinned at Mason's words. "Yes, she is smart. Sometimes too smart for her own good." It was obvious that Blake could push April's buttons at times, but Blake was usually a well-behaved young lady.

As the two of them talked in the hallway near the elevators, Claire and the girls exited from the one that was closest to them. "Oh, hey, you two. How's it going?" Claire asked.

"Excellent," Mason answered, "Blake is doing very well at chess."

Mason said hello to Emily and Brie, whom he was introduced to the day before. "Good to see you again."

Claire had given them the 4-1-1 about Mason and April so they were smiling as they glanced at him and April.

Claire then asked April if it was alright if Shelly and Rose stopped by to see Blake as well. They were going to all cram together in the room and watch a movie with Blake. It wasn't going to be for another hour or so.

"Sure, I guess so. If Blake feels up to it," April said thinking about Blake.

"Cool, thanks," Claire said. "It was Blake's idea to begin with. I think she wanted to feel like it was a slumber party or something," she added.

Claire, Emily, and Brie headed towards Blake's room, leaving April and Mason alone in the hallway.

April sighed and then smirked, "Great, I get to spend my night at a slumber party."

Seeing the look of non-excitement on April's face, Mason thought of an idea that might help her with her evening.

"I know it's short notice, but would you like to go to dinner with me?" Mason asked. "It looks as if Blake will be well taken care of for a few hours. What do you say?"

April paused, thinking it over. It would be nice to get to spend some quality time with Mason. Besides, the girls were all going to be with Blake tonight. Plus, Blake was doing better today than she had done the previous two days.

Nodding her head, April said, "Sure, sounds like fun. What time do you want to go?"

Mason looked at his watch and thought about it. "How about six o'clock? That will give me time to finish up a few work things, and then I'll pick you up here?" Mason asked.

"Six o'clock will be perfect." April agreed. "I'll spend a little time with the girls before that and then I'll have dinner with you."

Mason smiled and pushed the button for the elevator. "Great. Sounds like a plan. I'll see you at six then." The elevator doors opened, and Mason stepped inside. "See you soon," he called out just before the doors closed.

April turned to walk back to Blake's room. Acting like a teenager, she pulled out her phone and called Crystal. "Don't overthink this," April began before Crystal could even speak, "but guess who is taking me out to dinner?"

"Hot guy? Am I right? The hot guy, right?" Crystal exclaimed, giddy as a schoolgirl, but before April could answer, Crystal joked, "Of course, it's Mason. I know it is. You know why I know? Because I am a detective, that's why."

April had to chuckle at Crystal's excitement. "Yes, it's Mason. He just asked me out to dinner tonight. Claire and a couple of her friends are going to watch a movie with Blake in her room so the date just kind of happened out of the blue."

"That's awesome, April. It's about time you started dating again. Seriously, you are a wonderful woman who has a big heart. It's time you open yours up again." Crystal's tone turned from jovial to direct.

April shook her head at the phone as if Crystal could see her shaking her head. "It's just dinner. Don't get fitted for a bridesmaid's dress just yet, ok?" April jokingly chastised her best friend.

"Ok, ok, maybe not tomorrow; but, remember, it was me who saw him at the coffee shop and wanted you to get up and talk to him," Crystal said for the record. "So, I will accept some credit during your wedding vows. Just saying."

April was amazed at how Crystal's mind worked. "Sure, when I marry him I will surely mention your name. I promise."

"Of course you will, because I'll be standing up there next to you." Having been the maid of honor during April's marriage to Nick, Crystal naturally figured she would be in bridal party at April's next wedding.

"Yes, Crystal. You will be up there with me. I just want my daughter to be around to be my maid of honor, you know?" April concluded as she rounded the corner, and was almost at Blake's room. "Hey, I'll call you later tonight after dinner. I'm just about to go in and check on Blake."

"Oh, sure thing, tell her that I love her and that I will be seeing her tomorrow morning," Crystal said. April knew that Blake's cancer diagnosis had affected Crystal immensely. Crystal was for all purposes her Aunt, and treated Blake like her own niece.

April told Crystal that she loved her, and that she would see her tomorrow when she came to see Blake. It was now around 5:00 p.m. so April had an hour or so before Mason came to pick her up.

Brie and Emily were seated in chairs next to the bed while Claire was in the bed next to Blake. If you had walked into that room not knowing any of them, you could have sworn that they had all grown up as best friends. You wouldn't have imagined that both girls sitting in the chairs were basically responsible for bullying Claire and causing her so much anguish. Claire had certainly taken the high road, and now they were all friends.

April told Blake that Crystal was going to drop by in the morning to see her and that she loved her. She then told her that she was going to go to dinner with Mason because of the amount of girls who were going to be in her room.

"Sure, that's the reason mom," Blake said, as she grinned at Claire. "It's because us 'girls' didn't want to make room for you and you decided to leave."

April knew that Blake was kidding, but kept up with the reasoning. "Yes, of course, my girls don't want me around anymore so I have to find solace with another adult."

"Whatever floats your boat, mom," Blake smiled. "It's ok, mom, I'll be fine with everyone here, so go and enjoy yourself."

April was happy to see that Blake didn't mind, and it did seem like Blake really enjoyed Mason's company. April talked with the girls until Mason arrived.

April looked at Blake one more time and she still looked tired and a little pale, but seemed well enough for her to leave for a little while.

"Call me if anything happens, ok guys?" April told the roomful of girls. Claire could see that April was worried and looked a little guilty for wanting to leave for dinner.

"I will, April, I promise," Claire answered April sincerely. "I'll keep a close eye on her."

April nodded her head, and then said, "Ok then, see you in a little while."

April and Mason left the room and headed for the elevator. He told April on the way down that he wanted to take her to an Italian restaurant that was just a couple blocks away from the hospital. April agreed and the two of them walked out into the chilly February evening air. The cold air hit April's face and even though it was freezing, it felt shockingly refreshing to her.

The restaurant was full, so they had to wait for fifteen minutes to get a seat. During that time, Mason found a couple of seats at the bar and ordered them each a glass of wine. As they became engrossed in conversation, Mason became fascinated by how the lights behind the bar reflected off of April's eyes. It was as if they were glowing.

Their discussion covered topics such as Mason's company and what projects he was working on, April's parents, and her friends, like Crystal and Gina.

The hostess came over and then took them to a table that was near the window. As they sat down, Mason's cell phone went off—it was his sister, Charlie. He picked it up and said, "Hello." Mason informed her that he was out to dinner with April, Charlie's voice instantly changed from normal to one that was filled with excitement. "Oh, sorry to bother you." April could hear Charlie's voice over the phone. "Have fun. Call me later." She quickly disconnected the call so that her brother could go back to his date.

"Your sister sounds really nice," commented April, as it was obvious that she could hear her voice.

"She really is," Mason agreed. "It was basically just the two of us during her teenage years." He didn't elaborate any more, but then turned his attention to the menu. "What do you feel like having for dinner?"

April picked up her menu and scanned it. She had dined at this restaurant quite a few times in her life and she already knew what she was going to order. "The chicken Parmesan is my favorite here." April commented as she set the menu down and looked over at Mason. He was already looking at her and when their eyes met, it was as if they were locked, glued to each other.

After a few moments, April blushed and said, "I'm sorry," and then turned her attention to the hustle and bustle that was going on outside their window.

"I love it here," April suddenly said about the city landscape that she was staring at. "I've lived in the city most of my life, and I love the buildings, the streets, and all the people wandering around and going about their lives."

Mason smiled at her, and said, "Me too. I think that is one of the reasons that I wanted to start my own company here is that there are so many things to do and it is never dull in the city. There is always something going on."

The waitress came up and took their order. This was the most relaxed that April had been in a couple of weeks and even then, her mind was constantly thinking about Blake.

As the dinner proceeded, April was becoming more and more attracted to Mason. Maybe it was the way that he could engage in quality conversations or the way that he looked at her. They were obviously attracted to each other physically, but it was deeper than that. As they talked, April thought that it could be that they both had had to deal with a loss of a loved one. Nick had died, while Mason and his wife were divorced. Whatever it was, there was something between the two of them that was undeniable.

When they finished dinner, Mason walked her back to the hospital, and up to Blake's room. Only Claire and Brie were still around. Rose and Shelly had taken Emily home when they had left. Brie and Claire were sitting on the two chairs that were pulled away from Blake's bed, looking at the screen of Claire's laptop. When April and Mason walked in, Claire put her finger up to her lips to signal them to be quiet. Blake had fallen asleep halfway through the movie.

Mason said goodbye to everyone, and then told April that he would see her tomorrow after he finished playing chess with Blake. Because they were standing so close to each other in the room, April's hand brushed against his as he turned to leave. It was one of those moments when you don't know if you should hug or kiss, or simply just say goodbye. Mason glanced down at her hand and for a moment, didn't know what the intention was. Being the classy gentleman that he was, he politely reached down and grabbed her hand and held it, not as if to shake it, but bringing it up about chest high, and said, "Till then, my dear."

April grinned at Mason's ability to make her feel at ease. "Till then, Mr. Steele."

April quietly closed the door behind Mason, and then turned to Claire and asked, "How was she tonight?"

"She was doing good, but then just got really tired. She fell asleep about an hour ago." Claire closed her laptop, and got up from her chair. "We decided to stop the movie and the others went home. Brie wanted to keep me company until you got back from dinner." Claire stretched her arms in the air, and then asked, "By the way, how was dinner?"

"It was good," said April, as she remembered when their eyes locked during dinner. "It was really good."

April and Claire said goodnight to Brie a few minutes later when her mom came to pick her up. April was tired, but didn't want to leave the hospital just yet. April and Claire sat there, talking quietly about their day. Finally, April got up and told Claire that they better get going. She carefully went up to Blake, and kissed her softly on her forehead. "I love you, honey," she whispered, as tears began to well up in April's eyes.

As she sat there, her cell phone went off—the call was from Addison James. She told April that she was sorry to hear about Blake, and that if there was anything that she needed, to let her know. April spent the next half-hour telling Addison about finding Claire and what an impact Claire had made in their lives. Before the conversation ended, Addison informed April that she was at her New York office, but would be flying out to Chicago tomorrow morning to spend the day with her and Blake. April thanked her and said that she would meet her at the hospital.

* *

IT WAS NOW VALENTINE'S DAY. TREVOR WAS TAKING CLAIRE out on a dinner date, while April and Mason had planned to go out for dinner and dancing. Claire told Trevor to pick her up at the hospital at 5:30 p.m. because she was going to go see Blake beforehand.

Because Blake was losing her hair more rapidly, she had made the decision a couple of days ago to shave her head. That was one of the roughest and most traumatic days for Blake so far. It was like she was giving in to the cancer by cutting her hair. Claire and April were the only ones there when she had shaved it off.

Today, Blake was wearing a white head covering with red hearts spread evenly throughout. Claire, of course, was wearing a matching headband. "I'm here," Claire said to Blake as she entered her room. Blake looked a little pastier than she had the previous day, but her eyes lit up when she saw Claire. It was Valentine's Day, and she was going to help Claire pick out her dress. Blake had narrowed it down to two different outfits, but wanted Claire to try on both in front of her so that she could see them in person.

Blake chose the hot red dress with the headband that Claire was currently wearing. Claire used the bathroom in Blake's room to change, and then apply a little more makeup.

Claire told Blake that Trevor was going to take her to a fancy restaurant downtown and then a walk by the Navy Pier. Even though it was cold outside, it was still a beautiful place to be.

Just then, April and Mason came into the room. "You look beautiful," April said to Claire, as she checked out her dress. "Thanks April," Claire grinned. "It was Blake here who helped me, of course."

Blake gave her a thumbs–up sign as she tried to move herself further up in the bed. It was obviously a struggle for her, so April stepped over to help her. "Are you sure it's ok if we go out tonight?" April asked feeling guilty about going out while Blake was stuck in her room.

"Definitely, mom. I want both you and Claire to have a great time," Blake said, doing her best to smile. "Besides, I will just be here watching a sappy movie anyways." Blake didn't want them to know that she was feeling exhausted and was getting nauseous. If she did let on about how she was feeling, they would cancel their dates and stay here with her. She couldn't allow them to give up their evening just to sit by and watch her vomit all night.

Trevor came to pick Claire up. He said 'hi' to Blake, and then the two of them left for their date. A few minutes after that, Blake told her mother to leave and enjoy her night. Mason said bye to Blake and waved goodbye. As she watched them go, Blake thought that she really liked Mason and totally could see him with her mom. As if on cue, the feeling of nausea could no longer be ignored and she quickly pressed the nurse call button.

Trevor drove Claire to a fancy restaurant that she had never heard of before. Because it was Valentine's Day, the streets were packed with couples and families going to dinner. Trevor had made reservations a few weeks earlier, thanks to his mother's idea, and was seated at a romantic table for two by a water fountain on the left side of the restaurant.

From the outside, Trevor gave the appearance of a thorough charming gentleman. On the inside, he was the teenage boy who had trash talked with Jordan, and he definitely had a certain plan in mind for the evening.

After they ordered, Claire reached into her purse, and pulled out a card and a little wrapped up box. Trevor blinked in surprise, but then said, "Oh... We are doing this now. Ok, then." He then reached into the pocket of his coat that was hanging on the chair next to him and pulled out a little box as well as a card. His box was a little bit bigger than hers, but was still small.

"You first," Claire offered.

Trevor smiled, and then opened the card. It was your basic boyfriend card but Claire had written a couple of heartfelt paragraphs about how much he meant to her, and that she never thought the new girl would find a boyfriend in the school's top jock. It was cutely written and she had signed it with her name circled in a heart.

Trevor then opened up the box and discovered that Claire had gotten him a leather men's bracelet that had the word 'Perseverance' engraved on the top with her and his name inscribed on the inside of it.

"Wow, cool, this is really nice," Trevor said, as he hadn't expected a gift like that. It was a word that his dad used to say when he was on the football team in high school. In fact, the trophy showcase had a plate that states "Perseverance" under one of the pictures of his dad in uniform.

Claire was glad that Trevor had liked his gift, and then she opened her card. It was a Valentine's Day card that was your typical girlfriend card. But, unlike Claire, Trevor had just signed his name at the bottom. Claire didn't care because she knew that most boys at this age didn't really get into the mushy stuff. She was glad that she had got a card, to begin with.

She then opened up the small box, and it was a necklace. It was a pretty red ruby necklace, and it made Claire really happy. It was the first gift of jewelry she had ever received from a boy.

"Thank you so much. It's beautiful," Claire beamed, as she pulled it out of the box and put it around her neck.

"You're welcome, baby," Trevor said, as he smiled at her. He took out his bracelet and put it on his right wrist.

The night felt like a dream for Claire. She felt so grown up, having a romantic dinner with her boyfriend at a fancy restaurant. Even though she was only sixteen, she still felt like a princess being courted by her prince.

They talked throughout dinner, and every time that Claire started talking about Blake, it seemed that Trevor managed to turn the discussion around, and they would end up talking about school or some game that was coming up. Claire didn't immediately get upset because maybe he didn't want to talk about Blake because it was a depressing topic, and maybe he wanted to keep things on more of a jolly note. It was, after all, Valentine's Day.

After dinner, Trevor drove Claire around the city, showing her more places that she didn't know about. Eventually, they drove up to Navy Pier, and Trevor picked a parking spot that was somewhat secluded and away from the few other parked cars that were nearby. Trevor kept pushing the scan button on the radio, until he finally settled on a Tenley Moore's song, *Until You Know*.

Tenley Moore rose to fame, when as a little girl of ten years old, she was recorded in her town's local church belting out a powerful rendition of *Amazing Grace* at her mother's funeral. Now, in her mid-thirties, Tenley Moore had released over fourteen studio albums and sixty-three singles. To many in the industry, it seems like her voice was only getting better as she got older.

Claire hummed to the melody of the song, and thought how cool it would be if she and Blake could attend one of Tenley's concerts one day. Claire had never been to a real concert before, and the idea of a Tenley Moore concert being her first one, appealed to her. She made a mental note to find a way to make it happen.

Trevor turned to Claire, and said, "Claire, I just want to know that I love you, and I think that you are awesome." He put his hand in hers, and continued, "You are the best thing that has ever happened to me." He then slowly went in for a kiss.

Claire, who was caught up in the moment, started kissing Trevor back. They made out like that for several minutes. Then, Trevor's had started to caress Claire's leg and was inching its way upwards.

Even though Claire's hormones were on fire, the way that Trevor touched her made her recall Roger's attempt to rape her. The memory of that dreadful time when she feared for her life, and knew that Roger was about to violate her hit her, and she involuntarily pushed Trevor off of her.

"What's wrong?" Trevor asked, annoyed as he looked at her with disbelief in his eyes.

"I can't do this right now," Claire said bleakly, ashamed of the emotions that had engulfed her.

"It's not you, it's me," Claire said, trying to offer an explanation.

"What does that mean?" Trevor demanded, his frustration turning to anger. "It's not like I don't love you."

"It's not about that," Claire tried to say. "I... I thought that I was ready, but there is something that you don't know..." Claire didn't want to tell her boyfriend that she had almost been raped, but didn't know if anything but the truth would appease him.

"What don't I know?" Trevor asked. "Is it someone else?" he demanded.

Someone else? Claire couldn't believe that Trevor thought that she would cheat on him. "No, of course not," Claire replied. "It's just something that happened a while ago, and I didn't know that it still affected me."

"Is it because of Blake?" Trevor asked grasping at straws. "Are you so emotionally upset over the illness of your foster sister that you don't want to make love to me?" Claire didn't know how Trevor could connect the dots like that. It wasn't like she didn't want to. She did, but the raw emotions that had just erupted in her mind and the thought of Roger's attempt to rape her, made it impossible for her to even think about sex.

Dumbfounded by his question, Claire blurted out, "No, it's because I was almost raped!" As soon as those words came out, she immediately started to sob. "Around seven months ago, I was attacked by my foster dad. If I hadn't smashed his head with a lamp, he would have raped me and done who knows what else!" The shame that Claire felt then, came flooding back to her now. How could a sixteen-year-old boy understand the gravity of her situation?

Even though the car was warm from the heat flowing from the vents, a chill washed over Claire.

The look of frustration that was on Trevor's face slowly turned to that of remorse.

"Look, Claire," Trevor began slowly, "I had no idea that you were almost raped. I'm sorry that happened to you. How could I have known this?" Trevor looked out of the driver's side window, starting at his and Claire's reflection. "I just wanted to prove to you that I love you—that's all," Trevor justified his actions. "I wouldn't have tried more if I had known."

Claire grabbed Trevor's hand and with tears still in her eyes, said, "I'm sorry too. I didn't think that it would have affected me like this. I love you too." Claire wiped the tears from her face with her jacket sleeve, and then said, "I do want you, and Trevor, and I just need a little time."

Trevor smiled at her and thought about it for a few moments. "Ok, baby. I'll give you more time. I love you and want us to be happy together."

Claire was begging to feel a little better, and said, "Thanks Trevor. I love you and thanks for being patient with me."

Trevor went in and gave Claire a hug and a kiss on the cheek. "Sure thing," he said to Claire, as he started the car to take her home, *but I'm not going to wait forever,* he thought to himself as he drove his car out of the parking lot.

* *

TREVOR DROPPED CLAIRE OFF AT THE HOSPITAL AND SHE went up to Blake's room. When she got there, two nurses were in the room, and Blake looked really weak. Before Blake realized that Claire had returned, one of the nurses asked her to wait outside.

Claire began to pace back and forth as she wanted to know what was going on. A minute later, one of the nurses came out and talked to Claire. "Blake has been vomiting for the past couple of hours. She is extremely weak right now, and the doctor is coming in shortly to see her," the nurse said with slight concern in her voice. Claire had already been emotional over the Trevor situation and she began to tear up. The nurse tried to comfort Blake by saying that they are looking at changing her medications again to help her.

Claire took a seat down the hall in the waiting area, and picked up the phone.

"April, it's me. I'm sorry to ruin your date, but Blake has been sick for several hours, and she looks weak. They won't let me in to see her," Claire informed April as she got a tissue from a Kleenex box on the end table to wipe her eyes.

"Ok, honey, we will be right there," Claire could hear the concern in April's voice as she hung up.

Claire sat there, feeling guilty for not being there for Blake. She never should have left her.

Twenty minutes later, April and Mason showed up. April was a little flustered, and you could tell that she probably had come running all the way.

Claire saw them exiting the elevator and went up to them. "She looked really weak, April," Claire began. "She looked extremely pale from throwing up." April hugged Claire, and then said, "Let's see what's going on."

April walked to the nurse's station just outside Blake's door, and wanted to know what was happening. The nurse told her that the doctor was in there with her right now and would be out shortly. The three of them stood by Blake's door and waited. After about five minutes, Dr. Powell walked out of the room. She was wearing a black cocktail dress with a diamond necklace. It was clear to April that she had been called in from her dinner to see Blake.

"What's wrong?" April asked Dr. Powell before she could utter a word.

Dr. Powell walked the three of them to an area of the waiting room that was quiet. "Her leukemia is progressing faster than we had predicted. The combination of the leukemia and chemo treatments is causing Blake's condition to worsen.

"Worsen?" April's voice cracked, as she repeated the word. "What can we do?"

"Like I mentioned before, Blake's only option of survival is a bone marrow transplant. We have searched the database, and as of now, there is no perfect match for her," Dr. Powell explained.

"So you mean to tell me that no one in the world is a match for Blake?" April asked, trying to keep from screaming.

"As of today, no," Dr. Powell said, "But every day thousands of people are being added to the 'Be the Match' registry, and we are hopeful her match will turn up soon."

April's fears were coming true. Blake was dying, and there was no one who could stop it. Dr. Powell said that she would be keeping a close eye on Blake tonight and then would see what the change in medications did for her.

As Dr. Powell left to go back to Blake's room, April tried to be strong, but it was too much for her. She broke down crying. "I can't lose her, Mason. I can't," she sobbed. Tears were running down Claire's face, as she turned to look towards Blake's room. Mason wished he could fix Blake for April, but knew that he couldn't. He did the only thing that he could do at that particular moment to help April—he reached out to her and allowed her to cry on his shoulder.

The next day, Claire went to the hospital in the morning to check up on Blake. She was doing a little better than the night before, but was still weak. Claire talked with her for a few minutes until Blake fell asleep. April told Claire that she should go to school. Blake was responding to the medications and said she would call her if her condition changed.

By the time Claire got to school, it was lunch hour. She made her way to the table where Brie, Shelly, and Rose were eating. They could tell that Claire was concerned about Blake. "How is she now?" Shelly asked.

"The new medications are helping, I guess, but she still looks terrible. The only thing that is going to save her is a bone marrow transplant, but of all the millions of people in the system, not one is a match," Claire explained, the frustration apparent in her voice.

"That really sucks!" Rose said, as she slammed her burger onto her plate. "What else is there?"

"Nothing," Claire said sadly. "Absolutely, fucking nothing. Chemo is killing her. Leukemia is killing her. The medicine that she is taking is making her sicker," Claire vented as the helplessness overwhelmed her. "Only a perfect match can save her, and as of now, and there isn't one."

The girls stood for a few moments, not knowing what else to say. Then Brie's eyes lit up as an idea popped into her head. "Hey, why don't we have 'Be the Match' come to our school and have students provide samples so they can get registered? I mean, if we can start having rallies and going to places to have people sign up, Blake's odds of finding someone will increase. Right?"

It was a really good idea. Claire looked at Brie, and said, "That's it. The more the number of people who sign up, the better chances she has." Jumping up, Claire exclaimed, "Brie, you're a genius! I'm going to go down to the principal's office and ask if I can call 'Be the Match' and have them come to school."

As Claire got up from the table, Brie got up and said, "I'll go with you." Claire smiled and the two of them ran all the way down to the office.

It took a little convincing but Claire and Brie talked the principal into it. Because it was short notice, he would make an announcement as soon as they found out if 'Be the Match' could come to school the next day, which was a Friday.

Claire called 'Be the Match' in front of the principal on speakerphone, and asked if they could come over. They told Claire that they did have a team available, but could only come between the hours of 10 a.m. and 2 p.m. Claire was happy to get what she could get, and thanked them profusely.

Brie's idea was quickly becoming a reality. When school was done for the day, Claire called back 'Be the Match' and inquired about other places and venues that they were planning on going, so that she could get the word out. This was a cause that Claire and her friends were going to get behind.

April had texted Claire earlier and informed her that Blake's condition was just about the same with no major changes. Despite that, Claire still hurried to the hospital to be with her. April was in the room with her. Blake's eyes looked sunken, and she looked skinnier than she did yesterday.

"Hey, Blake," Claire said, as she entered the room.

"Hi, Claire Bear," Blake answered, grinning with white thinned lips as she said it. "How's it going?"

"School sucks," Claire said jokingly to her, trying to make her laugh.

"How's it with you? Time to get better so that we can get out of here," Claire said to her.

"I'm trying," Blake said defiantly as she coughed. Blake was starting to cough more and more, and it was not a good sign.

"Now that you are here, there is something that I want to tell you guys," Blake said to her mom and Claire.

April sat up in her chair, and asked, "Ok? What is it?"

Blake looked from her mom to Claire, and then began, "I know that I am really sick. I'm trying my best to beat this, but I know that I am dying." Tears began to swell up in her eyes as she spoke about her potential fate. A sob escaped April's lips when Blake said the word 'dying', but she let her continue.

Still looking at Claire, Blake said, "I know that you have only recently come into our lives, but if I should die, I want you to be my replacement. I need to know that you are going to take my place, and be there for my mom."

Claire couldn't believe what Blake was saying. "No." Claire cried, as her eyes widened. "I'm not going to be your replacement because you're not going anywhere." Claire looked at April for reassurance. Claire put her head on Blake's chest, sobbing. "You are my best friend, and I need you to get better! We are going to fight this together." She picked her head up and looked into Blake's eyes, "I could never replace you, so you better not leave us!" At this point, April got up from the chair and was standing behind Claire. "Blake, honey," April said between sobs. "Claire won't be going anywhere, but neither will you. I need you to be strong and beat this."

"I'm trying mom," Blake explained through tears. "But, I want to know that you two will be there for each other if I don't make it. Please mom. I need to hear it from you," Blake said and then started coughing again, most likely due to the tears and the emotion of what she was saying.

"Fine," Claire conceded. "I will always be there for April, but I will never be your replacement. You aren't going anywhere to be replaced. Get the picture?"

Blake knew that all this was very upsetting, but the way that she had been feeling the last couple of days, she felt like she had to say it before it was too late.

"Good enough for me," Blake tried to grin. "I just want to let you know that I love the both of you, and want to be sure that you will be alright when and if I go."

April's heart was broken. Her daughter knew that she was dying. How could April go on living if Blake died?

As the three of them slowly started to recover from their tears, a nurse came in to bring in a change of medication for Blake's IV. "What do you want for dinner tonight?" the nurse asked Blake once she finished hooking the bag on the pole.

Blake thought about it for a few moments, and said, "I just want a soup and salad. I'm not that hungry."

The nurse wrote it down and then left the room. April didn't like the fact that her daughter wasn't eating that much, and the constant vomiting was taking a toll on Blake.

Claire then told April and Blake about how 'Be the Match' was coming to the school tomorrow, and how she was going to help them with driving up participation at their other collection sites. It sounded awesome as Claire was saying it, but the odds of finding a perfect match still seemed like a long shot.

* *

THE LINE WAS LONGER THAN CLAIRE HAD ANTICIPATED FOR the 'Be the Match' collection booth in the gym. They had set up a few booths and were collecting samples. Shelly, Rose, and Brie had posted the event on Facebook and Instagram. They had placed Blake's picture on it saying that she needed a life-saving bone marrow transplant.

Claire was in line with Brie, Shelly, and Rose as they waited to fill out the paperwork and have their cheeks swabbed. Trevor had gotten the entire team together and had just walked into the gym with a group of them. *This is truly remarkable,* Claire thought to herself, as she gazed around the gym. More and more students and teachers were filing in to get in line.

After they were finished, Claire and Trevor sat together for lunch. Ever since Valentine's Day night, they were good, but there was something different between them. Claire couldn't quite put her finger on it, but it was there. Claire knew that she had probably overwhelmed Trevor by opening up to him about her attempted rape, but at the time, she hadn't had much of a choice. Maybe he just needed more time to process it. Hell, she needed more time to process it.

Claire sat next to Trevor with her hand on his leg. She was eating a ham and cheese sandwich and was almost finished when Jordan came up to the table.

"Hey, Trev, Claire, what's happening?" Jordan asked, as he set his tray down on the table.

"Nothing much," Trevor answered, "just eating lunch. What's up with you?"

"I just heard that Darrell and Susie just broke up. Do you know what that means?" Jordan asked, as if Claire or Trevor could guess the answer.

When neither one of them could offer up a guess, Jordan said, "It means that I can go out with Susie now. God I would love to tap that!"

Before Jordan could say another word, Claire spoke up, "Really? You would like to tap that?" Almost immediately, Jordon knew that he should not have said that in front of Claire, but of course, he wasn't dating Claire, so he didn't care what she thought.

"Oops, my bad," said Jordan, then he looked over to Trevor and said, "See ya, bro." Jordan picked his tray back up, and went to find another table to sit at.

"God, Jordan can be an ass sometimes," Claire said, just after he got out of earshot. She looked over at Trevor, and for a second, almost thought she caught the glimpse of a smirk. Because he was looking in Jordan's direction, she couldn't be sure. "Yeah... He's an ass," Trevor agreed, but Claire couldn't tell if he was ok with that fact or not. Claire didn't have the energy to potentially start an argument with Trevor over Jordan, so she decided to drop it for now.

It was Friday night, and Crystal had just left April. They had dined together at the hospital cafeteria before Crystal had to go back to work. April had told Crystal about what Blake had said about her impending death. Crystal knew that Blake was a tough cookie and was doing her absolute best to fight this.

April was alone and on her way back to Blake's room. The elevators that she usually took to the cafeteria were closed due to a routine system check, so she had to take the ones on the other end of the hall.

Just before she got there, she stopped at a double door entryway. It was the hospital's chapel. She quietly peered inside to see if anyone was in there. She couldn't see the entire room, but it seemed empty. April slowly walked in and went up to the front row. She sat down and just stared at the big cross that was hanging on the wall in front of her. There were stained glass windows throughout the room but the windows did not really have an outside view.

"Why?" April suddenly said out loud. "Why her!" The sound of her voice echoed slightly as it reverberated off the curved walls. "You took Nick away from me! Now you want to take Blake!"

It was the first time that she had really talked to God since her husband had died. Deep down, she blamed Him for taking Nick away from her.

"Please, God," April begged. "Please don't take Blake from me."

April bent down and placed her head in her hands. She sat there for several minutes, repeating over and over in her mind, "Please don't take her."

* *

IT WAS SUNDAY MORNING AND APRIL WOKE UP BEFORE HER alarm went off. She looked at the time and saw that it was 7:45 a.m. The day before had been a dreadfully long day. Blake was sicker and couldn't hold any food down. The medicine that they had changed a couple of days ago was changed again. The chemo treatments were destroying Blake's immune system, and she couldn't fight off anything. The antibiotics were doing their best to ward off infections, but it was just a matter of time.

April got up and took a long hot shower, as if it could wash away all the anxiousness that she was feeling for Blake. She got dressed and then looked at her phone to see if she had any missed calls from the hospital. Seeing that no one had called, April headed towards Claire's room.

Before she got there, she heard a noise coming from Blake's room. Sitting cross-legged on the bed was Claire. She was holding a picture frame in her hands. It was the first selfie that the two of them had taken together. April walked into the room and sat down on the bed next to Claire.

Claire turned to look at April and with tears in her eyes said, "I can't lose her, April. I just can't." Claire tilted the frame to show more of it to April. "Look at us. Since my first day here, Blake has treated me with respect and kindness. She took me under her wing and showed me how to be a proper girl," Claire used the sleeve of her robe to wipe away the tears. "I mean... I didn't know how to put makeup on, and she took the time to help me. You know?"

"Oh, honey," April, said, "Blake loves you like a sister, and I know that she appreciates you just as much as you appreciate her." April could feel a sense of despair coming from Claire, and it was heart-wrenching.

"I miss playing video games with her," Claire said, as she looked at the gaming console on Blake's desk. "She used to kick my butt, and I used to still be happy sitting in here playing with her," Claire said, as the memory of the countless hours of gameplay invaded her mind.

"I'm sorry, April," Claire finally said. "I don't mean to be so sad when you have a lot to worry about." Claire got up from the bed and stood by it for a moment. "I just never had a family that I loved so much, and I can't see my life without Blake in it."

April stood up, and gave Claire a hug. She began to say something to her but her cell phone went off. It was Dr. Powell. April quickly pushed the button to answer it.

"Hello, Dr. Powell?" April said apprehensively, fearing the worst.

"Hi, April," Dr. Powell said, "I wanted to call you right away."

"Oh, my God," April began, "What's wrong?" The words were filled with worry and despair.

"Nothing. In fact, something wonderful has happened. We have located a perfect match for Blake's bone marrow," Dr. Powell said excitedly.

"Oh my God," April said, putting her hand over her mouth. Claire could hear only April's part of the conversation so she looked at April with concerned eyes.

Dr. Powell then added, "You are not going to believe this... it's Claire."

April almost dropped the phone. "What?"

Dr. Powell repeated what she had just said. "Blake's perfect match is Claire."

"Oh my God," April said again, realizing what was happening.

It was Claire from the beginning. That was why Nick wanted April to go talk to her. It was the reason why in Blake's dream, he didn't want her to let her go. He knew about her cancer. He knew that Claire was the match. April's eyes widened when she understood what all this meant—Claire was here to save Blake.

April began crying into the phone as Dr. Powell went over a few more details. April told the doctor that she would come to the hospital soon.

Claire was beginning to cry again because of April's reaction to Dr. Powell's phone call. When April got off the phone, she reached for Claire and grabbed her, holding her tight.

"It's you!" April told Claire between sobs. "You're a perfect match! You are Blake's perfect match!'"

"What?" Claire questioned, as if someone had just told her that unicorns were real. April was smiling, crying happy tears now. "It's you, Claire. You're the match!"

"I am?" Claire asked, as the news hit her like a ton of bricks. "I'm going to save her." Then she began smiling, and jumping up and down. "I'm going to save Blake! Oh my God, I'm going to save her!" Claire couldn't believe it. Of all the millions of people in the world, it just so happened that she was Blake's match.

"Are you sure?" Claire asked in disbelief, but wanting desperately for it to be true.

"Yes," April answered. "Dr. Powell said she double-checked the results. You're the one."

"But how is that possible?" Claire wanted to know.

April truly didn't have an answer for her, but she knew in that moment that it was time to tell her about Nick.

"I don't know," April honestly said. "But there is something that I've been wanting to tell you from the first day we met, and I didn't know until this very moment how to do it," April said, sitting down on Blake's bed and asking Claire to sit next to her.

April took a deep breath and began telling Claire everything. She told her how she had heard Nick's voice twice in her mind telling her to stop and turn around to go back to her. She told her about Blake's dream, and how Nick didn't want Blake to let her go. She told her that after Blake's dream, she had told Blake about Nick's voice.

"I didn't know why until this very moment," April tried to explain. "I think that Nick knew that Blake was going to get cancer, and I believe that he knew that you would be the match."

Sitting next to April, taking it all in, Claire could hardly believe it. "So, Blake's dad knew that I was going to be the one to save her, and that is why he brought me into your lives."

"I think so," April told her. "I didn't have a clue as to why he would have me go back to you, but then I thought it might have been to save your life when you got the flu. Then, when you told me about Roger trying to rape you, I thought it might have been to help save you from the life that you had been living."

April shrugged and looked towards the ceiling. "Whatever the reason was, Blake and I have loved having you in our lives, and when you told us that you loved us, I knew that day that no matter what the reason was or could have been, I loved you for you, Claire."

Claire looked into April's eyes, and said, "I love you so much, April. I can't believe this is happening, but I don't care. I love Blake like a sister, and now I am the one that gets to save her. It doesn't matter how I got to be here in your lives... I know that I am loved and that I am now part of a family that I truly care for."

Claire had a thought and then asked April, "Can I be the one to tell Blake?"

"Of course you can," April said, as she hugged Claire one more time. "You absolutely can!"

CHAPTER TWENTY-THREE

"BLAKE?" CLAIRE WHISPERED INTO BLAKE'S EAR. SHE WAS sound asleep, and when she finally opened her eyes, she was weak and lethargic.

It took Blake a few seconds to realize that it was Claire kneeling next to her. "Oh, hi, Claire," Blake said, as she tried to clear her throat. Her lips were chapped and her throat was sore.

"Blake," Claire began, "I've got something to tell you."

Blake focused her eyes on Claire's face, and said, "Yeah?"

"You're not going to believe this but... I'm your match," Claire paused for a few moments to let it sink in.

Blake blinked her eyes and they widened with surprise.

"My bone marrow is a perfect match to yours," Claire was grinning from ear to ear as she spoke.

Blake thought about it for a second, and then a smile formed on her face, "You're the one that is going to save me?"

Claire was still smiling but when Blake said that, tears began to form as she replied, feeling a little choked up, "Yes, I'm going to save you."

April then told Blake all that she had told Claire about her father's voice and Blake's dream, surmising that that was why her dad had wanted Claire in her life—to save her. As the news sank in, Blake became more excited and wanted to sit up. Claire grabbed her shoulders to help her up. Once Blake sat up and put her glasses on, a funny look came over her face as she thought of something.

She slowly picked up her finger and pointed at Claire. "I told you so," she said.

Claire had a quizzical look on her face. She quickly glanced at April, shrugging her shoulders indicating that she didn't know what Blake was talking about.

"You told me what?" Claire questioned Blake.

With a big, all-knowing smile on her face, Blake said, "That you're my 16-year-old, blonde, blue-eyed purpose," Blake said, "Don't you remember?"

Claire looked into Blake's eyes and as the true meaning of the words that Blake had uttered those many months ago on Thanksgiving night came to light, Claire's emotions swelled up again.

"Yeah, I guess you're right," Claire whispered, barely able to get words out, "I am your 16-year-old, blonde, blue-eyed purpose."

Just then Dr. Powell walked in with a couple of other doctors. "Good morning, everyone," she said. She introduced the others and informed April that they were going to be assisting with Blake's case.

"So what happens now?" April asked.

Dr. Powell took the lead and answered, "Well, Blake will have to go through several days of what we call conditioning. She will be subjected to more chemo and radiation. This will help get rid of all the bad stuff that is hurting her. However, because she is already reacting to chemo negatively, we have to be careful." She looked at Blake and then continued, "After that, we harvest the bone marrow from Claire in a simple procedure, and then we transplant them into Blake."

"So, if everything goes well, when can we know that it has worked?" April asked.

"Well, it's going to take about five to six days for Blake's conditioning. If all that goes according to plan, then on the same day as Claire's harvest, we will transfuse the bone marrow into Blake. Blake will need about thirty days after that for the new marrow to do its job. Realistically, it will be about a month and a half before we can think about Blake leaving the hospital."

Even though it sounded dreadful for Blake to go through, the light at the end of the tunnel was there.

Blake looked at her mother, and said, "Don't worry mom, knowing that Claire is my match, I'll try my best to get through this." Blake just got the hope she needed to make herself stronger.

Dr. Powell and her team spent the next few hours telling Blake and her family what to expect over the next ten days. Nurses came in to change Blake's IV and prep her for a round of chemo and radiation.

April took a few minutes to step out of the room and call Gina. She told her that Claire was Blake's match and they were going to condition Blake in preparation for the transplant. She told Gina that maybe she should take a leave of absence because over the next month or so, she had to be by Blake's side.

Gina scoffed at the idea, and told April that she could take an off whenever she needed to and not to worry about her clients. When she finished with Gina, she called Crystal and told her the good news. Crystal cried happy tears for Blake, and told April if she needed anything she would be there for her.

April had called her parents and told them the news when she and Claire were on their way to the hospital. Of course, they were overwhelmed with joy and said that they would be there shortly.

Mason was the last person that April called.

"Hey, good morning," Mason said. "Is everything ok with Blake?"

April told him how she got the call that morning, and how Claire was the match. She told him that Blake had a rough road ahead, but hopefully this was her cure.

"Do you want me to come to the hospital to be with you?" Mason asked.

April was hoping that he would ask her that. "Yes, if you don't mind?"

"Of course, April. I'll be there in half an hour," Mason said, as he ended the call.

April smiled and knew deep down that this was part of the reason why she had called him. She wanted him there with her. Not since Nick had she ever felt this way with another man before. April realized that she thought about him constantly and wanted to be with him. The two of them had this undeniable connection that was almost impossible for April to ignore. She knew that Mason genuinely cared for Blake and Claire. You could see it in his eyes. It was a tragedy that he couldn't produce any children of his own because he would have made a remarkable father.

The waiting room down the hall was filling up with people associated with Blake Turner. Anne and Joseph Turner had shown up shortly after April got off the phone with Mason. Gina, Wanda, and Monica stopped by to show their support and to offer April any help that she might need. Monica Towers had visited around noon. She had pulled April aside and told her that she wouldn't work with any other editor and to take the time that she needed. Monica considered April one of her best friends, and wanted her to know that she was there for her.

Claire was making the calls to all of Blake's friends. She started with a group call to Shelly, Rose, and Brie and told them that she was the match. All three of them were blown away with the news, and told her that they were coming down to see her. Claire then reached out to Emily and informed her. Emily began to cry on hearing the news and told Claire that she wanted to come to the hospital to see Blake.

Finally, Claire called Trevor. She told him that she was the match, and was going to be the one to save Blake. He sounded excited and happy for her. She wanted him there with her, but by the end of the phone call, it didn't sound like he was going to offer to come. He ended the phone call by saying that he would see her in school tomorrow and that he loved her.

Somewhat disappointed, Claire turned her attention to all the people that were starting to arrive to support the family. As she greeted everyone, it became clear that she was truly a part of the family. They were coming up to her and giving her hugs and smiling. The love and support that she was receiving from everyone made her want to cry.

The morning turned into afternoon, and Claire was sitting with Shelly, Brie, Rose, and April's parents. April and Mason had just gone down to get some coffee and were going to bring up some donuts for everyone.

Emily came around the corner and asked if she could go in to see Blake. The nurse told her that she could, but only for a few minutes. Emily had to put a mask and protective gear on before she was allowed into the room.

Emily spent about ten minutes in the room and was asked to leave because the nurse had to check some vitals and adjust medications. Emily took off her mask and gear and then walked out to the waiting room. She sat down next to Claire, and then after a few moments, asked if she could speak to her in private.

"Sure," Claire said, as she got up from her chair, and followed Emily around the corner to another hallway.

"So, what's up?" Claire asked politely, wondering what Emily wanted to say.

Emily had been crying with Blake in the room, so her eyes were still a little red and swollen. She looked at Claire with apologetic eyes, and then said, "Claire, I just want to say to you that I am so sorry for the way that I treated you when we first met. I was jealous of the way that Blake talked about you and I thought that you wanted to take advantage of her." Emily paused to think about what she wanted to say next. "You didn't deserve what happened to you with Brie, and because I was the one that told her about you, I take full responsibility for it." Claire had heard Emily apologize for this the day it happened, and had considered it water under the bridge. She started to say something to that effect, but Emily wanted to finish. "No, please, I have to say this," Emily said holding up her hand to signal Claire to hold on before she talked. "And now, here you are; the only one in the world that can save my best friend, and I just wanted to tell you how thankful that I am that you are in her life. I can't imagine losing my best friend right now. So, I want you to know how sorry I truly am for being mean to you, and how thankful that I am that you are here."

Claire hadn't expected all this, but she was glad that Emily was remorseful for the way she had acted in the past and that she was grateful for Claire.

"Listen, Emily," Claire responded to Emily's apology. "I have forgiven Brie, and I forgive you for everything in the past. Blake needs us right now to be strong for her, so I am glad to hear that you will be there for her. I think that we can all work together as friends to help her through the next month or so."

Emily looked relieved to hear Claire say she had forgiven her. Claire looked at Emily, and then said, "We're good now, the two of us, we're good," Emily knew in that moment that she was going to do whatever she could to help Claire with Blake. "Thanks, Claire," Emily said with a sigh of relief. Claire gave Emily a hug, and then the two of them walked back to the waiting room to join the others.

As Claire looked around the room, all the girls were wearing matching headbands. It was such a nice idea that Blake had had, and it was nice to see the support. When they sat down, Claire went into her book bag, and took out a headband for Emily to put on. Emily smiled, placing it on her head.

April and Mason returned from the cafeteria with coffees and donuts for everyone. The entire waiting room was electric with excitement and hope. Even though Blake was really sick and most of the people gathered didn't get to go in and see her, it didn't matter. They were all there to show support for her.

April and Mason sat in chairs that were facing Claire and her friends. It was the first time in a month that April felt hopeful for the future. April handed Claire a coffee and thinking about the six weeks ahead, she looked at Claire, and said, "Here we go."

* *

THE NEXT SEVEN DAYS WERE BRUTAL FOR BLAKE. IT WAS BY far the sickest that she had ever been. There were times when she felt like giving up, but she didn't voice those thoughts to her mother. On one of the really bad days, she let it slip to Claire that she wished it were over, and for God to just take her. Claire immediately squashed that idea by telling Blake that she had to stick around so that when the day ever for Claire to get married, Blake would be the one to design her wedding dress. That seemed to help push Blake back from the edge.

The day finally arrived for them to harvest Claire's bone marrow. It was a simple process that took only a few hours. It was basically like getting a blood transfusion. There were some side-effects that Claire had to be aware of, such as pain and soreness, as well as possible flu-like symptoms. Claire didn't care if the side-effects meant that she had to grow a third eye or even grow a tail. Nothing was going to stop her donation.

Dr. Powell said that it was ok if she sat in Blake's room during the donation. A donation chair was set up next to Blake's bed. Claire had to put on a hospital gown and wear a mask the entire time that she would be in there. Before they hooked Claire up, Blake wanted to get a picture of her and Claire. April was going to be in the room as well, masked and gowned, just to be safe. April took out her cell phone and stood at the foot of Blake's bed and took a few pictures. The last one she took was both Blake and Claire posing as they did a thumbs-up sign facing the camera.

It took the nurse ten minutes to hook Claire up, and then it was basically just a waiting game. April looked at Claire and Blake, gowned and hooked up to IVs, which both broke and warmed her heart. To see both of your children in the hospital like that made her feel sad. But, on the other hand, Claire was in the process of giving Blake the gift of life. It was a moment that April would never forget.

The harvesting took a little longer than they anticipated, but it went well. Claire was hooked up for several hours, and it was early evening by the time she had finished. Blake was asleep when the nurse unhooked Claire from the machine. Claire sat in the chair next to April.

"It's done," Claire announced proudly to April. "I can't believe that the time has finally arrived."

April reached out and grabbed Claire's hand and held it. "Thank you for everything. I don't know what would have happened if it wasn't for you and what you have just done for Blake."

"Blake is my best friend, and I would do anything for her, you know? I just can't believe that it's me," Claire answered as she leaned back into the chair.

April and Claire sat in the room for several more minutes, and then decided to leave Blake alone to let her sleep. Claire was starving, but she felt a little light-headed. She told April about how she felt and April got the nurse. After a few minutes, the nurse brought Claire a bottle of orange juice and bottled water. She told her to stay seated for a few minutes while she drank the juices.

April started pacing as she began to worry about Claire. Not only was she feeling dizzy but she had started to look a little pale as well. Fortunately, after fifteen minutes, Claire began to feel better and the dizziness subsided. The two of them exited Blake's room and went to change out of their gowns.

April took Claire to the cafeteria for some dinner. Even though they had both been sitting all day, it still felt like a long day. Claire and April spoke about school, novels, and, of course, Blake. April found it easy to hold a conversation with Claire. Most sixteen-year-old girls would have their eyes buried in their phones, and not really cared to talk with their parents. Conversely, Claire enjoyed the time that she spent with April. It was like they could talk about books, school, current events, or just about anything. Part of the reason was that Claire had never had that growing up. The other part was that there was a special connection between the two of them since the first day that they had met. It wasn't because Nick had sent her to Claire, but more of a mother/daughter connection that was uncanny. April genuinely cared for Claire.

So, there they were, sitting in the cafeteria, dining on some sandwiches and talking about the future.

Blake received Claire's bone marrow the next day. It was a simple process, almost like a blood transfusion. The next few weeks were still rough for Blake. Her recovery was slow. At first, it felt as if nothing was happening. Blake was still severely sick and incredibly weak, but Dr. Powell told April and Claire that they had to wait for the process to work. Claire experienced mild aches and pains the day after the donation. Unfortunately, she did develop some flu-like symptoms and missed a couple days of school. She had to FaceTime Blake at the hospital during that time.

After the fourth week, Blake started feeling better, and was on the road to recovery. Mason visited her on a regular basis, and Blake was becoming quite proficient at chess. Of course, Mason was spending more and more time with April. One of those times, April made dinner for Mason.

Claire was in the kitchen helping April make the final preparations when Mason came up the elevator.

"Hi, Mason," Claire smiled as she waved with a glove-shaped hot pad in her hand. "Come on in."

April opened up a bottle of wine when he walked in. She went up to him and gave him a quick kiss on the lips. Claire pretended not to notice, but she was so happy for April. Claire took the pork chops out of the oven, and then put them on a platter that was already sitting on the counter.

"Is there anything that I can do to help?" Mason asked the two women in the kitchen.

"Nope," Claire happily replied. "We are almost ready. Have a seat at the table and take a load off."

"No problem," Mason smiled, "It sure smells good in here." The combination of the uncorking of the wine and the smell of the pork with raspberry sauce made Mason's stomach growl in hunger.

Claire then told April to have a seat, and that she would bring the rest to the table. April had lit the candles on the table a few minutes before Mason's arrival, so, as April sat down, the flickering flames created shadows across April's face. Mason couldn't help but stare at April's beauty.

Claire noticed how they were looking at each other, and offered, "Are you sure you want me to join you? I can totally eat my plate upstairs if you want to be alone."

Mason quickly replied, "No, of course not. I wanted to have dinner with both of you tonight. I enjoy your company very much, Claire, and I like the time that I spend with both of April's daughters."

Claire liked spending time with Mason as well. Over the past four weeks, he would talk with her at the hospital, and he had also started to teach her how to play chess. Claire and Blake had partaken in many discussions about Mason when it was just the two of them alone in her room. They both agreed that they really liked him and wanted him for April.

Claire grabbed the roll basket, and then got the salad bowl and set them both on the table. Looking one last time to make sure that she didn't forget anything, she finally sat down at the table across from April and Mason.

"Everything looks amazing," Mason said earnestly. "Thank you for this wonderful dinner."

"You're very welcome, now dig in," Claire said eagerly, as she picked up a roll for herself, and started diving into the mashed potatoes.

The conversation during dinner was mainly about how well Blake had just started doing.

"You know Claire?" Mason began, "It's a miracle that you were the one to be the cure for Blake. It must feel so awesome being able to give a part of yourself to your foster sister." Of course Mason didn't know that Blake's deceased father had basically pointed her out for the job.

Claire looked at April, and grinned, "Yes, it certainly was a miracle. Right, April?"

"Absolutely," April began batting an eye at Claire as if to say, '*Don't let the cat out of the bag.*'

"Claire is our little, blonde miracle," April finished, trying to remember what Blake had called her in the hospital room on the day that she had informed Blake that she was the match.

The three of them indulged in some more conversation, as they continued through dinner. Claire had baked a pie and it was unanimous that they were going to let their dinner settle before cutting into the pie.

As Claire cleared off the table, Mason whispered something into April's ear. She looked at him and nodded her head. When Claire had placed the last of the dirty dishes in the dishwasher, and was about to excuse herself to go upstairs, Mason stood up from the table, and said, "Would it be ok if you joined me for a quick game of Overwatch? I think that I am getting pretty good at it, but I would really like your opinion."

Claire glanced over at April to see her reaction. "It's fine with me," April said with a smile, as Claire's face lit up. "I'll be here sitting here on the couch watching the fire in the fireplace."

"We will just play a couple of quick rounds. What do you say?" Mason said, asking permission from Claire.

"Ok. Let's kick some ass," Claire exclaimed, as she ran upstairs to turn on her computer.

Mason followed Claire upstairs but before he got all the way up, he turned around and blew April a kiss.

April smiled and waved at him as he disappeared down the hall towards Claire's room. April made herself a cup of coffee, and walked over to the couch and sat by the end that was next to the La-Z-Boy. She was constantly amazed at what a perfect man Mason was. She found it hard to believe that any woman in their right mind would want to divorce him. April loved the fact that she as well as her two girls were completely captivated by him. April knew that she was falling hard for him, and even though her mind kept trying to look for red flags, her heart knew that Mason was the one.

April snorted when she heard Claire exclaim loudly from the bedroom, "We're kicking some major ass!" Obviously, Mason knew quite well what he was doing on *Overwatch*. Twenty minutes later, Claire and Mason came down, and it appeared that they were victorious.

"Mason is a monster at *Overwatch,* mom," Claire said with admiration. "He can kick some serious butt. You know what I mean?" Claire held up her fist for Mason. "Good job. Thanks for playing with me."

Claire was headed back upstairs when April called out after her, "Don't you want any pie?"

She put her hand on her belly, and said, "No, I am still full." Then she looked at both April and Mason, and said, "You guys can have some alone time. I'll be upstairs reading." Claire winked at April, not bothering to hide it from Mason, and then disappeared upstairs.

Mason watched Claire vanish from view, and then turned to April, "I guess we are alone now..."

April grinned at Mason, and agreed, "Why yes, Mr. Steele, I do believe that we are," Mason walked up to April, who was sitting on the couch and stopped in front of her. He put his hands out towards April's, and she put her hands in his. He gently pulled April to her feet and into his arms. There was a brief moment in which his eyes trapped hers. Then he leaned forward and kissed her on the lips. April leaned up as well, as if meeting him halfway. They kissed for several seconds before he released her.

He kept a hold of one of her hands as he sat down next to her on the couch. He leaned into the back of the couch as April laid her head onto his chest. They both sat there, enthralled by the flames of the fire.

After a few minutes, April picked up her head so that she could look at him. "What is it about us that makes me feel that I have known you?" April asked him, trying to understand the connection that they shared.

"You know, I don't really know for sure," Mason admitted, "but what I do know is that the moment that I saw you by the vending machine, I couldn't stop thinking about you. It was like I found the one person that I have been searching for, but not realizing that I was even looking. If that makes any sense?"

April placed her right hand on his left cheek and said, "It makes perfect sense." She leaned her head towards his and kissed him. When they stopped kissing she leaned back so that both of their heads were leaning on the back of the couch.

"You know something?" April said as a thought occurred to her, "You're one of the best things to have happened to me, and it was on one of the most terrible days of my life." April said thinking back to the day that she had to take Blake to the hospital. "Why do you think that is?"

Mason paused for a second to reflect on the question. "If I had to wager a guess about it..." Mason began, "I would have to say that God puts people in our path, at the right time in our lives, helping us find our way." He waited a few moments, and then added, "I suspect that He works in mysterious ways, and that we may not always know what He has in mind for us." Mason turned to her, and said, "That is my take on it. What do you think?"

April really didn't know, but said, "That sounds like as good an explanation as any."

Mason grinned, as he looked at her, and said, "I thought it was a pretty inspired answer for basically a few seconds' notice."

April smiled at him, and replied, "Yes, Mr. Steele, you were inspired," Then she kissed him again.

After several more kisses, they released each other and decided to watch a movie. The two of them sat together on the couch and enjoyed each other's company.

When the movie ended, April called Claire down to have some pie with them. She came running down to join them at the table.

"So, how was the movie?" Claire asked mischievously. "Did you even watch it?" she asked naughtily.

Mason made a funny face at her, and replied in a lighter vein, "Of course we watched a movie, it was, it was... Hell, April, I can't remember. What did we watch?"

April smirked, and said, "We watched a movie?"

"Very funny, you two," Claire chastised them, as she took a forkful of pie. "Seriously, what did you watch?"

"We saw *Safe Harbor*—it was a pretty good movie," Mason finally answered.

Claire nodded her head and agreed, "It was a good movie. Good choice, Mason."

The three of them sat at the table and ate pie. It was a nice way to end the evening. Claire said goodnight to Mason, and then headed back upstairs. April and Mason lingered in the kitchen, not wanting the night to end. The two of them ended up sitting on the island, sipping the remains of wine from a bottle leftover from dinner.

Finally, Mason stood up, and said, "I better get going." It was getting late, and Mason had a lot of work to catch up on in the morning.

"Thank you for a fantastic dinner and evening," He told April as he put on his coat. "I adore Claire and Blake, and I love spending time with them." He paused as April stood in front of him. "And of course, I love spending time with you, April." She smiled and kissed him. "I love spending time with you too."

"I'll see you tomorrow at the hospital," Mason said to April, thinking about how he had planned on spending time with Blake.

"Yes, absolutely," April said. "Thanks for being there for us. I really don't know what I would have done without you in our lives."

"I know that the circumstances were horrible, but I am glad that I could help with and be there for the girls," Mason honestly said. "I've had a remarkable time with both of them."

They kissed one more time, and Mason left the apartment.

April walked slowly back to the kitchen and put away the two wine glasses and then the two pie plates. She turned off the lights and went upstairs to retire for the evening. When she walked into her room, Claire was on the bed waiting for her. "So, April, how was your evening?" Claire asked, obviously digging for juicy details of the time that she and Mason spent alone together.

"It was great," said April, as she tried to avoid more of Claire's questioning.

"Super great or just great?" Claire teased, enjoying every second.

April sighed and confessed, "It was super great," She reached for her robe and asked Claire, "Aren't you tired, shouldn't you be in bed already?"

"Nope and nope," Claire informed April.

April got ready for bed as Claire remained in the room. When April was ready to get into bed, Claire had a serious look at her face. "You know, April," Claire began. "Both Blake and I absolutely adore Mason."

April had a feeling where this was going, but it was nice to hear her say it. Claire continued as April sat down on the bed beside her, "And we have been talking, and Blake and I are totally on board with what happens between you and Mason."

"Why thank you for that. I will have to keep that in mind," April teased.

Claire looked at April with eyes filled with conviction, "April, Blake wanted me to tell you that she loved her father with all her heart and soul, but she realizes that it has been years, and she doesn't want you to spend the rest of your life alone."

When Claire mentioned Blake's father, it caused her heart to skip a beat. Claire could see that April was taken aback with the direction of this conversation, but this is what Blake wanted Claire to convey to her mom.

"Blake doesn't want you to live in the past but wants you to move on. She will always love her dad, but she knows how Mason makes you feel," Claire paused for a moment to lean against April with her head looking up to see her face. "She can see you with Mason and she is totally fine with it," Claire gave

April a quick hug and then said as she got up from the bed, "And I think Mason is great for you too," Claire waved and wished April a good night.

April sat in her bed for a few moments, contemplating what Claire had just told her. It was obvious to the girls that she was falling in love with Mason, and Mason was falling in love with her. April turned off the light and pulled the covers to her shoulders.

April fell asleep and dreamt of a future that was filled with images of Mason and her two daughters.

* *

THE MONTH OF APRIL WAS ALL ABOUT BLAKE'S RECOVERY. She finally got the clearance to leave the hospital on Monday, April 24. Claire had let the school know that she wasn't going to be in that day, and of course, Emily was with Claire to help bring Blake home.

Blake's hair was slowly growing back. She had about an inch of newly grown hair that gave her a buzzed look, but she didn't care. She was alive and her hair had started to grow back. Instead of head coverings, she was wearing headbands on the top of her head.

Blake thanked and hugged the nurses who had cared for her during her stay there. She had grown really fond of them and promised that she would come back and visit them. April and Mason were walking hand and hand behind the nurse who was pushing Blake in the wheelchair while Claire and Emily were walking on either side of the chair. When they got to the sliding doors of the hospital's entrance, Blake stood up and slowly looked around the hospital's main floor. She turned back around to face her mother, and said, "Let's go home."

April smiled as the doors opened to allow the group to exit. Waiting next to the curb was a big black SUV with Derek standing next to it. Blake saw him and gave him a big hug.

"Nice to see you, Blake," Derek said affectionately. "I've missed seeing you around."

"Me too," Blake said, shielding her eyes from the sun. She realized that this was the first time that she had been outside since the end of January. The group piled into the vehicle with Claire up front next to Derek, Blake and Emily in the middle row of seats, and April and Mason in the third row behind Blake and Emily.

On the way home, Blake wanted to have Derek go through the drive thru at McDonalds so that she could get a large chocolate shake. It had been several months and she was craving for it.

When they arrived at the apartment, Blake's grandparents were there with several others, including Blake's friends and family. Wanda and Gina had hung a large banner that read, "Welcome Home, Blake!"

"Wow, you guys!" Blake exclaimed, "This is amazing," Everyone was so glad to have Blake alive and back home. There was a huge cake on the kitchen counter that had the picture of Blake and Claire giving a 'thumbs-up' on the day Claire had donated her bone marrow. That was the first time that Blake had seen that particular picture, and it caused a joyful tear to form in her eye.

"Look at this," Blake said to Claire, pointing at the picture baked on the cake. "That is awesome."

Claire stepped up to Blake and put her arm around her. "It was my idea. I loved that picture of us, and wanted to do something special with it."

Blake eventually ended up on the couch seated between Claire and Emily. April and Mason were standing in the kitchen talking with Anne and Joseph, snacking on one of the *hors d'oeuvres* platters.

April was smiling and laughing in response to the conversation that they were having. Blake tapped Claire's leg and whispered for her to look towards the kitchen.

"They are so great together," Blake told Claire. "He has been totally amazing with me the entire time that I was in the hospital. I could tell that he really loves her. Not to mention, I loved spending time with him too. There were days that he just sat there with me when you and mom were at work or at school, and we would just talk."

"Yeah, I know," agreed Claire. "He is so good for her and he truly makes her happy. I love to see them together."

April just happened to look in Blake's direction and noticed that both the girls were looking at her. Both girls smiled mischievously, and then waved. April could only guess what they were talking about, but she suspected that it was about her and Mason. April waved back, giving them a big grin. She then put her hand on Mason's shoulder as she turned her attention back to the kitchen conversation.

After a couple of hours, some of the guests began to leave because they didn't want to overwhelm Blake all at once. Blake was becoming a little tired, but she was so happy to be home that she didn't care.

Eventually, only Mason and Emily were left. Blake was resting in the La-Z-Boy while the rest were on the couches near her. Mason got up and retrieved his backpack by the elevator doors. He brought it over to the group, and he removed a giftwrapped box with a beautiful pink bow.

"This is for you Blake," Mason said, as he handed her the present. Blake took the gift and looked at him with appreciative eyes. Blake carefully unwrapped the paper from the box and then opened the lid of the box. Inside, was a fancy oak box that was engraved with the words, "Never give up." The box had hinges on the side with a fancy latch on the other. Blake slowly opened it up, and it was an exquisite chessboard with crystal chess pieces. It was more of a work of art than a play set.

"Oh my gosh," Blake couldn't believe what she saw. It had meant so much to her during her illness that Mason had spent time with her, teaching her how to play. During chess matches, when it looked as if she was about to lose, he would say, "Never give up." It wasn't till after she had received the transplant that she began to understand that he was saying this not only for the chess game, but about her fight to stay alive as well.

"I love it!" Blake exclaimed as she stood up to give Mason a hug. "This means the world to me."

April could tell that Mason was a little choked up and put her arm around him.

"Me too," Mason said as he helped Blake look through all the ornate chess pieces. "Even though you are out of the hospital, it doesn't mean that we are finished with playing chess, young lady."

Blake looked at Mason, and grinned, "The thought never crossed my mind."

After a few minutes, the doorbell rang—Crystal was down in the lobby wanting to come up. Crystal would have been there earlier, when Blake first got out of the hospital, but she had informed April the night before that she was working on a case and had to go out of town to interview witnesses.

Crystal came in, immediately rushing towards Blake. "Hey honey! So glad you're home!" She gave Blake a huge hug and it felt like forever until she let go. Even though Crystal was a tough cookie, she always had a soft side when it came to her best friend's daughter.

She squeezed herself in with Claire and Emily, and sat and talked for a few minutes with everyone. Eventually, she got up and asked April to join her in the kitchen.

"I've got some news for you and Claire that I just found out on the way here," Crystal told April, sounding a little cryptic. "It's about Roger."

When she spoke that name, it sent chills up April's spine. "What about him?"

Crystal looked at Claire, and asked politely if she could join her and her mom in the kitchen.

Claire got up from the couch and walked into the kitchen asking, "Yes?"

Crystal looked at Claire, and said, "I got some news this morning with regard to Roger Bower."

Claire's face changed, and she asked, "What about him?"

"We have been investigating him since the first week that I met you. Seattle Police Department has been monitoring his internet searches and his participation in chat rooms. Detectives in Seattle PD targeted his involvement in several interactions with teenage girls." Crystal paused to get out her phone to look at the report that had been emailed to her.

"They set up a sting operation involving an undercover woman who was posing as a sixteen-year-old runaway from California. He took the bait when she said that she wanted to hook up with him."

April put her hand on Claire's shoulder as Crystal kept talking.

"Well, you can imagine his surprise when we busted him with condoms and all sorts of sexual devices in his travel bag."

"Oh my God," April gasped at what Crystal had just said. Blake heard her mother's gasp and looked at them in the kitchen. She could see that they were involved in a serious conversation, and it was most likely about Claire.

"What is it?" Blake politely demanded as she got up from the couch and headed towards the kitchen. She came up and stood next to Claire on the opposite side of her mom.

"It's about Roger Bower, Claire's previous foster parent," Crystal said, filling Blake in on what she had just told Claire and April.

"So what's going to happen to him?" April asked.

"After his arrest, they obtained a search warrant for his house. They discovered multiple laptops and a secret compartment hidden in the wall of his bedroom's closets that contained pictures of naked teenage girls that he had apparently printed off from various websites." Crystal now looked squarely at Claire, and said, "You know what else they found in the hidden compartment?"

Thinking for a second, it dawned on her. "The wallet?" Claire asked, already knowing that was the answer.

"Yes," Crystal smiled with satisfaction, "The wallet."

Blake looked over at Claire with a look of victory. Roger was finally going to go to jail.

"So, it's over," Claire asked, sounding extremely relieved.

"Yes, it's over. Roger Bower will be going to jail for a long time," Crystal then added as she put her phone back into her pocket, "If it weren't for you telling us what he did to you, he may have been left unchecked for months or even years. Think of all the possible girls that you have saved from him."

Claire stood there staring at Crystal. She really hadn't considered that she had potentially helped girls from a fate that might have been worse than hers.

"It's over, Claire," April said overjoyed for the girl that she now considered one of her own, hoping that she could now get closure from this horrible ordeal.

Claire hugged Crystal as she began to tear up. "Thank you for believing me. I can't believe that he will be getting what he deserves."

"Oh, he will get what he deserves," Crystal said sounding positive. "There are multiple charges beginning with falsifying a police report when he said that his wallet was stolen by you, and ending with soliciting minors for sexual acts. Fear not, he won't be getting out in his lifetime."

Crystal was proud of Claire for being a strong young lady who had stood her ground, and had stopped a monster from violating her. Crystal knew that Claire possessed courage that was well beyond her years.

By this time, Mason and Emily ventured into the kitchen noticing that something was going on in there. Mason came up from behind April and put his arm around her waist. He didn't want to interrupt but he wanted her to know that he was there for support.

April spent the next few minutes alone with Mason telling him all about what had had happened to Claire and how she had managed to run away. Mason was sickened by what had happened, and wished he could be locked up alone with Roger for just two minutes.

The afternoon turned into evening, during which time Mason thought that he had better get going. He kissed April several times on the lips when they were alone before he went out to the living room.

Blake and Claire were sitting on the couch watching a YouTube video when Mason came up to them. "Good evening, you two," he said, as he bent down and kissed them both on the forehead. "Great to see you home, Blake," Mason said, as he departed.

"Bye, Mason," Blake and Claire almost said in unison.

April walked Mason to the elevator and pressed the button. The doors opened and he stepped in.

"Good night, April," Mason said, as he looked affectionately into her eyes.

"Good night, Mason," April said, as the doors began to close. But then, Mason put his hands to stop the doors from closing. He then pulled April into the elevator with him and she gasped with surprise.

Claire and Blake looked towards the source of the sound and saw that she Mason was holding her inside the elevator.

"Your mom will be right back," Mason informed the smiling girls looking at him. The last image that Claire and Blake saw was Mason, wrapping April up in his arms, kissing her as the elevator doors closed.

CHAPTER TWENTY-FOUR

SUMMER VACATION WAS NOW IN FULL SWING AND CLAIRE and Blake couldn't be happier. A week had already passed since the last day of school and it was a hot, sunny, June afternoon. Blake was in her bedroom picking out several outfits to pack. April had announced the day before that she was going to take Mason and the girls to Gina's Lake House for a long weekend. So, here was Blake, packing like she was going to be gone for a week, instead of just three days. Blake's hair had continued to grow, and instead of looking like it was shaved, she was rocking more of a pixie cut. Blake's hair had a long way to go, but it was coming along nicely.

Claire walked into Blake's room holding several T-shirts and shorts combinations, wanting Blake's opinion. It wasn't as if Claire couldn't dress herself, but it was almost a habit now to ask Blake to choose for her.

"Definitely the one on the left," Blake said, pointing at Claire's left.

Claire looked surprised, but then asked, "You don't like the one on the right?"

Blake wrinkled her nose, "It's ok, but the other one will 'wow', if you know what I mean."

"Ok then. It's your call... Miss I-Can-Dress-Claire-Turner," Claire joked.

"Hey... Have I ever let you down?" Blake questioned seriously. Then to answer her own question, she replied, "No, I haven't."

Claire put the outfit that Blake picked and put it on top of the other one in her hand.

"So, the Lake House is pretty neat?" Claire asked Blake, getting excited at the thought of vacationing on a lake.

"Oh my God, yes," Blake said excitedly. "It's so beautiful there, and Gina has a dock with a sandy beach that is on her property. We are going to have so much fun there." Blake sounded like a little kid filled with joy.

"I can't wait to go," Claire said sincerely. "This will be like my first actual vacation trip."

Blake sometimes forgot that Claire's upbringing had been completely different from hers. Blake was used to celebrating holidays, going on vacations, doing normal family things that Claire never had had the opportunity to do.

"Well, this is going to be a great first vacation," Blake smiled, as she picked up an outfit from her pile on the bed and threw it at Claire. "Bring this, it will look amaze-balls on you."

Claire caught the outfit, and sighed, "Are you sure?" But then saw the look on Blake's face and knew that she better not disagree with the expert. "You got it boss," Claire grinned. "It's going right on top of the pile."

"Darn right, it is," Blake laughed, as she threw another outfit at Claire. This time however, Claire didn't see it coming. The shirt and shorts landed squarely on Claire's face, messing up her hair.

"Hey!" Claire exclaimed jovially, "watch it." But before Claire could say another word, Blake threw another outfit, and it landed almost on the exact same spot.

"That's it," Claire yelped as she took the clothes that she was holding and threw them at Blake, the force of which almost knocked her over. Suddenly, Claire jumped onto Blake's bed and started throwing every piece of clothing that Blake had just packed in her suitcase at Blake. All Blake saw was an explosion of clothes flying towards her. She tried to duck, but the majority of the outfits found their mark. She started laughing in surprise at what Claire had just done, and was trying to fight back with clothes from the dresser drawers next to her. After Blake had exhausted most of the clothes from the dresser, she dashed towards her closet.

April was in the middle of putting a few outfits of her own in her travel bag, when she heard the commotion from Blake's room. She figured that the girls were probably up to no good, but curiosity got the better of her, and she walked towards Blake's room to see what was going on.

As she looked into the room, Blake and Claire were on the bed laughing and giggling, almost unable to breathe, as a cloud of Blake's clothing lay scattered throughout the entire room. Some of Blake's underwear and bras were hanging from the ceiling fan. Almost every piece of clothing was either on the bed or on the floor. April peeked at Blake's closet, and it was almost half empty.

"What the heck is going on in here?" April curiously exclaimed, as she walked in.

Just the way that April had said those words made the girls explode with even more laughter. When they managed to strip away all the clothes from the pile that they were under, and saw the look on April's face, they immediately began laughing hysterically again.

Claire tried to stand up, but slipped on a pair of Blake's black tights that was on the floor, and fell face first onto the bed. If Blake had any control over her laughter, it was now gone. Tears were running down her face and she couldn't catch her breath. Claire's muffled laughs could be heard from beneath the pile of clothes on the bed.

April just stood there, trying not to laugh as the girls tried to regain their composure. After about thirty seconds both girls could breathe and maybe start forming coherent words. Claire held out her hand to help Blake up off the bed. When she did, Claire looked at the mess that blanketed the room, and said, "Holy shit!" That was it. Blake and Claire were gone again. This time, April couldn't hold her laughter in any longer. She began to laugh with the girls. In between bouts of laughter, Claire said, "I only came in here for her opinion on an outfit." Finally, after about sixty full seconds of laughter, all three were calming down.

"Oh my God, that was funny," Claire said, gasping for air and wiping tears from her eyes.

"How did this happen?" April asked, looking at the pile of clothes on the floor.

Claire looked April in the eyes, and firmly said, "I am going to be completely honest with you, Blake started it," and then she started laughing again.

It took both girls about half-an-hour to clean up the mess that they caused in Blake's room. Claire had to search for the outfits that she had brought in because now they were somewhere deep in the pile.

Claire and Blake were finally ready to go. Both had their suitcases packed and were waiting by the island in the kitchen. April was making coffee, so that she could put it into her Yeti mug and take it with her on the way. They were going to pick up Mason on their way out of town.

April had just put the top on her mug and was reaching for her suitcase when her phone went off.

Seeing it was Crystal, she answered it with a smile, "Hi Crystal. We are just getting ready to leave for the Lake House. What's up?"

"April," Crystal said, in a voice that was filled with sadness.

"What is it?" April asked, as she began to feel concerned.

"It's Claire's mother, Melanie Forrester," Crystal said, "She's dying."

"What?" exclaimed April.

Crystal told April that Claire's mother was dying of pancreatic cancer. She was diagnosed just a little over four months ago, and she didn't have much time left. She had reached out to CPS in Seattle to see if they could locate Claire.

"She doesn't have much time left, April. We have got to get Claire to Seattle quickly," Crystal said with desperation in her voice. Put Claire on so that I can tell her."

"Oh, my God," April said with a look of shock and dismay on her face.

Claire and Blake looked really concerned, not knowing what was going on.

April handed the phone over to Claire, and said, "Honey, it's Crystal. She has to tell you something."

Claire took the phone from April and asked, cautiously, "What's going on Crystal?"

Crystal told her about her mom's cancer diagnosis, adding that she didn't have much time left.

"No, please no," Claire whispered, as she began to cry. She hadn't seen her mom in years.

April told Blake what was going on, and Blake could see the devastation in Claire's eyes.

Crystal told Claire that she was going to arrange a flight ticket for her as soon as possible so that she could get to her mother quickly. Claire handed the phone to April, and hugged Blake for support.

"My mom's dying," Claire wept into Blake's shoulders. Claire and Blake sat down on the island as April continued to talk to Crystal.

April informed Crystal that she and Blake would be going as well. Crystal said that she would take care of it and that they should get to the airport as soon as possible.

When she got off the phone, she gave Claire a hug, and said that they were going to go with her.

The three of them headed out to the streets of downtown and hailed a cab to get them to the airport. On the way there, April called Mason and told him about Melanie and how they had to go directly to the airport. He asked April if she wanted him to come with her, but she said that it would be better if she just went with Claire. He agreed and told her to keep him posted.

April then called Gina, and said that they were flying to Seattle, and that the lake house would have to wait. Gina said that it would still be hers whenever they got back and not to worry.

When they got to the airport, the found that the flight leaving for Seattle wasn't leaving until 2:00 p.m., so they had to wait for several hours. Claire had told April and Blake stories about how bad her mother was as a parent, but Claire managed to inform them about a few good times that she had had with her mother. Claire was feeling incredibly guilty for not going to see her earlier. Even though her mother had told her years before not to come, she should have made the journey when April had discovered her. Claire was sure that April would have flown out to Seattle if Claire had wanted to go. Claire didn't have anyone to blame but herself.

Crystal met them by the terminal an hour before the flight took off. She was going with them so that things would go more quickly for them when they reached the hospital. Melanie Forester was, after all, still a prisoner. Crystal had been in contact with the Seattle Police Department and had arranged for quick transportation from the airport to the hospital.

At exactly 2:00 p.m., Claire, Blake, April, and Crystal were seated in the plane that would take Claire to be with her mother for her last and final time.

* *

"MOM?" CLAIRE SAID IMMEDIATELY AS SHE WALKED INTO the hospital room. There had been a female guard placed outside the door as per policy, but it was obvious that the guard knew that Mel Forester would not be able to escape.

The frail woman lying on the bed turned her head towards the sound of Claire's voice.

Claire knew it was her mother but she looked so much older now. Mel had lost weight and her face looked aged.

"Claire? Is that you?" Mel said, coughing a little as she spoke.

"Yes mom. It's me," Claire began to weep, as she knelt down next to her hospital bed.

"Claire, sweet little Claire," Mel said, recognizing the young lady in front of her. "Oh my, you look beautiful." It had been several years since she had seen her, and visions of her just starting her teen years filled Mel's mind.

April and Blake had entered the room right after Claire, but stood just inside the door. Crystal remained outside for a while talking with the police officer.

"Claire, sweetheart, how have you been?" Mel asked, trying to sit up. Claire grabbed her gently to help her up, but was stunned by how light and frail her mom was.

Claire's mind swirled with everything she wanted to tell her. So much had happened to her since the last time they had seen each other, most of which was bad.

"I had a rough life, mom," Claire began, "I'm not going to lie." She wanted her mom to know that life wasn't better without her in it. "I got bumped from foster home to foster home. My life was a mess," Claire could see that Mel was getting upset, but she needed to hear it.

"I had to run away from my last foster home to avoid getting abused, mom," Claire said, trying hard to maintain her composure. "I hitched a ride with a truck driver all the way to Chicago. I was homeless on the streets for months. I didn't have a place to stay, I didn't have any money, and I was so lonely, mom," Claire exclaimed, letting it all out for her mother. Claire didn't want to upset her, but Mel needed to hear all of it.

Mel's facial expression turned from despair to horror as she listened to the ordeal that her daughter had gone through. "I am so sorry, Claire," Mel began to cry. "I never wanted this life for you. I was just so messed up for so long." Tears were running down Mel's face.

Claire was sobbing as she spoke to Mel. Claire used the sheet of the bed to wipe her tears.

"I know, mom," Claire conceded. "I know you were."

"But," Claire said, in a lighter tone, "I was there, alone on the streets, hungry and cold, when this wonderful woman and her daughter walked by and decided to help me. They brought me into their home. I got really sick with the flu, and would have died if April hadn't nursed me back to health," Claire looked behind her and waved April and Blake over.

"Mom, this is April and her daughter, Blake. They took me in, mom. They made me feel at home with them." Mel looked at April and Blake, and she held up her hand for April to take. April gently grabbed her hand as Mel spoke softly, "Thank you for saving my baby girl." April had tears coming down from her eyes as well. "You're very welcome. Your daughter has brought such joy and love to our lives. It has been an absolute pleasure having her with us."

Claire said, "They love me mom, and I love them. I am part of a family that cares for me." Claire wanted her mom to know that she was now happy and was going to be ok.

Mel looked up at April and Blake, trying her best to smile, "Do you love her? Do you love my Claire?" April, who still had Mel's hand, squeezed it tighter, and said, "Yes, very much so. I love her as if she was my own daughter." Blake was standing behind Claire, and said to Mel, "Yes, I do too. I love her like a sister. She is my best friend, and I love her with all my heart." Mel's face seemed to relax a little, as they confessed their love for her daughter.

Blake then went on to tell Mel how Claire had saved her life by donating her bone marrow. Blake explained how she was diagnosed with leukemia, and that only a bone marrow transplant could save her life, and that Claire had been her perfect match.

"She will forever be a part of me," Blake whispered, trying to talk between tears.

April could tell that Mel was becoming extremely weak and that she was struggling to stay awake. There was a peace that was settling over Mel as she learned that Claire was loved and had a great family that she was a part of.

The doctor came in to look at a few of the monitors and made a few notes. She asked Mel if she was in any pain. Mel said that it was getting harder for her to breathe. The doctor knew that Mel's organs were shutting down, and that it was only a matter of time.

The nurse had brought in extra chairs so Crystal, Blake, April, and Claire could have a place to sit while they waited for the inevitable. An officer from the women's prison stopped by to drop off a box that contained all of Mel's personal items from her cell.

Over the next couple of hours, Claire told her mom all about her life with April and Blake. She told her about Thanksgiving dinner, Christmas, the conflict with Brie, how she had a boyfriend named Trevor, the Winter Formal, and how she was the perfect match for Blake.

Mel just lay there taking it all in. Having Claire there, telling her all about the good things that were happening now, made Mel's heart whole again.

As they were sitting there, a question occurred to Claire, and she just had to ask.

"Mom, I am so happy with April and Blake, and I know that they love me and would never let me go, but I think that I want to know who my real dad is. This may be the only chance I will get to ever try to find him." Crystal, who was looking at an email in her phone, raised her head up to look at Claire and her mom, hoping that Claire would get the answer that she always wanted but never knew she needed.

A smile came to Mel's face as she began to remember Mel's dad, but then a look of guilt flashed across her face. "Claire, I lied to you about your father. When you were younger, I lied."

"What do you mean?" Claire wanted to know, as she thought back to what her mom had said about him.

Mel tried to clear her throat and then took a deep breath, "I lied when I told you that he left us when I got pregnant. The fact is: I left him before I knew that I was pregnant. So, when I found out about you, I was still so angry and bitter that I never told him." Mel looked so ashamed of what she had done.

"So," Claire tried to reason out what her mom was telling her, "My dad doesn't know that I even exist?"

Mel shook her head. "No, he doesn't. I'm sorry honey, but I never thought that life would turn out like this for us."

Claire felt overwhelmed and confused. Her dad was out there somewhere, not knowing that he had a daughter in the world.

Because Mel was getting emotional, it was becoming harder for her to breathe. Claire sat there for a few moments, waiting for Mel to recover.

"So, who is my father?" Claire asked with determination.

Mel was looking into her mind's eye, remembering the only guy that she truly loved. She began to remember the good times with him; the day they met, the time spent at the bar, and the camping trip.

"His name is Sammy," Mel said in a whisper, grinning at his memory, looking at Claire with wide eyes.

Mel looked at Claire as if she should know that name. After a few seconds of staring at Claire's confused expression, Mel remembered that she had hidden a picture of him in a picture frame. Mel pointed at the box in the corner, and in a raspy voice, she said, "Get the box and bring it closer."

Mel instructed Claire to take out the picture frame of her and Claire when Claire was a little girl.

Claire actually remembered when that picture was taken. It was one of the few times in Claire's life as a child that she was happy. It was at a neighborhood park, and Mel was kneeling down with Claire playing in a sandbox.

Mel kept pointing at the back of the picture frame. Claire kept flipping it over, not understanding what her mom was getting at.

"Take out the picture," Mel whispered, "it's behind that one."

Claire finally realized what she meant and removed the back of the frame. Underneath the backing, hidden behind the picture, was another picture that was folded.

Claire's hands began to shake as she pulled out the hidden picture. She carefully unfolded it and gazed upon the image.

Claire's heart skipped a beat. As her eyes examined the picture before her, Claire's brain couldn't comprehend what was going on. There, standing beside her mom, was Nick Turner. They were posing with each other inside a bar. Nick's eyes were lovingly gazing upon Mel's, while Mel had one of the happiest looks that Claire had ever seen on her mom's face. Claire knew immediately that the man standing next to Mel was April's husband. She had seen his picture over the last eight months scattered throughout the apartment walls, sitting on Blake's dresser, on his driver's license in the wallet on Blake's desk, and all the pictures organized within albums. There was no denying that it was Nick Turner standing with Claire's mom in that picture.

Claire's face turned white as she turned to April. "Oh, my God," she exclaimed handing the picture to April.

April took the picture from Claire, and when she saw the man standing next to Mel, a sob escaped her lips. It was Nick, her beloved husband Nick. He looked younger, almost like the day they met. Contrary to the shadow of a woman that lay before her now, Mel looked very pretty, and the two of them seemed like they were in love. April could tell by the way that Nick's eyes gazed upon Mel that he loved her. Likewise, Mel had this look of glee on her face, and her eyes were beaming with joy.

Claire was beginning to feel light-headed with shock. Her hands were still shaking, and her knees felt like they were about to buckle. She looked at April, "How can this be?"

Blake took the picture from April to see what was going on. There, imprinted on the paper, was her dad.

"Mom?" Blake said, confused, as shock set in. "What is going on?" Blake wanted to know.

April took the picture from Blake to show Mel, and said, "This is Nick. His name is not Sammy."

Mel squinted her eyes to look at the picture, and then she was confused for several seconds. Then the explanation dawned on her, and she said, "I used to call him Sammy because his middle name was Samuel. For some reason, I started calling him that instead of Nick. I can't remember why, but I think it had something to do with an ex-boyfriend. So I began calling him Sammy." Mel smiled as she relived an old memory. "He didn't like it at first, but it grew on him, and he ended up loving it when I called him that."

April's mind went numb. Her husband's name was Nickolas Samuel Turner. Claire was looking from her mom, to April, to Blake.

"Mom," Claire said confused, "Nick was April's husband and Blake's father. He died over four years ago. Are you trying to tell me that Nick was my father too?"

Mel looked at April, and then her eyes moved to Blake. Mel then looked at Claire expressing a look of sadness upon hearing that Sammy had passed away.

"Yes," Mel pointed to the picture adamantly. "Sammy is your father," Mel said, with absolute conviction that the man in the picture was Claire's father.

Blake went up to April, and couldn't believe that this was happening. "Oh my God," Blake said, as a thought washed over her like cold water flowing down a stream. "Claire, you're my sister, my actual sister."

Claire looked at Blake, as if she was being introduced to her for the first time. "My dad was your dad."

Blake took two steps towards Claire, and hugged her like she had never hugged her before. "You were my sister this entire time! Since the day we brought you home, you were my sister!"

April felt like someone had turned the world upside down, and she had to sit down as a wave of realization washed over her. That was the final piece as to why Nick had wanted April to stop and go back to Claire that day in November. He knew that she was going to get the flu, he knew that she was the match for

Blake, and he knew that Claire was his daughter and wanted April to make her a part of his family.

Crystal was standing a few feet away listening to the revelations about Nick when she had finally made the connection. On that first day that she had met Claire, she had thought to herself that there was something about Claire that she couldn't put her finger on. She now realized what it was. She saw Nick's features in Claire's face. The way she smiled, the same eye color. Hell, the more she thought about it, she realized they even had the same kind of voice. The detective part of Crystal's brain knew that there was something there, but no way could she have connected the dots until this moment.

April asked Mel how she and Nick had met. Mel explained to April that she lived in Seattle, but went to UCLA from time to time with her friends to hang out at their apartment near campus. During one such visit, she had met Sammy at a local bar, where he used to hang out. He was going to college for architecture. It was love at first sight for them, but then she explained how she got hooked on drugs and the relationship went downhill from there. Mel confessed that Sammy was the one that kept trying to get her help, but she kept refusing it, and she eventually left him because of it. Mel had walked out on him, and he went to Chicago to start a job in some building downtown. She never saw him again. Mel told April that her leaving him was the worst thing that she ever did.

As April thought back to the day that she and Nick met, she recalled that he had moved from LA, and had just finished college, and was starting an entry-level position. He had been open and told April that he had just gotten out of a bad relationship. Now April realized that he had been talking about Mel. They all just sat in silence for a few minutes, not knowing what to say. Then a couple of alarms went off, and Mel's body began to arch in pain. The doctors came in and adjusted the medication.

She looked at Claire, and whispered, "It's almost time."

Claire went next to her mother's bed, and held her with her face close to hers. Her mother was barely conscious, but knew that Claire was there.

"I love you, baby girl," Mel whispered, struggling to say each word.

"Mom!" Claire softly yelled. "I love you!"

Mel's eyes were just about to close when Claire exclaimed, "Mom, I forgive you." She kissed her mom on the cheek, and Mel grinned as if she had been clinging on to life just to hear her daughter say those three words. Mel whispered the words, 'I love you,' to Claire one last time, and then closed her eyes.

Before Mel took her final breath, a smile slowly formed on her face, and she whispered, "Oh Sammy?" as if he were standing in the room. And then, like a fleeting, gentle gust of wind, she was gone.

Claire stayed next to her mom, holding her hand. The nurse came in and turned off the machines. Claire got up from Mel's side and reached for April. Claire embraced her and held her tight, sobbing in her arms. April held onto Claire and didn't let go. Blake got up from her chair and joined in the embrace. After several moments, through tears and sobs, April whispered in Claire's ear, "I love you."

* *

THE AIRPLANE RIDE HOME WAS BITTERSWEET. THEY WERE all sad that Claire had lost her mom, but the realization that Claire was Nick's child was still overwhelming.

Claire and Blake were sitting next to each other, deep in discussion about their newly discovered sisterhood. It was incredible that they had connected over the last eight months, unaware of the biological bond that they shared. Now, with this newfound discovery, the two of them were inseparable.

Because the plane had only three seats across, Crystal had been seated directly behind April. She leaned forward and tapped April on the shoulder.

"I would have never guessed in a million years that your Nick would end up being Claire's father. It is just such an incredible turn of events," Crystal said, amazed at how things had turned out.

"I still can't wrap my head around it," April confessed. "My Nick had a daughter before we were married, and he never knew."

Crystal had this curious look on her face, and then she said, "You know something, that would make you Claire's stepmom."

April blinked again in surprise. "Wait, what?" asked April.

"Think about it. Nick had Claire, and then the two of you got married. That would make Claire your stepdaughter."

"Oh my God, you're right," April said, stunned by the way that everything had turned out.

Blake had heard part of Crystal and her mom's conversation, "Holy cow, you're right." She turned towards Claire, and said, "April is technically your stepmom." Claire blinked in surprise, realizing that Blake's comment was correct. She looked at April, and smiled, "I guess that is true, if you think about."

"Yes, I suppose it is," April happily agreed.

April sat back in her seat and thought about the entire stepmom situation. Then she thought about how they had found out that Nick was Claire's dad. April looked at Claire as she thought about something. Claire had just found out who her dad was, but he had died before she could ever meet him. She couldn't imagine how it must be like for Claire—she had wondered about who her father was for a long time, and then when she had finally figured out the answer, she found out that he had passed away.

April sat up, and said, "Hey, Claire, can I ask you something?"

Claire looked away from the airplane window, and turned to her, and asked, "Sure, what?"

Because Blake was sitting between April and Claire, she was looking at her mom too, wondering what she wanted to ask Claire.

"I know that we all just found out that your father was Nick, but how are you doing with the news? To know that he has passed away and you won't get a chance to meet him...?" April wanted to let Claire know that she was there for her to help her through her feelings.

Claire blinked at the seriousness of the question, and then looked at Blake as she thought about it.

"I am shocked, to be honest with you," Claire said. "I could never have imagined that he would have been my father, but thinking about it right now, I am happy to have found out who he was and the kind of dad that he was to Blake." Claire pushed her blonde hair back with her right hand, and continued, "I am relieved to know that he never knew that I existed. I know now that if he had, he would have loved me and cared for me. I wouldn't want it if my dad knew that I was alive, and didn't want anything to do with me. That would have been worse."

April was so impressed with how Claire was handling all of this. "Yes, I know that Nick would have wanted you, and would have loved you with all of his heart."

Blake looked over at her mom, and said, "Mom, he does love her, he brought her to us. Remember?"

The three of them looked at each other and knew that Nick had brought them all together.

After they landed, it was decided that they would still go to Gina's Lake House. A full-fledged family vacation was definitely in order. April had called Mason while she was still in Seattle, and had explained everything to him. She told him about hearing Nick's voice in her head, about Blake's dream, and now about finding out that Nick was Claire's dad.

Mason had taken it all in, and when April was finished, told her that he wanted to be with her now more than ever. She asked him if he could meet her and the girls at the Lake House because they were going to go directly there from the airport.

Crystal had parked her car in one of the secured lots, so she told the Turners to enjoy the Lake House. She had to get back to work because she had been working on a drug case that was about to wrap up soon. Not to mention the two days of paperwork that was sitting on her desk from her being in Seattle.

"Love you guys," Crystal said, as she took the shuttle to the parking structure.

"Bye, Crystal!" April and the girls waved to her.

Gina arrived shortly after Crystal left to pick them up. As Gina drove them to the Lake House, April filled her in on the revelation that had occurred in Seattle. Gina was almost speechless, and couldn't believe it. "That is so amazing how things turned out with Claire. You have had her with you, not knowing that she was a piece of Nick that he had left behind. How remarkable, don't you think?"

April sighed, and then said, "Yes, it is." But April couldn't shake a feeling that had come over her. April looked in the backseat to see what Blake and Claire were doing. Both of them had headphones in, and they were apparently watching the same video because they laughed at the same time. Turning her attention back to the front of the vehicle, April looked directly at Gina.

"Gina, what if he had known? What would have happened if Mel had told him? You know Nick—he would have stayed with her and taken care of Claire. He would never have met me and then Blake would not have been born." April was becoming a little anxious. "Claire had to live a messed up life so that Blake could be born. How is that fair? But, where would I be if Nick and I had never met?"

Gina glanced over at April in the passenger's seat, and said candidly, "Listen, you can't think about it like that. Nick directed you to Claire at the perfect moment in time for both of you. He knew that she would have died out there, and he knew that Blake had leukemia. You welcomed Claire into your home and she has never been happier. So, yes, things might have been different, but you have to believe that things happen for a reason, and that it was supposed to turn out this way."

"Besides," Gina continued, "You have another daughter that you may never have the opportunity to get to know. Claire loves you guys, and I know darn well that you love her. Claire is Nick's gift to you."

Gina had a way of making April see things in a different light. "You are so right," April said sweetly. "I guess I just needed to hear it that way. It was such a surreal experience—seeing your husband pictured with another woman, obviously so much in love, fathering a child together, and never knowing anything about it..."

Gina removed her right hand off the wheel and tapped April's thigh with it. "Don't worry about all that. It's over and done with. Focus on the future with your two girls, and Mason."

April smiled at the sound of his name. She was in love with Mason, and it felt so right. Even after she had found out about Claire being Nick's daughter, the first person she wanted to share the news with was Mason.

It was early evening when they arrived at the Lake House. The girls unloaded the suitcases and followed Gina inside. "This place is awesome," Claire said as she entered the front door. The 'Lake House', as it was referred to, was a huge log cabin that contained four big bedrooms, 3 full baths, and a hot tub room that consisted of one large inlaid hot tub with two other smaller hot tubs. There were two small log cabins outside next to the main cabin. They were just one room only cabins, but were still good-sized.

Gina had two hundred feet of frontage by the lake, and the cabin rested on three acres. Out on the water, was a long dock that went sixty feet into the lake. There was a boat house, but it was set up as a recreation room with a couch, table and chairs, and a full-fledged bar.

Gina told the girls if they wanted to, they could spend the night in one of the outside cabins. Of course, Blake and Claire thought that it was a great idea and took their suitcases to the far one.

Mason arrived twenty minutes after April and the girls. He walked up to April and gave her an affectionate kiss on the lips, and said, "I missed you."

April felt comforted by his embrace, and answered him with, "I missed you too."

Claire and April came running up from the cabin, and gave him a hug. After hugging Blake, he hugged Claire, and said, "Claire, I am really sorry for the loss of your mom. I just want you to know that I am here for you in case you need anything. Ok?"

Claire hugged him back, and said, "Thanks Mason. It means a lot."

Now that everyone was there, the five of them made their way to the kitchen where Gina and April started preparing dinner. It was almost 7:00 p.m. by the time dinner was ready. Gina was a really good cook, and she had prepared a pot pie casserole that was to die for. April had cut up pieces of meat and cheese, and had set them out with a bowl of chips.

After dinner, Gina took them to the boathouse. Blake informed Claire that she usually spent most of her time either in the boathouse or swimming in the lake. Because it was getting late and everyone was tired from their trip to the Lake House, it was decided that everyone would retire early so that they could get an early start tomorrow.

Claire and Blake tucked themselves in the outside cabin for the night, talking about how they were going to only use the candles to light it up to make it look as if they were camping outside.

April walked Mason upstairs to his room, which just happened to be across from her room. Gina's room was the master suite on the main floor of the cabin.

The three of them sat on the couch of the living room directly in front of the big stone fireplace, and mostly talked about what had occurred in Seattle. Even though there was talk about her deceased husband, Mason was at ease with it, and said only comforting things to April about the future.

Gina wished both April and Mason a good night and then retired to her room. April and Mason continued to sit in front of the fire, with April's head resting gently on Mason's chest.

After several minutes, April lifted up her head and looked into Mason's eyes. "Thank you for being here for me. I don't know how I would have handled it if it weren't for you."

Mason gazed into April's eyes and knew that this was the right moment to tell her how he felt. "You're welcome, honey." He put his hands on hers and pulled her a tiny bit closer. "The first day I met you I knew that I wanted you in my life. Even through the tragedy of Blake's illness, I knew that I never wanted to leave your side. Now, with the loss of Claire's mom and the news that Claire was your husband's child, my feelings for you couldn't be stronger." Mason's face was now only inches from April's. "What I am trying to say is that I love you, April. I've loved you since that very first day when I met you. I want to be in your life."

April's heart fluttered and she knew that she loved him too. "I love you too," April began. "I never thought that I would love another man again, but the moment I met you, all that changed. You have been my rock through everything, and I can't see my life without you."

Mason removed his hands from April's and wrapped his arms around her. He began kissing her passionately. There was no denying their love for each other any longer.

April led Mason upstairs with her hand cupped firmly in his. She stopped at her bedroom and opened the door. "Are you sure about this?" Mason asked April as the passion he was feeling intensified.

April reached up and kissed him fervently, "Yes, Mr. Steele, I'm sure," she said. He grabbed her by the waist and picked her up, still kissing her as he took her into the bedroom.

The next couple of days were filled with fun, sun, and sand. Mason noticed that Gina had two wave runners stored next to the boathouse. Mason and April got aboard one, while Blake and Claire took the other one. Because Blake had ridden them before, she was used to operating it. The first time out, Mason drove the one he was on, while Blake drove the other one. Blake showed Claire how to work the wave runner, and the two girls took them out alone.

The boathouse quickly became Mason's favorite place to hang out. It had a big barn door opening in the back that allowed a full view of the dock and the lake. April and Mason spent hours there, snuggling on the couch, playing card games, listening to music, or just sitting at the bar enjoying an adult beverage.

On their third day there, Claire and Blake were lying out in the sun towards the end of the dock. Gina, Mason, and April were in the kitchen thinking about what they were going to do for lunch.

Blake came up from the dock and asked Gina, "Can I borrow a pen, a piece of paper, and some scissors?"

Gina thought about it for a second and wondered where she had kept those items. "Sure thing, I think there are some in that drawer over there next to the refrigerator," she finally said. Blake went to the drawer and pulled out a pen and a pad of paper. Gina then looked in the drawer next to her, and mixed in with the spatulas and serving spoons was a black pair of scissors. She handed them to Blake, who then sat at the kitchen table.

"What are you doing honey?" April asked her daughter.

"I'm working on a little project. No biggie," Blake said, innocently as she began writing on the paper. Blake sat there for several minutes, then she started cutting bits and pieces from the sheet of paper. When Blake had completed 'her project,' she quickly cleaned up the mess of tiny shards of paper that were sprinkled on the table, and headed back down to the dock. She thanked Gina, and with a cut-up piece of paper in her hands, headed back down to the dock.

"I wonder what that was about?" April asked no one in particular.

"You know, Blake," Gina said, "always designing something."

April looked down at the end of the dock and noticed that Blake had taken her place in the sun right next to Claire, just like earlier. April's curiosity quickly faded as Mason came up behind her and wrapped his arms around her. "So, April, my dear," Mason said as he squeezed her with affection. "What would you like for lunch?" April closed her eyes and soaked in the moment. She slowly turned around, and with great regret said, "What I want is unfortunately not on the menu." She looked over at Gina who was searching in the pantry for ideas for lunch, so her attention was not directed at them. "But, I know what I want for dessert," April said, giving him a couple of quick kisses before Gina moved away from the pantry.

Later that evening, Mason gathered up some wood into a stack in the fire pit so that he could start a bonfire. The girls were inside the boathouse playing cards when April called them over to ask if they wanted to make S'mores. Mason and April had gone shopping to the nearby grocery store earlier that day and bought the ingredients for making them. However, April also got Keebler's striped fudge cookies as well. All you do is to toast your marshmallow and then place it between two striped fudge cookies—and you have instant S'mores.

As the fire crackled, a full moon presented itself in the clear starlit summer sky. Blake had hooked her phone to an external speaker, and was playing music from one of her playlists. Claire and Blake were laughing and dancing around the fire, having a great time. When a slower song began to play, Mason stood up from his chair, and held his hand out to April. "May I have the pleasure of a dance?" April smiled at him and put her hand in his. "Of course," April smiled as he pulled her into his arms.

With the full moon above them and the view of the lake behind them, they had the perfect backdrop for a romantic evening. To April's surprise, Mason was a really good dancer. He led her easily around the bonfire and towards the sandy beach. April had totally fallen in love with Mason. She felt safe and comforted in his arms.

Claire had made a mess of her T-shirt as several melted marshmallows had dripped from the S'more to her T-shirt. "I'm going to go to the cabin and change my shirt real quick. I'll be right back," she told Blake.

"Ok. I'll be waiting right here for you," Blake said, as she started to toast her final marshmallow for the night. Claire walked to the cabin and closed the door. After a minute, Claire came running out of the cabin, and heading straight to Blake, she asked, "What the hell is this?" Bursting into peals of laughter,

Blake couldn't disguise her guilt any more. April and Mason heard the commotion and walked over to the girls.

There, imprinted on Claire's belly, just a fraction of an inch above her belly button were the words, 'I love my sister'. Blake had designed those words on a paper template and then had set it carefully onto Claire's belly while she slept on the dock when she was sunbathing. Claire's skin had tanned around the paper, leaving 'I love my sister' in perfectly white, untanned skin.

April put her hand to her mouth to prevent her from laughing. Claire was standing in front of Blake holding her shirt just far enough so that you could see the suntanned tattoo. "Well, what do you have to say for yourself?" Claire demanded trying to sound mad.

Blake smiled and stood up. She lifted up her own shirt to show Claire that she too had used the suntan trick to tattoo her belly with the words 'I love my sister'. Blake had designed two sheets of paper and set one on each of their bellies.

What Claire thought was a typical Blake prank was not just a prank, but was an act of sisterly-love that she had created for both of them. Claire rolled her eyes, surrendering to the sweetness of it. "How can I be mad at you?" Claire asked, looking from her belly to Blake's.

"You can't, Claire Bear. It's almost impossible now to be mad at me. You know why?" Blake asked, knowing what the answer was.

"Why?" Claire asked, wanting to be enlightened. "What can't I be mad at you?"

Blake put her hand on Claire's belly and then back on hers, "Because, I have a piece of you inside me—and the fact that you're my sister, my actual sister!"

Claire hugged Blake, smiling as she told her, "You're right. I do love my sister."

* *

CRYSTAL WAS SITTING AT HER DESK WHEN SHE GOT A CALL from a uniformed officer about a suspect that he had picked up for a traffic violation. Apparently, the poor kid had been caught speeding, and when the officer pulled him over, he found all kinds of drugs in the car. Some were prescription drugs, while others were of the meth lab variety. Wanting to get into the least possible amount of trouble, the kid began to confess where he had got the drugs from. The cops at the station who were responsible for taking down his statement recognized a couple of the names and knew they were part of an investigation that Crystal had been working on.

Crystal told the officer that she would be right down to ask the kid a few questions. She hung up the phone and the right side of her lip curved into a grin. *This could be just what I need to blow the top right off this case,* Crystal thought to herself, as she opened her desk drawer and removed a couple of file folders. She took her time getting to the interrogation room. On the way, she stopped at the coffee machine and poured herself a fresh cup of hot coffee. Crystal stopped at the office of her captain to ask him a few questions about another case that she was working on. As she got closer to her destination, her pace slowed to almost a crawl. It was a tactic that she liked to use. Make the suspects sweat a little. Give them time to get in their own head and plant the seeds of doubt.

Crystal walked into the room slowly and sat down across from the kid. He was sweating and his eyes darted from side to side, examining the room as if he was a scared animal. He was definitely nervous as hell.

"Hey, buddy," Crystal began. "What's your name?" Even though it was printed on the paper she held in her hand, she wanted him to tell her what it was.

"It's Paul," the kid replied.

Sighing as if annoyed, Crystal asked, "Paul, what?"

"Oh, sorry, it's Paul Summers," the kid answered, as if Crystal was a drill sergeant.

Crystal paused for a few seconds, pretending to write it down. She then kept her attention on the paperwork as if reading it for the first time, without saying a word. After a minute or so, Crystal looked up from the file, and said, "Listen, Paul. You've got two choices. First, you tell me everything I want to know, and I mean everything, or you go straight to jail, and by the time you are out, maybe, just maybe, you won't need a cane to walk." Crystal could see Paul involuntarily swallow his spit that had been forming in his mouth, "Or you can choose the second option, which is... Hell, let me be honest with you. There is no second option," Crystal glared intimidatingly at him with her dark brown eyes.

Paul closed his eyes for a brief second, probably trying to keep from pissing himself, and then opened them back up. "Fine, what do you want to know?"

A half-hour later, Crystal walked out of that room with a name that she didn't have before. The name that Paul had supplied was 'Donald Adler'. He was a pharmacist near downtown Chicago. He was married with one son. His son's name was Owen Adler.

CHAPTER TWENTY-FIVE

A MONTH HAD FLOWN BY SINCE CLAIRE'S MOM HAD PASSED away. April and Mason were spending as much time as they could together while Blake and Claire spent the first part of summer hanging out with their friends.

When April wasn't with Mason, she was working with Monica Towers, editing her latest novel. The two of them had become best friends. In fact, Monica had planned a working party of sorts at April's home office. She was going to bring take-out over for dinner as they worked on the novel. It was a good night to spend with Monica because Mason was out of town for a business meeting. Claire was planning to go with Trevor to Jordan's birthday party at Jordan's house. Blake was spending the day with Emily, but had planned to be home sometime after dinner.

Claire and Blake had just left the apartment to go their separate ways. April sat alone on the stool of the kitchen island. She unlocked her phone and saw the time and date: 9:26 a.m. Sunday, July 8. *Where has the summer gone?* April thought to herself. Claire's 17th birthday was just two days away, and she and Blake had planned a huge celebration. *This is going to be the best birthday Claire has ever had.* April smiled to herself as she thought about it. April knew that Claire's last birthday ended with her almost being raped and with her fleeing her foster home.

April had ordered a huge cake, made reservations at one of Claire's favorite restaurants, and had bought and wrapped her gifts. The thought of Claire's party was making April giddy with excitement. Claire had been through a lot this past year, and April wanted to show her that there were a lot of people that cared about her and loved her.

April got up to make herself a cup of coffee before she retired to her home office for a few hours when her phone rang. "Good morning, Crystal," April said cheerfully, "How's it going?"

"Great! Glad you asked," Crystal said. "Hey, I planned on going shopping later today for Claire's birthday party. Give me some ideas on what to get her," Crystal asked curiously. "I have a couple of gift cards for her, but I want to get her something special, especially after the year that she has had."

April thought about it for several seconds and then offered, "I know, why don't you get her this beautiful bracelet that I saw her look at a few weeks ago. I'll send you a picture of it. We saw it at a department store downtown."

"Cool, you're the best," Crystal said, thankfully. "Text me the name of the store, and I'll go get it sometime tonight, hopefully."

April began to look through the pictures on her phone for the picture of the bracelet. "How late will you be working tonight?" April asked.

Crystal chuckled into the speaker of the phone, and replied, "I'm supposed to get out around 5:00 p.m., but I'm about to make some arrests on this drug case that I have been working on for months, so you never know what may happen."

"Well, if you can't get it today, text me and maybe I can get it for you," April offered, knowing how busy Crystal could sometimes get when she was working a case.

"Ok," Crystal said, "but I'll know more later. It should be alright, but I will keep your offer in mind, in case I need it."

Crystal said goodbye to April as she ended the call. As April walked to her office with her coffee, she noticed a red cardinal sitting just outside the window of the dining room. It was just resting on the ledge, looking in the apartment as if it wanted to come in and sit down with April.

April stared at it in quiet fascination for several moments, taking in its beauty and splendor. Even though the bird could see April looking at it, the cardinal seemed content, looking back at April.

April finally turned her gaze away from the bird, and smiled as she entered her office and took a seat behind her desk.

* *

OVER THE LAST MONTH, TREVOR HAD BEEN INCREASING the amount of steroids that he had been using. Because it was summer, he spent a lot of time working out and exercising. He ran every morning, he lifted weights during the day, and his father had paid for intense physical conditioning with a personal trainer five days a week.

Trevor's father could see that his son was changing rapidly, but credited it to the personal trainer he had been paying for. Unfortunately, he dad had missed all the red flags that had been popping up indicating his son's involvement in drug abuse. Only Trevor's mom was becoming increasingly concerned about Trevor's physical and mental transformation, but as she voiced her opinion to her husband, she knew that it was landing on deaf ears.

During the month of June, Trevor had seen Claire only a handful of times. They were still going steady, but it just seemed that their lives were drifting apart. It had started when Claire had to fly to Seattle to be with her dying mom. Then, she spent a week at a cabin on some lake several hours away. Sure, they had been texting and talking on the phone through most of that time that they were physically apart, but Trevor desperately wanted alone time with her. He was getting to the point where he wanted to have sex with her or he had to end it soon. Little did Claire know, but when Trevor was at the bonfire with Jordan the week before Valentine's Day, he had hooked up with the cheerleader with the black tights and the sexy blue sweater. He had hooked up with her three times since then, but it was merely sexual between the two of them. The cheerleader had a boyfriend who was a senior, and only enjoyed Trevor on those special occasions when both were available for a quickie.

Deep down, Trevor did love Claire. There was something special about her that he didn't want to let go of. Unfortunately, his hormones would often overrule this heart, so he would find his release in the arms of a cheerleader that he cared little for.

It was the Sunday of Jordan's birthday bash, and Trevor was taking Claire to the all-day party. There was a pond to go swimming in that had a floating dock with a ladder. Jordan's family had three ATVs and two four-wheelers, so there was going to be a lot of fun riding around the yard. Of course, a bonfire was planned for the afternoon and evening hours.

Over the two weeks leading up to his birthday, Jordon kind of gave Trevor an ultimatum of sorts—he told Trevor that he had to bang Claire by the end of the night of his birthday bash or he was going to make him end things with her. Jordan cared about his best friend, and wanted him to be able to close the deal. He was his wingman after all.

Trevor got into his bright red Mustang, and started the engine. He opened his glove box to make sure that he still had his box of condoms hidden below the plastic envelope that contained his insurance and registration. Of course, the box had been opened and two were missing from it.

He quickly glanced in the backseat to make sure that he had his backpack with him. Not only did it contain a change of clothes, deodorant, and other masculine items, it housed the secret compartment that hid his steroids and other illegal drugs that he had recently purchased from Owen.

Trevor opened the garage door, and peeled out of his driveway, leaving black streaks burned into the pavement. He felt as if he could take on the entire world and make it his bitch. He was grinning from ear to ear as he sped down the street on his way to pick up Claire.

"Hey, babe," Trevor smiled, as he pushed open the passenger side door for Claire. He just pulled up to her apartment building, and she was waiting by the front doors. Claire was wearing white shorts with blue pinstripes and a white lace V-neck blouse that had a thin blue line sewn into the collar. It looked amazing on her, and Trevor couldn't wait until tonight. Claire was carrying a large handbag that contained her swimsuit, towel, and other items that she had brought with her, just in case.

"Hey Trevor," Claire smiled as she entered the car. Trevor leaned over and the two of them kissed on the lips. "I'm excited about going to Jordan's house today. It should be really fun," Claire said, as she reached for her seatbelt to put it on.

"Yeah, it is," agreed Trevor, as he grinned and then put the car into drive.

It took Trevor about an hour to get to Jordan's house, partly because of the distance and the traffic that he encountered leaving the city. Claire had held hands with him most of the way there and the two of them talked about what had happened in their lives over the past week.

When they arrived, the party was just getting started. Cars were arriving steadily, and there were already twelve cars parked in the front yard on the lawn. It was partly cloudy as the temperatures were going to near the upper eighties that day. The weather station had suggested that there was a chance of severe storms popping up later in the day, but as of right now, the weather was perfect.

Shortly after getting there, Claire changed into her bikini when some of the other girls that she knew wanted her to go swimming with them. It was around noon and it was getting hot. Claire told Trevor that she would meet him by the pond after she had changed.

Claire was standing at the edge of the pond, slowly putting her feet in the water when Trevor walked up to her. "God, you're hot!" Trevor exclaimed, as he looked at Claire's scantily dressed body. Claire blushed slightly because he had announced it loudly, and several guys had looked over in their direction. Claire looked up at Trevor, and he was only wearing his light blue swim trunks. His abs and pecs were glistening with sweat from the hot summer day, and he too looked hot. "You're pretty hot yourself," Claire conceded, as he reached for her hand. He led her into the water where they floated in closer proximity to each other. The two of them made their way to the floating dock where Trevor used his left arm to hang from the dock and his right arm to hold Claire in an embrace. He started kissing her, as she was nestled in his legs, he used them to keep Claire afloat.

Claire and Trevor eventually found themselves sitting on the floating dock, just taking in the sun. Claire's suntan tattoo of 'I love my sister' could still be seen on her belly as she laid on her back. After a few minutes, Trevor stood up and dove into the pond. He swam around the dock a couple of times, and then stopped in front of Claire.

She stood up and then jumped into the pond, extremely close to Trevor, so that she could splash him with the wave that she created.

Trevor began splashing Claire with his hands, causing wave after wave of splashes.

"Ok, ok, I give!" Claire exclaimed, as she tried to stop the onslaught of water.

Trevor stopped splashing, and swam up to her and began kissing her. It started out tenderly, but was becoming more forceful as it continued. Claire broke from the embrace, and gave Trevor a concerned look. She rubbed her mouth, and said, "Not so rough, ok?" She knew that Trevor could become intense when they made out, but she didn't want that much right now, especially in front of everybody.

Trevor's face flashed a look of disappointment, but then he said, "Sorry, you look really hot today, and it's hard for me to keep my hands off of you."

"It's ok, I love kissing you, just try not to be so rough, that's all," Claire consoled Trevor so that he wouldn't think that Claire didn't want to kiss him.

"No problem," Trevor said, as he gave her a quick kiss and then began swimming to the shore.

Trevor and Claire continued kissing and hugging throughout the day. There were times that Trevor went off with Jordon to do whatever guys did when they were together as Claire hung out with some of the other girls that were there. Rose, Brie, and Shelly got to the party around 1 p.m. so Claire hung out with them as well.

Around 5:00 p.m., Jordan's family cooked up what seemed like hundreds of hotdogs and burgers. Claire and Trevor sat at one of the picnic tables that were set up near the pond. Trevor ate about three of them, and was heading up to the table to get one more. Claire had only consumed one hotdog and a handful of chips. As she watched Trevor go up to the table, she saw him stop to talk with Jordan. After a minute, the two fist-bumped and began laughing about something. Claire didn't think too much about it. Boys will be boys. Brie, Shelly, and Rose were sitting across from Claire and Trevor.

"This is such a blast!" Rose said to all of them. "I can't believe that we are about to be seniors this year."

"I know, I can't believe it either," Claire agreed. She looked at Trevor with Jordan at the food table, and then said, "You know something?" Claire told her friends, "I never had a group of girl friends like you guys in my entire life. This year has been the best of my entire life, and I feel so lucky to have all of you in my life." Claire looked from Brie, to Rose, to Shelly. "I am so looking forward to spending my senior year with all of you!"

All four girls made a circle of hands and Brie suggested, "Let's all agree that this circle of friends will be the absolute best friends that we can be and allow nothing to come between us for the entire year!" All four girls smiled and chuckled at the pact, but all agreed to uphold it.

Trevor had made his way back to the table, and noticed that all the girls were holding hands. "Am I missing something?" Trevor questioned, looking at his girlfriend. Claire released the hands that she was holding, and answered, "Yes, but it's ok," The four friends smiled at each other as Trevor consumed his fourth hotdog.

Jordan and Trevor started the bonfire at around 6:00 p.m. The sky was turning overcast and dark, a storm was threatening to blow over. Claire and her girlfriends had chosen a good spot on a log that was by the bonfire. Trevor had gone off with a group of guys into the pole barn.

Jordan, Trevor, Ben, Jose, Will, and Casey had made their way into the area of the pole barn that Jordan had sectioned off for himself. It had a couch, a few chairs, a table, and a huge television. It was like Jordan's man cave.

Jordan looked around to make sure no one else was in there, and he pulled out a box from under the couch. The box contained several pints of whiskey. He took one of them out and began pouring some into the 20oz plastic Coke bottles that each of the guys had brought with them.

"Happy birthday to me!" Jordan grinned, as he poured the rest of the pint into his bottle.

The guys guzzled down the 20oz rather quickly, so Jordan retrieved a second pint from the box, and took it with him so that he could add it to his friends' bottles when needed. The other three guys left the pole barn while Jordon and Trevor remained.

"So... Trev? You and Claire tonight?" Jordan questioned.

"You know, I don't know," Trevor admitted sheepishly. "I hope so, but there is something about the way that she acts when we start kissing. I don't know, dude. It's like she doesn't ever want to have sex." Trevor's frustration was building.

"I told you man," Jordan began, "If she doesn't give it to you tonight, then drop her man. You've got plenty of other girls that you can tap and you know it," Jordan chastised his best friend. "Time for her to commit to you dude!"

"Yeah, I know it," Trevor agreed. "It's time that I get what I deserve."

"Fuck yeah!" Jordan egged him on. He took out the pint from his pocket, and took a long swig. He handed it to Trevor. To Jordan's surprise, Trevor took a huge swig and emptied half the bottle.

"That's the Trevor I love man!" Jordan laughed as she took another hit from the pint. Jordan walked over to the mini-fridge that was seated next to the couch and took out a 20oz Coke bottle. He poured about half of it out onto the floor and then filled it back up with the pint. He handed it to Trevor with a smile. "Cheers, dude," Trevor grinned as Trevor accepted the bottle.

Trevor and Jordan exited the pole barn and went their separate ways, Jordan headed towards a group of girls who were near the tent, while Trevor headed to the bonfire. Before he got there, he took a handful of Funyuns chips that he grabbed from the snack table to help get rid of the smell of alcohol.

"Hey, Claire," Trevor grinned, as she sat next to Claire on the log. "Enjoying yourself?" He gazed at her as she looked into the bonfire. "It's been an awesome day. I've had so much fun," Claire admitted, as she put his arm around her. The wind began to pick up and thunder rumbled in the not too far-off distance.

Dark clouds were coming in from the west, and it was obvious that a storm was about to come in. Several kids headed for their cars, while most of them just waited until the storm began.

Shelly, Rose, and Brie got up from the log, and decided that they weren't going to wait until the storm let loose.

"Do you want to come with us?" Brie asked Claire. "The three of us will be watching a movie at my house." Claire was going to say no because she still wanted to hang out with Trevor, but Trevor spoke up rather loudly, and said, "Sorry girls, Claire's all mine tonight." As he said so, the words came out rather mean, almost as if he didn't want her friends to take her away from him.

Brie flashed a look of concern at Claire. She did not like the way that Trevor had come across just then, and was worried for Claire.

"No, it's cool, you guys," Claire reassured them. "Trevor and I are going to hang out a little while longer."

Trevor gave the girls a shit-eating grin, as if he was a little boy and had just been awarded the toy that he had been throwing a fit for at the toy store. "Good night, ladies," Trevor said, as if to tell them to get out of there.

Shelly gave Rose a sideways glance, as if to say, *what the hell is up with him?* The three girls got into Rose's parent's car, and then left Claire with Trevor.

"What was that about?" Claire asked Trevor, a little perturbed. "You didn't have to be mean."

Trevor was feeling like he wanted to explode on Claire, but managed to keep his cool without her noticing. "Listen, babe," Trevor said, "All I wanted to do today was to be with you and have a great time. Let's not spoil it, ok?" He flashed his charming smile that he usually flashed when he was trying to make Claire feel better about something.

Just then, a bright flash of lightning ripped down from the sky and then a loud crack of thunder erupted overhead. Almost immediately after that, the clouds opened up and released the rain. Huge drops led the curtain of water that was on its way down.

Claire and Trevor ran to his car and managed to get in and closed the doors before it started to pour. Trevor placed his Coke bottle in a cup holder and his cell phone in the other and then started to reach into his pocket to retrieve the key to the car. The wind had increased dramatically in the last couple of minutes causing the rain to come down in sheets. Trevor started the car and sat parked on Jordan's lawn, as other cars had begun to leave the party. After a few minutes, Trevor put the car in drive and then headed out.

"What do you want to do now?" Claire asked him after he started driving down the road. The storm was intensifying and it was clear that they would not be able to do anything else outside.

Trevor looked over at Claire and without skipping a beat, and said, "I want to make love to you tonight." Not allowing Claire time to resist, he continued, "I've waited long enough for you, and I love you. I want to take our relationship to the next level."

Taken aback by the forcefulness with which he was talking, Claire immediately began to feel apprehensive.

"Listen, Trevor," Claire slowly began. "You know that I love you and I do want to have sex with you, but something is up with you today. I don't know what it is but it's kind of freaking me out." A feeling of anxiousness was washing over her.

Feeling like he was losing control of where the night was going to lead, Trevor opened the 20oz of Coke and took a swig. As he set it back down in the cup holder, Claire caught a whiff of the whiskey that was mixed in it. "Have you been drinking?" Claire asked, raising her voice in shock.

Not caring if he admitted it or not, Trevor yelled, "Yeah. So what?"

"Are you seriously drinking and driving right now?" Claire couldn't hide her surprise.

Just then, Jordan, who was totally drunk, texted Trevor, and asked, "Hey Trev, did you get into Claire's pants yet?" The words appeared clearly on Trevor's locked screen. Unfortunately for Trevor, his cell phone display just happened to be facing Claire.

"Did you get in my pants yet?" Claire yelled, as she read the text from Jordan. "Seriously, Trevor!" Claire asked, now totally pissed.

Trevor's eyes enlarged with rage as he looked over at Claire. "It's a fair question, Claire! We've been dating for eight fucking months now, and it's way past time! I know that you were almost raped, but Jesus, Claire, the guy didn't actually do it, so what's the goddamn problem now!"

Claire was dumbfounded that this was coming from Trevor's mouth. She was scared and confused, and just wanted to get away from him.

As Trevor continued to yell, his driving became more and more reckless, and he was speeding down a wet dirt road. Thunder echoed as lightning flashed, making the road more treacherous to the drive on.

"I'm sorry," Claire said, trying to defuse the situation. "Please stop the car," Claire said, as she turned away from him, looking out the passenger window.

Just then, Trevor's phone rang—it was ringing through the speakers of the car. It was Owen Adler. Because of the emotional state that Trevor was in, and the amount of alcohol that he had just consumed, he tapped the 'Accept' button on the steering wheel instead of the 'Decline' button.

Owen's voice erupted through the speakers almost instantly. "We're fucked, dude. The police arrested my dad, and they're coming for me! It's over! I'm not going down alone!" Trevor tried to disconnect the call, but his eyes were focused on the road and the rain cascading over the windshield. So, instead of hitting the call disconnect button, Trevor kept hitting the volume increase button, allowing Owen's confession to be loudly heard. "Trash what drugs you have on you before the cops get you!" Owen said just before he hung up.

That was the last straw for Claire. Within a matter of sixty seconds, everything that she felt for Trevor had just been obliterated. "Stop the car now!" Claire yelled defiantly. She wanted to get as far away from him as possible.

Trevor's face turned red with rage. The steroids that coursed through his veins only added fuel to his rage. His world was collapsing in on itself, and he was acting like a trapped animal. "Fuck you, Claire!" he spat, as he pushed his foot down further onto the gas pedal.

"Fuck me?" Claire yelled. "Fuck you, Trevor! We're done!" Claire exclaimed as anger and fear welled up inside her.

As the speed of the Mustang increased, it was becoming more difficult to see the road ahead.

"Please stop the car!" Claire pleaded, as she could barely see the road amidst the rain and the darkness.

Trevor didn't say anything, but had this look of disdain on his face. He looked over at her as if she didn't exist, and continued to speed.

"Please Trevor, slow down!" Claire screamed, trying to reason with him.

Trevor's mind was racing. It was just a matter of time before the police came and picked him up. Claire was obviously done with him, and his college dreams were probably doomed as well. He couldn't concentrate as he saw his entire life's plan slip away.

"Stop the car, please!" Claire begged, as she began to cry. Tears were rolling down her cheeks as fear took over.

"I'll stop when I am good and ready!" Trevor yelled at Claire, as he looked at her. Because his reaction time had been compromised, as he focused his attention back to the road, he couldn't swerve his car in time to tackle the curve in the road ahead.

Trevor slammed on the brakes, but it was too late. Claire screamed as the rear end of the car fishtailed off the road, slamming into a mailbox on the driver's side. The car then ricocheted off the mailbox and flew back to the right side of the road, tumbling upside down into a ditch. As the car flipped into the ditch, branches from a fallen tree smashed the passenger side window. Entering the car through the now broken widow, the branches slammed against Claire's head on the left side.

Claire was upside down hanging from her seat belt. She began to scream in agony as the pain exploded through her entire body. The branch had hit her hard on the right side of her head, and blood was now gushing from the wound. Claire's hand and wrist were hurting, as well as her right leg. She knew it was bad.

As she tried to move her head to see Trevor, a sharp pain exploded from her shoulder and neck. She could smell blood as it ran down in front of her face, and could taste it as it ran down into her mouth.

"Trevor!" she screamed, wanting to see what had happened to him. She heard the door of the car creak open and then got a glimpse of Trevor. He was bleeding from his forehead and had blood on his hands. He looked stunned and in shock. After several seconds, he managed to escape from the driver's seat, and stand up on the road. He put his hand on his head and screamed. He looked over at Claire, and the look that he gave her made Claire's heart sink. It was clear to her that he thought Claire was in bad shape. He began to cry, more for himself, and then began to limp away from the car, forgetting that his backpack was still in the backseat of the Mustang.

Claire was in shock. She was severely injured and trapped in the car, and Trevor was leaving her there.

"Trevor! Don't leave me!" Claire cried out, begging through the pain. "Get me out of here!" The pain in Claire's head was intensifying as well as the pain in her leg. Tears mixed with blood as Claire sobbed uncontrollably.

Trevor couldn't look back at her, his cowardice took over his body. He slowly limped away, trying to get as much distance between himself and the car as possible. He feared that Claire was just minutes away from dying.

* *

FRED TANNER WAS YOUR BASIC TRUCK DRIVER. HE LIKED LIS-tening to music during long runs, and he, like millions of other drivers, texted while he drove.

On this particular evening, he had been sending his wife pictures of him-self stating that he would be home soon, and that they would spend a romantic night together. As he typed sexual innuendos about how the night was going to go down, he took his eyes off the road. Once he finished with an emoji that showed a smiley face blowing a heart kiss, he looked up from his phone. Unfortunately, there was a huge doe and its baby fawn directly on the road in front of him. He reflexively slammed on the brakes, causing his trailer to jack-knife. The trailer tore itself free from the tractor and flipped over, spilling its contents all over the road. The trailer lay sprawled out, blocking both directions of the road.

"Goddamn it!" Fred exclaimed, as the tractor came to a halt. He unbuck-led his seatbelt and got out of the truck. Standing on the road, he called 9-1-1 to report his accident. As he informed the operator about what had just occurred, he looked up to the sky to see the dark clouds of a storm approaching.

This is just great—just fucking great! Fred thought to himself, knowing that his wife was going to be really, really, pissed.

* *

THE SIGN

CALEB ALLEN HAD JUST GOTTEN OFF HIS SHIFT FROM WORK. He was 18 years old, and had graduated from high school in May. He had light brown hair and hazel eyes. He had played football during his junior and senior year, but wasn't the best player on the team. He just enjoyed the sport and was playing it because a lot of his friends were on the team.

He lived with his mom and dad in a subdivision just on the outskirts of town. Caleb's dad had been a paramedic for twelve years, but then decided to become a doctor. Caleb's mom ran the local diner, and was well liked by just about everyone in town. He was very close to his parents and had no plans to leave the house until he had enough money to buy his own house. Caleb's brother, Jacob, was a year older than him. Jacob had just left Illinois to attend college at the University of Idaho, to study Animal Sciences with the intention of becoming a veterinarian.

Caleb knew at an early age that he wanted to be a paramedic like his dad. When he was ten, he just happened to be with his dad when they witnessed a car accident. Caleb got to witness first hand his dad jumping into action and saving a life. Ever since that day, Caleb wanted to experience that same feeling of being able to help people during their time of need.

Caleb's dad had trained him on his own about emergency medicine and what to do during a crisis. By the time Caleb graduated high school, his knowledge was almost that of a fully trained paramedic. However, he still had to get certified, so he had to take classes during the summer to prepare for the boards. He worked at the fire station during the day and helped stock the EMS rigs with medicine and supplies.

As Caleb headed down the road in the direction of his home, driving his Chevy Silverado pickup truck, his thoughts dwelled on what he had just accomplished at work, and the dinner that he knew his mother was fixing at that very moment.

Caleb began to search through the country stations that were actually playing songs instead of commercials as he turned down the same road that he usually took to get home. The rain had begun to fall as thunder and lightning pounded the skies. Caleb had to put his wipers on high just to see where he was going. Towards the end of the road, he noticed flares and the flashing lights of a police car. As Caleb approached, he could see that there had been an accident. An eighteen-wheeler had tipped over in the middle of the road. He pulled up next to the police car and rolled down his window. Caleb recognized the patrolman as Officer Whitmore.

"Oh, hi, Caleb," Officer Whitmore said as he recognized him. "How's it going?"

"Good," Caleb answered, "What happened here?" Caleb asked, pointing at the mess on the road.

Officer Whitman sighed, "Goddamn texting driver again. When are people going to learn to keep their phones away while driving?" He paused a moment to gaze out onto the road. "Good thing that no one was coming in the opposite direction." Officer Whitman said thankfully.

"Yeah, no doubt," Caleb agreed.

"The road is going to be closed for most of the night," Officer Whitman informed Caleb. He then pointed towards the dirt road next to the police car. "Sorry, this is the only way through, and it has added an extra four miles to your trip."

"No worries, it's no big deal," Caleb told the officer. "I'm just on my way home anyways."

Caleb waved bye to the officer, and started driving down the dirt road. He was about two miles down when a flash of light ahead of him seemed to dance across the road. As he focused his eyes, he saw a red car sliding sideways across the road and flip into the ditch on the opposite side.

"Oh, shit!" Caleb exclaimed, as the adrenaline began pumping through his veins. By the way the car flipped and then crashed, he knew that it wouldn't be good. The crash was about a ¼ mile ahead so he stepped on the gas to get there.

As he approached the wreckage, he could see the driver exiting the car and start limping away.

Caleb pulled up close to the ditch and yelled after the driver, "Hey, come back here! You're hurt. Let me help." But then he heard a girl scream from inside the car. Caleb jumped into the ditch and went to the passenger side door. What he saw made his heart stop. There hanging upside down was a very pretty teenage girl who was bleeding profusely. She was in bad shape, and Caleb knew he had to hurry.

"Hey, Miss," Caleb called to her as he reached for the door. "My name is Caleb. What's yours?"

Claire looked up at the sound of Caleb's voice.

"Oh God, please help me!" Claire cried out in agony. "I'm trapped!"

Caleb opened the door and grabbed onto Claire. "What's your name?" Caleb wanted to know as he tried to release her from the seat belt.

"It's Claire, my name is Claire," Claire said through clenched teeth.

"Claire, nice to meet you," Caleb said. "I'm going to undo the seatbelt and then I'll hold you so you don't fall. It's probably going to hurt, but I will do my best to limit the movement, until I can get you out of the car. Ok?"

"Yes! Please yes! Get me out of here!" Claire yelled, gratefully.

"One... two... three..." Caleb counted and then he pressed the seat belt button. Claire was released and collapsed into Caleb's arms. Claire yelped out in pain as the movement jarred her injuries. The rain was still falling at a steady rate as he carried her to the bed of his truck. He had to examine her as fast as he could to evaluate the extent of her injuries.

Immediately he put his hand on her head to stop the bleeding from the gash. It was swelling up quickly, and Caleb knew it was severe. He looked at her right leg and saw the constant heavy flow of blood escaping from the wound. Caleb quickly removed his belt and wrapped it around her leg. "Claire, you are bleeding badly from your leg. I have to put a tourniquet around it or you're going to bleed out. It is going to hurt a lot, but I have to keep the belt as tight as I can."

"Ok," Claire whispered, as she started going into a state of shock.

As soon as he got the belt as tight as he could, he reached for his cell phone and called 9-1-1. While he was on the phone, he got his med kit from the cab of his truck and went back to Claire.

He told the operator where he was and the severity of Claire's injuries. Caleb informed the operator that he was trained as a paramedic, and that he had begun to attend to her with his med kit. He kept the operator on the line, but then told her that she better send for the medical helicopter—Claire might not make it otherwise.

Caleb removed gauze from the kit and taped a handful to Claire's head to slow down the bleeding.

Claire was shivering from the rain and loss of blood. She couldn't feel her legs anymore and could hardly move. As Caleb attended to her, she could feel her mind clouding up and her body become numb from the pain.

Tears continued to flow from her eyes as Claire faced the reality of death.

"Caleb," Claire whispered, holding onto consciousness. "Please tell April and Blake I love them."

"Stay with me, Claire," Caleb gently ordered, as he kept applying bandages on her bloodied wounds.

Claire didn't want to die, but wanted to make sure that April and Blake knew how much she appreciated everything that they had done for her just in case she did.

"Tell April and Blake that I love them," Claire pleaded again.

Caleb continued to work on Claire, as he said, "Have faith, I'm going to save you," Caleb told her, trying to keep her awake and alert for as long as possible. He then asked, "Who are April and Blake?"

Claire was soaking wet with rain, blood and mud. She tried to turn her head to get a better look at Caleb but he had just put some kind of neck brace on her. "They," Claire began, as she started to cough up blood. "They're my mother and sister," Claire's eyes were starting to close. "Tell April and Blake I love them," Claire said again, praying that Caleb would.

"Yes, I promise," said Caleb, as she gazed upon Claire's face. "So, what happened?" Caleb asked.

As she thought about what had led to the crash, Claire's face contorted in pain. "We were arguing," she tried to explain. "Trevor—he went crazy," Claire said, stopping to cough, and spitting up more blood. "I tried to get him to stop, but he wouldn't stop," Claire told Caleb, hoping that he understood what she was trying to say.

He could see that her eyes were beginning to roll in the back of her head. "Stay with me, Claire," he ordered. A long streak of lightning flashed across the sky, briefly illuminating Claire's face.

Claire could feel herself slipping away. She tried to hang on, but was too weak to mount any kind of serious effort. As the darkness closed in, Claire's last image was of Caleb, pleading with her to hold on.

* *

"HI GUYS," BLAKE SAID TO HER MOM AND MONICA AS SHE walked into the apartment. It was after 7 p.m., and they had just finished with their dinner. April was putting the dishes away as Monica was in the process of throwing away the empty take-out containers.

"How was your day?" April asked Blake, as her daughter entered the kitchen.

"Great," Blake smiled. "Emily and I went shopping, then we had dinner with her dad. He made this really good spaghetti and meatball dinner. It was fabulous."

"How was your night? Did you get a lot accomplished with the novel?" Blake asked Monica politely.

Monica grinned, and then looked at April. "Yes and no." Monica looked back at Blake, and said, "Yes, it was good night, and we did work on the novel, but then we got to talking about other things, and the night just got away from us." By the look on her mom's face, Blake surmised that the 'other things' referred to Mason.

"Well, that's good," Blake said, looking in the cabinets for a snack.

"Are you still hungry?" April asked Blake.

Blake continued to look for a snack. "No, not really. I just want something sweet, I think, but I don't know yet what I want."

April went up to her daughter and kissed her on the top of the head. "When you figure it out, let me know."

Just then, April's phone began to ring. It was Crystal. Before she picked it up, she thought to herself that Crystal was going to say that she had to work late and ask if April could pick up the bracelet.

"Hi, Crystal," April said, but before she could say anything else, Crystal interrupted her sounding frantic.

"April, Claire's been in a bad accident. You need to get to the hospital right away!" The urgency in her tone was undeniable.

"What?" April gasped, as a blanket of fear smothered her.

"Claire and Trevor were in a car accident. She is being airlifted to Chicago Med as we speak." Crystal's voice wavered as she told her. April burst into tears sobbing, "Oh God, no!"

Crystal kept talking, and urging her, "You've got to hurry, April—she's in bad shape. I am on my way there right now."

Blake turned to her mother, stunned by her mom's crying. "What is it, mom?" Blake asked, concerned.

With the phone quivering in her hand, April exclaimed, "Claire's been in a bad car accident." As she said those words, sobs were escaping from her lips. "Crystal says it's bad and we have to hurry to the hospital."

"No!" Blake screamed, as she began to cry. "Mom, please no!"

Monica ran for her purse. "I drove here. I can take you to the hospital right away! Let's go!" April didn't take the time to grab her purse on the way out. The three of them ran to the elevator as fast as they could, and raced to Monica's car.

On the way there, April called her parents and told them about Claire and asked them to hurry to Chicago Med as fast as they could. April knew that Mason was out of town, but needed to call him. He told April that he was going to book a flight as soon as they got off the phone and would fly back.

Blake called Emily, crying hysterically, and told her about Claire. Emily said that she would call Brie, Shelly, and Rose for her and that they would meet her at the hospital.

Monica was weaving in and out of traffic trying to get to the hospital as fast as she could. A storm had moved in, and rain was pouring down from the clouds. The sky was dark with flashes of lightning, creating an ominous backdrop. April and Blake were in the back seat. Blake's head was on her mother's chest. "She can't die, mom!" Blake cried, as she held onto her mother. "She just can't!"

The ride there only took about fifteen minutes, but it felt like two hours to April. Monica sped up the hospital driveway and right up to the ER entrance. April and Blake quickly got out of the car and ran into the building. The ER was filled to capacity. There were people bleeding, people coughing and wheezing, and there was even a kid who had apparently stuffed a matchbox car up his nose.

"Where's Claire?" April asked frantically of the nurse who was standing behind the first counter that she spotted. Before she could answer, Crystal called her name from down the hall.

"April, over here," Crystal said, walking towards her.

"Oh my God," April whispered, as Crystal embraced her. "What happened?"

Crystal hugged Blake, and then kept her arm around her as she explained the situation.

"Claire and Trevor were driving away from Jordan Stile's birthday party, and it had started to rain heavily due to the storm. Apparently an argument broke out, and he wouldn't stop the car. Trevor lost control and the car rolled and crashed into a ditch," Crystal said, tearing up.

"So what happened to Trevor? He is badly hurt too?" April asked.

A serious look flashed across Crystal's face. "He's in custody." April looked at Crystal for further explanation. "Remember when I told you about the drug ring that I was looking into today?"

"Yes? Why?" April replied.

"I arrested a pharmacist and his son today. The son, Owen, had been supplying Trevor Thomas with steroids and other illegal drugs. We found the drugs in his backpack at the crash site." Crystal informed April but continued with more bad news. "And Trevor had been drinking before he left Jordan's. His blood alcohol level was above legal limits."

"What!" April said dumbfounded. "Are you sure?"

Crystal shook her head. "Unfortunately, yes, he was drunk," Crystal could see April starting to realize that this was more than just poor road condition. "There is something else," Crystal needed to tell April. "Trevor left the crash scene. He left Claire trapped in the car."

"He did what!" April yelled. She couldn't believe what Crystal was telling her. "He left her to die?"

Crystal wiped the tears that were flowing down her cheek. "Yes, he tried to run away. He did nothing to help Claire."

Blake couldn't take it anymore. "That asshole!" she spat the word venomously. "How could he do that to her! She loved him!"

Crystal looked down at Blake, "I don't know, but he left her."

The thought that Claire's injuries were a direct result of Trevor's reckless behavior made April that much more upset.

"Where's Claire?" April wanted to know.

Crystal put her arm around both April and Blake as she guided them down the hall. "She is in emergency surgery right now. It's bad... She has blunt force trauma to the head and face, her hand and wrist were broken, and her right leg suffered severe damage, and she has some internal damage as well."

"Oh, dear God, Crystal," April's mind was reeling. "Is she going to make it?" she asked, afraid to hear the reply.

Crystal looked at April blankly, and replied, "They don't know."

The three of them took up seats in the surgical waiting room area. Crystal got up and went to get them coffee. Blake was fuming and couldn't believe that this was happening. "Mom, I can't take it! I don't want her to die! How can I live without her?"

Crystal returned with the coffees, and sat down next to April. After a few minutes, Caleb was walking by the waiting room on his way from talking with the police.

"Caleb," Crystal waved him over to them. As he approached, Crystal introduced him. "April, Blake, this is Caleb. He is the one who rescued Claire."

April stood up, and looked at Caleb. He was wearing a gray T-shirt and blue jeans, but he was covered in blood and mud. Then it occurred to her that it was Claire's blood that was splashed on his clothes. April reflexively started to put her hand on his shirt. "That's Claire's blood," she said. Then she looked at him, and said, "Thank you so much for helping her." April began to sob again as she hugged him.

Caleb hugged her back, and said, "You're very welcome. I saw the accident happen, and I rushed to the scene." Caleb told them that he was studying to be a paramedic, and that his dad was a doctor, so he was trained in what to do.

As he thought back to the crash, Caleb asked, "You are April and Blake, right?"

"Yes, we are," April answered.

Caleb cleared his throat, and said, "Claire wanted me to tell you that she loves you. She made me promise that I would let you know."

Blake began to sob again. "We love her too," Blake wanted it to be known to Caleb—as if he could convey her words back to Claire.

"She knew that she was in bad shape, and asked me to let you know that she loved her mom and sister. She also told me that she and Trevor were arguing and that he left her trapped in the car. When I came close to the accident spot, I saw him limping away from the crash scene. I tried to call him back, but he continued fleeing. I was going to go after him, but then I heard Claire's screams from the car, and I went to her immediately."

Crystal looked from Caleb to April, and said, "Caleb got her free from the wreckage, and applied a tourniquet to her leg. If it weren't for his quick action, Claire would be dead. As it is now, she has a fighting chance."

April could see by the blood on Caleb's clothing that he had tried his best to save her. "I want to thank you for saving my daughter's life. I don't know what would have happened if you hadn't turned up."

On hearing April thank him, Caleb couldn't help but feel emotional. A tear escaped from this left eye. Clearing his throat, he replied, "When I was there with her in the car, I looked into her eyes, and I knew that I had to save her. She looked so scared, but she wanted to fight to stay alive. I promised her that I would save her. She... she... had this love for her family, and all I could think about was to make sure that she saw you guys again."

Blake went up to Caleb, and gave him a hug, "Thank you for bringing my sister back to us," Blake's eyes were red from crying, and her tears were flowing freely as she thanked him.

Caleb's cell phone went off. It was his parents texting him that they had just pulled into the hospital parking lot. Caleb had called them after they got to the hospital, and informed them about what had happened. His dad said that he was going to pick his mom up from the diner and meet him at the hospital.

"My parents just arrived," he said, looking up from the phone. "Do you mind if I go get them? I told them what happened, and they wanted to come to see how I was doing."

"Of course," April said, as she gazed into Caleb's eyes. She knew that Caleb was the last person that Claire had seen, and was the sole reason why Claire was still alive.

Monica found them at the surgical waiting room, and April filled her in on what was going on. She wanted to stay with them to show her support for Claire. Caleb came back to the waiting area with his parents, and April told them what an outstanding son they had. Caleb's parents were very nice people, and they knew how special their son was. They sat there, comforting April and Blake to the best of their abilities. Rose, Shelly, Brie, and Emily soon arrived, and gave April and Blake teary hugs. The girls were in shock after learning what had happened, and were cursing Trevor for what he had done to her. April's parents arrived shortly after that, and they simply couldn't believe that Claire was now fighting for her life. Anne held her daughter tight in her arms as Joseph comforted Blake.

After several hours of waiting, the doctor finally came out to inform April about the situation. "Claire is out of surgery, but she is in critical condition. She lost over 65% of her blood. Our main concern is Claire's head injury. She has swelling in her brain, and is in a coma. We don't know for sure if she will wake up from it, so all we can do is wait. Time will tell if she will be able to pull through this." The doctor told April that he would keep her posted on her condition, and that the nurse would come out in a few minutes to bring April back to see Claire.

As the doctor turned to leave, April broke down crying. Claire was in a coma.

CHAPTER TWENTY-SIX

APRIL AND BLAKE WALKED INTO CLAIRE'S HOSPITAL ROOM and were horrified by what they saw. Claire was connected to several monitors, all of which were keeping track of several areas of her body. Her head was wrapped up in a bandage, and there was a piece of gauze that was taped on her cheek. Both of her eyes were black and blue. Claire's right leg and left arm were wrapped up. She looked like she was in bad shape.

"Mom," Blake's voice quivered as she gazed at her sister. "Oh God, mom, look at her."

April held Blake's hand, and the two of them stood there watching Claire.

"How could Trevor do this to her?" Blake asked viciously. "How could he?" she demanded.

Not taking her eyes off of Claire, April said, "I don't know, baby." April pulled the chairs close to Claire's bed. She sat down and carefully grabbed the hand that wasn't wrapped up in a bandage and held it. "Hi Claire," April said. "It's me, April. Blake is here too. We got your message from Caleb. We love you too. Do you hear me? We love you."

"We love you, Claire," Blake blurted out, trying to force the words into Claire's mind. "Please wake up," Blake insisted.

The two of them sat there, emotionally drained, hoping that Claire would wake up at any moment now. It was sometime around midnight when Mason walked into Claire's room.

"Oh, Mason," April got up, and wrapped her arms around him. "I'm so glad you're here," April said, beginning to tear up as she released him. Mason then hugged Blake and kissed her on her forehead. "I'm so sorry about Claire," Mason said to Blake, as he looked at Claire's motionless body lying on the bed. "Claire, sweetie. It's Mason. I'm here," he said. He stood there looking at the extent of Claire's injuries, and couldn't help but ask, "How could this have happened?"

April took his hand in hers, and said, "Trevor did this to her. He was on drugs, and he was drunk when they left the party." April paused as she explained. "When they crashed, he left her to die, Mason. How could he leave her?"

Mason didn't know how anyone could leave another person in such a way, especially if they loved that person. "I can't imagine what Claire must have felt knowing that he was leaving her there," Mason said, shaking his head.

The three of them sat in the room for another hour and Mason suggested that April and Blake could go lie down on the couch in the waiting room to get some rest. "I'll stay with her for a while," Mason said. "I'm still on California time, so I'm good for a while."

Reluctantly, knowing that Mason was right, April looked at her watch and then glanced up to check both Mason and Blake. "We'll be back in a couple of hours," she said, putting her arm around Blake to lead her to the door.

April and Blake left the room to lie down on the couches in the waiting room. Mason took a seat next to Claire, and started to speak to her. "Claire, I think it's time that we had a talk. Don't you?" he asked. Mason leaned back into the chair and crossed his legs. "I know that it is not a secret, but I love April. She is the best thing that has happened to me," Mason said, smiling at the thought of April. "With that being said, I want to confess that you and Blake are the second best things to have ever happened to me. You are a strong, beautiful young lady. I am so proud of the woman that you have become," he told her. Mason had planned on sharing how he felt with Claire at some point in the near future, but he figured he had to speak now.

"When Blake got sick, you stepped up and gave of yourself to be there for both her and April. Now, here comes the part that I really want you to know," Mason said, as if he was telling her a secret. "Had I had the opportunity to have a daughter of my own, I would have wanted her to be exactly like you."

Mason continued talking to Claire over the next couple of hours. He told her how he grew up and about his sister. He told her about his relationship with his dad, and about how he started his own business. He even told her about the movie that he saw on the plane flying to see her. He kept talking to her, hoping that she was hearing him.

The next day, Claire's room saw innumerable friends and family coming in to see her. April's parents had been at the hospital since she was brought in, and didn't want to leave. Brie, Rose, Shelly, and Emily took turns staying with Claire. At first, it was all four. Then it was Brie and Rose. Shelly and Emily played YouTube videos so that Claire could hear them. Crystal and Tripp sat in on her for a while.

Around late afternoon, April and Blake were in the room with Claire. Blake was sitting on the chair next to Claire, while April was standing at the foot of the bed. As she looked at Claire, April had a flashback of the past eight months. Scenes danced across April's memory as she remembered the day when she had first seen Claire holding the sign, and then when she had held Claire's hair back while she was throwing up due to the flu. April pictured Claire's face when she had brushed her hair for the first time. April smiled as she remembered taking selfies with Claire when she had first got her phone, and when Claire had walked down the staircase wearing the family's pearl necklace. April actually grinned when she remembered the whole Thanksgiving Day pancake batter incident.

"You can't go yet," April said aloud to Claire. "We've got a lifetime of memories yet to make. Do you hear me?"

Blake looked up as her mother spoke. "What mom?" Blake didn't hear the first part of what her mom had said.

"She can't go yet," said April to Blake. I was remembering all the special moments that I have shared with her, and I want to make more of them. She has been such a huge part of our lives. I'm not ready to let that go."

"Me neither, mom," Blake agreed. "I mean, we just found out that we were sisters, and we haven't spent enough time being sisters to each other."

Blake picked up the bottom of her shirt to reveal the area around her belly button. Her suntanned tattoo was still imprinted on her. "See mom, it's still there. I love my sister," Blake said, as she rubbed her belly where the suntan was.

There was a knock on the door. Caleb slowly cracked open the door a bit. "Caleb," April said, as she saw who it was. "Please, come on in." Caleb stepped into the room and gazed at Claire. "I just wanted to stop by to see how she was doing." April told Caleb that she was in a coma due to the head injury, and that the doctors were unsure if she would wake up.

Caleb didn't want to believe that the girl, whom he had fought so valiantly to save, might still die. "Can I talk to her?" Caleb asked April.

"Of course," April answered. "The doctors say that it might help to have people around talking to her. They don't know if she is able to hear us, but sometimes the patients who recover say that they got a sense that their loved ones were present."

Caleb stepped closer to Claire, and knelt down by her bedside. "Hi, Claire, it's me, Caleb. I'm the one that promised you that I would tell April and Blake that you love them. Remember? Well, I did it. I told them and they told me to tell you that they love you too." Caleb looked up from Claire and gave April and Blake a quick smile. Turning his attention back to Claire, he said, "But here's the thing, Claire. I also said that I was going to save you, and I have kept my end of the deal. Now it's your turn to promise me something. You need to promise me that you are going to wake up. Ok?" A tear had escaped from Caleb's right eye as he spoke. "I want you to fight. Do you understand?

The girl that I saw hanging upside down in that car is a fighter. So fight to come back." Caleb finished what he wanted to say, but continued to gaze at Claire. He couldn't take his eyes off of her. He didn't know her, but could feel that she was someone very special and wanted to get to know her.

He finally got up and stepped away from her.

"That was very touching," April told Caleb graciously. "I'm sure that she is fighting as hard as she can. Claire has been through a lot in her life, and I have never met anyone as resilient as the girl in that bed right there," April said as she pointed at her. "Her courage and compassion have amazed me from the first day that she entered our lives."

Caleb smiled at April, and asked if he could come back tomorrow to see her. "Of course you can. I think that she needs many people telling her that she is loved, and that we want her back."

"Thank you, Mrs. Turner, for allowing me to see her," Caleb said. As he was about to leave the room, he said, "Please keep me posted if her condition changes."

"We will," said April, as she went up to him. "Thank you again, for what you did for her," April said as she hugged him. As Caleb left the hospital and started his drive home, the only thing that he could think about was how much he wanted to talk to Claire again.

* *

"HAPPY BIRTHDAY, CLAIRE," BLAKE SAID TO CLAIRE, AS SHE still lay motionless in her hospital bed. It was July 10 —Claire's 17th birthday. The room was filled with Claire's family and friends. Blake was holding a small birthday cake with seventeen candles on it. Spelled out in pink icing on white buttercream frosting, were the words, "We love you, Claire!"

"Make a wish," Blake told Claire as she blew out her candles for her. Tears started to flow from Blake's eyes as she removed the cake from Claire's unseeing eyes. The gifts were stacked up in the corner of the room. April had made the decision to allow everyone to bring the gifts with them so that Claire could sense that they were holding a party for her.

Shelly had her phone out playing some of Claire's favorite music. Rose and Brie were sitting next to Claire describing the scene that was happening in her room, and how everyone was there. Emily had placed a banner above the door and in Claire's direct line of sight that said, "Happy Birthday!"

As April looked around the room, she thought to herself how Claire's birthday was supposed to be the best day of her life, and now it was filled with tragedy. Grief began to swell inside her, and she had to leave the room for a few minutes. She told Blake that she would be right back, and then quickly exited the room. She only got a few steps away when she couldn't hold it in any longer and broke down crying. April walked down the hall aimlessly, without any particular destination in mind. Not only was she grieving for what had happened to Claire, April was also extremely angry.

April followed a hallway and then turned the corner. Tears were pouring out of her eyes, as she sobbed uncontrollably. She was about halfway down the hall when she noticed the chapel was two doors away from her.

April wiped the tears from her eyes angrily, and marched into the chapel. Fortunately for her, it was void of any worship seekers. "Why!" April exclaimed, as she paced towards the front by the pulpit. "Why Claire!" She stared at the cross that was hanging from the wall in front of her.

"I begged you to save Blake and you did. Please do the same for Claire!" April begged, yelling at the cross. "Don't take her away from me," April put her hands in her face and continued to cry. She thought that she heard someone enter the chapel, but she didn't care. As April lifted her head, she became aware of the heart shaped locket that Claire had given her for Christmas. She opened it up to gaze upon the two girls pictured inside.

A dark thought occurred to April, and she began to yell, "So you saved Blake, but now you want Claire in return. Is that how it works?" April asked, wanting to know. "You took Nick away from me and now you want his daughter too?" April stood there, waiting for the cross to answer. She closed the locket and gently lowered it down, allowing it to hang freely from the chain.

"I don't think that it works that way," a voice resounded behind her. April spun around to see that Mason had followed her into the chapel.

"Mason," April said, as she went up to him and just about collapsed in his arms. "Why does He have to take the ones I love from me?" April was distraught with sorrow and bitterness.

Mason took April's hands and sat her down next to him in the first pew. "There is something that I want to tell you, and I think that it may help."

April looked into Mason's eyes, and she could tell that what he was about to say was important to him. Mason let a sigh escape as he began. "Do you remember when I told you that I lost my father when I was 20 years old?" April nodded, remembering that when they had first met, he had spoken about losing his parents in close succession.

"Well, I didn't tell you *how* he died," Mason said. "When I was fifteen years old, my dad was diagnosed with ALS." A small gasp escaped April's mouth, but she allowed Mason to continue.

"You see, my dad was a proud man. He worked for a financial firm and was well known throughout the community. Even though he loved my sister and me, he was too busy to really show his affection to us. He would often miss our sporting events or would arrive late on special days, like our birthdays and award ceremonies. When I was little, I got a kite for my birthday and asked him on several different occasions to help me put it together and fly it with me. He kept promising that he would make time, but he never did. I eventually built it myself and spent the day alone in the park flying it." Mason paused to clear his throat. "So, you can imagine the despair and frustration that he felt that fate had dealt him that particular disease. He went from a 5'10", 190 lbs. powerhouse of a man to one that weighed only about 120 lbs. who couldn't even speak," Mason said, wiping tears from this eyes, as the memory cut through him like a knife.

"You see, ALS takes almost everything from a person. It takes their ability to move. It takes their ability to eat. It even takes a person's ability to speak.

Unfortunately, it leaves the mind completely alone. It doesn't touch it. So, you are trapped in a useless husk of a body, with your brain as sharp as a tack."

Mason paused to let what he was saying sink in.

"The first couple of years were rough. My dad knew that there was no cure, and that he had to accept that he was soon going to die in a horrible manner. My family wasn't very religious at the time, but we did believe in God. In spite of that, I blamed God for giving my dad ALS, and wanted nothing to do with Him. But, after the first year, something amazing happened. My dad sat me down and taught me how to play chess. Even though his hands were shaky at the time, we spent countless hours sitting across from each other, playing match after match. We also began to engage each other in meaningful conversations. In fact, it was during one of those conversations that he told me that when I got older and wanted to marry, that it was ok not to have any biological children of my own. Knowing that I would be unable to ever produce children, he told me that being a father was more than just reproducing biologically. He said that if I should ever marry and wanted to adopt, that it wouldn't matter if the child was biologically someone else's, that as long as I loved them as my own and looked after them, that was all that mattered."

April was engrossed in Mason's testimony, and her heart was breaking for what he had had to endure as a teenager.

"As sad as it was to see my father's body decay as the disease progressed, I was thrilled with the time that we were spending together. The day I turned sixteen, he was there when I got my driver's license. In fact, we had the clerk redo my picture several times just so that my license reflected the perfect expression on my face. Afterwards, I actually got to drive him around town in my mom's convertible. On the day of my graduation from high school, he was there as I walked across the stage. Of course, he was in a wheelchair and could hardly move, but he got to see his only son receive his high school diploma."

Mason raised April's hands and then put them together, using both his hands to cover hers.

"Weeks before my dad passed away, he communicated to me by using letters on a chalkboard. As I would go over the entire alphabet with a pointer, he would nod when the pointer was over the letter that he wanted. It was almost as if we were playing hangman. One of the last things that my father spelled out to me was, 'There is nothing left unsaid.'"

Mason's voice wavered as he said those words. "I knew in that moment that my dad loved me, and had enjoyed every minute of the last four years of his life that he had spent with his family. There was nothing more to say, because through our talks and discussions, he had revealed everything that he had ever wanted to convey. We knew that he loved us, and he was well aware of our love for him."

Mason blinked away more tears as he tried to focus his eyes on April's.

"On the day he died, the entire family was present in the bedroom with him. We were all talking about his life, and what a great man he was. At one point in the conversation, everyone became quiet, and my sister and I just happened to look at my dad's face. We witnessed him take his last breathe, and with a smile on his lips, he was gone. As my sister and I sat there sobbing, a red cardinal appeared in the window of the bedroom. It was sitting there looking at us as if it knew that our dad had just journeyed to Heaven. To this day, my sister swears that when something life-changing happens, sometimes, she catches a glimpse of a cardinal.

Mason was gazing deep into April's eyes. April then remembered seeing a red cardinal on the night of Claire's car crash. Was Mason's dad there, signaling the tragedy? Or was it there to say that it was going to watch over her? Or was it just a coincidence?

"Oh, Mason," April sobbed at the thought of his dad suffering like he had. She didn't know what was worse? To lose someone you love quickly, in a car crash, or watching them waste away before your eyes. "I am so sorry about your father." She leaned over and kissed him on the lips and put her arms around his neck.

Mason allowed her to hold him for several moments, and then slowly removed himself from her grasp. He looked into her eyes, and said, "So, even though it seems like God is just taking from us, He is actually giving us what we need. I don't think that my dad and I would have ever been that close, if he hadn't gotten ALS. Now, I'm not saying that I am glad that he died or had to suffer, but the time that we spent together during his illness, I wouldn't trade it for the world. Unfortunately, I don't know the reason why Claire was in that accident, and maybe I will never know, but I believe in my heart that He does love us and will give us only what He knows we can handle. Maybe, just maybe, he has a plan for her?"

April was saddened with the thought of what Mason had had to endure as a child. She was sad that Claire was clinging onto life at this very moment, but she was happy that Mason had entered her life.

"I love you so much," April smiled through tears, as she kissed him repeatedly. "I don't know how I could handle all of this if it weren't for you," April said honestly. "You've been here to support me through it all. I need you in my life, Mason."

Mason knew in that moment that he wanted to spend the rest of his life with her.

"I love you too," he said, as he wrapped his arms around her and stood there, in front of the cross, thanking God for putting April in his life.

Brie had stayed at the hospital after Claire's birthday party, sitting in the waiting room, reading a book. After a couple of hours, she decided to go in and talk to Claire again.

As she entered the room, she realized that Claire was alone, and that everyone else had either gone home or was getting something to eat.

Brie walked up to Claire and carefully pulled back a strand of blonde hair that had fallen down across her forehead. "Claire, it's me—Brie," she said, as she pulled over the chair so that it was touching the bed. "I want to say a few things, now that we have some alone time." Brie pulled back her own hair, and began playing with the tips.

"Do you remember your first day of school?" Brie asked with a smirk. "I was so indifferent to you." Brie stopped playing with her hair because she wanted to be serious as she spoke. "I was so jealous of you and the way that Trevor was looking at you," Brie's eyes closed at the mere mention of his name.

"Then, I set up that stupid poster board and caused you so much pain," she said. Tears were welling up in her eyes, as she recalled how mean she had been to Claire. "But you stuck up for yourself. You put me in my place in front of the entire school," Brie said, grinning at the memory of Claire's tenacity that day in the lunchroom. "And yet, when it came to me being kicked out of the cheerleading team, you went to bat for me. You knew how much it meant to me, and even though I treated you like a piece of trash, you still showed me compassion and kindness."

Brie got out of her seat and sat on her knees so that she was just inches away from Claire's ear. "God, when Russell tore my dress and fell on me, you didn't hesitate, you came running up to protect me—me—of all people." Brie's voice was almost a loud whisper as her emotions swelled up inside of her.

"As I turned to walk away in humiliation, you embraced me as a friend— someone who was worthy of forgiveness," Brie continued. A few of her tears were now dripping from her face onto Claire's cheek.

"You became my best friend, Claire. Do you hear me? You're my best friend, and I owe you everything. I am a better person today because of you," Brie said, as she slowly stood up from her knees, and used her sleeve to carefully wipe her tears from Claire's face.

"As your best friend, I am begging you to come back to us," Brie pleaded with heartfelt emotion. "The world is a better place with you in it. So you better wake up soon."

Brie continued to sit with Claire for several more minutes before she decided to leave. "Happy birthday, Claire," she said one final time, before she left the room to go home for the night.

* *

"CHECKMATE," MASON SAID TO BLAKE, AS SHE MOVED HIS rook in a direct line with Blake's king.

Blake gave Mason an annoyed look and, said, "Seriously?" Blake's eyes swept the board one final time to see if there was any possible way out. Of course, there wasn't so she knocked down her king as a sign of surrender.

"How did you get so good at chess, anyways?" Blake asked, as she started to put the pieces back into her wooden box.

Mason grinned at the memory of his dad, and replied, "A lot of practice."

They had pulled two chairs together and were using the arms of both chairs as a makeshift table for the chessboard. Claire was beside them, still unconscious. It was now July 15—a week or so since the accident. The black and blue of Claire's eyes was slowly fading and about half of the color was turning yellow as it healed. The doctors still could not give April and Blake any definite answers as to when or if Claire would wake up. April had brought in several picture frames and set them out throughout the room. The picture of April brushing her hair as well as the folded picture of Mel and Nick that her mother had given her was among the frames.

April was sitting on a chair next to Claire on the opposite side reading to her from one of the books that Claire had wanted to read that was in April's personal library. In fact, April had spent countless hours in that very chair, reading passages from some of Claire's favorite books.

April had just finished a chapter and closed the book when Caleb stopped by. He had been dropping by every day since the second day of her accident. He would usually only stay for about half an hour, and tell her about his day and how nice it was outside. But today, he came into Claire's room carrying a guitar case.

Mason got up from the chair that he was sitting in, and stepped to the other side of the bed, standing next to April. Blake had just put the chessboard away and was seated in the chair next to Claire.

As Caleb unbuckled the guitar locks from the case, he asked April, "Do you mind if I sing her a song?"

April smiled at Caleb, and replied, "Please, I think that it would be wonderful."

Caleb removed the instrument from the case and sat down in the chair that Mason had just got up from.

"I am just learning to play, so please bear with me," Caleb politely warned Claire's family. "I only know this one song because I played it at my parents' 25th wedding anniversary party. It was one of the first songs that they danced to as a married couple. I thought that it would be appropriate for this situation."

Caleb spent a few moments tuning his guitar, and then after clearing his throat, began to play. The song was *How Do You Talk To An Angel* by a group called The Heights. As Caleb began to sing the words to the song, Mason put his hands on April's shoulders and the two of them became lost in the world of music. Caleb sang as if he were telling Claire how he felt through the words of the song. The first verse had words that he wanted Claire to hear: *"I see her voice inside my mind, I know her face by heart, Heaven and earth are moving.... In my soul... And I don't know where to start. Tell me the words to define, the way I feel about someone so fine."* And then the chorus followed: *"How do you talk to an angel? How do you hold her close to where you are? How do you talk to an angel? It's like trying to catch a falling star."*

Caleb sang the entire song, and when he was finished, he paused to look into Claire's eyes. He so wanted her to wake up so that he could tell her that she was like an angel that had crashed into his life over a week ago. He couldn't stop thinking about her.

"That was amazing," Blake told Caleb after he finished, "Claire would love it."

Caleb sat there with the guitar resting on his lap as he turned to address Blake, "Your sister seemed like an angel to me that day. I knew the moment that I spoke to her that she was someone very special." He looked down at the guitar in his hands, and confessed, "I am hoping that she will hear the words and come back, you know?"

Mason walked up to Caleb, and shook his hand, "It's a beautiful gesture, and I think that you should sing that song to her every day. She might just hear it and want to see who is singing to her."

Caleb nodded his head, and then said, "I would love to." Caleb ended up staying for over an hour, and Mason said that he was going to take Caleb down to buy him a cup of coffee in the cafeteria, and would take that time to get to know him better.

April knew that Mason knew Caleb had fallen for Claire. She just hoped that Caleb would get the chance to get to know her.

Another week went by, and it was now the evening of July 22. Caleb had visited Claire every day, and had sung that same song to her. Most days, he sang it over and over until his voice was hoarse from singing it. April and Blake were worn out, physically and emotionally. Because neither one of them could sleep well, they both looked exhausted and fatigued. Claire's brain activity remained the same, and the doctors were trying to be optimistic, but the reality of Claire's prolonged comatose state did little to fuel the supply of hope.

"I'm going to go and get us something to drink. Do you want a pop or coffee?" April asked Blake as she took out her wallet from her purse. Blake looked up from her iPad and she took several seconds deciding what she felt like to drink. "Coffee, I think," Blake answered indecisively. "You sure?" April asked again, noticing how rundown Blake looked.

"Yeah, coffee," Blake said, committing to her choice. "I think that I need the caffeine," Blake said as she tried to suppress a yawn. "You got it," April said as she left the room.

Blake turned her attention back to her iPad, and to the dress that she had been working on. It was a dress that she had begun to design for Claire when she was in the hospital recovering from leukemia. It was actually a wedding dress. Claire had challenged her when Blake had wanted to give up, and told her that she wanted her to design it for her. Blake had originally thought that it would be

Trevor marrying Claire, but in light of recent events, it was obvious the groom would be someone else. Over the past couple of weeks, Blake had spent more time on it, so that when Claire woke up, she could see the finished product.

Blake used her stylus on the display to fill in a spot that she wanted to highlight, and then she stood up and showed Claire the screen.

"What do you think about this?" Blake questioned her motionless sister. *What if she never sees this?* Blake thought to herself. As Blake looked at Claire's closed eyes, she set the iPad down and began talking to her.

"This isn't fair, Claire," Blake began as the thought of her never waking up again filled her mind. "When I was sick and close to death, you came along and gave me your marrow. You saved my life!" Blake grabbed Claire's hand and slightly squeezed it. "But there is absolutely nothing that I can do to save you, Claire Bear. I can't give you anything of mine to help. I can't give you my kidney, I can't give you blood, there is nothing that I have that will help you," Blake said, frustrated with her inability to help.

"But, there is something that I can say that might make you return to me," Blake suggested as she placed her hand on Claire's heart.

"Remember when I said that you were my 16-year-old, blonde, blue-eyed purpose? Well, your purpose wasn't only to be my bone marrow donor, at least not entirely. Your purpose is to be my sister. We need to spend more years together as sisters. Do you hear me? I need my big sister back," Blake said, as she gently placed her forehead on Claire's. "Please come back to me, I miss you."

April came in through the door and saw Blake put her forehead on Claire's. She heard Blake tell Claire to come back to her. April set the coffees down on the table next to Claire's bed and hugged Blake. "I miss her, too," she said.

Blake put her arm around her mom as the two of them stood next to Claire and looked at her for several moments. Blake reached for her coffee and took a sip from the cup as she faced her sister "I really miss you."

* *

CLAIRE COULD FEEL HERSELF SLIPPING AWAY. SHE TRIED TO hang on, but was too weak to mount any kind of serious effort. As the darkness closed in, Claire's last image was of Caleb yelling at her to hold on.

The pain vanished as the darkness engulfed Claire. She felt as if she was floating in the blackness of space with no direction or purpose. Despite not knowing what was happening, Claire felt at peace. Off in the distance was a glimmer of light pulsing as if it had a heartbeat. It was growing in intensity and size as it approached her. Claire raised her hands to try to block it as it overtook her.

Suddenly, Claire was standing on a sidewalk in front of a house. It took her eyes several moments to adjust to the bright light. As she looked at that yard in front of the house, Claire recognized where she was. Claire was standing in front of the house where she had lived when she was a little girl in Seattle.

Claire looked around and noticed that a couple was walking hand and hand towards Claire on the same sidewalk. The couple was about a block away, but even from that distance, Claire could tell that they were happy. The woman was giggling at something that the man had just said, and it was clear to Claire that they were in love. They stopped in front of a rose garden, and the man picked a flower for the woman. She accepted it with a smile and then gave him a kiss.

As they got closer, Claire recognized the woman as she focused on her face.

"Oh my God, mom? Is that you?" Claire yelled in the direction of the couple.

Mel looked directly at Claire, and said with a loving smile, "Yes, my darling. It's me."

Walking with her mother was Nick Turner. As they approached, Nick released Mel's hand and held out his arms to Claire. "Claire, it's me, Nick," he said, pausing to give Claire a welcoming smile, and then added, "your father."

"Dad," Claire smiled and wrapped herself up in his arms. Even though she had seen pictures of him, she had never heard his voice before.

"Claire, my amazing daughter." Nick smiled. "I've waited for this day for a long time." He kissed her on her forehead and gazed upon her body. "You are so beautiful," Nick noted with pride.

Claire couldn't believe that she was with her mom and dad. Both of them looked as if they had just walked out from the picture that Claire had discovered hidden in the picture frame. Nick was young and very handsome while her mother was absolutely gorgeous. This was the best version of her that Claire had ever seen. "You are amazing, too," Claire said to Nick.

Nick took Claire's hand, and Mel took her other hand as they started slowly walking down the sidewalk. Nick looked at Mel, and she nodded her head as if to say, 'it's ok,' and then he said to Claire, "Honey, I know that your mother told you how she never told me that she was pregnant with you. Even though I didn't' get the chance to get to know you while you were growing up, I want you to know that I love you and would have cherished every moment of your childhood."

Claire had this feeling of contentment wash over her. She was happy that her dad loved her and that he was Blake's dad.

"Dad," Claire began, "I want you to know that it's ok, because then you wouldn't have left to go to Chicago and met April, and then you wouldn't have had Blake."

Nick grinned at the mention of April and Blake. He had guided them to her, and knew that they would find love in each other.

Claire kept going, "And by the way, Blake is so wonderful. She is the best sister that I could have ever wished for." Then as Claire thought about April, she said, "April is amazing too. She took me in and welcomed me into her home. She took care of me and treated me with compassion and respect. I love her too." She looked at her mom, smiled, and said, "She loved me when you weren't able to." Mel stopped walking and turned Claire towards her. "April did a wonderful job, and I want you to know that I am so glad that she was there for you." Mel gave Claire a hug and said, "I love you so much, sweetie."

Claire hugged her mom back and said, "I love you too, mom."

The three of them were now walking towards the park that was across the street. It was a beautiful day, and there was virtually no wind. It was the perfect temperature and everything looked as if it was in HD. Colors were exploding from everything, and Claire felt like she was walking inside a painting.

Nick and Mel guided Claire down a path and into the park. As they walked, Nick told Claire stories about the time that he and Mel had dated. He explained to her how much he had cared for and loved her. As they walked around the bend, Mel saw an ice cream stand. "Come on, honey, let's get an ice cream cone," she said, as she excitedly pulled Claire behind her. Nick had to run to keep up. The gentleman behind the kiosk smiled, almost as if he was expecting them, and before Mel could say what she wanted, he handed them each a cone that was already prepared.

"This is so delicious," Claire smiled, as she consumed the frozen treat. It tasted better than any ice cream that she had ever had before.

The three of them continued to walk the path through the park and came upon a playground. Mel and Claire walked up to the swing set and sat in the seats. Nick walked up behind them and started to push them one at a time. Mel was giggling, and she smiled as Nick pushed her higher and higher. She looked over at Claire, and Claire realized that her mom was having just as much fun as she was.

Once they were done swinging, Nick took them over to the merry-go-round, and began spinning them round and around, faster and faster they went. Claire and Mel's hair was flowing in the wind as they spun in circles. Nick grabbed onto one of the poles, and the merry-go-round quickly slowed its momentum. Both Mel and Claire were dizzy and could hardly walk. Mel tried to use her daughter as support as they walked, but they both ended up in a pile on the soft, green grass.

Nick reached down and gently picked them up. Once they recovered from being dizzy, they continued their trek through the park.

It felt like they were in the park for hours. Claire and her parents spent the entire day enjoying every aspect of the park. Nick found a couple of soccer balls and the three of them took turns shooting shots towards the net. After scoring several times on her dad, Claire ran across the soccer field with her hands high in the air, celebrating her victory. They left the soccer field and proceeded down the path. Several minutes went by and a man walked up to Nick and offered him a kite. He then held out his hand for Nick to shake, as he introduced himself. Claire couldn't catch the name, but Nick grinned admiringly, and patted the man on the shoulder. The man was wearing khaki pants and a white polo shirt. There was an embroidered patch below his left shoulder of the symbol that Mason had on his backpack. The man and Nick were engaged in a conversation about how the man wished that he could have spent more time with his son and daughter when they were younger. He had never made time to take his children to the park and just play.

The man gave Mel and Claire a wave as he departed. Nick and Claire spent the next couple of minutes building the kite. While Nick held the kite high above his head, Claire, with the string grasped firmly in her hands, started running towards the open field. The kite majestically gained altitude as Claire ran faster and faster. Mel and Nick held hands as they watched their daughter guide the kite in whatever direction she wanted. Eventually, the kite was so high in the air that Claire thought that it looked like a bird flying high in the sky.

While Claire was in the middle of the field, with her kite high in the air, her peripheral vision captured a tiny flash of light. She looked over to her right and noticed a young woman, about fifty yards away, standing on top of a hill. The woman looked to be in her early twenties, and had beautiful, shiny, red hair that went down just below her shoulders. She was wearing a green dress that was low cut, about six inches above the knee, with opaque nylons and short black boots, with a small heel and a pattern of rhinestones at the tip of the toe to add a hint of glimmer. She was also wearing a lightweight, black leather jacket with a scarf that had a red, black, white, and green checkered pattern throughout it. As Claire gazed at her, she saw that the woman was holding out her arms, with her palms up and her fingers slightly curled up, as she was holding something in each hand. The woman's bright, sparkling green eyes focused on Claire and for a moment, and seemed surprised to see her. But, almost instantly, the surprised look changed to one of joy, and she smiled. Claire didn't know who she was, but couldn't help but to smile back at her. Claire wanted to wave, but she was holding the kite with both hands. Claire turned her attention from the woman to the kite for a moment so that she could reposition her hands, but when she turned back, the woman had disappeared.

Claire continued flying the kite for several more minutes, hoping to see the woman again, but she didn't return. After the kite had returned to solid ground, Claire walked back to her parents. Because it was getting late, the trio left the field and started walking back the way that they had come.

As they left the park, Mel and Nick were walking with Claire hand and hand again. They guided her towards the house where she grew up. Nick had a look of such joy about him. Claire gazed over at her mom, and for the first time, she was at peace. The way that she looked at Nick with such affection and warmth, made Claire's heart fill with zeal. With a parent holding each of her hands, Claire walked towards the front door.

Nick stopped them just before the door. He looked over at Claire, and said to her. "I love you so much, and I can't wait to start this next chapter with you." Mel looked at her daughter, and said, "I love you with all my heart, sweetie."

Claire looked up to her dad, and said, "I love you too, dad." And then, to her mom, she said, "I love you, mom."

The door to the house opened by itself allowing the bright light within to spill out onto the porch. An overwhelming sense of love and family poured around Claire's body. She knew that there was unbelievable love and peace just inside those doors.

As Nick led Claire through the threshold and into the light, he asked his daughter if she was ready to come home.

* *

BLAKE AWOKE WITH A START. IT WAS AROUND MIDNIGHT, and the room's lights were dimmed. Blake picked up her head from the chair and saw that her mother was asleep in the chair next to her. Unfortunately, Claire's condition seemed unchanged, as Blake stood up and gazed at her sister.

Blake stretched her arms in the air, trying to loosen her limbs from the awkward position that they had been in when she had fallen asleep. Suddenly, all the monitors and devices surrounding Claire's bed turned off. It was as if someone had cut the power lines.

At first, Blake thought that the hospital had lost power, but the dimmed overhead lights were still on.

"Mom?" Blake quickly nudged April to wake her up, and said, "Mom, the power went out."

April's eyes sprang open, her heart beating faster as she was jolted from her slumber.

"What?" April asked, her eyes trying to focus on her surroundings. "What's going on?"

Blake pointed at the powerless equipment at Claire's bedside, and exclaimed, "Everything just turned off, mom. It's as if someone pulled the plug." Confusion and concern filling her voice,

April looked at Claire, who was still motionless, and then back at the monitors. After a few seconds of continued silence from the equipment, April swiftly reached for the nurse call button and pressed it firmly. As the nurse raced into the room, the power was suddenly restored, and all the monitors and computers turned on at once. Immediately, the sound of alarms filled the room as the software rebooted to an unplanned shutdown.

Blake grabbed Claire's hand to hold it as more alarms continued to sound. Tears began to well in Blake's eyes as the nurses rushed into the room. *No, God, please don't take her.* Blake pleaded in her mind, *not now.*

Suddenly, Blake felt Claire squeeze her hand.

"Mom!" Blake yelled, as Claire's squeezed more tightly. April could see that Claire's hand was moving and looked at Blake.

"Claire!" Blake exclaimed. "Can you hear me?" Both April and Blake were looking at Claire's face when her eyes fluttered open. Claire didn't know where she was or what the sound of sirens meant, but she could see that April and Blake were standing before her.

"Blake?" Claire asked, confused by what was happening.

"Claire!" Blake yelled again. "Can you hear me?" Blake asked, as Claire tried to focus on Blake's face. "Yes," Claire said, slowly licking her dry lips, "I can hear you."

Blake began to sob joyous tears. Claire slowly turned her head from Blake to April. "April?"

"Yes, honey, it's me," April said, as she started to cry. "Oh my God, Claire, you're back!"

Claire didn't know what was happening, but she knew that something bad must have happened.

"Where am I?" Claire asked, as she examined the room that she was in. The nurse had turned off the alarms, and was checking her vitals as she spoke. One of the nurses paged the doctor the second that Claire had awakened.

Blake was still holding her hand, as she answered, "You were in a bad car accident. Do you remember?"

Claire stared at Blake as she tried to think. Her head was pounding and her body was radiating with pain from just about everywhere. "I was at the party," Claire began, as she partially remembered. "We were at Jordan's house," Claire grimaced as she tried to move her left arm and realized that it was bandaged up. She looked at the bandages as if someone had placed them there as a joke, because she didn't know why the arm was wrapped up.

"It began to rain," Claire muttered, as she had visions of running to the car. "We, we, I mean, he..." Claire's voice trailed off as she desperately tried to recall that memory. "There was thunder and lightning," Claire continued, trying to piece together what had happened.

"He was, yelling?" Claire asked herself, as if she could question her own thoughts to reveal the memories.

"Trevor was yelling at you?" April questioned softly.

Claire blinked as the horrible memory of Trevor came flooding back to her. Tears from Claire's eyes began to moisten her cheeks as she replayed the scene in her mind.

"He had been drinking. I didn't know it until he had already started driving." Then as Claire remembered what Trevor had been so out of control about, she put her good hand up to her eyes to cover them. Claire sobbed, "He was mad that I wouldn't have sex with him. He was so filled with rage."

April's heart filled with anguish as Claire recounted Trevor's treachery.

"He... was so mean to me," Claire whispered, as she remembered how scared she was of him.

Claire paused to blink away the tears that were filling up in her eyes. Her eyes turned more defiant as she continued to recount Trevor's actions. Claire was extremely weak, but the sound of her voice and the memory of her testimony gave her the strength to continue.

"I tried to make him pull over, but he just went faster. The rain was coming down so hard and it was difficult to see. He wouldn't stop the car!" Claire screamed through clenched teeth, trying to breathe, as it played back in her mind.

"Then Owen," Claire looked confused, as she said that name. She couldn't remember why it was important, but she suspected that Owen was the key to what had happened.

Claire's eyes flickered back and forth as she desperately searched her memory. "Owen... He... He called Trevor," Claire remembered abruptly. "Oh shit... He... and Trevor..." Claire croaked as the soreness in her throat threatened to silence her voice.

The nurse left the room to get a cup of water. She handed it to Claire and she took a few sips from the straw and it looked like it was difficult for her to swallow.

Claire looked up and squinted at the ceiling lights, trying to focus. Then, as if she was watching a YouTube video, the traumatic scenes of the crash filled her mind.

"No. No. Stop!" Claire screamed, as her eyes widened in horror. "We crashed, Trevor lost control of the car and landed in a ditch," Claire reached up with her good hand to feel the side of her head. "My head," she muttered, as she caressed her fingers over the texture of the bandages.

"I thought that I was going to die," Claire sobbed, as the severity of the accident overwhelmed her. April and Blake continued to look at her as Claire spoke. "He left me," Claire cried out as she remembered the fact that Trevor had walked away. "He left me there!" Claire gazed into April's eyes. "How could he do that to me? I thought he loved me!"

"I'm so sorry this happened to you, Claire," April said, trying to console her. She told Claire how he was picked up by the police shortly after, and how he was in some serious trouble.

"Where's Caleb?" Claire suddenly wondered, as the image of her rescuer popped into her mind. "He saved me, April."

April grinned at the mention of his name, and told Claire, "He's been stopping in to see how you were doing."

Claire remembered her last thoughts before she lost consciousness. "Did he tell you that I love you?" Claire wanted to know.

"Yes," April answered, as the memory of that washed over her. "Yes, he did," April's tears glistened on her face. "He made sure that we got the message."

Blake put her head down to Claire's ear and whispered in a low voice, "We love you too, Claire Bear." A couple of Blake's tears fell from her face and onto Claire's ear. "I have missed my sister!" Blake exclaimed, her voice filled with joy now that Claire was awake.

At that point, Dr. Powell came rushing in, and immediately went to Claire. "Hi Claire, I'm Dr. Powell, and I am the doctor overseeing your case," she said. As she looked into Claire's eyes with a tiny flashlight, she asked, "Can you tell me where you are?"

Claire had turned her attention to Dr. Powell when she came up next to her bed. "I'm in a hospital," Claire answered.

"Yes, you are. Can you tell me what happened to you?" Dr. Powell asked as she continued to examine Claire intently. "I was in a car crash," Claire admitted. "I... I... was hurt."

"Yes you were, sweetie," Dr. Powel said as she concentrated on a monitor that was to the right of Claire's bed.

"Do you know your name?" Dr. Powell asked.

"It's Claire," she answered without hesitation.

Dr. Powell pointed at April and Blake and asked, "Do you know who they are?"

Claire smiled as she answered, "Yes, April and Blake." Claire paused for a moment and added, "They're my family."

Blake joyously declared, "She is my sister! Claire is my big sister!"

Dr. Powell asked Claire several more questions, and was very satisfied with her responses. Before she left the room, she pulled April aside, and said, "It is a miracle that she appears to have her mental faculties about her. We are going to run a series of tests to see what kind of damage is lingering within the brain," Dr. Powell said.

"What do you mean?" April asked, feeling concerned about Claire.

"I just mean that there may be some things that are unknown at this point until I can see the results of her tests. She may have to learn how to walk again. Her arm and shoulder suffered severe damage as well as her leg," Dr. Powell said, as she listed the litany of damage that Claire had sustained. "She had massive internal bleeding so we have to keep an eye on her blood work to make sure everything is performing as well as we like."

Dr. Powell smiled, and then said, "It's going to be a lot of work for her, but at least she is here to go through it."

"Thank you so much, Doctor," April said appreciatively, as she looked at Claire. "I can't imagine what would have happened if she hadn't made it."

As Dr. Powell left the room, she asked one of the nurses to call the field tech on duty and ascertain the reason for the unexplained phenomenon that had caused only the equipment in Claire's room to lose all power.

April turned her attention back to Blake and Claire. April now realized that the road to recovery for Claire was more than likely to be long and filled with pain, but as she looked at both of her daughters, April couldn't worry about that now—at least Claire was alive. Blake couldn't stop telling Claire how glad she was that she had come back to her.

As Claire listened to Blake, she started wondering about her situation. Looking at April, she asked, "How long was I unconscious?"

CHAPTER TWENTY-SEVEN

APRIL AND BLAKE STAYED UP MOST OF THAT FIRST NIGHT, making calls to let friends and family know that Claire had woken up from her coma. April's parents told her that they would be down first thing in the morning to see her, and Mason said he was going to take a quick shower and would then go over to be with her.

By mid-morning, Claire's friends and family poured into the hospital as though she were a celebrity. Anne and Joseph came in, overjoyed that Claire had come back. They too had been through an emotional roller-coaster with Blake's leukemia and Claire's accident. Anne embraced April, and told her that she would be there to help them get through Claire's rehabilitation.

Around 9:30 a.m., a doctor and a nurse took Claire down to get a CAT scan, MRI, and some X-rays of her injuries. The doctor indicated to April and Blake that they would be gone for at least an hour, and if they wanted to go get breakfast, it might be a good time to do so since Claire would be occupied for a while.

Mason, April and Blake headed down to the cafeteria. Blake and April looked utterly exhausted as they sat down, but the adrenaline from when Claire had woken up, had been flowing through their veins all night. The feeling of relief had trumped the fatigue that had consumed their entire being over the past three weeks.

April took a sip of coffee and waited for the caffeine to enter her bloodstream. She looked at Mason as he took a bite from his bagel and set it back on the plate. "I can't believe that this day has finally come," April said, thinking about Claire. "I can't believe that she's going to be ok," she added, sounding grateful.

Mason smiled at her and set his hand on the table so that April could hold it. "It certainly is a miracle," he said.

Blake had just taken a forkful of eggs and agreed with Mason, "I know. Someone must have been looking over her." As soon as she said it, the thought of her dad came to mind and she quickly glanced at her mother. Blake knew that she had disclosed the fact to Mason that they had had communication from Nick, who had guided Claire into their lives.

Mason grinned at Blake, and offered, "You know, I truly believe that love never dies. If Nick had the opportunity to help both of his daughters overcome tragedy in their lives, then I think that he must have been an amazing husband and father to his family."

When they were almost finished with breakfast, Brie and Emily walked into the cafeteria. They had gone straight to Claire's room but since she was taken for tests, the nurse told them that April and Blake were down getting breakfast.

Blake saw them first, and jetted from her chair. She ran up to them and embraced them. "She's awake!" Blake said gleefully. Blake led them back to her table so that they could join her.

Over the past three weeks, April and Brie had engaged in conversations about Claire and their friendship. April knew that Brie cared deeply about Claire, and had visited the hospital every day since the accident. As they came up to the table, April stood up and hugged them both. Brie was smiling as she sat down. "I can't wait to see her," she said eagerly.

April told the girls that it was going to be a rough road to recovery for Claire, and that she would need the full support of her friends as well as her family.

"I am going to be there for her every day," Brie declared. "She didn't give up on me, and I certainly won't give up on her either," said Brie, as her mind replayed the night of the Winter Formal when Claire had forgiven her and wanted to be friends.

After breakfast, they returned to Claire's room and had to wait several minutes for her arrival. Brie was overcome with emotion when the nurse positioned Claire's bed and reconnected some of the monitors. Brie carefully hugged Claire, making sure not to put pressure on her left arm or bump against her bandaged head. "Oh Claire," Brie said as she looked at her, "I can't believe that you are awake."

Claire smiled and said that she was happy too. Brie had this look of sorrow on her face as she blinked away tears and said, "I remember how you said at Jordan's party that senior year was going to be the best year ever. When you got in the accident, I didn't want to think of the possibility of you not being here for it."

Claire signaled to Brie with her good hand that she needed another hug, and Brie held onto her for several moments, allowing all the sorrow and dismay that she had felt over the past few weeks to evaporate.

Releasing Brie, Claire said to her enthusiastically, "I told you, this is going to be the best year ever." Emily then told Claire that she was so glad that she was alright. As Mason and April looked on, the girls engaged in discussion about what they were going to do when Claire got out of the hospital. April watched Claire smile and giggle as they joked and had a good time. Claire was obviously in pain from her injuries, and as the day progressed, she grew tired and weary. Brie and Emily told Claire that they would be back the next day to spend time with her.

It was mid-afternoon when Mason said to April that he had to go to a job site for a computer installation. It was approximately an hour outside of downtown and that he would come back to see her sometime later that evening. She kissed him goodbye and gave him a hug.

"Love you," Mason said as he opened the door to leave.

"Love you too," April responded back. She slowly closed the door to Claire's room, as if to linger in Mason's presence for as long as she could.

It was just April and Blake in the room with Claire. Blake was in the chair next to Claire and April was lying back in her chair soaking up the silence in the room. Claire was beginning to nod off and her eyes just happened to focus on a picture in one of the frames that was in the room. It was the picture of Mel and Nick that she had got from her mom in Seattle. She gazed upon the image for several moments until her eyes sprang open and she exclaimed, "Mom... Dad!" April and Blake were both startled by Claire's outburst, and stole glances at each other.

"What?" April asked, sitting up straight.

"April," Claire began, unable to contain her excitement. "I saw them, my parents, Nick and my mom," Claire said, as the memory of their encounter came flooding back into Claire's mind. April and Blake were now listening intently to Claire.

"I was standing in front of my mother's house in Seattle. They came walking up hand in hand. I...," Claire paused as she realized something. "I heard his voice. He told me that he loved me," she said, and focused her attention on Blake. "I heard our dad's voice," Claire smiled as she recalled it.

"They took me to the park across the street and we spent hours there. We swung on the swings, he pushed mom and me on the merry-go-round," said Claire feeling almost giddy at the memory. "We played soccer on the field. I scored on him several times. Eventually, this guy came and offered my dad a kite. We put it together and I flew it."

Blake and April sat there mesmerized by Claire's account of her time with her parents.

Claire sat up as best as she could, as the excitement coursed through her body, and said, "We walked back to the house and they told me that they loved me again, and that we were going to go home." Claire's eyes looked inward as she remembered the bright light. "The light from the door... it was so peaceful. The feeling that flowed from it was like nothing that I have ever felt before," she said, and then Claire got this look on her face as she realized what Nick had meant.

"We walked through the door and into the light. He said that I was coming home. I thought that it was supposed to be with them," Claire choked, as she said, "but I know now that he meant for me to come back to you guys—that you are my home." Tears flowed onto Claire's cheeks as it became clear that Nick and Mel had sent her back to be with April and Blake. Claire knew that she had been in a coma, but being with Nick and Mel in Seattle didn't feel like a dream induced by it. She remembered how warm the sun felt on her skin, the way the green grass of the park felt incredibly soft—as if it were carpet. Claire could feel Mel and Nick's touch as they held her hand when they walked to and from the park. *It must have been a dream, right?* Claire wondered to herself, as she tried to rationalize what she had experienced.

"I miss them," Claire confessed as she sobbed. "I am so thankful for the time that we got to spend together in the park. I know now that they loved me with all their hearts and how proud of me they were; even if it was a coma-induced dream, it all seemed so real," she said dolefully.

Blake smiled through the tears, and said, "Wasn't our dad wonderful? He was the best dad ever and you got to see him." Even though Blake was still sad for the loss of her father, she was happy that he got to meet Claire."

Claire grinned, and said, "He was so amazing, Blake." As she remembered her conversation with him, Claire told Blake, "I told him what a great sister you are to me and he said that he was very proud of you for everything that you have done for me." Blake choked up as Claire said that. "Really? He said that to you?" she asked.

"Sure did," Claire confirmed. "He told me that he loved both of you unconditionally and how he wanted us to be a family."

April missed Nick terribly and even though she was in love with Mason, her heart was still in pieces over the idea that Nick was gone and had guided them all in directions that had brought them together

"I love you, Nicolas," April declared, as if he was standing in the room with them. Looking at both Blake and Claire, April said, "Thank you, for everything."

* *

LATER THAT AFTERNOON, APRIL HAD HER PARENTS TAKE Blake back to the apartment so that she could get some sleep. Blake was worn down and April didn't want to jeopardize her health. Claire had just finished lunch and the nurse came in to remove the lunch tray. April had pulled the two chairs together and she was using one as a leg rest. She was sitting upright though and was immersed in a hardcover book that she had brought with her from home.

Claire was skimming through the pages of a magazine when she started to hum. At first, she didn't realize that she was even doing it.

April looked up from her book and asked Claire quizzically, "Was Caleb here?" April had called him along with everyone else, and he told her that he was going to try to make it there before evening when he got off of his shift. As far as she knew, he hadn't been there yet.

At the mention of his name, Claire's eyes blinked with curiosity. "No. Why?" asked Claire. Her heart fluttered as the image of his face filled her mind. His was the last face that Claire had seen before she went into the coma and she knew that he had been the sole reason as to why she didn't die on that rain soaked road.

"Because," April said as she grinned, "That is the song that he has been playing on his guitar and singing to you this past week."

"Seriously?" Claire questioned, having no memory of his visits.

"Yes, sweetie. He came every day for over a week and hoped that you would hear the music and come back to us," she said. Claire didn't know the song but she could hum the melody and chorus as if she had written it.

"Wow," Claire said softly to herself. There was something about the way that Caleb told her to hang on and to stay with him. She didn't know if it was the desperation or the heat of the moment, but Claire wanted to see him so that she could thank him for saving her life.

"He is a remarkable young man," April said, "He graduated high school last year and is studying to be a paramedic. If he hadn't shown up when he did...," April's voice trailed off not wanting to finish her sentence.

"I know April," Claire said, trying to comfort April from what might have been quite a different outcome.

"I owe him my life," Claire said matter-of-factly.

There was a knock on the door and Gina, Wanda, and Monica entered.

"Hi Claire," Gina said as she put her hand over to mouth to keep from crying. "Glad you're back with us," she said.

"Me too," Claire replied honestly, as each one of them came up and gave her a hug. "Thank you all for your support. April told me that you were all there for her and that means a lot to me," she said.

Wanda's hair had changed since the last time that Claire had seen it. Wanda had dyed it red, similar to the hair color that Annie had in *Little Orphan Annie*. It looked really good on her. All three of them stayed for over an hour talking shop with April and Claire. They enjoyed Claire's take on storytelling and appreciated any input that she wanted to contribute. Claire was glad to see them there and became aware of just how hard it was for everyone that she had been so close to death.

April was exhausted and told Claire that she was going to go home and take a nap so that she could come by later. It was early evening so Claire told April that she didn't have to come back tonight and that she could just come tomorrow morning. Claire could see that April had been through a lot in the past few weeks and knew that she needed to get some rest.

Claire was actually pretty tired herself and dozed off a few minutes after April had left. A couple of hours went by when she was awakened by a soft knock on the door. Claire tried to say 'Come in', but her voice cracked. "Come in," Claire said again as she cleared her throat.

Caleb Allen walked into her room carrying a bouquet of flowers and his guitar case. "Hi, Claire. Do you remember me?" he asked.

Claire's eyes lit up. "Yes, of course I do," she said with a smile as she waved him in. Caleb set the flowers down on the chair next to the bed and stood the guitar near the foot of the bed. He looked into Claire's eyes and she waved him over to her. She held out her one arm to hug him as the overwhelming feeling of gratitude blanketed her. Caleb bent down so that she could hug him. "Thank you so much for saving my life," Claire said with tears streaming down her face. She knew that he was her savior that night.

"You're very welcome," Caleb replied. "As soon as I saw you, I told myself that I was going to do everything in my power to save you," he said.

Claire felt completely at ease with Caleb as if they had been friends for a long time. She told him to sit and tell her about himself. Caleb told Claire about how he was going to be a paramedic and how his dad had basically been training him for it his entire life.

Twenty minutes went by and Claire glanced towards the guitar at the foot of the bed. "April tells me that you sang to me when I was in a coma?" she asked.

Caleb smiled humbly and confessed, "Yeah, I did." He looked at his guitar and then turned his attention back to Claire and said, "I learned to play this song at my parent's wedding, and I thought that it would be something I could do to help wake you up."

"Can you play it for me now?" Claire asked bashfully. "Apparently, I have been humming the melody, but I don't know the words," she said. Caleb was somewhat taken aback by this because it seemed that she had heard him sing to her, at least subconsciously.

Caleb picked up the guitar case and as he opened it, he said, "I would love to." He sat in the chair and put the guitar on his knee just like he had done over the past week. He took out his pick and then, with a sheepish grin, said, "Here it goes."

Caleb sang Claire the same song that he had played over and over when she was in a coma. Unlike the other times, Caleb knew that she could hear him. As he sang the words and strummed the chords, Claire began to hum the melody as he played. In that moment, Caleb realized that everything that he learned as a kid with his dad, all the training that he completed to become a paramedic, all of it, had led him up to this point in time with Claire. His heart filled with joy at the prospect of getting to know the beautiful girl that he had rescued on that terrible night.

Caleb stayed with Claire and talked with her for several hours before she fell asleep. He quietly packed up his guitar and closed the case. He stood at the foot of the bed watching her chest slowly move up and down as she breathed. The rhythmic pattern of her breathing was hypnotic, and he didn't want to take his eyes away from her. Even though she was still in rough shape physically, Caleb thought to himself how much she looked like an angel.

* *

THE MONTH OF AUGUST WAS CHALLENGING FOR CLAIRE. Because of the blunt force trauma to her brain, she had temporarily lost partial control of her right leg and left arm, including her hand. She became frustrated when she tried to pick up objects and her hand couldn't obey the signals that her brain was sending.

Claire had to learn how to walk again by training her brain to communicate with both legs at the same time. Because her right leg had been severely damaged, it took longer than she had hoped.

The tree branch that had been responsible for Claire's trauma had caused two separate scars. The biggest one was underneath her hair towards the left side of her head. The second one was a tiny branch that had torn into Claire's right cheek on her face. Because of the shape and smaller size of the branch, it created a star-shaped scar on that cheek. It would end up being the size of a nickel, but it became a facial reminder of the accident, and how close she came from death.

True to her word, Brie was there most days at rehab with Claire, helping her push through the exercises. She was essentially Claire's rehabilitation cheerleader. In fact, there was one day that she and Emily were there, dressed in their cheerleading uniforms holding signs up that said, 'You can do it!' cheering Claire on.

Blake spent most of her time with her sister. It was crystal clear that Blake never wanted to be separated from Claire for that length of time ever again. Blake was now into full remission from her leukemia. Her hair had grown an inch from her shoulders and Blake knew that it was going to be a while until it was the original length. .

Caleb visited Claire at every chance that he could. He was a full-fledged paramedic and had gotten a job with one of the ambulance companies that were based out of the same hospital that Claire was in. Even though Claire was mentally traumatized by what Trevor did to her, her feelings for Caleb were undeniable. He had a wonderful heart and absolutely adored Claire. They loved spending time together, and Caleb actually enjoyed reading. Of course, he wasn't up to Claire's level.

Trevor was booked for a DUI and illegal drug possession. The state of Illinois suspended his driver's license and he was still facing charges, including leaving the scene of an accident and causing great bodily injury to another. His parents got him out on bond, but he was still in a lot of trouble. Most of his friends abandoned him and his social life was in shambles. Brie saw Trevor coming out of a store downtown and went off on him. In front of his parents, Brie yelled and cursed at him and asked how he could have possibly done that to Claire. She told him that she didn't know how Claire could have ever been in love with a douchebag like him, and finally told him that if she ever saw him within a mile of Claire, she was going to kick his ass. A short time after that, Brie heard a rumor that Trevor had switched schools and was going to be completing his senior year at Payton College Prep High, Jones College Prep High School's rival.

It was now the end of August and Claire was being released from the hospital. Claire had to use a crutch in order to steady her walk, but the doctor forecast that she would need it for only a week or so. With any luck, she would be crutch free by the start of school.

Ironically, it had started to rain the morning of Claire's release. The sky was swirling with dark gray clouds and thunder rumbled off in the distance. When the car pulled up to the exit doors of the hospital, Blake gave April a concerned look.

"Is Claire going to be okay?" Blake spoke softly into her mother's ear as Claire was being brought down by wheelchair.

April shook her head looking up towards the city skyline. "I think she'll be fine." The rain was falling at a steady rate but it wasn't pouring like it did that fateful day six weeks prior.

As the nurse brought Claire up to the car, April said to Claire, "Are you ready to go home?"

Claire stood up from the wheelchair and reached for her crutch. "Very much so." Claire grinned with eager anticipation. "I've missed waking up with you guys at home and coming down to make breakfast," Claire said honestly.

"Us too," Blake said. "I can't believe that you're coming home today. It's been a long six weeks, and I need my sister back." The look in Blake's eyes conveyed all the emotions that she had to endure since the accident, and Claire knew that Blake had been through the ringer.

Blake helped Claire in the car and then placed her crutch in the trunk of the car. Blake got in the seat next to her and then April sat up front.

"Where's Mason?" Claire asked as they drove home to the apartment. Claire stared out of the window as the raindrops cascaded upon the glass and distorted the diminishing view of the hospital. It was fitting to Claire that it was raining today. She felt that she arrived at the hospital in the pouring rain; she might as well leave it in the rain.

"He's in a meeting at his office," April lied. "He said that he is going to stop over after work today." April didn't want to let on that there were about two-dozen friends and family waiting for Claire at the apartment. Similar to Blake's homecoming from leukemia, April had banners, balloons and a cake waiting for Claire when she got home.

"Oh ok," grinned Claire, as she looked onto Blake's face to see her reaction to April's answer. For her part, Blake didn't even blink at the mention of Mason's name so it was apparent to Claire that she was trying hard not to show any reaction or give anything away. Claire had a pretty good idea that there was going to be some kind of welcome home party. Rose and Shelly were acting a little weird about today, which gave Claire the impression that something was going on. It didn't matter to Claire; she was thrilled to be going home, and if there was a party, so much the better.

By the time they made it back to the apartment, it was pouring rain and the rumble of thunder turned into loud explosions of sound. Despite this, Claire was happy to be walking into the apartment building that she had been absent from for over six weeks.

"Welcome home!" everyone yelled, as the elevator doors opened. Even though Claire had the feeling that this was going to happen, she still was startled and let out a tiny yelp of surprise. The main floor of the apartment was filled with friends and family that had come to show Claire support.

The entire room was covered with banners, balloons and streamers hanging from all corners of the apartment. Furthermore, there were three posters that contained the words 'Welcome Home' and were signed by the hospital staff, kids from school and associates from Priscilla Publishing.

Brie, Shelly, and Rose were standing up front and in the center and stepped up to Claire first. After giving Claire hugs, they guided her to the kitchen island where there was a big cake that said 'Welcome home, Claire'. Next to the island was a table set up with brunch. It consisted of all of Claire's favorites including scrambled eggs, sausage, ham, waffles, and a blend of donuts and Danishes. Mason was standing next to Caleb to the left of the kitchen. Claire hugged Caleb and he gave her a kiss on the cheek. Mason also hugged her, but then kissed her on the forehead. Claire made her way around the room allowing friends and relatives to show how happy they were for her return.

"Thank you so much everyone," Claire said appreciatively, adding, "It feels so good to be home." April stood behind Claire with her hand on her shoulder. "We've missed you so much sweetie and are so glad that you are with us," she said.

Claire and Blake were seated at the head of the table as everyone else gathered around. As Claire watched them get their food and talk amongst themselves, a feeling of content washed over her. Now that her mother was gone and the mystery of her biological father solved, Claire realized that all the people that were surrounding her in the apartment were her family. She had never felt more at home than she did in that moment. Blake was looking at Claire while she was lost in thought and whispered to her, "Are you okay?" To Blake, it looked as if Claire had zoned out for a moment.

Claire blinked as she smiled and looked at Blake. "Very much so," Claire said. "I was just thinking how great this family is... I mean, how great *our* family is and how wonderful it is to be a part of it. I wanted a family like this my entire life. I used to watch TV shows and fantasize that I could have a family like that one day," said Claire and turned her head to look at all the wonderful people in the apartment. She said, "They all care and love us, you know? I never could have imagined my life with so many loving people in it."

Blake was touched by Claire's assessment and was thankful for everyone that was there with her and Claire today. "When you were in the accident and we didn't know if you were going to make it, I never felt so lost in my life. I couldn't imagine my life without my big sister. It tore me up and I didn't know what to do. I thought that I could handle another round of leukemia if it meant that you would come back to us," said Blake, holding back tears. "I just want you to know that you are a huge part of this family and you won't ever have to worry about having a home again," she added.

Claire reached for Blake's hand, and said, "Thanks, sis, I love you."

Blake said with a deadpan expression, "I know."

Claire smirked at her sister and then held up her fist for a fist bump.

"Love you, Claire Bear," Blake said, as she bumped her back.

After almost everyone was done eating, Claire stood up at the head of the table and tapped her water glass with a butter knife and said, "Hey everyone, can I have your attention?"

Everyone turned to look at Claire.

Claire cleared her throat and began, "I want to say how much I appreciate everyone here for coming here today to welcome me home." With that, the room burst into applause.

"As most of you know, I am lucky to be alive right now and I know that I wouldn't be here with all of you today if it weren't for Caleb," Claire pointed at him and he looked a little surprised with the attention, but he graciously accepted more of the applause.

Claire reached April's hand and held onto it. "I can't imagine my life right now if it weren't for the love of April and Blake and how blessed I am for having all of you in my life," she said. Claire paused for a moment and then added, "I never had a family like this and when I look at the banner that is over the kitchen that says welcome home, it means a lot more to me than just coming home from the hospital." Claire blinked away a tear and concluded, "It means that I actually have a home... and a family that I love."

Claire sat back down. April leaned over and gave her a hug as she whispered in Claire's ear, "I love you, sweetie."

Claire eventually made her way to the La-Z-Boy in the living room and pulled the feet out so that she could rest her leg. It was starting to ache a little and she was becoming a little tired with all the excitement. It felt good to be sitting on the La-Z-Boy, where she had spent countless hours reading and watching TV. Caleb sat on the couch next to her and was talking with Brie and Rose, who were sitting next to him on the couch.

"I can't believe that school is starting in a couple of weeks." Brie said to Claire. "We are going to have the best year," she said excitedly.

"Yeah we are!" Rose declared and added, "We've got our Claire back so we are going to make this last year awesome!"

Shelly walked up from the kitchen and suggested, "I have a great idea. Why don't we make a pact that we have to stay at one another's houses every Friday night during the school year?" Shelly then looked over at Blake and added, "You too. You are part of this pact, don't you know." Blake looked up from her phone and said, "Really? That is going to be so cool!" The six of them—Claire, Blake, Shelly, Rose, Brie, and Emily decided that they would all rotate hosting every week, starting with the Friday of Labor Day. Brie volunteered her place for the maiden voyage of the Friday Night Sleep Over aka FNSO; which is what the girls later referred to it as in texts and tweets.

As Claire looked around the couch at her friends, she couldn't help but think that her life would never be the same again.

* *

BLAKE HAD JUST COME DOWN THE STAIRS WITH HER OVER-night bag and walked towards the kitchen. Claire was already downstairs and was making a cup of coffee. It was the Friday before Labor Day and the girls were getting ready for the first Friday Night Sleep Over. Because Claire was still using her crutch, the six of them decided to take it easy and spend the day relaxing on the beach and then going to Brie's house for a pizza party followed by binge watching scary movies.

"Good morning sis," Blake greeted Claire as she took a seat on the island. "Are you ready for a day of fun and excitement?"

Claire opened up a sugar pack and began to pour its content into the mug. "You bet I am!" Claire responded excitedly as she stirred the sugar with a spoon. "I feel like a little girl getting ready for her first slumber party."

The sun had just peeked out from behind a cloud, brightening up the entire downstairs as if someone had turned on a light switch. The weatherman on the local news station promised a partly sunny 81 degrees on Friday and if the morning sky was any indication, it was going to be a great beginning to the holiday weekend.

April came out of her bedroom with a towel on her head and walked down towards the girls.

"Good morning," April said, smiling as she walked to the kitchen. "How are my wonderful girls?" she asked.

"Fantastic," Blake declared as she looked at Claire. "We are getting ready to leave to spend the day with the girls. First we are going to the beach and will then spend the night watching movies," Blake explained.

Claire nodded her head in agreement as she sipped on coffee from her mug.

April subconsciously glanced at Claire's crutch and she had this worried look on her face. "Please be careful today," April said to both girls as she looked from Claire to Blake and added, "It's the holiday weekend and you know how the roads are going to be busy today."

Claire knew that April still worried about her and what had happened with the crash. Hell, she was even nervous at times being in a car, but she never let on.

"We will," Claire answered assuredly and added, "We actually have Derek taking us in the SUV and then picking us up to take the group back to Brie's. I called Grandpa and he offered to schedule him for us today."

April felt somewhat relieved at this news. Derek was a good driver and the Black SUV was as big as a tank and just as safe.

"That's good," replied April, visibly less anxious. "I feel better now that I know he is driving you guys," she said.

April took the chair next to Blake and set her phone down on the counter.

"Do you want a cup of coffee?" Claire asked April.

"Sure, that would be great," April smiled, as the smell of Claire's cup of coffee helped with her decision.

As April waited for her coffee, she asked Claire, "So, all of you are going to have breakfast at Brie's house tomorrow?"

"Yeah, I think that we are going to make pancakes with her mom." Claire said and added, "She apparently makes them really thick and fluffy."

"Sounds delicious," April agreed, as Claire handed her the freshly brewed mug of coffee.

April blew across the surface of the mug and then delicately took a sip of the hot coffee. After a few moments, she began to hum.

"What are you thinking about?" Blake asked as she listened to her mom humming. "You tend to hum when you're concentrating," she observed.

April was thinking about her date with Mason this upcoming evening. He had alluded to a romantically filled night that included dinner, dancing, and possibly spending the night since the girls were going to be away at Brie's.

"I was just thinking how lucky I am for having two wonderful daughters like the two of you," April responded, sidestepping her actual thought.

"Aww," Blake grinned and asked, "but seriously, what were you thinking about?"

"Nothing really. I am happy and content with my life and I love you two with all my heart, that's all," April said, as she smiled and got up to enter the kitchen. "Do you guys want breakfast?"

"You bet," Blake smirked, "I thought you would never ask."

Claire squinted her eyes at Blake as if to reprimand her. "We were about to make you breakfast, April," Claire said, wanting to let her know.

"That's ok. I'll make breakfast for my two favorite daughters," she said. April grinned as she opened the refrigerator door and asked, "Do you want scrambled eggs or French toast?"

Claire looked at Blake and said, "It's up to you sunshine, and it doesn't matter to me."

Blake thought about it for a few seconds and then asked, "How about French toast?"

"You got it," April replied, as she reached in and grabbed the eggs and milk.

While she cooked, April smiled to herself as she thought how nice it was to make them breakfast. The past year had been incredibly tasking for April, with Blake's leukemia and Claire's accident. Considering the fact that she could have lost both girls, it was a miracle that she came out of it mentally intact. April began to hum again, and this time it was because she was happy to be with her daughters.

After breakfast, Blake was putting her empty plate into the dishwasher and asked her mom, "So, what are you going to do tonight? Do you have plans with Mason?"

April grinned at the thought of it and replied, "As a matter of fact, we do. We are going out to dinner and then possibly a movie."

"Sounds romantic," Blake teased, grinning sheepishly at her mom.

April smiled at Blake but didn't really want to engage her any further with discussions about the date with Mason. She knew that the girls really liked him, but didn't feel the need to be completely open with them about the intimate portions of their relationship.

"Yes, it should be a really nice evening," April conceded, trying to end Blake's round of questioning.

Claire hobbled upstairs because she forgot her phone on the charger next to the bed and she wanted to conduct a final check to make sure that she didn't forget anything. Blake was double-checking her own bag because Claire's double-checking had made Blake unsure if she had everything.

"So, you guys will be home around noon tomorrow then?" April asked Blake.

Blake stopped rummaging through her bag and glanced up at the mother. "Yes mom, Claire and I will both be back tomorrow in the afternoon," Blake reiterated Claire's previous statement.

"Okay then," April said, seemingly satisfied.

Blake thought that it was odd that her mom was so worried if she and Claire were going to have breakfast tomorrow morning, but after a few moments decided that her mom was just being more anxious than usual, due to Claire's crash.

Claire came back down to the kitchen and held up her phone to Blake signifying that she had it and wasn't going to forget it. "Ready to go?" Claire asked her sister.

"Yuppers," Blake answered as she picked up her bag and laid it across her shoulder. "I'm all set," she said.

April went up to both girls and performed a quick mental examination. "Have a great day you two." April said as she hugged them. "Text me when you get there ok?"

"Yes, mom," both girls answered in unison, as they headed to the elevator.

"Love you, see you tomorrow at noon," April said, as she waved goodbye to the girls.

"Love you too," Claire managed to say before the elevator doors closed.

"What's with mom and breakfast tomorrow?" Blake asked as they headed down to the lobby. "She must have asked us two or three times when we were coming back tomorrow morning."

It didn't occur to Claire until she had heard it out loud from Blake. "Holy crap, Blake. I know why April is all nervous about us and tomorrow morning," Claire smirked, as she put two and two together.

"She plans on Mason spending the night tonight. That's got to be it. She wasn't very forthcoming with details about tonight and she kind of avoided talking about it," smiled Claire.

Blake started to grin at the realization of what Claire was saying. "Do you think?" Blake asked hopefully.

"I bet you that's it. She is making sure that we aren't coming back first thing so that we don't find him in her bed," laughed Claire.

Blake giggled at the prospect, but then looked at Claire with a little more favorable tone and said, "I think that is awesome if it's true. I really like Mason and I know that they are in love with each other. I don't know why mom has to try to hide it from us."

The elevator doors opened to display the majestic view of the lobby. The girls stepped out of the elevator and Claire responded, "I know that she is aware of how we feel about her dating and that we are totally okay with it, but I think that deep down she believes that we might think that she is cheating on Nick if she totally gives herself to Mason."

"I've told her before that I was okay with her dating and all that it implies. She should be okay with bringing Mason home if she wants. I am a big girl now and I just want her to be happy," said Blake trying to rationalize it for her mom.

The warmth of the sun hit them as if they had opened a door to an oven. As they walked to the black SUV, Derek opened the doors for them and bid them a hello.

As the SUV pulled away from the apartment building, Claire's eyes lit up and she tapped Blake on her arm for full affect. "I got it," Claire smiled, and added, "I know how we are going to handle this."

Curious about Claire's declaration, Blake looked at her and asked, "What do you have in mind?"

Before Claire told Blake the plan, she leaned up towards the driver's seat and asked Derek, "Hey, what are you doing tomorrow morning?"

* *

IT WAS FIVE O'CLOCK ON THE DOT WHEN MASON WALKED through the elevator of April's apartment. He was wearing khaki pants and a dress shirt, but no tie. Over that, he had on a navy blue sports jacket.

"Wow, you look beautiful," Mason said affectionately, as his eyes soaked in what April was wearing.

April had on a sexy black cocktail dress that had lace across the neck and was covered just above her chest. She had decided to wear a strand of white pearls that formed a choker. She also put on her favorite black Louis Vuitton heels that had red on the soles.

"You don't look too bad yourself," April remarked with a hint of mischief in her voice.

Mason went up to her and gave her a passionate kiss on the lips and then he bent his elbow and extended his arm so that he could escort her to the door. April smiled and looped her arm into his and said, "Why thank you Mr. Steele."

"You're very welcome, Mrs. Turner," Mason smiled back and asked, "Shall we depart for our fun-filled night?"

"We shall," April smiled, as Mason led her to the elevators. Once they got outside onto the street, Mason grabbed her hand and walked with her slowly on the sidewalks. They talked and laughed all the way to the restaurant. Mason knew that April had been wanting to go to this particular one for some time now and had reserved a private table in the most romantic part of the establishment.

After the waiter took their order, he brought over a bottle of wine for them to try. April took a sip and nodded her head in agreement. The waiter then poured two glasses and left the bottle on the table. Mason held up his glass for a toast. April picked up her glass and held it in front of her.

"To us," Mason said, adding "to the joy that I feel when I am with you and the anguish I feel when we are apart."

April smiled at his toast, but before she tapped her glass to his she added, "To us... and to the man that has been there for me through one on the darkest years of my life. You've helped me though Blake's illness and then Claire's crash. Never once did you flinch or shudder away from us. In fact, you became the glue that held us all together."

Mason smiled as April's words hit home.

"I love you April," Mason declared as he gently tapped his glass to hers.

"I love you too, Mason," April said as she took a sip of wine.

For the rest of dinner, Mason and April held hands across the dinner table. As April gazed at their hands intertwined, she realized how perfectly that they fit into each other, almost as if God had cast a mold and used their hands as the template.

After dinner, Mason took April dancing at a nightclub that was more suited for couples of their age. It wasn't like they were headed for the retirement home, but April and Mason were definitely not in the millennial category. They spent the next couple of hours twirling and whirling around the dance floor. April and Mason could really cut a rug and were often put on the spotlight by the DJ.

As they left the nightclub, April had this overwhelming feeling of tranquility. Her heart was filled with love again and it was intoxicating. For the first time since Nick had died, her heart was whole.

Mason put his arm around her waist and slowly walked with her as they headed back to April's apartment. The sun had retired for the night and was replaced with a bright full moon.

April looked into the sky and paused to take in the moonlight. "It's so beautiful," April said, as her eyes reflected the moonlight. Mason glanced at April's face and then up at the moon. "It certainly is," he said.

Mason turned his attention from the moon to April's lips. April slowly turned away from the moon and looked into Mason's eyes. In that moment, she knew he wanted her. He kissed her with deep passion. April wrapped her arms around his neck, and kissed him back as their two moonlit shadows became one as they embraced each other.

"I love you, April," Mason professed as they broke apart and she nestled her head on his shoulder.

"I love you too," April, confessed to Mason as her heart fluttered and her mind started to race.

The two continued their walk back to April's apartment, but this time there seemed to be a sense of urgency. Even though April's feet were starting to ache from the dancing, she was slowly picking up the pace.

They arrived at the apartment building and entered the elevator. April removed her shoes and held them in her left hand. As soon as the doors closed and Mason pressed the button for the top floor, he turned to April and scooped her up into his arms and kissed her.

As the doors opened, revealing the living room, Mason stopped kissing her and motioned her to go first out of the elevator. With her shoes still in her left hand, she grabbed Mason's hand and began leading him across the room. When they got to the staircase, he spun her around to face him and she dropped her shoes at the base of the stairs. He kissed her passionately and left no question as to what he wanted next.

April removed his sports jacket and tossed it on the floor. She pulled out his shirt and ran her hands up his bare chest. Before April realized what was happening, Mason scooped her up into his arms and headed towards the bedroom.

He carried April over the threshold of the bedroom and with his foot tried to kick the door closed. The door stopped about three inches from the frame, but neither one of them noticed. Mason gently placed April on top of the bed and then for a brief moment gazed upon her. "God, I love you," he said as he removed his shirt and leaned across the bed on top of her.

April's heart was pounding. She never wanted a man more than how much she wanted Mason right then and there. With a grin that was fueled by desire, she lustfully demanded, "Prove it."

April slowly opened her eyes as the sunlight from her bedroom windows shone brightly against the inner walls. She could feel someone sleeping next to her and the memory of last night came flooding back into her mind. She smiled as she thought about her wonderful evening and thereafter.

After a few moments, she gently turned to face Mason. They both were naked under the covers so as she moved, her hands lay on his somewhat hairy chest. She could feel his heartbeat and the rhythm of his breathing. April eyes were now inches from his as she took in the image of his face. He had this peaceful look about him, with his lips sculpted into a smile.

April slowly, softly, kissed him on the lips. Mason's eyes fluttered open and he smiled as April's nearness filled him with joy.

"Good morning, sweetheart," Mason whispered, as he grinned realizing that he had spent the night with the woman that he loved.

"Good morning," April smiled, as she kissed his lips again. "How are you feeling?"

Mason smiled at her and said, "Honestly, I feel perfect," He removed his right hand from underneath the covers and ran his fingers through her long brown hair. He started to massage her head as he simultaneously combed her hair with his hand.

"God, that feels good," April hummed as she became lost in Mason's touch.

"You feel good," Mason teased as he kissed her on her lips.

Mason propped himself up with his left elbow and gazed at April. He continued to run his hands through her hair as he slowly started to remove the sheets that were covering them.

Mason had just uncovered April's chest when his nose suddenly caught a whiff of bacon.

"I smell bacon." Mason said. "Did you make us breakfast?" he curiously asked April.

"No?" April replied, as her nose caught the scent of it as well.

"I smell eggs and coffee too," Mason added, smirking as he began to realize what was happening.

"Oh no, the girls are home!" April whispered horrified. She quickly picked up her phone to see what time it was. The display on the phone insisted that it was only 8:15 a.m.

"Oh, God," April said, pulling the covers up to her neck. "What are they doing home so early?" Mason was grinning at the sound of panic in April's voice.

Mason knew that they had been caught and that this was a way for the girls to call them out as it were.

April got up and began looking for her robe. "What are we going to do?" she stammered.

Mason stayed in bed watching April's mini freak out.

"April..." Mason began.

"Let's see, we can tell them... "April said, trying to come up with an excuse.

"April..." Mason said again.

"Maybe if we say that you were..." April tried to say.

"April..." Mason said again with a little more force. "It's ok," He smiled. "The girls wanted this for us."

"I know, but..." April whispered, feeling like a high school girl, getting caught by her mother.

"No buts, April. They wanted this for you. Both girls love you and want you to be happy," Mason got up from the bed and went to April. "Don't worry about it. They are perfectly fine."

Mason searched for his pants that were on the floor and picked them up. With them still in his hand, he kissed April and said, "Let's go down there and enjoy the breakfast that the girls apparently worked hard to prepare for us."

April sighed and she couldn't help but grin at Mason standing before her naked and extremely handsome. "You're right. Let's go face the music," Mason put on his pants and found his shirt on the floor in front of the bathroom. It was awfully wrinkled since it was lying in a crushed heap on the floor all night. He proudly put the wrinkled shirt on and with April in her robe, headed out the bedroom.

When they looked down from the top of the stairs, they saw Claire and Blake sitting at the dining room table with four place settings. All the food had just been cooked and placed in bowls and serving dishes on the table. The girls had presented breakfast family style. Somehow they knew that Mason would be joining them.

"Good morning," Blake said, grinning from ear to ear.

"Yeah, good morning," Claire said, "It's a beautiful day. Wouldn't you agree?"

Mason and April walked down the stairs hand and hand as they headed towards the table.

"Good morning girls," Mason proclaimed happily. "Nice to see you two up so early on this blissful Saturday morning."

"You too," Blake said mischievously. "Both of you," Blake playfully amended.

April's hair was disheveled and she had the after-glow of sex. She took a seat next to Blake and asked with slight bewilderment, "So, you guys are home early?"

"Are we?" Claire answered covertly for Blake. "I guess we didn't realize the time."

Mason took the seat next to Claire and looked at the food presented on the table. "This looks amazing, you two," Mason said, winking at the girls.

"Thanks Mason," Blake replied happily. "We wanted to have a family style breakfast. You know?" she said.

As the four of them began to eat, Claire turned to Mason and asked, "So, how was the date last night?"

Mason took a bite of toast and replied, "It was magical," as he smiled at April.

Both Blake and Claire giggled at that and April could feel her cheeks flush.

Claire smiled at April and asked, "So, how was dinner?"

April gave Claire a playful stare as if to say 'enough', but Claire only stared back with a look that this line of questioning was not quite over.

"Dinner was great. We ate a fantastic meal and then we went dancing," April remarked telling the girls about the first part of the evening.

"Cool," Claire replied, egging her on for more details.

"Then what?" Blake asked as she glanced from Mason to April.

April had this sheepish, bashful look on her face, but didn't want to reply.

"Then," Mason said with a smile as he sipped his coffee, "We came back here so that we could wait for you two to make us breakfast."

"So, that's how it went down?" Claire asked as she glared into Mason's eyes as if her stare was a lie detector.

"Yes. That's exactly how it happened. That's my story and I'm sticking to it," Mason said.

"Uh huh?" Claire said looking into his eyes and said, "I think that there is a detail, or two, missing from the story you speak of."

"Girls," April interrupted. "Let's just eat and enjoy this breakfast you've made. Ok?" April said hoping that it was the end of the inquisition.

Mason chuckled and said, "Ok, ok, I give up. I confess."

"I confess that I love your mom with all my heart." Mason admitted. .

"Not only that..." He said pointing at Claire and Blake, "But I love the both of you as well."

April's facial expression turned from bashful nervousness to love and admiration.

"I love you too," said April from across the table.

Mason stood up and kissed Claire on the forehead and then went up to Blake and kissed her on the forehead as well. Then he got to April and kissed her directly on the lips. His love for her was visibly apparent.

"If you guys would like, I would like to spend the day with all of you. Maybe we can go to the park and have a relaxing picnic? How does that sound?" Mason asked, still standing in front of April.

"Sounds amazing," Blake said, "Are you sure you want us all to go? You can spend some quality time with mom if you want."

Mason nodded his head, smiled, and said, "Yes, of course, I want all of us to go. I would love to spend the day with all three of you. Nothing else would make me happier."

April wrapped her arms around Mason and said, "That sounds lovely. I'm going to run upstairs and take a shower and get ready to go."

Mason watched her go upstairs and then he took his seat back at the table. Both Claire and Blake were smiling at him as he turned his attention from April to them.

Mason took a forkful of scrambled eggs and then a bite of toast as he grinned at the girls.

"Well played, you two," Mason chuckled at the unannounced breakfast and said. "Well played."

Claire held up a fist for Blake to fist bump and Blake immediately responded. Mason set his fork down and held up his fist too. Claire and Blake bumped it at the same time and the three of them giggled.

Mason looked up towards April's bedroom to make sure that April was in the shower.

Leaning back into his chair and with a look of eager anticipation he said, "Now that I have both of you alone, there is something that I want to ask you."

CHAPTER TWENTY-EIGHT

CLAIRE WAS SITTING AT THE DINING ROOM TABLE WAITING for April and Blake to return home. April had taken Blake to a doctor's appointment after school, and then was going to take her shopping. They had asked Claire to go, but she lied and said that she had made plans with Brie after school. It was supposed to be the night of the FNSO, but Claire had asked Shelly, Rose, and Brie if they could cancel it and make up some excuse to tell Blake.

Claire had dressed up for the occasion and was wearing a red plaid skirt that went down to her knees with black tights as well as a black sweater. She had taken out the white family pearls from Blake's drawer and was wearing those. Claire had spent about half an hour putting on her makeup and doing her hair. She was careful not to put too much foundation on so that it wouldn't cover up the star-shaped scar on her face. There was something about it that reminded her of receiving a second chance at life.

Claire had been anxious all day thinking about what she had planned for tonight and now as it was almost here, she actually was becoming a little nervous. She looked at her phone for the sixth time in the past ten minutes and it displayed 7:25 p.m. Claire knew that they would be home at any moment.

The elevator doors opened up and the sound of April and Blake talking filled the room. They were talking about an outfit that Blake had been designing when they noticed Claire sitting at the dining room table.

"Oh, hi Claire," April greeted, surprised by the fact that she was there and not at Brie's. She then noticed how dressed up Claire was and the look on Claire's face.

"Is everything ok?" April asked. "What's the matter?"

Claire stood up from the table and waved to both to join her. "Please sit, I want to talk to you both about something."

"What's going on Claire?" Blake asked her sister, giving her a quizzical look.

"Please sit," Claire asked. "I have something I want to say."

April looked at Blake and she gave her mom a look stating that she had absolutely no idea about what was going on.

Once they were seated, Claire placed a gift box on the table in front of April.

"Before you open this, I just want to tell you something," Claire said, the look in her eyes somewhat serious, "It's been almost a year since that day that you and Blake found me on the street and took me in..." Claire was holding back tears because she wanted to get through this without crying.

April looked at Blake and then looked back at Claire. "We know, sweetie. It felt like yesterday that you came into our lives," April said, the memory of that fateful day etched in her mind as if it were yesterday.

Claire smiled, and continued, "And ever since that moment, you have welcomed me into your home and have loved and cared for me. I can't imagine my life now if you hadn't accepted me as part of your family." Claire's voice was beginning to waver, but she continued with eager determination. "I have never loved anyone in my entire life the way that I love you and Blake. You just love me for me. Even before we found out that Blake and I were sisters, you loved me." Claire couldn't hold off her tears anymore and a few drops flowed from her eyes.

April and Blake had started to tear up too, feeling emotional for Claire, and also not knowing where this was heading.

"So, because I love both of you so much and because of the undeniable bond that we share, I want to..." Claire paused to wipe a tear away from her face.

April reached for Claire's hand and said, "It's ok, Claire, you can tell me anything."

Claire grinned through the tears, and said, "I don't want to tell you anything... I want to ask you something..." She then pointed to the box sitting on the table. "Open it."

April looked at the box before her and then glanced up at Claire with a nervous look in her eyes.

"Open it," Claire said calmly.

April slowly removed the lid of the box and then peered inside. She pulled away a few sheets of tissue paper to reveal a picture. April's eyes widened in disbelief and she put her hand up to her mouth to hold back a sob.

The picture was of Claire. Surprisingly, she was in the exact spot on the sidewalk in downtown Chicago where they had found her. She was sitting crossed legged and smiling from ear to ear, holding a sign just like she had done almost a year ago today. But, this time, the sign read, 'Please adopt me'. Underneath the picture was a clasp envelope that contained adoption papers.

"Oh, my word, are you serious?" April sobbed, completely stunned. She handed the picture to Blake who then looked at her sister.

"Holy cow, Claire Bear!" Blake exclaimed, "This is really cool."

Claire spoke to April as they both began to smile and cry at the same time. "You see, April, in the past year you have been more of a mother to me than I had ever had my entire life. I love you so much that I want to be yours. I don't want you as a foster mom... I don't want you as a step-mom... I just want you as my *mom*." Claire paused for a second and then looked directly into April's eyes, "Will you be my *mom*?"

April was overwhelmed with joy. Since that first day with Claire, she had felt an undeniable connection with her. She adored her and cared deeply for her. When Claire confessed her love for them when she had that nightmare, April knew then that she had felt love for her as well. In the morning she found out that Claire was Blake's bone marrow match; she loved her. When Mel died and they all found out that Claire was Nick's daughter, she loved her. When Claire was lying unconscious in a coma and no one knew if she was going to make it, April loved her. Now, in this moment, Claire wanted to be her daughter, and April loved her.

"Yes, oh my God, yes!" April exclaimed, as she stood up and grabbed Claire and held her tight within her arms.

"You have been a member of this family since the day we met, you know?" April said, still embracing Claire.

Blake came up and put her arms around both of them. "I love this family!" Blake said happily.

April released Claire and was laughing with happiness. Claire was smiling and wiping tears off of her face. "So, from now on, I want to call you 'mom'. Is that ok?"

"Yes, of course," April agreed. "I so wanted this for a while, but I didn't want you to think that I wanted to replace the memory of your mother."

Claire knew where April was coming from but she also knew what her own heart wanted. "I love my mother and I always will. But I believe that she and Nick know that you have been an amazing mom to me, and that it is going to be ok if we make it official. I want to be a Turner now."

Claire took out the paperwork from the envelope and showed it to April. "Not only are you going to be my mom, but I am going to change my last name to Turner. I love my dad, and it's time for me to take the name that I should have always been called."

"Claire Turner?" Blake said, trying to listen to how the name sounded out loud. "I love it," Blake decided with a smile.

It felt like Christmas morning. Claire was all set to go with the paperwork in the envelope. Apparently, Claire had called Duncan O'Rourke from Illinois Protective Services to help her set everything up. All April had to do was to sign the forms and it would be official.

April was looking through the forms and Duncan had put highlighted arrows where she was supposed to sign. Claire had placed April's favorite pens that she kept at her desk in the library office in the box.

April picked up the pen and turned a couple of pages until she got to the first highlighted arrow.

"You are sure you want me as your mom and to change your name to Turner?" April questioned Claire, knowing this would be her last chance to change her mind.

"With all my heart, *mom*," Claire whispered to April.

April blinked away the tears that threatened to splash on the forms. April quickly signed on all the places that she was supposed to, and held them so that both Blake and Claire could see.

"Welcome home, Claire," April exclaimed, as she embraced both her daughters for the first time officially. "Welcome home."

Claire took the forms and carefully placed them back in the envelope, and said, "Let's go, you guys, I am taking the three of us out to dinner."

"Where are you taking us?" Blake wondered looking at Claire.

Claire smiled and replied, "I thought that we would eat at the pizza place where you took me that first day. It's kind of symbolic, don't you think?"

April thought that was the perfect place to celebrate Claire's adoption. "Sounds great," April said as she picked up the picture of Claire asking to be adopted. She thought to herself how fitting it was for them to return to the very restaurant that they had taken her to almost a year ago. What a miracle it was that one hand-written sign could alter the course of destiny for an entire family.

As they headed out, April thought about how Nick's voice had led them all here to the very moment in time, in which, *his* daughter, had now officially become *her* daughter, and would now, forever, be a permanent part of *their* family.

* *

ON THE FOLLOWING FRIDAY NIGHT, CLAIRE AND BLAKE hurried home from school and packed their bag for FNSO. It was being held at Rose's house, and both girls seemed really excited. April was in her office when they came downstairs. Blake turned on the Christmas tree lights and the lights above the mantle before she went towards the kitchen. It was hard to believe that it was only a week or so until Christmas.

"What are you girls going to do tonight?" April asked curiously. She finished typing the last couple of words on the email that she was working on and then stood up and went out to say goodbye to the girls.

"We are going to get pizza takeout and stay up all night watching YouTube videos," Claire answered as she double-checked her bag. April didn't notice, but Claire was carrying more items than she usually did to the sleepovers.

"Sounds like fun," April said, as she walked into the kitchen.

Blake was texting Emily on her phone and looked up from it long enough to ask her mom, "So, what are you and Mason going to do tonight?"

April opened the refrigerator door and took out a bottle of water. "I think that we are going to have dinner at the new Italian bistro that just opened up near my office."

Blake caught a quick glimpse from Claire and then Blake replied to her mom, "Sounds amazing. Have fun and tell Mason we said 'hi.'"

April took a sip of her water and said, "I will, and it does sound like fun."

The girls gave their mom a goodbye kiss and headed to the elevator. "Love you, mom," Claire and Blake both said at the same time.

"Love you too," April smiled, as she waved to them. "Be careful and text me when you get there."

The doors closed and April was alone in the apartment. Mason was coming to pick her up in about an hour so she thought she'd head upstairs to get ready. Mason had suggested that she should dress up because it was a fancy place.

April looked at several dresses in her closet, but eventually settled on a stunning, red, short cocktail dress. She added a little more makeup and curled her hair. April checked her phone and saw the text from both Claire and Blake that they had made it to Rose's house.

Mason texted her and told her that he was running a few minutes late. April said that she would meet him in the lobby and then they could take off from there. April grabbed her winter coat from the closet and looked in the mirror one last time.

By the time she got to the lobby and walked near the door, Mason had just pulled up in a cab.

"Great timing, my dear," he said as she walked out into the snow. Mason helped her into the cab and they headed off to the Italian bistro.

"You look beautiful," Mason said as he leaned over to kiss her.

"You look amazing yourself," April said honestly. "I can't wait to try this new place. I've heard that it is out of this world."

"Me too," Mason agreed, as he placed his hand in hers. "It should prove to be a romantic evening."

The cab pulled up to the restaurant and they got out. After a ten-minute wait, the hostess found them a quiet table for two on the far side. The ambiance of the room was exquisite. It looked and felt like they were in Venice, Italy. There was a mosaic of St. Mark's Basilica on the far wall. The room had two actual gondolas placed in pools of water in the middle of it and the sound of water filled the air.

"This place is amazing," said April, as they took their seats. "It feels like we are in Italy."

"It sure does," Mason agreed, as he placed his napkin upon his lap.

Mason and April enjoyed a delicious dinner as they talked about their dreams and the future. April discussed how this was Claire's senior year and how she had been applying to colleges. It looked like she wanted to study English at college, and April couldn't be happier. Blake was a sophomore, but her area of study was surely going to be fashion.

Mason's business was expanding, and it was obvious that he was becoming very successful. He loved working with computers and having the time to do what he wanted, when he wanted to do it.

After dinner, Mason suggested that they walk around the town to look at the Christmas lights. There was snow on the ground but the sidewalks were cleared. As they walked, Mason had his arm around her, holding her close to him. Even though it was cold out, April enjoyed the walk. It was very romantic.

As they rounded a corner, the coffee shop where April had first 'seen' Mason, was all lit up, but the blinds were closed. On the door was a sign that said, 'Closed – Private Party'

Mason slowly guided April to the front door of the coffee shop.

"Let's go in," Mason said, sounding mischievous.

"We can't go in there," April said, matter-of-factly. "Someone is having a party. We just can't go in and crash it."

"Yeah, maybe you're right," Mason agreed, as he started to walk away from the door with April.

Suddenly, Mason turned back around and reached for the door.

"Maybe we can take a quick peek," Mason suggested, as he pushed the door open.

"No, wait," April started to resist, but Mason was in the process of pulling her inside the shop.

As soon as she entered the shop, she saw balloons and streamers... and pictures of her and Mason. Not only that, but there were pictures of her with Blake and Claire.

"What's going on?" April asked, clueless about what was happening.

Mason left her side and went to the center of the empty room. He called out and then Blake and Claire came out of the back, wearing party dresses.

"Blake? Claire? What are you doing here?" April questioned.

"You'll see," Blake said as she looked up at Mason. Claire was standing on the right and Blake on his left.

Mason was smiling as he looked at April.

"April..." Mason began, "From the moment our eyes locked onto each other at the vending machines at the hospital, I knew that I wanted to be a part of your life. What I didn't realize that day was that not only did I want to be a part of your life, but I wanted to be a part of the lives of Blake and Claire as well. As you know, I could never have children of my own, but when I fell in love with you, I fell in love with them as well. They love you April, with all their hearts." Blake and Claire nodded their heads in agreement to validate what Mason was saying, but didn't speak so as not to interrupt Mason.

April had a pretty good idea what was going on now, but she was too shocked to say anything. She just listened to Mason speak.

"So, when I decided that I was going to do this tonight, I wanted to make sure that I had asked their permission to be a part of their family. Obviously, they agreed whole-heartedly," He held out both of his fists and the girls fist-bumped him at the same time. "Then, I took your parents out to lunch and asked them if I could have the privilege of having their daughter's hand in marriage," Mason grinned and then continued, "Of course they said 'yes' because this was the happiest that they had seen you in a long time," Mason paused for a moment to think about how he was going to phrase the next line. He cleared his throat and said, "If my parents were alive, I believe in my heart that they would be filled with joy that I wanted to marry you. My parents would have enjoyed spending time with you and your daughters."

Mason turned around and reached for a small black velvet box that was sitting on the counter.

"April Turner... Will you make me the happiest man in the world and agree to marry me?" Mason got down on one knee, and opened the ring box as he held it up to her.

Mason had chosen a big beautiful diamond that was surrounded by several smaller diamonds. However, April barely noticed the ring as she leaned over and embraced him.

"Yes, yes, of course, I will marry you!" April exclaimed joyfully.

Immediately after she accepted the proposal, all of their friends and family exploded out of the backroom and filled the shop. "Congratulations!" everyone yelled, as they swarmed the newly engaged couple. April's parents were the first ones out, embracing their daughter and grandchildren. Crystal, Gina, Monica, and Wanda surrounded April and hugged her. All of Mason's friends were there as well.

One of Mason's friends had begun pouring champagne into flutes and was handing them out to everyone. Even Claire and Blake were handed a glass.

"A toast," he said holding up his glass. "To the engagement of April and Mason!"

"Hear, hear." Everyone cheered and raised their glass.

April clinked her glass against Mason's, and said, "I love you so much."

Mason smiled and replied, "I love you too, Mrs. Steele."

April liked the sound of that. As she sipped her champagne, Blake and Claire came up to her.

"I can't believe that you lied to me about going over to Rose's tonight," April said, pretending to be upset.

Blake grinned at Claire, and replied, "I know. It felt so wrong to lie, but I did it for the greater good."

April squinted her eyes and pointed a finger at Blake. "Just don't lie to me again. Get the picture?"

"Yeah, yeah," Blake said dismissively. Then she looked at April's face and amended, "I mean, sure thing... No lies, ever. I get it," April held her arms open so that both Blake and Claire would hug their mom.

"I love you. Both of you," April said, as she embraced her daughters.

"We love you too, mom," they said as they each kissed her on the cheek.

Mason wrapped his arm around April's waist and turned her slowly around to face him. "You've just made me the happiest man in the entire world and I can't wait to marry you. I love you with all my heart."

April wrapped her hands around his neck and looked longingly into his eyes. She could see her future in them, and it was amazing. For the first time in five years, her heart was completely whole again. Whatever damage Nick's death had caused was now healed by the unconditional love of Mason. April realized in that moment that she wanted Mason with all of her heart and soul.

April blinked as she thought about what Mason had just said. A grin appeared on her lips as she passionately replied to her fiancée, "Prove it." April pressed her lips against his and began kissing him as if they were the only ones in the room.

EPILOGUE

APRIL COULDN'T BELIEVE THAT THE WEDDING DAY HAD finally arrived. She was alone in one of the rooms above the church, admiring the dress that Blake had designed for her. April was so proud of Blake and her keen sense of fashion. It had taken her two months to completely design and make this particular dress for her mom, and it had undergone several revisions along the way.

April's parents had been up to see her and asked her how she was doing. April didn't deny her emotions, and told them that she was excited but still a little nervous. Anne and Joseph told her how beautiful she looked and told her that they would meet her downstairs.

There was a knock on the door and April sneaked one last glance in the mirror and walked across the room to open the door. It was Crystal.

"Wow, you look amazing," exclaimed Crystal, at her best friend. "Blake sure knows what she is doing, that's for sure." Crystal commended Blake's design abilities.

April spun around in her dress to show Crystal the entire ensemble.

"Very nice," Crystal said to reiterate her previous statement. "You are getting better with age, honey." Crystal teased as she whistled at April.

"Stop it," April chuckled. "I am feeling really old today and it just seems like yesterday that I graduated college and was looking to take on the world."

Crystal nodded her head in agreement, but then said admiringly, "You have succeeded in ways that you never would have thought possible," Crystal then took a seat on the couch that was next to her and waved April to join her. "Listen to me, you became one of the main editors of Priscilla Publishing within the first four years of working there. Then, after Nick died, you continued to work hard as you successfully raised and cared for Blake." Crystal paused to let that sink into April's mind for a second and then continued, "Furthermore, you took in a homeless girl from the streets of downtown Chicago and made her part of your family. You have survived a major tragedy with each daughter, and you came out of those situations stronger than before."

April could always count on Crystal to put things into proper perspective. April leaned in to give Crystal a hug. "Thank you for everything throughout my entire life. You have been there for me and I love you for it."

Crystal grinned and said, "That's what best friends do. They are there for each other; no matter what."

As the two best friends talked for several minutes, Crystal asked, "When are the girls coming up?" April looked at the clock on the wall and answered, "They should be here any minute. It's almost time."

Crystal stood up from the couch, and said, "Ok then, I'll see you down there, sweetie." She gazed at April one more time and then left the room.

April stood up too and had started to pace. Claire and Blake should be up in the room with her by now and even though it was only three minutes past 5:00 p.m., April was becoming concerned.

Then, at exactly 5:04 p.m., on Friday, October 23, 2020, Claire Turner entered the room, ready to be married—and her sister, Blake, walked in directly behind her.

Claire's wedding dress was beyond words. April stood in stunned silence as the bride-to-be revealed her wedding dress to her mother. Blake had spent years designing Claire's wedding dress. She had started it during her bout with leukemia and she had worked on it feverishly since then. Simply put, Claire looked like an angel walking through the door. Blake had spent the last hour doing Claire's makeup while Brie had styled her hair.

"Claire," April gasped as she gazed upon her daughter. "You are so beautiful!"

April then turned to Blake exclaiming, "Honey, your design is magnificent!"

Blake put her hand and forearm across her belly and took a bow. "Thank you, Mom. By the way, you look totally stunning in the dress that I designed for you, too."

"Thank you, mom," Claire said affectionately immediately after Blake. "I can't believe that I am marrying Caleb today."

Blake smiled at her handy work and walked over and gave her mom a hug. "Do you believe that my big sister is getting married today?"

April shook her head and it seemed like yesterday that she and Mason had tied the knot. Even though it was slightly over a year prior, on a beautiful Saturday afternoon on August 24, in downtown Chicago. Her dad had tears in his eyes as she gave her away for a second time. Mason was so handsome in his tuxedo as he stood there reciting his wedding vows that he wrote himself. During the vows, he had mentioned how blessed he was for not only being allowed to have the woman of his dreams, but to be able to be a father to her daughters. Not only would he be given the title of husband, but as a father as well. A title he never thought he would ever be granted.

Blake was her maid of honor with Claire, Crystal, Monica, and Gina as her bridesmaids. As promised to Crystal, April commented in her vows how it was Crystal who had first seen Mason at the coffee shop and wanted April to go talk to him. Addison James attended the wedding, of course, and as a wedding gift, presented the new couple with an all-expense paid trip to Cancun & Riviera Maya. Even though April had made plans to have all of her friends over at the apartment when they return from their honeymoon, Addison had to decline because she had to attend another wedding in Oregon.

April gazed at her two daughters and couldn't believe how they had grown up to become such beautiful young women. It's felt like Blake was born just yesterday, and like Claire had entered their lives almost in the blink of an eye.

Now, one year after her own wedding to Mason, April's daughter was marrying the man who had rescued her from certain disaster and literally saved her life. Like April and Mason, Caleb fell in love with Claire at first sight and he knew that she would be forever in his life.

April smiled and looked at Blake, and said, "No, I can't believe it. It feels like it was just yesterday that we brought her home to spend the night. I would have never guessed that fate would have taken us down that road that it did and bring us to this point in time."

Even though Claire was only nineteen, she knew in her heart that Caleb was the one. He had proposed to her on Valentine's Day of her senior year with plans to marry her in the upcoming autumn. He knew that he didn't want to wait and couldn't imagine his life without her.

After graduating high school Claire started working for April as a junior editor. It was as if all the books that she had read in her lifetime were stepping stones, directing her on a path that led to finding April and realizing her career passion. Claire had started online English classes, but they were more of a formality then actually needed. She was going to work slowly towards her Bachelor's degree in English and literature, but she was ok with it taking a while.

Blake, now a junior in high school, had started an online designing business. Even though it was in its infancy, she already had several orders from some of the seniors in her school, as well as a few in the surrounding area. Even though Blake had always wanted to go to places like New York or Paris to attend design school, her focus had changed after Claire's accident. She now wanted to be in close proximity to her sister, the fear of them being separated weighing heavy on her mind. Through fate, they had found each other and there was no way that they would be apart.

April looked at the clock again and it was now 5:10 p.m., "Ok, ladies..." April said to Claire and Blake. "Let's get situated," April stepped over one of the dressers in the room and pulled out the family pearls that Claire had worn only a couple times before.

"Here you go, sweetie," began April, as she held them out and stepped closer to Claire. "I know that you are aware that these are my grandmother's pearls. This is for *something old*." April then carefully placed the necklace around Claire's neck and sealed the clasp. "Claire... As of this moment, these pearls are now yours. Blake and I are giving them to you to keep."

Claire put her hand on the necklace, and said defiantly, "No, I can't keep them. These are Blake's. She should have them."

Blake held up her hand and replied candidly, "No Claire. We are giving them to you. You are my big sister and part of this family. I asked grandma and our mom if you can have them and they both said 'yes'. So, as of now, they are yours."

Claire's mind went back to that fateful Thanksgiving Day when Blake had made her put them on. She remembered how honored she was to wear something so meaningful to the family. Now, on her wedding day, they would be hers to cherish forever.

"Thank you, mom," Claire said appreciatively. "You know that I will treasure them forever."

April paused for a moment to admire the pearls on Claire, and then handed her a little ring box.

"Now, this is for *something borrowed,* and I thought that it would be appropriate on this special day." April opened the box and presented Claire with Nick's wedding band. "This is your father's wedding band that I gave him when we got married," April explained as a single tear formed in her eye.

Claire looked at April, and couldn't believe that she had thought of something that special.

"Thank you so much, mom," Claire said, as she carefully removed the ring from the box. "Where should I put it?"

"I got this." Blake said as she took the ring from Claire. "You see. I made a secret insert in your dress, just near your left breast. That way, it can be hidden, but it is still close to your heart." Blake tucked the ring inside the secret compartment and had a tiny piece of Velcro that kept the ring in place. No one would ever know by looking at her that it was even there.

Claire put her hand over her heart and then whispered, "I love you, dad." Both April and Blake blinked away tears so as to not ruin their makeup before the wedding.

"Ok, your turn," April said to both girls. "You were in charge of *something new and something blue.* What did you do for that?" April asked, curious as to what her daughters had picked.

Claire and Blake glanced at one another and then smirked, "Well, you see, mom," Claire began sounding a little sheepish, as she was about to reveal what they had picked for something new.

"Remember when all of us girls went to Gina's Lake House for the weekend last week for my bachelorette party?" Claire asked April.

"Yes?" April asked, feeling as little concerned.

Even though Claire was now nineteen years old, she felt a little bashful telling her mom.

"Well, it was kind of Blake's idea, and well, I thought it was really cool and appropriate for the wedding and…"

"Quit stalling, Claire," April politely reprimanded, "Just tell me."

Claire grinned and said, "It would be better if we showed you." Claire slowly lifted up her wedding dress just high enough to reveal her right ankle. There, tattooed, was a butterfly with the words 'Sisters' inscribed above it. Furthermore, Claire's own handwritten signature was inked in the top right wing, while Blake's signature was inked in the top left. Before April could say anything, Blake lifted up her dress and she had the exact same tattoo, but it was inked on her left ankle.

"Oh my God, you two," April put her hand to her mouth to try to hide the gasp. As she looked at the matching tattoos, she began to smile. "No...you didn't?"

"Yup, we did," said Blake, failing to suppress a smile.

"What a beautiful gesture," April confessed, though mildly taken aback, "You two have always had a special bond, and now the world will be able to see it as well."

"That's what I thought!" Blake admitted. She put her ankle right next to Claire's and said proudly, "Sisters forever!" Claire held out her fist and Blake gave her a fist bump.

"Ok, what have you done for *something blue*?" April asked suspiciously. "Please be something less painful." April asked.

Blake smiled and said, "You are going to like this, mom." Blake stood in front of Claire and bent down towards the bottom of her dress. Blake flipped up one of the inner panels of the dress and carefully sewn it into it was a small blue and plaid heart, about the size of a silver dollar.

"Do you recognize where it came from?" Blake asked her mother.

April looked at it but couldn't place it. April shook her head and looked at Claire.

Claire took April's hands in hers, and said, "It is from the Burberry scarf that you gave me the first day we met. You bought it for yourself, but then you gave it to a dirty, hungry, lonely, homeless girl because she didn't have warm enough clothes for the weather outside. She was cold and you just gave it to her."

April had to suppress a sob as the memory came flooding back to her. The look on Claire's face when April told her that she could keep the Burberry scarf was still one of April's fondest memories.

April ran her hand over the heart-shaped Burberry cut-out. "This is perfect," April said to Claire.

"I want to get a selfie of us before we go down," Blake said as she pulled out her phone. With April in the middle, Claire on her left, and Blake on her right, Blake snapped about three pictures.

The clock on the wall now displayed 5:21 p.m. "We better get down there," April said, smiling at the sight of both her daughters, just minutes away from Claire's wedding.

"Ok..." Claire said, "but before we go down, I just want to tell you how much I love you, mom. I am so proud to be part of this family that I am not fully giving up my name."

"What do you mean?" April asked, confused.

"Caleb and I talked about it and I didn't want to lose the name, Turner. I mean, I've only had it for a short while and out of respect for my dad, I didn't want to give it up," Claire explained. "So, we decided that I am going to hyphenate it. Once we are married, I will change my name to Claire Turner-Allen."

April didn't know what to say. "Are you sure?" April asked. Even she had changed her last name to Steele when she had married Mason.

Claire smiled and replied, "Absolutely. Caleb is totally on board with this, and so are his parents. I just wanted to be forever known by the name Turner, you know? I think that my dad would appreciate that."

Blake didn't know that Claire was going to do that either. "Classy move, Sis. Our dad would be overjoyed that you want to keep his name."

"I don't know what to say, Claire," April said, overcome with emotion. "What a wonderful thing to do."

"It just felt right," Claire said, blissfully.

Blake grabbed Claire by the hand and headed towards the door. "Let's go Mrs. Claire Turner-Allen, it's time for you to get married."

When they reached the bottom of the stairs, Mason was waiting for Claire. He was wearing a black tuxedo with tails. "Wow," Mason breathed, as he saw Claire. "You look stunning, my dear."

"Thank you, *dad*," Claire said. Ever since the day that April and Mason got married, Claire had started calling Mason dad. She loved him like a father, and he actually was the only father figure that Claire had ever known. On the day that she asked if he would give her away at her wedding, he had broken down crying. This was something that he had never expected to be able to do in his life. He never thought that he would be giving away a daughter.

Blake was her maid of honor, followed by Brie, Shelly, and then Rose. Standing up for Caleb was his brother Jacob as his best man, followed by three of his best friends from his paramedic group of co-workers. Mason and Claire stood in the back, just off to the side, hidden from view. They watched as the bridesmaids marched up to the front, one at a time. Mason looked at the crowd of guests, and after several seconds, noticed his sister, her husband, and his nephew. As Mason met his sister's gaze, he knew that she was thrilled that her brother had found his true love and was happy that he was able to be a father to two girls.

The music changed and then everyone stood up. Mason turned to Claire, and said, "Thank you for this. I love you."

Claire looked into Mason's eyes and replied, "No, thank you, for being the dad that I never had. I love you, too."

Mason proudly escorted Claire down the aisle. Everyone was in attendance. As they marched down, the faces of friends and family were all focused on them. Even though they both were walking very slowly, it felt as if only a few seconds went by and they were at the front.

Mason had stopped several feet away from the groom as the preacher asked him, "Who gives this woman to be married to this man?"

Claire turned her head to face Mason as he replied. However, before he replied, Mason pointed towards the first chair in the front row. Setting in that chair was a beautiful crystal frame that contained an 11x14 picture of Mel and Nick. Mason had enlarged and enhanced the original print so that it was a magnificent representation of her biological parents being present.

Once Claire saw the picture of her mom and dad, she let out a sob. She couldn't believe that Mason had done this for her. Not only were April and Mason there, but now Mel and Nick were represented right next to them in the front row.

Claire hugged Mason as tears of joy ran down her face. Mason embraced Claire and then handed her his handkerchief from his breast pocket.

Mason then cleared his throat to answer the preacher's question. "We do, April and Mason Steele, her mom and dad." He then looked at the picture and then added, "They do, too, Nick Turner and Melanie Forrester, her mom and dad as well."

By this time, it was hard to locate a dry eye in the entire church.

Caleb came up to Mason and Claire. Mason held out his hand for Caleb to shake.

"Caleb..." Mason said, his voice resounding through the church.

"To the man that gave Claire back to us..." Mason said, referring to the car accident in which Claire had almost died, "I now freely give her to you."

He held out his hand that was embracing Claire's, and presented it to Caleb.

Claire grabbed Caleb's hand and squeezed it tight. Caleb was in awe at the sight of the woman that he loved. He turned to Mason and responded, "Thank you, Mr. Steele. With love and adoration, I accept your daughter's hand."

Claire and Caleb turned to the preacher. It was then that Claire noticed another picture that was posted directly behind the bridesmaids. It was the picture of all of them when they had left the Winter Formal all those years ago. It was the first time that they all were friends, and were truly happy. Claire looked at all her bridesmaids with a look that displayed that no matter what happens, in their lives going forward, that they would forever be friends. After the couple said their vows and exchanged rings, it was time to kiss the bride. Through the thunderous sound of applause, Claire and Caleb were now married.

April and Mason Steele watched Claire and her husband, followed by Blake and her friends, as they walked down the aisle towards the doors. April and Mason walked hand and hand down the aisle among all their friends and family.

As they marched towards the doors of the church, Claire noticed the word 'faith' carved into each of the stones of the pillars of the archway heading out of the church. Above the carved word *faith* was a small plant, sitting on a shelf, that contained a carved wooden cross pushed into the pot with a tiny red cardinal perched on one of the small branches.

Faith? Claire thought happily as she squeezed her husband's hand. It was one of the first things that Caleb had said to her when she was in the car accident. *Have faith, I'm going to save you,* Caleb had told her, and now here they were, married, husband and wife, experiencing a love like no other.

Excited for the future that lay ahead, Claire couldn't help but to think that *'Faith' would be a great name for a daughter.* Even though they weren't thinking about having children in the near future, she mentally filed it away for safekeeping, for the day that they both decided the time was right to expand their family.

The bridal party all climbed into a horse-drawn carriage that would take them through the streets of downtown Chicago, and ultimately to the wedding reception. Claire and Caleb waved to everyone as the carriage lurched forward and began its voyage. Looking at April and Mason with huge smiles on their faces, Blake and Claire blew kisses at them, letting them know how much they loved them.

April threaded her arm around Mason's waist and planted her head on his shoulder as she watched the carriage slowly move away from the church. Securely fastened to the back of the carriage was a sign with the words, 'Happily Ever After'.